SOME DREAM FOR FOOLS

BOOKS BY FAÏZA GUÈNE

Kiffe Kiffe Tomorrow

Some Dream for Fools

SOME DREAM FOR FOOLS

FAÏZA GUÈNE

Mariner Books
Houghton Mifflin Harcourt
BOSTON • NEW YORK

First Mariner Books edition 2010
French © 2006 by Hachette Littératures
English translation © 2009 by Jenna Johnson

www.hmhbooks.com

Library of Congress Cataloging-in-Publication Data
Guène, Faïza.
[Du rêve pour les oufs. English]
Some dream for fools / Faïza Guène.
p. cm.
ISBN 978-0-15-101420-0
1. Immigrants—France—Fiction. 2. Family—France—Fiction.
3. Family—Algeria—Fiction. 4. France—Social conditions—Fiction.
5. Algeria—Social conditions—Fiction. I. Title.
PQ3989.3.G84D813 2009
843'.912—dc22   2008050167
ISBN 978-0-15-603292-6 (pbk.)

Book design by Brian Moore

Printed in the United States of America

DOC 10 9 8 7 6 5 4 3 2 1

For my family.
My father, Abdelhamid Guène.
My mother, Khadra Kadri.
My sister, Mounia Guène.
My brother, Mohamed Guène.
That you may be proud of me.
I love you.

For all those who have supported and encouraged me.
For the Courtillières, represent.
For my friends, thank you.
For those who have been imprisoned, stay strong.
For Algeria.
For all the crazy fools, here and over there.
For those who dream.

GLOSSARY

aâmi — my uncle; an honorific for a male elder

bakchich — tip, bribe

belâani — to pretend

bendirs — North African percussion instrument

bled — (1) a village; (2) a godforsaken place, the middle of nowhere, a wasteland; (3) a hole or dump; (4) countryside, terrain; (5) the interior of North Africa, the Maghreb (French, by way of Algerian Arabic *blad*)

bledard — a person from the *bled*

boléta — ball

châab — people; here, the North African people living in North Africa

chabin — Creole term for a person of mixed racial heritage or a person of Afro-Caribbean heritage with light skin; here, used in its feminine form, **chabines** (Caribbean, specifically the Antilles)

chétane — devil

djellabas — a loose-fitting outer robe

djoufs — here, girls whose heritage links them to parts of Africa that contain El Djouf, a region of sand dunes that is part of the Sahara. Countries containing or touching El Djouf include Mauritania, Algeria, Morocco, and Mali. El Djouf means "empty place."

el aïn — the evil eye

franssaouis — French

frotti-frotta — close, sensual dancing

gandouras — sleeveless, light dresses of Berber origin, worn in North Africa, often around the house

habs — prison

haïk — traditional outfit consisting of a piece of light-colored fabric which women roll or drape around the entire body

hanout — store

inchallah — var. *inshallah*; literally, "if Allah wills"; God willing

istiqlal — independence

Khoyya — brother; also a general term for a male friend or relative

Kiffe — to be really crazy about something

Kou yinkaranto — idiots (Sonninké)

labès — part of a traditional Muslim greeting, roughly, "How are you?"

miskina — the poor

miskine — poor guy; an expression of pity

naâl chétane — Curse the devil!

sadaqa — offering

salaam — the "hello" portion of the ceremonial Muslim greeting, often accompanied by a bow with the right palm placed on the forehead

starfoullah — May God preserve us!

toubab — a white person, particularly used in African countries to refer to white Europeans, somewhat pejorative (etymology uncertain, but probably from Wolof)

verlan — slang for *à l'envers*, literally, "inside out" or "back to front"; the name of a type of French slang that involves reordering syllables in a word or phrase

youyous — ululations

ziara — a disenchantment, the breaking of a spell

SOME DREAM FOR FOOLS

Big City Cold

IT'S FREEZING IN THIS *bled,* the wind makes my eyes water and I have to run in place to get warm. I tell myself that I'm not living in the right place, that the climate around here isn't for me, because in the end, climate's the only thing that counts and this morning the crazy French cold paralyzes me.

My name is Ahlème and I roam around in the middle of everybody, the ones who run, the ones who beat each other up, are late, argue, make phone calls, the ones who don't smile, and I see my brothers who, like me, are very cold. I always recognize them, they have something in their eyes that isn't the same as everybody else, like they want to be invisible, or be somewhere else. But they're here.

1

At home, I don't complain, even when they cut off the heat, or else Papa tells me: "Don't even talk, you weren't here for the winter of '63." I don't answer him, in '63 I wasn't even born. So I head out and wander around the wonderfully smooth streets of France, I pass rue Joubert where some hookers yell across the street to each other. You could say that these old, wrecked dolls aren't afraid of the cold anymore. Prostitutes are the climatic exception, location doesn't matter, they don't feel anything anymore.

My appointment at the temp agency is at 10:40. Not 10:45. Not 10:30. Everything's precise in France, every minute counts and I can't seem to make myself get into the rhythm. I was born on the other side of the sea and the African minute has more than sixty seconds.

On the instructions of M. Miloudi, the adviser at my neighborhood unemployment office, I went to talk to this new place: Interim Plus.

Miloudi, he's a real veteran. He's been at the agency for the Insurrection Housing Projects for years and must have seen through every case in the district. He's pretty efficient. But he's also always in a hurry. At my interview, he didn't waste a minute:

"Sit down, young lady . . ."

"Thank you, sir."

"And next time, mind that you knock before you come in, please."

"Sorry, sir, I didn't think about it."

"I'm telling you for your own good, because that sort of thing could cost you an interview."

"I'll remember."

"Good, so let's get started, no wasting time, we only have twenty minutes ahead of us. You are going to fill out the competency form in front of you, write in the boxes in capital letters and don't make any spelling mistakes. If there's a word that makes you hesitate, ask me for the dictionary. You brought your résumé?"

"Yes. Five copies, like you said."

"Very good. Here's the paper, fill it out carefully. I'll be back in five minutes."

He took a box of kitchen matches and his pack of Marlboros out of his pocket then left the room, leaving me to stare down my destiny. On the desk there were piles of folders, a mess of papers that blocked your sight, they took up all the space on the desk. And above it all, an enormous clock hung on the wall. Every tick of its hands knocked out a sound that reverberated in me as if it were my death knell. All of a sudden I was hot. I was blocked. The five minutes passed like a high-speed train and I hadn't written anything but my last name, my first name, and my date of birth.

I heard M. Miloudi's hacking cough in the hallway, he came back into the room.

"So? Where are you? Have you finished?"

"No, I'm not done."

"But you haven't filled out anything!" he said as he leaned over the paper.

"I haven't had enough time."

"There are lots of people who are waiting for appointments, I have to see other people after you, you saw them in the waiting room. We only have ten minutes left at the most to contact the SREP, because it won't help at all to go through the AGPA at this time of year, there aren't any more spots. We can try FAJ, the paid apprenticeship program . . . Why haven't you filled it out yet? It's pretty simple."

"I don't know what to put in the box marked 'life objective'—"

"Do you have any ideas?"

"No."

"But on your résumé, it's clear that you have a lot of work experience, there has to be something that you liked in all of that."

"I've only had little jobs as a waitress or salesperson. Just to make money, sir, not as part of my life objective."

"Fine, let's forget the form, we don't have time. I'm going to give you the address of our temp agency so you can go while we're waiting to contact FAJ."

Johanna, an office worker at Interim Plus, looks about sixteen, has a quivering voice, and speaks like every word hurts her. I realize she's asking me to fill out a questionnaire; she gives me a pen with their ridiculous office logo on it and tells me to follow her. The mademoiselle is wearing ultra-tight jeans that betray every violation of her Weight Watchers diet and give her the look of an adulterous woman. She points me toward a chair near a small table where I can settle in. I have trouble writing, my fingers are frozen, I struggle to loosen them. It reminds me of when Papa—The Boss, as we call him—used to get home from work. He always needed a little time to open his hands. "It's from the jackhammer," he said.

I scratch along, I fill out their boxes, I check things off, I sign my name. Everything is miniscule on their form and their questions are kind of annoying. No, I am not married, I don't have children, I am not a B-permit cardholder, I haven't done any higher education, I am not a Cotorep-verified disabled person, I am not French. Where do I find the box marked "My life is a complete failure"? At least with that I could just immediately check yes, and we wouldn't have to talk about anything else.

In a compassionate tone, Johanna, her jeans pulled so tight they could make her uterus explode, presents my first "interim mission." It's funny that they call them missions. It makes these shitty jobs feel like adventures.

She offers me a stock job at Leroy Merlin next Friday evening. I say yes without the smallest hesitation, I really need to work and I would take pretty much anything.

I leave the office all satisfied, proof it doesn't take much.

Later I head out to meet Linda and Nawel at La Cour de Rome, a bar near the agency over in Saint-Lazare. They've been trying to see me for a few weeks and I admit I dodge going out when I'm broke. And then the last few times, the girls have all been glued to their boyfriends and it wears me out, always feeling uncomfortable planted there alone in the middle of them. I'm not far from winning the Third-Wheel Championship title for all Europe and Africa.

The girls are set up in a banquette at the back of the room. I knew it, they're always like that, I know their old secret smoker tricks by heart. Back in the neighborhood, they even have their own headquarters. They're always fucking around behind the stadium, lighting one up. Their secret phrase for meeting up is: "Let's go play some sports."

As usual, they're all tricked out. I notice that they're always classed up and I wonder how they ever find enough time to get dressed, put on makeup, do their hair. Nothing is left to chance, everything matches, is calculated, chosen with care.

The few times I agree to make this kind of effort, it really takes it out of me, it's too much work. What won't we chicks do to draw just one nice look or a compliment in our days racked with doubt. And the ones who say that they do themselves all up like this just for their own pleasure, yeah, my eye!

When I get to the girls, they light their cigarettes in perfect unison and welcome me with a warm, smoky hello.

Just to keep things on script, this is followed by a "What's new?" with a few seconds' pause afterward to think about an answer before they jump right back into their conversation.

Then comes the inevitable question I always dread.

"And how're things with the boys?" A quick shake of the head does the trick. They understand right away. I wonder why, whenever they ask this question, they make "boy" plural. It's hard enough to find one love, why make things even more complicated?

Then, like always, the eternal refrain: "How can a pretty girl like you still be single? It's because you don't really want it . . . It's your fault, you're too difficult . . . We've introduced you to a whole mess of guys, from the beasts to the super-slick, there's nothing more we can do for you, you're all closed up."

I can't seem to make them understand that my life isn't as bad as they think, because if everything goes well menopause isn't going to come tomorrow. But there's nothing I can do, they're just going to keep hitting me with losers.

Guys with an IQ of 2, who talk themselves up to no end, all pretentious, guys who are incapable of conversation or who are chronically depressed.

So I manage a magnificent sidestep anyone would be proud of and change the subject—this is my real talent, I'm triple champion of all Africa and Europe at jumping over obstacles and problems.

Actually I think that, like most people, they already have their lives planned out in their heads, all the elements are there, like pieces of a puzzle that are just waiting to be put together. They split their time between work and play, go on vacation to the same place every summer, always buy the same brand of deodorant, have cool families and boyfriends that they have been with forever. Even their boys are "no-fault" guys, the kind I like but would never personally go away with for a weekend. Not one false note. They all come from the same village as the girls, back in the *bled,* so that's going to please their parents. You might say that we're living out a sort of return to incest. At least with your brother, you can be sure that he comes from exactly the same place as you, you can verify it, ask your mother. The girls find this very practical, because if your traditions are different, your families don't agree about everything; and then it's complicated when you're teaching your kids, when you're not even speaking the same language . . . Me, I say that these are just ridiculous details, and you shouldn't build a home on such practical questions.

Nawel just came back from vacation, she was in Algeria with her father's family, and I mentioned that she lost lots of weight, at least ten pounds.

"Oh yeah? I really got skinny?"

"You're practically dried up. I almost feel sorry for you, *miskina.*"

"It's the back-to-the-*bled* effect."

"The vacation diet, right?"

"Yeah, that's right. . . . The heat, the stuffed green beans at every meal, your grandmother's jokes, those Chilean soap operas. . . . Of course you lose weight."

"But how did you make it? Two months is plenty in the *bled,* I would have been completely depressed . . ." I asked Nawel, intrigued.

"Eh, it just passes. The only thing that was a little harsh was that on the TV there was only one channel. Even *Mr. Bean* is censored there."

8

"At least that means you don't have to put up with that annoying moment when the whole group is in front of the TV and BAM! there's a hot sex scene or an ad for douche. Then, the dad starts coughing and you have to be quick, take the remote, and shut that thing right off. This is why now, at my house, we have a satellite dish. It saves us all the time because on French television they love to put naked women all over the screen at the drop of a hat."

"And things were good with your family?"

"My cheap-ass family . . . The first week they loved us because the suitcases were packed full. As soon as we passed out all the gifts, it was over, we didn't rate with them at all. I told my mother: 'Next summer, I swear on the Koran, we'd better ask that discount store Tati to be our corporate sponsor.'"

Later it's time to catch up on the neighborhood gossip with Linda.com. She's a force of nature, a true talker. Linda, she knows what's happening with everyone, I don't know how she does it, sometimes she even knows people's stories before they know themselves.

"Do you know Tony Lopez?"

"No, who is he?"

"Come on, he's the new guy on sixteen."

"The blond?"

"No, the tall brunet. He works at Midas."

"Yeah, and what about him?"

"He's going out with Gwendoline!"

"The little one? The redhead in your building?"

"No, not her. The anorexic, the one who's covered with un-finished tattoos. Nawel, you have to know who she is."

"Yeah, I know the one, I see her on the bus every time I go to work. Hey maybe you know something that's always in-trigued me, do you know why she's never finished one of her tattoos?"

"How is she supposed to know that?" I said naively.

"No, no, I know—"

"Fuck, you freak me out, you're a real professional gossip you know? Tell us."

"She was with this really shady guy before, a tattoo artist. And that's it. He started all these tattoos on her and he never finished them before he dumped her for another girl."

"A true bastard. He could have at least finished the job."

"Okay, so the anorexic is going out with Tony Lopez, and what else?"

"And he wanted to break up with her. According to my sources, it's because he was messing around with the accoun-tant at Midas. And Gwendoline was so crazy for him, she gave him all this psychological pressure to stay with her. So he ended up staying with her but he made her pay . . ."

"What? Spill! Stop stringing us along."

"She's knocked up, the little thing. Pregnant up to her eye-balls. Crazy right?"

And there you go, every time she ends with "Crazy right?"

She told us two or three stories that had to be whispered be-fore she left us with a smile that made everyone wonder what our secrets were and that shields me from the outside world and its cold.

The platform is black with the crowds, there are service disruptions on the line. One train in four, I think, at least that's what they said on the radio.

So I'm forced up against the pole in this car. There's no air in the RER, everyone's pushing me, blocking me in. The train sweats and me, I feel smothered by all these sad silhouettes, all looking for a little color. You could say that all the air in Africa wouldn't be enough. They're phantoms, they're sick, contaminated by sadness.

Me, I'm going back to Ivry to see my neighbor, Auntie Mariatou, and her children. My asthmatic RER will cough me up in my zone where it's even colder. There are some days like that where you don't know anymore where you're going, you feel like you don't have any luck at all, and that's just too bad. It's true that it's sad, but fortunately, at the end, there's always this little thing that gets us up in the morning. No guarantee, but you think that one day, one day it will be better. Like Auntie says: "The most beautiful stories are the ones that start badly."

The Dollar Tree

I ENVY THE KIDS in this house. It's beautiful the way that they are surrounded by love and warmth, this family is a true poem. Auntie Mariatou is motherhood in all its splendor, so soft you might even say she was made of cotton itself—the better to wrap her little ones snug. I'm fascinated every time to see her teach them so firmly but always dripping with honey. When I talk about her I get a little carried away, it's true, but this is the woman I want to become some day. For me she is a model, all at once a woman, a mother, and a wife. Auntie is very beautiful, her lips are full, her hips broad, and her curves fed the dreams of more than one man in the village back in the day. And though she's a plump woman, she does have something in her that makes her naturally walk as light as an antelope. A certain je ne sais quoi, as the French would say, that would make those 60-pound mannequins tremble.

She and her husband, Papa Demba, have made four beautiful children who came one right after the other and resemble one another just like Russian dolls. The oldest is called Wandé, and she's eight years old. Today I came over to help her do her homework. She dreams of becoming a singer and complains that no *toubab* in her class wants to be her boyfriend because she has fake hair. Then come Issa and Moussa, the twins. They are too mischievous these two, and they scare me the way they will believe anything anyone says. As for the last one, he only knows how to scream for now—he's barely six months old. He's my pride and joy, the little one. It was me who whispered his baptismal name to Auntie Mariatou when she was at the end of her pregnancy and running out of ideas. I chose Amady because it's the name of the first boy I ever loved. I remember being so crazy about him. He would always play with me on the merry-go-round and push with all his strength. I would go so fast that my little pleated skirt would rise without anything to stop it because my hands would be glued to the bars. I was always too afraid of falling on my face to ever let go of them.

That devil Amady regularly used this little strategy in order to get a peek under my skirt. I didn't understand it until a long time afterward because I was only five years old at the time.

Anyway back to the subject of baby Amady. While Auntie was walking him in his stroller around the big park, she was stopped by the old Gypsy woman, the one everybody thinks is crazy. And she told her that this baby would one day become an exceptional man who was going to change history forever, that he would do something very great and that it would take everyone by surprise. She said that the baby carried the promise of an entire people in his belly.

Of course, like most of the people here Auntie Mariatou didn't take her seriously. She even laughed when she thought about it again later as she changed her son's diaper.

"If all the promise that this little one carries in his belly turns into crap, then those people are up shit's creek, no?"

Even if everyone says that she's crazy and just scares the children, me, I find the old Gypsy very interesting. From time to time I get to observe her from a distance, just as she is. In the morning, she takes herself for a walk, she marches along, her shoulders covered by a big black shawl, and stops sometimes to feed the birds. And honestly, deep down, she gives me the heebie-jeebies, especially when I see her talking to the pigeons. She tricks one of them, always the fattest. Then she puts the bird in her hand, and it's bizarre, because every time he stays calm, he doesn't even try to fly away. Then she begins murmuring things to him. From far away you might think that the bird answers her and that they settle in for a discussion, all natural. This lasts a little while and then, all of a sudden, she lets out a horrible, high-pitched scream and all the birds that she has invited to her bread-crumb party let fly in every direction. They take off like maniacs. It's anarchy in the gray Ivry sky.

When everything quiets down, the beating of wings a little farther off, you notice something very strange. The old woman is still there, standing, stiff as a stick, and in the hollow of her hand, up near her mouth, the fat pigeon stays peaceful. Usually, in the end, she leaves with the bird as if nothing happened, and gradually, the greedy little pigeons wait for the old lady to depart to come back one by one to get a little dessert.

Sometimes I imagine the after-party: she twists the bird's neck and crunches into it, sinking her canine teeth into it like a starving she-wolf. Then she finishes by swallowing the whole thing raw, feathers, head, beak, and all.

This old lady truly intrigues me. I wouldn't know what age she could be, or what era she's from either. It's like she exists outside of time.

I am sitting on a wooden chair in the middle of the room and waiting impatiently for the nightly episode of *Star Academy* to end so I can finally start working with Wandé. Impossible to get her to leave her post, she's stuck to it like a cockroach on a Raid strip. I think it's because she's in love with one of the contestants, the little blond who's made it to the finals. She makes me think of my little brother, Foued, when he's in front of the PlayStation playing his war games.

"Wandé! It's already seven-thirty, my love! I'm not going to wait all night for your homework."

"But it's the finals."

"I'm warning you—after this I'm going back to my house. Either you turn off the TV now, or you do your homework all by yourself."

"Let it go, Ahlème. She's just going to get a zero."

"Mama, shh! I can't hear anything!"

"What! Who did you tell to shh? Were you raised so badly?"

"It's because she's on a date with her future husband. He's going to sing," I said, trying to tease Wandé.

Auntie Mariatou, furious, ripped out the TV plug.

"Still, there are some things more important than television! This kid would rather piss all over herself than miss a second of this show, it's terrible."

Wandé starts to get angry and takes on this sulky air that she does so well.

Since she had her first braids, she gets such a funny puss when she sulks. Her face is all tight, pulled to the back. Cornrows are the African face-lift. Auntie Mariatou always pulls too tight. I know, she's done my hair too. The result is right pretty but, in order to achieve it, she pulls at your head like it's a carpet and this can last for hours. If you grit your teeth it goes a little better. At the same time, she knows what she's doing, it's her career and you should never correct someone who's working, that's what The Boss says. There are clients who come from far away for Auntie to do their hair because she has a steady hand and really knows what's in style, what will make them happy, and what will work for them.

Recently she started subscribing to an American magazine

on Afro hairdressing. She says that black women in America are fearless with their hair, they're likely to try the craziest things. In this magazine, they tell the secrets of the stars—like Mary J. Blige or Alicia Keys for example.

Auntie's funny when she talks about that, she gets all carried away.

"What do you think? This girl here, Beyoncé, the one who waddles around in those clips on MTV, you think she was born with blond hair as smooth as silk? The truth is that her hair is as frizzy as mine, my dear, except that she, she has the means to make everyone forget it, that's all."

Auntie Mariatou works four days a week at Afro Star 2000, a salon in Paris, in the Château-d'Eau neighborhood. Of all the heads she works on, mostly people from the Ivory Coast, many of them have become good friends.

Auntie loves doing hair and has had a passion for it for a long time. Her secret dream is to move over there, to America, and open a big salon.

"Big deal if I don't speak English, I will use the language of hair itself."

Her dream of America goes back to her childhood. She too had a face drawn tight from the back by the braids her mother gave her. And while everyone had nothing but Paris on their lips, she saw only New York. Sometimes she says that if she hadn't followed love and her husband, Papa Demba, to France, she would certainly have gone over there to join I don't know which distant cousin.

17

When Auntie Mariatou lived in Senegal, in Mbacké, whenever the time for the American soap operas would come, every neighborhood would gather in front of a little television installed in the middle of the courtyard. It was practically a religious ritual. Whenever it was super-bright and sunny out, someone would get up and put a palm leaf above the screen.

Sometimes the image would get scrambled or the worn-out set would even stop showing anything for a minute or two. An eternity for the little girl who had tears in her eyes and started cursing everything she could until one of the other viewers would get up and repair the receiver. Often it was her cousin Yahia, the one who was nicknamed Romeo in the village because he courted all the girls behind their parents' backs. He would go find a nice stainless-steel fork that he would plant in the ass of the temperamental TV. What's more, that same fork had, incidentally, served several days before to stem little Aminata's tetanus spasms.

It always happened that this D-list method worked very well and quickly enough would have its effect: the image returned in less time than it would take to say so and the entire assembly would cry out an "aaah" of relief. Mariatou always arranged to put herself in the front row so she had the best seat. Mouth wide open, fascinated by what she saw, she was so focused that she didn't even take the trouble to shoo the flies that came and landed on her face or that tickled her naked, dry feet.

Her cousin Yahia, alias Romeo, the one with the fork in the TV, amused by the fascination this little girl had for the big world on the other side of the ocean, fed her a line just to have a little fun with her. He told her a story that she believed in as hard as iron: The Legend of the Dollar Tree.

"This legend says that in America there are extraordinary trees. These magic trees produce bills for leaves, dollar bills. These trees thrive under any conditions, they don't need water because they water themselves, and they're in bloom all year long. Everyone has the right to profit from these trees, and it's for this reason that these people know neither hunger nor thirst."

Mariatou dreamed of the dollar tree from morning to night until she reached the age of reason.

I think she still believes in it a little and that we've all believed in it once. The Boss, he was convinced that in France all you had to do was dig into the soil to make your fortune. When he told us that, it hurt my heart but I smiled all the same.

Dignified and Standing Tall

"YOU OKAY, PAPA?"

"It's cold here. You know, I only have five cigarettes to last the whole rest of the evening."

"That's because they cut off the heat, I told you that yesterday, they're going to turn it back on in a week. And I'll go buy some more cigarettes at the store, they close late."

"Weren't you just out?"

"I was out since this morning."

"Oh, okay. I didn't hear you leave."

"By the way, Papa, do you keep up with Michel, our upstairs neighbor?"

"The one missing an arm?"

"No, the other one."

"Which other one? The skinny guy who's always fighting with his wife, the one who's as nasty as anyone?"

"No, the fat one with the glasses, the same one whose dog died last year."

"What about him?"

"It sounds like he tried to commit suicide."

"Again?"

"Yeah, it's the third time . . . no, the fourth, I think."

"Four times already? My God, that happened fast. And did he die?"

"No, he failed again, he's in the hospital."

"You see, I always told you he was a failure, that one. Couldn't even kill himself! It's not all that hard, dying."

"Yeah, sure."

"You know, I only have five cigarettes for—"

"Yeah, I know, I'm going down to find some. Where's Foued, Papa?"

"He's playing ball outside with the kids."

"Good, I'm going to find him, he should be home by this hour, and you know it, it's ten-thirty—"

"Ten-thirty? It's late, the smoke shop is going to close . . ."

The Boss, he's always like that, but lately I have the feeling it's getting worse. He's been like this ever since the accident, which will be three years next month. Three years, it's not a huge deal, but to see him in this state, in the middle of sentences that don't make any sense, sitting all day in his armchair, in pajamas, you

21

might think he had always been there. So he spends all his time in front of the TV, which has become a member of the family in its own right. It's the TV that regulates The Boss's new life, he doesn't need a watch anymore. *Morning TV,* that's time for coffee, news, and breakfast; *Derrick,* that's when he takes his nap; and the last shot from the evening movie, that's when he goes to bed. Since he went off the rails, he lives a never-ending day.

I remember, it happened very early in the morning, he was working at the building site and he was keeping his balance up there, like he had kept his balance his whole life.

Only that day, he wasn't wearing his helmet. Papa had given his to Fernandes — the one who never drank — because he was walking under the girders and Papa thought it was dangerous. If I know him, The Boss must have said: "Me, I'm all the way up here, so I'm not in danger of anything falling on my head except maybe lightning."

No one knows exactly why he fell from that bitch of a beam. The fall was so spectacular that all the boys thought he was done for. The truth is that his body didn't suffer anything truly horrible, two or three broken ribs and a ridiculous ankle sprain.

Only, as he fell over, his head hit a joist and because of the blow it doesn't turn all the way around anymore.

He wasn't wearing his helmet, so the boss refused to pay him damages. There was first the workers union, and then the lawsuit, the lawyer, the trial. Luckily he won the case in the end. Recognized disability, incapable of working. So he gets a pension and even a free transit card.

But I remember that with the lawyer we really had to do battle by shuffling papers in every sense, doctors' affidavits, declarations of one sort or another.

It's true that it was hard at first but afterward we managed.

During the first months following the accident, there were mornings when Papa woke up at 4:00, in the middle of the week, like usual, went through his ablutions, prayed, made his lunch, and dressed himself to go out. It seems to me he wasn't doing all this in a logical order anyway. When I realized that he was standing, I had to get myself up and explain to him that he wasn't going to work and it broke my heart because he answered me, confused: "Yes, it's true, you're right, I forget, it's Sunday."

Foued really doesn't like it that I go looking for him when he's outside with his buddies, he says that I embarrass him—he's Mr. Big, you understand. In general, I avoid it, it's true, but this time I warned him and noted that he doesn't really care about disrespecting the rules I make for the house. After all, he's a kid, he's only fifteen. He has to get up early to go to school tomorrow morning, and there's nothing for him to be doing outside at this hour.

He's probably at the other end of the neighborhood, at the Pierre de Coubertin Stadium. I've noticed that most of the sports fields are named after Pierre de Coubertin. What a lack of originality! Me, I propose that one day we rebaptize our stadium Ladji Doucouré.

Anyway, the stadium is at the foot of what everyone calls "The Hill," a sort of big rise that hangs over the whole neighborhood. I position myself at this strategic spot, and there an extraordinary view lies waiting. Lights come toward me from every side and it's so beautiful to me.

I am surrounded by all these buildings with all their crazy sides that hold in our noises, our odors, our lives here. I stand there, alone, in the middle of their strange architecture, their gaudy colors, their unconscious forms that have cradled our illusions for so long. The time has passed when running water and electricity were enough to camouflage injustices, the slums are far off now. I am dignified and standing tall and I'm thinking about a whole mess of things. The events that took place in our neighborhood during these last few weeks have stirred up the press around the world, and after some face-offs between the police and the kids, everything is newly settled down. But what can our three burned-out cars change when an army of maniacs are trying to make us shut up?

The only curfew worth minding is the one I, non-French citizen, will impose this evening on my fifteen-year-old brother.

I see Foued down below, right in the middle of the stadium, running around, agile, he's easy to recognize. He's playing with about ten other neighborhood boys around the same age. For the most part I know them, I've watched some of them grow up. I can see that even the Villovitch brothers are here. I haven't run into these two hooligans in an eternity. They've been avoiding me since our last encounter. They must have been so ashamed that they would willingly clear away like the fog if they could.

That night I had gone down to the basement to lock up Foued's bike. I opened the bulletproof door, which got jammed a little as I pushed the front wheel, and it was there that I took those two scoundrels by surprise. They were planted on this old two-seater couch that's been in retirement in the basement for years, and since they had their backs to me, they didn't immediately see my intrusion on their privacy.

Right in front of me, I discovered the ingenious contraption they had cooked up. Thanks to a pirated outlet, they had installed a little television, placed it on an upside-down cardboard box, and below it a game console served as their DVD player. It was some comic scene, I just saw what was happening on the couch, which was basically their little clammy necks and their right arms jiggling nervously.

At the heart of this little staging, an official episode of the Young Olympics was playing. On the TV, a busty blond bimbo was carrying out a perilous performance of rhythmic gymnastics, supported a little too closely by these guys on the parallel bars. The basement had been transformed into a screening room of Cinema Blonde-Trash.

> *O Puberty I write your name.*
> *On Concrete, I write your name.*

At this fateful moment, I decided not to laugh. I didn't want to take the risk of castrating these virile budding men and having the responsibility for all their future troubles. Then came the inevitable "ahem"—I had to interrupt this sketch in order to put the bike away.

I will never forget the expression on their faces. They were caught red-handed, with no desire to play any awkward word games. I did serious violence to myself to lock down and keep my cool, using sadness to fight back this irresistible need to laugh that was pestering me.

The villains didn't dare turn their heads in my direction, they put away their hardware, feverish with shame. I got out of that basement à la Ali Baba and His Forty Tools, leaving those two foxes with their remorse so I could finally let my wild laughter shake itself out on the elevator. I nearly went back down to thank them, it had been such a long time since I had laughed so wholeheartedly. And there it is, that's why they avoid me, those two disgusting little creeps.

I make my way onto the field and already my little Zizou-in-training is blasting me a look. He wants my hide for coming into his territory.

And respect for elders? I'm going to take him back to the house by the elastic in his underwear if I have to. Who does he think he is? I raised him, this kid, and even if his memory is short, I remember very well. He owes me obedience. Now that he's terminated his contract with Pampers he thinks he doesn't owe me any respect. That's the best shit yet.

"Foued! Come home right now!"

"One last little game and I'll be there. Go ahead, it's all right."

"This isn't a discussion. Let's go," I said.

"It's fine, okay! You're boring the shit out of me. I'll be home afterward."

"Shut up! Listen to how you talk to me! You want to act like the big man in front of your boys, yeah, well, you failed at that my old man. Get over here!"

He quits his leg tricks, ultra-pissed, and stays put. Suddenly there's a silence in the group. We're about sixty feet from each other, we're both standing straight up, and so begins a great battle of looks. It was like a Western of the this-town-isn't-big-enough-for-both-of-us variety.

To my great shock, at this critical point in the movie, one of the Villovitch brothers had the balls to speak up.

"Let him play one more game, please, it's not right!"

"You, little shit, no one asked you anything as far as I know. It's not your place to tell me what is or isn't right . . ."

Mr. Mini-glans lowers his head, humiliated. I confess, I hit him a little hard. But at the same time the dirty kids wanted to usurp power. I was the victim of a coup d'état, so I had to be firm.

Foued follows me without saying anything, he's even too ashamed to say goodbye to his friends. If at this exact moment he had a gun in place of his eyes, I bet he would have already put a bullet in my back. I don't need to talk either, I know that he knows. Papa should never be alone in the house, that's rule number one. Sometimes I get the feeling that I was born to take care of other people. Foued is young, he isn't responsible for all of it, but he needs to understand that he can't just do what he wants. He's at the age where you start to build—and not on construction sites, like The Boss, who spent his whole life earning practically no francs an hour, coming home dirty and exhausted, hands ruined and back broken with the strain. I would be thrilled to read a little motivation on Foued's face when he decides to do his homework. This pisser never does shit.

The Cat with Nine Lives

FROM NOW ON, I'll think twice before using the expression "That's not even worth a nail." Today I know better than anyone the exact value of a nail, this little object that seems without importance at first but which is in reality the source of all things. We don't think about them enough.

The night before my stock job started, I got a phone call from that dear Johanna, the girl from my temp agency. It's already an accomplishment to understand what she's talking about when you're in front of her, but on the phone it's practically a miracle. You almost want to give her speech therapy for her birthday.

So she called me to give me instructions for the "inventory" mission.

"Be a volunteer, be motivated, show your supervisor that you deserve the opportunity that you've been given in being hired, wear the employment agency's name with conviction."

Of course they don't send just anyone to their client businesses. Especially to spend an evening counting nails in an empty store.

I arrived at Leroy Merlin very early—I always do that just to be sure. Punctuality is like a sickness for me. I don't like people who always arrive late, especially the ones who don't think it's a big deal. When someone makes me wait a long time, I take off and that's that. The Boss often says: "If you wait for someone once, you'll be waiting for him your whole life."

Once on the premises, I had to talk to a certain Sonia, a thin, dry woman around thirty years old.

When the crew was finally at the meeting spot, she turned to explaining how our crazy evening would unfold.

One break—pee or cigarette—for a maximum of ten minutes, so it's impossible to smoke and piss, you have to choose, unless you do both at the same time. Then a formal prohibition against leaving the store with your bag or jacket during inventory. What are they afraid of? That someone will discreetly steal a sink?

So all the people are for the most part in their twenties, the majority are students, and it's a group composed mostly of boys.

Sonia assigns us to departments with partners.

With my luck, I end up in the hardware department with a little guy named Raphaël Vignon who didn't leak a single word the whole evening. Wonderful! There I am stuck in the festival of nails, screws, and bolts with a kid suffering from verbal constipation. Sometimes I feel his disturbing gaze on me, but I continue to count my nails as if nothing is happening, even though really I am a little creeped out—empty stores, like underground parking garages, call to mind murder scenes. At certain points in the evening, I nearly forgot he was there, but at that exact moment he starts whistling or hacking out a cough or something like that.

What a life! I could have ended up with another partner, the big brunet in the back for example, the cute one with the good body who I saw giving me little interested glances. But no, I had to be inflicted with this Vignon, with his domestic-animal-assassin demeanor. It's always like this anyway, I don't know why I'm still surprised to find myself in these kinds of situations. It's my destiny, I should get used to it.

Plus my back and my legs hurt. In the process of becoming glued to the stepladder, I had these ugly marks on both of my knees, and all for a payoff of 65 euros. With this pile of cash I can only go to the market twice.

I think I've been stuck with the stupidest little jobs imaginable. Except for maybe playing Santa Claus at the Galeries Lafayette.

I was a counselor for little kids at a vacation camp. I know all about pissed-in pants, untied shoelaces, boogers hanging out of noses, tantrums and fits of tears. And being paid in peanuts of course.

I've passed out balloons shaped like hearts on Valentine's Day at the Thiais shopping mall. I met the most wild-in-love couples in the entire Val-de-Marne that day, I remember, and it hit me hard because I'd been dumped the night before.

Then there was the wave of stints in restaurant work, McDonald's, Quick, Paul, KFC. I remember gaining at least five pounds that I lost right away when I was a waitress at the Nut House, the bar that makes you nuts.

I even worked for a phone chat line. It paid well and I worked under the charming pseudonym Samantha. I cracked quick enough though because it was too shady. I put a stop to it the night that a guy, one who called pretty regularly, asked me to imitate a hen.

I also went door-to-door selling prepaid cell phones. I can't count the times someone slammed the door in my face screaming: "I don't believe in God, I'm not interested."

Before that, I worked for a telemarketing company that sold surveillance cameras. We pulled our numbers primarily from stores in the super-luxe sixteenth, eighth, and seventh arrondissements. Every morning a guy the employees nicknamed Cocaine came to brief us in the office. He tried to put little disks in our heads, like: "You're winners, believe it! Today will be great!" And of course he always slid in there that the one who sold the most should get a bonus of half their salary. I was fired at the end of a week because I didn't secure a single contract. It was too hard, I felt like I was working for the minister of the interior. And no lie, the work we did helped the police. In any case, it was the only time in my life when I was thrilled to be laid off.

My last job was as a substitute at Pizza Hut. Even today this phrase resonates in my head like a Machiavellian echo: "Thank you for choosing Pizza Hut, goodbye and we'll see you again soon."

Obviously I aspired to better, but a person has to live. People who get to fill their refrigerators by doing what they love are very lucky. If that were the case for me, I would give thanks to God more than five times a day, it would deserve at least that much.

Sometimes I write things down in a little spiral notebook I lifted from Leclerc down on the avenue. In it I tell something about my life, what makes me happy and what really messes with my head. I tell myself that if one day I go crazy like my father, at least my story will be partially written, my children will be able to read what I dreamed. I'm kind of like a cat, it's as if I've already lived several lives. I'm twenty-five years old and feel like I'm forty.

A Person Needs Two Hands to Clap

IT'S LATE NOW and I'm on my way home. They're sleeping like big babies, no doubt, I heard The Boss's snores all the way from the lobby. So now I'm stuck with a situation I don't much like: open the door without making any noise, something that's not so simple with the kind of key we have, keys with CARE-FREE marked on them. They're ENORMOUS, twelve inches long, eight wide, all for a weight of about thirty pounds, they look like the keys to the dungeon from the time of the Roman Empire. Sure I exaggerate but that's pretty much the idea. Next, I undress in the dark so I don't wake anyone and I slide under my cold comforter. There, if I fall asleep right away, it's good.

To tell the truth I just barely avoided an ambush. My dear and unpredictable friends, Linda and Nawel, suggested we see a movie tonight. I knew that boys would be in the picture but I didn't imagine that they had a plan B and that the plan B was a setup. You know, the friend of a friend of a girlfriend. The guy in question, a certain Hakim, was supposed to serve as my partner for the evening. On seeing the girls arrive early, I suspected they were getting ready for something, I noticed that there was the smell of fish in the air. Usually with this sort of thing I see them coming with my naked eye, I should have caught that they were arranging a *Love Boat* evening for me behind my back. As soon as I saw the individual in the hat get out of his car to join us, I got the whole thing and I tried to do an about-face because I don't like surprises too much. Then seeing that, on the surface, the young man had some selling points, I stayed. Unfortunately, as usual, the barrels for this vintage knock hollow.

I had the honor of choosing the film; to the great despair of the rest of the group I then chose a Belgian art film that lasted two hours (which turned out to be excellent anyway). During the whole screening I had the privilege of hearing the intensely stupid commentary of this scam artist Hakim, I was ready to choke him just to shut him up. I could see perfectly well that the film basically didn't interest anyone but me and two old folks (if you're good at mental math you'll note that there were only eight of us in the darkened room) but at least the others kept themselves busy. They were playing a game of "oral exploration," a pastime that simultaneously develops the senses of taste, touch, hearing, and eventually smell.

Bizarrely, on leaving the theater, everyone was really hungry, so we went to get something to eat, and this time, it's funny, but no one asked me to choose the place. Mouss, Nawel's boyfriend, a man of good taste, had the hype idea of taking us to a trendy restaurant near Montparnasse, decorated '70s-style: the Space Shuttle. Everything was perfect, but Hakim the Scammer's manners clashed so much with the classiness of the place . . . one word came to mind and that word is "wrong."

The highlight of the evening came as we placed our order. Of course, Hakim put himself in charge. He called to the waiter, a tall, skinny, distinguished blond who held himself straight up like you learn at hotel-restaurant management school.

"Hey! Hey there, chief! Come over here would you? Can you take our order please, cuz?"

You would have thought we were at the fish stand in the outdoor market. In another context I would have definitely laughed, but then, I wanted to hide. At that precise moment if someone had offered I would have said okay to a burka. I swallowed my meal like it was a day of mourning then I faked a surprise migraine so they'd drop me off at home. So then I drank some coffee with Auntie Mariatou and told her the unwinding of the whole crazy evening, and instead of sympathizing she clucked like a turkey during my whole tale. Then she concluded with one of those magic phrases that have the ability to unravel the most serious situations and defuse the most charged atmospheres.

"Man is a jackal but what woman can do without him? A person needs two hands to clap . . ."

Auntie's husband, Papa Demba, still looks at her with eyes filled with admiration and love, he's one adorable person, solid and gentle, the ideal spouse. Their story, the one he told me anyway, is mad extraordinary. Of all the young women in the village, she was the one he noticed. One morning, when he was passing by in a wagon, he saw her crossing a field. The view from that day never left him — I think he was making a subtle reference to her unforgettable backside — and then he swore to himself that she would be his beloved. He belonged to the blacksmith caste and she belonged to the noble caste so the union was impossible, but Papa Demba's strength and determination won out over everything else.

I love that Auntie tells me these coupling stories, they make you laugh so hard you piss yourself. She always says that it's the woman who makes the couple a success and the man will be its downfall. Maybe that's a little extreme but it's about right. She also says that love is like hair, you have to take care of it.

Since I was thirteen or fourteen, I have entrusted all my stories to her. She's a woman who gives very good advice. She always consoled me when I had heartaches, encouraged me to have confidence in myself, and pushed me to become more feminine, which was no small task because I was a true little tomboy. Auntie's horrified by my big sweatshirts, long shorts, and tracksuits, so when I have the misfortune of wearing a cap, we don't even speak of it, I exasperate her. She introduced me to women's magazines, high heels, and makeup. It's taking me a while to stick to it.

At sixteen or seventeen, when boys started to get interested in me because I finally resembled a young woman more than a thug, I thought they weren't sincere, that they were making fun of me. Auntie was reassuring, telling me: "You are very pretty and very intelligent, let the boys drool over you. Watch the other girls a little and you'll see how much you're worth. As they say, you have to watch a lot of empty plates go by before you can appreciate your dinner."

I must have been ten or eleven when I lost Mama and left Algeria with Foued in my arms. Over there, it was the complete reverse, I never saw men. I was glued to my mother's underskirts, and all the other women in the village too, who stuck together and were responsible for the education of the children. I could get fifteen different smacks for one single mistake. I lived among a crew of women who spent their lives hiding themselves from men. I worked whole days sorting through beads and ribbons for Mama, who was the village seamstress. I stayed shut up in the hut. Luckily there was school, where I could talk to the other kids, and the little garden in the back of the house. I passed my free time at the foot of our little orange tree and watched the street on the other side of the chain-link fence, inventing stories about the people passing by. For example, I thought it was loads of fun to try to recognize through their djellabas the fat women I had seen at the hammam the day before. Once I saw the one who had the misfortune of scrubbing my back with a bristly glove that ripped up my skin, so I took devilish pleasure in throwing some stones at her.

Settled in Ivry with The Boss, I was shocked by the immense liberty, the fresh air. He always left me alone to play outside and often took me to the OTB bar. I remember, while he filled out his trifecta tickets, he let me play some rounds of pinball. Afterward, if I won, I was entitled to one big cup of hot chocolate. If I lost, I was entitled to one anyway. This is why I'm still unbeatable today. I played ball with the boys in the neighborhood and, like them, I pulled the girls' hair and stole their jump ropes to whip them. I went nonstop, no layover from an exclusively feminine universe to a world of men.

At the beginning of adolescence, everything got complicated because I matured early.

I was truly ashamed of my chest, which I hid under gigantic sweatshirts ten times too big for me, all the more so because I was the only one in the class already fully equipped. The other girls, extremely flat in every way, envied me. If they had known that I was smashing the goods down so they would seem smaller . . .

My first true trauma went down the first time I bled. I was convinced that I didn't have long to live. I remember writing goodbye letters, thinking about terrible things, the kind of things you consider only at the twilight of your life, like confessing to Elie Allouche that I had a crush on him. Elie Chelou, we called him, Elie the Weird, all the girls at school thought he was a big loser, but me, I thought he was sweet. Sure that my bleeding was a symptom of my imminent death, I also made the big mistake of giving all my Boyz II Men tapes to Bouchra, a smart kid in class whom I extorted money from and bullied into doing my homework for me. I was lost with all of it.

Luckily Auntie Mariatou was there to guide me through these moments, she's done a lot for my brother and me, trying to do what she can to fill up the absence left by our mother.

I know that around fourteen or fifteen is the "critical period"—that's why I do my best to be behind Foued a hundred percent. I remember that once I was a real mess. I spent my time outside, stepping and scrapping like some street kid. When the neighbors told Papa, he laid into me, but it didn't do any good, I started back up the next week.

I was tough and I fought like a man. I didn't scratch, I didn't slap, but I got in my blows: with fists, feet, knees, and eventually my head.

In Algeria, I spent the beginning of my education in a little communal school where girls and boys weren't even allowed to sit next to one another. We had a profound respect for the school and always showed great deference toward our teacher. For example, in class, when he asked a question, the student being asked was required to stand up to answer. Also, if one of us was caught cheating or gossiping, she was immediately disciplined with a cruel metal ruler; the sound was so horrible we felt a collective pain.

My mother and my aunts often said that a teacher was like a second father and that it was right for him to discipline me; they added that they should even discipline me one more time to show they agreed with him. A second father, that could be strange. I already barely knew the first one. He was the man who lived in France to work, who sent us money so we could eat well and so we would have pretty dresses for the Aïd el-Kebir celebration. I saw him two weeks every year during his vacation. He didn't talk much but he gave me hundred-dinar bills all the time so I could buy myself pretty things. I often asked him what it was like to fly, how the planes could stay up there . . . He didn't give me any scientific explanations and always answered me saying something crazy, that I remember . . .

When I arrived in this cold, scornful land I was a little girl, enthusiastic and polite, and in less time than it would take to say so, I became a true parasite. I quickly let my good old habits slide, like standing up to speak to the teacher, for example. The first time that I did that here, the other students broke up laughing. I got all red and they called out in chorus: "Teacher's ass-kisser!"

I quickly understood that I had to take control of myself and that's just what I did. Ever since, I haven't made bad progress. Like they say, I've become a perfect model of integration.

Practically French. The only thing missing for my costume is a stupid piece of laminated sky-blue paper stamped with love and good taste, the famous French touch. This little thing would give me the right to do anything and would get me out of waking up at three o'clock in the morning every trimester in order to go to the line in front of the prefecture, in the cold, to obtain for the umpteenth time a renewal for my residency permit.

On the other hand, you can meet some interesting people in these long lines. The last time I talked to a guy from I don't know what country in the East. Tonislav was his name. He offered me some Diesel jeans that he was running some game out of selling for half the retail price. We spent some time in line together, and the more I looked at him the more I found him cute in his old Perfecto jacket. But fine, it would be stupid, if you're going to hook up with some guy he should at least have his papers. I've had enough of being a foreigner.

There are also two guys I see often, two Turks from Izmir, brothers. One day when everyone was waiting in a driving rain, one of these two was nice enough to lend me his umbrella—it really touched me that he would get wet for me. Ever since then whenever we run into each other we talk and they always invite me to come eat kebabs where they work. "Free. No problem. Greek, skewers." I'll go one of these days, I know where it's located, just across from the train station, the Bodrum Sun it's called, like three-quarters of the kebab joints in France . . .

I've had some cool encounters, but you can't say that there's rich ambiance in front of the prefecture every day. In general the cops deal with us like we're animals. The bitches, behind this fucking window that keeps them far from our realities, talk to us about our residencies, more often than not without even looking us in the eyes.

Last time, an old man, from Mali I think, missed his turn because he didn't recognize his name. The good woman called out Monsieur Wakeri, one time, two times, then three times before scrupulously going on to the next person. He'd been waiting there since dawn and his name was Monsieur Bakari, which is why he didn't get up. A woman told him in Bambara that they had definitely already called his name; she tried to negotiate his way to the window because he didn't speak much French himself, but it was too late. He had to come back the next morning.

I remember one day when I was full-out ready to collapse. I was extremely tired. I had finished working at the bar at one in the morning and the customers had been particularly shitty that night. I was on edge. At four o'clock, I was already in line in a pitiless cold and it wasn't until one in the afternoon that my number came up. So I had a really hard time bearing the disdain that this old hooker behind the glass threw at my face. Lucky for her I had lost the impulsiveness of my fourteen-year-old self, if not she would be dead, drowned in her own saliva. I just let loose like some poor bitch, for nothing because all she had to do was gesture for the uniforms to come and throw me outside.

When my temperature went back down I felt pretty stupid. I hadn't even sorted out the story with my papers in the end. Result? I went back the next morning, eyes to the sky, and lucky thing that I am, I landed on the same employee as the day before. Obviously she didn't remember me at all.

Ever since the February 2006 circular and its goal of 25,000 expulsions in a year, there's a gas-like odor around the lines in front of the prefecture. Going right along with the trouble-some echoes of wartime ambush is this crazy little story a woman told near the counters. Her cousin had received a summons from the prefecture. He was very happy because he'd been waiting for it for months. He thought he was finally going to get legalized but it was a trap. They took him to the retention center and now he's back in Bamako. He didn't even have the time to say goodbye to his loved ones or to pack his belongings. Ever since I heard her tell that story, when I'm sitting on one of those hard, uncomfortable chairs at the prefecture, I imagine men with little mustaches in the offices who only have to push a button for it to become an ejector seat and for me to find myself back in the village.

A Rainbow After Weeks of Rain

TODAY IS THE BOSS'S birthday. I made *kerentita* for the occasion, a recipe that comes from my grandmother Mimouna—she taught me when I was living in Algeria. This cake, with its chickpea-flour base, is a specialty from the west of the country. I still remember when, early in the morning, the traveling salesman took his tours of the block on his old bike, calling: "It's here, the *kerentita* has arrived!" Then all the cousins and me, wanting to buy something from him, would leave the hut running, barefoot, dressed in simple gandouras, and not giving a shit about anything. Our uncle Khaled would go crazy: "Get right back in here you wild girls! You want someone to see you? The men are going to look at you, for shame! Come back!"

That made us crack up but if you were a straggler you couldn't laugh too much because he would throw his legendary plastic sandal at you. I still haven't cracked his technique, but he never missed his target. It didn't matter where he was throwing it, the shoe would turn over and over and finish by landing exactly where he intended. In your back, usually. He was too talented, Uncle Khaled. After so many years of experience, he was Africa's champion of throwing plastic sandals.

"How old am I anyway?"

"Sixty-one, Papa."

"Oh no, no no, we can't celebrate that!"

"And why not?"

"It's a fool's party, a party for whities who clap for themselves because they're one step closer to the grave—"

"No, don't say that, it's a chance to have a party with the three of us all together."

I handed him his best outfit and his most attractive tie. I could see that he was happy, The Boss. Foued and I pulled out all the stops: cake, candles, and even the song. Meanwhile our witch of a neighbor banged on the ceiling with her broom. Did she think she was going to keep me from singing? If she keeps pissing us off, I'm going to go down and break her body in half. Anyway we don't give a shit about her and we sang even louder to rile her up, the bitch, and that made all three of us happy. I love these rainbow moments after weeks of rain.

After that, I went and shut myself up in my room to listen all-out to the Diam's CD that I jacked from Leclerc last week —that said, I have to stop stealing, I'm way too old. I'm in front of my mirror with my roll-on deodorant for a mic, and I sing like a crazy person. Oh, if anyone saw me! It doesn't take much to be happy. I'm happy, I know that it won't last very long but it's good while it's here. I'm like a lunatic, I sing louder and louder, I turn up the volume on my hi-fi and I jump with all my strength. The music takes me over and I'm dreaming I'm at a Diam concert: she invites me onstage for a duet, we rap together in front of a euphoric crowd, I'm loving it, I raise my arms, my throat's killing me, my heart's racing. She lets me be the star a little and gets the crowd chanting my name, so everyone shouts: "AHLÈME! AHLÈME!" When it's all over we go backstage, exhausted but wild with joy. Diam's is still keeping it together, her mascara hasn't run, she's not sweating. As for me, three staff guys bolt in my direction with towels and makeup-remover wipes. Later we trade impressions while sipping a glass of Tropicana in the skybox.

A run of knocks brings me back to reality. This nasty-ass neighbor—a bitch *and* public servant, it's too much—is thumping again. I made her angry with my tall tales of rap concerts, but I don't give a fuck. She can uncross her arms or even call the police, I'll invite them all to dance with me. We'll produce a remake: *Dancing with the Cops.*

Then the ringing of the phone brings me back to earth. It's this brat again who won't stop calling the house to talk to Foued. I always tell her he's sleeping, he's taking a shower, or that he went out even if he's in his room. She's getting on my nerves with all this calling. I don't like her voice and she doesn't bring out anything good in me. She sounds like a little twat who stuffs her bras and who treats her mother like a stupid bitch. I have no faith in her. Sometimes Foued asks me: "Who was on the phone?" And so I swallow my saliva and lie, telling him: "It was city hall" or "My friend Linda." You should always swallow your saliva before you lie, it works much better.

I can't explain why I do that. Maybe I shouldn't, but I can't seem to stop myself. With my little brother, I believe in always doing what's necessary. As far as girls go, there's no rush. For the moment, he has to think about school. He can have girlfriends in the summer when he's far from home, like at summer camp. That way I at least won't know anything about it. Until then, he'll be putting some more software on his hard drive. So for now, the little bitch can keep running her psych tests and screwing with my brother's peace and quiet.

Right now it's tight for him at school. Just last week I was called in by the guidance counselor and things didn't go very well. I don't know, there just wasn't a particular affinity between us. At first I wasn't going to take any advice from anyone. And then I hated how this poor woman in the over-ironed blouse approached the whole thing. She was full of good feelings and ready-made expressions that you find in books, like: "the work of the suburbs," "to change the world," or even "for the poor to thrive." She read me, not without a certain enjoyment, some disciplinary reports from teachers who had excluded Foued from their classes. "Insolent," "violent," "disrespectful" were the three adjectives used most often. I couldn't believe they were talking about my little brother, but on examining some of the reports, I recognized his stamp and had to confess that it was sort of funny.

Student Foued Galbi urinated in the wastepaper bin at the back of the classroom when my back was turned, a disgusting odor invaded my class. I will no longer tolerate this animalistic behavior.

M. Costa, math teacher

Foued G. is a loudmouth. He plays the clown and only thinks of how to amuse the gallery instead of doing his work. He waits for a moment of silence during work with the plan to modify his voice and pronounce vulgar and shameful things like "DICK" or "PENIS." Then the whole class breaks out in laughter and I have to play policeman to calm the ruckus.

Mme Fidel, Spanish teacher

Report from M. Denoyer, earth science teacher:
Foued Galbi threatens me in the middle of class. I quote: "I know where you live, bastard!," "I'm going to punch you in the mouth, bugger, go!"
What's more, yesterday, Wednesday the 16th, hidden in the hallway behind a deceptive post, he called out serious insults toward me, I quote: "Denoyer has an ass face," "Denoyer has a fat ass," "Denoyer, your wife is fat."

Before that, on an exam day, he put a piece of chewing
gum in the classroom door's lock. I couldn't open my
classroom and had to postpone the test. I demand the highest
sanction for the seriousness of the deeds and intentions
of this young person, that is to say at least a disciplinary
committee followed by complete expulsion.

I asked the counselor of this random education if kicking a kid of fifteen out of school because he said his teacher
had a big butt wasn't kind of an extreme decision. She simply
responded that in any case in a few months school would no
longer be compulsory for him and that if he continued on this
path his dismissal would be the final outcome.

I ended the meeting by telling her exactly what she hoped to
hear: I was going to let him have it, that this would never happen again, and within a week, he'll even be an algebra genius.
Promise, swear, spit. Pttthhht.

These teachers, I swear . . . I had the same sort of ball break-
ers who do the job because of the vacation, it's convenient for
them, and it has their favorite time of day—the sacrosanct
coffee break.

I finally got out of that creepy office with the walls covered
in public-service posters and photos of domestic animals. After half an hour in there I had that woman's number. It's crazy
that in the end she's all alone, watching the collapse of one
after another illusion she's created for herself about her job.
So she makes a big show and that's what is noticed. She tries

to convince herself that she's really useful here. She believed it until a few days ago, just before they found Ambroise, the school goldfish she had nourished with love, dead in the back of that slut Madame Rozet, the gym teacher's, locker. With a little luck this poor counselor will be transferred to Sarthe and everything will work out for the best.

When You Love Someone, You Stop Keeping Count

I SEE THE MEN in green who are getting dangerously close to me.

"You're completely screwed! We told you that you should have used one! You're really in deep shit now—"

"All right, I know, don't make it worse, I get it. I'm going to assume responsibility for my stupidity and that's that. It was a mistake, an accident, I wasn't thinking."

"But I hope that you realize that this is some crazy shit. You got into this so idiotically, you even have one on you. All you had to do was use it, that's all! And you don't even have the means to take care of your mistake. What are you going to do?"

"Yeah, okay, thank you, it's already done, stop giving me shit, it's not going to change anything. I'll get myself out of it, it's fine . . ."

The girls are right, I really messed up. It's fucked, too late to take back my slip-up, I'm going to pay the price for my carelessness.

"Transit pass."

I give him my ID card right out so he can give me the fine. It's not worth the trouble to argue, I can already see in his depressed bird face that all exits are blocked.

Linda and Nawel, model citizens, ass-kissers to the system, meekly offer their Navigo cards. They salvage their reputations with girl-next-door smiles that respect the law too.

I surrender and hold out the magnificent green passport that justifies my existence. His sickly bird eyes land on the exotic inscription: PEOPLE'S DEMOCRATIC REPUBLIC OF AL-GERIA. I see that this distresses him, his head spins around, he is distracted, he needs his drops right away.

"Don't you have a document written in French?"

"If you open it you'll see that it's bilingual, your language is inside."

"Don't get cheeky with me or this could go badly, let me remind you that your things are not in order."

All this because I didn't feel like putting their damn purple paper in their fucking machine.

So I shut up because here like everywhere else when you're out of line you keep your mouth shut. I had no desire to spend my afternoon at the station because the cops, well that's another story . . .

The RATP agents break off, happy to do their work as they must, leaving me with this little blue paper that condemns me to pay sixty-two euros. And so I'm obligated to inject this scandalous sum into our drug addict of a state that always needs more. The girls offer to help me pay. I refuse, that just isn't right, but at the same time I notice that they don't really insist either. Then they start telling me about their Valentine's Day evenings, their candlelit dinners, their gifts and other things that you don't normally discuss on a bus, particularly at this hour on a shopping day.

At first I listen to them and participate. Then when they start talking about love, I tune out. While the chicks are trading impressions of their pampered Valentines, I notice a young couple to my right. They're well dressed and smell like perfume. The guy has a little bit of gel in his hair and the girl, she has a little eyeliner under her eyes. They're in a state of osmosis, it's impossible to describe it. It hits me that they love each other, they stare into each other's eyes all the way to the back of their retinas, and seeing them like that, I'd bet they could do it for hours. They touch each other a little, discreetly, they smile at each other. Then he starts kissing her neck and the girl wriggles around like a chicken, it looks like it makes her feel good. The guy plunges into her gorgeous bosom with the air of an orphaned baboon. You would think you were watching an animal documentary.

I was in love once too, but not in public, not like that, at least I don't think so or maybe I don't remember it anymore. That already seems like so long ago . . .

Right now I see couples everywhere. They come out especially when it starts to get nice outside. They go to the parks, the cafés, the movie theaters, and they go on like everything's normal, these places crawling with people in love. Who act as if nothing exists outside of themselves.

In such a state, there's such a tiny part of your lucidity left that a person could do pretty much anything. From my perch and by my count, I'd say we lose at least half of our intellectual capacity, maybe even more.

It's true that if you are stupid in love then you are truly stupid in your grief for a love . . . You spend your time blubbering, you cry until you destroy every last inch of your Kleenex, and then you begin to lose weight, burning some incredible number of calories.

It's wild that sadness is an efficient diet, but it works ten times better than any of these miracle recipes for "How to Lose Weight Before Summer" that stuff all the magazines.

At times like this your people worry like crazy and never stop asking if things are going better—and not just how things are going, like before.

You multiply your consumption of coffee, cigarettes, alcohol, and eventually drugs . . . You take up listening to sad songs and watching weepy films. You need to talk often and find yourself with phone bills ten pages long. Most of all you think only about one thing. At work you're reprimanded almost to the point of being laid off, and it's strange but you'd almost like it to happen. At home, you break dishes, and often enough you unintentionally fuck up the nicest piece in the cupboard, a gift from the family. In front of the mirror you have trouble confronting the tear-puffed face that you've never seen so ugly. And when you're obligated to make some effort, it's all you can do to put a little lipstick on without brimming over completely. At a time like this, you're at the end of your rope, and you can only find the strength to say bluntly to your chatty neighbor who has been breaking your balls since forever, really, that you honestly don't give a shit about her stories of the sick uncle in Brittany or the heat cycles of her cat that are so spectacular even the vet can't do much.

You don't give one shit about this or the rest either.

And then, one merciful morning, you notice that there it is, the load is lighter, you feel better, you sleep through the night, you go out during the day and give yourself the courage to move on.

A little while later, you happen to run into the relevant party in the street. And on this day exactly, you happen to look straight-out awful, and I'm talking about the kind of ugliness that you suffer just once a year. And there you go, that's the day you run into him.

It always happens like that. Nothing like every other way you've imagined this moment, the movie of your meeting that you projected in your head hundreds of times and remade over and over to infinity, running back through without forgetting a single detail. No scenario can possibly resemble this catastrophic reality. You are dressed like a sack, you have dark circles that reach all the way to your cheeks and a haircut fit for an '80s TV series. There you have it, validated theory as true as "the other line always moves faster" or "whatever your neighbor ordered smells better." There it is, no other solution but to run, to avoid him at any cost while pleading with the heavens that he saw nothing.

Me, in order to avoid ever being in that situation, I had myself vaccinated. I swore to myself that in the future I wouldn't trust nice guys, the ones who hold the door open, pay the check, and listen to you when you talk; because all of this is inevitably hiding something. A guy like that, I dodge him like the plague, he'll always be the one who leaves you in the worst state, who crushes your heart and your Kleenex.

He says that he loves you, then shows you the photo of his wife surrounded by kids that he keeps in a special place in his wallet in the middle of all his credit cards.

He says that you're the woman in his life, then brutally leaves you because you're supposedly too good for him. You don't understand a thing until the day when you see him walking around the complex with his ex—well, you're the ex now.

He thinks you're beautiful, intelligent, sweet, and funny, and borrows money from you often—but when you love someone, you stop keeping count. Then one morning, like every other morning, you call him to tell him that you love him but, surprise, the cold, cynical voice of the lady phone operator answers. She lets you know that the number is no longer in service, you will never hear from or speak to him again.

Or then he comes to pick you up at the entrance of your building in his metallic-gray Ford Focus, opens the door for you, asks you if you had a good day, and compliments you on your outfit. You, you feel beautiful, you look at him lovingly and tell him that you're good when you're with him. When you get out of the car he adjusts his balls and burps. You find this repulsive but too bad, you like him too much—you kiffe him. Then he uses the remote car lock, passing it over his shoulder, beep beep. You think this is super–high class, he's glamorous and you like that, and long story short, you love him. He announces that he's taking you out to a restaurant—see, that doesn't happen often. Since you're a Sunday-afternoon made-for-TV-movie addict, you think that he's going to ask you to marry him. But in the middle of your diet salad, he explains that he's met someone else, that she's a really nice chick and that he's going to head off to Grenoble with her. He's packing his bags next week so would you be a sweet girl and bring him back the drill he loaned you and all his Barry White CDs? And while we're at it, can we split the check?

I've cried plenty for guys. I often regret it after the fact when I think about how they are all assholes—and I mean all of them—and that none of them is worth a single one of my tears. At the same time, I cry for just about anything. I'm even capable of crying in front of fool TV shows like where the child finds her mother or the unemployed guy finds a job, that stuff melts me.

The day Auntie Mariatou went into labor not only was I the only white girl in the clinic waiting room, but I was also the only person who cried. The others looked at me sideways, wondering if I was there for the same thing as them. It's like I'm making up for all those years when my eyes were stingy with the tears.

When Mama died I didn't cry. I think I didn't understand what was happening, simple as that.

It was the wedding day for Fat Djamila, a distant cousin who lived in a neighboring village. Mama was in charge of sewing all the outfits for her trousseau. I can still see myself squatted down nearby observing. I could spend hours watching her work, she fascinated me. With her thin, delicate fingers she embroidered the Algerian jacket with gold thread, following precisely and carefully the curves of the design, never going outside the lines, never having to start over. During some long months, she created the seven traditional outfits for a bride. This was no small task: it took plenty of fabric and beads, because the bride in question weighed more than two hundred pounds.

I remember those long afternoons when the village women would talk about nothing but the grand event. Zineb and Samira in particular, the cooks who were always making fun of Djamila, couldn't do anything but jaw on about it.

"You'll see, the day of the wedding, it's going to rain the whole day. You know what they say: if a girl opens her lunch box in the kitchen to snack before mealtime, hiding from her mother, it brings unhappiness and it rains on her wedding day. She had to have done that a bunch of times, you know, since she's fatter than the Belbachirs' cows."

"Yeah, it's true, I wonder if she's going to fit into the dresses that Sakina has killed herself to make . . ."

And then they cackled like chickens. I thought it was kind of nasty on their part and wondered how they could dare to make fun of Djamila so viciously and open their venomous mouths without a second thought when those mouths held only a few rotten teeth. Mama let loose on them and told them that they were just two smug, jealous, bitter old biddies and that God would punish them for saying things like that. In the middle of the yard she yelled: "One morning, you're going to wake up without your tongues, *inchallah*."

I wanted to go to that party so badly I would have done anything. I was only eleven and I begged Mama to take me. But she refused, with no chance for negotiation. I even proposed that I sort her ribbons and all the fabric scraps, clean the barn, milk the cow every morning, go to Aïcha the witch to get back some wool, but there was nothing I could do, I had to take care of my little brother who was still just an infant and also she wouldn't be able to sit with me because she would be too busy dressing the bride. The thing that worried her most, though, was the long trip to the village. "These days the roads aren't safe, the whole country is infested with fake roadblocks, and I don't want something to happen to you."

And nothing could happen to her? I could sense that the climate was tense. I remember that you couldn't listen to music too loudly, especially love songs, and that certain words weren't supposed to be spoken outside of your house. People were afraid all the time, the curtains were taken down from windows and replaced with wire mesh. Uncle Khaled didn't want anyone to step foot outside of our house, not even to buy our *kerentita* ingredients—from then on the traveling vendor no longer came by our house anyway.

The date of the wedding arrived and death struck savagely. It came as a crew, setting its heart on this little village in which, at least once for one evening, joy had reigned. It was a true massacre, no more *youyous*—no more cries of joy, only cries. They killed everyone, even the children, even some babies as small as Foued. And it was not the only village that was razed. So then no one would really celebrate marriages anymore, the people were traumatized by these images of mutilated bodies and blood-drenched baby bottles. I remember having this dream where the dresses that my dear little mama had constructed with so much care were splattered with blood. It was Mama who chose to call me Ahlème. My name means "dream" in Arabic. Mama's dream was to see me have my turn parading in the seven traditional bridal outfits one day. I've never set foot in Algeria again, I don't know whether it's out of fear or something else. I hope that I'll have the strength to return one day, to feel anew the earth of the *bled*, the warmth of the people, and to forget the scent of blood.

Luck Aside

THE BOSS IS TAKING a siesta, me, I'm dreaming of a better life, and students are protesting in the streets of Paris. The local precinct calls the apartment for someone to come get Foued. My little brother hanging with the blueboys, that gave me a shock. At his age if I'd had a simple RATP ticket The Boss would have had an epileptic fit and beaten me enough so that I wouldn't forget it; he taught us to respect authority. Well, he tried anyway.

It has always surprised me, this strange gratitude that The Boss and the other men his age have for their new country. They keep their heads down, pay their rent on time, keep their records clean, not five minutes of unemployment in forty years of work, and after that, they take off their hats, smile, and say: *"Merci, France!"*

I often wonder how The Boss, who considers his pride a vital organ, could lower his head all these years without losing it completely. I'm not about to wake him up to tell him that his only son is down at the five-o, it's not worth it, I let him rest. I watch him sleep and he looks old and tired to me. My poor Boss seems worn out, bled out from having waltzed with his partner the jackhammer without relief, played out from having led this tumultuous tango with "Franssa" for nearly forty years. He doesn't so much as hold a bitter taste in his mouth for all this, but just all this nonsense in his head . . .

Why does Foued have to hand me such a complicated mess? Recently he promised to calm down, to make a little effort at school; he knows perfectly well that he can't fuck around, I thought he understood but, as Auntie Mariatou says, "Just because the snake is still doesn't mean it's a branch."

And now because of this little pissant I'm going to have to set foot in uniform central and that gives me some serious rage.

At the station entrance I run into a familiar face that I had already seen once in an office full of strangers. It's Tonislav, the hot guy with the old leather jacket. Right as I'm heading straight for him, I see him, frowning. I grab his arm as we're passing and, anxious, he jumps.

"You scared me, pretty girl. How's it going?"

"Okay, thanks! And you, Tonislav, things are good?"

"Me, I'm always good. What are you doing here?"

"I have to go find my little brother, he must have been doing some bullshit."

"Ouch! Don't be too hard on him—"

"Yeah, yeah, we'll see soon enough . . . Anyway, I'm so happy to see you—what luck to run into you here!"

"Luck? I'll teach you one thing today: luck doesn't exist —it's for fools."

"Is that right—just for fools?"

"Yeah, but maybe you'd like it if we saw each other not by chance . . ."

He raises an eyebrow and looks at me without blinking. It gets me laughing—him too. His big blue eyes squint and two sweet little dimples write themselves into his cheeks while I see, for the first time, a gold tooth appear that draws attention to itself and mocks all the others. He got to me, this guy. I have to admit he's attractive. I give him my phone number and he slides it, all proud, in his beat-up leather pocket. He's right, I would like to see him again, all luck aside.

I speak to a chubby, perverted cop who looks at my chest like it's my eyes. He reminds me of that zouk singer Franky Vincent, with his thin mustache and his even more lewd attitude. He asks me to be patient and points to the right at a coffee machine, signaling that I'm definitely going to wait longer than five minutes. I could have really used a little shot of espresso but the machine is broken—that would have been too easy. I pace, I turn the other direction, my heels make an unpleasant noise when they hit the tiles. It echoes everywhere and drives me nuts. I end up sitting down. I think about Tonislav and get myself dreaming of love in the middle of a police station lobby.

A crowd of people parades past me. There's a woman who came to lodge a complaint against her boss. In a loud voice she says it was sexual harassment because he put his damn hands on her ass and said: "Bitch! Get me a coffee. Bitch! Make me a copy." It was then that I realized there's a real fucking lack of privacy in a police precinct. Even if you're just waiting for a piece of paper, you hear everyone's stories.

And then I see my brother's friends the brothers Villovitch, handcuffed with a band of smug jakes, and I get that this was a family affair. My brother was arrested for a stinky plan that, as far as I know, he was entirely capable of organizing it, because Foued's real problem is that he's no follower.

Franky shoots me little languorous looks from time to time. I've been waiting well over an hour. I decide to ask him again when it will be possible for me to collect my brother, and then, all cheeky, he confesses with no remorse that he had forgotten why I was there. So after he gives me directions I hurry toward a door and don't bother to guess whether his hungry eyes are following my ass. I'm trying to keep my cool at the max but God knows that it's not easy. There Foued sits, on a bench in a little office that's way too bright. Seeing me walk into the room, he doesn't dare meet my gaze, preferring to lower his eyes. He's ashamed and he should be. My brother is handcuffed to a radiator against the wall and it hurts me like these guys in blue can't even imagine. Starsky and Hutch take me out of the office to run over the story, a big mix-up among the kids at Insurrection, between Foued and his associates and some guys from Yuri Gagarin, the projects next door. According to the cops it was all part of some amateur scam. My little brother and his accomplices resold a bunch of DVDs for one of the guys next door, someone a little older, but they didn't give back the right amount because the other guy didn't want to pay them enough, or some bullshit like that, a dirty trick by some kids who don't understand anything about anything. Then Navarro the TV detective and his whole crew searched Foued's bomber jacket and found a tear-gas bomb, a shard of glass, and a big steak knife. I could have told them that my-self—I turned the whole kitchen upside down looking for that knife.

That said, the idiot squad is right, it could have turned out really badly. One of the kids is in the hospital; according to my brother he has a broken nose and his mouth is super swollen. You'd think he'd been injected with collagen or something.

The little shit in question, I don't let loose on him at all. It isn't that I don't want to—at this precise instant I would like to make a bow tie out of his body. But I can't bring myself to react. I'm too overwhelmed. I gave all of myself to this little Foufou, who used to watch cartoons and drink hot chocolate with me before school, so I don't even have the strength to bend him in half, the little jerk.

I hope that The Boss is still sleeping when we get back.

1st d8

I FIXED MYSELF up for my date. I spent two hours in the bathroom. I put on mascara to lengthen my lashes, a padded bra to round out my chest. I used a blow dryer to straighten my hair, a mask to hydrate my skin, and a prayer to ensure my salvation. I thought about wearing a skirt, but I don't know how to carry myself in those things. I would have to constantly think about keeping my legs crossed when I sat and adjusting my walk if it rides up too high. In the end I opted for jeans, otherwise there's too much to worry about.

Of course I don't forget the final touch and bombard myself with perfume. Objective for the day: remind him of his favorite childhood candy. I went all out, I'm even going to wear high heels. I have a knot in my stomach, I'm hurrying and so I bump into something and then I stop myself for a second and ask myself why I'm doing all this.

On the telephone he told me to meet him at five o'clock in a café on the place d'Italie and then he added that he would be there at 4:45. So I'm clocking in at 4:40.

The café's called Le Balto, like a lot of cafés. Maybe later this place will be "our" café. Maybe, in a few years, we'll remember this day, and we'll reminisce about it with great emotion. Yes, I'm getting carried away, so what? Don't I get to do it at least once?

I settle in and order an espresso. Next to me, a very fat woman with an enormous bun is counting out some two-centimes pieces on the table. "Eighty-eight, ninety, ninety-two, ninety-four, ninety-eight, one hundred two . . . uh . . . oh crap! Shit! Two, four, six, eight . . ." I burn my lips with the boiling coffee while the barman methodically wipes the glasses. He whistles a song I don't recognize and then he starts singing some Brel, and then, that's when things get complicated. I feel the fat woman with the bun getting annoyed and then, all of a sudden, she tosses up into the air all the change that she has been carefully arranging into little piles in front of her.

"Shit, Diego. Sing in silence, you're making me lose my concentration."

"It's my bar, isn't it? I'll sing if I want."

"You're bugging the shit out of me, I'm trying to count."

"You just have to stop drinking, Rita, and you'll see, you'll count more quickly!"

This fat, hysterical woman turns brusquely toward me.

"And you, young lady? Do you count quickly?"

Without leaving me time to come up with my response, she takes all the change by the handful and scatters it on my table. She puts it everywhere, a coin even falls into my cup. Rita plunges two of her fat, bulging fingers into my coffee to salvage part of her fortune. Then I carry out The Big Bun's orders. I conscientiously sort out the change and make the calculation: there is exactly four euros and thirty-eight centimes. Satisfied, the lady gathers the kitty into a plastic Monoprix bag, leaves eight centimes on the table, and throws me a "Keep that, beautiful, you deserve it."

Right then Tonislav pushes open the door. Like a scene from a movie, he enters Balto's in a beam of light, I see everything in slow motion and I even hear music in my head. All the elements are there to make his arrival sensational. He has disheveled hair, a three-day beard on his face, jeans covered in holes, and the battered Perfecto he'll never give up. If with all that I still manage to find him attractive then it's well worth the trouble of spending weeks in the bathroom. I feel a little awkward and superficial now . . .

After that everything goes very fast, he shoots me his romantic poet smile, comes over and kisses me like it's the most natural thing in the world, almost like it's something he does every day, a common thing like tying his laces or lighting up a smoke. You could say he's straight-out direct, this guy, he has me traumatized, in shock, on the spot. Then he installs himself near me on the banquette with an astonishing calm.

I stay wide-eyed for a minute before The Big Bun explodes into a fat laugh that makes me feel like an even bigger fool.

Suddenly it's all too much, I feel feverish. Then I see Tonislav's laughing and I start laughing too and the atmosphere relaxes.

When I tell the girls this story, they'll never believe me because, and I swear on my mother's grave it's true, in normal circumstances I would never let myself be kissed on a first date! And then, holy-son-of-a-baobab-pipe, a guy comes and pops me one on the mouth as if it's no big deal . . . No signing any papers first, no one sent me anything in the mail to warn me, and I was just not ready, not one bit.

So then we talk for hours and I soak up his words like a true beginner. He tells me all sorts of crazy stories and I believe them the way you believe in Santa Claus when you're four. He tells me about his life in Belgrade, when he organized savage dogfights to earn his living when he was a broke teenager, or later, how he taught violin lessons at a school for girls. They must have drooled all over him like little slugs. If I had a teacher that looked like Tonislav, I certainly wouldn't have stopped going to school at sixteen.

In fact he's a great musician, he's played the violin for years, and he learned all by himself, with his father's old instrument, according to what he told me. He stole scores from the national conservatory and managed to get along fine.

What has me completely stumped is that in front of this man I barely know I completely lose my shit, not one point of reference left, content to laugh stupidly at everything he says. What the . . . ? What's happening to me? This isn't me, this dumb bitch with all the makeup who clucks like a chicken in the yard.

The Boss's Honor

TODAY MY FATHER is no longer a man. Our world is collapsing.

The Boss wanted to trim his generous mustache, he miscalculated his stroke, his mind must have been somewhere else, and he messed it up. When I got home I found that imbecile Foued rolling around on the ground laughing his ass off. As for the poor Boss, he was in his bed lying on his back with a piece of his mustache in his hand. Above his lips there remained only a formless patch. He was too pitiful, stretched out like that, you could say he looked like an old cancer patient on his deathbed.

"What happened, Papa?"

"Someone gave me *el aïn*! Someone gave me the evil eye!"

"No, no one gave you the eye, you just shaved wrong, that's all."

"And the other one is over there laughing!"

From the living room we heard the little shit's high-pitched cackles.

"Foued! Shut up! Papa, come here and I'll shave it all, that way it will grow back like new."

"I am no longer a man! My son has more of a mustache than I do. I'm never going outside again and I'm not going to work anymore."

"It's no big deal, your mustache will grow back."

"I've lost my honor! All I had was honor! I carried the flag high! I was proud and looked toward the sky!"

And so he started singing the Algerian national anthem while staring at the ceiling. Then he signaled at me to come closer.

"Me, I prefer the egg on the plate when the white is well cooked and the yolk runs a little, so I can dip my bread into it. I always did that at Slimane's café at the Goutte-d'Or when I first arrived in Paris. There were eggs every day. At that time I had the most attractive mustache in the place, I was proud, you know . . . I want to go back and see Slimane. As soon as I can, I'll go visit him at his café, soon, *inchallah*. But I'll wait for my new mustache. If Slimane sees me like this he'll make fun of me. Slimane smokes at least two packs of Gitanes a day, so he'll light a Gitane and laugh at me, and say: 'Monsieur Moustafa Galbi, without his mustache, he might as well be dead!' Listen to that spoiled ass still laughing, mocking his father, he has no shame! Tell him to shut up or I'll slit his throat, I'll take my Opinel razor and give him the Kabyle smile."

The Boss is sad but, tomorrow, he certainly won't remember the sketch that he gave me about his mustache. And then he'll maybe tell me again about the first time he went to the movies in Paris.

He and his friends Lakhdar and Mohamed got a kick out of sneaking in, entering by the emergency exit in order not to pay for their seats. It was the thing to do back then, it seems. Anyway that's what The Boss said.

He spent all his free time there. He loved American movies, Westerns, Robert Mitchum . . . He would have liked to have been an actor too, or a musician, or something like that. In the '70s he played the guitar for his friends at Slimane's famous café at the Goutte-d'Or and called himself Sam. He had some success, the devil. From time to time, when the mood strikes him, he still sings to himself a little but all that is way in his past now . . .

The next day I woke up tired. I didn't sleep enough because I spent the whole night consoling Linda who had a talk with her boyfriend. This sort of Big Talk always ends in a mess or even a slaughter in certain cases. While they had been together five years and engaged for a couple months, the guy explained to her that he wasn't completely sure of his feelings, that he didn't feel ready to commit. What a dumb move on his part . . . I know Linda, she can be a true witch, and she will make him pay for this one over and over. Sometimes it's better to keep your doubts to yourself and pray that they're just temporary.

Linda has loved Issam since middle school and she sees herself with him for the rest of her life, imagines him the father of her children, has fantasies about his socks and boxers and that she'll wash them by hand with "delicate wash" fabric softener, and especially, up until now, she placed a blind confidence in him. Seems like a mistake to me.

"Fuck this shit! He's crazy, this guy, talking to me like that about commitment. What does he think? I'm a telephone operator? He must have thought he was going out with a phone company like SFR or Bouygues or something to talk to me about commitment like that!"

I think that she still doesn't fully realize it, she's too mad right now.

Linda works at Body Boom, a beauty salon that offers body treatments and hair removal. Since she was a little anxious today a couple of clients complained about her.

She told me that she made one bimbo cry this afternoon. The chick came in to have some hair removed and asked for a Brazilian bikini wax, and Linda, because her mind was somewhere else, she did the job all crooked. This had me rolling because according to Linda it was more like a Nike symbol than a Brazilian wax.

I think she needs to unwind and she's going to benefit from this little couple's hot flash to let herself go some. She even suggested that we take a ride out to the Tropical Club Saturday

75

night. I like it when she talks like that because you can tell that it's going to be a good time. The Tropical Club is a real one-of-a-kind nightclub, there's nothing like it in the world, you have to see it to believe it. When the girls decide it's time to go there it's usually for a good laugh. There you have to forget about the chic, flirty end of the evening. A mass of losers in an exotic-provincial ambiance is a thing to experience at least once in your life. The deejay, Patrick-Romuald, a West Indian guy around thirty with an accent that fell straight out of a palm tree, has the art and the style to give the floor some atmosphere. He intros each piece and never forgets to rally the troops.

"Come on, gentlemen, get up and move your booty. Go find the ladies, now is the time to ask the *chabines* to dance! I'm the emcee tonight, the life of this extraordinary evening, so let me introduce myself: Patrick-Romuald, aka 'the Alligator with teeth sharpened for grabbing *chabine* bumps . . .' Oooh! A little joke from Pointe-à-Pitre, West Indies . . . Good night and I promise you some *frotti-frotta* tonight!"

When you ask Patrick-Romuald why the nights he runs the Tropical Club end at four A.M. instead of six A.M. like most other clubs, he answers with a malicious smile:

"Young ladies, you already know that the parties at the Tropical Club are nothing like 'most other clubs' and if Patrick-Romuald parties end specifically at four A.M. it's simply because anyone who hasn't found a piece to take home by four A.M. is a loser! And anyone who has found someone, after four A.M., well, he wants to do more than dance . . ."

· · ·

Now all we have to do is convince Nawel to unglue herself from Mouss, her leech of a boyfriend, whom I actually like but who's a little sticky-clingy for my taste. Never one without the other, even worse than a couple—they're like a pair of socks.

Mouss, he's THE hot thing in the neighborhood, he's always provoked passions around Insurrection. When he walks by, the girls whip their claws out, rip their panties, break chairs over each other. One smile, one look from him and a crowd of women are at his feet, even more than for Claude François, more than Patrick Sabatier. You have to be brave to take on a guy like that and not be afraid of all the competition. Nawel was tough, she even fought with Sabrina Achour for this guy. And if you know Achour's record and animal physique you can consider Nawel's feat a proof of a great love. I hope she'll be on for the Tropical Club and that she won't play the little woman of the house this Saturday night.

The Gibbon

I SPENT THE AFTERNOON at Auntie Mariatou's house. She gave me braids flat on the top of my head, American style, with strands that cross each other. I ask for this hairstyle often, especially since I saw the clip of Alicia Keys on MTV, the one where she sings for the guy who's in jail while she's playing the piano with her eyes closed. While she's doing my hair we watch a program on TV about a couple torn apart by jealousy, Auntie's comments were so delicious I laughed until it made me tired. The man's name was Tony and his wife was Marjorie. Tony is tall, handsome, muscular, and he loves his mother very much. Marjorie is little, plump, stutters, riddled with complexes, and very, very jealous. She checks her man's cell-phone messages, calls him every five to eight minutes when he goes out with his boys, and when they walk in the street together she never stops watching him to make sure that he doesn't cruise other women, that is the ones who aren't little, plump, stutterers with complexes. If he ever had the misfortune of getting caught looking at a woman, there you'd have it, the drama of the century, a public scandal, a real bloodbath. Then, in the program, each of them tells the camera about their unhappiness, with the tears to prove it.

Auntie was one hundred percent into the program. So when we were watching she was really irritating me and pulling at my head like a savage. I thought she was going to end up scalping me. She spoke to Tony like he was right in front of her.

"But you're crazy for staying with a lunatic like that! She's really sick! Are you a man or not? You let her go, a handsome man like you, tomorrow you leave her, tomorrow you find another woman better than her . . . Ooooh, and then he goes back to her, that's serious . . . He's a victim, this guy, as they say, 'The lizard's tail is tough, the more you cut it the faster it grows.'"

So we were in the middle of an intense, refreshing cultural activity when, all of a sudden, Papa Demba shot into the apartment like an arrow. He charged toward the bookcase in the living room, pounced on the dictionary, and started turning the pages like a wild man. Auntie and me, all surprised, watched him out of the corner of our eyes. He ripped through the dictionary pages with a finger he wet with his tongue, his eyebrows knit together, as if his life depended on the definition he was seeking.

He quickly raised Auntie's sugar levels, irritated enough already, she couldn't stop herself from asking him what he was looking for in his frenetic quest.

"What has you springing on the dictionary like a rabbit on the run? What are you looking for?"

"I'm looking for the word 'gibbon'!" he said, carefully articulating this mysterious word.

"Gibbon?"

"Yes, exactly."

"*Starfoullah!* And why? Where did this fever come from?"

"Just now at the square near the Vitry city hall I was questioned by the police, they verified my papers, as usual, standard operating procedure and all . . . fine, and then, when they let me go, they were snickering to each other and said: 'Go on, gibbon!' I would just like to know what they were talking about because I don't know that word."

"And so, what does it mean?"

"Wait a second, I'm only in the *F*s."

He didn't want to read the definition all the way through. "Species of anthropoid monkey from Asia that has no tail, with a large black face, they climb trees with agility due to their extremely long arms . . ."

Papa Demba closed the French dictionary with a sigh that contained within it not a few other stories like this one.

Then he left the room. And Auntie Mariatou said: "Well there you go. All that fuss for that! For some nonsense like that you got your whole body in a sweat . . . Tell me what you gain from listening to this drivel?"

To which Papa Demba replied from the other side of the apartment: "I gained nothing just like I lost nothing, but I'm used to looking things up, that's all!"

Papa Demba, the gibbon in question, is a math teacher in a high school in Vitry-sur-Seine and he's pulled aside for questioning a little too often if you ask me. When the cops ask him where he's coming from, he responds that he's coming from the high school because he's a teacher. And so then comes the final play where they add: "For sports?"

Auntie Mariatou went to join Papa Demba. "Listen to me! Monsieur Demba N'Diaye, teacher, son of Diénaba N'Diaye and Yahia N'Diaye, you are the glory of the village Mbacké, it is not worthy of you to give importance to a word you learn from a red face in a blue cap! Don't listen to them, those *kou yinkaranto*!"

I love it when she gets up on her high horse. She said all this while holding her hand at her waist and rolling up her boubou with the other. She looked like a character on that comedy show *The Clowns of Abidjan* that Auntie loves to watch. Then she put on some music—Prince so she wouldn't have to change it —and finished doing my hair in some furious rhythm.

I'm at the Café des Histoires now, a little bit beyond Porte de Choisy. I stupidly came here because I liked the name. I set out with my little spiral notebook and installed myself at the back of the room on the banquette, like Linda and Nawel. I ordered an espresso from the nice waitress and borrowed a pen from her. I've never kept a journal because I always thought it was stupid and egocentric. I prefer inventing stories, at least they're fun to reread.

Actually, there are plenty of people who write. Even Linda writes when she's sick of everything. The day when she heard that her boyfriend had cheated on her, she wrote at least fifteen pages, it was called "The Travels of a Vicious Cuckold." She was touched by a real delirium that day, I was actually worried about her. Then she tore the pages to pieces and never spoke about it again. If I ever brought that up to her I think she would be ashamed.

The nice waitress, whose name is Josiane, brought me my espresso with the kind of smile that makes you want to come back even if the coffee is disgusting. Curious, she asked me what I was writing with such an air of concentration. So I invented a whole life for myself, I imagined I was someone important, to see what that would make me in the eyes of a person I didn't know. I just wanted to know what kind of feeling it would stir in others and I decided that Josiane would be my guinea pig for this idiotic exercise.

"Are you doing homework?"

"No, not at all."

"Ah. So what are you writing then?"

"I write stories that are published every week in a magazine."

"Really? Wow, that's cool . . . What sort of stories? Love stories? Stories about crimes of passion? Because I love reading, I know all the books of Pierre Bellemare practically by heart . . . And also every Wednesday I buy *Detective,* I don't know if you know it but it's full of sordid stories, assassinations, rapes, children shut up in closets. If you want to give them a peek there are the last ten issues over on the bar. My boss wants me to take them away because he says they give our customers bad ideas, but people ask for them, they like them so much. And like I say, the ones you find leaning at the bar here are often the ones who don't have much to say, and they give them something to talk about. Don't you think?"

"Yes, miss, you're certainly right about that—"

"Oh but you can call me Josiane! My name's Josiane Vittani and I've been working here for at least ten years. Everyone knows me around here."

"I'm Stephanie Jacquet, but I sign all my articles Jacqueline Stephanet, just to keep myself anonymous."

"Delighted, Stephanie," she said as she gave me her hand covered in rings.

"Pleased to meet you, Josiane!"

"So if it's not love stories or crime stories, what is it?"

"They're more like social stories, I'd say. Stories about people who struggle sometimes because society hasn't given them the choice, who try to pull themselves through and find a little bit of happiness."

"And people find that interesting?"

Good question, Josiane. I hope so, deep down, but all the same I should have told you that I wrote love stories, of obsession and betrayal. It's safe to assume that interests people. But the story I want to write looks something like this:

It would be 1960, on a beautiful, sunny afternoon. A MAN would come looking for a WOMAN. They would have a date.

While he would be in the middle of parking his Vespa below her house, she would be watching him from the bathroom window and saying quietly: "Oh, he's so handsome." She would powder the tip of her nose one last time before going down to join him. He would be thrilled to see her, she would have missed him enormously these past days and you'd notice a stain on his jeans. Then they would kiss fervently. Then they would both get on the Vespa and take to the road. A light breeze would caress their faces and they would tell each other about the grandeur of their love.

Arriving at the roundabout at the shopping center, ANOTHER MAN would suddenly intercept them. In his hard face you would know right away that he was the villain in the story. He would say something like: "Hey! You two! Stop!" Then the young WOMAN would get worried all of a sudden and say something like: "Oh shit! Fuck! It's my asshole brother!" At that point a terrible brawl would break out between the brother and the MAN, all hits would be allowed, dirty punches, sucker punches, Trafalgar punches—punches that will have unknown consequences for years to come . . .

The brother suddenly takes the MAN by the neck and
says: "Listen to me good, coward, this·is the last time
I'm going to see you running around with my sister, you
understand?" And then he would turn to his poor sister:
"And you little slut! I don't want you going out ever again
with a guy like that—black, illegal, Muslim, orphaned,
unemployed, with a record! Otherwise I'll kill you, you little
whore." Then she would try to defend herself: "But I love
him!" And the brother, pigheaded, would reply: "I don't
give a shit!" So the two lovers would be separated by the
villain-brother, a militant member of the National Front, but
the lovesick and valiant MAN would swear to return to his
beautiful girl . . .

The moral of the story, it has to be truly sappy, is that this
sort of love has no color, no religion, no social security number . . . I'm deep in my own world and it's very nice. Josiane
offers me an espresso and invites me back whenever I want. I
think that the Café des Histoires will become my regular spot.
I'll come back with my little notebook, stolen from the Leclerc
store down the avenue, or with my friends, or with Tonislav if
he decides to call me again. I would never have believed that I
would fall for an illegal Yugo with a gold-capped tooth.

There's No Point in Running
if You're Chasing a Cheetah

"WHERE ARE YOU GOING now?"

"Out."

"Don't mess with me, I can see that you're going out, so stop trying to be slick. Answer my question, Foued, where are you going?"

"I'm going to the basement to play video games with everyone. I'll be back in half an hour . . ."

"Who's everyone?"

"Shit, you're annoying. Everyone is the same as always: Abdoullah, Bensaïd, Hassan, and the brothers Villo, Nikolas and Tomas. I don't understand why you have to play the big heavy, the boys don't report to anyone—"

"I already told you that I don't like it when you hang out with them, they make you hateful, it's a bad crew, they're idiots and you're getting worse than them—"

"Their mothers say the same things about me."

"Fine, go, get lost, and I hope that it's not to go watch your porn DVD, you band of dirty little thugs."

"Whatever, I don't need to go to the basement for that, I have a TV in my room—"

"Ahhh! Get out, move it! Go on, get out! Don't tell me the story of your life, you little pig. You think that you can spread your wings because you're sixteen? Don't forget that you pissed the bed until you were eight and eight is only half of sixteen! And don't forget either who cleaned your little piss-covered swizzle stick back then!"

Around then he galloped across the apartment hallway like a crazy person, stuck on his sneakers, letting his mocking laugh ring out. The shit pellet is getting his jollies at the idea that he could have made me sick of him and runs off carrying his soccer and combat games under his arms. All the same there's no risk that I'll get tired of my only brother whom I raised since he was just a baby. On the other hand, the more he grows, the more I want to slap him every morning, the *chétane*. And he plays it close to the wire because he's completely aware of his powers of seduction. It's true that Foued is a very attractive kid, he has nice skin that doesn't get shiny, black mischievous eyes, nice teeth, a reasonably toned body for his age, and his golden rule, summer and winter, hair shorn almost to a shave. And if I ask him why he doesn't let it grow out a little he says to me:

"If I let my hair grow, it'll look nasty. With my frizzy Arab hair, it would be like I had a carpet on my skull. It's for street cred."

When he turned sixteen I let him pierce his ear but he had to earn it. He wanted it, that's for sure. When he came back to it a little later he had improved his grades at school and sometimes even did the dishes for me.

"You want me to dry, Ahlème?"

"Ahlème who?"

"Ahlème the sister I love with all my heart."

"What else . . . ?"

"The most wonderful, the most intelligent, and the hottest chick in all of Insurrection."

"Good, that's enough, not bad but I think you went a little too far this round, you degraded yourself. You shoved your pride way down deep into your ass, I can see that you really want this piercing don't you?"

"Yeah, I want it and I'm going to have it, no matter what happens!"

"You must be pretty sure of yourself to say that—"

"I mean, if my dear sister says I can do it, of course."

"There, I like that better."

So I ended up agreeing. Against my will, of course, but I agreed. All the same he deserved to be rewarded for all his work. The day that he came home with a diamond in his ear, I took it hard, I admit. I had a hard time swallowing it. It bothers me that my little brother looks like all those R&B singers and, honestly, less masculine than me.

But then I didn't give in on everything. Foued wanted to go to Leclerc together and have me buy him a blond rinse—L'Oréal Excellence Crème. That one, my good man, is out of the question. I would rather he tattoo a scorpion on his abs like Joey Starr, that would be less traumatizing.

He does take care of himself, the little idiot. Mornings are hell, he has a whole ritual, he races to the bathroom. He spends hours in there. He wastes all his pocket money and his school money on clothes and creams. I tell him all the time that it's shameful for a boy his age. My brother's generation, it's the "G" generation, which in their lingo means a fine thing, a tight guy . . . And not only is Foued a real, clean G but he also only hangs with G's. Their slogan is: "G or nothing." And when they pass by girls, the *djoufs* as they call them, they make like peacocks and the girls go into raptures in front of them: "Aww, look at the boys, look at the tenda G's!" which does nothing but inflate their already abnormally overdeveloped narcissism.

My brother is so bigheaded that sometimes I could really thump him. His tango with the blond rinse, I found the whole thing a little too much. Under the influence of the pop-psych books Nawel lends me now and then, I even told him that if he didn't know who he was anymore he could ask himself some questions about what felt out of whack and we could talk about it. He answered me, laughing: "Don't worry, I'm not gay, is that what you think?"

Bleached hair has been the style for a few years. As summer nears you see all these blond heads rise up from nowhere, a wave of little chicks walking around the neighborhood. That can make a style "fresh-groovy-smooth-now," but it can also scare little children too. It cuts both ways. I'm afraid that Foued will wreak havoc later. He's my little brother, it was me who raised him, but I think that he will be a real bastard with the ladies. I can tell. The phone rings a lot more these days and I regularly hear the voices of the little honeys who want to speak to him.

Today, despite myself, I had to referee a ping-pong match, a real pro event, like the ones with the super-quick Chinese who play so fast that you have trouble following the ball. Two chicks called one after the other, it felt like the words passed each other, except that Foued wasn't there right then. I cracked fast enough when one of the two took the liberty of telling me her life story and I sent her packing. I was cold, it's true, but at the same time she had some serious nerve.

"Excuse me, it's Eva again, I already called just now for—"

"Yes, I remember that you already called, you're not teaching me anything there. What do you want now?"

"Uh . . . I wanted to know if Foued came back yet or not?"

"You called no less than ten minutes ago and I told you that he would be back in around half an hour, true or false?"

"Uh . . . true."

"So if you know how to count to thirty, he'll be back in

about twenty minutes, so please be a good girl and stop calling because it's really starting to bug me."

"You his sister?"

"Yes, exactly, his sister, not his secretary."

"Does a girl named Vanessa also call your house?"

"Am I asking you questions? We don't know each other, I'm not your friend, I am not even your age! Did I ask you the color of your underwear? There is no Vanessa who calls here and soon there won't be an Eva either."

"There's no reason to talk to me like that, I won't call anymore."

"Great news. Bye."

I had forgotten how painful it was to be sixteen. The second honey called a few minutes later. Her name was, in fact, Vanessa. It's a good name for a little breezy. I didn't even let her have the time to introduce herself before I hung up.

I'm taking advantage of Foued's absence to clean up his bedroom a little bit because he doesn't really appreciate my intrusions into his "sector," as he calls his room. Fatal error. Tell me about the mess in your room and I will tell you who you are. And so I can tell you that Foued is a little oblivious fuckhead. Just thinking that I would clean up the cracked drawer filled with useless things, I find packages of multicolored condoms. I see that the Monsieur denies himself nothing. Getting ready to sort through the clothes all jumbled in the closet, I take out three big trash bags filled with women's handbags—Lancaster, Vuitton, Lancel—and as I go past them . . . I find a shoe box under the bed with bundles of bills. Not two bills, not three, not ten, not twenty or more. Bundles.

I can't even believe it when I discover all this. I'm crushed. It's impossible that this is his. But yes, it has to be his.

The first idea that comes to me is to take it all, put it in the toilet, and pull our old friend the flusher. As for the bags, I would burn them in the empty lot behind the hill. But this sort of nonsense is vigilante justice, the kind you see in moralist American movies where honesty wins out over everything. Only here, it's real life, and in real life I don't really want my little brother to shoot himself. So I don't touch anything without knowing more.

I prepared something for The Boss to eat, read him the newspaper, listened to him talk about the endless domino games he played at Lakhdar when he lived on the rue des Martyrs. The Boss was very good, he won every round, every time he had the best combinations. The others envied him, especially Abdelhamid, who always tried to figure it out: "But Moustafa, how in the devil do you beat your opponent and win all the points? Maybe you have a special technique that you don't want to share with us? Or maybe you put a spell on the domino games at Lakhdar?" Nothing of the sort. The Boss's only technique was to trust in luck. Someday I would like to succeed in following this life philosophy, only, too bad for me, I don't believe in luck, or trust either. Today I don't believe in much. I believe in Allah who is my only guide and in public aid too, thanks to which I survive.

The Boss is finally sleeping. Everything is almost getting peaceful again.

Foued's been gone for nearly four hours, not "half an hour" like he promised before he went down to the basement. Though now I'm not at all sure that he really went down to the basement, I'm no longer certain of anything to tell the truth.

He came into the apartment, playing cool, whistling the tune from some ad for pickles that runs all the time lately. He doesn't know what's waiting for him, the poor thing, I'm going to fry him up like a sausage. Sitting on his bed in the shadows, I watch him come in.

"Ahlème! Ahlème! Where are you? Is The Boss sleeping?"

He moves into his room, feeling his way in the dark and pressing the light switch. He jumps, surprised to see me there.

"Fuck! I nearly shit myself! You scared me! What happened? Why are you kicking around here in the dark?"

I say nothing in reply, just look at him. I want to rise up and annihilate him.

"Answer! What are you on? It's like you're possessed! *Naâl chétane.*"

I stand up, grab him by the neck, flatten him against the wall, and then shake him wildly like I have a rag doll in front of me.

"You little shit! Where does it come from—all the crap I found in your room?"

"What are you talking about? Let go of me! You're sick!"

"I'm not letting go! And stop fucking around with me! You want me to choke you? You know exactly what I'm talking about, asshole. The paper in the shoe box, the handbags in the closet! And the jimmies in the drawer, what's all that?"

Caught off-guard, he violently pushes me away. I lose my balance and find myself back on his bed. I stand up again and throw myself at him even harder. The energy with which I catch him by the throat shocks even me. I squeeze his neck and start wailing with rage.

"I asked you where it came from! Answer me before I kill you! Answer me!"

"Stop! Please stop! You're hurting me—"

"And me? You think that I'm just all right? I kill myself for you, I did everything for you!"

"I can't breathe, let go—"

The Boss is awake. His voice drags me out of my mania.

"I can't sleep. Turn off the television!"

"Go to sleep, Papa! It's fine, don't worry, the TV's off."

I take Foued by the shoulders and push him so he's sitting on his bed. He touches his neck like he's trying to make sure it's still there, that his head is still really attached to his body. I must have gone at him pretty hard, he's all red and his eyes are popping out of his head.

"It's not worth getting all bent, I'm going to tell you. The money's not mine. It's the big dogs', I'm holding it for them, that's all . . . I swear to you it's not mine, I swear—"

"You're holding it for them?"

"Yeah, I'm holding it for them. They pass it to me to keep

for a few days and afterward they come pick it up and in exchange they slip me an ace, leave me fifty euros or something like that—"

"Are you joking? What about the bags?"

"That's one of the bigs who trusted us with a little deal, that's all."

I sit down near him—if I stay standing up much longer I'm going to die.

"What do you mean, 'deal'? And who are they, these bigs?"

"It means that they give us some stuff and we have to clear it out, so we sell it and there you go. Then at the end they give us some cash. It's like that."

"Like with the DVDs?"

"Yeah—"

"Yeah . . . That's all you say . . . Last time didn't teach you a lesson? I swear you're completely oblivious! Did you think about the cops? What would happen if you got picked up? They'd want to come and do a search of the house. What did you think, my friend? The big guys are bastards, they'll use you as a cover, you understand? You want The Boss to have a heart attack when the cops come here, is that it? And me too, while we're at it? Fuck . . . I want to kill you! What do you want?"

"It's nothing, it's fine. And the big dogs, you don't know them. Don't call them bastards, you're judging them when you don't even know them!"

"Who are they? What are their names?"

"You don't know them, let it go!"

"Names, I said! Spit them out!"

"Champs, Cockroach, Poison, the Vif, Lépreux, Magnum are the bigs you don't know . . . It's a family, that's the ghetto."

"They're your family, you dog? Say it to me again, you asshole!"

"Stop crying, please—"

"It's the only thing left for me to do, blubber like a fool, I'm going crazy . . . But think about it a little would you? Did it ever occur to you to use what God put in your head disguised as a brain? You thought that I would never notice anything?"

"Fuck, what about me? You don't think there are times when I want to cry too? Even if I act like there's nothing wrong, it's only because I don't want you to worry about me, that's all. Just because I eat and sleep doesn't mean everything's okay. That's the street, that's how it is. I'm not the only one, and me, I'm nothing compared to the others—"

"You're not the others! I don't give a shit about the others!"

"You think I'm not tired of watching you work like a dog? Always running to scratch up some money here or there. The clothes I wear, I lied to you, no one gave them to me, the TV in my room, I didn't really borrow it, and the game console isn't Jimmy's, it's mine. All of it is mine. I bought it with *my* money—"

"You're not ashamed?"

"No, I'm not ashamed! You have to figure out how to make it, everyone does it here. You don't see. You think that you know everything but you don't know anything! You're just a chick, anyway, so it's not the same."

"That has nothing to do with it!"

"It's got plenty to do with it! You don't understand, it's like the jungle! It's eat or be eaten, fuck or get fucked. The ones on top, the chiefs, those are the lions and us, down here, we're the hyenas, we only get the leftovers—"

"SHUT YOUR MOUTH! IT'S NOT TRUE! STOP! Was it those big dogs who put this bullshit in your head? And you swallow all their programming like a chump! Just because they fucked up their lives they have to fuck up other kids'. They want you to believe that it's already a lost cause, the bastards! We have to fight twice as hard as others, that's the truth! I know that, so stop thinking that you're going to teach me about life! Who do you take me for? I thought you wouldn't be like the others . . . And school? What's school for?"

"Stop it already, you know well enough that it's useless. Even you quit when you were sixteen, so don't try to teach me that lesson. The bigs, even the ones who went to school, they don't have jobs anyway."

"Do you want to end up in the *habs* or what? If you keep going and that's your goal, you're going to end up achieving it, you'll have your place in the joint, don't you worry. What do you think I'm doing all the time? Huh? I'm working my ass off, I'm making it work. Your way is too easy. You're weak. Your money is dirty. You're going to take back all this crap. You're going to give back the cash and tell the big dogs that you don't want to work like that. If you don't do it yourself,

I'll go find them and tell them. You hear me? You know me and you know that I'm capable of going to see them, I've got balls, right, but it'll ride better for you if you go yourself!"

"I can't do that, I can't—"

"You're going to do it! This isn't open for negotiation!"

"It's going to cause me some trouble!"

"You're going to have bigger trouble if you don't do it. And the jimmies? What the hell's wrong with you?"

"That's something else, and it's my life. If you had a guy I wouldn't say anything to you!"

"Let me point out I'm not the same age as you. You're still a dirty little brat, nothing but a little piece of shit! You want to knock up one of your little hoochies? Is that what you're after?"

"I'm careful."

"Yeah, right . . . With all the dirty bills you should have at least bought yourself a cell, so your little honeys would stop driving me crazy calling here."

"I already have one."

"Oh yeah, breaking news . . . That's the best yet. Great! You really take me for a complete nucker! I'm outta here, I can't look at you anymore. I'd better go to my room. I would never have believed it, I can't even stand the sight of my own brother anymore—"

"Stop acting like you're my mother! You're not my mother!"

"SHUT YOUR MOUTH! SHUT IT!"

Then I couldn't stop myself from giving him the pounding of his life, the final blow, the ultimate bolo. I slapped with all my soul, used the last of my strength. I nearly took his cap off, a little more and his head would have just flown right off.

I can't look him in the eyes anymore. I stand up and go into my room, beside myself. I lie on my bed without even bothering to put on my pajamas, hoping to fall asleep fast and for a really long time.

Then an IAM song jumps into my head, one I used to listen to on a loop maybe ten years ago:

Little brother left the playground, he's just learning to walk and wants the ogre's magic seven-league boots. Little brother wants to grow up fast, but he forgot that there's no point in running. Little brother . . .

Yeah, there's no point in running, "especially when you're trying to catch a cheetah . . . ," as my dear Auntie Mariatou would say.

Tales from Below

I WENT TO AUNTIE'S house, beaten. I felt like a worn-out rag used for mopping the floor. I told her the whole story, crying, I was in a truly sorry state. She made me a coffee with the percolator that Papa Demba gave her for her birthday — since the acquisition of this machine she makes coffees all day long. She told me to calm down, take a minute to breathe a little, because she said I looked like a Kenyan at the end of a marathon.

Everything I told Auntie about the fight seemed to dumbfound her, she could hardly believe it. At one point I even suggested sending Foued to the *bled* so he could chill, but clearly this was a ridiculous idea.

"It's no good, he doesn't know that country, he shouldn't

discover it for the first time as part of some punishment. Even you haven't set foot there for at least ten years, right?"

"Yeah . . . You're right. I don't know what to do anymore. At the beginning I told myself all his bullshit was normal. It's not all that serious, it's just the age. But now he's already chasing after money. I don't understand it at all."

"If he keeps it up and gets caught by the police, they're not going to do him any favors, he's grown up now. You heard about the double penalties?"

"I know, Auntie. It bugs me because he doesn't get it. He doesn't see what he's diving into. He loves the take-home too much."

"He got caught in a vicious circle, that's all, what can you do? You can't let go of him. Get behind him. Talk to him."

"He's not stupid. He's a good guy, my brother, but he wants to be big, he wants to be rich. Sure, I'll talk a pretty game, but I won't be able to do anything. The more he has, the more he wants."

"As we say in Africa, 'money calls for money.'"

"I hear you . . ."

"Money calls money but the rich call the police."

So she managed to break me down. Just then her daughter, Wandé, came into the living room carrying her little school notebook in her arms, which she'd wrapped carefully in craft paper.

"Ahlème, can you please help me with my French homework? I'm having trouble with the calculations—"

Auntie jumped right in, I wasn't in any kind of state . . .

"Go do your homework by yourself in your room, and figure it out! You think we don't have enough problems out here so you should bring us some more?"

The whole rest of the evening, Auntie Mariatou tried to dissuade me from going down to the bottom of the building to talk to the big dogs. I didn't see much point in standing around with my arms crossed waiting for it to rain, but at the same time she wasn't wrong, it wouldn't be a good thing to walk into.

All calmed down, I thank dear Auntie for always being there for me and I leave. I'm like a bag lady with my cheap flip-flops and my light robe, my pajamas torn at the thigh. I have a horrible headache. My eyes are red and swollen, I feel like I drank gallons of alcohol. I feel like a walking hangover.

Of course, instead of going back to my house, I went downstairs.

I went directly to block 30, the most high-risk spot in the neighborhood, the place where people are usually afraid to go out, the place where even the special anticrime brigade dreads going when they have to train someone.

I take a hesitant step into the poorly lit hall. There are three guys leaning their backs against the wall. I stand petrified for a few seconds in front of them, not knowing what to say to them or at least not knowing how to begin. The slight odor of shit is already starting to suffocate me and, mixed with the open Dumpsters, I'm afraid it's going to make me puke. The first gentleman, the one whose head is just below the inscription FUCK SARKO, speaks to me:

"What are you looking for? What are you doing here?"

"I'm looking for some people."

"What do you want?"

"It's for my little brother."

"Who's your little brother?"

"His name's Foued."

"Oh yeah, the little Orphan Arab?"

"His name is Foued."

"Who do you want to see?"

"Magnum, Lépreux, Cockroach, and I don't know who else . . ."

He's bizarre, this guy, he seems high and he looks me up and down in a funny way. I don't know what made me rush down here at this late hour, they're going to think that I came looking for something shady.

Then one of the guys at the pulls back his hood and comes toward me. The moment he gets into the nasty neon light, I recognize Didier, the ice cream maker's son, a boy I grew up with, I cheated at school with, who stole with me at the supermarket, who slipped me my first tongue kiss, even. I'm dumbstruck. He seems stunned too.

"No way! Back from the past! Ahlème, the Bomb! What the hell are you doing here?"

"And you, what the hell are you doing here? I haven't seen you for years and years."

"I was doing some time . . ."

What happened to me out there was a like a bad scene from a TV movie, but it went down exactly like that. So then he slipped me a kiss full of fraternity and good memories. It all got so sweet that I didn't know how to bring up the problem anymore.

"You know this *djouf*, Cockroach?"

"Yeah yeah, I know her, don't worry."

As if it wasn't obvious. And I hate it when people talk about me in the third person when I'm standing right there.

"So you're the one they call Cockroach?"

"Yeah."

He lowers his head, a little embarrassed.

"Crazy . . . and when people call you Cockroach you respond?"

"Well yeah . . . I don't know."

"Where does that nickname come from?"

He starts laughing and the other guys crack up too. One of them asks for some rolling papers from Didier. He gets them out of his pocket and gives them to the guy, a little ashamed in front of me.

"Cockroach, it's a trip you know, they've been calling me that for a long time . . . Because these bastards here, one day, they were giving me shit and there was a little cockroach that crawled out of my jacket, right. It's like that in the apartments around here . . . ever since they stopped sending the guys who do their thing with the spray, they're all over. And afterward, there you go, it just kept on from there . . . But that doesn't mean that I have bugs in my pockets, and I'm not dirty either, it's just a joke . . . They've got ghetto names too: he's Stray Dog and that one over there, that's Escobar."

"Escobar? After Pablo Escobar?"

"Yeah, that's right, like that . . . His real name's Alain, the great myth!" he says, laughing. "You know that fucker is a legend! Alain my brother!"

"Fuck you, asshole, you're nothing but a dirty dog, and your name is Didier!" answers the other guy straight off.

"Yeah but Alain is worse! And your mother's name is Bertha!"

"Shut your mouth, I didn't say anything about your mother, let it be—"

"He's right, it's worse! It's true!"

The other guy who was quiet up until then can't resist his turn.

"Don't even talk, Mouloud, Moulud the Grinder, with your grocery-store name."

"I'm going to fuck you up."

"No, I'm going to fuck you up—"

"Uh . . . excuse me, Didier, can I speak to you about something?"

We stepped outside so we could get away. I didn't have a jacket, I shivered a little.

"You don't have to be scared, what is it?"

"I'm not scared."

Tonight it's not Cockroach I'm talking to but Didier. In simple words I explain the situation that's got me angry and indignant. I tell him all my worries and fears, I tell him how my brother and me, we keep hopping from one foot to the other in this *bled*, because we have to be careful, we weren't

105

born here. He must have heard talk about people getting expelled. What I was telling him was the real story, no legend. If Foued didn't keep quiet from now on the cops would be merciless with him. And my big speech, it wasn't just for my brother. I asked Didier and his boys to stop ruining the kids' lives like they ruined their own. I know that I'm not going to change the system, it's bizness and everything, but Foued's only sixteen. Shit.

Didier's not a bad guy. He's done some low-down shit, that's for sure, but the really bad guys don't hang out in the hall at number 30. The real villains, sitting in their comfortable armchairs, decide *who* is going to troll the halls at number 30. They're the ones who can decide to chuck a guy like Foued out of France for any little thing. Didier, he can understand that. He had wishes, dreams, those kinds of things . . . He probably doesn't even remember having told me, but he wanted to have a boat, one with white sails, ever since the time when his father gave us Italian ices behind the backs of all the other kids. Only Didier, he thought he could never sail a boat because in Ivry there's no ocean.

When we start to break it down, I notice that he is in all the schemes that my brother was mixed up with. He apologizes, swears on his mother's head that he's sorry, promises me that he didn't know that Foued was my brother. I wonder if he isn't just talking out of his ass, maybe it's just the spliff that he's smoking that's making him say all that. But I believe at heart, he's sincere.

"We'll keep him at a distance, your little brother, you're right. I guarantee it, and I'll be paying attention. Everyone around here knows who I am, and don't worry, they'll listen. Cockroach, he's not just anybody. And if you need me, I'll be there. I'll watch over him, I swear to you on the life of my race, I give you my word, Ahlème. No one will give him shit, no one will mix him up in the business. Sorry. I didn't know that you were the little Orphan's sister—"

"And stop calling him the little Orphan, he has a name."

"All right, that's out of bounds . . . Okay. Sorry."

I leave, dying of cold. We agreed that I'd come back tomorrow at the same time and bring Didier the money and all the shit that was lying around my house. I thank him warmly and I thank God too, I thank him for having to do business with Didier rather than the other shady rat who calls himself Escobar, because that guy, he was liable to ask me to give him a favor in return, something disgusting in exchange for letting Foued safely out of the business. I was ready to do anything for my brother, even the worst, so I'm happy not to have to face that.

The Breathless One

THE TELEPHONE RANG. I picked it up and right away I recognized Tonislav's voice. His simple "hello" seemed like a spell to me, or even better, a blessing. He asked to meet for a date at Châtelet–Les Halles at the foot of the fountain, at Carrée square. For the first time in my life, I understood what it could mean to "need someone." Why him in particular? I have no idea at all. I am completely turned upside down, my heart beats ten thousand times an hour just at the thought of seeing him. My knees wobble, I feel like I'm a clueless teenager going on her first date. I must be a pitiful thing to see.

On my way to meet him, sitting in my RER, I tell myself that I'll be bold when I see him.

I give myself the goal of greeting him with a kiss and asking him the favor of holding me hard in his arms, even at the risk of traumatizing him and having him not call me ever again. Today, without really understanding why, I just want to abandon myself to the sort of thing that I usually think is too sappy. I will let him discover all the weaknesses that I kill myself to hide from the whole world, and from myself most of all. And too bad if he freaks. That would just tell me that he's a jerk like all the others and he's not worth the trouble in the end. This time I'm not all tricked out. I'm just me and I don't give a shit about the rest.

At Carrée square I sit down on the steps near the fountain, I'm on time but I don't see him.

There's a crowd here. It feels funny to be here in the middle of all this activity that I can watch as if I'm not even there. I look at the people passing by, running, just hanging around. I have the strange feeling that they're all happy except me. You could say that they live, thrive, dangle their joy in front of me on their faces without a lick of shame. Of course I know it's wrong but at this exact moment I'm having trouble convincing myself. It's like all these people had piles of dreams that I was denied. There they are strolling around, taunting me. I know what they're trying to do, they want to make me crazy with rage. And, well, they succeeded.

At this moment I feel like I've lost a game of dice. You throw the dice on the rug dozens of times believing so strongly in each toss. You imagine yourself already stopped at the glorious number six, but it's no good, the score is always low. One, two, or three at the most, never more. You shake them well in the small of your hands, blow on them, close your eyes and whisper a prayer, always nothing. I think at the end of enough setbacks, you have the right to be discouraged.

I feel like a little kid being punished. I am in the corner of Carrée square and I'm hoping for just one thing: to see a stranger arrive and to huddle myself into his arms. I am in a complete fever, it's really some kind of crazy shit.

A group of Mexican musicians set up their equipment on the square. They started messing around with their foot pedals while finishing up their last little adjustments. They're laid out a few feet from me and they're mad funny with their gigantic sombreros. I thought listening to them would let me distract myself a little. I didn't have any trouble guessing what they would start playing. In general, it always starts with "Guantanamera." As soon as they let out those first notes, I recognize the tune and tell myself: won, that wasn't hard to figure out. A few happy people are gathered around and partially block my view, while I'm getting impatient waiting for a nasty character who is incredibly desirable . . .

The worst is that I can't get hold of him because he doesn't have a phone. Every time he called me it was from a telephone booth. It's too horrible to have no control. This guy doesn't even know it but he holds all the strings for my marionette. I have no mercy for latecomers usually, but him, I'll wait for him. More than once to give myself courage I tell myself: "Fine, go, I'm getting out of here, I'm no victim waiting thirty years for a guy I barely know, this pisses me off!" But for all that, I don't get up. I stay planted there like a sad rusty nail. And during this whole painful wait, I can't count how many guys, including boys who haven't even hit eighteen, came to hit on me, asked me for a light, told me I was charming, asked me if I had a minute to let them get to know me . . .

With a cynicism that comes from the depth of my guts, I tell them: "I don't have a light, I'm sexy on the outside but inside I have AIDS, you still interested?" and also "If you think you can get to know me in a minute, I must not seem all that interesting . . ."

And then there it is, I see a familiar silhouette from afar, wandering in the middle of the crowd. He's running. He was just a little late, after all, a good hour anyway . . . I start to seriously worry about myself in this whole scenario, not only did I stay here, alone, waiting nearly an hour in total turmoil, but on seeing him arrive I didn't even want to scream at him or make a scene. I only want him to wrap me up in his arms with all the passion in the world. Maybe I've seen too many TV movies but I don't care, I'm grabbing on to him and I've decided that I don't want to let go. He comes closer and in one jump I get up like a starving person you're holding a chunk of bread out for and I walk in his direction thinking of all the most beautiful wedding-march scenes in the movies. In truth, this guy could be a hustler with no kind of conscience, an assassin, a rapist, a slasher, or a guy who carves up his victims to steal their kidneys and sell them on the Internet . . . And me,

I continue walking toward him, a smile on my lips, my arms spread, and my heart in my hands. Then, just at this minute, I realize for the first time: "I'm in love with this stranger, he can make jelly out of me."

Before I even had to make the first move, he surrounds me in his reassuring arms and squeezes me hard, not too much, and not just enough, just hard, like I imagined. He smells like musk, his hair's flattened in the back, a single strand falls on his forehead and then there's his breath that I feel in his neck . . . all that sets my head spinning. You could say that he knows exactly what I've been waiting for from him.

The afternoon we spent together was surreal. If he hadn't needed to leave, I would have even spent the evening with him, maybe the night, or even my whole life. He read the lines in my hand, invented a life for me. In my opinion he doesn't know how to read palms, or even the lines in your feet. But I let him keep going anyway, it was nice, it tickled my palm.

And then just before we were about to part, he took off his old chain and put it around my neck. I kissed him with all of my one hundred percent sincerity to thank him for the gift. Afterward, he told me that I was a princess and that it was right for a princess to be treated like one.

It was very smooth but in my head all I could manage to think was: "You're very sweet, my man, but could you tell that to the slut from the employment agency, the woman at the family benefits counter, or even to the fat bitch who I had as a boss the other week at my last temp job at the Paris Bakery, I'm not sure that all these people share your opinion."

He left a little quickly for my taste, promising to call me the next day, which I believed without question, without even being tempted to shoot him my legendary "Yeah, yeah, right" like I always do with all the guys. I was on a cloud . . . My God, please let me stay there a little while.

Love Goes Around and Comes Around

SINCE SHE MADE UP with Issam, Linda has disappeared from circulation a little, she's now more scarce than a solar eclipse. According to Nawel, I get the idea that she is even more glued to her man than she ever was before. I talk to them both on the phone because they still think about getting all my news, but I get the feeling that they're drifting apart a little bit. We don't do as much together lately. The little cash I managed to get my hands on, I blew on physical-therapy appointments for The Boss, who's been complaining a lot about his back pain for a while. I told myself oh well, I'd rather let the girls enjoy themselves, take advantage of these beautiful days coming to them without my holding them back. And anyway it hurts me a little

114

that they feel guilty every time they're with me, that they feel bad spending their money, telling themselves I'm jealous, even if they never stop offering me their help.

Foued and me, we're slowly getting back on speaking terms after our big fight. We're doing our best at pretending, but I can see that it's all for show, all *belâani,* as they say around here. A few syllables here and there, some jokes, asking to go buy some bread, to change the channel on the TV, or to take the trash downstairs. He doesn't hang out much outside anymore, I think it's been hard on him. His boys must be a little pissed at him, but they're not paying him much mind anymore because he was pushed out by big dogs. So he's home a lot, he doesn't even go play soccer at Coubertin.

This morning I received a letter from my aunt Hanan. Every time she writes, she never stops giving me a hard time, telling me to come back to Algeria with my brother and The Boss, and using her favorite technique: the guilt trip. In our family it's the fundamental basis for any education.

Your grandmother is old and sick. What are you waiting for? For her to die without seeing you again? We miss you enormously. Every time we reminisce about you here, it's the whole house that cries, with tears even pouring down the walls. Come see us, so we can get to spend some time with you and finally reunite our whole family. Our sister, whose soul is with God, left you orphaned, she surely didn't want us to be separated for so long. We wait for your return with great impatience, this great day, inchallah, when we will celebrate before God and joyfully make our reunion. My oldest children are all married, you haven't been here for a single wedding, and they have sincerely regretted your absence. According to my youngest children, they have grown up not even remembering their own cousins . . . So if God wishes, maybe this summer, fate will reunite us again. Please, Ahlème, can you send us a package with some medicine for your grandmother, the blue bottles like last time, because you know that it's too expensive here?

May God give you mercy, dear Ahlème, you will be rewarded, inchallah, your cousin Souriya wants to ask you to think about putting in two or three bras, Playtex Cross Your Hearts in lace, please, may God keep you safe, you know that she's going to be married soon. Sabrina and Razika, our Kabyle neighbors, the ones who work at the Aïn Témouchent hair salon, say hello, they would like you to look at the prices for turbo blow dryers, they promise to pay you back as soon as they can. Naïma, who celebrated her seventeenth birthday last season, asks you for something she's calling "strings," I don't know what that means but she said that you would surely know and then just to finish, I would like you to send me the French cream for fighting aging that I asked for, I think the brand is Diadermine. May God protect and guide you, may he compensate you for all your kindness, and may he send good luck to your house. Take good care of our little brother and your poor father.

I wonder if this letter was really meant for me or if she should have had it expedited directly to Santa Claus. As usual, it looks more like a birthday list than anything. I feel like I didn't share anything big with them, just a few memories. All that seems pretty far away.

The day we left, I wore a little blue dress that Mama had sewn. I remember that I begged her for something that "turned."

It was Uncle Mohamed who drove us to the Oran airport. He turned us over to the hostesses, who were covered in makeup and who promised to take good care of us until we arrived in Paris. Then he squeezed me in his arms very hard. I think it was only at this moment that I really understood, while his beard tickled my neck and he whispered that I had to be brave. I realized that it would be really hard because before that day, Uncle Mohamed, out of modesty, had never allowed himself any display of affection toward me, except one kiss a year at Aïd el-Kebir.

I left my country, leaving behind me a whole part of my life. For the last time, I watched the Algerian sky from the window and I thought I would be going back soon. Since I arrived in France, I never took the road back to the *bled*, and if I decided to return, I don't know how but I would make a big comeback. But lately, I'm seriously considering it.

Nawel's maybe going to pull some strings so I can work in her uncle Abdou's shoe store on the boulevard de la Chapelle. He's about to fire his saleswoman because he found her in the stockroom with a customer. If the tip comes through, I could maybe finally get some long-term work and manage to save a little bit. With this I could take The Boss and Foued to Algeria, to our mother's village, near Sidi Bel Abbès, to our family home, Dar Mounia.

Right now I'm spending most of my time with The Boss because I'm not working. I savor these moments with him, I read his life in the lines of his hollow face, in his moist eyes, in his falling eyelids, in the curls of his hair that's gone all white, I tell myself that I would really miss him if he kicked it. When we spend this time together, exchanging pleasantries, he tells me his stories, and me, I sing him some songs. I listen to him with attention and I wait for him to take his siesta before I run off to the Café des Histoires to write down all his little tales. I've become a regular at this place, and it's rare that I get familiar with anything. When I arrive, Josiane already knows what I want to drink. She brings me my espresso and most of the time, if it's empty in the afternoon, she sits down at my table. She says that I listen well, that I inspire confidence quickly, and that it's a wonderful quality to be interested in others like I am.

The problem is that she continues to call me Stephanie Jacquet and bug me for copies of the papers where my stories are published. I can't bring myself to confess everything I've been brewing for so long.

Josiane never wanted to have a child, and when I asked her if she ever regretted it, she answered very precisely: "At forty-eight it's a little late to have regrets and then I know that I'm not stable, and it's better not to have kids if you're not giving them a real family. Anyway, you know that a pregnancy completely changes your body . . . I think that was part of it too, I didn't want to have flabby skin and hopeless breasts."

It's true that she's a pretty woman and that she's very stylish. Now and then she brings to mind old, bygone France, but I like that a lot. Josiane is on her fourth marriage and admits that she's thinking about divorce again, but she doesn't exactly know why she wants to do it. She says that she has never had a single valid reason for her previous divorces. I think she loses herself a little in all her stories. She wants to keep her first husband's name because she thinks that Josiane Vittani sounds like the name of a movie star from the '6os. She's funny and she's open. So like that, at the café, it's all good, but I tell myself that to live with her every day, that must really be something else.

"And anyway, at my age, it's not so easy, I'm getting senile, my poor girl! Just take the other day, he made the effort, the poor guy, to make a surprise and bring me breakfast in bed, and because I love surprises you would think I was very happy! Coffee, croissants, apple juice, the whole works! Oh! It was a beautiful spread, I'm telling you. The problem is that early in the morning, my head's all a jumble, like anyone. So when I wanted to thank him, I don't know why, I didn't know my memory played hide-and-seek with my mouth, but instead of saying 'Thanks, Arnaud!'—because my husband's name is Arnaud. Anyway, guess what I said to him: 'Thanks, Bertrand!'—except that Bertrand, oh God, he's my ex-husband. But I didn't tell you what happened after. Fortunately, I didn't make any other mistakes, I didn't add Frédéric and Gilles, the two before, the first ones. And the cherry on the top is that I didn't say I was sorry because I don't like to do that and it wasn't such a big deal anyway. Yes, that's right, I didn't even take the trouble to say that I acted poorly on that front. I never say 'I offer you all my apologies' because if I offer all of them, there won't be any left for afterward, for more important things . . ."

Then she plays out a sketch from the marriage service. She tells me about her husband's older son, who is, according to her, a sublime young man of twenty-five. She's certain that I'll like him and he would like me too. If I know what she's talking about, he's a subtle cross between Brad Pitt and Bill Clinton. Josiane says that she can introduce me to him. After all why not? I can give it a shot. I already wasted my time dozens of times letting the true social-work cases that Linda and Nawel insisted on bringing over to me try their luck, it would be hard for this to be any worse. And as far as Tonislav goes: no news.

After that, Josiane goes back to work, and me, I write in my little spiral notebook.

This is the story of a girl who grew up too fast and who was often sad. The littlest pleasant things were what saved her from her everyday worries, things that other people would think were boring, but her, they made her crazy with joy. She often dreamed of something else and she hoped that this something else would come soon.

*One day, in the middle of a long waiting line, she met
a foreigner, a violinist whom she liked in fast-forward. This
poor girl, a little sheltered, grabbed on to him like the girl
on the* Titanic *grabbed on to her plank of wood in the frozen
water. She believed in him, in their story, something that had
never happened to her before, and she told herself that maybe
finally it was her turn to know the rapture of love.*

*Alas, just when she thought she was waiting for nirvana,
when she had allowed her heart to beat a little, that heart she
thought had been rusty for a long time, it happened that the
violinist disappeared without leaving a trace. She was so sad
that she discovered it didn't even do any good to be sad and
she promised herself to forget him forever.*

I told Auntie this story, in its full length, in its full breadth,
and in *verlan*. She thought it was unbelievable, knowing me
so well, that I could have succumbed so quickly, so hard. Usually I nitpick for months and months before I crack, lots of
people put down their weapons before the end of the battle.
Anyone interested in me has to be extremely patient and motivated to win a little of my heart, a little of my trust, or to finally start a story together . . . And once it starts, in general it
never lasts for very long. Either the guy runs off before I can
even learn his number by heart and give him several ridiculous
nicknames, or I bolt first, because I got bored with him too
quickly. So now it looks like Tonislav broke the record. Euro-
pean Champion of Rapid Exits, in the heavyweight category
for mysterious disappearances . . .

Honestly, I have a real dazzling hatred in me. I don't usually need to cry at night before I go to bed because some clandestine tramp from the East didn't call me back. It's ridiculous . . . Nothing but bastards, all the same and, like Linda said the other day, "It's when you believe you've found the exception that you risk the biggest raid." In other words, it's when you least expect it that they give you the biggest fine.

Auntie Mariatou says that I have to let it be for a while, but I've been left hanging for two weeks already. For someone who was supposed to call me the next day, I think that's a little long . . . And she has an answer for everything, she makes an inventory of everything that could have happened to him, poor Tonislav, like he misplaced my number, had an accident, or fell ill . . . Maybe he had to go swimming or something, while she's at it. I've had enough of making excuses for everyone. And me, I don't give myself any. There's no reason.

I insulted him with all my soul, this crazy bastard, I used all the worst words that I knew, I even worked them into a few languages. I cursed him and his descendants, I prayed for the next seven generations to be born eunuchs, with four eyes and seventeen fingers.

Auntie says that I'm acting like I'm in a movie, that I'm not even thinking about what I say, because I'm not a bad girl and I'm only capable of giving people the benefit of the doubt.

Me, I say that he should never come back. And I am almost sure to run into him at the town hall one day or another. I didn't even notice in all this that my appointment date isn't here yet. I persuaded myself that if I see him, he will die of fear in front of me, and he will be ashamed, so ashamed that he will hide. And then, finally, I tell myself that it's all for nothing. The only thing I'm going to be able to do is to make myself more ridiculous in his eyes. If I do that, I will have given up my dignity for good, I will have condemned my pride to death. Negative. I'm forgetting him. Besides, I promise never to talk about him again, I won't even call up his memory anymore. I've decided to totally eject him from my mind, as if he never existed. Between Tonislav and me, there will be no regrets, a little like between the Danone factory and its two hundred laid-off employees.

The Life of a Stray Dog

I'M STARTING TO LIKE the fact that I have a real job.

I was hired for totally unjust reasons, nothing to do with my qualifications. I have this job only because I'm friends with Nawel, the boss's dear niece, and also because I speak fluent Arabic, and it's true that in this neighborhood, that can always be very useful. For once I can benefit from knowing people, and I'm not going to cry. Nawel's uncle Abdou is a very nice man, I like him a lot—at the store I call him Monsieur Kadri, because it's important not to get everything mixed up anyway.

From now on, my job is to sell shoes.

I spend my days among feet and I'm remembering that I really hate that. I think a foot is a truly disgusting thing. I'm seeing long ones, large ones, bizarre ones, dirty ones, old ones, fat ones, thin ones, and rarely some handsome ones. Some are actually infected. Sometimes I get the idea to take photos of the most horrible ones and make an album or create a list of the most unbelievable feet. Anyway I think I can even organize this whole idea into a commercial strategy: the winner of the contest for the ugliest foot will receive a free pair of shoes. All that just to say that I have some trouble with them, even my own, I even think they're horrible too. I can't bring myself to look at them. When I have to help a customer try on a shoe, sometimes I think about the Cinderella story and tell myself that if she had disgusting feet, with dirty nails and toes covered in blisters, the story wouldn't have turned out the same. The prince would have turned on his heels and run after throwing that dirty glass slipper at the bitch's face.

Now I spend my life in the middle of shoe boxes and unknown feet but I'm holding up. Uncle Abdou's store is really well placed, it's on the boulevard de la Chapelle, at the heart of the wild neighborhood of Barbès. I love this place. As soon as I have a break, I go walk around. I even make up little rituals for myself. Every day at noon, I eat at Monsieur Yassine's, the old Algerian who has a sandwich place a little farther up. His halal toasts are truly extraordinary.

Afterward, I walk by Kaïs's kiosk, a really special guy who seems like he's messed up somehow. It's very strange, this man never finishes his sentences but he makes them seem like they're naturally that way. I buy the newspaper from him and go drink a coffee in the tobacconist and bar across the street.

One day, on a whim, I went looking for Slimane's famous café at the Goutte-d'Or that The Boss talked about so much. I was convinced that I would recognize it right away if I passed it because it was at the heart of so many stories and he described it in such detail . . . I looked in the whole neighborhood, making the rounds many times in vain; finally I finished by asking two old Algerians sitting on a bench if they know whether this place or this Slimane even existed. One of them, wearing a checkered cap, told me that some years earlier the café had been bought and turned into a Chinese restaurant. As for the Slimane in question, the previous owner, he surrendered to cancer maybe a few months ago according to what the old man said, and his children decided to bury him back in the *bled* because that was always their father's wish. I stirred up something very delicate in their spirits because the two old guys started into a big nostalgic dialogue.

"Slimane, may God rest your soul, *miskine*. You see, my brother, those of us still waiting will finish the same. After having worked here all our lives like stray dogs, someone will send us there dead, between the four planks of wood in a coffin."

"Don't talk of unhappiness, God will provide and that's all, you know well enough that we don't decide anything."

"I know it, my brother. My only dream was to return to my home. Every year I said: next year. Then I said: when I retire. And then I put it off even more saying: when the kids are grown. Now they're grown, thank God, but they don't want to follow me there. They say they're French and their lives are here."

"What can you offer them in that country? There isn't even work for *châab* children and you think that *franssaouis* children are going to find any?"

"They haven't found any here either."

One of them turns to me.

"Tell me, my girl, why are you looking for Slimane? Are you family?"

"No, but my father knew him."

"Who's your father?"

"Moustafa Galbi."

"Moustafa Galbi . . . Galbi . . . Where's he from?"

"He's from Tlemcen, sir."

"Your father is Galbi the mustache?"

The two old guys break out laughing. The one wearing the checkered cap starts coughing like an asthmatic pig. He was laughing so hard that at one point I told myself: "We're going to end up losing him."

"I don't believe it, my friend. You remember him?"

"Who doesn't remember Sam! The old rascal, I never managed to beat him in a single game of dominoes!"

"You know, my girl, your father played in the café, I remember he played the guitar . . ."

"Yes, he told me about that."

"Oh, it's a strange omen that you passed by here. Tell your father that Najib and Abdelhamid the Oranais say hello."

"I'll tell him, *inchallah*."

"And tell the old loon he can come see us here, we sit here quite often."

It's possible that the old loon, as monsieur so affectionately called him, doesn't remember them at all, but I will tell him about our meeting anyway. I told them goodbye and ran off because if not, they would have talked to me for hours about a time I didn't know and had a hard time imagining. Since I'm too emotional, I think I would have been able to shed a little tear or two in front of them. And they would have thought I was the loony one.

I have to be a little crazy, deep down, because I always think I recognize that bastard Tonislav when I pass in front of the little Serbian bar on the other side of the street. My heart beats as loud as the Tlemcen *bendirs* and then, as I get closer, I realize it's not him. The worst part is that I'm disappointed.

The Right to Dream

WHAT I DREADED MOST has ended up happening and Foued has been permanently expelled from his high school. They didn't even really hesitate much. There was a hurried disciplinary council to which I was kindly invited and then the decision came down after some deliberation even if, it seems to me, it was made already in advance.

Here are the facts: during the year-end interview with his teachers and the guidance counselor, Foued explained that he would like to follow a sports-studies program with a section on soccer because it has been his passion forever—he has played on the Ivry team since the age of six. He loves it and what he would like is to become a professional. Here's the advice that the counselor thought appropriate to give him: "Don't go dreaming, it's unrealistic. I can't take the responsibility of sending you over there, not everyone can become Zidane. You should take a technical track in mechanics or electronics instead. I think that will suit you best."

Result: Foued, who was a little nervous, got worked right up. He stood up, started insulting them with every name in the book, most notably *catin*, which clicked particularly well with his French teacher—a real bastard if you ask me—who thought it was very ironic that he used a term for "slut" from fourteenth-century Old French when he wasn't capable of writing a sentence without spelling mistakes. He said this in a loud voice and it made some of his colleagues laugh. And there you go, no doubt it made him happy to put my little brother down at a moment when his future was at stake. Foued was expelled from the school system because they condemned his dream in advance.

I contacted Thomas, one of the special youth teachers who work around Insurrection, to see if he could help my brother find another high school. He explained that at this time of year that's no easy thing, especially given the weight of Foued's file. He said the best plan would be to repeat his grade and for us to look for a place for him starting next year. So that leaves us a little time. I asked Uncle Abdou to give me two weeks off. To convince him, I told him I was ready to never take another day of vacation in the next twenty years for these fifteen days now. He understood the importance that these two weeks had for me and gave me my vacation without any fight. I think now's the time. I reserved three tickets on Air Algerie.

I had to tell my brother that we were going. I think he was pretty surprised. He was in the middle of drying the dishes and he broke a glass from our Nutella service. It's sensible and practical, their being glasses. We also have a set that came from Maille mustard and another from Garnerth cocktail olives.

"But I don't really speak Arabic," Foued objected.

"Most of the people in the *bled* speak French, don't worry."

"Are we going to stay long?"

"No, not long. Two weeks or something like that."

"What are we going to do with The Boss?"

"He's coming with us. We can't just drop him down the garbage chute."

"He knows? You told him that we're going over there?"

"Yeah, I just told him. Ask him, you'll see, you'll get a laugh out of it."

We head into the living room to The Boss, who's in the middle of making little paper chicks out of the pages from the TV guide.

"Papa?"

"Here I am. Who wants me?"

"Where are we going, Papa? Do you know?"

"Gambetta, Les Andalouses, Bel Air . . . to Oran. Yes, I know where."

"We're going to the *bled*, right? We're going to the village too. I told you. Do you remember?"

"Yes. I've had it with the commercials on Channel One. Always commercials."

"Foued's going with us. We're taking a plane."

"Those crooks! Nine hundred thirty-four euros roundtrip. We're not rich. I can swim. It's not far."

Foued and me, we cut up at that. The Boss is unpredictable.

I have a date with Linda and Nawel. It's been forever since I saw their faces, I've missed them. We're meeting up at the Babylon Café near the mall in Ménilmontant where Nawel works. She knows the bar well because she goes there a lot with her co-workers. She says that it doesn't look like anything much but it's a tight spot.

I get there first, and from the outside I spot that it really doesn't seem all that special. I push open the door and take back what I was going to say, I liked the atmosphere right away: the lighting is soft, the colors are hot, and I hear a Manu Chao song playing. All the ingredients are here. So I'm a fan right off. Near the bar I see a strange character, a man around forty, with sort of a wild feeling about him, an extraordinary appearance, long legs, a sailor cap, and immense blue eyes, the kind of big eyes that tell stories. He sees me and shouts over: "Hello princess! Welcome! Sit down! What can I get you?" I ask him for an espresso.

"Why an espresso?"

The wild man has completely thrown me off. It's the first time anyone has ever asked me to justify my order in a bar.

"Uh . . . I don't know. It's what I always order, out of habit."

"Habit, that's what kills men. My name is Jack. But everyone calls me Jack the Weasel."

"Mine's Ahlème."

You'd think he's trying to make me crazy.

"Welcome. You know, I say 'welcome' because you're here for the first time."

"Yeah, sure. I'm going to order a tea instead for a change."

He shoots my order to the bartender like a tennis player serves a ball into play.

"A tea!"

Then the bartender, who has a smile Scotch-taped to his face, repeats it to himself like he wanted to remember it for the rest of his life. "A tea! A tea!"

I like that he's smiling. In general, when I go to cafés in Paris, I get the feeling that the waiters have a slot hidden somewhere in their bodies, where you have to slip a coin to get anything that could be like the hint of a grin. And there's nothing gross about that at all, is there?

The Weasel comes back toward me with the tea, which he puts on a paper coaster that's made to look like the globe.

"Thanks a lot, Jack."

"You've got some luck, you're going to drink your tea on top of the world."

"Yeah . . . I hadn't seen it like that."

"You must be waiting for someone you really like, it shows."

"I'm waiting for my friends."

"Ah! I was right! If you had a date with a court bailiff or an accountant, I would have known that too."

With these great lines, the Weasel abandons me as suddenly as he first started questioning me and leaves me to meditate quietly on top of the world. Shit, I spilled a little drop of tea on Africa, that's not cool, like they didn't have enough crap like that already. For someone who calls himself Jack, I think his accent sounds a little Algerian around the edges. But I would never ask him where he comes from, even if I became a regular at the café, because that's just something you don't ask. Me, for example, I don't like it when people ask me so I won't ask any questions, first of all because Jack works well for him and that's enough for me, and second of all . . . well, no, there isn't any second of all.

Linda and Nawel finally arrive at the Babylon Café. They're all tricked out, as always, they make a stunning entrance in a cloud of smoke from their cigarettes and their sophisticated perfume, the scent of springtime. They play the scene like girls who know the place, kiss cheeks, go behind the bar like they're at home, and smile to the right, smile to the left. I notice with great regret that Linda has dyed her pretty brown curls; she went all through with these kind of light, bleached, burned streaks and it looks absolutely messed up to me. What a waste. Worse: a crime against humanity. They come toward me in a pair. I think they missed me too, so we give each other big hugs and I invite them to sit on the banquette, like always.

"Didn't you notice something?"

"Your hair?"

"Yeah!" she says enthusiastically.

"You talking about this piss-blond dye-job? This stickup your hair surrendered to?"

"No! You're playing with me! You don't like it?"

"Not at all!"

"You see! I told you!" adds Nawel.

"But why? You don't think it's pretty?"

"Fuck, Linda, you're too much. You had the most beautiful hair in the world and you had to go color it with paint so it would look like all these little grungy super-skanks who go buy their panther-print thongs at the Clignancourt market every Saturday morning?"

"Oh shit! You're too cruel . . . I was aiming for a blond between golden and ash, it's going to be summer soon, that's why I did it."

"Man, you make me crazy! But what about the hairdresser, you had to see that she missed your color: it's not golden or ash, it's . . . smoky, like an old yellow."

"Fine, forget it. I am disgusting, I can see that it's ruined, but I wanted to convince myself that it was beautiful, but shit, I'm not a very good actress, so there . . . It's true, it's out of hand, I admit it. This stupid bitch of a stylist at Jean Louis David, she put these fat round disks in my brain, and I was so bored, she managed to convince me that it was going well. And then I went and left her a five-euro tip! Come on, we're going back there and slap her shit, right? I'm hatin' her now . . ."

At that, Nawel the little thug breaks out laughing. Fortunately Linda is far from sensitive. With the girls, you can say anything. Since we aren't villains at this point, we suggest buying her a Movida rinse and giving it to her at home so she can be reborn as the beautiful, dark brunette who causes riots wherever she passes, the one men dream about in the middle of the day, the one who conjures up princesses of a thousand and one nights.

Maybe I'm exaggerating a little but it's just to emphasize the fact that she's much prettier as a brunette.

Probably just to give us a change of subject, Linda told us a piece of gossip all fresh, all hot, all wrapped up in golden paper. This one deserves to be relayed by the most successful American soap opera. They could do something with it, true.

A few days ago, Magalie, her boss at Body Boom, on the occasion of her husband's birthday, decided to go back to her house earlier than expected to surprise him. She asked Linda and the other aestheticians to hold down the fort without her and to close up for her just this once. Of course, like in all the stories that begin with "she decided to go home earlier than expected to surprise," the end is horrible, you can guess that already. So the poor Magalie goes home, she makes all the efforts in the world so that her surprise can be a success: she doesn't take the same way as usual, she's discreet, climbs the stairs without a sound, etc., etc. But of course all these precautions are useless since the husband in question isn't supposed to be there . . . You had to imagine too that when Linda told it, she set the whole scene in place, the tiniest details. Me, I prefer to pass over them because it doesn't take anything of the punch out of the punch line.

Magalie, confident and full of herself, enters the dining room to prepare this magnificent table that she had planned to set up so she could give her loving spouse a romantic, candle-lit dinner. But so much was her shock on discovering, on the couch that they had bought together at the giant Swedish furniture store, her pig of a husband in the arms of a young Asian boy of seventeen years! If I remember right, the end of the story, it's that she has an epileptic seizure, or maybe that she strangled the Chinese boy . . . or maybe that the Chinese boy strangled her instead . . . I don't remember anymore.

After that, Nawel, with no warning, took her turn strangling me. Without wanting to, she killed me. She always keeps really up to date on the news in the world, contrary to Linda who favors news that we'd call more local. On the phone Nawel told me about an article she read a few days ago that talked about a new expulsion of people without papers. She takes the newspaper out of her bag and starts reading out loud.

"You're going to see, it's some crazy shit. 'The man, twenty-seven years old, presented himself in the morning at the immigration office in the Val-de-Marne prefecture in answer to an ordinary summons. He came with no fear, in possession of a promise of employment that would allow him to obtain the much-coveted ten-year visa. Someone pointed him to the room where he had to wait for someone in the administration but, to his stupefaction, there were two policemen who had come to pick him up. Headed for the local retention center. Then the first plane for Belgrade—'"

I rip the newspaper from Nawel's hands. The article is titled "When the Prefectures Set Ambushes."

"Quietly, calm down—"

"I need to see! I need to see!"

I immediately landed on the passage I was dreading.

". . . the minister of the interior denies 'having set traps for just anyone.' But the case of Tonislav Jogovic isn't unique. According to the organization Papers for All, his would be the thirteenth case of this kind since the February regulations."

The Other Side

THE FIRST STEP I take on Algerian soil is difficult, my body goes tense. I'm wearing a dress that spins and, since there is a little wind, I'm being careful to hold it. The sun in the *bled* shames my white legs that I never show.

The thing that comes back to me first is the odor, the scent of the earth, the hot air hitting your face. And always that letter missing on the sign: AÉRO ORT ORAN-ES-SENIA.

The mustachioed customs officer nervously rifles through our bags, he turns over—in every way—the bags I spent hours organizing, and shoots me a little shady look. No doubt it's the word *bakchich* I read in his eyes. Not a chance. I'd rather die in this airport than feed the beast of corruption. So he continues his performance, he settles our papers and continues to watch us in the hope that one of us will take a magnificent bill out of our pockets. Best-case scenario, one in the right currency — euros — and worst-case, a stack of two hundred dinars cash. He makes us wait with unconcealed pleasure, searching as if the eighteen passages to the customs booths and automatic doors since Paris-Orly weren't enough. Determined to achieve his objective, he calls one of his co-workers over for a "ferification." In reality, he makes a slight signal with his head and she understands right away. The good little woman comes over with a firm step, the mustache speaks into her ear — from what I see, they want to keep it on the DL. The woman has an enormous head that you'd think was screwed onto her bust. It's like she doesn't have a neck, she looks like the tortoise in the cartoon *Big Turtle* that used to run on Channel Five when we were little. She talks to me in a serious voice: she would like to know what the objects are that I have wrapped up in newspaper. I explain to Big Turtle that these are boxes of pills for my suffering grandmother. She wants to know more, so I tell her that she can open them if she wants. What does she think, this one? That I'm bringing ecstasy to my grandmother in the *bled*? She feels the boxes through the paper, rudely munching her gum, then I see her stop at a piece of paper. She gets jammed up there for several minutes. It's the best, this one, she's in the middle of reading, as if that's all anyone had to do. We're still waiting . . . But what the hell is she doing?

"What date is this? Is it today's horoscope?"

Then she returns to her post, looking dissatisfied. The predictions must not have been very good.

The Boss, knocked out by the heat, is even more out of it than usual. So he can make it through, I gave him a brochure on the security procedures that I stole from the plane. Foued seems straight-out lost. He looks everywhere, like a child loose in a shopping mall. The guy in uniform keeps insisting, then noticing that he can't manage to push us over the edge, he finishes by closing our bags and marking them with little white chalk crosses, which signifies that everything is okay. He grudgingly lets us leave, a little like a fisher would let a big salmon go. We take our bags and steer ourselves toward the exit. I catch him giving us one last dirty look, all the while twisting his mustache between his thumb and his index finger. I wonder what he's saying to himself, maybe: "These immigrants, what a bunch of cheapskates! With all that money they make in France . . ."

In front of the arrivals gate, people wait under the palm trees. The sun bangs against the windshields and bald skulls of the taxi drivers, who intercept travelers from every direction. They shout their destinations, the little villages they're going to pass through. Then the people climb up into the vehicle, throw their suitcases in the trunk themselves, and vroom, it makes a big American getaway.

We're waiting for our cousin Youssef. I'm not sure I'll recognize him, but he will recognize us for sure.

For the past few minutes, Foued is ready to follow every taxi driver who comes toward us calling The Boss "*aâmi*," thinking he's the cousin we're waiting for. I explain to him that it's just a polite expression and that here all the guys who call each other *khoyya* aren't necessarily brothers. It's a little like the boys in the city and the way they call each other cousin.

Youssef finally arrives. The reunion is emotional but a little strange because, actually, none of us remember anything about the other at all. Anyway, it's no big thing. He's a man now, his worries have made him age earlier than expected, and except for the bit of an evil glint in his eye, the mischievous little kid I learned forbidden games with has disappeared. We get into the taxi and our cousin tries to make conversation with The Boss. He's having trouble but he keeps trying. I warned him, I explained everything to him so he wouldn't be too stunned at the difference. Besides, I warned them all that Papa was sick. They're used to it because of Uncle Kader, he's been like this too since he came back from the army—I wonder what they did to him over there. According to Aunt Hanan's letters, it must have been tough. He really bugged out. Apparently he pissed himself in the middle of the market and decided to get undressed in the street and started dancing around. Youssef asks us some questions, asks what we do, shows an interest in our lives. I tell him I'm working, but he seems disappointed when I explain exactly what I do for a job. As for Foued, he lies and says that he's going to school and that he works hard. He swallowed his saliva before lying: I can see we have the same technique. He avoided my eye while he was doing it. Maybe he was afraid that I would expose him, that I would shame him in front of a *blédard*, as he calls them.

"You still play *boléta,* Foued, like your sister wrote to me in her letter?"

"Yeah, that's right."

"Why don't you ever write us a letter?"

"Because I'm not so great at French."

"What about mine? It's worse than yours, but I write all the same. You're putting me on, little *Franssaoui* . . ."

That makes one point for the *blédard,* I'd say.

It's too hot around here, drops of sweat run down my forehead. The air is dry and the dust comes in through the lowered window and gets into the corners of my eyes. The taxi driver drives like a crazy freak and I'm going to spend two weeks with these people that I haven't seen in more than ten years and I don't know all that well.

The day before we left for Algeria I went to say goodbye to Auntie Mariatou. I told her some of my worries about the trip. I was really afraid of having nothing in common with my relatives, I was afraid that France has stamped me to the point of making me feel even more of a foreigner over there. So she gave me one of her succulent sayings, which I brought in my suitcases: "A wood plank can stay a hundred years in the river, but it will never be a cayman."

Just like I imagined, the entire village is on watch, a crowd is posted in front of the house. I don't know all these people expecting me, all these faces waiting for me, I wonder what I'll have to say to them. I feel lost like a fledgling bird who doesn't know where his nest is anymore.

The taxi parks in a cloud of dust and, on seeing the family house, Dar Mounia, something grips my heart. I'm short of breath, everything is moving too quickly for me. This is where I grew up, and the first sensation I have is that everything is small. My memory is right in front of me, only in a reduced version. We get out of the car and, while Foued and cousin Youssef take the suitcases out of the trunk, The Boss decides to make a real entrance. I don't know what came over him but he burst out of the car and set himself crying with joy, raising his arms, clapping and whistling. The craziest part is that the people picked up his vibe, it was like the audience at the beginning of an NTM concert in their glory days.

"Long live Algeria! The people of Algeria are free! We won! Algeria is ours! *Istiqlal! Istiqlal!*"

People are laughing, the children surround us. They cling to us, to our clothes and our arms. It's craziness. They start shouting:

"The immigrants! The immigrants! Where is Jacques Chirac?"

Then I recognize some familiar faces coming toward us. Aunts, uncles, and cousins throw themselves on us, hug us, embrace us with all their hearts. We are welcomed in a mad crazy euphoria, their shouts and *youyous* take us up, the village is in full celebration because a piece of France is paying them a visit. Then the ceremonial greetings, the "*salaam*" and the "*labès*," begin. I feel like a week has passed between our arrival and the moment when we finally enter the house.

As time goes along more details come back to me. I rediscovered my little secret corner. For me, all of Algeria could be found here. The fence through which I watched the passersby and invented stories for them had been replaced with a low stone wall. My beautiful orange tree has disappeared. Someone cut it down, replacing it with a water spigot and some huge ceramic sinks for doing laundry. Except for these things, Dar Mounia hasn't really changed.

My grandmother's grown old, she is sick. Having lost all her teeth, she can only eat soup and vegetable purée now. She spends her time sleeping because she gets tired too quickly. The poor woman is sweet for Foued. She has a particular affection for him because she was the one who rocked him as a baby, murmuring the traditional songs, and she was the one who chose his name too. The problem is that the little shit dodges her, because I think she frightens him: "She freaks me out with all the drawings on her face, and her mouth stinks too! She's like the killer in *Saw*!" He's talking about the tribal tattoos she wears on her forehead and chin. No one does them anymore, but in the old days it was a horrible test, it seems. In the village, there are some elders who used to be in charge of it, with heated needles, and apparently these elders weren't very fun, more like real hyenas. You could always try to escape, fight them off, but no way, they held your face good and tight. Grandmother told me that when they wanted to do it to Mama while she was still a little girl, she ran into the forest to hide. She laughed when she told the story, opening her empty mouth wide.

My memory of Aunt Hanan was true enough. She's melodrama personified, she cries all the time, for anything and everything. When I see her eyebrows start to wriggle and her lips start to twist from top to bottom, I think: "Oh shit! There she goes, she's doing it again for us!" Fortunately she's never seen *Titanic*.

She talks to me a lot about the time when I lived there. She makes me look at old Polaroids, she even shows me the spot where I slept . . . It's like she wanted to bring me all the little things I would have lost along the way. She tells me that France tore me from the arms of my country like a baby is ripped from its mother. There you have it, she says something and so it starts, the wiggling eyebrows and the trembling lips . . . She has quite a few other magic formulas like this. Aunt Hanan, she could make a truck driver cry.

I spend my days listening to people, trying to remember who I come from. I have a hard time admitting it, but the truth is that my place is no longer here.

My young cousins have one word on their lips: marriage. They prepare their trousseaus, and at Foued's age they're already real women. Their lives are stitched into their straw rugs as surely as mine is engraved into the concrete of Ivry's buildings. In the afternoon, they let themselves fantasize about another life, far away and impossible, when they watch the Mexican soap opera, drenched in orange-blossom water, clumsily dubbed into Arabic—minus the slightly hot scenes, censored, because they can dream, but not too much all the same. This nonsense happens every day at one o'clock. So in the village at one o'clock, life stops. And after the viewing, it's time for the siesta.

It's exactly at this hour that poor Foued cracked.

"Shit it's dead here, I want to go outside—"

"But there's no one out there."

"What's with this *bled* where everyone sleeps?"

"It's too hot outside at this hour. You think you're in France, or what? If you go out now, you're going to fall down dry, you'll see. The sun is going to scald your skull."

The "cousins," the ones who live in France and are in the *bled* for vacations, talk about nothing but their new country. They talk about it like a close friend who sometimes reaches out to them, sometimes kicks them away. They relay the stories they hear, the accounts of those who have slipped through the mesh in the net, and they add some, never admitting their failures or their misery. They never tell their family in the *bled* that they work at night, that they wash dishes at nasty Chinese restaurants, and that they sleep in miserable little maids' rooms. They embellish everything because they're ashamed, but they still prefer all that over coming back forever.

Cousin Youssef, he'll never know France. He told me that half the population is at least twenty-five and, destitute, doesn't know what to do about its dreams.

I would like to tell them that over there, in France, it's not what they think, that through the distorting window that is the television, they know nothing real. The French channels they pirate to watch the TF1 summer shows don't show them the truth. As the young people here say, the satellite dishes hooked on the buildings of Oran are the ears of the city, stretched toward the north, ready to hear it all. But these ears are clogged.

But I don't let myself tell them all that, I don't want to be taken for Madame Know-It-All. These people have known a civil war, hunger, and fear, and even if France isn't what they believe, it's not so bad there, because here it's maybe actually worse.

After the traditional diarrhea of the first days, Foued has managed to strike up a friendship with some of the little neighbors. The kids around here have already nicknamed him "the Migrant." Together they spend their days in the area, hanging out in front of the *hanout*. His new hellmates, they're *bled* kids, real resourceful guys, guys who sell plastic bags, peanuts, or cigarettes by the piece in the street, who are going to spend their days digging through the trash in search of an eventual miracle or a pair of shoes. Even if we don't stay here long, I hope that Foued will see that money, it's not so easy to get, that these kids who march their dirty, aching feet in counterfeit "Mike" shoes, and who are beaten by adults all day long, including by their parents in the evening when they haven't earned enough dinars, these kids, they suffer but they get by and don't often complain. I hope seeing life here is going to make him think.

Today we're going to the city, to the ocean, and then to the cemetery where Mama's buried, while the brothers Djamel and Aïssa drive The Boss to the marabout's house in the neighboring village to do what they call a *ziara*, a sort of disenchantment.

The ritual is the same for curing insanity, for setting a curse, or for treating troubled children. We'll see what good it can do, anyway it can't make it any worse.

While everyone is getting ready, I plant myself under the olive tree in front of the house. I listen to Algeria, I smell its odor, and I write in my little spiral notebook to describe it all.

I even talk about the small wooden comb my aunts use to smooth out my hair. I talk about Isis, the brand that has the monopoly on laundry detergent here, and also shampoo, soap, dish soap, toothpaste, sanitary napkins . . .

I tell the story of the big party the first night that was organized in our honor, the sheep they fattened and then roasted on a spit, all these new heads I have to memorize in such a small amount of time.

I talk about my cousin Khadra who sticks to me all day and who never stops complimenting me on the Agnès B. cardigan I wear. She touches it, saying she would love to have one like it, that she looked all over the Oran boutiques, that she thinks it's soft, new . . . She certainly hopes that I take it off and leave it with her, but it was a present from Linda and Nawel for my birthday. Cousin Khadra practices psychological pressure on me. Foued was the first to notice her little game and he hasn't stopped himself from warning me.

"That's some bullshit, I've never seen the like, it's a sweater yo, you'd think she'd never seen a sweater."

"It's not just a sweater. It's my Agnès B. sweater."

"Oh yeah . . . So then the cuz, she knows that she can smell it."

In my notebook I don't forget to write down what makes Foued happy. His thing is to speak French in front of the cousins who don't understand it at all, the poor things, and to drive them especially crazy by teaching them a little slang. So then I hear Aunt Norah's little ones playing in the courtyard singing at the top of their lungs: "Fuck the po-po, fuck the po-po."

I talk about my cousin from Aïn Témouchent who asked for my hand after three days here. His name is Bilel, and it's like he's the sex symbol in the village, a real G, as Foued says. He has blue eyes and that's his trademark around here. All the honeys in this *bled* want him for a husband just for his beautiful eyes. He comes to Dar Mounia every day to see me, he struts around, shows his stuff. He thinks he's impressing me but he forgets that I live in France, and that I just have to take the metro to see some blue eyes. If he keeps flossin', God is going to punish his arrogance, and one morning without knowing how, he will wake up with brown eyes. And they'll be the most common brown in the world. That will teach him.

They've even vaguely talked to me about marriages of convenience they would have for me. Guys offering unbelievable sums to marry a girl with a CIF, a French identity card, the bids go up to seven thousand euros. I wonder where they find all this dough, it's alarming to see what they're ready to pay to know the other side.

The sardine vendor passes in front of me on his moped. The noise of the motor distracts me. It sounds weak, he should train with Speed Pizza—there, if your order doesn't arrive in half an hour, the pizza is free, so they're mostly interested in moving it fast. It's funny how life unwinds in slow motion here. Even if we haven't been there for a long time, Paris and its restlessness seem far away already. I get the feeling that my little brother would like to be there, but I hope that he understands too that his life isn't here in the *bled* and that he'll calm down when he gets back, because his expulsions worry me more and more. I think about them nonstop, even here. I dwell on the Tonislav story in every sense, I realize every day that those fuckheads aborted my love story and didn't give a shit about lighting up this poor guy's straw dreams. And then they think they're going to take my little brother?

Finally we leave for the post office in the city. We enter a huge room, armored by rows of phone booths, smothered by a hellish brouhaha, flooded by a whirlpool of djellabas and haiks. I would like to just call Auntie Mariatou to reassure her and to get some news of her little ones. So we go to the VIP corner, reserved for international calls, and there I see the fate of those who are brought here to disappear, to serve their second sentence. Their expression is the same as the one worn by the brothers I cross early in the morning at Saint-Lazare station, the ones who are cold and who walk with lowered heads. Crammed around these booths, these guys, as French as Foued or me, hold their handsets nervously, and watch the meter with anxiety. Sometimes they want to buy just a little more time, they scratch the bottom of their pockets to put in one last coin—they always say it's the last one . . . They call their mothers, their boys, maybe their girlfriends, they try to talk loud to cover the noise and I get the feeling that they actually try just to talk at all. I explain all this to Foued, he watches them and I think he's as overwhelmed as I am. When we get back into Uncle Mohamed's car, no one says a word. We stay quiet all the way to the cemetery.

The rusty gate is wide open. The whiteness of the place hits me first, and its reach. It's striking.

But the most frightening is the birth dates, too recent, all the rows of tombs, these stars with five points looking east. It's hard to think about, but there are children under there. I realize then that Foued and me, we could have been buried here. That doesn't add up to much really. There were two hundred deaths that night, so two more . . .

The Boss is crouched down in front of the tomb, silent, stroking the ends of the white stone fingers. From time to time a sigh escapes from him and you would think that he understands everything, that he knows. I'm convinced that at this very moment he is all back in his head.

Foued stays standing, his eyes lowered, I hear him sniffling but I don't dare look at him to see if he's crying.

And me, I'm sitting on the same red earth, my palms flat on the ground, as if I wanted her to give me strength, the courage to leave again and face life.

We've prepared a prayer for her, for the others who rest here, and also for those who mourn them, for us, for the ones from over there. We will make a *sadaqa* in her memory this afternoon at the mosque.

·   ·   ·

Time doesn't work the same in Algeria, the hour of our departure sneaks up on us. I promise to come back very soon and not to forget. There are some things in this *bled* that I wouldn't find anywhere else. The atmosphere is strange, the odor is too and it's especially hot, maybe too hot. After all, it's only a question of climate and the Algerian heat anesthetized me.

Foued wants to stay a couple more days with The Boss. We work out the tickets so they can postpone their return. Me, I have to get back because Uncle Abdou put his foot down and he's waiting for me at the store.

Truce

I'M TKOed, I busted my body all night on the dance floor at the Tropical Club, it was blazing thanks to the talents of deejay Patrick-Romuald. I'm taking advantage of my time alone. I still have a week of liberty before Foued and The Boss come back. I have the apartment all to myself.

Yesterday evening with Linda and Nawel, we really let ourselves go. They managed to escape their boys, Issam and Mouss. It was easy, there was a soccer match on TV.

We spent the evening with some Brazilian dancers, Coco, Miguel, and Sadio. They had real class. Three handsome guys who danced mad well. They taught us two or three steps and bought us two or three fruit cocktails. Coco, the finest of the three, followed me the whole night and it was pretty nice. We danced all freaky and tight, glued together, sweating. It was exquisite.

Around four o'clock in the morning, me and Coco decided to leave the Tropical Club. The others wanted to stay. In the lobby while we were getting our stuff the girls gave me the thumbs-up and winked at me from afar. It was embarrassing.

Coco told me about another party nearby. The boy seemed like he was high, he seemed like he was built to go all night. We climbed into his Golf and it was like it was all custom made for him: the cream-colored leather seats, the Marvin Gaye CD in the stereo, the smooth ride . . . It's the Coco way. During the drive, he put his hand on my knee, smiled at me, and asked me in a suave voice if everything was cool.

We finally arrive. He parks the car and gives me a sweet, polite kiss. From here I can see the line. There are a hundred people. I'm too lazy to deal with that whole line. In the end we're not even guaranteed to get in. And now my feet hurt, I'm wearing shoes from the store. I have to remember that I spend my days selling low-quality shoes. Uncle Abdou's a crook after all.

Getting out of the car with Coco, I hear the birds. I hate hearing morning birds.

Coco waves to me and moves away. It's nice of him to drop me off. He seemed disappointed that I wasn't going with him to his party. He promised to call me tomorrow, but if he doesn't, it's no big thing for me. As Auntie often says: "You have to kiss a lot of toads before you can find your prince."

I move toward the line. Always the same tired faces. These weary people. Strangers, foreigners, who come at dawn for a ticket.

It's six o'clock in the morning and I'm in front of the prefecture.

THE AMERICAN CONGRESS

Sixth Edition

The American Congress provides the most insightful, up-to-date treatment of congressional politics available in an undergraduate text. Informed by the authors' Capitol Hill experience and nationally recognized scholarship, this book presents a crisp introduction to all major features of Congress: its party and committee systems, leadership, and voting and floor activity. *The American Congress* has the most in-depth discussion of the place of the president, the courts, and interest groups in congressional policy making available in a text. The authors blend an emphasis on recent developments in congressional politics with a clear discussion of the rules of the game, the history of key features of Congress, and stories from recent Congresses that bring politics to life. No other text weaves into the discussion the important ideas of recent political science research. The book includes the most comprehensive list of suggested readings and Internet resources on Congress to date.

Steven S. Smith is Kate M. Gregg Professor of Social Sciences and Director of the Weidenbaum Center at Washington University in St. Louis. He has authored or coauthored seven books and many articles on congressional politics, including *Call to Order: Floor Politics in the House and Senate, Party Influence in Congress*, and *Politics or Principle: Filibustering in the U.S. Senate*, and has coauthored several articles and a book on Russian parliamentary politics. He is a former Senior Fellow at the Brookings Institution and has taught at the University of Minnesota, Northwestern University, and George Washington University.

Jason M. Roberts is Assistant Professor of Political Science at the University of North Carolina at Chapel Hill. His research interests include American politics, the U.S. Congress, elections, and Supreme Court nominations. He is the co-author of *Why Not Parties?: Party Effects in the United States Senate* and has published articles in the *American Political Science Review, American Journal of Political Science*, and the *Journal of Politics*.

Ryan J. Vander Wielen is Assistant Professor of Political Science at Temple University. He was previously a Fellow in the Political Institutions and Public Choice Program at Michigan State University and at the Weidenbaum Center at Washington University in St. Louis. He has recently been published in *Political Analysis* and *Loyola of Los Angeles Law Review*.

The American Congress

Sixth Edition

Steven S. Smith
Washington University

Jason M. Roberts
University of North Carolina

Ryan J. Vander Wielen
Temple University

CAMBRIDGE
UNIVERSITY PRESS

CAMBRIDGE UNIVERSITY PRESS
Cambridge, New York, Melbourne, Madrid, Cape Town, Singapore, São Paulo, Delhi

Cambridge University Press
32 Avenue of the Americas, New York, NY 10013-2473, USA

www.cambridge.org
Information on this title: www.cambridge.org/9780521749060

First published 2009

Printed in the United States of America

A catalog record for this publication is available from the British Library.

Library of Congress Cataloging in Publication data

The American Congress / Steven S. Smith, Jason M. Roberts,
Ryan J. Vander Wielen. – 6th ed.
 p.   cm.
Includes bibliographical references and index.
ISBN 978-0-521-74906-0 (pbk.)
1. United States. Congress.   2. United States. Congress – Evaluation.   3. United
States – Politics and government – 21st century – Public opinion.   4. Public opinion –
United States.   I. Smith, Steven S., 1953–   II. Roberts, Jason M.   III. Vander Wielen,
Ryan J.   IV. Title.
JK1041.A617   2009
328.73 – dc22   2009010737

ISBN 978-0-521-74906-0 paperback

Contents

Preface

The American Congress has long been one of the most powerful legislative bodies in the world. Congress is now struggling with momentous issues such as health care and worldwide environmental problems, the stabilization of the world financial system, the rehabilitation of America's infrastructure, funding the U.S. system of retirement security, the war against terrorism, and the place of the United States in the post–Cold War world. These issues present a serious challenge. They affect the interests of all Americans, they are highly controversial, and they involve complex public policies.

Major Features of *The American Congress*

Understanding the Place of Congress in American Democracy. Our primary goal in writing this edition is to instill in students and general readers an appreciation for the importance of a strong legislature in the American democracy. Such an appreciation requires an understanding of the constitutional setting in which Congress operates, the basic rules of the electoral and legislative processes, and the resources and strategies of members of Congress and other key players. Each chapter is designed to contribute to the reader's understanding by introducing key concepts, describing essential details of the process, and outlining general principles for understanding the subject.

The Changing Congress. In our efforts to introduce you to congressional politics, we emphasize the evolving nature of Congress. In writing a textbook, it is easy to describe current arrangements and create the impression that the rules and processes described have long been as described and are likely to stay that way for some time. We do not want to create that impression. Congress is created by its members and frequently changed by its members. Consequently, we emphasize the factors that influence legislators' thinking about their institution. Party conflict, competition with the executive branch, the drive for reelection, and other forces in congressional politics are discussed.

Important Ideas About Congress. We also highlight important ideas in recent public commentary and political science research about Congress and its members. Although we do not organize our discussion around debates in the professional literature on Congress, we do not hesitate to observe differences of opinion among our colleagues in political science on important subjects. Political scientists have offered competing and insightful perspectives on the sources of the incumbency advantage, the importance and motivations of legislative parties, the power of committees, and other subjects. We provide an accessible and balanced discussion of the deserving perspectives.

A Starting Point for Your Research on Congress. We provide a starting point for most undergraduate research projects by including an extensive bibliography on congressional politics at the end of the book. The bibliography emphasizes both classic and recent books, includes major journal articles, and contains major Web sites that include useful information on Congress and related subjects. Because we have provided a lengthy bibliography, we have limited references to literature in the text.

We have not hidden our enthusiasm for congressional politics. To be sure, Congress is easy to dislike and often difficult to defend. The rough-and-tumble world of legislating is not orderly and civil, human frailties too often taint its membership, and legislative outcomes are often frustrating and ineffective. Still, we are not exaggerating when we say that Congress is essential to American democracy. We would not have survived as a nation without a Congress that represented the diverse interests of our society, conducted a public debate on the major issues, found compromises to resolve conflicts peacefully, and limited the power of our executive, military, and judicial institutions.

Organization of the Text

Chapter 1 begins with an overview of the condition of the modern Congress. The chapter gives the reader a look at the general trends in American politics that are shaping the character of congressional policy making. It also reviews recent developments that have changed partisan control of the institution and altered the distribution of power within the institution.

Chapters 2 and 7 survey both constitutional and internal legislative rules to give an integrated perspective on the legislative game. The special character of American national legislative politics is the product of the Constitution, which created three institutions – the House of Representatives, the Senate, and the president – and set rules governing their interaction in the process of enacting public laws. In addition, the House and the Senate have developed different rules and practices that have a substantial effect on public policy.

Chapter 3 focuses on congressional elections. It covers the fundamental rules that govern elections and details the advantages enjoyed by congressional incumbents in their efforts to stay in office. The chapter concludes by evaluating the importance of election outcomes for the policy choices made by Congress and the president.

Chapter 4 focuses on individual members. It begins by reviewing the variety of political goals that members pursue. It also considers the resources that members may mobilize in pursuit of their goals and the political actors who influence members' behavior. The chapter concludes by looking at the strategies that members pursue in the case of voting and policy leadership.

Chapters 5, 6, 7, and 8 concern the central components of the legislative process – parties, committees, and the chamber floors. Parties and committees are not mentioned in the Constitution, yet the interaction of parties and committees defines the decision-making process in the modern Congress. The emphasis is on both the development of congressional parties and committees and recent changes that have altered the character of congressional decision making in important ways. Chapter 8, while detailing the activity that takes place on the House and Senate floors, concludes with an overall perspective on how parties, committees, and the floors are related to each other.

Chapters 9, 10, and 11 consider the major institutions and organizations with which Congress interacts – the president and executive branch, the courts, and interest groups. In each case, the emphasis is on the way in which resources and strategies of the institution or organization affect its relations with Congress.

Budget politics and process are the concern of Chapter 12. Budget politics has become a nearly dominant feature of congressional politics, and many important procedural developments have occurred in recent years. This chapter emphasizes the importance of the evolving budget process for the distribution of power in Congress.

A Special Appendix

We have added an appendix on spatial theories of legislative politics. Spatial theory now plays a central role in the political science of legislative politics.

Students at all levels benefit from understanding the basic ideas in spatial theory. We suggest that you read the relevant sections of the appendix along with the core chapters. We think it will enrich your understanding of the political strategies pursued by legislators and presidents and give you some basis for understanding the determinants of legislative outcomes.

Acknowledgments

We are very pleased to be publishing this edition of *The American Congress* with Cambridge University Press. Cambridge editor Ed Parsons has championed this project, provided wise advice to us, and shepherded the review and editorial processes with great skill.

This edition would not have been possible without the support and motivation provided by the Weidenbaum Center at Washington University in St. Louis. Chris Moseley provided superb administrative assistance.

Over the years, members of Congress have been remarkably generous with their time. Smith is particularly indebted to the late Speaker Thomas P. "Tip" O'Neill, with whom he spent a year under the auspices of the Congressional Fellowship Program of the American Political Science Association. He learned a great deal about congressional politics from Speaker O'Neill and his top aides, Ari Weiss and the late Spencer Smith.

We thank our many colleagues who teach about Congress for their encouragement.

Steven S. Smith, Jason M. Roberts, and Ryan J. Vander Wielen

Above: Members of the Congressional Black Caucus participate in the CBC ceremonial swearing in event at the Capitol Visitors Center Congressional Auditorium on Tuesday, January, 6, 2009. **Below:** WASHINGTON, DC – Nov. 17: House Representatives-elect on the East Front steps of the U.S. Capitol for a freshman class photo. Democrats bolstered their majority with a gain of 20 seats in the House in national elections in November. (Photo by Scott J. Ferrell/Congressional Quarterly)

1

The American Congress: Modern Trends

C ONGRESS IS AN EXCITING PLACE. REAL POWER RESIDES IN ITS MEMBERS, real social conflicts are tamed or exacerbated by its actions, and thousands of people – most of them good public servants – walk its halls every day. Much good work is done there. In recent years, Congress has passed widely applauded bills that have, among other things, approved new security measures for airports and funding for the war against terrorism; granted important civil rights to women, minorities, and the disabled; given parents job protection so they can care for sick children; forced states to reduce barriers to voter registration and supported reforms of voting processes; expanded funding for college students; and limited what lobbyists can give to legislators.

Congress is a frustrating place as well. It is not easy to understand. Its sheer size – 535 members and more than 25,000 employees – is bewildering. Its system of parties, committees, and procedures, built up over 200 years, is remarkably complex and serves as an obstacle to public understanding. Perhaps most frustrating is that its work product, legislation, is the product of a process marked by controversy, partisanship, and bargaining. Even some members of Congress are uncomfortable with the sharp rhetoric and wheeling and dealing that are hallmarks of legislative politics.

But Congress is also important. No other national legislature has greater power than the Congress of the United States. Its daily actions affect the lives of all Americans and many people around the world. It checks the exercise of power by the president, the courts, and the bureaucracy. If you want to understand the forces influencing your welfare, you must understand Congress.

Congress is always changing. It changes because it is a remarkably permeable institution. New problems, whatever their source, invariably create new demands on Congress. Elections bring new members, who often alter

1

the balance of opinion in the House and Senate. Elections also frequently bring a change in majority party control of Congress, which leads to a transfer of agenda control on the floor and in committees from one party to another. And each new president asks for support for his policy program. Members of Congress often respond to these demands by passing new legislation. But as lawmakers pursue their personal political goals, compete with one another for control over policy, and react to pressure from presidents, their constituents, and lobbyists, they sometimes seek to gain advantage or to remove impediments to action by altering the procedures and organization of Congress itself. The result is nearly continuous change within the institution.

Explaining the ongoing changes in Congress is the central focus of this text. We begin in this chapter by highlighting several developments in American politics that have changed congressional politics. These developments – including changes in the way Congress is covered by the media, evolving standards for public ethics, the rise of plebiscitary politics and new information technologies, new forms of organized efforts to influence Congress, new kinds of issues, and the war on terrorism – have altered the context of congressional policy making in basic ways.

Low Public Confidence

The popularity of Congress ebbs and flows with the public's confidence in government generally. When the president's ratings and trust in government improved after the tragic events of September 11, 2001, Congress's approval ratings improved too. Still, Congress's performance ratings are almost always below those of the president and the Supreme Court. The legislative process is easy to dislike – it often generates political posturing and grandstanding, it necessarily involves compromise, and it often leaves broken promises in its wake. Also, members of Congress often appear self-serving as they pursue their political careers and represent interests and reflect values that are controversial.

Scandals, even when they involve a single member, add to the public's frustration with Congress and have contributed to the institution's low ratings in opinion polls. Some of the highlights are provided in the box on page 3. A consequence is that Congress is a never-ending source of comic relief, like the joke about the senator who dozed off during a roll-call vote, was jerked awake when his name was called, and reflexively yelled out, "Not guilty." There also is the joke about the member who kept referring to the presiding officer as "Your Honor."[1] But seriously . . . it seems fair to say that a large majority of today's members behave ethically. It is even reasonable to argue

HIGHLIGHTS OF RECENT CONGRESSIONAL ETHICS SCANDALS

• In 1989, House Speaker James Wright (D-Texas) resigned after Republicans charged him with ethics violations for receiving extraordinarily large royalties on a book.

• In 1991, Senator David Durenburger (R-Minnesota) was condemned in a unanimously approved Senate resolution for a book deal and for seeking reimbursement for expenses for staying in a condo that he owned.

• The disclosure that many House members had repeatedly overdrawn their accounts at the House disbursement office led people to believe that members enjoyed special privileges.

• Questions about the propriety of campaign contributions were raised in the "Keating Five" affair, which concerned the relationship between five senators and a prominent savings-and-loan owner seeking to block an investigation of his financial dealings.

• In 1995, a long investigation of sexual harassment charges against Senator Robert Packwood (R-Oregon) led to his forced resignation from office.

• In 1995, Representative Dan Rostenkowski (D-Illinois), former chairman of the House Ways and Means Committee, was found guilty of illegally receiving cash for personal use from the House post office. He later served a prison term.

• In 1995, Representative Enid Waldholtze (R-Utah) retired after her husband was charged with felonies in conjunction with raising funds for her campaign.

• In 1997, Speaker Newt Gingrich (R-Georgia) agreed to pay $300,000 in fines based on charges that he used nonprofit organizations for political purposes and misled the House Committee on Standards of Official Conduct.

• In 1998, Representative Jay Kim (R-California) pleaded guilty to charges involving more than $250,000 in illegal campaign contributions.

• In 2002, Representative James A. Traficant, Jr. (D-Ohio), was convicted of receiving bribes in exchange for helping businesses get government contracts and of engaging in a pattern of racketeering since taking office in 1985.

• In 2004, House Majority Leader Tom Delay (R-Texas) was issued letters of admonition by the House ethics committee for improperly promising to endorse the son of Representative Nick Smith (R-Michigan) in exchange for Smith's vote on a bill and for attending a fundraising event with lobbyists for a company that was lobbying him on pending legislation.

• In 2005, Representative Duke Cunningham (R-California) resigned and pleaded guilty to taking more than $2.4 million in bribes and related tax evasion and fraud, the largest financial sum involving an individual member.

• In 2006, Representative Tom Delay (R-Texas) resigned after being indicted in Texas for laundering money through a national party committee in his effort to redistrict Texas congressional districts.

(*continued*)

HIGHLIGHTS OF RECENT CONGRESSIONAL ETHICS SCANDALS (*continued*)

- In 2006, Representative William Jefferson (D-Louisiana) won reelection to the House but was denied a Ways and Means Committee assignment after FBI agents videotaped him appearing to solicit a bribe and later found $90,000 of the marked cash in his freezer – making this the cold cash scandal. Jefferson was defeated for reelection in 2008. The prosecution continues at this writing.

- In 2006, Representative Mark Foley (R-Florida) resigned after it was disclosed that he sent sexually explicit email messages to underage House pages.

- In 2006, Representative Bob Ney (R-Ohio) pleaded guilty to making false statements and participating in a conspiracy, receiving thousands of dollars in gifts from lobbyist Jack Abramoff. A Ney aide pleaded guilty to receiving gifts. Separately, Abramoff pleaded guilty to charges of conspiracy, fraud, and tax evasion.

- In 2008, Senator Ted Stevens (R-Alaska) was convicted of seven counts of failing to disclose gifts related to the renovation of his Alaska home on his Senate financial disclosure forms. His conviction was later overturned due to prosecutorial misconduct.

- In 2008, Representative Tim Mahoney (D-Florida) confessed that he had had an extra-marital affair with a staff member. Shortly after, news reports indicated that Mahoney attempted to buy the staff member's silence, his wife filed for divorce, and he was defeated for reelection.

that today's cohort of members is at least as ethical as any past cohort. No doubt the ethical standards applied by the public, the media, and Congress itself are higher today than at any other time. Yet, there is no denying that the seemingly regular flow of scandals harms Congress's standing with the American people.

Congress suffers generally from low ratings, which some observers believe represents a long-term trend. Political scientist Norman Ornstein notes that changes in the electronic and print media have led to a greater emphasis on the negative and sensational side of Congress. He refers to this as the "tabloidization" of media coverage:

> The drive to emulate the *National Enquirer* and the *Star* has spread to the most respectable newspapers and magazines, while network news divisions have begun to compete with tabloids like "Inside Edition" and "Hard Copy" with their own tabloid shows like "Prime Time Live" and "Dateline: NBC," and with changed coverage on the nightly news.

Stories or rumors of scandal – both individual and institutional – have dominated news coverage of politics and politicians in recent decades more than at any time in modern history, and not just in terms of column inches or broadcast minutes, but in emphasis as well:

> The expansion of radio and cable television talk shows also seems to have increased the speed with which bad news about Congress is disseminated and the frequency with which bad news is repeated. On many of these programs, there is a premium on a quick wit and a good one-liner and little time for sober, balanced commentary.[2]

Groups supporting term limits for Congress and other reforms probably have influenced public opinion too. Term limits advocates argue that congressional incumbents are a privileged class. Incumbents, in this view, have created a system in which various benefits of office – including biased districting, free use of official resources, fundraising leverage, and cozy relations with lobbyists – give them an unfair advantage that can be overcome only through radical reform. The more extreme versions of this argument suggest that incumbents have been corrupted by their experience in Washington. Incumbents are said to have developed an "inside-the-beltway" mentality (the Beltway is the freeway that encircles the District of Columbia and its inner suburbs) or to suffer from "Potomac fever" (presumably a condition brought on by proximity to the famous river).

Politicians, of course, quickly latch on to themes that resonate with the public. As a result, running for Congress by running *against* Congress, an old art form in American politics, has gained an even more prominent place in recent campaigns. Indeed, many recent arrivals on Capitol Hill promised to end "business as usual" in Washington and to push through reforms to "fix" Congress – to end the system of congressional perks, to stop the influence of special interests, and so on. The repetition of anti-Congress themes undoubtedly contributes to the low ratings for Congress and its members in public opinion polls.

The public's generally low evaluations of Congress have been observed for years. The Gallup Poll has regularly asked the question, "Do you approve or disapprove of the way Congress is handling its job?" Figure 1.1 shows that less than a majority of the public approves of Congress's performance most of the time. In the last few decades, the only time Congress's approval rating reached significantly above 50 percent was in the months following the terrorist attacks of September 11, 2001, during which anti-terrorist legislation was quickly approved.

While Congress languishes with mediocre approval ratings, individual members of Congress continue to do quite well. Typically, Gallup finds that about 70 percent of the public approves of the way its own U.S.

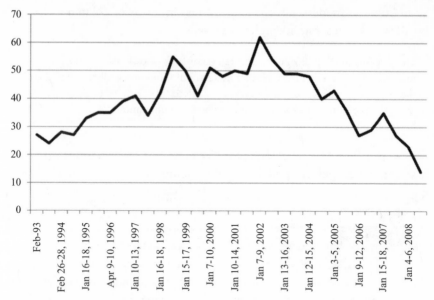

Percent Approving Congressional Performance, 1993–2008. *Source:* Gallup Poll.

representative is handling his or her job. Running *for* Congress by running *against* Congress works well.

Plebiscitary Politics

Political scientist Robert Dahl argues that Congress suffers from the increasingly plebiscitary nature of American politics. By a movement toward plebiscitary politics, Dahl is referring to the trend toward more direct communication between the public and elected officials and the demise of intermediaries – such as parties and membership organizations – that once served to represent or express public opinion to elected officials. Directly observed, rather than mediated, public views are more important than ever – which could not be further from Madison's aspirations for the national legislature.[3]

Plebiscitary politics is facilitated by new technologies. Advances in transportation allow most members of Congress to be back home in their districts or states most weekends. Public opinion polls, which allow the public's views to be registered with legislators, have become more affordable because of advancements in digital technology. Leaders and parties sponsor focus groups to learn about nuances and shadings in public attitudes. Radio and television call-in shows enable nearly every constituent to talk directly to a member of Congress from time to time. Satellite technology allows members

a vote of the people on a proposal submitted to them

to communicate easily and inexpensively with groups in their home state or district from Washington.

Members of Congress, and certainly candidates for Congress, find the new information technologies irresistible and contribute to the trend. Members love to demonstrate their commitment to keeping in touch with their constituents by being among the first to use a new innovation in communications. To be sure, members face real problems reaching constituents in districts and states with ever-growing populations. The average House district is approaching 700,000 people, up from about 300,000 in 1940 and 400,000 in 1960. Still, the political value of appearing to be connected to constituents drives elected officials to exploit new technologies.

On its face, plebiscitary politics might seem to be a good thing: It seems better to have public opinion influencing members' decisions than to have highly paid lobbyists representing organized interests swaying their votes. But as Dahl notes, the effects of direct communication between the people and their representatives on Capitol Hill may not be so desirable. For one thing, elected officials and special interests might manipulate direct communication to their advantage. If the politicians are the ones who choose the time and place for direct communication, the process may create nothing more than a deceiving appearance of responsiveness.

More important, plebiscitary politics may undermine both representation and deliberation in legislative policy making. With respect to representation, the "public" that is likely to communicate directly to members may not be representative of members' larger constituencies. They will be people who are intensely interested in politics, generally or in a single issue, and can afford and know how to use new information technologies. If so, then members' impressions of public opinion may be distorted by such communication.

With respect to deliberation, direct communication with more constituents could lead members to make premature public commitments on more issues and reduce their flexibility in negotiating compromises in the legislative arena. The possible result is that demagoguery and grandstanding would take precedence over resolving conflicts and solving problems. Public opinion may win out over the public interest, which is what Madison sought to avoid.

Governing as Campaigning

A close cousin to the rise of plebiscitary politics is the weakening distinction between governing and campaigning. Of course, we hope that there is a strong linkage between governing and campaigning. Elected officials' desire for reelection underpins our ability to hold them accountable. Broadly speaking, campaign promises are (and should be) related to governing, and election outcomes are (and should be) shaped by performance in office. Inevitably, then, the line between governing and campaigning becomes blurred.

In recent decades, campaigning has become more fully integrated with governing. No longer is governing done in Washington and campaigning done at home. The daily routines of members and top leaders are now geared to the demands of campaigning.

Few members retire from Congress without complaining about how much it costs to mount a campaign for reelection. Returning members may not have time to complain. In recent years, the average victor in a Senate race spent more than $8 million, and the average House victor spent more than a million dollars. Many races were far more expensive. For an incumbent seeking reelection, that is an average of more than $25,000 for each week served during a six-year Senate term and almost $10,000 for each week served during a two-year House term. These sums do not include additional millions spent by parties and independent groups on congressional campaigns. Competitive pressures, between incumbents and challengers and between the two parties, have produced a never-ending search for cash.

Congressional leaders have changed their ways, too. To assist their party colleagues, most party leaders spend many evenings and weekends at fundraising events. Many leaders have developed their own political action committees (leadership PACs, they have been called) to raise and distribute money. Leaders have formed public relations task forces within their parties, and the campaign committees of the congressional parties have greatly expanded their activities. Perhaps most important, congressional leaders now often use technology developed for campaigning in legislative battles. Professional consultants and pollsters help fashion legislative priorities and tactics. Opposition research – digging up dirt on your election opponent – is now conducted by the congressional campaign committees against congressional incumbents of the opposite party. Media campaigns are now planned for major legislative proposals with the assistance of television advertising specialists. Money, media, and partisanship feed on each other.

New Forms of Organized Influence

The number of interest groups in Washington and the rest of the country multiplied many times in the last half century. By one count, the number of groups increased from about 1,000 in the late 1940s to well more than

PAC: Political Action Committee

Congressionally Speaking...

Each Congress has a two-year life span. Federal law sets the date for federal elections, but the Constitution specifies the starting date for each Congress. Before 1935, congressional elections in November of an even-numbered year preceded the convening of a new Congress the following March. Since 1935, after the ratification of the Twentieth Amendment to the Constitution, a new Congress convenes on January 3 unless Congress otherwise provides by law, as it often does to avoid weekends. Each two-year Congress is given a number – the 111th Congress convened in January 2009 – and is divided into two one-year sessions. Congressional documents are often numbered 111–1 or 111–2 to combine the Congress and session numbers.

7,000 in the early 1980s.[4] Due to lobbying registration requirements that were enacted in 1995, we know that the number of registered lobbyists has more than doubled since 2000 to more than 35,000. This increase is primarily a by-product of the expanding scope of the federal government's activity – as more interests were affected by federal programs, tax policies, and regulation, more interests have sought representation in Washington. Technological developments in transportation, information management, and communications have enabled scattered people, corporations, and even state and local governments to easily organize, raise money, and set up offices and staff in Washington. The process feeds on itself, with new groups forming to counter the influence of other recently formed groups. The result has been a tremendous increase in the demands placed on members of Congress by lobbyists from organized groups.

Not only have interest groups proliferated, they have also become more diverse. Economic interests – corporations, trade associations, and labor groups – greatly outnumber other sectors among lobbyists. In addition, many groups represent new industries, and "citizens" groups sprouted in the 1960s and 1970s and continue to grow in number. These groups are often outgrowths of national movements – such as those for civil rights, women's rights, children's rights, the elimination of hunger, consumers' rights, welfare rights, gay rights, environmental protection, and the homeless. Many of these groups now enjoy memberships numbering in the hundreds of thousands.

Along with their increasing number and diversity, groups have become more skilled in camouflaging their true identity. For most major legislative battles, coalitions of interests form and take all-American names, pool their resources to fund mass media campaigns, and often dissolve as fast as they were created. Many of the coalitions are the handiwork of entrepreneurs in law firms, consulting outfits, and public relations shops who are paid to coordinate the activity of the coalitions they spearheaded.

The roots have been taken out of grassroots lobbying. New technologies provide the ability to make highly targeted, highly efficient appeals to stimulate constituency demands on Washington. By the late 1980s, computerized telephone messages allowed groups to communicate with many thousands of people within a few hours. Technology now allows a group to telephone its own members, a targeted group (such as one House member's constituency), or the general public; briefly interview the respondents about their views on a subject; and, for respondents who favor the group's position, provide a few more facts to reinforce their views, solicit them to write letters to members of Congress, and quickly transfer the calls to the appropriate Capitol Hill offices before the respondents hang up. Several groups have developed television programs – some shown on the many cable television channels that are available in most communities – as a way of reaching specific audiences. Lobbyists exploit email and interactive video technologies to motivate citizens to flood Congress with messages. As a result, for a group with money, the absence of a large membership is not much of an obstacle to generating public pressure on members of Congress.

New Issues

New issues – such as the war against terrorism and global warming – always present some difficulty for Congress. They often create problems for congressional committees, whose official jurisdictions were defined years earlier when the new issues were not anticipated. Committees scramble to assert jurisdiction, and party leaders sometimes are asked to referee. After some amount of infighting and delay, committees eventually manage to adjust. In the view of some observers, however, Congress's ability to adjust in a timely way is becoming more and more strained.

It is nearly hackneyed to say that the issues facing Congress are becoming more technical and complex, but it is true. Increasingly, expertise in science, engineering, economics, or other fields is required to understand policy problems and alternatives. Congress often solves this problem by setting broad policy goals and delegating the power to make the necessary technical decisions to experts in the executive branch.[5] In this way, Congress is able to respond to demands for action. However, it does so at the cost of enhancing the executive branch's power over the details of public policy.

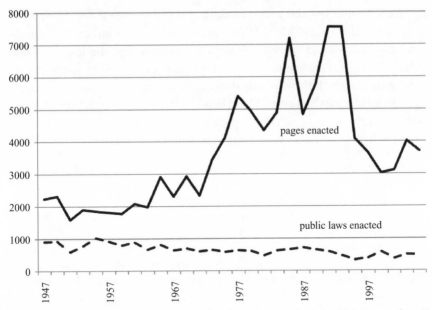

FIGURE 1.1. Number of Public Laws Enacted and Pages Enacted, 1947–2006. *Source: http:// www.gpoaccess.gov/statutes/browse.html.*

At other times, Congress seeks to legislate the technical details. The cost then is that only a few members and staff assistants can understand the legislation and participate effectively in making important decisions. Scientific and medical research, defense programs, environmental protection, the regulation of financial institutions, international trade, and many other fields of public policy are no longer within the common experiences of elected officials. Thus, most members must look to competing interpretations of proposed legislation offered by staff specialists, lobbyists, and a wide array of outside experts.

The new policy challenges result from an increasingly complex American society coupled with the integration of international and domestic economies. Fewer major policies can be debated in isolation from other major policies. Health care reform, for example, concerns employer-employee relations, economic growth, welfare reform, and tax policy, among other things. This complexity leads Congress to craft unwieldy bills, often written by multiple committees, laden with technical language, and reaching several hundred pages in length. Figure 1.2 shows the increasing length of the average bill enacted by Congress in recent decades, at least until the Republicans gained congressional majorities in 1994. Between 1995 and 2006, the total number of bills and the number of pages enacted into law declined sharply, but the average length of a bill remained several times as long as for the 1950s. More than issue complexity underlies the increasing length of bills, as we will see in later chapters, but the length of bills presents a serious challenge to legislators who might want to understand the legislation on which they are asked to cast votes.

Political scientist Lawrence Dodd believes that Congress, at least as it now operates, cannot cope with the important issues of our time. In his view, the problem lies in the relationship between members and their constituents:

> The voters may see the decay of urban infrastructure, sense the declining educational and job opportunities of their children, acknowledge the ecological damage of industrial pollution, and worry about the long-term effects of a mounting deficit. But as they consider their vote for senator and representative, the citizens override any broad concerns they may have with collective issues and vote in accord with ensuring immediate benefits; they do so by voting for the powerful local incumbent who can assist with a desired local defense contract or who can help them with their veterans claim or Medicare benefits. They do so because of the immediate influence that a powerful incumbent legislator can have on their particularized interests . . . The emerging collective problems of the new era thus go unacknowledged and tear away at the fabric of society.[6]

If Dodd is right, then the public's ratings of congressional performance will continue to be low while incumbent legislators will continue to be routinely reelected.

Congress's tendency is to allow the president to define solutions to the nation's problems and then to criticize those solutions from narrow, often parochial perspectives. Unfortunately, plebiscitary politics, the proliferation of interest groups, and the new ways of influencing members of Congress of interest groups, and the new ways of influencing members of Congress reinforce this tendency. Modern politics puts more pressure than ever on members to explain themselves in terms that are readily understood by the folks back home. Scholar and congressman David Price (D-North Carolina) observes, "Members must constantly explain themselves and their actions in terms of ordinary knowledge. A decision that does not lend itself to such an explanation often has a heavy burden of proof against it. In the era of television journalism, of thirty-second ads and negative advertising, a defensive deference to ordinary knowledge has probably become more important in congressional behavior than it was before."[7] The gap between what legislators do and what they can explain seems to be widening.

Congressionally Speaking . . .

Every 10 years, the Census Bureau counts the number of people living in the
United States. On the basis of that count, the Census Bureau allocates seats in
the U.S. House of Representatives to each of the states according to a formula
set in law. This allocation is called *apportionment*. States then draw the
boundaries of districts for the House of Representatives, a process known as
districting. Districting is controversial because it may advantage one of the
parties or certain incumbent legislators. Districting was very controversial in
Texas following the 2000 census. The original districting plan enacted by a
Democratic majority in the state legislature was replaced by a plan enacted
by a later Republican majority in the legislature. As the Republicans hoped,
the new districting plan helped to elect more Republicans to the U.S. House of
Representatives in 2004.

Changing Membership

Regional Shifts

In recent decades, demographic and social changes in American society
have altered the composition of Congress in important ways. One important
change has been in the allocation of House seats to the states. The 435
seats of the House are reapportioned every 10 years to reflect changes
in the distribution of the nation's population across the states. A formula
established by law guides the Census Bureau, which calculates the number of
districts for each state every 10 years after the decennial census. Population
shifts have allowed certain states in the South and West to gain seats in the
House of Representatives at the expense of several eastern and midwestern
states. The regional shifts are visible in Table 1.1. The South and West gained
even more seats after the national census in the year 2000 – again at the
expense of the industrial Northeast and Midwest.

The redistribution of seats away from the northern industrial states has
reduced those states' political clout at a time when they could use it. The
need for infrastructure repairs, worker retraining, low-income housing, and
other government services is severe in the old industrial states, but the
declining influence of these states is reducing their ability to acquire financial assistance from the federal government. Indeed, the shift of power to
the more conservative regions of the country has undercut congressional

TABLE 1.1. Changes in the Apportionment of House Seats, by Region, After Census of 1960 and 2000.

Region	Post-1960 Seats	Post-2000 Seats	Difference
East	108	83	−25
Midwest	125	100	−25
South	133	154	21
West	69	98	29
Total	435	435	

Source: Census Bureau.

support for a major federal role in the rehabilitation of the industrial cities of the northern-tier states.

The population growth in the South and West is the result of that region's economic growth, an influx of workers from the older industrial states and other countries, and the expansion of the region's middle class. The most obvious consequence of these developments is that the South is no longer a one-party region, as it was just three decades ago. Republicans are now competitive in Senate races throughout the South and hold many House seats as well. As recently as 1960, Republicans held no Senate seats and only six of 104 House seats in the states of the old Confederacy. After the 1992 elections, Republicans held 13 of the 22 Senate seats and 48 of the 125 House seats in the region, with the largest numbers in Florida and Texas. The southern Senate seats were critical to Republicans between 1981 and 1986, when they controlled the Senate, and again after 1994.

Preliminary population estimates for 2010 promise a continuing shift of House seats away from the East and Midwest to the South and West. New York and Ohio may lose two seats each, while Illinois, Iowa, Michigan, Minnesota, and Pennsylvania may lose one each. Texas may gain four seats, Arizona may gain two seats, and Florida, Georgia, North Carolina, and South Carolina may gain one seat each.

Women and Minorities

Beyond the changes in regional representation and partisan composition in Congress, Capitol Hill has also acquired a sizable contingent of women and minorities. The growing strength of women's and minority groups, the acquisition of political experience by women and minority politicians in state and local government, and new voting laws have contributed to the

TABLE 1.2. Number of Women and Minorities in the House and Senate, 1971–2007.

Congress (first year)	Women		African Americans		Hispanic Americans	
	House	Senate	House	Senate	House	Senate
92d (1971)	12	1	12	1	5	1
93d (1973)	14	0	15	1	5	1
94th (1975)	18	0	16	1	5	1
95th (1977)	18	0	16	1	5	0
96th (1979)	16	1	16	0	6	0
97th (1981)	19	2	16	0	6	0
98th (1983)	21	2	20	0	10	0
99th (1985)	22	2	19	0	11	0
100th (1987)	23	2	22	0	11	0
101st (1989)	25	2	23	0	11	0
102d (1991)	29	2	25	0	10	0
103d (1993)	48	6	38	1	17	0
104th (1995)	49	8	39	1	18	0
105th (1997)	51	9	37	1	18	0
106th (1999)	58	9	39	0	19	0
107th (2001)	59	13	36	0	21	0
108th (2003)	62	14	39	0	21	0
109th (2005)	68	14	42	1	24	2
110th (2007)	67	16	40	1	24	3
111th (2009)	77	18	41	1	25	2

Source: *Vital Statistics on American Politics* (Washington, D.C.: Congressional Quarterly Press, 2000), p. 201; entries for the 107th–111th Congresses collected by the authors. Numbers reflect membership at the start of the Congress.

recent improvement in these groups' representation in Congress. In 1993, the Senate gained its first Native American, Ben Nighthorse Campbell (D-Colorado), who later switched parties, and its first black woman, Carol Moseley-Braun (D-Illinois). Table 1.2 shows the gains that women, African Americans, and Hispanics have made in Congress in recent years, and even more – many more – women and minorities have been running for Congress. More than 100 women have been major party candidates for Congress in each election since 1992. In 2006, 139 women ran for the House. Only three Native Americans have served in the Senate.

Women and minorities are still underrepresented in Congress relative to their proportions in the population, but few doubt that women and minority

1.) Speaker of the House
2.) Whip
3.) Chairman

lawmakers have already had a substantial impact. Most obviously, the Congressional Caucus for Women's Issues, the Congressional Black Caucus, and, to a lesser extent, the Congressional Hispanic Caucus have become important factions within the House Democratic Party. Women and blacks comprise about 20 percent of the House Democratic Caucus. In 2009, the Senate began with 17 women and three Hispanics, and after he was appointed to replace President Barack Obama, one African American, Roland Burris (D-IL). In fact, in winning his 2004 bid for a Senate seat from Illinois, Democrat Barack Obama became only the third African American popularly elected to the Senate since the early twentieth century when the Seventeenth Amendment to the Constitution, providing for direct election to the Senate, was ratified. Only one Native American, Tom Cole (R-Oklahoma), a member of the Chickasaw Nation, remained in Congress in 2009. Cole was elected chair of the National Republican Congressional Committee, his party's campaign committee, in late 2006, which he gave up after the 2008 elections.

The presence of more women and minorities has changed the mix of voices heard in congressional debates. Social and economic problems seem to be more frequently discussed in the first person today – that is, more members refer to their personal experience when addressing their colleagues and constituents. In addition, more legislation reflecting the issues that are given greater emphasis by women and minorities is introduced. Generally, issues important to these groups have been given higher priority by party leaders, particularly Democratic leaders.

Only one woman, Rep. Nancy Pelosi (D-California), has been elected the top leader of a congressional party. Pelosi was elected Speaker in 2007 after the Democrats won a majority of House seats in the 2006 elections. She had been elected the Democrats' Minority Leader in late 2002 after serving in the number two position, Democratic Whip, for two years. The other women in party leadership are Representative Cathy McMorris Rogers (R-Washington), the House Republican Conference Vice Chair, Senator Patty Murray (D-Washington), the Senate Democratic Conference Secretary, Senator Debbie Stabenow (D-Michigan), the Senate Democratic Steering and Outreach Committee Chairwoman, and Senator Barbara Boxer (D-California), the Senate Democrats Chief Deputy Whip. Many women have gained sufficient seniority to chair important committees and subcommittees.

Only two African Americans have served in one of the top three leadership positions in a congressional party. J. C. Watts of Oklahoma served as House Republican Conference chair in 1998–2002, but he retired from Congress in

2002. James Clyburn of South Carolina was elected the House Democratic caucus vice chairman and chairman in 2002 and 2004, respectively, and then was elected Democratic Whip in 2006. When Rep. Robert Menendez of New Jersey became the House Democratic Caucus chair in 2002, he became the highest ranking Hispanic legislator in the history of Congress. Menendez was appointed to fill a Senate vacancy in late 2005 and was elected to the seat in 2006.

Previous Occupations

Notable changes have occurred in members' occupational profiles. Congress is still dominated by lawyers and business people, with over 200 lawyers and about 200 members with business backgrounds in the House and Senate in 2009. The number of farmers has declined – down from about 75 in the 1950s to just over two dozen in recent Congresses. Educators have become more numerous – over 90 in 2009. Overall, the occupational backgrounds of members are now somewhat more diverse than they were three or four decades ago.

These trends in the membership of Congress – the shift to the Sunbelt, the increasing numbers of women and minority members, and the greater diversity in members' previous experience – are likely to continue. The professions of law and business still dominate, but a wider range of experiences are reflected in the membership of Congress now than a generation ago.

Changing Party Control

Perhaps the most conspicuous changes in Congress in recent years were the changes in party control. During the 1955–1980 period, Democrats enjoyed majorities in both the House and Senate. In 1980, the Republicans gained a Senate majority but lost their majority in 1986. In 1994, Republicans won majorities in both houses, which they maintained until 2001 when Senator James Jeffords of Vermont gave up his Republican affiliation and created a short-lived Democratic majority. Republican victories in the 2002 elections produced Republican majorities in both chambers, which they retained and expanded in the 2004 elections. Democrats won narrow majorities in both houses in the 2006 elections, which they retained and expanded in 2008. With an evenly divided electorate, we have experienced a prolonged period of narrow majorities in both chambers of Congress in the last decade (see Figure 1.3).

Lost in 2012

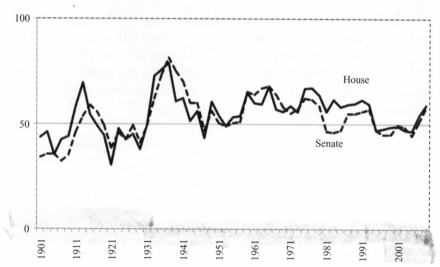

FIGURE 1.2. Percent of House and Senate Seats Held by Democrats at the Start of Each Congress, 1903–2009.

Political scientist Richard F. Fenno, Jr., argues that frequent changes in party control keep the arrogance of the majority party in check.[8] Fenno contends that the uncertainties created by frequent change in majority control reduce the temptation for a new majority to overreach itself once in office. According to Fenno, because the Democrats had dominated the House for 40 years, when the Republicans took over in 1994, they were both inexperienced and impatient. The Republicans overstated their mandate from the 1994 elections, translated that inflated mandate into rigid and ultimately unsuccessful legislative strategies, and perhaps contributed to the reelection of Democrat Bill Clinton to the presidency in 1996.

Fenno also observes that the long era of Democratic rule led the Republicans, prior to their 1994 takeover, to adopt radical measures to end it. The Republicans assumed an uncompromising stance in Congress, making legislating more difficult and intensifying partisanship. After the Republicans gained control, Speaker Gingrich led a rhetorical assault on the very institution his party had fought to control, contributing to a further loss of public support for Congress.

If Fenno is right, then alternating control of Congress produces greater flexibility in party policy positions, more pragmatic party strategies, greater civility in political discourse, and perhaps greater public support for the institution. Early evidence may have supported his argument. In late 1996, hoping to do well in the upcoming elections, a House Democratic leader was quoted as saying, "Our themes will be to make the institution look reasonable, to take moderate steps for average Americans and to make sure that the public understands what we are doing."[9] In 1997, after experiencing a lopsided defeat in the presidential election and a scare in the House elections of 1996, congressional Republicans proved considerably more willing to bargain with the president over the single most important matter before Congress, the budget (see Chapter 12). After the 2006 elections, leaders of both parties promised to turn down the level of partisanship. A political "uncertainty principle" – that an uncertain electoral future breeds political moderation – seems to contribute to these proclamations.

The moderating effect appears to have a very short half-life. By many accounts, the Congress has been more partisan since the turn of the new century than it had been for a hundred years. Poor personal relations among leaders of the two parties, the exclusion of minority party legislators from some conference committee meetings, minority obstructionism on judicial nominations, personal campaigning against incumbents of the opposite party, and other developments are cited by insiders as evidence of deteriorating relations across party lines. Moreover, after 10 years of Republican control of the House, many Democrats asserted that they need to follow the approach of the Republicans of the late 1980s and 1990s, that is, to better define differences between the parties, intensify public relations campaigns against the majority party, and gear legislative tactics to winning a majority in the next election. With new Democratic majorities in Congress, the Fenno hypothesis will get another test.

The War on Terrorism and Congressional Power

Perhaps the most serious challenge to Congress's role in the American constitutional system is secret government necessitated by national security. The war against terrorism has revived fears that secrecy in the national security agencies of government will threaten Americans' civil liberties and undermine Congress's ability to influence the direction of policy, to oversee the expenditure of public funds, and to hold executive officials accountable. Executive branch officials are hesitant to reveal certain information to members of Congress because they do not trust legislators to keep the information secret. For their part, legislators cannot know what information is being withheld from Congress, so secret government tends to breed distrust on Capitol Hill.

In the 1970s, in the aftermath of the Vietnam War and disclosures of misdeeds by intelligence agencies, Congress enacted a variety of laws to require notification of Congress, and sometimes to grant the power to approve or disapprove to Congress, for the commitment of armed forces abroad, arms sales, and covert operations. Congress also created intelligence committees and established other mechanisms for handling classified information. Presidents of both parties have not liked to be constrained by these laws, at times arguing that the laws unconstitutionally impinge on the president's powers. Many members of Congress, on the other hand, have been unwilling to assume some responsibility for national security policy by exploiting new laws or insisting on presidential cooperation. The result is continuing uncertainty about when congressional approval is required. Congressional participation in national security policy making varies from case to case, driven by political calculations as well as legal and national security considerations.

The fight against terrorism poses special challenges for members of Congress. More classified activity, more covert action, and a bewildering array of technologies are involved. More domestic police activity is conducted under the umbrella of national security. The need for quick, coordinated, multi-agency action is intensified. Congress is not capable of effectively checking such executive action. Congress is open and slow, its division of labor among committees is not well matched to the executive agencies involved, and its members are hesitant to challenge the executive branch on high-risk policies and in areas where the public is likely to defer to the president.

Congressional participation in policy making related to the war against terrorism tends to be limited to a few members. The president consults with top party leaders, while agency officials brief members of the intelligence and defense committees. Average members are not regularly informed about developments in the war. They are asked to support funding for the war without access to all relevant information.

With Republican majorities during much of the period since the 9/11 attack, Congress did not actively pursue oversight hearings and investigations of Republican administration's conduct of the war against terrorists or the war in Iraq. Democrats, after winning majorities in both houses in the 2006 elections, were more active.

Tempered Decentralization within Congress

The partisanship, concentration on budget, and national security issues have produced a Congress that behaves differently from what was predicted in the 1970s, when Congress last changed its organization and rules in major ways. Political scientists call this period the "post-reform" era. This term requires some explanation.

The House and Senate went through a period of reform in the early 1970s that led observers of the day to warn about the dangers of fragmentation in congressional policy making. In the House, new chamber and party rules were adopted to guarantee that committees operated more democratically and that subcommittee chairs were given greater independence from full committee chairs in setting their agendas and proposing legislation. Power appeared to be flowing away from central party and committee leaders and toward subcommittees and individual members. In the view of some members and outside observers, Congress seemed to be losing whatever ability it had to enact coherent policy. This occurred at a time when the pressures brought by new interest groups, new lobbying strategies, and new issues were mounting. Although Congress had become a more open and democratic institution, its capacity to manage the nation's affairs seemed diminished.

By the mid-1980s, however, Congress – particularly the House – had not turned out as many observers had expected. Individualism had moderated a little, the congressional agenda had become more focused, party leaders and party organizations showed signs of revitalization, and the decentralization of power to the subcommittees had been tempered. Although Congress did not revert to its old ways, it acquired a new mix of characteristics that justified a new label – the "post-reform Congress." A brief review of the characteristics of the post-reform Congress serves as an introduction to many of the topics addressed in later chapters.

Tempered Individualism

Whatever other changes occurred after the 1970s, the entrepreneurial spirit of individual members remained strong. In fact, it is almost a cliché to call members of today's Congress political entrepreneurs. The term is used to indicate members' relative independence from local and national parties. Candidates for congressional office now develop their own campaign organizations, raise their own money, and set their own campaign strategies. This independence from the political parties tends to carry over when the winners take office. Once in office, members use official resources and exploit their relationships with interest groups and political action committees for political advantage. Knowing that they are on their own when it comes to getting reelected, they take full advantage of taxpayer-supported travel opportunities and communications technologies to maintain a high profile at home. These topics are addressed in Chapters 3 and 4.

By the late 1970s, members had become weary of the surge in committee and floor activity that was the by-product of reforms and unchecked individualism. Part of the concern was that members were spending longer days on Capitol Hill, away from their families and their home states and districts. And part of the concern was political – members faced more numerous and more hazardous political choices as their colleagues forced recorded votes on more legislative proposals. In the House, some members, even some of those responsible for the reforms, began to ask committee and party leaders to assert more control. The most conspicuous response was to put more restrictions on floor amending activity in the House, a topic that is addressed in Chapters 7 and 8. But more generally, both representatives and senators now seem to appreciate leaders who are willing to set some direction, narrow the agenda, and reduce scheduling and political uncertainties. Individualism appears to have tempered somewhat.

Budget Constraints

A large federal budget deficit has a dominant force in legislative politics in most Congresses of recent decades. Other than in national security, few new federal programs were initiated, and much, if not most, of the period's important legislation consisted of large budget bills, particularly budget reconciliation bills. These bills, which are discussed in Chapter 12, are the handiwork of many congressional committees and affect the full range of federal programs over multiple years. This emphasis on large, all-encompassing budget bills further reduced the ability of committees and individual members to pursue policy initiatives.

In the late 1990s, it appeared that the federal budget would be in balance for the foreseeable future and that the politics of blame may be supplanted by a politics of claiming credit. At the start of 1998, the Congressional Budget Office, Congress's budget and economic forecasting agency projected no deficits and measurable surpluses to the year 2008. Predictably, new policy initiatives were proposed by Democratic president Bill Clinton, but few stood a chance of passage with the Republican majority in Congress. After George W. Bush was elected in 2000, Republicans enacted a tax cut bill was passed in 2001, one that seemed quite affordable to many observers until a recession settled in the economy and the terrorist acts of September 11, 2001, motivated large spending initiatives for New York, the war against terrorism, and the war in Iraq. Suddenly, the president and Congress were facing long-term deficits once again.

President Barack Obama and larger Democratic majorities elected in the 2008 elections occurred just after the Wall Street crisis of that fall and created budget challenges that were more serious than ever. The Democrats brought plans for a wide range of new domestic initiatives, all of which were expensive, just at the time the federal government was committing far more than a trillion dollars to bail out Wall Street and other corporations and hundreds of billions were being spent to address a deteriorating economy. The resulting budget constraints greatly limit the policy options of the president and Congress.

Revitalized Parties

In the post-reform era, parties and their leaders have taken on greater importance than was predicted in the 1970s. Frustrations with unrestrained individualism and an emphasis on balancing the budget – issues that had long divided the parties – also contributed to the assertiveness of top party leaders since the 1980s. The replacement of some conservative southern Democrats by conservative Republicans made the Democratic cohort in Congress more liberal on balance and reinforced the conservatism of congressional Republicans. Divided party control of Congress and the presidency seemed to intensify partisanship during much of the period since the 1970s, as each institution and party tried to avoid blame for ballooning deficits, unmet demands for action on social problems, and economic hard times. Top party leaders began to speak more authoritatively for their parties, and party regulars looked to their top leaders to aggressively promote party views in the media. For a year or so after the Republicans gained a majority of House seats in 1994, Speaker Gingrich came to be recognized as the most powerful Speaker since Joseph Cannon (R-Illinois) in the first decade of the twentieth century. Gingrich's successor, Speaker Dennis Hastert (R-Illinois) remained remarkably active in all major policy decisions and Speaker Nancy Pelosi (D-California) has proven to be even more pro-active in structuring the Democrats' legislative program. These developments are detailed in Chapter 5.

The heightened partisanship of recent decades is evident in the use of the Senate filibuster (Figure 1.4). Because the Senate lacks a general rule limiting debate, senators can refuse to stop talking in order to allow the Senate to vote on a pending motion or measure – a tactic called a filibuster. A filibuster

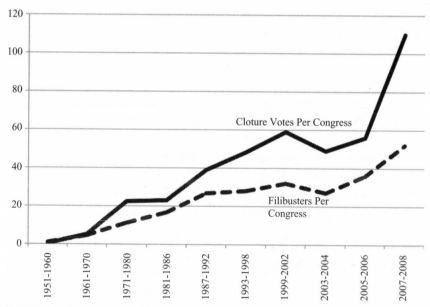

FIGURE 1.3. The Increase in Filibusters and Cloture Votes in Recent Decades. *Source:* Adapted from Barbara Sinclair, "The New World of U.S. Senators," in Lawrence C. Dodd and Bruce I. Oppenheimer, eds., *Congress Reconsidered,* 9th ed. (Washington, D.C.: CQ Press, 2009), p. 7.

obstructs Senate action and can be overcome only with a three-fifths majority of senators voting on most matters – a procedure called cloture. In the highly partisan Senate of recent Congresses, the minority party has more frequently attempted to block majority party legislation and the majority party responded with more cloture motions. This parliamentary arms race has contributed to sharper partisan rhetoric about which party is to blame for legislative outcomes.

Less Autonomous Committees

Chapter 6 details the substantial changes that have occurred in the role of the congressional committees in making law. Multiyear budget pacts, more assertive party leaders, and less deferential parent chambers have altered the place of committees and their subcommittees in the policy-making process. When committees may act and the kinds of legislation they may propose are now more highly constrained, and when they do act, committees are quite likely to act after receiving guidance from party leaders. Although committees remain central features of congressional policy making, they do not enjoy the autonomy that they once did.

The Changing Congress

The ways in which representation and lawmaking are pursued in Congress have evolved in important ways in recent decades. As this chapter has implied, not all of these developments have improved representation or lawmaking. In the chapters that follow, many of these developments are given a closer look. However serious we judge the problems of today's Congress to be, we should remember that Congress is a remarkably resilient institution. Its place in the political process is not threatened. It is rich in resources; critics even charge that it is too strong. Despite the attacks on Congress from many quarters, the legitimacy of its decisions is not seriously questioned by the chief executive, the courts, the states, or the American people.

POLITICAL PASSIONS LEAD TO VIOLENCE IN CONGRESS

Above: The caning of Charles Sumner (R-Massachusetts) by Preston Brooks (D-South Carolina). Brooks was upset by Sumner's speech against slavery.

Below: Cartoonist rendition of the first brawl on the House floor between Matthew Lyon (Democratic-Republican-Vermont) and Roger Griswold (Federalist-Connecticut). Lyon allegedly spit in Griswold's face after a heated debate, Griswold responded by attacking Lyon with a cane. Mayhem ensued as Lyon fought back with a fireplace poker as other House members looked on.

2

Representation and Lawmaking in Congress: The Constitutional and Historical Context

I N REPRESENTATION AND LAWMAKING, RULES MATTER. THE CONSTITUTION creates both a system of representation and a process for making law through two chambers of Congress and a president. One constitutional rule determines the official constituencies of representatives and senators; another determines how members of Congress are elected and how long they serve. Other constitutional rules outline the elements of the legislative process – generally the House, Senate, and president must agree on legislation before it can become law, unless a two-thirds majority of each chamber can override a presidential veto. More detailed rules about the electoral and legislative processes are left for federal statutes, state laws, and internal rules of the House and Senate.

Although the constitutional rules governing representation and lawmaking have changed in only a few ways since Congress first convened in 1789, other features of congressional politics have changed in many ways. The Constitution says nothing about congressional parties and committees, yet most legislation in the modern Congress is written in committees. Committees are appointed through the parties, and party leaders schedule legislation for consideration on the floor. In this chapter, we describe the basic elements of the representation and lawmaking processes and provide an overview of the development of the key components of the modern legislative process.

Representation and Lawmaking

Congress serves two, not always compatible, purposes – representation and lawmaking. Members of the House and Senate serve individual districts or states, yet they must act collectively to make laws for the nation as a whole. Collective action on divisive issues entails bargaining and compromise – among the members of each chamber, between the House and the Senate, and between Congress and the president. For compromise to be possible, members sometimes must retreat from their commitments to their individual states and districts. Determining who must compromise – and how to get them to do so – is the essence of legislative politics. The process can be messy, even distasteful, but, if it is to serve the nation, it is unavoidable.

Congress can be properly evaluated only by understanding our own conflicting expectations about the institution and about the politicians who work within it. To sort out the issues, we begin with a brief introduction explaining how representation and lawmaking occur in practice on Capitol Hill. As we shall see, achieving both perfect representation and perfect lawmaking, in the ways we desire each of them, is impossible.

Representation

REPRESENTATION BY INDIVIDUAL LAWMAKERS. Members of the House and Senate are expected to be *representatives* of their constituents back home. That is not a very precise job description. We might think that a representative's job is to faithfully present the views of his or her district or state in Congress – that is, to serve as a *delegate* for his or her constituents. But a delegate-legislator would not have an easy job because constituents often have conflicting or ambiguous views (or none at all) about the issues before Congress. Alternatively, a member of Congress might be considered a *trustee* – representing his or her constituents by exercising independent judgment about the interests of district, state, or nation. But it is impossible to be a both a faithful delegate and a true trustee.

A third possibility is to see the representative as a *politico* – one who behaves as a delegate on issues that are important to his or her constituents but on other issues has leeway in setting personal policy priorities and casting votes. Unfortunately, for many members of Congress, constituents are not likely to agree either about which issues are important or about when legislators should act as delegates and when they should exercise their own discretion. The challenge of the politician is to balance these legitimate, but often competing, expectations.

REPRESENTATION BY CONGRESS. Even if individual legislators can be considered good representatives for their own constituents, we might still wonder whether Congress can adequately represent the nation as a whole. Congress could be considered a delegate or trustee of the nation. As a delegate institution, Congress would be expected to enact policies reflecting nationwide public opinion, but public opinion often is conflicted,

TABLE 2.1. Two Forms of Aggregating Policy Preferences in the Public and in Congress.

District	District's policy position on a 5-point scale	Legislator's policy position on a 5-point scale	Difference between district and legislator
A	5	1	4
B	4	2	2
C	3	3	0
D	2	4	-2
E	1	5	-4
	3.0	3.0	0.0

Adapted from Robert S. Weissberg, "Collective vs. Dyadic Representation in Congress," *American Political Science Review* 72 (1978): 535–7.

ambiguous, or undeveloped. As a trustee institution, Congress would be expected to formulate policy in a manner consistent with its members' collective judgment about the nation's interests, whatever the state of public opinion. Members regularly invoke public opinion (a delegate perspective) or claim that Congress must do what is right (a trustee perspective) in their arguments for or against specific legislation.

COLLECTIVE VERSUS DYADIC REPRESENTATION. In practice, the correspondence between the quality of representation at the district or state level and that at the national level might be quite weak. To see this, imagine an issue on which five legislators from different districts take varying positions. As Table 2.1 illustrates, even if the legislators are not well matched to their districts, they can collectively represent the nation well. That is, *collective* representation can be good even when *dyadic* representation is not. Congruence between policy and public opinion may be poor at the state or district level but perfect at the national level. As a general rule, a legislative body will be at least as good a delegate for the nation as are individual members for their district or state.[1]

The logic of Table 2.1 does not guarantee that the House, the Senate, and the president will be able to agree on legislation. Indeed, James Madison, the chief architect of the Constitution, hoped not. Madison argued that policy should not necessarily reflect the majority's views. He justified the creation of an independent executive branch (the presidency) and a bicameral legislature (the two chambers of Congress) on the grounds that policy should not simply reflect majority public opinion. He gave the president and the members of the two chambers terms of different lengths, specified different means of selecting them, and gave the president the power to sign or veto legislation. Madison expected the two chambers and the president to reflect different interests, which would reduce the likelihood that a majority could capture all three institutions and impose its will on a minority.

PARTY AND GROUP REPRESENTATION. We often think of political parties and other groups as representing parts of the nation. Nearly all members of Congress are recognized as either Democrats or Republicans and often are identified with other groups based on their gender, race, occupation, age, and other personal characteristics. Legislators, presidents, and the public usually see Congress in terms of its party composition. We speak of a "Republican Congress" or a "Democratic Congress," reflecting the importance of party control of the institution. Although voters choose between congressional candidates only in a single district or state, and no one votes directly for a Republican or Democratic majority in Congress as a whole, the party of the candidates and voters' views about which party should control Congress influence many voters and election outcomes. In turn, legislators tend to join with others of their own party to enact or block legislation; to develop and maintain a good reputation with the public; and to seek or retain majority control. Plainly, a great deal of representation occurs through the party mechanisms.

Although we do not often speak of a white-male, lawyer-dominated Congress, many people are conscious of the composition of Congress beyond its partisan or ideological makeup. A farming background is important for candidates in many areas of the country, whereas a union background is important in other areas. Organized caucuses of women, blacks, Hispanics, and other groups have formed among members of Congress, and groups outside Congress have developed to aid the election of more members from one group or another. It is said that increasing the number of women and minorities in Congress is essential because legislators' personal experiences shape their policy agendas. Moreover, the presence of role models in Congress may help motivate other members of these groups to seek public office.

THE TRADEOFFS OF REPRESENTATION. We cannot hope for perfect representation in Congress. Our multiple expectations for representation can all be met only if Americans hold uniform views on questions of public policy. They do not. Tradeoffs and compromise between the different forms and levels of representation are unavoidable. Neither the individual legislators nor the institution as a whole can simultaneously be a perfect delegate and a perfect trustee. In practice, we muddle through with mixed and changing forms of representation.

Lawmaking

For Madison, representative government – also known as republican government – served two purposes. One was to make the law broadly responsive to the people. The other was to allow representatives, not the people themselves, to make law. This second purpose was, and still is, controversial. Madison explained in *Federalist No. 10* that he hoped representatives would rise above the inevitable influence of public *opinion* to make policy in the public *interest*.

THE UNITARY DEMOCRACY MODEL. Madison's argument assumes that the common or public interest can be discovered by an elected representative through deliberation. In this view, the purpose of the legislative process is to discover those common interests through a process in which legislators share information, offer policy alternatives, and move toward a consensus on action to be taken. Building a consensus, rather than resolving conflicts by force of majority vote, is the object of this process. The emphasis on a common interest has led scholars to label this decision-making process *unitary democracy*.[2]

THE ADVERSARIAL DEMOCRACY MODEL. Madison's view may not be reasonable. Inherently conflicting interests may lead legislators to articulate those interests and decide controversies by the power of a larger number of votes. From this perspective, deliberation is viewed as needless delay to a majority that has no interest in compromise and has the votes to impose policies of its choosing. The majority naturally emphasizes the importance of efficiency and majority rule. The presence of conflicting interests leads us to call this decision-making process *adversarial democracy*.

THE TRADEOFFS OF LAWMAKING. Congress cannot easily harmonize the ideals of both adversarial and unitary democracy. Deliberation and consensus building may seem to be the preferred model of decision making, but time and the compromise required will frustrate a majority eager to act. In practice, as for representation, Congress will make tradeoffs among the ideal forms of lawmaking. Congress sometimes looks quite deliberative but will be pushed by majorities to be more efficient and look, at least to outsiders, as quite adversarial and partisan. Moreover, the two chambers of Congress need not make the same tradeoffs. As we will see in later chapters, the smaller Senate continues to look more deliberative than the larger House, due in large part to significant differences in the rules that the two chambers have adopted over the decades to govern themselves.

The struggle to balance alternative models of representation and lawmaking never ends. Contending forces in American politics usually favor different models as they seek to define democratic processes that give them an advantage. An implication of our discussion is that most sides can find theoretical justification for their positions – to better represent Americans in Washington (usually meaning to increase the influence of one group or another) or to reform lawmaking processes (also usually meaning to increase the influence of one group or another). This is not to say that common interests do not sometimes exist or that the nation as a whole cannot be better represented at times. It is to argue that the history of Congress is not one of smooth progress toward "better" representation and lawmaking processes. Rather, it is a history of political conflict as parties and ambitious politicians sought to appeal for votes and determine policy choices.

The Predecessors of Congress

The First Congress convened on March 4, 1789, under the Constitution drafted in Philadelphia in the summer of 1787. Despite the newness of their institution, the members of the First Congress were not new to legislative politics. The American Congress shares the same roots as Great Britain's parliament. The colonists brought with them British parliamentary practices and quickly established legislatures that governed in conjunction with governors appointed by the British crown. Beginning with Virginia's House of Burgesses in 1619, the colonial legislatures became both elected representative bodies and important lawmaking institutions almost immediately. Most of the legislatures followed procedures similar to those used in Parliament. Representation and lawmaking were well-accepted features of self-governance long before the Constitutional Convention of 1787. Eventually, the usurpation of the powers of the colonial legislatures by British governors became a critical motivation for the Revolutionary War.

Besides their experience from the colonial era, the members of the First Congress had more recent legislative experience from participating in the Continental Congress and in their state legislatures in the years after independence. The first Continental Congress met in 1774, at the time of the

Boston Tea Party and British assertion of military and political control over Massachusetts, as a step toward jointly working out differences between the colonies and the British government. The Continental Congress was not intended to be a permanent body but rather a temporary convention of delegates from the colonies. The crisis with Britain extended its life into the Revolutionary War, and its role in the new nation was formalized in 1781 with the ratification of the Articles of Confederation.

The Continental Congress was severely handicapped by its own rules. Very open floor procedures and a weak presiding officer undermined efforts to coordinate the diverse interests of the states and encouraged factionalism.[3] The Articles of Confederation did nothing to change that. Although they legitimated the national government that the Continental Congress constituted, the articles gave the Congress little power. The Continental Congress could not regulate commerce or raise taxes, and without executive and judicial institutions to implement and enforce the laws it passed, it was wholly dependent on the willingness of state governments to carry out its policies.

In contrast to the weak Continental Congress, most state legislatures were very powerful. The state constitutions adopted after independence gave the legislatures the power to appoint the state governors, guaranteeing that these officers would serve at the pleasure of the egalitarian, popularly elected branch. The new governors were not granted the power to veto legislation, and most were denied the power to make executive branch appointments, which were left to the legislature. Governors, it was hoped, would be mere administrators.

Soon legislative tyranny came to be viewed as a major problem. In the 1780s, an economic depression led debtors to demand relief from their creditors, and because debtors greatly outnumbered creditors, the legislatures obliged them. This undermined financial institutions, creating instability. Thomas Jefferson referred to the situation in Virginia as "elective despotism." Majority rule itself came to be questioned, and people began to wonder whether republican government was viable.

The practice of having a bicameral, or two-house, legislature was well established in the states by the time the Constitution was written in 1787. Britain had evolved a bicameral parliament based on its social class system, with the different classes represented in the House of Commons and the House of Lords. All of the American colonies except for Pennsylvania and Georgia had bicameral legislatures in 1776. Even after the Revolutionary War, when the British model was called into question, most states continued with a bicameral legislature. Debate over the proper relationship between

Congressionally Speaking...

The terms *unicameral* and *bicameral* come from the Latin word *camera*, which means "chamber." Under the Articles of Confederation, the national Congress was unicameral – one chamber – but many state legislatures were bicameral. The Constitution, of course, provided for a bicameral Congress. Among today's American state legislatures, only Nebraska's legislature is unicameral. Nebraska adopted the unicameral form in 1934 after using the bicameral form until then.

the two chambers was frequent, and the states experimented with different means for electing their senates. Representing different classes in different institutions had lost its appeal, but the idea of preventing one house from becoming too powerful was widely discussed. By 1787, most political observers were keenly aware of the strengths and weaknesses of bicameral systems.

The Constitution's Rules of the Game

Against the backdrop of an ineffectual Continental Congress and often tyrannical state legislatures, the framers of the national Constitution sought a new balance in 1787. They constructed a stronger national government with a powerful Congress whose actions could be checked by the president and the Supreme Court.

For the making of public law, the Constitution establishes a specific process, involving three institutions of government, with a limited number of basic rules. The House of Representatives, the Senate, and the president must all agree to enact a new law, with the House and Senate expressing their agreement by simple majority vote. If the president vetoes the measure, two-thirds of the members of the House and of the Senate must agree to override the veto. If any of the three players withholds consent or if a presidential veto is upheld, the legislation dies.

The Constitution also provides for the election of members of Congress and the president, prohibits legislation of certain kinds, specifies the size of majority required in Congress for specific actions, and identifies the player who must make the first or last moves in certain circumstances. In addition, the Constitution allows the Supreme Court to determine whether Congress and the president abide by its rules.

The framers of the Constitution gave Congress tremendous political power. Article I, Section 8 of the Constitution grants to Congress broad discretion to "provide for the common defense and general welfare of the United States." It also specifies the basic powers of the national government and grants to Congress the authority to make laws to implement those powers. This general grant of power is supplemented by more specific provisions. Congress is given the power to tax, to regulate the economy, to create courts under the Supreme Court, to create and regulate military forces, and to declare war. Section 9 grants Congress control over government spending: "No money shall be drawn from the treasury, but in consequence of appropriations made by law."

The Constitution entrusts the Senate with the authority to ratify treaties and confirm presidential nominations to executive and judicial offices. Congress can regulate congressional and presidential elections and must approve agreements between individual states and between states and foreign governments. The breadth of Congress's powers is reinforced in the "elastic clause," which provides that Congress can "make all laws which shall be necessary and proper for carrying into execution" the powers enumerated in the Constitution.

To protect members of Congress from personal intimidation by executive, judicial, or local officials, the framers of the Constitution devised several important clauses. First, beyond the age and citizenship requirements, the Constitution leaves to each house of Congress the authority to judge the qualifications of its members, to rule on contested election outcomes, and to punish or expel members for inappropriate behavior. Second, the Constitution protects members from arrest during and en route to and from sessions of Congress. And third, no member may be questioned by prosecutors, a court, or others about any congressional speech or debate. Members may be arrested and tried for treason, felonies, and breach of the peace, but they cannot be held personally liable by other government officials for their official actions as members of Congress.

Legislative Procedures

With respect to the details of the legislative process, the Constitution offers little guidance, with a few important exceptions. First, the framers of the Constitution were careful to provide that each chamber keep a journal recording its actions (Article 1, Section 5). Further, they required that the votes of individual members on any matter be recorded in the journal upon the request of one-fifth of the members present. A successful request of one-fifth of the members is known as "ordering the yeas and nays." In the Senate, the yeas and nays are taken by having a clerk call out each member's

THE LEGACY OF 9–11 FOR THE CONSTITUTION, STATUTES, AND HOUSE RULES

The terrorist attacks of September 11, 2001, led members of Congress and other congressional observers to worry about how the institution would function if an attack on the Capitol complex killed a large number of legislators. In 2002, the resolution providing for the adjournment of the 107th Congress provided that representatives and senators designated by the Speaker and Senate majority leader be allowed to call Congress into session in the event that those two leaders were killed or incapacitated. Without the provision, only the president could have called the Congress into special session, as the Constitution provides, but legislators believed that Congress should be prepared to act as an independent branch of government. In 2003, the House adopted three rules to address such a possibility. One rule requires the Speaker to establish a list of members who, in order, could serve as Speaker Pro Tem if the Speaker died or was incapacitated. This provision would allow the House to convene to elect a new Speaker. A second rule allows the Speaker to recess the House if there is an imminent threat to members' safety. Previously, the Speaker was not allowed to recess the House if business was pending. A third rule allows the Speaker to lower the number of members counted for the purposes of a quorum when a member dies, resigns, or is expelled. Without the change, a majority of the 435 possible members would have to be present for the House to conduct business. The new rule allows the total possible to be reduced to the number of seats that are currently filled.

In the view of some observers, the measures taken to date are inadequate. Enacted legislation to require special House elections of substitute legislators within 45 days of a deadly attack is considered ineffective – no states have altered their laws to conform to the requirement. In 2005, the House adopted a rule that allows the House to act temporarily without a full quorum by empowering the Speaker (or his designee) to reduce the number required for a quorum after a series of lengthy quorum calls. Many observers doubt that this rule is constitutional because it appears to violate Article I, Section 5, of the Constitution, which provides that "a majority of each shall constitute a quorum to do business." A private study group recommended an amendment to the Constitution that would provide for quick and temporary appointment of replacements by state governors in the event of the death or incapacity of the incumbent, or by declaration of a national emergency by the House. The proposed amendment received only 63 votes in the House in 2004 and has not received a vote in the Senate.

The Senate is less of a problem. In nearly all states, governors are authorized by law to appoint replacement senators upon the death of the incumbents. Still, senators have expressed concern that the inability to gain a quorum in a national emergency would incapacitate the Senate. Legislation has been introduced to provide for temporary appointments if the majority and minority leaders jointly determine that the absence of a quorum to conduct business was caused by the inability of senators to discharge the duties of their office. States would determine how the temporary appointments would be made. No action has been taken on the proposal, which its sponsors recognized would have to be preceded by a constitutional amendment authorizing the process.

name and recording the response by hand. In the House, the yeas and nays have been recorded by an electronic system since 1973.

Second, the framers provided that tax bills originate in the House. Because the Senate was originally to be selected by state legislatures, with only the House directly elected by the people, it was thought that the initiative for imposing taxes should lie with the House. The Constitution provides that "all bills for raising revenue shall originate in the House of Representatives; but the Senate may propose or concur with amendments as on other bills." The Senate has used a variety of gimmicks to circumvent this restriction, but the House generally has jealously guarded its constitutional prerogatives and spurned Senate efforts to initiate tax bills.

Third, the Constitution requires that "a majority of each [house] shall constitute a quorum to do business" (Article 1, Section 5). In principle, a majority of the members of a chamber must be present at all times, but like many other rules, this one is not enforced unless a member raises a point of order – that is, unless a member asks the chair for a ruling that a quorum is not present. This is sometimes used as a dilatory tactic. In the Senate, quorum calls have become a routine way to take a time-out – while the clerk calls the roll of senators' names, senators can confer in private or wait for colleagues to arrive. The most important implication of this constitutional provision is that a majority of members must be present and vote on a measure for the vote to count. To prevent absence from being used as an obstructionist ploy, the Constitution further provides that each house "may be authorized to compel the attendance of absent members."

Finally, the framers outlined the process of presidential approval or disapproval of legislation (Article 1, Section 7). After each chamber has passed a bill, it must be presented to the president, whose options depend on whether Congress has adjourned in the meantime. Congress has an opportunity to override a president's veto only if Congress remains in session (see box, "Constitutional Procedures for Presidential Approval or Disapproval of Legislation"). If Congress adjourns, the president can kill a bill by either vetoing it or taking no action on it (which is known as a pocket veto). Congress may pass a new bill if the president successfully kills a bill.

Constraints on Congressional Power

Although the framers of the Constitution intended Congress to be a powerful policy-making body, they also feared the exercise of that power. This concern produced (1) explicit restrictions on the use of legislative power; (2) a system of three separate institutions that share legislative powers; (3) a system of direct and indirect representation of the people, in Congress and by the presidency; and (4) a Supreme Court that judges the constitutionality of legislation and interprets ambiguities in legislative outcomes. The result is a legislative process that cannot address certain subjects, is motivated by political considerations, is likely to involve bargaining, and is biased against enacting new legislation.

EXPLICIT RESTRICTIONS. A list of powers explicitly denied Congress is provided in Article I, Section 9 of the Constitution. For example, Congress may not tax state exports, pass bills of attainder (pronouncing guilt and sentencing someone without a trial), or adopt *ex post facto* laws (altering the legal standing of a past action). The list of explicit limitations was extended by the 1791 ratification of the first ten amendments to the Constitution – the Bill of Rights. Among other things, the Bill of Rights prohibits laws that abridge freedom of speech, freedom of the press, and the freedom to peaceably assemble (Amendment 1) and preserves the right to a jury trial in certain cases (Amendments 6 and 7). And the Bill of Rights reserves to the states, or to the people, powers not delegated to the national government by the Constitution (Amendment 10).

In practice, the boundary between allowed and disallowed legislative acts is often fuzzy. Efforts by Congress to exercise its powers have often conflicted with individual rights or with powers asserted by the president and the states. The Supreme Court has resolved many ambiguities about where the lines should be drawn around the powers of Congress, but many remain for future court consideration. In some cases, particularly in the foreign policy realm, the Supreme Court has left the ambiguities to be worked out between Congress and the president.

SEPARATE INSTITUTIONS SHARING POWER. Rather than creating a single legislature that represents the people and determines laws, the framers of the Constitution created three institutions – the House, the Senate, and the presidency – that share legislative powers. Formally, legislation may originate in either the House or the Senate, with the exception of bills raising revenue. The president may call Congress into special session and is required to

CONSTITUTIONAL PROCEDURES FOR PRESIDENTIAL APPROVAL OR DISAPPROVAL OF LEGISLATION

If Congress remains in session, the president may sign a bill into law, veto the bill and send it with a statement of his objections back to the house in which the bill originated, or do nothing. If the president vetoes the bill, two-thirds of both houses must vote to approve the bill (and thus override the veto) for it to become law. If the president does nothing by the end of 10 days (excluding Sundays), the bill becomes law.

If Congress adjourns before 10 days, the president may sign the bill into law, veto it, or do nothing. Because Congress has adjourned, it cannot consider overriding a veto, so a vetoed bill will die. Likewise, if the president takes no action by the end of 10 days (excluding Sundays), the bill will die. Killing a bill by failing to take action on it before Congress adjourns has come to be known as making a pocket veto.

There have been disputes between Congress and recent presidents about the meaning of a temporary congressional recess. Presidents have argued that they may pocket veto a measure while Congress is in recess for a holiday or another purpose, even though Congress has not adjourned *sine die* (formally adjourned at the end of a two-year Congress). Many members of Congress disagree. Lower courts have ruled against the presidents' position, but the Supreme Court has not written a definitive opinion on the issue.

recommend measures to Congress from time to time. The president's recommendations carry great weight, but the president cannot formally introduce legislation or compel Congress to act on his recommendations. Legislative measures are formally initiated in Congress, and once passed by both chambers, they must be sent to the president for approval or veto.

A special arrangement was established for treaties with foreign governments, which also have the force of law. The Constitution (Article II, Section 2) provides that the president "shall have power, by and with the advice and consent of the Senate to make treaties, provided two-thirds of the senators present concur." Thus, the president formally initiates legislative action on a treaty by submitting it to the Senate, and a two-thirds majority of the Senate must approve it for the treaty to be ratified. The House is excluded from formal participation. Nevertheless, the House participates in foreign policy making by sharing with the Senate the power to restrict the uses of the federal treasury, to declare war, and to regulate foreign commerce. The House also participates in foreign policy decisions that require congressional appropriations or changing in American domestic law, such as trade agreements.

Just as the president is an integral part of legislating, the Congress is central to implementing laws. The Constitution obligates the president to "take care that the laws be faithfully executed" and grants to the president the authority to appoint "officers" of the United States. But the Constitution requires that the president's appointees be confirmed by the Senate, allows Congress to establish executive departments by law and to establish means for appointing "inferior" officers of the executive branch, and grants Congress the authority to remove the president or other officers for "treason, bribery, or other high crimes and misdemeanors."

Interdependence, then, not exclusivity, characterizes the powers of the House, Senate, and president.

DIRECT AND INDIRECT REPRESENTATION. The framers of the Constitution wanted the government to be responsive to popular opinion, but they also wanted to limit the possibility that some faction could gain simultaneous control of the House, Senate, and presidency and then legislate to violate the rights of others. Only members of the House of Representatives were to be directly elected by the people. Senators were to be chosen by state legislatures, and the president was to be chosen by an electoral college composed of individuals chosen by the states. Furthermore, House, Senate, and presidential elections were put on different timetables: The entire House is elected every two years, senators serve six-year terms (with one-third of the seats up for election every two years), and presidents stand for election every four years.

The result was a mix of constraints and opportunities for the legislative players. By providing for direct or indirect election of members of Congress and the president, the framers of the Constitution increased the likelihood that electoral considerations would play an important part in shaping legislative outcomes. Political competition could be expected to motivate much legislative action. But the framers hoped that indirect election of senators and presidents, along with their longer terms of office, would desensitize them to narrow interests and rapid shifts in public opinion. This safeguard was considered particularly important in the case of treaties and major appointments to the executive agencies and the judiciary, which are left to the president and the Senate.

Concern about the responsiveness of senators to public opinion led to the adoption in 1913 of the Seventeenth Amendment to the Constitution, which provided for direct election of senators. Direct election of senators reduced the difference between the House and the Senate with respect to their link to the electorate. Nevertheless, because senators represent whole states and representatives are selected from small districts regulated by size, along with the differences in term of office, it continues to be likely that the House and Senate will have somewhat different preferences about public policy and can frequently be controlled by different parties. The requirement that both chambers approved legislation creates a bias against the enactment of legislation and increases the probability that successful legislation will represent a compromise among competing views.

JUDICIAL REVIEW AND STATUTORY INTERPRETATION. Since 1803, when the Supreme Court issued its opinion in *Marbury v. Madison*, the federal courts have assumed the power to review the acts of Congress and the president and to determine their constitutionality. This power of judicial review gives the courts, and ultimately the Supreme Court, the final authority to judge and interpret the meaning of the Constitution. The courts' interpretations of the Constitution serve to limit the policy options that can be considered by Congress and the president. For example, the Supreme Court's interpretation of the freedom of speech provision of the First Amendment bars policies restricting how much of her own money a candidate for elective office can spend on her campaign.

In addition, the federal courts interpret the meaning of laws passed by Congress – statutory interpretation. Individuals, organizations, and governments that are disadvantaged by executive branch interpretations of laws often file suit in federal courts. The courts are asked to resolve ambiguities or conflicting provisions in statutes. For guidance about congressional intentions, the courts rely on previous cases, congressional committee reports, the records of floor debate, and other sources on the legislative history of a statute. Court interpretations are often anticipated by legislative players and subsequently shape the legislative language employed by these players. Legislators, in turn, often take court rulings into account when drafting legislation.

The powers of judicial review and statutory interpretation are exercised by federal judges who themselves are partially dependent on the legislative players. The Constitution provides that Congress may establish federal courts below the Supreme Court and that the president nominate judges to the federal courts with the consent of the Senate. Congress also has required that lower court judges be nominated by the president and confirmed by the Senate. But to protect federal judges from the influence of presidents and members of Congress, the Constitution insulates them from potential sources of presidential and congressional manipulation by granting them life terms (although they may be removed by Congress for treason, bribery, or other high crimes and misdemeanors) and preventing Congress and the president from reducing their salaries. The effects of these provisions are discussed in Chapter 10.

Congressional Development

Since the ratification of the Constitution, the United States has been transformed from a small, agrarian nation with little significance in international affairs to the world's largest industrial power and sole military and political superpower. The most rapid changes occurred during the industrial revolution of the late nineteenth century, when industry was transformed by new technologies, many new states were added to the union, modern political parties took form, and federal policies gained greater significance. These conditions changed public demands on members of Congress, who in turn changed their expectations of their institution. By the early twentieth century, many features of the modern Congress had taken form.

The Constitution provided only limited guidance to the House and Senate concerning how they should organize themselves. The House, according to the Constitution, shall elect a Speaker to preside, whereas the vice president shall serve as the Senate's president. The Senate is also authorized to elect a president pro tempore (or "pro tem") to preside in the absence of the vice president. And the Constitution requires that the House and Senate pass legislation by majority vote.

The Constitution says nothing about how legislation is to be prepared for a vote. Instead, it grants each chamber the authority to establish its own rules. Since their origin in 1789, the two chambers of Congress have each accumulated rules, procedural precedents, and informally accepted practices that add up to their own unique legislative process. The two chambers have developed similar legislative processes, but their parliamentary rules differ in important ways, which are detailed in Chapter 7.

The modern Congress has parties and committees that organize nearly all of its activities. Nearly all legislation passes through one or more committees in each house. Members of those committees take a leading role in writing the details of bills, dominate floor debate on those measures, and represent their house in conference committee negotiations with the other house. Parties appoint members to committees, give order to floor debate, and are given proportional representation on conference committees. The majority party in each chamber takes the lead in setting the agenda. But the Constitution is silent on the role of parties and committees in Congress. Both were created to meet the political needs of the members.

Congressionally Speaking...

In the context of the legislative process, *rules* can be a confusing term. While the Constitution outlines the basic features of the legislative process, each house of Congress has lengthy rules governing its internal affairs. In addition, Congress has placed rules governing its proceedings in many statutes, such as the Budget Act, which sets a timetable and special procedures for considering budget measures. Standing committees have their own rules, such as rules establishing subcommittees and providing procedures for committee meetings and hearings. Each of the four congressional party organizations (House Democrats and Republicans, Senate Democrats and Republicans) has its own rules to govern the election of party leaders, create party committees, and govern meetings. Chamber, committee, and party rules have been elaborated in many ways in recent decades as reformers have sought to reduce arbitrary rule by committee and party leaders.

Parties

We now assume that the presiding officer of the House, the Speaker, will be the leader of the majority party and will be responsible for setting the legislative agenda of the House. Similarly, we assume that the Senate's majority leader will set the agenda for that house. But in the early Congresses, no formally recognized party leaders existed. In fact, it took nearly a century for the House to develop something like its modern party-based leadership structure and the Senate took even longer. The Constitution, of course, is silent on the role of parties in Congress. Congressional parties developed only gradually, as parties outside Congress formed to compete in elections. Politicians and others seeking to get elected or to elect others have always taken the lead in forming political parties. Congressional party organizations have formed among newly elected members of the same party or, as has happened a few times, when sitting members form new parties to compete for reelection. They have varied in strength and influence as the degree of consensus about policy goals and political strategies has varied among their members.

EARLY FOUNDATIONS. Groups of legislators have collaborated to influence policy outcomes from the beginning. By the time of the Third Congress, shifting coalitions within the legislature had settled into polarized partisan groups, which began making organized efforts to get like-minded individuals elected. In the administration of George Washington, these groups were led by opposing cabinet officers (Jefferson and Madison versus Hamilton).

For a generation, the parties remained groups of elites, largely members of Congress and executive branch officials who shared party labels – at first, Republicans and Federalists. The congressional and presidential elections of 1800 initiated a period of Republican dominance that lasted until 1824. During that period, when the Federalist party faded away, members had clear party affiliations and gradually developed party caucuses to coordinate party activities. But there were still no formal party leadership posts in the House or Senate.

Speaker Henry Clay (R-Kentucky) was an effective leader, largely by force of personality, during his six nonconsecutive terms (the first starting in 1811). Remarkably, Clay gained the speakership during his first term in the House, which reflects as much on the weakness of the position as on Clay's popularity among his colleagues. But party factionalism, and sometimes assertive presidents, kept speakers relatively weak; indeed, small shifts in the balance of power among factions often led to the election of a new speaker. After Clay, strong personalities and factional leaders served as informally recognized leaders in both houses. Speakers enjoyed the power to make committee assignments, but this ability was insufficient to provide a foundation for party leadership because the most coveted committee assignments were promised in advance during the multicandidate contests for the speakership itself.

During the nineteenth century, the Senate did not have party leadership positions at all, except for caucus chairmen, whose duties and powers amounted to little more than presiding over caucus meetings. Strong regional leaders, like John C. Calhoun (D-South Carolina), Clay, and Daniel Webster (Whig-Massachusetts), tended to dominate Senate parties without holding formal leadership positions. But the first steps toward more party-based control of the chamber were taken in the middle of the nineteenth century. Conflict over control of standing committees led the parties in 1845 to rely on caucus meetings to prepare committee lists, and in 1847 the Democrats created a "committee on committees" to coordinate the task of making committee assignments for the party. In late 1859, the new Republican party formed its own committee on committees.

PARTY GOVERNMENT. The Civil War was an important turning point in the organization of the parties in Congress. Republicans became the dominant party during the war and began to use task forces and steering committees to coordinate the work of the House and Senate. After the war, the two major parties – now the Republicans and the Democrats – settled into broad regional divisions, with the Republicans powerful in the Northeast and the Midwest and the Democrats dominating the South. House Speakers during the 1860s and 1870s were not particularly strong, but they were the recognized leaders of their parties.

In the early 1890s, under Speaker Thomas Brackett Reed (R-Maine), rulings of the Speaker and new House rules gave the Speaker more power to prevent obstructionism and allowed House majorities to act. These changes, stimulated in part by intensifying partisanship on major issues, firmly established party-based governance in the House. For the next two decades, House decision making was highly centralized and under the control of the majority party's leader, the Speaker. Speakers Reed and "Uncle Joe" Cannon so firmly controlled the flow of legislative business that they were known as "czars." By the end of the first decade of the twentieth century, the press referred to Cannon's heavy-handed style as "Cannonism."

In the Senate, the presiding officer – the vice president – may not share the same party affiliation as the Senate majority and so was never granted powers similar to those of the House speaker. During most of the 1800s, the parties had caucus chairmen but they did not acquire genuine leadership duties until very late in the century. Arthur Pue Gorman (D-Maryland), the Democratic caucus chairman, emerged as his party's floor leader in the 1890s, but Republicans did not follow his example. Instead, by the late 1890s and into the new century, a group of four Republican senators, led by Finance Committee chairman Nelson Aldrich (R-Rhode Island) dominated the party.

"Aldrichism" was sometimes paired with Cannonism in the press, but the absence of rules limiting debate or amendments in the Senate prevented the majority party from changing rules to bolster the authority of its leaders. As a result, minority-party obstructionism was not overcome, as it was in the House. Any change in the rules that disadvantaged the minority party could be filibustered – that is, the minority could prevent a vote on a proposal to change the rules by refusing to conclude debate. Efforts by Aldrich and others to limit filibusters were themselves filibustered. Consequently the ability of even the strongest majority party leaders to bring legislation to a vote was severely constrained by the possibility of a filibuster (see Chapter 7).

THE TWENTIETH-CENTURY PATTERN. In the first decade of the twentieth century, a fragmenting Republican party altered congressional party politics for decades to come. Republican reformers in and out of Congress challenged Cannonism and Aldrichism. In 1910, a coalition of insurgent Republicans and minority-party Democrats forced changes in House rules that substantially reduced the power of the Speaker. The Speaker was stripped of the chairmanship of and power to make appointments to the Rules

Committee, which controlled resolutions that put important bills in order on the floor. In the next Congress, with a new Democratic majority, the Speaker's power to make committee assignments was turned over to a party committee.

In the Senate, with few formal chamber or party rules relating to leadership, the fading of Aldrichism was more gradual than was the revolt against Cannon. By the time the Democrats had gained a majority in 1913, no leader dominated either party, although Gorman and his successors as caucus chairs were known as the top party leaders. At a time when his party and the new president, Woodrow Wilson, wanted firmer Senate leadership, John Kern was elected Democratic caucus chairman and, in that capacity, also became known as majority leader, the first recognized majority leader in the Senate. Soon afterward, the Republicans created the position of minority leader, and both parties appointed "whips" to assist the top leaders in managing their parties' business on the floor.

For decades, neither House Speakers nor Senate majority leaders enjoyed the level of influence that Speaker Cannon and Senator Aldrich had possessed at the turn of the century. Committees became more important, as neither party, when in the majority, seriously challenged committee decisions. With a few short-lived exceptions, top party leaders fell into a pattern of supporting and serving the needs of committees more than trying to lead them. This pattern was maintained until the 1970s. Developments since that time are discussed in Chapter 5.

Committees

Members of the first Congresses were influenced by their experiences in the Continental Congress and in their colonial and state legislatures. They devised mechanisms to allow congressional majorities to express their will, while maintaining the equality of all legislators. They preferred that each chamber, as a whole, determine general policy through discussion before entrusting a subgroup of the membership with the responsibility of devising detailed legislation. Because legislators feared that committees with substantial policy discretion and permanence might distort the will of the majority, House committees in the first eight or nine Congresses usually took the form of special or select committees that dissolved when their tasks were completed.

EARLY FOUNDATIONS. The House took the lead in developing the foundations of a standing committee system. By 1810, the House had created 10 standing committees for routine policy areas and for several complex policy areas requiring regular investigation. The practice of referring legislation to a select committee gradually declined thereafter.

In its formative years, the Senate used select committees exclusively on legislative matters; it created only four standing committees to address internal housekeeping matters. A smaller membership, more flexible floor procedures, and a much lighter workload – with the Senate always waiting for the House to act first on legislation – permitted the Senate to use select committees in a wider variety of ways than did the House and still maintain full control over legislation. But beginning in 1806, the Senate adopted the practice of referring to the same committee all matters relating to the subject for which the committee had originally been formed, creating implicit jurisdictions for select committees.

In the decades leading up to the Civil War, the standing committee systems of both houses became institutional fixtures. Both houses of Congress began to rely on standing committees and regularly increased their number. In the House, the number of standing committees increased from 10 to 28 between 1810 and 1825 and to 39 by the beginning of the Civil War. The Senate established its first major standing committees in 1816, when it created 12. It added 10 more by the Civil War.

The expansion of the standing committee systems had roots in both chamber and party needs. A growing workload and regular congressional interaction with an increasing number of executive departments combined to induce committee growth. And the House began to outgrow a floor-centered, decision-making process. The House grew from 64 members in 1789 to 241 in 1833, which made open-ended floor debate quite chaotic.

In the House, partisan considerations also were important. Henry Clay transformed the speakership into a position of policy leadership and increased the partisan significance of committee activity. Rather than allowing the full House to conduct a preliminary debate, Clay preferred to have a reliable group of friendly committee members write legislation. The Speaker's control of committee appointments made this possible. During Clay's era, two procedural changes transformed committees' places in the sequence of the House bill process and further enhanced their value to the Speaker. First, the practice of allowing standing committees to report at their own discretion was codified into the rules of the House in 1822 for a few committees. Second, Clay made referral of legislation to a committee before floor debate the norm. By the late 1830s, after Clay had left the House, all House committees could introduce new legislation and report it to the floor at will. Preliminary debate by the House came to be viewed as a useless procedure. In fact, in 1880 the House adopted a formal rule that required newly introduced legislation to be referred to committee, which meant that the participation of the full membership was reserved for review of committee recommendations.

Changes to the Senate's committee system came at a slower pace. The Senate tended to wait for the House to act first on a bill before it took up a matter, so its workload was not as heavy as the House workload. Additionally, the Senate did not grow as quickly as the House. In 1835, the Senate had only 48 members, fewer members than the House had during the First Congress, and, in sharp contrast to the House, factionalism led senators and their weak party leaders to distrust committees and avoid referral to unfriendly committees. As a result, the Senate's standing committees, with one or two important exceptions, played a relatively insignificant role in the legislative process before the Civil War. The Senate retained a more floor-centered process.

PARTY CONTROL. In the half-century after the Civil War, the role of committees was strongly influenced by new issues associated with industrialization and the dramatic population growth, further development of American political parties, and the increasing careerism of members. Both houses had a strong tendency to respond to new issues by creating new committees rather than enlarging or reorganizing existing committee jurisdictions. When dealing with important issues, party leaders often liked the opportunity to appoint friendly members to a new committee within their jurisdiction. And committee chairs, who acquired offices and clerks when they were appointed, resisted efforts to eliminate committees. By 1918, the House had acquired nearly 60 committees and the Senate had 74. Nearly half of them had no legislative or investigative business, but allowed their chairmen to be assigned an office and hire a clerk.

The rapid growth in the number of committees in the late nineteenth century did not lead to a more decentralized Congress. Because of the stabilization of the two-party system and the cohesiveness of the majority-party Republicans in the late 1800s, majority-party leaders of both houses used the established committee systems as tools for asserting control over policy choices. In the House, the period between the Civil War and 1910 brought a series of activist Speakers who aggressively used committee appointments to stack important committees with friendly members, sought and received new bill referral powers, and gave the Rules Committee, which the Speaker chaired, the authority to report resolutions that set the floor agenda. With these powers, the Speaker gained the ability to grant a right-of-way to certain legislation and block other legislation.

Senate organization in the years after the Civil War was dictated by Republicans, who controlled that chamber for all but two Congresses between 1860 and 1913. The Republicans emerged from the war with no party leader or faction capable of controlling the Senate. Relatively independent committees and committee chairs became the dominant force in Senate deliberations. By the late 1890s, however, elections had made the Senate Republicans a smaller but more homogeneous group, with a coterie of like-minded members ascending to leadership positions. This group controlled the chamber's Committee on Committees, which made committee assignments, and the Steering Committee, which controlled floor scheduling. These developments made Senate committees agents of a small set of party leaders.

Party dominance did not last, however. After the revolt against Speaker Cannon in 1910, party cohesiveness and party leaders' ability to direct the legislative process declined substantially. With less central coordination and weaker party leaders, the bloated, fragmented committee systems became intolerable. Besides, the more independent members began to acquire small personal staffs in the 1920s and no longer needed the clerical assistance that came with a committee chair. As a result, both houses eliminated a large number of committees, most of which had been inactive for some time. Some formal links between party leaders and committees were broken as well. Because of reforms within the House Republican party organizations and similar policies adopted by the Democrats, the majority leader no longer chaired a major committee, chairs of major committees could not serve on the party's Steering Committee, and no committee chair could sit on the Rules Committee.

THE MODERN SYSTEM. The broad outline of the modern committee system was determined by the Legislative Reorganization Act of 1946. By 1945, most members shared concerns about the increasing size and expanding power of the executive branch that had come with the New Deal programs of the 1930s and then World War II. Critics noted that the large number of committees and their overlapping jurisdictions resulted in unequal distributions of work and participation among members, caused difficulties in coordination between the House and the Senate, and made oversight of executive agencies difficult. Committees also lacked adequate staff assistance to conduct studies of policy problems and executive branch activities.

The 1946 act reduced the number of standing committees to 19 in the House and 15 in the Senate, by consolidating the jurisdictions of several groups of committees. The standing committees in each house were made nearly equal in size, and the number of committee assignments was reduced to one for most House members and two for most senators. Provisions dealing with regular committee meetings, proxy voting, and committee reports constrained chairs in some ways. But the clear winners were the chairs of the standing committees who benefited from expanded committee jurisdictions and the addition of more committee staff, which they would direct. Chairs also continued to control their committees' agendas, subcommittee appointments, the referral of legislation to subcommittees, the management of committee legislation on the floor, and conference delegations.

Committees appeared to be quite autonomous in both chambers for the next decade and a half. Committee chairs exhibited great longevity. More than 60 percent of committee chairs serving between 1947 and 1964 held their position for more than five years, including approximately two dozen who served more than a decade. And, by virtue of southern Democrats' seniority, chairs were disproportionately conservative. Southern Democrats, along with most Republicans, constituted a conservative coalition that used committees to block legislation favored by congressional and administration liberals.

A set of strong, informal norms seemed to govern individual behavior in the 1940s and 1950s. Two norms directly affected committees. First, members were expected to specialize in matters that came before their committees. Second, new members were expected to serve an apprenticeship period, during which they would listen and learn from senior members and refrain from actively participating in committee or floor deliberations. These norms emphasized the development of expertise in the affairs of one's own committee and deference to the assumed expertise of other committees. The collective justification for these norms was that the development of, and deference to, expertise would promote quality legislation. By the mid-1960s, new cohorts of members, particularly liberals, proved unwilling to serve apprenticeships and to defer to conservative committee chairs. Many members began to demand major reforms in congressional operations.

A five-year effort yielded the Legislative Reorganization Act of 1970. It required committees to make public all recorded votes, limited proxy votes, allowed a majority of members to call meetings, and encouraged committees to hold open hearings and meetings. House floor procedures were also affected – primarily by permitting recorded teller votes during the amending process and by authorizing (rather than requiring) the use of electronic voting. These changes made it more difficult for House and Senate committee chairs to camouflage their power in legislative jargon and hide their domination behind closed doors. As we will see, however, the reform movement did not end with the 1970 act. Indeed, the act only set the stage for two decades of change in the role of committees in congressional policy making. The developments since the early 1970s are discussed in Chapter 6.

Conclusion

Congress's place in the constitutional scheme of representation and law making was shaped by the experience with the Continental Congress and the state governments in the years following the Revolutionary War. The Constitution made Congress more powerful than the Continental Congress had been, but it also limited its power by dividing the policy-making process among the two chambers and the presidency and by imposing explicit constraints on the kinds of law that can be made. The Constitution provided only the most rudimentary instructions on how the two houses of Congress were to organize themselves to make law. Gradually, as members struggled to control policy choices and to meet changing demands, legislators created the key features of the modern Congress:

- legislative parties, which gather legislators with common political interests;
- committees, which write the details of most legislation;
- leadership positions in both parties and committees, which are held by elected and appointed legislators who organize most legislative business; and
- rules, which are now very complex and govern the activities of individual legislators, parties, committees, and the parent chambers.

By the 1920s, Congress had taken its modern form, with a full complement of party leaders and standing committees.

Above: Democrat Kay Hagan, standing in front of her family, from left, daughter Carrie Hagan, son Tilden Hagan, and husband Chip Hagan, celebrates winning a U.S. Senate seat for North Carolina in a race against Elizabeth Dole at the Greensboro Coliseum in Greensboro, North Carolina, Tuesday, November 4, 2008. (Ted Richardson/Raleigh News & Observer/MCT)

Below: MINNEAPOLIS, MN - NOVEMBER 19: A ballot that was challenged during the election recount in the Senate race between Al Franken and Sen. Norm Coleman is seen at the Minneapolis Elections Warehouse in Minneapolis, Minnesota on November 19, 2008. Ballots circles are supposed to be filled in completely which is why this ballot was challenged. (Photo by Cory Ryan/Getty Images)

3

Congressional Elections and Policy Alignments

T HE YEAR 2008 MARKED THE SECOND CONSECUTIVE DIFFICULT ELECTION year for congressional Republicans. The 2006 midterm elections saw the Republicans lose control of both the House and Senate for the first time since 1994. This election continued a pattern of midterm elections being tough for the president's party in Congress – especially those occurring in a president's second term. Complicating matters further for Republicans going into 2008 was the declining popularity of President Bush, based in large part on the public's declining view of the war in Iraq. In contrast, national Democrats were excited about the possibility of winning back the White House and padding their congressional majorities. Republicans saw a number of incumbents retire rather than seek reelection, while Democrats had a seemingly unlimited supply of good challengers willing to target vulnerable Republicans. As the fall campaign shaped up, Republicans were forced to play defense in vulnerable states and districts, while leaving potentially vulnerable Democrats without seriously funded challengers. When the dust settled, Democrats had increased their majority by 21 seats in the House and at least 7 seats in the Senate. The 111th Congress thus began with large Democratic majorities in both chambers and a Democratic president, presenting Democrats with unified control of government for the first time since 1994.

The general policy preferences of the key players – the House, the Senate, and the president – are a product of elections. Elections are selection devices. They are intended to be competitive processes in which some candidates win and others lose. The winners arrive in Washington with certain personal policy views and an idea of what their supporters expect of them. Collectively, the winners give shape to the balance of policy preferences within the House and Senate and determine the broad contours of agreement and disagreement among the House, the Senate, and the president. Policy alignments change to some degree with each congressional and presidential election.

The connection between elections and policy is far from perfect. For one thing, election outcomes are influenced by factors other than the policy views of voters and candidates – such as personalities and scandals. For another, forces beyond constituency opinion and members' personal views are at work on most issues before Congress. Organized interest groups, expert and editorial opinion, and vote trading can influence policy choices. Moreover, most of the specific policy questions faced by Congress and the president do not arise in election campaigns, yet elections determine whether the same party controls the House, the Senate, and the White House, whether they lean in a liberal or conservative direction, and whether they are likely to agree on major policy questions.

Elections influence the legislative game beyond the party affiliations and policy positions of members of Congress and presidents. Most members seek reelection, and they seek legislative opportunities and resources that will further that goal. As we see in later chapters, the structure and function of virtually every major feature of Congress – committees, parties, rules, personal offices, and staffs – reflect the influence of electoral considerations. As political scientist David Mayhew wrote in 1974, and it is surely more true today, "[I]f a group of planners sat down and tried to design a pair of American national assemblies with the goal of serving members' reelection needs year in and year out, they would be hard pressed to improve on what exists."

Modern candidates for Congress face an electoral system that is highly decentralized and candidate-centered. The system is governed as much by state law as by federal law. Political parties endorse candidates for Congress, but they do not formally control the selection of candidates to run in the general election. Rather, any person who meets basic eligibility requirements may run in a primary election to gain a place on the general election ballot under a party's name. With few exceptions, candidates build their own campaign organizations, raise their own campaign money, and set their own campaign strategies. They do so in 435 different districts and 50 different states, each with a unique blend of economic, social, and political conditions. The winning candidates often emerge from their campaigns with strong individualistic tendencies, which they bring with them to the halls of Congress.

In this chapter we describe the formal rules and informal practices that shape congressional election outcomes. We then look at different types of candidates and at the advantages of incumbency. Next, we will consider national patterns in congressional elections, including the forces underlying divided party control of Congress and the presidency. Finally, we discuss the effect of elections on policy.

The Rules Governing Congressional Elections

More than 2,000 candidates run in congressional primary and general elections in any single election cycle. Their candidacies are governed by a web of rules provided by the Constitution, federal and state law, and, for incumbents, House and Senate rules. The rules have become increasingly complex as Congress and state legislatures, as well as the federal courts, have sought to prevent election fraud, to keep elections fair, and (on occasion) to tilt the rules in favor of one type of candidate or another. The rules concern eligibility for office, filing requirements, campaign finance restrictions, use of congressional staff, and many other matters. By shaping the strategies of candidates seeking election or reelection to Congress, these rules influence election outcomes and the political composition of the House and Senate.

The Constitution: Eligibility, Voting Rights, and Chamber Size

ELIGIBILITY. The Constitution requires that members of both chambers be citizens of the state from which they are elected, though this rule does not always prevent individuals from running to represent states that are not their primary residence. For example, Elizabeth Dole (R-North Carolina) had not lived in the state in decades before winning a Senate seat there in 2002. Members of the House must be 25 years old and must have been a citizen of the United States for seven years, while members of the Senate must be 30 years old and must have been a U.S. citizen for nine years. Candidates may be younger than the age requirements at the time they run for office, although they must have reached the required age before being sworn into office. Current Vice-President Joe Biden was only 29 when he first ran for the U.S. Senate. House members must reside in the state but not necessarily in the district they represent, though most do. Representatives serve two-year terms. Senators serve staggered, six-year terms, with one-third of the seats up for election every second year. Representatives' and senators' terms begin at noon on January 3 following each election or as soon thereafter as the House and Senate may determine by law.

VOTING RIGHTS. The Constitution leaves the "times, places, and manner of holding elections for senators and representatives" to the states, although Congress may enact (and has) certain federal regulations concerning

FILLING VACANT SENATE SEATS: VARIATIONS IN STATE LAW

The Seventeenth amendment gives state legislatures the option of allowing the governor to appoint a replacement or having a special election if Senate seats become vacant. The amendment reads in part, "When vacancies happen in the representation of any State in the Senate, the executive authority of each State shall issue writs of election to fill such vacancies: *Provided*, That the legislature of any State may empower the executive thereof to make temporary appointments until the people fill the vacancies by election as the legislature may direct." Recent events highlight the controversy that can arise with these appointments.

In Alaska, Senator Frank Murkowski (R-Alaska) resigned from the Senate upon winning the governorship of Alaska in 2002. He subsequently appointed his daughter, Lisa Murkowski, to fill the remaining two years of his term. Charges of nepotism surrounded Ms. Murkowski throughout the remainder of her father's term and her own campaign for the seat in 2004, but she was able to secure a full term for herself by narrowly defeating her Democratic opponent. Alaska law was subsequently changed to provide for a special election in lieu of gubernatorial appointments.

In Illinois, Senator Barack Obama (D-Illinois) resigned from the Senate upon winning the 2008 presidential election. By law, Illinois Governor Rod Blagojevich (D) was permitted to name a replacement. Controversy erupted however, when federal prosecutors arrested Blagojevich and charged him with numerous counts of corruption, including trying to trade the Senate seat for campaign contributions or a job for himself or his wife. Federal prosecutors released recordings from telephone wiretaps that included Blagojevich stating in relation to the Senate seat, "I've got this thing and it's [expletive] golden, and, uh, uh, I'm just not giving it up for [expletive] nothing." As Illinois legislators began to consider impeachment proceedings against Blagojevich he appointed Roland Burris, a longtime Chicago politician, to the seat. Senate Democrats initially indicated that they would refuse to seat Burris given the controversy surrounding the appointment, but he was eventually allowed to join the Senate.

elections. For example, in 1845 Congress fixed the date for congressional and presidential elections as the Tuesday following the first Monday in November, although this change was not fully implemented until 1880. Constitutional amendments have added several rules limiting the ability of states to regulate the right to vote in federal elections. The Fourteenth Amendment (ratified in 1868) bars restrictions based on race, color, or previous condition of servitude (slavery); the Nineteenth Amendment (ratified in 1920) bars restrictions based on gender; and the Twenty-fourth Amendment (ratified in 1964) prohibits poll taxes (a tax that must be paid before a person can vote). Most recently, the Twenty-sixth Amendment (ratified in 1971) guaranteed the right to vote to persons 18 years of age or older.

CHAMBER SIZE. By implication, the Constitution sets the size of the Senate – each state has two senators. Since the late 1950s, when Alaska and Hawaii joined the union, the Senate has had 100 members. The Constitution guarantees at least one representative for each state, but the specific size of the House is not dictated by the Constitution and instead is set by law. For more than a century, the House grew as the country's population grew and states were added to the union. Since 1911, federal law has left the House at 435 voting members. With the House's size fixed, a growing population has produced districts of growing size – most districts now contain more than 600,000 citizens, a far cry from the 30,000 originally provided by the Constitution. A House vacancy because of death or any other cause must be filled by a special election, which is called by the state's governor. A Senate vacancy, according to the Seventeenth Amendment, may be filled by election or appointment by the state's governor, as determined by state law (see box, "Filling Vacant Senate Seats"). Generally, state laws provide for a temporary appointment followed by an election at the time of the next regularly scheduled federal election to fill the remainder of the term. A bill to give the District of Columbia a House seat has been debated in recent years. The Senate passed a bill in early 2009 that would expand The House to 437, with D.C. receiving one seat and Utah the other. As of this writing, the House has not passed the bill.

Federal Law: Apportionment and Campaign Finance

APPORTIONMENT. After each decennial census, changes in the distribution of population among the states must be reflected in the allocation of House seats. Fifty seats are allocated automatically because of the requirement that each state have at least one representative. But the constitutional requirement that seats "be apportioned among the several states according to their respective numbers" leaves ambiguous how to handle fractions when allocating all other seats. Congress, by law, establishes the formula for apportioning the seats. Population shifts over the past half-century have resulted in a redistribution of power from the industrial Midwest and Northeast to the South and Southwest (see Chapter 1). In addition, since 1967 federal law has required that states with more than one House seat must create districts from which only one representative is elected (single-member districts).

CAMPAIGN FINANCE. The Federal Election Campaign Act (FECA) of 1971, and important amendments to it in 1974 and 1976 created the Federal Election Commission (FEC) and established limits and disclosure requirements for contributions to congressional campaigns. The regulations were a response to scandals involving secret contributions to presidential candidates of large sums of money from wealthy individuals and corporations, some of which was used for underhanded activity. FECA restricted the size of contributions that individuals, parties, and political action committees (PACs) could make to candidates for Congress. FECA created no restrictions on how much congressional candidates may spend, and the Supreme Court has barred limits on how much a candidate or family members may contribute to their own cause. The law required groups and candidates to report contributions and expenditures to the FEC.

Under the law, membership organizations, corporations, and labor unions may create PACs to collect money from organization employees or members in order to pad resources for campaign contributions. Because PACs may contribute more than individuals, there is a strong incentive to create PACs, which grew in number from 608 in late 1974 to more than 4,000 in the mid-1980s and was just over 4,000 in 2003. The largest growth was in PACs tied to corporations, which numbered 1,552 in mid-2003, but growth has occurred in all categories – labor union PACs, trade association PACs, PACs formed by cooperatives, and PACs not connected to any organization.

The limits on contributions reflect a judgment that contributions from the wealthy and corporations may be harmful to the system and that party participation is more desirable. The basic rules on contributions provide that

- individuals may contribute larger sums to candidates and parties than to PACs;
- parties may contribute larger sums directly to candidates than may PACs;
- parties may coordinate a certain amount of spending with candidates, while PACs cannot.

The law emphasizes public disclosure of contributions and expenditures by candidates, parties, and PACs. Full disclosure of all contributions must be made in reports to the FEC, all contributions of more than $50 must be individually recorded, and the identity of donors of $100 or more must be provided. Detailed reports on expenditures are required as well.

FECA has loopholes. Contributions may be bundled, for example, by gathering many individual or PAC contributions and offering them as a package to a candidate. Lobbyists and other interest-group leaders can use bundling, without violating the limits on the size of individual contributions, to make very conspicuous contributions to candidates who might not pay much attention to much smaller, separate contributions. The Honest Leadership and Open Government Act of 2007 did require disclosure of the identity of bundlers and the amount bundled. Furthermore, the law did not regulate "soft money" contributions, which by the late 1990s had taken on increasing importance in congressional and presidential campaigns. Soft money was contributed by wealthy individuals and corporations to political parties, to be used for television ads for the party (not specific candidates), party staff and office expenses, voter registration and GOTV efforts, and other purposes that are not directed by, but obviously benefit, the party's candidates. This loophole allowed individuals and PACs that had reached their limit in direct contributions to a candidate's campaign to contribute money to a party organization that can work on the candidate's behalf.

By the late 1990s, many had come to believe that the soft money loophole was allowing candidates, parties, and donors to circumvent the rules established by FECA. After almost a decade of bitter debate, proponents of campaign finance reform, including Senators John McCain (R-Arizona) and Russ Feingold (D-Wisconsin), succeeded in convincing Congress to ban most uses of "soft money" with the Bipartisan Campaign Reform Act of 2002 (BCRA) – sometimes known as "McCain-Feingold." In addition to the ban on soft money, the BCRA increased the amount of hard money that individuals could contribute to campaigns, created exceptions to the hard money limits for candidates facing self-financed candidates, and restricted "issue advocacy" by independent groups in the 60 days prior to an election (see Table 3.1).

A separate loophole was generated by a 1996 Supreme Court ruling that eliminated limits on how much parties could spend on congressional campaigns, as long as the spending was not coordinated with individual candidates' campaigns. The ruling paved the way for a sharp increase in fundraising and spending by the congressional campaign committees. The Senate Republicans immediately set up a special unit to raise funds for these "independent" expenditures. Total expenditures by the parties' congressional and senatorial campaign committees exceeded $900 million for the 2006 election cycle, which was up from slightly more than $500 million in 2004.

There are many legal obstacles for any new campaign finance reform law and the BCRA has been subject to many of them. The Supreme Court ruled in *Buckley v. Valeo* (1976) that the free speech clause of the First Amendment to the Constitution applies to campaign spending. The argument is that individuals and groups must be free to spend money to express themselves. Many observers thought that this interpretation of the First Amendment meant that the Court would not let stand the BCRA restrictions on when groups can spend money to advocate issues. However, the Court initially did just that in *McConnell v. FEC* (2003), on the grounds that the restriction of free speech was minimal and justified by the government's interest in curbing corrupt practices. However, the Court reversed itself in *FEC v. Wisconsin*

TABLE 3.1. Congressional Campaign Contribution Limits under the Bipartisan Campaign Reform Act of 2002, for the 2007–2008 Cycle.

Type of contributor	Limits	Additional provisions and explanations

Limits on Contributions from Individuals	• $2,300 per candidate for primaries
	• $2,300 per candidate for runoff
	• $2,300 per candidate for general election
	• $108,200 total per two-year election cycle
	  ○ $42,700 to candidates
	  ○ $65,500 to parties and PACs
	• unlimited independent
		The $2,300 limit on contributions to a candidate for the general election triples if a House candidate faces a self-financed opponent. A more complex formula raises the limit for Senate races.
		Independent spending is spending by an individual or political action committee for or against candidates without coordinating with a candidate

Limits on Contributions from Political Parties	• $10,000 per House Candidate (Combined National, State, Local) • $39,900 per Senate candidate • Parties can either spend independently or in coordination with a candidate, but not both • National party committees have no limits on donations to state & local party committees ○ 2 cents per voting-age person in the state in coordinated spending.	The Senate limit of $39,900 applies to House candidates in single-district states. Coordinated spending is party spending for services provided to a candidate without coordinating
Limits on Contributions from Political Action Committees (PACs)	• $5,000 per candidate for primaries • $5,000 per candidate for general election • $15,000 per calendar year to a political party ○ unlimited independent spending	Independent spending is spending by an individual or political action committee for or against candidates with a candidate

Source: Federal Election Commission, www.fec.gov.

Right to Life (2007). In a bitterly divided 5–4 opinion, a majority held that the restriction of so called "issue ads" in the weeks prior to an election amounted to unconstitutional censorship. This ruling is likely to increase the amount of corporate and union money used to indirectly campaign for or against candidates – which could effectively circumvent the soft money ban in the BCRA.

Even before the Court gutted many of the restrictions on advertising prior to a campaign, other loopholes in the BCRA had been exploited. Most notably, a number of so called "527" and "501(c)3" groups, named for the section of the tax code that permits their existence, formed during the 2004 election cycle. These groups, with names such as "MoveOn.org," "American Coming Together," and the "Media Fund" spent hundreds of millions of dollars seeking to influence the outcome of recent elections. In many ways, these groups filled in the void left by the soft money ban in the BCRA. 527 groups spent more than $200 million during the 2006 congressional elections.

THE "MILLIONAIRES' AMENDMENT". The Supreme Court's ruling in *Buckley v. Valeo* (1976) that money spent on gaining political office is protected speech invalidated restrictions on candidates' use of personal wealth that were contained in FECA. In recent years, many candidates for Congress and other offices have spent a considerable amount of their personal fortunes in their quests for office. Jon Corzine (D-New Jersey) is the most notable, having spent in excess of $60 million in his successful quest for the Senate. However, he is not alone. Maria Cantwell (D-Washington), Mark Dayton (D-Minnesota), and Peter Fitzgerald (R-Illinois) each spent in excess of $10 million from personal sources in their successful bids against Senate incumbents. Despite the fact that most self-financed candidates are not successful – Blair Hull spent more than $28 million in a losing effort to capture the Democratic Senate nomination from Illinois in 2004 – many observers have raised questions about the impact of self-financing on the electoral process. Critics argue that self-financing allows the wealthy to "buy elections," thus excluding citizens of more modest means from elective office. For their part, self-financed candidates often argue that by paying for their own campaigns they assure the public that they are not influenced by campaign contributions from organized interests.

The Bipartisan Campaign Reform Act of 2002 (BCRA) attempted to address the issue of self-financed candidates in the so called "millionaires' amendment." First, the act restricted the amount candidates can raise to repay themselves to $250,000 for loans to their campaign. Advocates of this restriction argued that candidates would be discouraged from self-financing more than that if they cannot repay themselves later. Second, the act allowed candidates running against self-financed candidates to raise additional hard money. Under the BCRA, candidates can only accept donations of $2,300 per election from an individual donor, yet if they were facing a self-financed candidate this limit tripled for House races and possibly more for Senate races. Advocates pointed out that this provision will "level the playing field" for candidates facing self-financed opponents. The Supreme Court ruled that this provision was unconstitutional in the case *Davis v. FEC* (2008). A narrowly divided court ruled that the unequal treatment given to candidates under this rule violated the first amendment to the Constitution. This continued a trend whereby the Supreme Court has continually chipped away at BCRA provisions, causing many to worry that the law will soon become ineffectual.

State Law: Redistricting and Primaries

State laws continue to regulate many aspects of congressional elections. They exhibit a bewildering array of provisions. Two sets of state laws – those governing the drawing of district lines and those governing the process of gaining a place on the ballot – are particularly important.

REDISTRICTING. Among the most sensitive issues governed by state laws is the drawing of district lines for House seats. Because the composition of House districts can make the difference between winning and losing, the two major parties and individual politicians, particularly incumbents, often fight fierce battles in state legislatures over the alignment of districts. These battles are renewed at least every 10 years, after the decennial census.

Following the 2000 census, the seven least populous states – Alaska, Delaware, Montana, North Dakota, South Dakota, Vermont, and Wyoming – were each allocated a single at-large House district, so redistricting was not an issue. Of the other states, 37 began by using the normal process of having the state legislature enact redistricting legislation. But in response to the controversial character of redistricting decisions, the other states adopted some special procedures – an independent commission, a combination of commission and legislative action, or some other special rules. Incumbent members of Congress often seek to influence state redistricting decisions, but their influence varies. Redistricting is likely to be most controversial when a state loses one or more seats and must pit incumbent members against one another in consolidated districts.

States face two significant constraints when drawing district lines. First, federal law – the Voting Rights Act – requires certain states to submit their plans to the U.S. Department of Justice or a federal district court for approval before implementing them. These are states where discriminatory barriers to voting were or now may be a problem – a total of 16 in 2001. Since 1982, the Voting Rights Act has barred districting plans that have the effect of diluting the voting power of racial minorities by splitting their vote among districts, even if there is no evidence of deliberate discrimination.

Second, the Supreme Court has moved to set standards to limit certain kinds of gerrymandering – the manipulation of district lines for political purposes – as well as some unintentional districting outcomes. The clearest court directive is that House districts must be equal in population – within a very narrow margin. In addition, the Court indicated in 1986 that districting plans designed to advantage one political group (such as a party) over another may be unconstitutional. But just what constitutes impermissible "political gerrymandering" remains unclear as of the Court's latest decision on the topic, *Vieth v. Jubelirer* (2004), in which the Court did not intervene in the case because it recognized that it could not offer a concise solution.

Racial gerrymandering is another matter. Following the 1990 census, the federal courts at first let stand very oddly shaped congressional districts created to give racial minorities a voting majority. These new districts were critical to the election of more African Americans and Hispanics to the House of Representatives in 1992. But between 1993 and 2001, the Court made a series of confusing rulings concerning the constitutionality of districts drawn with racial motives. The decisions have forced federal courts to determine whether other factors justified the redrawing of those districts' lines. By 2001, following the new Supreme Court rulings, courts had ordered "majority-minority" districts to be redrawn in Florida, Georgia, Louisiana, New York, North Carolina, Texas, and Virginia. In early 2009, a narrowly divided court ruled in *Barrett v. Strickland* that the Voting Rights Act only required protection against minority vote dilution in districts in which racial minorities make up a majority of the population. It is too early to know if this case will affect redistricting following the 2010 census, but if the past is any guide, more litigation over the composition of districts is likely.

Political and legal complications abound in redistricting. Failure to adopt a timely redistricting plan or to meet legal standards often leads a federal district court to design and impose a plan. After the 2000 census, federal courts became involved in redistricting in at least 10 states, and state courts became involved in several others. Several states did not have settled district lines until the summer of 2002, forcing some of them to extend the filing deadline for congressional candidates for the 2002 elections.

PRIMARIES. State laws that govern the placement of candidates on the November general election ballot are remarkably varied. All states provide for primary elections as the means for choosing candidates from the two major parties for the November ballot. In 2008, the earliest standard primary elections for House and Senate seats were in Illinois on February 5. The last standard primary was in Hawaii on September 20. But 10 states require that a candidate receive a specified percentage of the primary vote (more than 50 percent in most cases) before being placed on the November ballot; if no candidate wins the specified percentage, a run-off primary election is held soon thereafter.

Furthermore, states vary in the way they regulate voting in primary elections. Most states have closed primaries: Voters must register in advance as either a Republican or a Democrat and may vote only in that party's primary. Open primaries, used in nine states, allow voters to choose to vote in either party's primary at the polling place on election day.

Nearly all states have a system of plurality voting in the general election. That is, the candidate with the most votes wins, even if that candidate receives less than a majority of the total vote. Consequently, if more than two candidates are on the ballot (usually a candidate from each major party, plus minor party candidates), the winner may receive far less than half of the votes.

Louisiana has the most distinctive system. It puts all candidates for a House or Senate seat, regardless of party, in a single primary election. Prior to 1997 this primary occurred in October, and if a candidate received more than 50 percent of the vote, they were elected to office without a general election. If no candidate won a majority, the two candidates with the highest votes share, regardless of party, were placed on the ballot in the November general election. Because only two candidates would compete in the general election, if a general election were necessary, one candidate would win a majority (in the absence of a tie). In late 1997, the Supreme Court struck down the Louisiana primary election law. Because a candidate could be, and often was, elected in the October primary, the Court ruled that the Louisiana law conflicted with the federal law setting the date for congressional elections as the Tuesday following the first Monday of November. Following this ruling, Louisiana shifted the primary to the date for the general election with a runoff following if no candidate attains a majority.

THE CHANGING CONGRESS: REDISTRICTING EFFORTS HIGHLIGHT NEW PARTY STRATEGIES

Republicans in the Texas legislature found themselves in the majority for the first time in over 100 years when they convened in 2003. With some urging from then U. S. House Representative Tom DeLay (R-Texas), Texas Republicans began considering various plans to redraw the state's U.S. House districts to increase the number of districts likely to elect Republicans.

The drawing of House district lines is one of the most controversial and partisan issues faced by state legislatures, and the ensuing Texas episode was no exception. Aside from the requirements of equal population and certain restrictions found in the Voting Rights Act, states are free to draw their congressional district lines as they see fit. For much of the early part of the twentieth century, states redrew lines infrequently, if at all. Following the Supreme Court's decision requiring equal population in *Wesberry v. Sanders* (1964), redistricting became a decennial event in states, occurring prior to election years ending in "2." Nothing in federal law prohibits states from redrawing districts more frequently; in fact, in the late nineteenth century, states often redrew lines after each legislative election. Ohio, for example, once had six different sets of lines in six consecutive elections.

In the Texas case, Democrats fought the redistricting efforts for much of 2003. On two separate occasions, Senate Democrats fled the state to prevent the quorum necessary to enact the plan. After months of delay, a quorum was eventually attained after one of the Democratic senators relented and came back to Texas. After a skirmish among themselves, Texas Republicans eventually enacted a plan that significantly altered the partisan composition of many districts. The results were drastic for the Texas delegation. In the 108th Congress (2003–2004), Texas sent 17 Democrats and 15 Republicans to the House. Under the new districting system, the 109th Congress began with 20 Republicans and 12 Democrats, a net gain of five seats for the Republican Party.

In the wake of the Texas "re-redistricting" Colorado and Georgia enacted new districting plans. Colorado Republicans attempted to enact a plan that would have increased the proportion of Republicans in their U.S. House delegation, but were rebuffed when the Colorado Supreme Court ruled, and the U.S. Supreme Court affirmed, that Colorado law only permitted redistricting once per decade, while the new Georgia planned produced less net change in their congressional delegation.

ELECTION PRACTICE REFORM. In the wake of the 2000 presidential election controversy, Congress sought to expand the federal role in national elections by making it "easier to vote and harder to cheat." Congress enacted legislation in 2002, the Help America Vote Act (HAVA), which authorized almost $4 billion to aid states in improving the mechanics of the election process. Close to $1 billion of this authorization was to assist states in replacing the infamous "punch card" voting machines that were the source of controversy in Florida in 2000, as well as replacing other outdated voting technology. The law also required that states must allow voters to cast "provisional ballots" in federal elections if their registration status is unclear. Upon demonstrating that the voter is properly registered, these provisional ballots are then to be counted as actual votes. The law seeks to reduce voter fraud by requiring identification for first-time voters, and a state-issued identification is now required in order to register to vote.

House and Senate Rules: Office Accounts, Staff, and the Frank

The House and Senate have established rules to limit incumbents' use of their official offices, accounts, staffs, and other privileges for campaign purposes. Generally, incumbents may not use their offices or staffs for campaign purposes. For example, they may not accept campaign contributions in their official offices. Staff members are required to take leave without pay to work on their bosses' campaigns.

Dating back to the first Congress, members have been permitted free use of the mail by using their signatures in place of stamps. The use of their signature, called the frank, is now regulated by a 1973 law that prohibits the use of the frank for purposes "unrelated to the official business, activities, and duties of members" and for "mail matter which specifically solicits political support . . . or a vote or financial assistance for any candidate for any political office." In 1989, the House limited the number of district wide "postal-patron" mailings that could be sent. The rules forbid explicit partisan and campaign references and allow only a limited number of references to the member per page.

The rules also bar mass mailings within 60 days of a primary or general election in the Senate and within 90 days in the House. Many members still use the frank within the 60-day period for multiple batches of mailings of fewer than 500 pieces each to target certain groups within their districts or states, and members still use the frank more in election years than non-election years. However, the 1989 rule change combined with a further tightening of member allowances in 1995 have reduced the amount of money spent on franked mail from over $100 million in 1988 to less than $20 million in 1999.

Until 1992, House members could send mass mailings at taxpayer expense to individuals living outside their district. Responding to a court ruling of that year, the House banned all mailings to more than 500 persons outside a member's district. The restriction is a problem for members whose districts are redrawn in an election year and seek to quickly communicate with their new constituents. The restriction also constrains members who are contemplating running for a statewide office, such as a Senate seat or governorship, who want to reach a larger electorate.

The Candidates

Personal ambition, more than any other factor, seems to drive people to run for Congress in the modern era. In recent years, party organizations have become very active in recruiting candidates. Interest groups, ranging from environmental groups to women's groups to manufacturing associations, seek candidates who reflect their viewpoint to run for Congress as well. Nevertheless, the initiative for the vast majority of candidacies rests with the candidates themselves. They are self-starters – independent political entrepreneurs who personally assess the costs and benefits then assume the risks of running for Congress.

Conventional wisdom suggests that Congress is an ossified institution filled with well-entrenched incumbents. As usual, conventional wisdom is half right and half wrong. Incumbents are advantaged and usually win reelection when they seek it. But it does not take very many voluntary retirements and electoral defeats in each election for substantial change in the membership to occur over just a few elections. Despite the fact that 90 percent or more of incumbents seek reelection, it takes only a few years for substantial turnover in the membership to occur. In 2003, for example, 245 of the 435 members of the House had been first elected in 1994 or later. In the Senate, 45 of the 100 senators serving in the 107th Congress (2001–2002) had served less than one full six-year term.

Three types of congressional candidates should be distinguished: incumbents seeking reelection, challengers to incumbents, and candidates running in districts or states with an open seat (that is, where the incumbent chose not to run or was defeated in the primary). As Figure 3.1 illustrates, several clear patterns have emerged in recent decades:

- most incumbents run for reelection and win;
- House incumbents are more successful than Senate incumbents in the typical election;
- in the House, the percentage of incumbents who successfully seek reelection has reached new highs in recent elections.

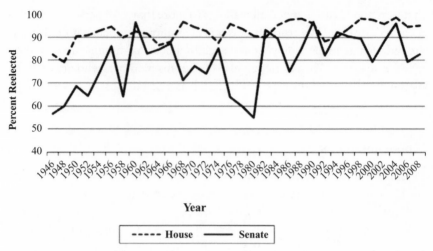

Year

| ----- House   ———— Senate |

FIGURE 3.1. House and Senate Reelection Rates, 1948–2008. *Sources:* Ornstein et al. Vital Statistics on Congress, 2001–2002; Abramson, Aldrich, and Rohde, Change and Continuity in the 2000 and 2002 Elections. 2004–2008 calculated by the authors. *Note:* The percentage includes only those seeking reelection.

Clearly, the odds are stacked against challengers, although challengers for Senate seats are more successful as a group than are challengers for House seats. The high rate of success for incumbents seeking reelection has led observers to note an incumbency advantage – something intrinsic to incumbent officeholders, their office and campaign resources, or the electorate that gives incumbents a built-in advantage over challengers.

One indicator of the strength of incumbents' advantage is the percentage of incumbents reelected with at least 60 percent of the vote. As Figure 3.2 indicates, this percentage was higher in the 1980s than in the previous three decades. The percentage dipped in the 1990s when incumbent Democrats suffered losses, but in 2002 and 2004, the percentage was back to levels seen in the late 1980s. This measure can be misleading. Any national shift in voter preferences favoring or hurting the majority party will affect most incumbents' margin of victory even if nothing associated with incumbency played a role – this appears to have been the case in 2006.

A better measure would provide a statistical adjustment for how well the candidate did in the last election and how advantaged or disadvantaged his or her party is nationwide. Such a measure indicates the advantage of incumbency corrected for the local and national advantages enjoyed by the incumbent and his or her party. Using a more refined measure, the House incumbency advantage shifted upward from 1964 to 1966. In the 1950s and early 1960s, the incumbency advantage was something less than five

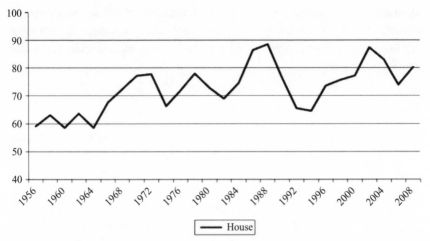

FIGURE 3.2. Percentage of House Incumbents Winning with At Least 60 Percent of the Major Party Vote, 1956–2008. *Source: Collected by authors.*

percentage points in most elections. Since then, the incumbency advantage has averaged close to 10 percentage points.

Senators' constituencies are often larger and more diverse than representatives' constituencies, and thus Senate races are often more competitive than House races. Incumbent senators find it more difficult than do incumbent House members to build a large base of support that will sustain them from election to election. The long six-year term may contribute to the inter-election variability in support for senators. Whatever the reason, Senate incumbents face a much higher probability of defeat than do their House counterparts.

In contrast to the pattern in elections involving incumbents, contests for open seats have become more competitive in recent decades. Between 1946 and 1964, only 20.3 percent of House open-seat contests produced a change in the party that controlled the seat; between 1966 and 2000, the percentage rose to close to 30. The trend is sharper in Senate open-seat races – 41.3 percent yielded party change between 1954 and 1964, and more than 50 percent did so between 1966 and 2000. In 2008, all three open Senate seats saw a change in party control.

Explaining the Incumbency Advantage

Political scientists have worked hard to identify the causes of the declining competition for seats held by incumbents and have discovered that many factors contribute to it. Influences include the declining importance of party identification in voting, an expanding incumbent advantage in campaign resources, more nonpartisan constituency service, imbalances in campaign funding, the quality of the candidates challenging incumbents, and more contact with voters.

The Decline of Party Identification

A major factor in incumbents' success is that their party holds the advantage in the district or state they represent. Democratic constituencies tend to elect and reelect Democrats; Republican constituencies tend to elect and reelect Republicans. For House districts, according to one estimate, the expected vote for incumbents, subtracting the vote attributable to their incumbency has varied from between 55 and 60 percent for most of the period since the late 1940s.

But party is a major element of the story of incumbency. The decline of party identification in the general electorate in the latter half of the twentieth century probably contributed to incumbents' advantage. As voters' psychological attachment to a major party weakened, the proportion of the electorate voting for congressional candidates in a reflexive, partisan way declined. This enlarged pool of "floating" voters and weak partisans produced more ticket splitting. The proportion of the electorate voting for the candidate of one party for one office and the candidate of the other party for another office – whether measured for House-Senate splits or House-president splits – nearly tripled from the 1950s through the 1980s, before declining in recent election cycles.

For congressional incumbents, weak partisanship and ticket splitting presented both danger and opportunity. The danger was that incumbents' natural base of support among fellow partisans was weakened, as there are fewer votes guaranteed for their party. This shift made the electorate more unpredictable. Indeed, for much of the 1960s–1980s there was more election-to-election volatility in incumbents' vote margins than there was in the 1950s – so much more that it nearly offsets the average incumbent's margin of victory. The increase in volatility accounts for the fact that incumbents were receiving a larger share of the vote but not actually winning at a much higher rate.

Expanded Perquisites of Office

The decline in party loyalty in the 1960s–1980s certainly contributed to the incumbency advantage, but incumbents have continued winning even in this era of renewed partisanship. Another important factor is that incumbents exploit their individual resources to combat electorate volatility and expand their base of support into the enlarged pool of independent voters. Their resources, which are discussed in Chapter 4, include a sizable personal staff distributed between their Washington and home offices, their committee staffs, office and stationery budgets, the use of the frank, a travel allowance, access to and influence over the White House and executive agencies, access to the media, and the expertise of the congressional support agencies.

All of these resources have grown since the 1960s and legislators can use them to attract favorable publicity at home. Staff members, often with the assistance of experts in support agencies, help members write legislation and timely amendments that are popular at home. Committee and subcommittee staffs assist their bosses in organizing hearings, some of which are held away from Washington and many of which attract media attention. Stationery allowances and the frank permit members to send mass mailings directly to their districts or states. Travel allowances make it easier for members to return home more frequently to appear before groups. And Congress's own radio and television facilities now permit members to make live and taped appearances on local television more frequently.

Expanded Constituency Service

Incumbents' official resources also can be used to improve their personal standing with their constituents. Additional staff and home offices have allowed members to provide personal services to constituents. Many of these services fall under the heading of "casework" – efforts to solve constituents' and local governments' problems with federal agencies. Perhaps the most common problem involves a constituent's eligibility for social security benefits. The expansion of federal programs since the mid-1960s has fostered this ombudsman role for members. Unlike legislating, which forces legislators to take sides on controversial issues, casework is a nonpartisan activity for which members can gain credit. The emphasis on personal service and de-emphasis on controversial issues facilitate more candidate-oriented and less party-oriented campaign.

Of course, the expansion of members' resources and the growth of constituency service have another side. In a large country with a large, complex federal bureaucracy, members perform a genuine service on behalf of constituents with real problems with government agencies. Legislators often justify their resources on the grounds that they are meeting the needs and

Congressionally Speaking . . .

Political scientists often use the *swing ratio* to gauge the bias of an electoral system. The swing ratio is the percentage change in seats won by a party for a 1 percent increase in its average nationwide vote. In a system of perfect proportional representation, the number of seats a party wins is proportional to the number of votes received, so the swing ratio is 1.0. A party winning 55 percent of the vote, for instance, would win 55 percent of the seats.

For single-member districts, a small percentage increase in the vote for a party may produce a large increase in the number of seats it wins (narrow defeats might be turned into narrow victories). The swing ratio for House elections has been about 2.0 in the twentieth century, indicating that a party gains two seats for each additional one percent of the nationwide vote it gains. The increasing incumbency advantage has reduced the House swing ratio in recent decades. Incumbents, who average more than 60 percent of the vote, can lose 5 or 10 percent of the vote and still retain their seats. This means that the system is less responsive – seat changes are smaller for the same change in nationwide vote.

expectations of their constituents. It is not surprising that members advertise their good works and get credit from voters for doing them.

Redistricting

One seemingly obvious explanation for the increase in the incumbency advantage is redistricting. With the Supreme Court ruling in *Wesberry v. Sanders* (1964) that districts had to approximate a "one person one vote" standard, many states had to redistrict for the first time in decades. In 1962, Michigan's largest district contained more than 800,000 residents, while the smallest contained less than 200,000. This massive wave of redistricting in the wake of *Wesberry*, is timed almost perfectly with the increase in the incumbency advantage.

For many years political scientists were unable to demonstrate that redistricting in the aftermath of *Wesberry v. Sanders* was responsible for the increased incumbency advantage. Recently, political scientists Gary Cox and Jonathan Katz have demonstrated that redistricting in the 1960s played a significant role. They point out that redistricting was dominated by Democrat-controlled state legislatures and federal courts staffed by Democratic judges. These authorities "packed" Republican voters into a few overwhelmingly Republican districts while spreading Democratic voters across more districts so as to increase the number of seats Democrats could be expected to win. This packing of Republicans produced a large number of seats that were virtually guaranteed to elect Republican members, but decreased competition in many other seats that were controlled by Democrats. Thus, they conclude that the increase in incumbency advantage was largely attributable to this increase in the number of safe Republican seats.

The post-2000 census redistricting has surely contributed to the lack of electoral competition in the 2002 and 2004 elections and helped prevent further Republican losses in 2006 and 2008. In addition to locking in more Republican seats, this round of redistricting considerably reduced the number of districts with a competitive party balance. By one count, 75 percent of the seats that had been competitive in 2000 were no longer competitive after redistricting. The most extreme of these "incumbency protection acts" was the new districting system in California, where all 53 districts had at least an eight percentage point registration advantage for one party.

Biased Campaign Funding

Changes in campaign finance laws and the introduction of PACs have been a mixed blessing for incumbents. The expanded resources and activities of party committees and PACs create a potential threat to incumbents. By recruiting, funding, and providing campaign services to challengers and even organizing mass mailings and media campaigns against incumbents, PACs and party committees can neutralize some of the advantages of incumbents. Republicans have proved to be especially adept at this strategy, but the Democratic party successfully used this strategy against them in 2006. Rep. Rahm Emmanuel (D-Illinois) and Sen. Charles Schumer (D-New York) successfully recruited and raised funds for many of the candidates who were key to the Democrats gaining a majority in the 2006 elections.

Of course, incumbents generally do not sit idly by as potential challengers are recruited and trained. In fact, by using their committee and subcommittee chairmanships, party posts, and other sources of influence, incumbents have done a good job of staying ahead of challengers. The incumbency advantage over challengers in PAC contributions, as well as in total contributions, is huge and has been growing since the 1970s.

Further, as the competition over majority control in Congress has intensified, the parties themselves have turned more attention to bolstering the resources of their own incumbents. Following the controversy surrounding the impeachment of President Clinton in 1998–99, House Majority Whip Tom DeLay (R-Texas) created a fundraising plan dubbed ROMP (Retain

Our Majority Program) in which incumbent Republicans donated over $1.5 million to the campaign funds of Republicans who were thought to be vulnerable during the 2000 election cycle. The stated goal of ROMP was to insure that vulnerable incumbents had enough money to "scare off potential challengers." Democrats instituted a similar program in 2004 called Frontline, which sought to funnel money from members in safe seats to endangered Democratic incumbents. In attempting to keep their newly expanded majority beyond the 111th Congress (2009–2010), the Democratic party had already identified 21 endangered incumbents for the Frontline program by February of 2009 – more than 19 months ahead of the 2010 election!

The flip side of contributions is expenditures. Figure 3.3 shows the historical record of spending by congressional candidates. The incumbent-challenger spending ratio increased from 1.5:1 in 1978 to 3.7:1 in 1990 for House races and from 1.9:1 to 2.1:1 in Senate races for the same years. By the year 2000, challengers improved their competitiveness, reducing the ratio to 2.2:1 in House contests and 1.6:1 in Senate contests, but in both 2004 and 2006 the ratios were over 4.5. In Senate campaigns, the gap between incumbents and challengers has grown, but generally it is not quite as large as the gap for House campaigns. Expenditures by open-seat candidates for the House show increases that parallel those of incumbents. In fact, open-seat candidate spending consistently runs ahead of incumbent spending. Without an incumbent to scare away candidates, open seat races tend to attract quality candidates and stimulate more spending on both sides.

The fundraising capacity of incumbents gives them a tremendous advantage over challengers. Indeed, incumbents now raise large sums early to deter potential opponents from entering the next race and to protect against unforeseen challenges. Incumbents' emphasis on deterrence and risk avoidance is evidenced in their efforts to raise far more money than they end up spending. These surpluses, along with fundraising efforts initiated just after an election, give the incumbents a huge – and growing – head start on any potential challengers for the next election. Figure 3.4 shows just how costly it has become to defeat a House incumbent. In 2000, the average winning House challenger spent approximately $750,000, but by 2006 that number had more than doubled to $1,800,000 – an increase of more than $1 million!

Candidate Quality

Congressional elections are primarily contests between local candidates, each of whom has a mix of personal and political attributes that influences voters' evaluations of them. If one party fails to field a quality candidate, or

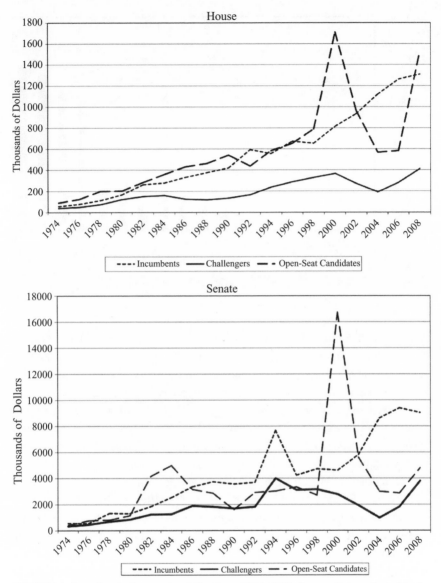

FIGURE 3.3. Spending in Congressional Elections, 1974–2008. *Source:* Data collected by the authors from FEC data and the Center for Responsive Politics.

perhaps any candidate at all, the other party is greatly advantaged. In fact, candidate quality, as measured by candidates' previous political experience, is strongly related to electoral success for both challengers and open-seat candidates. Members of Congress have always known this.

Declining quality among challengers may underpin incumbents' increasing margins of victory in recent decades. Over the past four decades, the

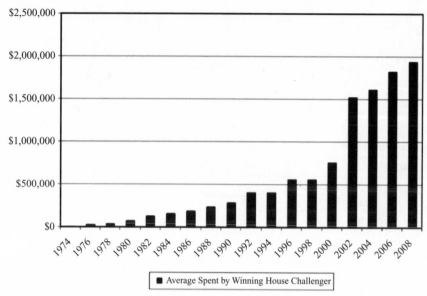

FIGURE 3.4. Average Spent by Winning Challenger, 1974–2008. *Source: Opensecrets.org.*

quality of challengers has declined, which may be a partial explanation for the growth of incumbent vote margins. Contributors, quite naturally, may have been less willing to give money to candidates who seemed unlikely to win. The party with the best set of challengers typically does a much better job of winning elections in the aggregate. Republicans attracted far more quality candidates to challenge Democratic incumbents in 1994, when they dislodged the Democrats as the majority party, but Democrats were able to turn the tables on them in the 2006 and 2008 election cycles.

The record in House open-seat contests, in which no incumbents are present to scare off potential opponents, is very different. In recent decades, the quality of open-seat candidates in general elections has improved. By one estimate, the number of high-quality, open-seat candidates (those with experience in elective office) has nearly doubled since the 1950s. This pattern, which contrasts sharply with the pattern for challengers, helps explain why open-seat races have become more competitive as races between incumbents and their challengers have become less competitive.

Contact with Voters

Incumbents' increasing advantage appears to be the product of several mutually reinforcing developments in the electorate's partisanship, incumbents' resources and behavior, campaign finance practices, and the decisions of potential candidates. Note also that scholars have eliminated several other possible explanations for incumbents' increasing vote margins.

The incumbency advantage, the competitiveness of open-seat elections, and House-Senate differences are all revealed by patterns in voters' contacts with candidates. Voters have somewhat more contact with small state Senate incumbents than with House incumbents, but the big difference lies between House and Senate challengers. Voters report far less contact with House challengers than with most Senate challengers, reflecting the vast difference in visibility and campaign resources for challengers at the two levels. In fact, Senate challengers do not lag much behind Senate incumbents in voter contact. One reason for this is the notoriety of many Senate challengers. People of wealth, celebrities, and well-known politicians make up a larger proportion of Senate challengers than House challengers. Many Senate challengers simply have a head start on their House counterparts.

The form of voter contact for which incumbents enjoy the biggest advantage over challengers is contact through the mail. This is true of both House and Senate incumbents, which suggests that incumbents' franking privilege and funding for mass mailings give them an important edge over the competition. Open-seat candidates have more contact with voters than do challengers, but have less contact than do incumbents. This is expected. After all, in comparison with challengers, open-seat candidates tend to be better qualified, more familiar to voters, and more successful at raising campaign funds. For the same reasons, Senate open-seat candidates are more successful than House open-seat candidates in reaching voters.

National Patterns in Congressional Elections

Although the local candidates and their personal and political characteristics are the major determinants of congressional election outcomes, national forces appear to be an influence worth at least several percentage points in some congressional races. Such a small effect may seem quite unimportant, but it is more than enough to determine the outcome in many close contests. The state of the national economy, the public's evaluation of the president's performance, and the public's tendency to be conservative are typically strongly related to which party is most successful in congressional elections. When the economy is weak, the president's performance ratings are low. When the public mood is out of sync with administration policy, candidates of the incumbent president's party are less successful. By influencing the outcome in at least a few races, such forces can shape the partisan and ideological balance in the House and Senate.

National forces may be felt in congressional elections in several ways. Voters and financial contributors sometimes reward or punish congressional candidates for national conditions. To the extent that they do, potential candidates have reason to assess the odds of winning. In any given year, potential candidates of one party may decide to stay out of congressional races when conditions do not seem favorable, reducing the pool of quality candidates that the party is able to field. Weak candidates, of course, attract few contributions, build ineffective campaigns, and are not likely to win. Thus, anticipated and actual choices made by voters, contributors, and potential and actual candidates combine to reward the candidacies of the party credited with good times and to punish the party blamed for bad times.

This description of the influence of national forces has one serious weakness: It cannot account for the frequency of divided party control between Congress and the presidency. The influence of national conditions generally pushes voters in the same direction for congressional and presidential elections. To be sure, idiosyncratic factors – a presidential scandal, for example – might occasionally produce a Congress and president of different parties. And yet, in 18 of the 29 two-year Congresses between 1952 and 2008, divided party control existed. All of the Republican presidents in that period served with a Democratic House and, usually, a Democratic Senate. In 1995–2000, Democratic president Clinton served with a Republican Congress.

It turns out that the effects of national forces, including presidential popularity, on congressional elections are not invariant. In fact, important changes have occurred in recent decades.

Presidential Election Years and the Coattail Effect

The "coattail effect" refers to the ability of popular candidates at the top of the ticket to attract voters to candidates of the same party for other offices. The coattail effect is thought by some to be generated by a spillover process – the popularity of the top candidate becomes associated with all candidates from the same party in the minds of voters. Such coattail effects may amount to rewarding all candidates of the same party for good times (or blaming all candidates of a party for bad times). Or perhaps the party of a strong top candidate, whose strength may come from favorable economic conditions, attracts better candidates for lower offices. Conversely, the pull might actually be in the other direction – popular congressional candidates draw support to their party's presidential candidate. Whatever the mechanism at work, coattails, when they exist, have an important con-sequence: They produce a change in voting in the same partisan direction for presidential and congressional elections, and they encourage the election of a president and congressional majorities of the same party. The best evi-dence mustered by political scientists indicates that the presidential coattail effect is irregular but has declined since the mid-twentieth century.

The weakened coattail effect is consistent with the expanded incumbency advantage. Incumbents may have been able to insulate themselves from negative public evaluations of presidents of their own party. They do so by working hard to associate themselves with the needs of their local district or state, distancing themselves from party labels, and advertising their personal attributes. How much they can divorce themselves from their party is lim-ited, however, because they are listed with a party label on most state ballots, and challengers work hard to show the connection when it is advantageous to do so.

Midterm Elections

For congressional elections held in the middle of a presidential term – called midterm elections – there is no concurrent presidential contest. Yet for House midterm races, the number of congressional seats the two parties win is predicted well by the state of the economy and the public's evaluation of the president's performance. But candidates of the president's party are not credited or blamed for economic conditions in midterm contests as much as they are in presidential election years, when the choice of a presidential candidate is also on voters' minds. In Senate midterm elections, economic conditions are even more weakly related to partisan seat gains or losses than they are in the House.

Midterm elections are distinctive for two reasons. First, turnout among voters is lower in midterm elections than in presidential elections. Without the stimulus of a highly visible presidential contest, turnout is often 10 to 15 percentage points lower in a midterm election. In recent midterm elections, less than 40 percent of the nation's adult population has voted. Turnover varies widely among states and districts, however, and surges in midterm election turnout are related to the competitiveness of congressional races. Incumbents must be wary of challengers who can stimulate turnout and create uncertainties about the size and composition of the November electorate in midterm elections.

Second, for most of the twentieth century, political scientists could safely predict that the president's party would gain seats in Congress in presidential election years, but lose seats in midterm elections. This pattern held for House seats in every midterm election from 1938–1994 and for Senate seats in all but three midterm elections during the same period. In 1990, for example, the Republicans lost a net of eight House seats and one Senate seat. Between 1946 and 1996, the president's party suffered an average loss of about 24 seats in midterm elections, compared with an average gain of about nine seats in presidential election years.

The election outcomes in 1998 and 2002 bucked this familiar trend. In 1998, Democrats managed to win a net gain of five House seats and lost no Senate seats, whereas in 2002 Republicans gained seven House seats and three Senate seats. The common thread running through both of these elections is that both occurred while the president enjoyed extraordinarily high public approval ratings.

Furthermore, the president's party tends to lose more House seats in the midterm election of the president's second term than in the president's first term. By one estimate, which took into account other factors that influence House elections, the president's party does about twice as poorly in the second term as in the first term. The 2006 election is an excellent example of this as the Republicans, weighed down by an unpopular president, lost 30 seats in the House and 6 in the Senate.

A reasonable explanation of the difficulty confronted by the president's party in midterm elections is the exposure thesis. This thesis holds that the more a party gains in one election above its average or natural level for recent decades, the more seats it is likely to be holding in states and districts that generally favor the other party. The party that gains in a presidential election year becomes vulnerable to losing seats two years later in the midterm election. The number of seats won in the presidential election year that are above the party's average indicates how "exposed" the party will be to seat losses at the midterm. Actual results are influenced by national conditions and the president's popularity.

Congressional Elections and Policy Alignments

Assessing the effects of elections on public policy is tricky. We can never be sure what kinds of policies would have been enacted had the cast of players within Congress and the White House been different. Moreover, some of the factors that influence election outcomes, such as changing public attitudes, directly affect both old and new decision makers and might produce policy changes even if little turnover in Congress occurs. To complicate matters further, we usually cannot determine the policy preferences of members

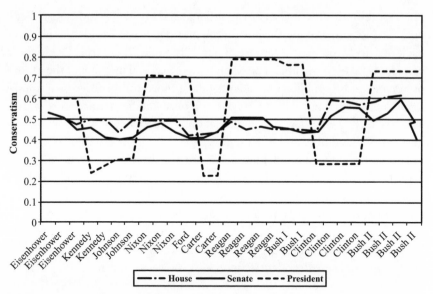

FIGURE 3.5. House, Senate, and Presidential Conservatism, 1955–2008. *Source: Data provided by Keith Poole and Howard Rosenthal,* http://www.pooleandrosenthal.com.

until they cast roll-call votes. This means that we usually cannot distinguish members' policy views immediately after an election from positions they take later on, which are influenced by new events, presidential demands, interest group lobbying, and other political forces.

Even when election results appear to predict future policy directions, there is no simple one-to-one correspondence between election outcomes, the ideological alignment of the three lawmaking institutions, and eventual policy outcomes. For example, the 1986 elections clearly produced a more liberal Senate – Republicans lost eight seats and gave up majority control. But the White House remained in the hands of Ronald Reagan, a conservative Republican president, whose concurrence was required to get liberal legislation favored by Congress enacted into law. Thus, although the Constitution provides the means (elections) for changing the policy views represented in Congress and the White House, it also established rules for the electoral and legislative systems that reduce the chances that changing views will be translated directly and immediately into new public policy.

Ideological Outlook

Figure 3.5 demonstrates the effect of elections on the changing ideological position of the House, the Senate, and the presidency in recent decades.

High scores indicate a conservative outlook, and low scores indicate a liberal outlook. Not surprisingly, the line for the presidency varies widely as it moves back and forth between Democratic and Republican control. Democratic presidents take a more liberal position than the typical member of the House or Senate, and Republican presidents take a more conservative position. In contrast, the ideological positions of the House and Senate are more stable, which reflects the tendency of single elections to produce only a small change in the overall membership of Congress.

The patterns revealed in Figure 3.5 are consistent with what might be expected. During most of the period since the 1950s, all presidents have faced challenges in gaining cooperation from the two chambers of Congress. As we might expect, Republican presidents Nixon (after his first two years), Ford, Reagan, and Bush differed from the Democratic houses of Congress by a larger margin than did Democratic presidents Kennedy, Johnson, and Carter. Republican President Eisenhower, however, did not differ a great deal from the Democratic Congresses that he faced in the late 1950s.

Moreover, the 1980 and 1986 elections, which produced a change in party control of the Senate, are associated with changes in the ideological placement of the Senate relative to the House and the presidency. The Senate became more like the Republican White House after the 1980 elections, although still not as conservative as the administration. After the 1986 elections, the Senate reverted to its usual place, close to the House, with Presidents Reagan and Bush taking far more conservative positions.

The patterns in Figure 3.5 are important because they show that elections shift the ideological alignment of the three institutional players. They indicate that the House and Senate are usually not too distant from each other, and the president is often the outlier. If left to their own devices, presidents probably would produce more radical shifts in policy than they are allowed to do in the three-player game. Nevertheless, important shifts do occur within Congress as well. For example, Congress moved considerably farther away from President Clinton following the 1994 election, leading to a conflict-ridden six years of divided government, while the 107th through 109th Congresses were very sympathetic to President Bush's legislative agenda, whereas the 110th Congress produced two years of acrimony between President Bush and congressional Democrats.

The extended period of divided party control of government under Presidents Ronald Reagan, George H. W. Bush, Bill Clinton, and George W. Bush have rekindled a debate about the policy consequences of divided control of government. Many observers have characterized the period as one of political deadlock: Conservative presidents have checked the initiatives of a liberal Congress, and the liberal Congress has blocked the proposals of conservative presidents (and, under Clinton, vice versa).

Partisan competition exacerbates the already difficult task of gaining agreement among the House, the Senate, and the president. This depiction of the state of American national government has led many critics to recommend radical reforms, so we must know whether it is accurate. Does divided party control of government make any difference?

The Divided-Government Debate

THE MAYHEW THESIS. Political scientist David Mayhew investigated the question of divided control in his book *Divided We Govern*. He examined the frequency of major congressional investigations of the executive branch and the enactment of major legislation for the period between 1947 and 1990. During that period, one party controlled both houses of Congress and the presidency for 18 years and neither party controlled both houses and the presidency for 26 years (including 1981 to 1986, when Republicans controlled the Senate and White House but not the House). He found that "unified as opposed to divided control has not made an important difference in recent times" with respect to either the undertaking of high-profile investigations or the rate at which important laws are enacted. Mayhew concluded that "it does not seem to make all that much difference whether party control of the American government happens to be unified or divided."

Mayhew's somewhat surprising findings call attention to the forces in American politics that lead to cooperation between the House, the Senate, and the president. All three institutions must respond to the same national problems, and they share many constituents. Furthermore, members of Congress and presidents both have strong electoral incentives to establish a positive record of accomplishment. And even if public opinion varies greatly among different congressional constituencies, shifts in public mood, which are produced by changing conditions and events, tend to propel all elected officials in the same direction.

OTHER EVIDENCE. Nevertheless, evidence seems to show that divided party control does make some difference. To make sense of patterns in the direction of public policy over time, we must take into account the ideological distance between the House, the Senate, and the president at specific points

---

TABLE 3.2. Presidential Success on Roll-Call Votes: The Effect of Divided Government, 1953–2008.

Unified Government	76.6
	(16)
Divided Government	64.2
	(40)

Percentages reflect average success rates of presidents on roll-calls that they took positions on. Data collected by the authors from *Congressional Quarterly Weekly Report*. Number of years indicated in parentheses.

---

in time. After all, divided control may not always cause a large gap between the policy positions of the president and the two chambers of Congress, nor is it true that unified control insures ideological alignment between the president and Congress. We have seen that ideological distance between the House, the Senate, and the president is related to party control. In addition, we can examine direct measures of policy agreement and disagreement among the three institutions. In fact, three such measures – the rate of success for presidential proposals, presidential success on congressional roll-call votes (see Table 3.2), and presidential vetoes – show the expected differences between unified and divided control. The president's recommendations are adopted less frequently under divided party control, the president's position on roll-call votes wins less frequently, and the president resorts to the veto more frequently under divided control than under unified control.

Others have pointed out that differences between the president and Congress are not the only causes of legislative gridlock. Factors such as the level of consensus between the two chambers of Congress and within each chamber of Congress, along with the strength of congressional parties are also important determinates of legislative productivity. Scholars have also pointed out that many institutional features of the lawmaking process, such as the bicameral nature of Congress and the two-thirds majority required to override presidential vetoes, impact the lawmaking process as much if not more than partisan affiliation of the players.

A fair conclusion is that the party balance in Congress, a direct product of elections, is an important force among the many different forces that shape relations between the House, the Senate, and the president. Because party control is related, albeit imperfectly, to ideological distance, it affects the degree to which the president's policies are accepted by Congress and vice versa. Other forces are at work as well, and many of them push the House,

Senate, and president in the same direction even when partisanship divides the three institutional players.

Conclusion

The electoral arena has changed in important ways in recent decades. New laws and court decisions have greatly complicated the rules governing congressional elections and are sure to continue to do so in the coming years. The power of the president's coattails has declined, PACs have blossomed and gained a critical role in financing campaigns, and parties have taken on a greater role in financing campaigns. Campaigns have become more candidate-centered and less party-oriented, with candidates often spending large sums of their own money to gain a seat. Perhaps most importantly, congressional incumbents, particularly House incumbents, have gained important advantages over challengers.

Although congressional elections are primarily contests between local candidates, they have had critical national consequences. Time and again, national conditions and elections have altered the ideological alignment between the House, the Senate, and the president. Since the mid-twentieth century, elections have regularly produced divided party control of government, which has increased conflict between the branches of government and has made it more difficult to assign credit and blame for government performance.

Above: Don Cravins, staff director for the Senate Small Business and Entrepreneurship Committee, speaks to Roll Call in his Russell Senate Office Building office on Thursday, Feb. 5, 2009. **Below:** Administrative Assistant Art Estopianan talks with interns, from left, Ashley Hacker, Jenny Urizar and Sara Susnjar in the Washington D.C. office of Rep. Ileana Ros-Lehtinen (FL). (KRT) NC KD 2001 (Horiz) (Ide)

4

Members, Goals, Resources, and Strategies

I N TODAY'S WORLD, WE MAKE SEVERAL REASONABLE ASSUMPTIONS ABOUT members of Congress. We assume that most of them will seek reelection, and, if they do not, it is because they are seeking another elective office or are retiring. We expect that legislators have the ability to get back to their districts and states on most weekends to attend civic functions and meet with constituents. We take for granted that legislators can answer the mail, deal with the government problems of constituents, and address the policy concerns of House districts that average about 675,000 people and states that average nearly 6 million people.

These assumptions are fairly accurate, but Congress has not always been this way. Only in the last few decades have nearly all legislators sought reelection. In the late 1800s, it was common for two-thirds or less of House members to run for reelection. Even in the 1940s, two out of 10 legislators sat out the next election. But in recent Congresses, 90–95 percent of incumbents sought reelection. Moreover, the technology, resources, and staff required to make frequent trips home and to be responsive to ever-expanding constituencies are of recent vintage. Since the 1950s, office budgets have quadrupled and personal staffs have doubled in size.

This chapter looks at Congress from the members' perspective. Legislators exhibit a range of personal goals, but most modern legislators see politics as a career and view reelection as essential to the achievement of their goals. Over time, they have granted themselves the resources to pursue their electoral, policy, and other objectives simultaneously. Still, legislators do not pursue all goals all the time, but rather they exploit resources and opportunities selectively. We will see that there are important patterns and generalizations that can be made.

Setting Personal Priorities

Legislators have well-established policy attitudes by the time they arrive in Washington for the first time. For example, most of them can be characterized as liberals, moderates, or conservatives, with some variation on specific issues. Those attitudes are the product of many factors – personal experience, a track record in politics, the necessities of the campaign, and so on. In general, therefore, the voting behavior of most members is quite predictable. And yet members face many decisions for which their general ideological outlook offers little guidance – how to vote on hundreds of roll-call votes on narrow issues, which committee assignments to request, how to allocate staff, which issues to emphasize, and how much time to spend in Washington versus the home state or district. Members' choices about these matters mold their legislative careers.

Members have wide latitude in setting their personal priorities and choosing strategies for pursuing their goals. No party leader or president dictates how members vote, what issues members pursue, how much time members spend in their home districts and states, or how members organize their staffs. To be sure, members are subjected to pressure from leaders, presidents, and many other people and groups, but members of the modern Congress are remarkably free to shape their priorities and determine their own strategies.

There is a catch. Time, staff, and budgets are limited so members must exercise care in allocating their resources. New members face the most difficult choices. They must worry about organizing a staff, selecting and arranging new offices, requesting committee assignments, and responding to appeals from senior members competing for leadership posts – all while trying to find a place to live in a new city. Members do these things with incomplete information. In requesting committee assignments, for example, a member might like to know the career plans of committee and subcommittee leaders: Whether they plan to retire soon or to run for higher office will affect how quickly the member might rise to chair a committee or subcommittee. In hiring staff, a member might like to know what issues will be hot in the coming years so that he or she can appoint people with relevant expertise. In nearly every aspect of setting priorities, a member would like to know who future opponents are likely to be and whether economic and world conditions will favor his or her party. And most members would like to know if and when opportunities to run for higher office will arise. With the passage of time, members gradually resolve some uncertainties, acclimate themselves to others, and settle into routines that reflect their personal priorities, campaign experience, and style.

Members' Goals

Members of Congress tend to be quite purposeful in their professional activities as elected officials. Most of what they do as legislators is connected to some goal or goals – political scientists would label this *instrumental* behavior. They do not always articulate their goals, but they usually can explain how particular decisions affect their own political objectives. Moreover, they usually see connections between their goals and what they do every day. They try to use their limited resources effectively, if not always efficiently, and consciously move toward achieving their personal political goals. To be sure, not every move is calculated, but members generally think and act in ways that make it reasonable to characterize them as strategic politicians.

What are members' goals? For our purposes, focusing on the political goals that members mention when explaining their many decisions makes sense. Political scientist Richard Fenno, in studying differences among members sitting on different committees, found that three categories – reelection, good public policy, and influence – accounted for most of the goals expressed by members.

Reelection

Members of Congress are like the rest of us – most of them want to keep their jobs. They gain personal satisfaction from making contributions to public policy and serving the interests of people they care about, as well as from the prestige of holding high public office. Perhaps a few members like the income, have a craving for power, enjoy the attention given to them by lobbyists and others, or simply like to see themselves on television.

Members face a test for retaining their jobs that most of us do not. Periodically, at times fixed by law, they must seek the approval of a very large number of citizens they do not know personally. The opinion voters hold of their representatives and senators can turn on factors beyond the members' personal control. And campaigning, even for members who have won by wide margins in the past, involves a large commitment of time, money, and energy. Most of the rest of us do not face such an extraordinary test to retain our jobs once we have established a career.

We should not be surprised that many, if not most, members make obtaining reelection a high priority in their daily activities. In the view of critics, members care too much about reelection. Some critics assert that members ignore the general welfare of the country while pursuing the narrow interests of financial contributors, the special interests of organized groups, and the parochial interests of their home constituents. Furthermore, critics contend that the reelection drive has become more intense in recent years. Supporters of term limits, in particular, claim that members have become obsessed by reelection, have become excessively insular in their political outlook, and have built up staffs and perks – the resources that come with their office – that virtually ensure their reelection.

Even scholars often assume, at least for the sake of argument, that members are single-minded seekers of reelection. And for good reason: In recent decades nearly all members of Congress seek reelection, and much of what members do is best explained by the drive for reelection. Requesting assignment to committees with jurisdictions affecting their constituents, introducing popular legislation, winning federal funds for projects in their states and districts, solving constituents' problems with federal agencies, evaluating legislation for its impact on their constituencies, and soliciting media attention are common activities that members pursue to enhance their chances of reelection. Political scientist David Mayhew neatly summarized these activities as credit claiming, position taking, and advertising. And political scientist R. Douglas Arnold has shown how congressional leaders take into account the electoral calculations of members when designing strategies for building majority coalitions.

Still, great care must be exercised in declaring reelection to be the sole motivating force of congressional action. Reelection is probably better viewed as a means to an end rather than as an end in itself. As we see it, people seek election and reelection to Congress primarily because they value membership in Congress in some way. If other goals were not served by membership, or if running for office were too onerous, few people would make the effort. Those other goals, whatever they may be, surely influence members' daily activities as well.

Moreover, reelection plays little role in many decisions and activities of members of Congress. Many committee and floor votes have no consequences for reelection, and actively advocating legislation and building coalitions involves much activity that is unseen and unappreciated at home. David Price, a political scientist and a Democratic representative from North Carolina, explains that "most members of Congress, most of the time, have a great deal of latitude as to how they define their roles and what kind of job they wish to do. If they do not have the latitude, they can often create it, for they have a great deal of control over how their actions are perceived and interpreted."[1]

One way a member gains latitude is to earn the trust of constituents. Political scientist Richard Fenno observes that trust is earned only over time, as a member's constituents come to see him or her as qualified, as a person who

---

Congressionally Speaking . . .

The *pork barrel* is the term used in politics for local projects funded by Congress. The term is thought to originate in the pre-Civil War practice of serving slaves salted pork in large barrels. When the pork barrels were set out, slaves would rush to grab as much of the pork as possible. In the early twentieth century, journalists began to comment that members of Congress behaved similarly in an effort to distribute pet projects to their constituents.

Each year Congress approves funding for hundreds of local projects ranging from a university building to a youth center to a new dam or bridge. Legislators take credit for the projects by issuing press releases, including stories in their newsletters, and appearing at ground-breaking and opening ceremonies. As nonpartisan public works, almost everyone at home appreciates the "pork" projects and the legislators' efforts, a perfect combination for legislators eager to please voters.

Earmarks are provisions in bills or committee reports that direct funding to individual projects. In 2007, the House and Senate passed rules changes to reform earmark practices. As a result, both chambers now require committees and other sponsors of legislation to list earmarks and their sponsors in accompanying reports. Moreover, the chambers compel members to certify that they do not have a personal financial interest at stake in an earmark they sponsor. In 2009, the House also passed a rule prohibiting appropriations conference committees from inserting additional earmarks.

---

identifies and empathizes with them, and as someone who can defend his or her actions in Washington credibly. In seeking to develop such trust, members develop distinctive "home styles," tailored to their own personalities and skills as well as to the nature of their constituencies.

For one member of the House, Barney Frank (D-Massachusetts), wit has become a trademark. During his reelection campaign of 1992, a year in which a large number of members retired from office, Frank wrote a letter to supporters saying that

> I feel somewhat apologetic about what I am going to tell you: I do not plan to quit Congress. As I read the praise which the media lavishes on my colleagues who are retiring, I'm afraid my eagerness to keep working on a broad range of public policy issues may be taken as a character defect. So I hope that as character defects go, this one will be considered sufficiently minor for you tooverlook.[2]

Apparently, it was. Frank was reelected in 1992 with 72 percent of the vote and has been reelected every two years since then.

Nearly all members of Congress seek reelection, so it is reasonable to assume that concern about reelection plays a part in many, if not most, decisions that legislators make. Because it is a goal that must be achieved periodically if a legislator is to continue pursuing other goals in public office, it is not too surprising that reelection dominates all other considerations. Yet for most members, reelection does not explain everything.

Good Public Policy

Among the other goals members pursue is to make good public policy. The cynics are wrong: Most, if not all, members care about the country's future. Many members come to Congress with preexisting policy interests and often are deeply committed to certain policy views. These commitments influence members' committee preferences, staffing decisions, and legislative activities.

A good illustration of a legislator's background shaping his or her legislative interests is Representative Carolyn McCarthy (D-New York), who has developed a national reputation as a staunch advocate of gun control. In 1993, McCarthy's husband was killed and her son seriously injured by a gunman on the Long Island Railroad. When McCarthy's representative, Dan Frisa (R-New York), voted against a federal ban on assault weapons, she decided to run for office. Despite being a lifelong Republican, she ran under the Democratic label in 1996 and won by a decisive margin. Since her initial election to office, McCarthy has fought for stricter gun control laws. She has sponsored or cosponsored dozens of bills proposing more stringent regulation of guns and ammunition. She has won reelection six times – most recently with 64 percent of the vote in 2008.

Political scientists have shown that personal experience motivates involvement in the legislative process. For example, studies demonstrate that African American members of the House of Representatives devote more legislative effort to the issues that are particularly important to African Americans even when the composition of their home districts is taken into account. Similar findings are reported for women, although, on the whole, their behavior is not as distinctive as African Americans in Congress. More casual observations about other groups – farmers, veterans, business leaders, and so on – are made with some frequency, too.

Many legislators acquire policy interests, sometimes quite accidentally, while serving in Congress. It could hardly be otherwise. Members are introduced to many subjects in the process of listening to constituents, sitting through committee hearings, and discussing issues with colleagues, staff, and outside experts.

Political Influence

Many members also want political influence. Influence may be an end in itself, or it may be a means for pursuing certain policy goals, constituency interests, or even reelection. Most members try to develop a base of power within Congress so that they have more influence than other members do.

Influence can be acquired in many ways, but earning formal party and committee positions is particularly important in Congress. Party and committee leaders often enjoy certain procedural prerogatives and additional staff, both of which may give them an edge in influencing policy outcomes. Members striving for broad influence pursue party leadership posts by first seeking appointment or election to low-level party positions, in the hope of gaining a top post in the future. Holders of committee and subcommittee chairs also are advantaged, at least within the jurisdiction of their committees and subcommittees. Members also might try to gain a seat on committees with broad and important jurisdictions, such as House Appropriations and Ways and Means. Because the work of these types of committees is important to all members of Congress, and many special interests, a spot on one of them puts a member in a position to help fellow members. As Representative Norm Dicks (D-Washington) described the House Appropriations Committee, "It's where the money is. And money is where the clout is."[3]

Serving Constituents   delegate v. trustee role

Many members feel a strong obligation to look out for the interests of their home constituents, even when doing so has little effect on their reelection prospects or when there is little connection between their constituents' needs and their own policy interests. Political scientists have sometimes called the duty to behave in accordance with the wishes of constituents the delegate role. The delegate role is often contrasted with the trustee role, in which the member exercises independent judgment about questions of public policy. Of course, members seldom make a conscious philosophical judgment about whether to act as a delegate or as a trustee. For many members, behaving as a delegate comes naturally, at least on many issues. After all, most members grew up in the districts or states they serve. They often identify and empathize with their constituents, and believe that their constituents deserve good representation. But because their constituents have opinions about only a small fraction of the many policy questions Congress must confront, every member must behave like a trustee much of the time, no matter how committed he or she is to serving constituents' interests.

Political scientist Christopher Cooper and Representative Daniel Lipinski (D-Illinois), a former professor of political science, suggest that members strategically communicate their dedication to the delegate role. Using rhetoric, members signal to constituents the extent to which they are acting as a delegate or trustee, although the rhetoric may not be an accurate depiction of their legislative behavior. The use of this rhetoric for this purpose appears to be systematic. Members are more likely to emphasize the delegate role when they are in their first term or when they represent a district that contains a large percentage of blue-collar workers, senior citizens, or friendly partisan voters – groups that appear to prefer a more home-oriented form of representation.

Not all constituents are of equal importance to members. It goes without saying that virtually every member would prefer a happy constituent to an unhappy one, but members know that they are choosing which constituents to give priority to when they select their committee assignments, set their personal policy emphases, and cast votes on divisive issues. Members naturally give priority to constituents who supported them when they were forced to make tough choices, and this makes it difficult for the outside observer to distinguish between members who are genuinely committed to their constituents' interests and members who are motivated by reelection alone.

Higher Office

Higher office is on the minds of many members of Congress. They may not see their current position solely as a stepping-stone to higher office, but many members are clearly ambitious. In 2008, for example, 9 sitting House members left their seat to run for higher office. This number is particularly low in part because there were only 11 gubernatorial races, and only three of those races were open seats. Despite this, the number of House members that pursue higher office is quite large when we aggregate across several congresses. For instance, by one count, a total of 225 House members ran for the Senate between 1960 and 2008. Moreover, this surely understates the number of members with progressive ambition over this period of time. Counting only those that ran for higher office overlooks the potentially sizeable number of members who desired higher office but made the strategic decision not to run, at least for the time being. Table 4.1 details the political background of members of the 111th Congress (2009–10). Progressive ambition is quite apparent. In both chambers, the vast majority of members bring to their current positions experience in elective office. Nearly half of

TABLE 4.1. Highest Previous Elective Office of Representatives and Senators, 111th Congress (2009–2010).

Current Office	Previous Elective Office						Percent with Previous Elective Office
	U.S. Representative	U.S. Senator	Governor	State Legislator	Mayor	Other Elective Office	
House of Representatives[a]	–	0	1	214	15	54	65.6
Senate[b]	47	–	10	8	3	15	83.0

[a] At time of writing, Illinois district 5 and New York district 20 remain vacant.
[b] At time of writing, the Minnesota Senate seat is being contested.
Source: Congressional Biographical Directory. Coding done by authors.

all senators previously served in the House. And ambition does not stop with the Senate: For the general elections between 1960 and 2008, 29 of the 52 major-party candidates for president and vice president had served in the Senate.

Several factors contribute to a member's decision to run for higher office – comparative value of the higher seat to the current seat, probability of winning the higher seat, and cost of running for the higher seat. The relative value of seats is an important aspect in any member's decision to run for higher office, and it is often visible in Senators' determination whether to run for governor. Incumbent senators seldom run for small-state governorships but are more inclined to run for large-state governorships. The probability of winning is a factor that is frequently illustrated after the redistricting of House seats. House members who find their district lines changed radically anticipate that gaining reelection to their seat may be difficult and often choose to run for higher office.

Legislating

The work of legislating seems to have an intrinsic appeal to many legislators. The legislative game can be fun. Formulating strategies, mastering complicated issues, learning the complexities of the policy-making process, building majority coalitions against talented opponents, making a lasting contribution to public policy, and associating with other bright and energetic people appear to motivate many members. Former senator Dan Quayle (R-Indiana) is a case in point. A close observer of Quayle reports that "in recounting his first year's activities [as a senator] he exuded enthusiasm for legislative work in general. 'I had fun on all of them,' he said after canvassing his first-year interests. 'There was no one highlight. The highlight is getting involved and accomplishing a whole lot of things.'"[4]

Multiple Goals

Most members appear to be motivated by more than one goal. In fact, much of what they do is consistent with pursuing several goals. After all, the more goals served by a particular activity or decision, the more valuable it is likely to be. For example, using a committee hearing to draw attention to a policy problem and to oneself may simultaneously further a member's reelection chances, prospects for higher office, and public policy objectives. Furthermore, the media attention generated by a hearing may help influence colleagues' views about the member's intelligence and leadership ability as well as their views on the issue at hand.

Members can pursue a multifaceted strategy to avoid having to select among competing goals. For example, Senator Sherrod Brown (D-Ohio), an educator prior to entering politics, sought an assignment on the Agriculture Committee, which has jurisdiction over farm programs important to large parts of his state, but also gained a seat on the Health, Education, Labor, and Pensions Committee, where he can pursue issues of personal and national interest.

With limited time, money, and staff, members often face making tradeoffs among goals. Generally, representatives face more severe tradeoffs than senators do. With fewer committee assignments, a smaller staff and office budget, and a shorter term of office, representatives must carefully allocate resources among the various activities they would like to pursue. Fortunately for them, over the past few decades, all members have benefited from an expanding base of resources.

pursue multiple goals

Members' Resources

power to vote is best resource

Pursuing goals requires resources. A member's most important resource is the power to vote – in subcommittee, in committee, on the floor, or in conference. Members also have many nonprocedural resources. As managers of numerous offices – personal, committee, and perhaps even party offices – with their sizable staffs and budgets, members might even be thought of as heading small political enterprises. *gain resources w/ influence (experience)*

Over the long term, a member's resources may expand. As a legislator takes on more important party or committee leadership positions, he or she will gain more influence and additional budget and staff support. Because many committee leadership posts are allocated on the basis of seniority, these additional resources are acquired by winning reelection repeatedly. In this way, the value of a House or Senate seat – to the member and to home constituents – increases with time.

Personal Office and Staff Allowances

For the first time in 1893, the House voted to permit the use of government funds to hire personal staff assistants. Until then, members either paid for assistants with their own funds or relied on family members, usually wives and daughters. Even committee aides were rare until the mid-nineteenth century. Only after office buildings were built adjacent to the Capitol early in the twentieth century did rank-and-file members acquire personal offices. Before then, only top party leaders and committee chairs were given separate rooms in the Capitol.

In the modern Congress, a spending bill for the legislative branch is passed each year. It specifies a certain amount of money for members' personal offices. In recent decades, members in both chambers have been given more discretion over the use of these funds. In 1987, the Senate adopted reforms that consolidated senators' office and staff allowances into a single, fungible account called the Senators' Official Personnel and Office Expense Account (SOPOEA). Whereas the previous system limited the portion of a senator's total personal budget that he or she could allocate to staff or office expenses, the reforms lifted those constraints. Senators now receive a single allowance from which they can determine the mix of resources that best suits their needs. In 1996, the House followed the Senate's lead by putting into place the Members' Representational Allowance (MRA) system. Prior to the MRA, members were required to pay for resources from three separate accounts – the clerk-hire allowance, the official expenses allowance, and the official mail allowance. The MRA puts these allowances under a single, flexible account, and permits members to interchange funds freely.

Although members in both chambers have a single account, the different needs of the members require that components of the accounts be calculated separately. In the House, members are allocated identical amounts for personnel, and are entitled to hire up to 22 employees – 18 full time and four part time. That limit is up from eight in 1955, 10 in 1965, and 18 in 1975. Although there are a few restrictions on how office funds may be used, representatives are largely free to allocate staff as they see fit. Members adopt a wide range of strategies in choosing staff (see Table 4.2). The office and mailing expense components of the account vary from member to member depending on a variety factors, such as the cost of traveling to his or her district from Washington, long-distance phone costs to the district, and the cost of renting office space in the district. In calendar year 2008, the MRAs ranged from $1,299,292 to $1,637,766.

In the Senate, there is no explicit limit to the number of staff aides a senator can hire. Personal staff funding varies according to state population. Senators from large states have funding to hire many more staff assistants than do senators from small states. In addition, each senator receives an equal amount of funds above the clerk-hire allowance for the hire of three legislative assistants. Senators also have an official expense allowance to cover office, telephone, travel, and mailing costs. This allowance varies from

TABLE 4.2. Frequency of Staff Titles in Personal Staff Offices and Location of Staff, 2006.

Position title	Mean number per office	Typical location of staff member
Chief of Staff	1.00	Capitol Hill Office
Counsel	0.05	Capitol Hill Office
Legislative Director	0.78	Capitol Hill Office
Senior Legislative Aide	0.55	Capitol Hill Office
Legislative Assistant	1.28	Capitol Hill Office
Legislative Correspondent	0.55	Capitol Hill Office
Office Manager	0.33	Capitol Hill Office
Press Secretary	0.68	Capitol Hill Office
Executive Assistant	0.23	Capitol Hill Office
Scheduler (D.C.)	0.36	Capitol Hill Office
Systems Administrator	0.13	Capitol Hill Office
Staff Assistant (D.C.)	0.68	Capitol Hill Office
Staff Assistant (District)	0.60	District Office
Constituent Services Representative	1.80	District Office
District Director	0.56	District Office
District Scheduler	0.27	District Office
Field Representative	0.80	District Office
Grants and Projects Coordinator	0.14	District Office

Source: "2006 House Compensation Study," Chief Administrative Officer, U.S. House of Representatives, 2006.

one Senator to another, as it does in the House. In fiscal year 2008, these accounts ranged from to $2,757,743 to $4,416,993.

In addition to their personal staffs, many members enjoy sizable staffs in their capacity as committee leaders – chairs or ranking minority members. Committee staffs are particularly important to senators, nearly all of whom are committee or subcommittee leaders. From time to time, members shift staff between their committee and personal offices in response to changing priorities. The combined personal and committee staffs responsible to a member can be quite large. A large-state senator who chairs a committee can have more than 100 staff assistants reporting to him or her.

The total number of congressional staff workers grew steadily between the 1930s and the 1980s. The 1960s and 1970s marked a period of particularly rapid expansion of personal and committee staff in both chambers. The numbers have remained relatively stable since the early 1980s, as shown in Figure 4.1. The Senate, having a smaller membership, employs fewer total

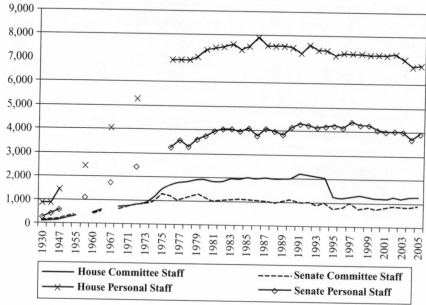

FIGURE 4.1. Number of Personal and Committee Staff in the House and Senate, 1930–2005. *Source:* Norman J. Ornstein, Thomas E. Mann, and Michael J. Malbin, Vital Statistics on Congress 2008. Washington, D.C.: Brookings Institution.

staff, although senators have more personal and committee staff per capita than representatives. In fact, the per capita advantage held by senators is substantial. In 2005, for example, the average senator had approximately 2.5 times more personal staff than the average representative. And the average senator's committee staff was more than three times as large as the average representative's.

One of the first decisions new members face is how to divide their staff between their home and Washington offices. Since the 1960s, as the size of lawmakers' personal staffs has increased, more members have placed staff aides in their home district or state. New members led the way in exploiting larger staff allocations to develop a more visible presence at home. As seen in Figure 4.2, the percentage of personal staff working in district or state offices has gradually increased since 1970. In recent years, approximately half of the personal staff of House members and over a third of the personal staff of senators have worked in district or state offices. Members have shifted more responsibility for constituency service to their home office staffs, allowing their Washington staffs to devote more time to legislative and policy work. Senators, with larger staffs, keep a larger percentage of their staff in Washington.

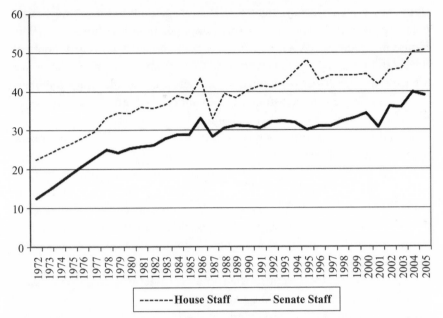

FIGURE 4.2. Percent of Personal Office Staff Located in District or State Offices, 1972–2005. *Source:* Norman J. Ornstein, Thomas E. Mann, and Michael J. Malbin, Vital Statistics on Congress 2008. Washington, D.C.: Brookings Institution.

Enlarged staffs have helped members meet increased demands for case-work while at the same time more vigorously pursuing their legislative activi-ties in Washington. Of course, members still differ in how they allocate their staff resources. First-term members seeking to solidify their hold on their seat often concentrate staff in their district. Senior members, who developed their staffing practices when members could not hire as many assistants and now have greater responsibilities in Washington, often are accustomed to having fewer local offices and tend to devote more staff resources to their Washington offices. In the House, a few committee and party leaders focus their personal staffs almost exclusively on constituency service and rely on committee or leadership staffs for their legislative work.

Travel and Recesses

Just as an increase in staff has reduced the severity of the tradeoffs mem-bers must make in setting priorities, expanded travel allowances and official recesses have enabled members to spend more time with constituents at home without fear of missing meetings or votes on Capitol Hill. Since the 1960s, the amount of time incumbents spend in their home districts and states has grown steadily. Before 1970, for example, House and Senate members averaged about two or three days per month at home. By 1980, House members were spending an average of about 10 days each month at home, and senators spent an average of six or seven days a month at home, a pace that they have maintained since then. In general, senior members spend less time in their districts, but members of both houses and at all levels of seniority make more trips home during an election year.

Both the House and the Senate have moved to accommodate members' need to travel to their home districts and states. The House, for example, rarely holds votes on Mondays or Fridays. Members are thus free to fly home on Thursday evenings and return to Washington in time for Tuesday votes. Members of the "Tuesday-Thursday club" can maximize their time at home among constituents without great cost to their performance in Washington. Many members of Congress do not even own or rent homes in the Washington area because they spend only two nights a week there. Several legislators have slept in their offices, sometimes for several years, before finding a residence in the D.C. area.

In both chambers, but particularly in the House, the number of official recess days increased significantly in the late 1960s and has remained high since then. In most years, official recesses now consume more than 100 days, not including weekends. The houses compensate for the increased number of recess days by concentrating their sessions into somewhat longer days. For instance, the 110th Congress (2007–08) was in session 52 fewer days than the 88th Congress (1963–64), yet was in session for 1,118 more hours, suggesting that the average workday was extended by approximately 4 hours and 40 minutes between these congresses. No committee markups or floor sessions are held during recesses so members know that they are free to go home.

Congressional Mail

Mail is a resource members use to remain visible in their districts between elections. By placing their signature where a stamp would go on an envelope (the "frank"), members of Congress may send mail through the Postal Service. Congressional offices are given budgets for this specific purpose. Members can maintain a presence at home by sending their constituents franked mail at the taxpayers' expense. Since World War II, the amount of mail sent by House and Senate members has grown steadily. Mail totals surge during election years and then drop in off years, a pattern that reflects members' efforts to advertise themselves as elections draw near.

THOSE NASTY LETTERS FROM CONSTITUENTS[5]

Most famous among the many witty responses that members and their staff have devised for constituents is the standard reply to critical letters of Ohio Representative Wayne Hays:

Dear Sir:

Today I received a letter from some crackpot who signed your name to it. I thought you ought to know about this before it went further.

Some of the increase in mail from Capitol Hill in recent decades is due to an increase in opinion letters from constituents and in requests for assistance from congressional offices (casework). As the population grows and constituencies become larger, legislators must respond by mail to a larger volume of demands. But that's only part of the story. Members more actively solicit opinions and casework in their newsletters and personal appearances – they are happy to be of service to voters. Moreover, most of the increase in outgoing mail is due to the vast increases in mass mailings from members' offices to their home districts and states. In fact, by one estimate, more than 90 percent of the mail sent by Congress consists of mass mailings of newsletters. Critics of the practice frequently cite the use of the frank for campaign-related publicity as an unfair incumbent advantage, and there is some evidence to support their view. Incumbents, on the other hand, argue that newsletters are essential for keeping their constituents informed about members' activities as their representatives. Despite lawsuits that have called into question the constitutionality of the franking privilege, the practice has withstood legal scrutiny.

Other Resources: Party Organizations and Support Agencies

The resources made available to legislators (at public expense) have expanded in many dimensions. A very conspicuous development is the expansion of House and Senate radio and television studios. Legislators use satellite up-link equipment to make appearances on local stations without leaving Capitol Hill. The congressional parties have their own facilities, too. These facilities are used heavily – nearly four out of five House members send regular radio programs to district stations. These programs are aired mostly, if not exclusively, by small-town stations with limited budgets and staff to purchase or produce their own programming. In addition, members sometimes can convince local television stations to use video news releases beamed in from Washington.

The addition and expansion of congressional support agencies (see box, "The Changing Congress") have made more expertise available to members seeking assistance and advice on policy questions. The assistance of policy analysts, scholars, lawyers, and other professionals in the support agencies makes it easier for rank-and-file members without large committee staffs to write bills and amendments, conduct studies, and meet constituents' requests for information.

Members are further aided by the computerization of Capitol Hill. Information networks give members and their staff instant electronic access to the text of bills and amendments, legislative summaries and analyses prepared by the Congressional Research Service, and a variety of databases on economic and social conditions and government programs. Computers also allow members to transmit large volumes of information among their Washington and home offices.

The tremendous expansion of the interest group community in Washington has also bolstered rank-and-file members' access to experts and information. By various counts, the number of lobbyists and others employed by interest groups doubled during the 1970s and 1980s, after having grown substantially in the preceding decades. Interest groups regularly distribute information favorable to their causes and make policy and legal expertise available to friendly members. Think tanks – non-profit organizations that produce studies and policy recommendations – also have expanded the availability of expert advice and assistance.

Influences on Members

Members act strategically. Their actions are not only a product of their own preferences and resources but also the actions and anticipated actions of others. Members care about other political actors – constituents, interest groups, party and committee leaders, presidents, and colleagues – because members rely on these actors to achieve their goals. Similarly, other actors place demands on members of Congress because members have something they want: influence over policy choices affecting them. The nature of the demands placed on members is the subject of this section.

Constituencies

Most members share the perspective of most constituents on important issues. This connection between legislators and their constituents is perhaps

THE CHANGING CONGRESS: CONGRESSIONAL SUPPORT AGENCIES

Congress has created a number of support agencies within the legislative branch to provide a variety of functions that are not conveniently provided by standing committees and their staffs. These units serve as nonpartisan servants of Congress and cost more than a half billion dollars each year.

Congressional Budget Office (CBO). Created in 1974, CBO provides economic forecasts, cost estimates for legislation, and other fiscal policy studies. CBO works most closely with the budget, appropriations, and tax committees and has more than 200 employees.

Congressional Research Service (CRS). Created in 1970 from the Legislative Reference Service, CRS provides policy research in nearly all policy areas and functions as a library reference service. CRS has nearly 700 employees. It responds to requests from committees and individual members and often lends policy experts to committees.

Government Accountability Office (GAO). Created in 1921 as the General Accounting Office, the GAO audits executive branch agencies, sets government accounting standards, settles certain claims against the government, gives legal opinions, and conducts policy studies as requested by formal acts of Congress, committees, and individual members. The GAO was renamed in 2004 (previously the Government Accounting Office) and has approximately 3,300 employees.

After the Republicans gained new House and Senate majorities in the 1994 elections, Congress closed the Office of Technology Assessment (OTA). OTA, with nearly 150 employees, was created in 1972 to provide analysis of scientific and technical issues.

the most important force in congressional politics. It originates in the process by which legislators are selected. Voters tend to favor candidates whose views are close to their own. Liberal, Democratic districts tend to elect liberal Democrats to Congress, just as conservative, Republican districts tend to elect conservative Republicans. As a result, legislators represent their constituencies' views fairly well simply by following their own political dispositions. In this way, legislators' personal views, the views of their constituents, and even partisanship tend to be mutually reinforcing influences on members' decisions.

Nonetheless, constituents' views are an important component of most members' decision-making process. Constituents, and more specifically voters, have something members want: votes in the next election. However, defining a member's constituency can be difficult. After all, the public rarely speaks with one voice and is rarely attuned to what is going on in Congress. Fenno proposes that members perceive constituents in four categories that

MEMBERS' PERCEIVED CONSTITUENCIES

Political scientist Richard F. Fenno, Jr., observes that many members view their constituencies as a set of concentric circles, ranging from their closest political confidants (the intimates) to their strongest supporters in the electorate (the primary constituency), to voters who vote for them (the reelection constituency), to their whole state or district (the geographic constituency). A great source of uncertainty for members is the variable composition of the primary and reelection constituencies.[6]

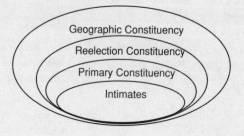

Geographic Constituency

Reelection Constituency

Primary Constituency

Intimates

can be conceptualized as concentric circles (see box, "Members' Perceived Constituencies"). A member's strongest political friends (intimates) are at the center, and they are encircled by a larger group of constituents who support the member in primary elections. Next is an even larger group that supports the member in general elections, but whose support is more tenuous. The entire district population stands as the fourth, or geographic, constituency. Fenno observes that legislators develop styles – home styles, he calls them – for relating to each of these constituencies.

Concern about how activities in Washington will play at home often preoccupies legislators. Members have to anticipate whether a roll-call vote or other public action will come back to haunt them in a future campaign. Party and coalition leaders, lobbyists, and presidents seeking support from a member must consider how that member's vote will be regarded back home. All participants know that high-profile issues – abortion, tax increases, social security, and congressional pay raises – always attract a more attentive public, whose views must be considered. On some issues, only a narrow constituency takes an interest, but its interest may be so intense that members are compelled to pay attention to it. On other issues – perhaps, even on most matters that come before Congress – members need not be overly concerned about the electoral consequences of their decisions. Still, the uncertainty of electoral consequences may keep some members guessing about the political costs and benefits at home of their actions.

Representatives and senators have several ways to gauge constituents' opinions. When a particularly controversial issue comes up, a wave of letters, phone calls, and emails is likely to flood members' district and Washington offices. Much of the incoming post takes the form of preprinted letters or cards supplied by lobbying groups. Because it takes little effort to send that kind of mail, legislators may not put much stock in it. Still, members are attentive to groups of constituents with intensely held preferences. In such cases, members usually take note of where the letters are coming from and bear in mind the level of interest expressed.

Members also learn constituents' opinions from interacting with them at home and in Washington. Most members hold town meetings or other forums in their district to give constituents a way to express their views. While at home, attentive members are almost always asking questions of and listening to their constituents. And in Washington, many members schedule regular events, such as weekly coffee, to provide an additional outlet for constituents to voice their opinions. The internet has facilitated the interaction between members and constituents by reducing the need for the two to communicate in person (see box, "Changing Congress"). With increasing frequency, legislators commission public opinion polls with campaign funds, most often at campaign time.

Interest Groups and Lobbyists

For many people, lobbyists and interest groups represent the unseemly, even corrupt, side of congressional politics. "Money talks," "the best Congress money can buy," and "the golden rule of politics – whoever has the gold rules" – are among the clichés that capture common fears about who really runs Congress. Just where the line between legitimate representation and bribery falls is one of the ambiguities confronting every democratic system of government. On the one hand, lobbying is protected by constitutional guarantees of free speech, free association, and the right to petition the government for redress of grievances. Lobbying often involves building support for a position by bargaining, providing assistance to legislators, and even providing timely campaign contributions. On the other hand, lobbying can cross the line into bribery when cash or other material considerations are traded for certain official actions, such as introducing a bill or casting a particular vote. The whole business of lobbying seems tainted to many.

Perhaps the most important change in Washington in recent decades has been the great expansion and fragmentation of Washington's interest group community. The best study of the subject indicates that most interest groups were formed after World War II, that the formation of groups has accelerated in recent decades, and that more and more groups are locating in Washington, D.C. (see Chapter 11). Many single-issue groups have been

THE CHANGING CONGRESS: MEMBERS AND THE WORLD WIDE WEB

The Internet has become an invaluable resource to members of Congress, as it provides a relatively low cost means of interacting with constituents. In addition, it offers members another platform for disseminating an image or message. Member websites have proliferated over a reasonably short period of time. Today, every member of Congress has a website and many of them are quite sophisticated. While there is considerable variation in website features, a common feature is an email form for constituents to communicate with their member.

Not surprisingly, large volumes of e-mail pour into Capitol Hill computer networks every day. Each house receives more than 100 million e-mails directed to legislators' personal offices each year. When email became popular in the 1990s, congressional offices were not prepared to deal with it. Most offices sent automatic responses saying that they could not respond to email, and the writer should send a letter by regular mail. That has changed. According to a 2001 survey of House offices, more than a quarter of members' offices were responding to email with individualized email responses.

Members have even begun to capitalize on the proliferation of social networking websites, such as Facebook, Twitter, and YouTube. Until 2008, there had been a long-standing rule prohibiting members of Congress from posting official communication on websites outside of the house.gov and senate.gov domains, in part because third-party websites may contain advertising and politicking. Led by Representative John Culberson (R-Texas), who openly violated the rule during a 2008 debate over off-shore oil drilling by tweeting "I just learned the Dems are trying to censor Congressmen's ability to use Twitter QuikYouTubeUtterz etc – outrageous and I will fight them," the House and Senate changed their rules to allow members to post communication on external websites provided that the members and the websites themselves abide by certain guidelines. By one count, some 19 senators and 50 representatives post on Twitter. YouTube has also launched *House Hub* and *Senate Hub*, which allow members to create and manage their own channel.

created and nearly every industry group has professional representation in Congress. In the health care industry, for example, the older American Medical Association is joined by associations for hospitals, medical schools, medical equipment manufacturers, health insurance companies, and a variety of professional associations of nurses, dentists, and others.

Particularly noteworthy is the rise of "citizens' groups" or "public interest groups," organized around a general cause rather than a narrow economic interest. Good-government groups such as Common Cause, environmental groups such as the Sierra Club, and consumer product groups such as the Consumers' Union are examples. About one-fifth of all lobbying groups counted in 1980 were citizens' groups. In addition, more corporations, state and local governments, universities, and other organizations have established Washington offices for in-house lobbyists. By one estimate, the number of corporations with Washington offices increased tenfold between 1961 and 1982. One consequence of this expansion in Washington-based representation of organized interests is that the clout of individual lobbyists and groups has actually declined. Often, large coalitions of lobbyists and interest groups pool their resources to overcome the fragmentation in the interest group community.

Party Leaders

Party pressures in congressional politics are weaker in the United States than in most other national legislatures. Representatives and senators rarely are dependent on party organizations – national or local – to secure reelection. Moreover, party leaders in Congress have relatively few ways to compel rank-and-file members to comply with their wishes. Indeed, party leaders generally want their party colleagues to pursue legislative strategies that will enhance their chances of reelection. When members of a congressional party vote in unison, it is due more to their shared policy views and similar constituency expectations than to pressure from party leaders.

Still, partisan pressures are ever-present in Congress. Many decisions members make have no direct electoral consequences, so members are free to meet the demands of party leaders. The high level of party loyalty on procedural matters provides some evidence of this. Moreover, much of the influence of party on legislators' behavior is indirect. For example, party leaders set the floor agenda and, particularly in the House, shape the alternatives from which members must choose. But occasionally, particularly on close votes, the direct pressure of party leaders can be critical. Even then, the leaders target just a few members whose votes will make the difference between winning and losing.

The President

Presidents need support from legislators for their own legislative programs, and they can wield considerable influence in their efforts to gain it. Much of the support presidents get from lawmakers comes from their partisan ties to members. Because members' own electoral fortunes are affected by the popularity of the president, members of the president's party have a stake in the president's success and thus provide a natural base of support. The size of that base of support depends on past congressional election outcomes, the diversity within party coalitions, and the president's popularity. Every member must decide when to stick with the president and when it is safe to ignore the president's wishes.

Presidents also influence members' choices by influencing the congressional agenda. By pushing major legislative proposals, presidents can help define the issues that dominate the congressional agenda and how the major alternatives are debated. A successful president draws the attention of the media, the public, and legislators away from issues that hurt him and toward issues that help him. An effective president also knows that his influence over the congressional agenda is tenuous. Presidents, after all, cannot require either house of Congress to vote on their proposals, or even to take their proposals seriously.

The task of presidents is primarily one of persuasion. Presidents have a variety of tools for influencing individual legislators (see Chapter 9). Presidents' primary source of influence is their formal power to sign or veto legislation, which gives them a source of leverage over members who want to see their own legislation enacted into law. Presidents' ease of access to the media gives them an advantage over members and other actors in shaping public opinion. In addition, their influence on agency decisions, which can have widespread implications for policy implementation, gives presidents more clout. That clout can be used to coax interest groups to work in support of presidents' legislative proposals or to prod legislators whose constituents are affected by executive branch decisions.

Staff

A popular theory is that members of Congress have been captured by their staffs. Michael Malbin's book, *Unelected Representatives*, lends credence to this view. Malbin, a political scientist who worked for many years as a Capitol Hill reporter and staff member, argues that "the staffs – individually well educated, hard working, and, in general, devoted to what they perceive to be the public good – collectively create a situation in which many of the elected members fear they are becoming insulated administrators in a bureaucratized organization that leaves them no better able to cope than they were when they did all the work themselves."[7] Malbin observes that staff assistants do a good job of representing their bosses, but, he continues, members delegate to their aides too much authority to initiate legislation, negotiate compromises, and narrow the range of policy choices offered to them. Staff assistants have created more work for members, distanced members from one another, and turned members into office managers. Staff influence is

TYPES OF CONGRESSIONAL STAFF

There are numerous types of congressional staff. Because legislators organize their own office staffs, there is tremendous variation in organization and titles. Some positions (e.g., legislative counsel) are quite rare in personal offices but quite common in committee staffs. Among the most common types of staff positions on Capitol Hill are chief of staff, legislative director (LD), legislative assistant (LA), constituent services representative or caseworker, and legislative correspondent (LC).

The top personal aide to a member is usually a chief of staff or administrative assistant (AA). This position oversees the entire operation and manages all staff. The legislative director supervises the policy staff and typically works closely with the member to devise legislative strategies. Legislative assistants are responsible for the legislator's work on specified policy areas and assist with committee work. Those charged with responding to constituent communications are often given the title of legislative correspondent.

All personal offices have constituent service representatives or caseworkers. These assistants are primarily dedicated to *casework*, the term used to describe constituents' problems that members are asked to solve. Casework ranges from getting a problem with social security checks solved to arranging for a leave for a soldier who just had a death in the family. These assistants usually are located in district or state offices where they can deal with constituents directly. They communicate electronically with federal agencies and the Capitol Hill office. Most legislators consider an effective caseworker essential to building a good reputation.

pervasive: It is felt both in the early stages of the legislative process, in the setting of members' and committees' agendas and at the late stages when the final details of legislation are worked out (see box "Types of Congressional Staff").

Choosing Strategies

Political scientists have no comprehensive theory to explain how members' goals, resources, and political environment combine to produce their strategies. Nevertheless, they have done a reasonably good job of describing and explaining members' behavior in one decision-making arena: roll-call voting on the floor. A newer area of research looks at policy leaders' coalition-building strategies, which focuses on how members solicit support from their colleagues. This section briefly reviews what we know about the typical member's approach to roll-call voting and coalition leadership and contrasts the strategies in these two areas of legislative activity.

Roll-Call Voting on the Floor

Casting roll-call votes is one activity members consider mandatory. Members want a good attendance record so that future opponents will not be able to charge that they are shirking their responsibilities. Maintaining a good attendance record is not easy, and maintaining a perfect record is nearly impossible. In recent Congresses, the average member voted on about 95 percent of the roll-call votes held, which have numbered between 500 and 1,000 per Congress. Plainly, members are forced to cast votes with such frequency that they cannot possibly study each issue with care. Yet, they are aware that they may have to explain a vote to some constituents, perhaps in response to a challenger's charges in some future campaign, or to some party or committee leader. Therefore, most members develop a general strategy for how to approach roll-call voting.

From time to time, members are confronted with particularly difficult choices. There is no question that the Emergency Economic Stabilization Act of 2008, more commonly known as the Wall Street Bailout Plan, put virtually every member of Congress in a very uncomfortable position, especially considering elections were right around the corner. The bill forced members to weigh the possibility of a financial crisis against a hastily constructed bill with a $700 billion price tag. Voting on the wrong side – voting against a bill that proved necessary or supporting a bill that ultimately failed – would be a political liability. Weighing his options, Senator Judd Gregg (R-New Hampshire) saw little political advantage to being on the winning side of a successful bill, stating "If we do this and it works right, it's most likely that people will never appreciate how close we came to the brink." Despite this, Gregg eventually supported the bill, having assessed that the United States was "facing a crisis of proportions that are almost incomprehensible."[8] Given the grave economic circumstances, he presumably calculated the costs of obstructing the bill to be too great. Clearly Gregg was not alone in considering the electoral ramifications of this difficult vote, as vulnerable members and members representing conservative constituents from both parties were significantly more likely to oppose the legislation.

Political scientist John Kingdon conducted an ingenious study of the vote decision. Kingdon interviewed members about how they had made up their minds on a series of fairly important votes on controversial issues that had been the subject of substantial political activity. Kingdon asked a simple question about each vote: "How did you go about making up your mind?" He then noted whether the members mentioned their constituencies spontaneously, only in response to a follow-up question, or not at all. For

TABLE 4.3. The Frequency with which Legislators Mentioned Political Actors as Factors in Their Voting Decisions (Percent of Voting Decisions).

| | Political actors involved in vote decision | | | | |
	Constituency	Fellow members	Interest groups	Administration	Party leaders
Mentioned Spontaneously	37	40	31	25	10
Mentioned in response to a question	50	35	35	14	28
Not Mentioned	13	25	35	60	62

Source: Kingdon, John. 1981. *Congressmen's Voting Decisions*, 2nd ed. New York: Harper & Row.

most members, the votes concerned issues that fell under the jurisdiction of committees on which they did not sit. Thus, most members interviewed by Kingdon had not had the benefit of listening to expert testimony in hearings.

Members' responses to Kingdon's questions show several important patterns (see Table 4.3). First, constituency considerations are frequently involved but are not always the most important factor. Members mentioned constituencies spontaneously 37 percent of the time. While members spontaneously mentioned fellow members more frequently than constituents, constituents ranked above every other group in this category. Members mentioned constituencies in response to probes 50 percent of the time and failed to mention constituencies altogether only 13 percent of the time.

Kingdon also found that the more salient the issue, the more likely members were to consider constituents' wishes to be of major importance in making their decisions. Consequently, they were more likely to vote in agreement with the constituency opinion they identified. Nevertheless, even on issues of low or medium salience, members were likely to give weight to, and vote in agreement with, constituency opinion. On most issues, members rely on trusted colleagues for cues about how to vote. In response to Kingdon's questions about their voting decisions, members mentioned their colleagues either spontaneously or after prompting 75 percent of the time (Table 4.3). As one member noted, "On a run-of-the-mill vote, on an obscure bill, you need some guidance. You don't know what's in it, and don't have time to find out."[9] Fellow members serve as informants who reduce uncertainty about the policy and political implications of a roll-call vote.

With so many staff assistants and lobbyists circulating on Capitol Hill, why do members rely so heavily on one another? Members turn to certain

colleagues because they trust that their fellow representatives and senators, professional politicians with problems similar to their own, will make
comparable calculations about which course of action to pursue. Indeed,
members tend to rely on colleagues from the same party, state, and region –
colleagues who can help them assess the political consequences of their
votes – and committee members who know the issue well. Fellow legislators
also are in the right place at the right time – on the floor as roll-call votes
are being conducted.

Members obtain guidance from fellow members in many ways. One way is
to read the "Dear Colleague" letters that are routinely sent to all members,
explaining bills and soliciting support for amendments. These letters are
usually concise arguments in favor of a bill, and they often explain how a bill's
opponents plan to distort the bill's true intent. For more detailed information
on a bill, members or their staffs are likely to turn to the written reports that
accompany most bills when they are reported by committee.

After constituents and fellow members, interest groups and the administration rank as the most important influences on members' voting decisions.
Most interest group influence, Kingdon found, came from groups connected
to members' constituencies. For example, farm groups played an important
role for members from agricultural districts. Presidential influence is greater
for members of the president's party – members who are politically connected to the president and have the highest stakes in the president's success.

Finally, party leaders and staff aides appear to have influence only at
the margins. In more recent years, party leaders probably have become
more important than Kingdon found in the late 1960s, when he conducted
his study (Chapter 5 describes the revitalization of party leadership in
Congress). Similarly, as roll-call votes have become more numerous, other
burdens on members' time have grown, and staffs have expanded in the
decades since Kingdon's study. Thus, members may have become more
dependent on staff assistants for guidance.

In summary, members adopt strategies in response to the unique character of individual voting decisions. Roll-call voting is repetitive, very public,
consumes little time and few resources, is well documented, and is considered politically compulsory. Members rely on cues from colleagues to simplify their decision-making process and assess the political risks of specific
votes. Members appear to be heavily influenced by constituency opinion and
electoral considerations, which they assess by seeking advice from trusted
colleagues and information from interest groups. At the same time, constituency considerations are seldom the sole or even the decisive influence
on members' votes.

Coalition Leadership

Serving as a coalition leader on a legislative issue lies at the other end of the spectrum of legislative activities. In contrast to roll-call voting, assuming a leadership role on an issue may not be very visible to the general public, is difficult to document, consumes more time and resources, and is normally discretionary. Consequently, the strategies of policy leaders may be shaped by a different mix of considerations than are voting decisions.

Political scientist David Mayhew observes that the goal of reelection, although nearly universally held by members, motivates little leadership activity within Congress. The effort to mobilize colleagues for or against legislation is worthwhile for a reelection-oriented member only if constituents or important financial contributors are paying close attention to the member's behavior. On most matters, merely advertising one's position and token efforts – citing speeches made, legislation introduced, and amendments offered – may be all that is required to receive maximum electoral benefit from an issue. Certainly, members do not actually have to win legislative battles as long as the people who affect their reelection prospects – people with votes, money, or endorsements – believe they have put up a good fight.

If Mayhew is right, most genuine leadership is motivated by goals beyond reelection. A member aspiring to higher office may seek special distinction and media attention by championing a legislative cause. A committee chair, seeking to preserve a reputation for influence, may assume the lead in writing legislation and soliciting support simply to avoid being overshadowed by a rank-and-file member who would otherwise take over. That same rank-and-file member may pursue a policy leadership role because no one else seems equally committed to his or her policy views.

Senator Pete Domenici (R-New Mexico), who was a prominent legislator in budgeting and fiscal policy, is a good example of a policy leader motivated by objectives beyond reelection. Fenno, in his book about Domenici's rise as a Senate leader, explains:

> From the beginning of his Washington career, Pete Domenici's most transparent goal was to become a policy-making "player" inside the Senate. The chairmanship [of the Budget Committee] brought him that influence. His first two years in that position, he said later, "made me a senator." He wanted to keep or expand the policy influence he had gained. A second goal – institutional maintenance – has been imposed on him by this chairmanship. And Domenici adopted that one, too – to protect and to preserve the budget process itself. The two goals did not always lead to the same decision. . . . In the two years ahead, he would

often be forced to choose between his desire for inside policy influence and his desire to keep the budget process alive.[10]

Domenici's reelection prospects, Fenno recounts, were greatly enhanced by his prominence in the Senate. He won reelection easily in 1984, 1990, 1996, and again in 2002, with vote shares of at least 65 percent.

Domenici's story seems typical in many respects. Electoral concerns did not seem to drive his leadership activity in Washington, even though that activity paid dividends at home. Thus, partly by good fortune and partly by personal skill and dedication, Domenici's multiple goals of obtaining influence, making good public policy, and gaining reelection were served by his leadership activities. And yet his goal of reelection cannot account for the priority he gave to his chairmanship and the legislative tactics he pursued as chairman.

Some relevant evidence about members' goals in pursuing leadership responsibilities is available. In one study, a political scientist asked top legislative aides of a sample of 121 members of both houses to identify issues on which their boss had taken a central leadership role and to offer explanations for their boss's involvement in those issues.[11] All aides reported that their boss had taken a leading role on some issue, large or small. But few members had taken on more than two or three issues at one time. Senators' aides tended to mention more issues than did representatives' aides, reflecting important differences between the two chambers. In the Senate, members have more committee assignments and staff, and they receive more demands from larger, more diverse constituencies.

For each issue the aides mentioned, the researcher asked them, "Why did (Senator/Representative –) take the lead on this issue?" They often mentioned several reasons. For 52 percent of the issues mentioned, they noted the importance of the issue to the member's district or state, although for only 17 percent was reelection or some other constituency-related reason the sole motivation mentioned. For 72 percent of the instances of policy leadership described, the aides mentioned their boss's personal interest or policy commitments as a motivating factor. In addition, 28 percent of the issues pursued by members were related to their responsibilities as committee or subcommittee leaders. Only 3 percent of the instances of policy leadership were described as being connected to a member's pursuit of higher office.

We are led to this conjecture: Leaders – whether they are party, committee, or self-identified coalition leaders – are motivated by more than reelection, whereas their followers are motivated primarily by reelection. Followers, most of whom are not sufficiently motivated to assume a leadership role on most issues, allow their default goal – reelection – to orient their behavior. Of course, if members' reelection prospects seem unaffected by a particular issue, as they often are, they are free to pursue policy positions for other reasons. Nevertheless, it seems fair to say, coalition building on most important issues typically involves interaction between policy- or influence-oriented leaders and reelection-oriented followers.

Concluding that members ignore their reelection interests when they pursue other objectives would be a mistake. On the contrary, members often discover issues that fit them well – issues that allow them to pursue multiple goals simultaneously, including reelection. Indeed, 47 percent of the staff assistants in the study readily identified more than one goal served by their boss's policy leadership activities. Forty-eight percent reported that reelection in combination with some other goal, usually good public policy, motivated policy leadership activities.

A good example of a member who discovered an issue that fit is former senator Dan Quayle (R-Indiana), who was vice president under President George Bush (1989–1992). In the mid-1980s, congressional liberals were pushing legislation designed to reduce the effect of political influence on decisions about the acquisition of military equipment, to introduce more competition into the process of bidding for defense contracts, and to limit the ability of former Department of Defense officials to take jobs in defense industries. Quayle was chair of the Senate Armed Services Subcommittee on Defense Acquisition Policy, so the task of resisting the liberal onslaught and developing legislation acceptable to the Republican administration fell to him. Quayle had become the chair of the procurement subcommittee in 1983 because more senior Republicans had chosen other subcommittee chairmanships.

Two considerations appeared to motivate Quayle's initial eagerness to take on procurement reform. The first was his concern that bad publicity about procurement practices might undermine the nation's commitment to defense spending, which he had worked to increase in the early 1980s. The issue was getting some media attention because of a few highly publicized cases of wasteful defense spending (a $700 toilet seat for a military transport plane, for example). The second was his interest in reinforcing his developing reputation as an effective legislator. He saw an opportunity to assume a leading role on an emerging issue and he took it. Quayle asked the Armed Services Committee chairman, John Tower (R-Texas), to create a task force on procurement, which he then chaired and later turned into a regular subcommittee. Taking the lead and being reasonably successful were important

to Quayle for reasons beyond his reelection prospects. He devoted considerable personal time, as well as the time and energy of his senior aides, to
the issue.

Quayle soon saw new angles to the procurement reform issue. Developing
his own reform legislation was a good way to score political points at home.
Quayle also realized that Indiana had a number of defense contractors and
subcontractors whose business might be affected by radical reforms. By
working to protect Indiana businesses and jobs, Quayle was doing himself
a favor. In a press release issued just before the 1986 election, Quayle's
press secretary listed eight major accomplishments of Quayle's first term.
The seventh was this:

> Senator Quayle had consistently supported the long-overdue strengthening of
> our national defense to meet the threat to our freedom. The help he has provided
> Indiana defense contractors and subcontractors in their dealings with Congress
> and the Pentagon has contributed substantially to the Hoosier State's economic
> development over the past six years; during that period, Indiana's share of
> defense procurement dollars has more than doubled – from $1.43 billion in
> FY 1980 to $3.16 billion in FY 1985. Quayle also succeeded in protecting the
> jobs of more than 800 federal workers in the drive to reform the Pentagon's
> purchasing practices to make sure our essential investment in national security
> is prudently managed.[12]

Pairing support for more defense spending with the procurement reform
effort allowed Quayle to deflect Democratic criticism that he and other
Republicans were throwing money at defense. The paired issues were mentioned in radio and television ads as well. The procurement issue was not
given the highest priority in Quayle's advertising, but he obviously found a
way to use his Washington activity effectively at home. In addition, taking the
lead on more moderate reforms than those proposed by liberal Democrats
yielded an influx of campaign contributions from defense contractors.

Just as important, Quayle developed a personal interest in procurement
politics and policies. Mastering procurement procedures, mediating bureaucratic battles within the Department of Defense, and dealing with powerful
defense contractors proved challenging. He appeared to develop a personal
commitment to devising good reform legislation.

Assuming a policy leadership role, then, is far more discretionary than
casting a roll-call vote. In addition, taking a leadership role on an issue
requires an investment of resources far in excess of those involved in casting
a vote. Members cannot afford to take on more than a handful of issues at
a time. Because such efforts may have only small direct electoral benefits

and take up time and resources that could be devoted to other activities, the potential value of the effort must be high in terms of policy objectives, personal influence or reputation, or other goals.

Conclusion

In this chapter, we have viewed the legislative process from the perspective of the individual member. Members' goals, resources, and strategies combine to shape their policy positions and political careers. We have seen how those goals, resources, and strategies evolve as a function of members' own choices, changes in members' institutional positions, and the evolution of Congress's political environment.

The roll-call voting and policy leadership examples in this chapter illustrate the two broad political purposes of members' strategies – avoiding blame and claiming credit. Avoiding blame seems to be the dominant situation in roll-call voting. The fact that roll-call voting is politically mandatory creates many hazards for members. Particularly in the House, where individual members have little control over the issues on which they must vote, members must frequently choose between groups of constituents in casting their votes. In contrast, claiming credit is the more dominant motivator in policy leadership. Senator Quayle's experience with procurement reform illustrates how goals, resources, and strategies can be combined opportunistically and give a member more control over the choices he or she confronts.

Since the late 1970s, members' opportunities for policy leadership have declined as budget constraints have limited new policy initiatives. Most members have not been as lucky as Senator Quayle. As a result, members have found that it is more difficult to counter the inevitable criticisms associated with voting by promoting one's own legislative successes. It certainly has contributed to the greater dissatisfaction with service in Congress that members have expressed in recent years and has intensified pressure on leaders to structure floor decision making more carefully.

Above: U.S. Senate Majority Leader Harry Reid (D-Nevada) answers questions from the news media as (L-R) incoming Minority Leader Mitch McConnell (R-Kentucky), Sen. John Ensign (R-Nevada), and Sen. Charles Schumer (D-New York) look on.
Below: Speaker of the House Nancy Pelosi (D-California) receives the Speaker's gavel from Minority Leader John Boehner (R-Ohio) after being elected as the first woman Speaker during a swearing-in ceremony in 2007.

5

Parties and Leaders

E LECTION OUTCOMES OFTEN MOTIVATE CHANGE IN THE ORGANIZATION
and strategies of congressional parties. After the 2006 elections, in
which Republicans lost seats in the House and Senate, there were important changes in their leadership. In the House, Speaker Dennis Hastert
(R-Illinois), who was blamed for excessive partisanship and ineffectiveness
in some quarters, quickly announced his retirement from leadership. In the
Senate, Senator Bill Frist (R-Tennessee) had earlier announced his retirement from the Congress. Spirited leadership contests followed the elections
in which candidates for the Republican leadership offered diagnoses of their
party's failings and new approaches to legislating and public relations. The
newly elected leaders of the two houses promised joint meetings, a unified communications strategy, and a common legislative program. Republican leaders promised to coordinate their efforts to reestablish an attractive "Republican brand," as one leader defined the task. At the same time,
Senate Democratic leader Harry Reid (D-Nevada) created a new post, conference vice chairman, to reward Senator Charles Schumer (D-New York)
for leading the Democratic Senatorial Campaign Committee during the
2006 campaign and to bring Schumer into the legislative leadership circle.

Republicans lost additional seats in the 2008 elections and discussion of
replacing some leaders resurfaced. Two top House Republican leaders, the
whip and conference chair, retired from their posts after it became clear that
they would be challenged. Senate Republicans retained their top leaders. In
both chambers, Republicans believed that an unpopular president, rather
than ineffective congressional leadership, caused their losses in the 2008
elections. Nevertheless, the relatively new Republican leaders clearly were
aware that their colleagues expected them to improve their party's image
and win back seats in the 2010 elections.

The recent experiences of Republicans are typical of congressional parties throughout history. Unhappiness with the party's popularity, more than anything else, motivates legislators to seek change in party strategy, organization, and even leadership. And when one party's innovations seem to be successful, the other party tends to follow. Over time, the two parties in each chamber of Congress have developed more elaborate organizations – and they tend to look alike.

In recent years, congressional parties have become more important avenues of participation for members and their leaders have been more active in shaping policy outcomes. This chapter considers the nature of congressional parties, outlines their organization, and describes the activities and resources of congressional party leaders and their organizations. It concludes with a discussion of the factors contributing to the intensified partisanship of recent years.

The Nature of Congressional Parties

Congressional parties exist to serve the interests of their members. The Constitution does not mention congressional parties. Just as candidates and their supporters created electoral parties outside of Congress to effectively compete in elections, legislators created congressional parties to serve their ends. The four congressional parties (House Democrats, House Republicans, Senate Democrats, and Senate Republicans) convene separately before each new Congress begins, and they meet with some frequency while Congress is in session. No formal joint organization of House and Senate Democrats or House and Senate Republicans exists, although party leaders of the two chambers often discuss matters of mutual concern.

Congressional party organizations are independent of the national and state political parties. Members of Congress have chaired and served in other capacities on the parties' national committees, but the four congressional parties have no formal relationship with the national party committees. Moreover, members of Congress usually are considered important party leaders in their home districts and states, but they are seldom officials of their local party organizations. Members' candidacy for office usually is endorsed by the local party organizations, but, as members know, winning the party primary, not the endorsement, gets them on the general election ballot in November. The bond between the local party and an incumbent representative or senator can be weak. National committees, congressional party organizations, and local party organizations do not directly control who is nominated through primaries and eventually elected to Congress. Party organizations may recruit candidates, contribute money, and offer campaign advice and expertise. They do not have the power to prevent someone from running in party primaries and gaining a seat in Congress.

A reasonable characterization of congressional parties is that they are relatively stable, but loose, coalitions of legislators that exist to serve the common interests of their members. Both electoral and policy interests appear to motivate party activity.

Common Electoral Interests

Members of each congressional party share a party label – a political "brand name." The party labels hold meaning for voters and influence their decisions at the polls, so members of the same party have an incentive to build and maintain a positive reputation for their party. This collective interest encourages legislators to develop party organizations and select party leaders who work to enhance the party's image. Leaders choose issues to emphasize, develop public relations strategies, and work with presidents and committee leaders to shape the content of legislation. They also work more directly to aid election campaigns by raising and contributing money, making appearances at fundraising and campaign events, disseminating information, and playing a role in recruiting candidates. In election years, top leaders spend several weeks traveling to support the electoral efforts of fellow partisans.

By building a favorable party reputation, leaders help their colleagues get reelected and help their party gain and maintain majority party status. A majority party controls committee and subcommittee chairmanships, which legislators covet, has more influence over the agenda, and, with more votes, is more likely to win legislative battles. Electoral failures have caused the defeat or led to the resignation of several party leaders (see box, "Electoral Trouble for Leaders").

Leaders are expected to promote their party's electoral interests, but tensions sometimes arise between leaders and rank-and-file members whose personal or political interests motivate them to vote differently than leaders and other party colleagues would like. Even congressional party leaders, whose job it is to rally support for their party's policy positions, are sensitive to the personal political needs of deviant colleagues. After all, most party leaders would prefer to give a deviant party member some leeway to vote as he or she chooses rather than lose that member's seat to the other party. Imperfect support for party positions is the typical pattern for most members. These differences in members' home constituencies are an important source of conflict over party strategy within all congressional parties.

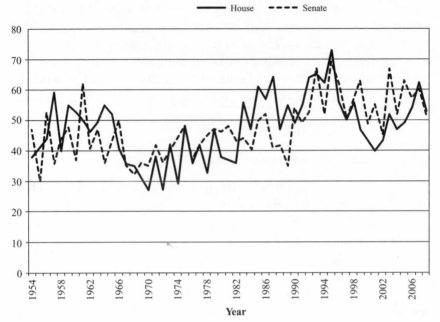

FIGURE 5.1. Percent of All Votes that Were Party Votes, 1954–2008. *Source:* Congressional Quarterly.

Shared Policy Preferences

Members of each party hold distinctive views on most important policy questions. The shared policy views among legislators of the same party are grounded in the similarities in the views of their home constituencies. Liberal-leaning districts tend to elect more Democrats than conservative-leaning districts, which elect more Republicans. Shared policy views create an incentive for members to choose leaders and coordinate their strategies.

   Majorities of the parties have taken opposing positions on roll-call votes about half of the time in most recent Congresses. Figure 5.1 indicates the percentage of roll-call votes that were party votes – those on which a majority of Democrats voted against a majority of Republicans. In the recent past, party voting has tended to be higher in odd-numbered years than in even-numbered years, particularly in the House. This trend may reflect political pressures associated with the two-year electoral cycle of the House. In the odd-numbered years immediately after congressional elections, the winning side may feel emboldened to push a partisan agenda. But as another election approaches, members and party leaders may avoid issues that polarize the parties and create problems at home for some members.

ELECTORAL TROUBLE FOR LEADERS

Members of Congress expect their leaders to guide their parties to electoral success. Major failures, or even unexpected losses, as well as other embarrassing developments, can lead to the demise of a leader, as is evident in several episodes described in the following section.

After his party suffered unexpected losses in the 1998 elections, Speaker Newt Gingrich (R-Georgia) took the extraordinary step of resigning from the speakership and Congress. His party had lost five seats in the House of Representatives, narrowing the Republican advantage to 223, just five more than a majority of 218. Rarely does the party opposing the president lose seats in a midterm election. In fact, 1934 is the only other midterm election of the twentieth century in which the president's party won additional seats. Gingrich was blamed for failing to provide needed leadership.

In 2002, just after his party failed to win seats in the midterm election, Democratic Minority Leader Dick Gephardt chose not to seek reelection as the party leader. Gephardt soon announced his intention to run for president, but many viewed his decision to retire from the post a wise move. Gephardt had served as party leader since 1994, when House Democrats lost their majority for the first time since 1954, yet he had not managed to lead the party back to majority status.

After his party regained a majority of Senate seats in the 2002 elections, Senate Republican Minority Leader Trent Lott (R-Mississippi) was expecting to become the majority leader as soon as the new Congress convened in January 2003. However, in December a video recording of Lott's comments at a birthday party for retiring Senator Strom Thurmond (R-South Carolina) were aired on television. The recording showed Lott saying that the country would have been better off if Thurmond had won the presidency when he ran in 1948. Thurmond was the pro-segregationist candidate of the Dixiecrats in 1948. It was soon learned that Lott had made similar comments two decades earlier. The public uproar caused by these disclosures led many of Lott's colleagues to conclude that he had to step down as party leader. Lott stepped down as party leader but remained in the Senate.

In 2006, after his party lost its House majority, Speaker Dennis Hastert (R-Illinois) stepped down as his party's leader. In 2008, after his party lost additional seats, House Republican Whip Roy Blunt (R-Missouri) retired from his post.

The percentage of party votes was relatively high in the late 1980s and 1990s. We consider this trend later in this chapter. But why aren't more votes in Congress aligned along party lines? The primary reason is that Congress addresses many programs and issues that do not involve partisan considerations, such as the merchant marine, veterans' health programs, and flood

FACTIONALISM WITHIN CONGRESSIONAL PARTIES

Intra-party factionalism in Congress is reflected in the presence of named groups. In the Senate, owing to its smaller size, members appear to see less benefit and some cost in becoming associated with formally organized factions. In recent years, a handful of Senate Democratic liberals formed the Democratic Study Group, a bipartisan group of moderates formed the bipartisan Senate Centrist Coalition, and a group of Senate Democratic centrists and their staff met on a regular basis. Only the Steering Committee, the informal organization of Republican conservatives, has been in existence for long.

In the House, factions representing liberals, moderates, and conservatives have formed and reformed in both parties. Liberal Democrats comprise the Progressive Caucus, which had over 70 members in 2008 and is the largest of the Democratic member organizations. The New Democratic Coalition, organized in 1998 by a group of self-proclaimed centrists, had nearly 60 members in 2008. The Blue Dog Coalition is an organization of conservative or moderate Democrats with 51 members in 2009. In addition, the Congressional Black Caucus and Hispanic Caucus represent Democrats who generally are liberal.

On the Republican side in the House, the Republican Study Committee, which dates back to 1973, is the major faction and is comprised of about two-thirds of the party. In 1994, Republican moderates organized the Tuesday Group, which numbered about 35 in 2008. Both the Republican Study Committee and the Tuesday Group hired staff aides to assist the groups.

The one inter-chamber group of prominence is the Main Street Partnership, comprised of Republican moderates from both houses. In 2008, six senators and 46 representatives were members, along with two governors.

insurance. Congress considers a greater volume of legislation – and more detailed legislation – than do most other national legislatures. Most of the legislation enacted into law each year is routine or concerns matters of little political interest. The parties are not motivated to play a role in shaping such legislation.

Even on votes that generate partisan divisions, the two parties are seldom perfectly cohesive. In most recent Congresses, an average of 70 to 80 percent of members have voted with a majority of their party on party votes – meaning that a 20 to 30 percent rate of defection is common even when party majorities oppose each other. Indeed, nothing in the way that members are elected or reelected guarantees that members of the same party will agree with one another on important issues or that Democrats and

Republicans will take opposing views. To the contrary, variation in political views of members' constituencies promotes variation in the voting behavior of members of the same party. Factionalism often has made it difficult to use the party organizations to promote policy ideas and solicit support.

Party Identification

Most members, like most political activists and many citizens of the United States, identify with their parties and have a psychological and emotional attachment to their parties. This attachment reinforces a sense of group identification and enhances group cohesiveness. These bonds lead members to turn to party colleagues for cues on how to vote and for other forms of assistance and advice. Party leaders further strengthen party bonds by emphasizing common loyalties, policy commitments, and personal ties in their appeals for support from their colleagues. Furthermore, most members of Congress face another reality: Legislators are dependent on voters who, for the most part, share the same partisan affiliation and vote in party primaries. Members who vote against their party's position on major issues or, even worse, actively work to undermine their party's institutional position may face challenges from within their party in a primary. Few members are willing to take such a risk. In this way, the partisan connection between a member and his or her electoral base constrains members who might otherwise work to form inter-party coalitions within their chamber.

Most Common Coalitions

Although congressional parties are not perfectly cohesive, they have an important advantage over other groups that might seek to influence legislative outcomes: They are the most common basis for building majority coalitions. Because party-based coalitions are so common, members have an incentive to organize formal party organizations and identify leaders to work on behalf of their common interests. That is, over the long run, members believe that they are better off joining an enduring party organization than operating as freelance legislators. Once established, parties acquire important institutional advantages that make it difficult for other coalitions to establish formal organizations in Congress. By using their procedural and appointment powers, as well as by making a few concessions to dissident factions, majority party leaders have been able to defuse the few intra-party disputes that have threatened party control of their chambers.

Stable but Loose Coalitions

For all of these reasons, the House and Senate depend on party leaders to perform many basic organizational functions, but do not give them too much independent power. Members of the *majority* party choose the presiding officers of both chambers (the Speaker of the House and, to preside in the absence of the Vice President, the Senate President Pro Tempore), select committee leaders, and assume responsibility for scheduling activity at all stages of the legislative process. The parties assign members to standing committees and subcommittees as well as to all select, joint, and conference committees. The majority party in each house reserves for itself the majority of seats on nearly all committees. And within the committees, most activity is organized by party – the questioning of witnesses at hearings, the hiring of staff, even the arrangement of seats in committee rooms. Seating on the House and Senate floors is also arranged by party: The Democrats are on the left and the Republicans are on the right when facing the front desk. Partisan elements pervade the organization of the modern Congress and have done so since the first half of the nineteenth century.

Yet, American congressional parties are not as strong as parties in many other national legislatures. Congressional parties in the United States usually are not as cohesive on questions of public policy as are parties in other systems. U.S. congressional party leaders have little power over who is elected under their party's label and few resources to compel loyalty from members once they are in office. Equally important, state and national party leaders have no formal authority over legislators sharing their party label.

Congressional party leaders sometimes struggle to balance the diverse policy and electoral interests of their party colleagues. In their efforts to do so, they may delay action on a bill until the timing is more convenient for a legislator or urge their colleagues to be tolerant of a legislator whose political circumstances necessitate a vote against the party position. Still, there are situations when leaders seek the vote of every party member. Such situations usually involve legislation that is a high priority for a president of the same party, whose success or failure will reflect on the party, and for which there are not enough supportive members of the opposition party to muster a majority. Leaders may seek to accommodate some members by compromising provisions of the legislation or by promising certain actions on unrelated legislation. Explicit or implicit threats of retribution for disloyal behavior are sometimes issued, typically in the form of warnings about future committee chairmanship or appointment decisions made by party committees and leaders. These tradeoffs reflect the loose organization and

---

Congressionally Speaking . . .

Among the four congressional parties, only House Democrats call their organization a *caucus*. House Republicans, Senate Democrats, and Senate Republicans call their organizations *conferences*. The difference in labels dates to the 1910s, when the House Democrats used their caucus, the so-called King Caucus, to make policy decisions and required party members to support those positions. The Democrats' binding caucus was so distasteful to House Republicans that they chose an entirely different label for their organization. Senate parties followed suit and use the term conference.

---

discipline of congressional parties and the long-term importance of party affiliations to members.

Party Organizations

Each of the four congressional parties (two in each house) has three major organizational features: a caucus (or conference) comprised of all party members in the chamber, party committees, and elected and appointed leaders. All four party caucuses meet in late November or early December after each election to organize for the new Congress, which begins in January. They elect their leaders, may adopt and revise their rules, and begin to make assignments to standing committees. In recent Congresses, all four caucuses have met weekly or biweekly while Congress is in session. These meetings usually serve as forums for the discussion of party strategies. To facilitate candid discussion and avoid media reports of party infighting, caucus meetings are generally not open to the public or the press.

Each party has a set of committees (see Table 5.1). The policy committees discuss (and, infrequently, endorse) policy positions; the campaign committees provide advice and money to party incumbents and candidates; the committees on committees assign party members to standing committees. For several decades, the policy committees of the House and Senate Republicans have sponsored weekly luncheons that serve as forums on matters important to the party. Senate Democrats adopted the practice of weekly luncheons in 1990.

Party staffs provide a wide range of services to members. Services include timely reports on floor activity, briefing papers on major issues, media advice and technical assistance, newspaper-clipping services, recorded messages on current floor activity, personnel services, and limited research assistance.

TABLE 5.1. Party Committees, 111th Congress (January 2009).

House Democrats

Steering	Makes committee assignments; sometimes endorses policy positions; discusses party strategy
Democratic Congressional Campaign Committee	Provides money and other assistance to Democratic House candidates
Organization, Study, and Review	Recommends changes in party organization and rules

House Republicans

Steering	Makes committee assignments
Policy	Discusses and recommends policy proposals
National Republican Congressional Committee	Provides money and other assistance to Republican House candidates

Senate Democrats

Steering and Outreach	Makes committee assignments; formulates political strategy
Policy	Recommends policy priorities; provides a forum for conference discussion; staff provides research
Democratic Senatorial Campaign Committee	Provides money and other assistance to Democratic Senate candidates

Senate Republicans

Committee on Committees	Makes committee assignments
Policy	Discusses and recommends policy proposals; staff provides research
National Republican Senatorial Campaign	Provides money and other assistance to Republican Senate candidates

Source: Collected by authors.

The Senate parties operate closed-circuit television channels that provide senators and their staffs with informative details about floor action. They also provide radio and television studios that allow senators to appear live on home-state stations. Over the last two decades, most new party leaders have found additional services to promise and deliver to the membership. As a result, the party staffs have become large and expensive, with nearly all of the funding provided through appropriations.

TABLE 5.2. Top Party Leaders, 111th Congress (January 2009).

House Democrats

Speaker	Nancy Pelosi, California
Majority Leader	Steny Hoyer, Maryland
Majority Whip	James Clyburn, South Carolina
Caucus Chair	John Larson, Connecticut
Caucus Vice Chair	Xavier Becerra, California

House Republicans

Minority Leader	John Boehner, Ohio
Minority Whip	Eric Cantor, Virginia
Conference Chair	Mike Pence, Indiana
Conference Vice Chairman	Cathy McMorris Rodgers, Washington

Senate Democrats

Majority Leader (and Conference Chair)	Harry Reid, Nevada
Assistant Floor Leader (Whip)	Richard Durbin, Illinois
Conference Vice Chair	Charles Schumer, New York
Conference Secretary	Patty Murray, Washington
President Pro Tempore	Robert Byrd, West Virginia

Senate Republicans

Minority Leader	Mitch McConnell, Kentucky
Assistant Floor Leader (Whip)	Jon Kyl, Arizona
Conference Chairman	Lamar Alexander, Tennessee
Conference Vice Chairman	John Thune, South Dakota

Party Leaders

The Constitution provides for presiding officers in Congress but says nothing about parties or leaders. It provides that the members of the House "shall choose their Speaker," makes the vice president of the United States the president of the Senate, and requires that the Senate select a president pro tempore ("president for the time being") to preside over the Senate in the absence of the vice president. Although the Constitution does not explicitly require the Speaker or the Senate president pro tempore to be members of Congress, all have been.

Only in the House is the presiding officer, the Speaker, also the leader of the majority party (Table 5.2). At the start of each Congress, the majority and minority parties nominate their top leaders for Speaker. The majority party leader is then elected on a party-line vote. In the Senate, presiding over daily sessions is normally a routine activity, so the vice president is seldom present. Since the 1940s, the majority party has named its most senior member president pro tempore. The president pro tempore is usually busy as a committee chair and assigns the duty of presiding over the Senate to junior senators of the same party. All four parties choose a floor leader (known as a majority or minority leader), assistant floor leader (or whip), conference chair, and other leaders.

Major Responsibilities of Party Leaders

No specific statements about party leaders' jobs can be found in chamber or party rules. Rather, leaders' responsibilities have developed in response to their colleagues' expectations that leaders must promote the common electoral and policy interests of their parties. These responsibilities are primarily assigned to the top leader in each party, although the burden is shared among the top three or four leaders in each party.

BUILDING COALITIONS ON MAJOR LEGISLATION. Building coalitions in support of party policy positions is a large part of the job of leaders. Because the majority party is often divided to some degree on controversial issues, such majorities do not automatically materialize. Rather, leaders carefully count votes, craft legislation, and use various means of persuasion to try to unify their own party and attract votes from members of the opposition party to pass or block legislation. Leaders also work to build majority coalitions in committees and conference committees from time to time, but they tend to be deferential to committee leaders at those stages. Party leaders are most active on the floor.

Extra-large majorities must often be mustered as well. In the Senate, 60 votes must be secured to invoke cloture on a filibuster, unless the matter concerns the Senate's standing rules, in which case a two-thirds vote (67, if all senators vote) is required. On a few other occasions in the Senate, such as to waive a budget restriction, a 60-vote majority must be found. In both chambers, a two-thirds majority of members present and voting is required to override a presidential veto. In such cases, support from at least a few minority members is usually required for the majority party leaders to win.

MANAGING THE FLOOR. Managing floor activity is primarily the responsibility of the majority party leadership. This responsibility includes scheduling sessions of the chambers and arranging for the consideration of individual pieces of legislation. The stark differences between House and Senate floor scheduling practices are noted in Chapter 7. In the Senate, minority members' power to obstruct proceedings requires that the majority leader work closely with the minority leader. In fact, nearly continuous consultation between the two leaders and their staffs is typical in the Senate in midsession. A much more distant relationship between the majority and minority party leaders is found in the House. As a result, the Senate majority leader has more difficulty gaining a tactical edge by careful scheduling than does the House Speaker.

SERVING AS INTERMEDIARY WITH THE PRESIDENT. Serving as intermediaries between the congressional party and the president has been a regular duty of party leaders since the early twentieth century. Leaders of the president's party normally meet with the president once a week while Congress is in session, and they often report on those meetings at party luncheons or caucuses. On matters central to the president's legislative agenda, the leaders work closely with executive branch officials to build majority support in Congress.

Congressional leaders of the president's party often have divided loyalties. Their most immediate obligation is to their congressional colleagues, who elected them, but they also feel an obligation to support the president. Tensions frequently arise as congressional leaders seek to balance the competing demands of the president and their congressional party colleagues.

Leaders of the out-party – the party that does not control the presidency – meet sporadically with the president, usually to be briefed on foreign policy matters. The relationship between a president and out-party leaders is not often one of genuine consultation, for obvious reasons. Occasionally, political circumstances or personal friendship may strengthen the bond. Senate Republican leader Everett Dirksen, for example, was a confidant of Democratic president Lyndon Johnson during the 1960s, and Dirksen's support for Johnson's civil rights and Vietnam War policies was crucial to the president's legislative success.

ENHANCING THE PARTY'S REPUTATION. Public relations is a central leadership responsibility in the modern Congress. Skillfully managing media relations is now considered an essential element of a good legislative strategy. The objectives are to win public support for legislative positions, to persuade undecided legislators of the political support for party positions, and to persuade voters that the party's legislative efforts deserve to be rewarded at election time.

REPLICATING SUCCESSFUL INNOVATIONS

In preparation for the 1994 elections, House Republican leaders prepared a 10-point legislative agenda – known as the "Contract With America" – that they promised to pass in the first 100 days of the new Congress if they gained a majority of seats. Republicans won a House majority in the 1994 elections for the first time since the 1952 elections and credited the new Speaker, Newt Gingrich, for enhancing the importance of national issues in House contests and ultimately for their success.

Ten years later in 2004, the House Democratic leader, Nancy Pelosi (D-California), organized a similar effort for her party. Drawing on the advice of outside consultants and citing the need for a clear message like the Contract With America, the Democratic leaders produced the "New Partnership for America's Future" in which they identified their party's six "core values." The effort did not lead to a new Democratic majority, at least not in the 2004 elections. In 2006, when the Democrats won back a House majority, Pelosi and the Democrats prepared a "Six for '06" agenda that included six legislative initiatives that were passed in the first 100 hours of legislative session in 2007.

Media skills were seldom a major consideration in leadership selection in the 1950s, 1960s, and early 1970s. Service to colleagues, mastery of the mechanics of the legislative game, and position among party factions were given greater weight. Perhaps because of their weak institutional position and lack of national media coverage, only House Republicans made media skills much of an issue in leadership contests. In general, party leaders took a back seat to committee leaders as opinion leaders on matters of policy. In fact, the leading studies on party leadership of the 1960s did not catalog service as party spokesperson or anything similar among the major functions or techniques of leaders.

Expectations have changed. The increasing importance of television as a medium of political communication, presidents' domination of television news, and the larger number of news programs seem to have intensified demand for telegenic leaders. Since the mid-1960s, out-party congressional leaders have sought and been granted time on the television networks to respond to presidential addresses. By the early 1980s, the role of party spokesperson had become so prominent as to warrant listing it among leaders' primary responsibilities.

Congressional party leaders realize that to compete with the president, television pundits, interest group leaders, radio talk show hosts, and other opinion leaders, all of whom actively court public opinion in an effort to

SWITCHING PARTIES, CHANGING PARTY CONTROL

In late May 2001, Senator Jim Jeffords (I-Vermont) announced that he was leaving the Republican Conference, becoming an Independent, and joining with the Democrats for the purpose of organizing the Senate. Since the 1880s, there have been 25 instances of party switching in the Senate, but Jeffords' move was the first time that such a switch caused a party to lose majority status in either chamber. The Senate had been divided 50–50 between Democrats and Republicans; the Republican Vice President Dick Cheney allowed the Republicans to be considered the majority party, for the Republican floor leader to be recognized by the presiding officer as the majority leader, and for the Republicans to control the committee chairmanships.

Republicans attempted to keep Jeffords in the party by offering more money for education programs, his favorite cause, giving him a seat in the leadership circle, and granting him an exemption to the party conference rule limiting the number of terms he could serve as chair of the Health, Education, Labor, and Pensions Committee. The new Democratic majority gave Jeffords a committee chairmanship. In the 2002 elections the Republicans gained additional seats and reassumed majority status. Jeffords lost his chairmanship. Jeffords did not seek reelection in 2006.

There have been 81 instances of party switching in the House since the 1880s.

generate pressure on legislators, they need media strategies of their own. All top leaders have daily contact with print, radio, and television reporters. The House Speaker and Senate leaders usually have brief press conferences before their chambers' daily sessions. They employ experienced press secretaries and speechwriters. They sometimes commission their own public opinion polls to gauge how well their party's message is being received. On a few major issues, they even create special party task forces charged with carrying out a media strategy.

CAMPAIGNING. Providing campaign support to colleagues is a regular part of leaders' activity. All modern leaders help their colleagues raise money and join them at campaign events. Leaders' efforts are not altruistic, of course. Party leaders want to see party colleagues reelected in order to maintain or gain a majority for their party, and they hope that their kindness will be repaid in loyalty. Even candidates for top leadership posts now spend time and money on their colleagues' campaign to attract support and demonstrate the kind of leaders they will be. All leaders, and most aspirants for leadership posts, form political action committees so they may receive contributions that they can donate to the campaigns of their colleagues.

MANAGING THE PARTY AND THE CHAMBER. Organizing the party and chamber is an important duty of party leaders. Obvious political aspects of this job include making committee assignments and appointments to various party positions. More administrative in character are the selection and supervision of chamber officers and other employees. For example, the majority party leaders in the two houses nominate and supervise the chief clerks and sergeants at arms, whose appointment must be approved by the houses, and they share responsibility for choosing a director for the Congressional Budget Office.

Selection of Leaders

The party caucuses elect their top leaders. The leaders are not chosen on the basis of seniority, although most recent leaders have been very experienced members. A candidate's place among factions and regional groups within the party, record of service to colleagues, personal friendships, intelligence and policy expertise, and other factors play a role in leadership contests. As noted, skill in managing relations with the media has become increasingly important. Members who have been serving in lower party posts may be advantaged because they have been in a position to demonstrate their skills and to perform favors for colleagues.

Only in the ascension to House Speaker is there much routine in leadership selection. A vacancy in the speakership is typically filled by the previous floor leader – the majority or minority leader – without opposition. The majority or minority leader generally has already won several leadership elections and has substantial support for the move to Speaker. Challenging the heir apparent would be pointless. Contests for the speakership have not occurred since the 1800s.

The election of Republican Speaker Dennis Hastert in early 1999 was a special case. After Speaker Gingrich announced his resignation shortly after the 1998 elections, in which the Republicans did unexpectedly poorly, the immediate favorite to replace Gingrich was Rep. Bob Livingston (R-Louisiana). But, after the media disclosed that Livingston had an extramarital affair years earlier, Livingston chose to resign from the House. Somewhat anxious to find a new leader, House Republicans asked Hastert, who had held only low appointive positions in the party and was not well known. Hastert was replaced by Nancy Pelosi, who had been the Democratic Minority Leader, after the Democrats won a House majority in 2006.

For other party offices, hotly contested races are common, usually to fill vacancies. As contests among fellow partisans, the races are often filled with intrigue. They involve intense campaigns as the candidates make personal appeals to colleagues to solicit support. Organized factions sometimes choose a favorite; in fact, faction leaders often are the candidates. Wild speculation, personal grudges, and conspiracy are the standard fare. The behind-closed-doors campaigning and secret-ballot voting always generate a great deal of speculation and second-guessing among Washington insiders. A potentially close outcome heightens the suspense.

Challenges to incumbent leaders occur only occasionally. Most incumbent leaders do the kind of job their party colleagues expect. Challenges to an incumbent tend to be particularly divisive, and even disgruntled members usually try to avoid a fight within the party family. Of course, taking on an incumbent may be risky. Leadership contests are expensive in terms of time and effort. Running and losing may undermine future leadership hopes, to say nothing of incurring the wrath of the winner.

House Party Leaders

Today's House party leaders are much more visible and active than were their predecessors of the 1960s and 1970s. Personality is one reason, but more important are the power of television and demands of rank-and-file party members for aggressive, media-oriented leadership. Partly for those reasons, somewhat younger and more assertive members have been promoted to top leadership spots in recent years. Greater party cohesiveness has liberated leaders to be more pugnacious and partisan without alienating major factions within the party.

The Speaker of the House

The Speaker of the House possesses more formal authority than does any other member of Congress. House rules and precedents grant the Speaker important prerogatives concerning floor scheduling and procedures, bill referrals, and appointments to select and conference committees and to various commissions. One of the Speaker's newest prerogatives is the power to remove a member from a conference committee delegation and replace him or her without the approval of the House, a power that is intended to make majority party members of a conference delegation accountable to their party's top leader. In addition to the rules of the House, both parties' internal rules give their top leaders control over the party's appointments to the Rules Committee, extra influence over other committee assignments, and power to make appointments to party committees. It is the combination

TERM LIMITS FOR LEADERS

Since the early 1990s, term limits for party leaders and committee chairs have been a popular reform proposal. Congressional Republicans have moved farther in adopting limits than Democrats. The known limits on leaders' service in key positions appear to have stimulated ambitious legislators to announce their candidacy for leadership posts earlier.

House Republicans led the way among congressional parties to set limits on the number of terms a legislator could serve in a particular leadership post. Soon after they gained a majority in the 1994 elections, the House Republicans limited all party leaders to six-year terms in any given office, with the exception of the speakership for which an eight-year limit was established. House Republicans eliminated the limit on the Speaker in 2003 and Democrats did not reimpose a term for the Speaker when they gained a House majority in 2007.

Senate Republicans followed their House counterparts by setting a six-year limit for holding any leadership position with the exceptions of floor leader and President Pro Tempore for which no limit was set.

House Democrats limit their caucus chair, caucus vice chair, and elected regional whips to two consecutive terms, but do not set term limits for other party leaders.

Senate Democrats have not imposed term limits of any kind on party or committee leadership posts.

of powers granted under House and party rules that make the Speaker more powerful than the Senate's majority leader, who enjoys few special powers under Senate rules.

The Speaker's most important source of power is his or her control of the flow of business on the House floor. By precedent, the Speaker has the power to recognize members on the House floor without appeal. That means that the Speaker may choose to ignore members who seek recognition to call up legislation that the Speaker prefers to consider later or to block. Scheduling prerogatives give the Speaker control over the timing of floor action, which may affect the legislative outcomes and political impact of House votes. Among other things, the Speaker can keep from the floor legislation he or she opposes or wishes to delay. Also, the Speaker may use scheduling to reward or punish legislators.

As presiding officer and the majority party's top leader, the Speaker must exercise great discretion in making public appearances and statements. For example, Speakers make floor speeches on only a few occasions each year, for important issues and close votes. On the momentous occasions when a

Speaker does speak on the floor, nearly all members are in attendance and the galleries are packed. Speakers are granted the privilege of speaking last.

Recent Speakers – Thomas P. "Tip" O'Neill (1977–1986), James Wright (1987–1989), Thomas Foley (1989–1994), Newt Gingrich (1995–1998), Dennis Hastert (1999–2006), and Nancy Pelosi (2007–present) – have been more active in using their formal powers than were the Speakers of the middle decades of the twentieth century. The speakership gained particularly high visibility after the 1980 elections, in which Republican Ronald Reagan was elected to the White House and the Republicans gained a majority in the Senate. O'Neill, as the highest elected Democrat, became the chief strategist and spokesperson for his party. After Reagan's initial year of great legislative success, the Democrats united in opposition to the president's conservative agenda, with O'Neill taking the lead in challenging Reagan's program and presenting Democratic alternatives. In doing so, O'Neill was responding to the demands for leadership from the frustrated liberal rank-and-file members of his party.

O'Neill's activism paled in comparison with the boldness of his successor, James Wright. Upon gaining the speakership, Wright insisted that committees to act quickly on a range of domestic legislation, leading Republicans to complain about a new House dictatorship. In the foreign policy arena, Wright broke through unwritten limits on congressional involvement by negotiating directly with representatives of the contending governments and factions in Central America.

Wright resigned from the House in 1989 after the House Committee on Standards of Official Conduct charged him with several violations of House ethics rules. Thomas Foley, who succeeded Wright, had been caucus chair, whip, and majority leader. Compared with Wright, he was less assertive, more deferential to committees, and less inclined to make partisan attacks on Republican leaders. Like O'Neill, Wright was unlikely to take the lead on controversial issues unless a consensus had already crystallized within his party.

Republican Newt Gingrich became the most proactive Speaker since the first decade of the twentieth century after he was elected to the post in January 1995. A well-developed agenda, called the Contract With America, provided an unusually concise 10-point policy platform for Gingrich. Gingrich was given much of the credit for these developments – he had championed aggressive Republican strategies in the House, coauthored the Contract With America, raised money, and recruited candidates to challenge the incumbent Democratic majority. Gingrich, backed by his House Republican colleagues, became the leading spokesman for his party, dominated the selection of committee leaders and other committee appointments, directed the actions of committees, set the floor agenda, and pushed legislation associated with the Contract With America through the House in the first 100 days of the 104th Congress (1995–1996).

Gingrich's speakership was a lightning rod for partisanship and ended in political tragedy. Gingrich had leveled the initial charges against Jim Wright that eventually led to Wright's resignation and later, as Speaker, was at least as aggressive as Wright in leading the majority party. His political downfall began with his 1995 strategy to hold hostage debt ceiling increases and funding for executive departments in order to get President Bill Clinton's approval of the Republican's budget plan. Clinton refused to budge and eventually the Republican Congress accepted Clinton's compromise legislation. The episode produced sharply weaker approval ratings in public opinion polls for Gingrich and much stronger ratings for Clinton. After that point, Gingrich became far less aggressive, setting aside his confrontational strategies. Following Clinton's reelection in 1996, Gingrich maintained a low public profile and appeared to be somewhat less heavy-handed in directing the work of the House, an approach that has received mixed reviews from his colleagues. In the summer of 1997 there was serious discussion among senior Republicans of replacing him. Gingrich continued to be subject to criticism for ineffective leadership, and he eventually resigned his post when challenged by Bob Livingston in the aftermath of the 1998 elections.

In 1995, the Republicans instituted a new House rule limiting the number of consecutive terms that a member could serve as Speaker. In December 1994, newly elected Republicans proposed a three-term limit for the Speaker, just as they proposed for committee chairs. At Gingrich's insistence, they approved a four-term limit instead, which was incorporated into the House rules in January 1995. Gingrich did not survive long enough for the rule to apply.

Hastert's style contrasted sharply with Gingrich's, at least at first. Hastert consulted more frequently with his fellow partisans and granted more independence to committee chairs. He successfully healed some of the rifts among Republicans left from the Gingrich years, and, for a while, he held regular meetings with the Democratic leader. He campaigned endlessly for his colleagues, earning their respect and indebtedness, and, in the view of some observers, used this support to gain the upper hand with other party and committee leaders.

However welcome Hastert's more accommodating style was initially, by late 2002 Hastert became more aggressive in his enforcement of party loyalty. He denied committee chairmanships and choice committee assignments to several Republicans who had opposed the leadership position on campaign finance reform, patients' bill of rights, and other issues. He endorsed Majority Leader Tom Delay's (R-Texas) proclamation that a Republican member of the party's organization who voted against the party on any procedural matter be excused from service. In 2003, the Republicans' package of House rules changes dropped the eight-year term limit for a Speaker. Democrats did not reimpose a term limit for the Speaker when they gained a majority in 2007.

After the Democrats won a majority of House seats in the 2006 elections, they elected their floor leader, Nancy Pelosi, the first woman Speaker. Pelosi, a liberal Democrat from San Francisco, had worked hard as minority leader to build support among moderate and conservative Democrats. During her first few months in the speakership, she proved to be an aggressive leader who set the agenda for her party and showed a willingness to work around committee chairs who were not in sync with her agenda. While she worked hard to win the support of fellow partisans on controversial issues, she created more opportunities for the minority party to offer alternatives and gave her own partisans somewhat more freedom to vote as they chose. Nevertheless, Pelosi has proven quite willing to have the most important legislation developed within her party with little minority party participation.

House Floor Leaders

Both House parties elect a floor leader – that is, a majority leader or a minority leader – at the start of each Congress. As the label suggests, floor leaders are the chief spokespersons for their parties on the House floor. The majority leader is considered the second-ranking leader of the party, just behind the Speaker. The minority leader is the minority party's top leader and is always that party's (losing) nominee for Speaker at the beginning of each Congress.

There are few duties formally assigned to the majority leader in party rules. Recent Speakers have relied on the floor leader to receive and screen requests to schedule legislation for floor consideration. The majority leader consults with the Speaker (normally several times a day), works with the Speaker and others to promote party unity, and increasingly serves as a party spokesperson. Recent majority leaders have been loyal to the Speaker and have seldom publicly disagreed with him or her. As the person who is next in line to become Speaker, and an individual with a strong voice in scheduling

---

Congressionally Speaking . . .

The term *whip* originated in the British House of Commons. It is derived from the term whipper-in – the fellow who keeps the dogs in line during an English foxhunt. In the American Congress, the use of the term reflected the responsibility of the whip to get party members to the floor on time. Today the term is often used as a verb – as in "the undecided members were whipped" – to refer to the process of persuasion and arm-twisting.

---

and all other leadership decisions, the majority leader is considered very powerful.

The minority leader generally is the minority party's chief spokesperson and strategist. The minority leader sometimes consults with the majority leader about the floor schedule, although more often he or she is merely informed of the majority leadership's scheduling decisions. Keeping the minority party united and attracting majority party votes are the central tasks of the minority leader's job. The job is made easier when the minority leader's party controls the White House, and the president's resources can be drawn upon. The minority party can do little to obstruct a cohesive majority in the House, so the minority floor leader's job tends to be quite frustrating. The minority leader, like the Speaker, is an *ex officio* member of the Permanent Select Committee on Intelligence.

House Whips and Whip Organizations

The third-ranking majority party leader and second-ranking minority party leader in the House are the whips. Both whips are now elected, although the Democratic whip was appointed by the majority leader until late 1986 when the position was made elective. Both whips head large whip organizations, whose purpose is to collect information for the leadership and persuade colleagues to support party positions. To facilitate the communication process, the whip offices maintain systems of recorded messages and email about floor actions, issue whip notices about the upcoming schedule, and use automated telephone and paging systems to reach members about pending votes. Whips also try to keep track of the whereabouts of members, particularly on days when important, close floor votes are expected.

The Democratic whip organization has been large for many years. In recent Congresses, the House Democrats had as many as nine chief deputy

EVOLVING PARTY ORGANIZATIONS

Congressional party organizations have become much more elaborate in the past generation, a result of competitive pressures and the desire to include more members in party activities. A good example is the elaboration of the Senate Democratic leadership following the 2006 elections. Senator Charles Schumer (D-New York) was praised by his party colleagues for recruiting candidates, raising money, and aiding in the creation of a new Democratic majority. He was rewarded by Majority Leader Harry Reid (D-Nevada) with an appointment to a new party position, conference vice chairman, that Reid created for him. Reid said the position would be the third-ranking leadership post under the majority leader and assistant majority leader (whip). Schumer continued to hold the position in 2009.

whips, 12 deputy whips, and 70 at-large whips, all appointed by the party leader. In addition, there have been 24 regional whips elected by groups of Democrats from specific regions and one ex officio whip (the ranking Democrat on the Rules Committee), for a total of 88 whips. The whip system has grown rapidly as the top leaders have responded to demands for whip appointments from party factions and individual members.

The Democratic leaders often appoint task forces to collect information and generate support on specific issues. This approach has been called a "strategy of inclusion," because it gives a large number of members an opportunity to work closely with the leadership. By working hand-in-hand with the party rank-and-file, party leaders are able to persuade some members who otherwise might oppose the leadership to join the team.

The House Republicans have a more modest whip system, although it also has expanded in recent years. The Republican whip system has been comprised of a chief deputy whip and about 17 deputy whips – all appointed – and nearly 50 assistant whips elected by groups for regions of the country. The Republican whips meet irregularly. The Republicans maintain several subcommittees on their Policy Committee that serve purposes similar to Democratic caucus task forces.

Appointment or election as a whip, policy subcommittee, or task force member gives a member some prestige, an additional office to add to his or her letterhead, and access to informative weekly whip meetings. For some members, service in these party posts provides an opportunity to prove their leadership abilities to their colleagues, which can be important to a member who aspires to the top leadership posts. For all members, these posts provide an opportunity to learn more about the politics of key issues and of their party. Nearly all members advertise their assumption of these "leadership" positions at home.

Senate Party Leaders

Traditionally, the Senate's smaller party organizations have had fewer formal leadership posts, committees, and staff than have their House counterparts, although Senate party organizations have become more elaborate in recent years. The Senate's chief leaders are the majority leader and minority leader. These two leaders have historically been prominent politicians, frequently mentioned in the newspapers and seen on television.

Senate Floor Leaders

The majority leader is the principal leader of the Senate. The majority leader sets the Senate's schedule and plans the order of business for the Senate floor. Critical to that function is a procedural advantage granted to the majority leader by precedent: the right of first recognition. The presiding officer recognizes the majority leader to speak or to offer a motion before recognizing any other senator, a practice that dates back to the 1930s.

Like House Speakers, Senate majority leaders vary in their assertiveness. Lyndon Johnson (D-Texas), who served as Democratic leader from 1955 to 1960, set the modern standard for aggressive leadership. Recent majority leaders of both parties have played a more important role in enacting major legislation – negotiating the content of many important bills, pushing committees to bring legislation to the floor, and taking a leading role in managing controversial legislation on the floor.

A majority leader's ability to set the floor agenda depends on the cooperation of his or her Senate colleagues. To call up a measure for consideration on the floor, the majority leader normally must gain approval of a "motion to proceed." Although the motion requires only a simple majority for approval, it also may be debated and so may be subject to a filibuster. Thus, on a controversial measure, the majority leader may require 60 votes to invoke cloture on the motion to proceed and get a measure to the floor for debate and amendment. Once the motion to proceed is adopted, the measure itself or any amendment to it may be filibustered. Consequently, the Senate's schedule is often quite unpredictable.

The majority leader usually seeks to limit debate and often seeks to limit amendments without going as far as invoking cloture. But to do so, the

TIME FOR REFORM?

In 2009, Senator Robert C. Byrd (D-West Virginia), who turned 91 in late 2008, was reelected president pro tempore of the Senate. The 1947 presidential succession act provides that the Senate's president pro tempore is third in line to the presidency behind the vice president and speaker of the House. Because of the modern practice to give the position to the most senior member of the majority party, the president pro tempore often is quite old and may not be capable of managing the duties of the presidency. In 2001, Strom Thurmond served as president pro tempore at age 98 and surely would not have been an effective president. Concerns about an act of terrorism incapacitating national leadership have stimulated new questions about the age of presidents pro tempore, but there has been no serious effort to change the informal seniority practice or the 1947 law.

leader must receive unanimous consent – that is, the leader's request will be rejected if one senator objects. Objections are common from senators who want to protect their right to speak, do not want to give up opportunities to offer amendments, or simply do not want to be inconvenienced. Of course, leaders of both parties entertain requests from colleagues not to allow certain measures to be called up for consideration on the floor (see box, "Congressionally Speaking"). As a result, scheduling in the Senate is much less routine and more a process of negotiation than it is in the House.

The minority leader works closely with the majority leader on scheduling matters. The minority leader protects the parliamentary prerogatives of party members when the majority leader seeks unanimous consent to call up measures, schedule floor action, or limit debate and amendments. Like majority leaders, minority leaders differ in their aggressiveness, and their success depends on the size and cohesiveness of their parties. Unlike the House Speaker and floor leaders, the Senate floor leaders may retain committee assignments. Both Senate leaders are *ex officio* members of the Select Committee on Intelligence. Floor leaders do not hold full committee leadership positions, however.

In late 1996, Senate Republicans set a three-Congress term limit for party leadership positions except for the floor leader and President Pro Tempore. The term limit forced several leaders to give up their positions for the first time at the end of 2002. Senate Democrats are alone among the four congressional parties in not placing term limits on any leadership positions.

Congressionally Speaking . . .

The predicament of the Senate majority leader is illustrated in the practice of holds. A *hold* is an objection to considering a measure on the Senate floor. Senators usually communicate their objections by letter to their party's floor leader. For several decades, these communications were considered confidential so the name of the senator placing the hold often is not known to his or her colleagues. When senators place holds on measures, they sometimes merely want advance warning of floor action, but at other times they seek to change the bill or even prevent Senate action on the bill.

Working to remove holds is time consuming and involves bargaining with contending factions. Holds are not formally recognized in Senate or party rules, but rather are effective because they constitute notices to object to a unanimous consent request to move to the consideration of a bill or other measure. A leader may call the bluff of a colleague and seek to bring up a bill without clearing the hold, but leaders generally observe holds because they need the cooperation of their colleagues on other matters.

In 2007, a provision requiring public disclosure of the name of the senator placing a hold was included in the ethics reform legislation. The sponsors hoped that disclosure would limit the practice by allowing the public and fellow senators to hold accountable those senators who place holds. The rule proved toothless (requiring senators to disclose their hold *after* an objection to considering a bill was made), but holds did seem to become less frequent. Filibusters and gaining cloture proved to be far more serious problems for the majority leader in recent years.

Senate Whips and Whip Organizations

Both Senate parties call their whips assistant floor leaders to reflect their chief responsibility: standing in for the floor leader in his or her absence. The Senate whips conduct few head counts. One reason is that bill managers – committee leaders or others who take the lead in the floor debate – often do their own head counting, owing to the Senate's smaller size. Senate whips' specific duties depend on the needs of individual floor leaders. Senate party whips have sometimes named assistant or deputy whips to help with head counts and floor duties, but, as a general rule, the deputy whips have not played a regular or important role in the smaller Senate, where the top leaders, bill managers, and their staffs can manage most duties.

Party Leaders' Resources

The influence of the top congressional party leaders flows from their use of several important resources: (1) their parties' voting strength, (2) the procedural powers granted them by the formal rules of their chamber and party, (3) the tangible rewards that they can grant to members, (4) information, (5) their access to the media, and (6) their staffs. Generally, the combination of party strength and formal powers accorded to him or her makes the House Speaker the most powerful member of Congress, followed in descending order by the Senate majority leader, the Senate minority leader, and the House minority leader.

Party Strength

The relative size of the parties' delegations in Congress determines their majority or minority status and thus which party will enjoy the procedural advantages conferred to the majority. Figures 5.2 and 5.3 show the size of the two major parties in each house since 1900. But a party's ability to pass or block legislation involves more than its size. A majority party must also be fairly cohesive, or at least benefit from a fractured opposition, for its potential strength to be realized. Seldom are majority parties so large that they can afford to lose many votes from their own ranks and still win on the floor. Votes that require supermajorities, such as the two-thirds majority required to override presidential vetoes or the three-fifths majority required to overcome a Senate filibuster, are particularly troublesome for majority parties. As a general rule, there is uncertainty about a majority party's prospects of prevailing on important issues. Hard work is required to build winning coalitions on most important legislation. Not all party colleagues can be trusted to support their leadership, and ways of attracting support from members of the minority party often must be found.

Formal Rules

The standing rules of the House and Senate, as well as the written rules of the congressional parties, grant party leaders certain procedural advantages over other members. Of the four top leaders, the Speaker of the House is, by far, the most advantaged by standing rules and precedents. The Speaker enjoys powers that far exceed those of the most comparable Senate leader, the Senate majority leader.

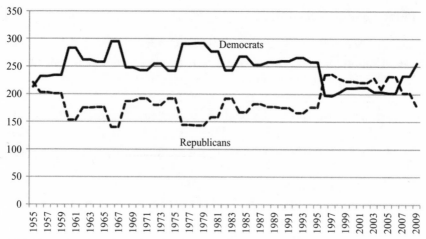

FIGURE 5.2. Number of Democrats and Republicans in the House of Representatives, 1955–2009.

The Senate majority leader, by virtue of the right of first recognition and a few other privileges, comes in second behind the Speaker in formal powers, but the Senate minority leader is not far behind. The Senate's cloture rule and its reliance on unanimous consent agreements to organize its business require the Senate majority leader to consult and gain the consent of the minority leader on most scheduling matters. No such consultation

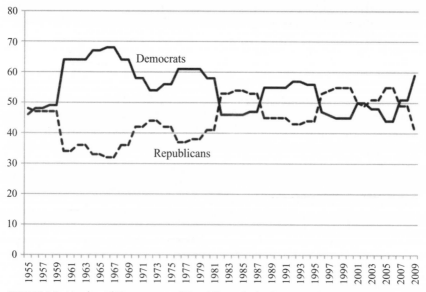

FIGURE 5.3. Number of Democrats and Republicans in the Senate, 1955–2009.

is necessary in the House if the Speaker has the backing of his or her party, making the House minority leader the weakest of the top congressional leaders.

In 1974, the formal power of the House Speaker was bolstered under House rules by granting the Speaker the ability to refer legislation to multiple committees or to propose the creation of an ad hoc or temporary committee. Previously, the Speaker was required to refer each measure to the single committee that had predominant jurisdiction over it. The Speaker now may send legislation to committees sequentially, with one committee identified as the primary committee, or can split legislation into parts to send to different committees. The Speaker may set time limits on committee action when more than one committee is involved. This flexible referral rule has substantially enhanced the Speaker's ability to control the flow of legislation in the House – even to direct legislation toward friendly committees and away from unfriendly committees. On only one occasion, for a large multi-faceted energy bill in 1977, whose content spanned the jurisdiction of many committees, has an ad hoc committee been used successfully.

The powers granted to the Speaker created the prospect of a more centralized, Speaker-driven, policy-making process in the House. That possibility certainly was not realized in the 1970s. Speakers Albert and O'Neill continued to defer to committees and did not attempt to manipulate committees by using their referral powers. To the contrary, the 1970s were a period of remarkably fragmented, decentralized policy making. This was the product of simultaneous reforms that diffused power from full committee chairs to subcommittee chairs (see Chapter 6). And it reflected the expectations of rank-and-file Democrats. Only in the last year or two of the 1970s did Speaker O'Neill begin to use his new referral powers with some vigor.

The power of the Speaker was enhanced in 1993 when the House, over the objections of minority party Republicans at the time, adopted a rule that allows the Speaker to remove members and appoint additional members to select and conference committees after initial appointments have been made. The new rule, which covers minority party appointees as well as majority party appointees, is aimed at majority party conferees who pursue positions that will obstruct outcomes favored by the leadership. Such conferees cannot be confident that their place on a prominent select committee or important conference committee will be protected once they have been appointed. Instead, the Speaker is free to correct errors in judgment made at the time of the initial appointments. In practice, the Speaker is likely to continue to defer to the minority leader on the appointment of minority party

ANOTHER STORY OF SWITCHING PARTIES

In 2004, with no advance notice, freshman Democrat Rodney Alexander (then D-Louisiana) filed for reelection to his seat as a Republican. Not only were House Democratic leaders surprised, they soon became upset when Alexander did not promptly return approximately $70,000 in contributions that he had received from the political action committees of several Democratic colleagues. Democratic leaders threatened a lawsuit for fraud after failing to hear from Alexander for a month. Alexander began to refund the contributions about two months later, just a month before the November elections, which, at least one Democrat complained, was so late that it limited the value of redirecting the money to other campaigns. Alexander won the seat and was rewarded by his new party with a seat on the prestigious Appropriations Committee, a move up from the Committee on Agriculture and Committee on Transportation and Infrastructure assignments he had as a Democrat. Alexander was reelected in 2006 as a Republican.

members to select and conference committees. The Republicans retained the rule once they became the majority party after the 1994 elections and it has remained in place since then.

With respect to intra-party rules and practices, the House parties give their top leaders considerable power. They have a strong influence over their party colleagues' committee assignments, appoint their parties' members of the Rules Committee, and appoint members to a variety of party positions. Through the Rules Committee, the Speaker, the majority party's leader, controls the flow of major legislation to the floor. In combination, the powers granted under House and party rules make the Speaker exceptionally influential.

Tangible Rewards

Party leaders have a few resources at their disposal that provide direct political benefits to their colleagues and can be used to reward friends and punish enemies. Influence over committee assignments is the most prominent of these resources. An assignment to a committee with jurisdiction over legislation important to a member's home constituency or to well-financed special interests may be important to the member's electoral prospects. Other committees are coveted because of their jurisdiction over important legislation and place their members in the middle of the most important legislative battles. Because party leaders play a major role in their parties' committees

THE LIEBERMAN SAGA

Senator Joseph Lieberman (I-Connecticut), a lifelong Democrat and the Democratic candidate for vice president in 2000, lost his party's primary election in 2006, largely over the issue of his support for Bush administration policy on the war in Iraq. Nevertheless, he successfully won reelection as an Independent. After the election, he continued to caucus with Senate Democrats and, by virtue of his seniority, continued to hold his committee and subcommittee chairmanships as a Democrat. His relations with some people in his party were strained because they had advocated the election of the official Democratic nominee.

In 2008, Lieberman endorsed and campaigned for the Republican presidential candidate, Senator John McCain, a longtime friend. His active support for McCain upset many of his Democratic colleagues, some of whom advocated that Lieberman be excluded from the Senate Democratic Conference or at least be stripped of his committee chairmanship.

After the election, in which the Democratic Senator Barack Obama won the presidency, no serious consideration of excluding Lieberman from the party conference was contemplated. Although he lost a valued committee assignment (see Chapter 6), Lieberman found Democratic leaders eager to find a way to keep him in the party. Party leaders did not want to alienate Lieberman more than necessary to appease rank-and-file Democrats. Party leaders surely figured that it was better to have a larger party and that Lieberman's support might prove critical on many issues.

on committees, where committee assignments are made, they can offer or withhold favors from colleagues.

Tangible rewards come in many other forms, too. The expanded use of task forces by the congressional parties has increased the number of opportunities for leaders to bestow special status on party colleagues. Leaders can appoint members to special commissions and approve international travel plans.

Leaders can be supportive of their colleagues' campaign efforts. They can influence the allocation of funds from the party campaign committees. In recent decades, party leaders have created political action committees of their own and contributed to colleagues' campaigns. Even candidates for leadership posts seek to demonstrate their leadership abilities by raising money that is directed to their colleagues' campaigns. And in recent years, leaders have become very active in attending the fund-raising events of their colleagues, sometimes even choosing not to attend an event to make clear their dissatisfaction with a member's behavior. In a few cases,

leaders have intervened to discourage primary challenges to an incumbent
colleague.

Information

Information is critical to legislative success. Devising effective legislative
strategies requires information about the specific policy issues and alternatives that will arise during the Congress, the policy preferences of the
membership, the administration, the other key players, and how others plan
to act. Advantages from chamber or party rules, or even party strength,
remain only potential sources of leadership power if they are not matched
by useful and timely information.

The top leaders navigate in a sea of information. With the help of their
staff, leaders collect and absorb information about committee schedules and
actions, floor scheduling, presidential requests, members' political circumstances, and interest group activity. The top leaders do not have a monopoly
over most kinds of information, of course, but they are uniquely placed to
assimilate information from many different sources. Requests are made of
them on such matters as scheduling, committee assignments, and campaign
assistance, and leaders can sometimes pry information from members, lobbyists, and others who want something from them. The whip systems and
party task forces are often activated to gather and disseminate information.
And the time they spend on or near their chamber floor gives leaders and
their staffs opportunities for casual conversations and informal exchanges
of information.

Because information flows to the top leaders so readily, few other members
can compete with party leaders as coalition builders. To be sure, committee
leaders and bill sponsors master information relevant to their own legislation.
But from time to time even committee leaders turn to party leaders for
assistance in gathering and distributing information. By exercising care in
granting access to their information, party leaders can affect the strategies
of other important players.

Leaders' informational advantage is stronger in the House than in the
Senate, owing to the House's larger size. In the House, the seemingly simple task of counting members planning to vote for or against something is
onerous. For the majority party, this means reaching more than 218 members, many of whom might be away from Washington when the information
is needed. Consequently, House bill managers often must rely on the services of the party leadership – whip offices and task forces – for timely
information. In contrast, Senate bill managers are more self-reliant because
they need to count fewer heads. Thus, Senate whip organizations are not

critical to the collection and dissemination of information on most important matters.

The overall trend in recent decades has been toward a diffusion of information across Capitol Hill. Junior members have benefited from the expansion of committee, personal, and support agency staffs and from the growth of the interest group community and informal members' caucuses. Party leaders now have more competition in the market for information than they did just a few decades ago.

Access to the Media

Although top party leaders cannot compete with the president for media attention, they enjoy far better access to the media than do most other members. The media often turn to top leaders for their reactions to events or to presidential decisions or statements. This phenomenon is natural: Leaders are presumed to represent their parties and to be in a position to act on their views. Even when there is no breaking story, leaders' routine press conferences attract reporters on the chance that the leaders will say something newsworthy. Few other members can count on such attention. Thus, leaders gain media attention because they are powerful, and, at least in part, they are powerful because they gain media attention.

Party leaders' media access serves as an important resource in the legislative game. Leaders can share their access with colleagues: They can mention a colleague's legislation, invite a colleague to join in a press conference, or refer reporters and television producers to a colleague. They can selectively divulge information about the plans of friendly and unfriendly factions. They also can increase the ease or difficulty of reaching compromises by intensifying or softening the rhetoric of claiming credit and avoiding blame.

Until recently, Senate leaders generally had an advantage over House leaders in their access to the media. The greater public prestige of the Senate and greater public interest in senators than in representatives encouraged the national media to pay more attention to Senate leaders. The advent of televised floor sessions in the House in 1979, about seven years before the Senate permitted television coverage of its sessions, seemed to make little difference.

Recent House Speakers have been as visible as the top Senate leaders on network news programs. In the 1950s through the mid-1970s, Senate leaders were far more visible on television news programs than were House leaders. The Speaker of the House has gained prominence since the 1970s. For a couple years in the mid-1990s, Speaker Gingrich was second only to the president in media visibility. The House minority leader generally lags

ONE NAME, TWO PARTIES

House and Senate Democrats and House and Senate Republicans have separate
organizations and elect their own leaders, but there are still good reasons
for fellow partisans in the two houses to coordinate their activities. In fact,
periodically a party's House and Senate leaders, usually from the "out party"
(the party that does not control the White House), promise to work together on
an agenda and public relations. A president tends to dominate congressional
leaders in defining the party's policy agenda and shaping the party's public
image. Soon after the Republicans lost the White House in the 2008 elections,
their congressional leaders promised greater coordination. Coordination tends
to fade quickly as leaders in each house struggle to meet the expectations of their
own party conference.

far behind other top leaders in media visibility, reflecting the relatively weak
formal powers and informal influence of most House minority leaders. In
contrast, the power of the Senate minority to obstruct bills, coupled with
the Senate's prestige, gives the Senate minority leader a big advantage over
his or her House counterpart in attracting media attention.

Recent party leaders in both houses have made a concerted effort to
shape the message communicated through the media to the general public.
They have expanded their press office operations, hired media specialists,
consulted pollsters, created party committees or task forces to shape party
messages, and sought new ways to communicate to the public. All recent
top leaders have sought to fashion coherent policy programs, to advertise
their programs, and to develop a common argument or theme for the parties
on major issues.

Leadership Staffs

Top leaders' staffs have expanded as leaders have sought to meet colleagues'
expectations and extend their own influence. These staffs now include policy
specialists, public relations personnel, and experts in parliamentary procedures, as well as people who assist the leaders with daily chores. With the
help of expanded staffs, leaders can more carefully follow committee deliberations, more rapidly respond to political events, and more frequently take
a leading role in the negotiation of legislative details.

Organizational arrangements for the staff of the four top party leaders
vary, reflecting both differences in the leaders' positions and historical accident. The House Speaker's leadership staff is spread between the Speaker's
office and the Steering and Policy Committee. Similarly, the Senate

Democratic leader's staff is located primarily in the Policy Committee. The House and Senate Republican leaders' staffs are housed within their leadership offices. Both Senate leaders manage the activity of the party secretaries, who are staff members, and the secretaries' assistants.

An Era of Reinvigorated Parties

The role of parties and their leaders in Congress is not written in stone. Indeed, members of the early Congresses could not have envisioned modern congressional parties. The development of congressional parties has occurred in response to the changing needs and demands of members, who elect the top party leaders and are free to write and rewrite the rules of their chambers and party caucuses. New issues, turnover in the membership, new presidents, new political cleavages in American society, the nature of electoral parties, and changing rules sometimes alter members' calculations about the kind of legislative party organization and leadership that will best serve their interests.

In recent decades, stronger parties and leaders have emerged. This development would have surprised most observers of the mid-1960s. At that time, the House and Senate caucuses of the majority party Democrats were inactive; today, all four congressional party caucuses (or conferences) are active and meet regularly. In the mid-1960s, the top Democratic leaders were deferential to committee and subcommittee chairs; today, party leaders frequently name party task forces, composed of members both on and off the standing committees of jurisdiction, to devise policy and strategy on major issues. In the mid-1960s, party leaders assumed that committee leaders would speak for the party on policy matters; today, party leaders themselves are clearly expected to assume a prominent role in the media on nearly all important matters. In the 1970s, extreme individualism was the most common description of Congress; during the last 20 years, unrestrained partisanship has been the dominant theme.

These developments appear to be the products of change in the several basic elements of the legislative game –what the issues are, who the players are and what they want, and the rules. Each of these elements contributed to forming the parties' coalitions inside and outside of Congress and deserves brief consideration.

The Issues

Large federal deficits in the 1980s and early 1990s dominated the policy agenda of Congress and exacerbated long-standing differences between the parties over the appropriate size and function of the federal government. Such matters as tax hikes and cuts, the allocation of money between defense and domestic programs, and government commitments to entitlement programs for the elderly, the sick, and the poor stimulated pitched battles between the parties. Few issues were perceived to have as direct a connection to electoral fortunes as aggregate spending and tax choices, so the incentives for the parties to seek credit and avoid blame were high. The partisan electoral consequences of fiscal politics produced demands on the top leaders to be more assertive in public relations and to work harder to bolster their parties' public images. Partisan differences over fiscal policy reemerged as a central issue after the 2000 elections and remain important. Contributing to partisanship is the use of omnibus legislation for the federal budget. As a consequence of procedures authorized by the 1974 Budget Act, budget policy was wrapped into two major pieces of legislation each year – a budget resolution and a reconciliation bill. The stakes are particularly high for reconciliation bills, which typically package the proposals for spending cuts of more than a dozen committees. These high-stakes bills force party leaders into all negotiations and encourage members and outside observers to judge outcomes in terms of party winners and losers.

To make matters worse, this high-stakes contest, between a Congress controlled by one party and a president of the other party, tended toward stalemate. Blaming the other party – and the other institution – for the lack of action became the chief political strategy. Only top party leaders and the president could overcome the gridlock, but that only increased the stakes and enhanced the perceived partisan consequences of the outcome.

In this environment, party leaders were expected to be aggressive and outspoken. Some leaders were not especially comfortable or capable in that role. Only after Jim Wright assumed the speakership in 1987 did House Democrats have a Speaker who relished a prominent place in the media. When Senator George Mitchell took over after Byrd relinquished his leadership post, also in 1987, Senate Democrats had a leader who saw being a party spokesperson as a high-priority responsibility. Since then, leaders of both parties and in both houses have aggressively promoted their party's views.

Contributing to a stronger role for party leaders have been issues that cut across the jurisdictions of multiple standing committees. When party interests dictate action on issues such as global warming and energy that fall under the jurisdiction of many committees, their chairs cannot be expected to act promptly and effectively to coordinate legislative action. The majority party's interests dictate that central party leaders coordinate the development of legislation, take the lead in finding compromises among party colleagues, devise public relations strategies to sell the legislation to the public, and concentrate the resources required to build majorities on the floor.

Members' Demands

Former Senate parliamentarian Floyd Riddick once observed that "the position of the floor leader is not that of an army general over a multitude of soldiers. Unlike army officers, the floor leaders must maintain continued support. They are subject to periodic reelection by the same persons they have been leading."[1] That is, party leaders are appropriately viewed as agents of their party colleagues, and their success depends largely on the cooperation of those colleagues. Consequently, leaders' goals and strategies are shaped by the demands and expectations of their party colleagues, whose own political goals and needs change over time.

Many observers have commented on the individualism that has characterized members of Congress in recent decades. This "new breed" of lawmaker, as it is often called, is a product of the 1960s. New-breed members are anti-establishment, intolerant of traditional norms and authority, and more national, or even worldly, in their orientation. They are more independent, outward-looking, issue-oriented, media-oriented, and entrepreneurial. Their individualism is encouraged by expanded opportunities outside Congress – a swelling interest group community, broader single-issue constituencies facilitated by new forms of electronic communication and greater ease in cross-continental and intercontinental travel, and the growth of computerized mass mailings and telephone solicitation techniques. In addition, individualism among legislators is encouraged by the necessity of personally raising large sums of money to gain reelection.

In the late 1960s, the Senate's new breed began to produce presidential candidates. In the 1970s, new-breed members contributed to a redistribution of power within House committees from full committee chairs to subcommittee chairs (see Chapter 6), the distribution of more resources to rank-and-file members in both chambers, and a surge in floor amending activity. They also contributed to the demise of such waning norms as deference to committee recommendations and serving a quiet apprenticeship period to learn the ropes before actively seeking to influence policy choices.

Unrestrained individualism created several problems for party leaders. Surveying, coordinating, and scheduling chamber activities became more complicated. No longer could majority party leaders rely on consultations with a few senior committee leaders. Individualism meant that leaders were less certain about who wanted to participate and who expected to be consulted, that committee leaders could expect more challenges to committee bills, and that floor sessions would be longer and less predictable. Of course, many bill managers faced difficulties because of their inexperience. In the House, individualism also meant less restrained tactics on the part of minority party members.

As members struggled to adapt to the new conditions, many majority party members turned to their party leaders for assistance. More and more frequently, majority party leaders were called on to resolve intra-party conflicts that had once been negotiated or squelched by committee chairs. Even before legislation was ready for floor action, conflicts between committees and between committee members and nonmembers led some members to ask top leaders to intervene. And majority party frustration with minority party tactics – calls for votes, redundant amendments, and so on – resulted in calls for a crackdown on the minority by the majority party leadership. The Speaker responded with some rules changes and more creative use of special rules to limit floor amendments. Ironically, then, from the chaos of unrestrained individualism came demands for stronger central leadership.

Policy Alignments

At the same time that policy making was becoming further complicated by individualism, members' positions on major policy questions became more polarized by partisan affiliation. Electoral forces and changes in Congress's policy agenda contributed to greater partisanship in voting during the 1980s.

The budget-oriented agenda produced intensified conflict among legislators. Large deficits increased the difficulty of finding funds for new or expanded programs, and old programs became targets for budget cutters. Consequently, legislation that in the past had seemed to produce far more winners than losers, such as student aid and environmental protection measures, was evaluated less on its own merit and more on the basis of its impact on the deficit during the next few years. Attention shifted from individual programs, which often attract support across party lines, to the overall spending and taxation patterns of the federal government – just the kind of issue that taps deeply held ideological beliefs and most differentiates the two parties.

Electoral forces also contributed to party polarization. The largest changes appeared in the South, where the expansion of the African American voting

LEADERSHIP IN ANOTHER ERA

Sam Rayburn (D-Texas) was the most beloved twentieth-century Speaker of the House. He served as Speaker from 1940 to 1961, with the exception of four years when Republicans controlled the House. Rayburn listened well and was always kind to his colleagues, and because he was sheepish about his bald head, he shied away from cameras. He exercised his power quietly. A Rayburn biographer reported an incident on the floor of the House that was typical of the way he ruled:

"[W]hen a bill providing for a cooling-off period to stave off labor strikes came to the House floor, Rayburn wanted it debated fully. Experience and instinct told him that with feelings running high an attempt might be made to shut off debate and go directly to a vote. This proved correct when Jennings Randolph of West Virginia, a member of the Labor Committee, won recognition and started to make a motion to do this.

While he was still talking, Rayburn walked down from the dais and headed toward him. With each approaching step Randolph's voice grew weaker. Finally he stopped talking when Rayburn reached him and put a hand on his shoulder. For a short time, with his face set sternly, Rayburn spoke in a low, gruff tone to Randolph, whom he liked. Then still talking, he removed his hand, plunged it into his jacket pocket, and his body rocked back and forth from his heels to his toes. Then he turned suddenly and walked back to the rostrum.

Laughter swept the chamber as embarrassment crossed Randolph's face. When silence came, Randolph announced he was withdrawing his motion, and he added, 'As a legislative son I am always willing to follow the advice of my legislative elders.'"

Rayburn was special, to be sure, but no recent Speaker, in an age of televised floor sessions and independent-minded members, would have dared embarrass a colleague in that way.

base for Democrats and the suburban, white base for Republicans altered the electoral coalitions for the two parties. Southern Democrats became more moderate and sometimes quite liberal, making the Democratic contingents in the House and Senate more homogeneous. Southern Republicans, a scarce breed before the 1970s, fit the traditional conservative Republican mold, so they reinforced the homogeneity of the Republican party in Congress. Southern Republicans now hold many of their party's top leadership posts.

A change from less to more polarized parties has characterized developments in the House and Senate since the late 1970s. Increasing intra-party cohesiveness, reinforced by increasing inter-party conflict, has altered the demands placed on party leaders. That partisanship has led members to insist that their leaders actively pursue party interests, and at the same time it has reduced resistance to strong central leaders from the remaining but shrinking minority factions within the parties.

Rules of the Game

The reinforcement of the Speaker's powers, beginning in the early 1970s, represents an important development in the distribution of power in the House. The House party leaders appoint the members of the Rules Committee, which, in the case of the majority party, gives the Speaker effective control over the content of special rules governing the consideration of major legislation on the floor. Furthermore, the Speaker now has the power to refer legislation to multiple committees and set deadlines for committee action. In the House, therefore, the majority party leader can exercise a good deal of control over the process by which legislation is brought to the floor, debated, and subject to amendment.

In many cases, the House Speaker's new powers have been exercised in routine ways. The Speaker does not seek to influence most committee assignments, for example, because many committees have little relevance to partisan concerns or few members are competing for the available seats. For more routine legislation going through the Rules Committee, the committee relies on past experience to guide the design of rules, without consulting with the Speaker. Similarly, the parliamentarian makes recommendations on multiple referral based on established precedent and inter-committee agreements and the advice usually is followed. The Speaker seldom gets personally involved. The development of such standard operating practices is a natural product of the gradual accumulation of precedents under new rules and the desire of members and their staff to lend predictability to the process.

The new powers become a political tool only when the Speaker deliberately calls them into play. In the 1970s, Speakers Albert and O'Neill generally let their procedural tools sit idle. But since the late 1970s, the nature of the policy agenda and members' demands led speakers to employ their powers more often and aggressively. In fact, the speaker's bill referral and special rules prerogatives are a regular part of strategic calculations by most members on important, controversial legislation. As a result, the speaker frequently is brought into discussions about strategy by other members at early stages in their planning so that the speaker has regular opportunities to influence the policy directions taken by House committees and subcommittees.

Strategies of Adaptation

Party organizations and leaders are much more important to congressional policy making now than they were three decades ago. Four aspects of party responses to the changing conditions deserve summary.

EXPANDED SERVICES. Since the 1970s, congressional party organizations and leaders have greatly expanded the services they provide their members. In doing so, party leaders seek to both gain or maintain majority status and earn the gratitude of party colleagues. Secondary leaders – whips, the chairs of the campaign, policy, and research committees, and conference chairs and secretaries – who, in their effort to demonstrate their fitness for even higher positions, have led the way by diversifying services. As members compete for votes to get elected to party posts, they solicit ideas for new services and move to expand services once elected. While doing so, secondary leaders expand party staffs that they control and extend their own reach to a broader range of issues.

Party staffs now provide quite varied services: publications on the chamber schedules, legislation, policy problems, and political matters; email communications; clearinghouses for job applicants; analyses of floor voting records; assistance in the production of newsletters and graphics material; and facilities and staff assistance for the production of radio and television messages and programs. In the Senate, the parties maintain in-house cable television systems to provide senators' offices with up-to-the-minute information on floor developments and satellite up-link equipment so that senators can make live appearances on local stations or at meetings away from Washington. On a personal basis, leaders work harder to meet the scheduling demands of party colleagues and to assist colleagues in fundraising, campaigning, and attracting media attention.

STRATEGY OF INCLUSION. All leaders want fellow party members to feel that they have influence on party policy stances and tactics – a strategy of inclusion. All four party caucuses (or conferences) and many of the party committees meet regularly. Whip organizations have grown and task forces have multiplied to give more members an opportunity to participate in policy making beyond the confines of their assigned standing committees. Leaders also call together informal groups of members to solicit their views and encourage their participation through party channels. These developments contribute to leaders' efforts to gather information, promote a party spirit, solicit support, and build majority coalitions.

PROCEDURAL STRATEGIES. Leaders have expanded their repertoire of procedural strategies. The standard committee-to-floor-to-conference process remains, but variations on that process are now more common. Discussions in party councils are more likely to occur before action is taken in standing committees. Leaders more frequently engage in negotiations with committee and faction leaders after committees have reported legislation but before floor action. Party task forces have added a layer of party members who influence both the content of legislation and coalition-building strategy. At times, task forces even initiate legislation, and their proposals are taken directly to the floor by party leaders. Flexibility, not rigidity, characterizes the legislative process in recent Congresses.

Majority party leaders, particularly in the House where their formal powers are the strongest, use their procedural tools to set the agenda in a way that favors their party. This happens at two levels. On the first level, leaders more actively seek to set detailed policy agendas for their chamber, including a general schedule for action on major legislation. On the second level, leaders work harder to control the specific alternatives that are considered on the floor once legislation gets there. In the House, this is done through special rules written by the Rules Committee. Controlling alternatives is more difficult in the Senate, where unanimous consent must be obtained to structure the consideration of alternatives, a requirement that severely limits the ability of the majority leader to manipulate the floor agenda. Nevertheless, pressure to lend some structure to the process comes from members of both parties, all of whom have busy schedules and an interest in avoiding embarrassing or repetitious votes. At times, negotiating unanimous consent agreements becomes a full-time job for the majority leader.

PUBLIC RELATIONS. Leaders work harder to influence the image of their party that is communicated through the mass media. Such efforts are aimed at creating a climate of public opinion favorable to the party, which makes it easier for party members to support their leaders and explain their votes at home. If successful, leaders' media strategies produce support for party positions from independent-minded members who are not readily pressured.

Congressionally Speaking...

In 2004, Senate Democrats created a "war room" to coordinate public relations and legislative strategy on a bill to extend unemployment benefits. Party leaders and staff met there to respond to the rapid flow of attacks from the other side by utilizing the full range of media outlets. The war room operation was made a regular part of the Senate Democrats' leadership structure after the 2004 elections, when Democrats lost four Senate seats, to improve the "message strategy" of the party. The term was used in a political context by the campaign strategists in the 1992 presidential campaign of Bill Clinton to describe their headquarters and was made famous as the title of a film documentary on the campaign. The official name for the Senate Democrats' operation is the Senate Democratic Communications Center. All four congressional parties now have some form of war room operation.

Conclusion

The environment of the late twentieth century and early twenty-first century pushed congressional party leaders to the forefront of policy making. Party leaders are now central strategists and coordinators of policy development in Congress. It has not always been so. In the mid-twentieth century, party leaders coordinated the floor schedule and worked closely with committee leaders on strategy, but, for the most part, they left the development of legislative details to the standing committees and their chairs.

Party leaders are not all-powerful. Far from it. Congressional parties still lack the capacity to deny nomination or election to Congress and so have limited influence over their members, far less influence than exists in most other national legislatures. To be sure, the parties elect leadership, organize the standing committees, and structure floor and conference action. More-over, congressional parties' internal organizations and staffs have become more elaborate. And in the last two decades leaders have been prime movers in the legislative process on major issues. Nevertheless, diverse constituency interests across a large, heterogeneous country, the weakness of the parties in candidate selection, the fragmentation of American party organizations across several levels of government, and the difficulty of coordinating House and Senate activities stand in the way of party-directed policy making over the long term.

Above: Sen. Charles Schumer, D-NY, introduces Sen. Hillary Rodham Clinton, D-NY, prior to her testimony before the Senate Foreign Relations Committee regarding her nomination by President-elect Barack Obama to be Secretary of State on Capitol Hill in Washington on January 13, 2009. (UPI Photo/Roger L. Wollenberg)

Below: WASHINGTON, DC – Dec. 05: General Motors Chairman Richard Wagoner Jr.; Chrysler CEO Robert Nardelli; and Ford Motor Co. CEO Alan Mulally; during the House Financial Services hearing on potential financial aid legislation for the U.S. auto industry. (Photo by Scott J. Farrell/Congressional Quarterly)

6

The Standing Committees

O NE OF THE MOST VISIBLE AND ENDURING FEATURES OF CONGRESS IS
its committee system. From hearings to investigations to legislative
activity, committees are the congressional darlings of the mass media. And
considering the central role that committees play in modern-day lawmaking
and oversight, there is little wonder why they garner so much attention.
Most important legislation originates in a standing committee, most of the
details of legislation are approved in committee, and standing committee
members usually dominate floor and conference action. When legislation
dies, it usually does so in committee.

The significance of standing committees in the policy-making process
varies over time. In the mid-twentieth century, committees were often
described as nearly autonomous policy makers (see Chapter 2). The tremendous growth in government and power of the presidency that characterized
the New Deal and World War II era of the 1930s and 1940s led Congress
to reevaluate the way it did business. The Legislative Reorganization Act of
1946 reduced the number of standing committees, provided detailed, written committee jurisdictions, guaranteed a professional staff for each committee, and directed committees to conduct oversight of executive agencies.
As a result of the 1946 act, most of the key features of the modern committee system were put into place. Moreover, the leadership of the internally
divided Democratic majority usually preferred to defer to committees rather
than risk open divisions on the House and Senate floor. In fact, prescrip-
tive norms deference to committees and senior committee leaders – were
articulated by leaders to bolster the power of committees.

In recent decades, committees have lost much of the autonomy they had
gained in the middle of the twentieth century. A more assertive membership,
increasingly polarized parties, stronger party leadership, and new checks on

committee leadership, among other factors, reduced the level of independence once held by committees and their leaders. Still, committees retain a considerable amount of power within their issue domains; they process the vast majority of legislation that is approved by the House and Senate. In this chapter, we profile the House and Senate committee systems and then examine the foundations of committee power and how these powers have evolved over time.

Types of Committees

Modern congressional committees have two formal functions: (1) collecting information through hearings and investigations and (2) drafting and reporting legislation. Committee hearings are Congress's primary means for formally receiving the testimony of representatives of the executive branch, organized interest groups, independent experts, the general public, and, occasionally, movie stars. Congress usually relies on committees to investigate disasters (natural or human-made), scandals in government or elsewhere, or policy crises. Informally, congressional hearings provide opportunities for legislators to publicize causes and receive media attention. On the legislative side, the vast majority of bills and other legislation introduced by members are referred to the committee or committees with the appropriate jurisdiction. In committee meetings for considering legislation, called markups, the details of legislation are reviewed or written.

The House and Senate have developed several types of committees to perform these informational and legislative functions. All committees can hold hearings and investigate policy problems that fall within their jurisdiction. However, not all committees have the right to receive and report legislation, and not all committees are considered to be standing or permanent committees (Table 6.1).

Standing committees have legislative authority and permanent status (standing committee are listed in Table 6.2). Their legislative jurisdiction is specified in chamber rules and precedents, and they write and report legislation on any matter within their jurisdictions. Committee members, and particularly chairs, are territorial about their committees' jurisdictions and resist efforts to reduce or reallocate their jurisdictions. As a result, with a few important exceptions, change in the committee systems of the House and Senate has been incremental.

Ad hoc committees may be created and appointed to design and report legislation, but they are temporary and often dissolve either at a specified date or after reporting the legislation for which they were created. Since 1975,

TABLE 6.1. Types of Committees.

Permanent Status?	May report legislation to the floor?	
	Yes	No
Yes	standing committees	some select committees joint committees
No	conference committees most select committees ad hoc committees	

the Speaker of the House has been permitted to appoint ad hoc committees with House approval, but this authority has been used infrequently.

Conference committees are temporary and have legislative responsibilities. They are appointed to resolve the differences between House and Senate versions of legislation. The Constitution requires that legislation be approved in identical form by both chambers before it is sent to the president. While the Constitution is silent as to how the two chambers are to resolve their differences, conference committees were an almost immediate solution to this problem. Although inter-chamber differences can be resolved in other ways, conference committees are formed for most important legislation. Conference committees have wide, but not unlimited, discretion to redesign legislation in their efforts to gain House and Senate approval. In theory, conference committees are bound to the differences between the House and Senate legislation. In practice, however, it is not uncommon for conference committees to insert provisions into legislation that did not appear in either chamber's final legislation and remove provisions that were agreed upon by both chambers. When a majority of House conferees and a majority of Senate conferees agree, a conference committee issues a report that must be approved by both houses for the bill to be sent to the president. Conference committees dissolve as soon as one house takes action on the conference report.

Joint committees are permanent but lack legislative authority. Joint committees are composed of members from both chambers, and the chairs alternate between the chambers from Congress to Congress. The Joint Economic Committee frequently conducts highly publicized hearings on economic affairs, and the Joint Committee on Taxation serves primarily as a holding company for a respected staff of economists whose economic forecasts and reports on fiscal policy matters are frequently cited. The Joint Committee on

TABLE 6.2. Standing Committees of the House and Senate, 2009–2010.

House of Representatives Name (Number of Subcommittees)	Dems[c]	Reps[c]	Ratio[d]
Agriculture (6)	28	18	1.56:1
Appropriations (12)	37	23	1.61:1
Armed Services (7)	37	25	1.48:1
Budget (0)	24	15	1.60:1
Education and Labor (5)	29	19	1.53:1
Energy and Commerce (5)	36	23	1.57:1
Financial Services (6)	42	29	1.45:1
Foreign Affairs (7)	28	19	1.47:1
Homeland Security (6)	21	13	1.62:1
House Administration (0)	6	3	2:1
Judiciary (5)	23	16	1.43:1
Natural Resources (5)	28	20	1.40:1
Oversight and Government Reform (5)	25	16	1.56:1
Rules (2)	9	4	2.25:1
Science and Technology (5)	27	17	1.59:1
Select Committee on Intelligence[a] (4)	12	9	1.33:1
Small Business (5)	17	12	1.42:1
Standards of Official Conduct[b] (0)	5	5	1:1
Transportation and Infrastructure (6)	45	30	1.50:1
Veterans' Affairs (4)	18	11	1.64:1
Ways and Means (6)	26	15	1.73:1

Senate Name (Number of Subcommittees)	Dems[e]	Reps	Ratio[d]
Agriculture, Nutrition, and Forestry (4)	12	9	1.33:1
Appropriations (12)	17	13	1.31:1
Armed Services (6)	15	11	1.36:1
Banking, Housing, and Urban Affairs (5)	13	10	1.3:1
Budget (0)	13	10	1.3:1
Commerce, Science, and Transportation (7)	14	11	1.27:1
Energy and Natural Resources (4)	13	10	1.3:1
Environment and Public Works (6)	11	8	1.38:1
Finance (5)	13	10	1.3:1
Foreign Relations (7)	11	8	1.38:1
Health, Education, Labor, and Pensions (3)	13	10	1.3:1
Homeland Security and Governmental Affairs (5)	10	7	1.43:1
Select Committee on Indian Affairs (0)	8	6	1.33:1
Judiciary (7)	11	8	1.3:1
Rules and Administration (0)	11	8	1.3:1
Select Committee on Intelligence[a] (0)	8	7	1.14:1
Select Committee on Ethics[b] (0)	3	3	1:1
Small Business and Entrepreneurship (0)	11	8	1.3:1
Veterans' Affairs (0)	9	6	1.5:1

a = The two intelligence committees are officially named select committees but have authority to report legislation. b = The House Committee on Standards of Official Conduct may report legislation; the Senate Ethics Committee does not have legislative authority. c = Numbers include only full members of the chamber and vacant seats allotted to the party. d = Party ratio is (Democrats: Republicans). Ratios in House and Senate chambers are 1.43:1 and 1.41:1, respectively (counting the independent senators among the Democrats). e = Independent Senators Bernie Sanders (I-VT) and Joseph Lieberman (I-CT) are counted among the Democrats. *Source:* www.house.gov; www.senate.gov.

Printing performs the more ministerial duty of overseeing the Government Printing Office; the Joint Committee on the Library oversees the Library of Congress. Bills are not referred to joint committees, and joint committees cannot report legislation to the floor. The Joint Committee on Atomic Energy (1946–1977) was the only joint committee to date with authority to report legislation.

Select, or special, committees are, in principle, temporary committees without legislative authority. They may be used to study problems that fall under the jurisdiction of several standing committees, to symbolize Congress's commitment to major constituency groups, or simply to reward particular legislators. Select committees have been used for seven prominent investigations since 1970, including the Senate's 1973 investigation of the Watergate break-in and cover-up and the 1987 House and Senate investigation of the Iran-Contra affair. Major reforms of congressional rules and organizations have originated in select committees.

Unfortunately, committee nomenclature can be misleading. For example, the House and Senate have each made their Select Intelligence Committee permanent and granted it the power to report legislation. Some select committees, such as the House Committee on Homeland Security, began as select committees and gained standing status later. In 1993, under pressure to streamline the legislative process and reduce spending, the House abolished its Select Committee on Aging, Hunger, Narcotics Abuse and Control and its Select Committee on Children, Youth and Families. The Senate maintains a Special Committee on Aging, which studies issues relevant to the elderly, in addition to the Select Committee on Ethics, which handles ethics violations of senators and staffs.

Standing committees are the primary concern of this chapter. In the modern Congress, standing committees originate most legislation, and their members manage the legislation on the floor and dominate conference committees. Unless otherwise indicated, the following discussion concerns standing committees.

The Nature of Congressional Committees

The Constitution makes no provision for committees. Yet, committees emerged early in congressional history. And across time the committee system has undergone considerable change. At different points in history the House and Senate have adopted rules to expand and reduce the number of committees, as well as to modify their structure and authority. Given the emergence and longevity of committees, it is clear that the division of labor that allows each chamber to pursue multiple hearings and legislative efforts simultaneously has proven useful.

To whom are committees responsible? What interests do committees serve? Such questions have motivated an important literature in political science. Three prominent perspectives offer rationale for the existence of committees – the information, distributive, and partisan perspectives.

Informational Politics: Committees Governed by Floor Majorities

One view of congressional committees is that they are designed to meet legislators' need for information about policy problems and solutions. Given Congress's large workload and the complexity of issues, it is unrealistic to expect members to have the capacity to make informed decisions on all matters. By focusing on the issues before their own committees, legislators gain expertise that is applied in a committee setting to improve the fit of policy solutions to policy problems. The expertise serves the interest of the larger membership by generating information that is useful to all legislators in evaluating the recommendations of committees.

In this view, committee experts serve the interest of a majority of the parent chamber. If committee recommendations diverge too much from the preferences of the floor majority or prove misleading, floor majorities will reject committee recommendations and may even reform the committee system. Under normal circumstances, the better-informed arguments of committee experts will guide the behavior of other legislators.

Distributive Politics: Autonomous Committees

A classic view of congressional committees is the distributive theory. This perspective suggests that committees exist to help members secure gains from trade of policy benefits across constituencies with diverse interests. Committees are created to address the legislative interests of constituencies who are important to legislators' reelection efforts. The multiple committees of each chamber allow legislators to gain membership on the committee or committees most relevant to their own constituencies.

By empowering committees, each chamber gives legislators with the strongest constituency interest in a policy area the most influence over legislative action. Because members represent diverse constituencies, the committee system institutionalizes a mutually beneficial arrangement for legislators who want to do favors for home audiences. Public policy is then

SOMETIMES A SENSE OF HUMOR IS REQUIRED

Senators do not always get their first choice of subcommittees. In an interview, Senator Amy Klobuchar (D-Minnesota) told a reporter about her first day on the Subcommittee on Oceans, Atmosphere, Fisheries, and Coast Guard:

Somehow I got placed on the Ocean Subcommittee. I didn't ask for that. But it does have jurisdiction over the Great Lakes, which is important, and so I can be a voice for the Great Lakes. But when I got there the first I realized all the other senators had an ocean. Olympia Snowe (R-Maine) was on there, John Kerry (D-Massachusetts) was on there. And I wrote a note to Frank Lautenberg (D-New Jersey) and I said, "I am the only senator on the Oceans Subcommittee without an ocean." And he wrote back, "Just come back next year and ask for one."

Source: http://blog.washingtonpost.com/sleuth/2007/06/post 1.html

the product of a giant "logroll" – each committee of legislators getting what it wants.

From the perspective of distributive politics, committees serve the interests of individual legislators and their home constituencies (see box "Sometimes a Sense of Humor Is Required"). Therefore, the committee system reflects the pluralism of American politics and permits legislators to focus on the political interests that matter most to them. The distributive perspective considers committees to be relatively autonomous units to which parties and the parent chambers defer. Each committee operates in a community of executive branch agencies and interest groups with similar interests. The larger public interest may suffer as the demands of the disparate constituencies are addressed by committees.

Partisan Politics: Committees Governed by the Majority Party

The partisan perspective posits that parties create committees to better ensure the success of party programs. On committees whose jurisdictions matter to the majority party, party leaders make committee assignments to enhance the party's policy prospects. This, along with expectations of loyalty, constrains the behavior of committee members. And since the majority party has a numerical advantage on committees, it ultimately dictates the policies that emerge.

From this perspective, committee members serve the interests of the parties. While each chamber approves committee membership lists, each party determines which of its members are on each committee list. Parties structure the internal organization of committees – the majority party assumes the chairmanships and controls most staff. And the majority party leadership schedules committee legislation for action on the floor.

In Practice: Committees Governed by Multiple Principals

In practice, committee members must balance conflicting demands placed on them by their parent chambers, parties, and constituencies. While seeking to satisfy the expectations of constituents, they must stay on good terms with party colleagues to retain important committee positions and must meet chamber majorities' expectations to get legislation passed. Fortunate legislators find that the demands of constituents, party leaders, and the chamber majority are aligned most of the time, but real-world politics require many committee members to take risks, balance interests, and struggle with difficult choices.

The extent of independent committee influence over policy outcomes varies over time and across committees. Three sets of factors stand out for their impact on the relationship between committees and their principals: The character of the policy agenda, party strength, and institutional context.

SIZE AND SALIENCE OF THE POLICY AGENDA. The size and salience of the congressional agenda affects the importance of committees to the parties and all chamber members. A large policy workload requires the division of labor that a system of committees provides, but only issues that are salient to a large number of legislators will attract the attention of party leaders or rank-and-file members on the floor. Committees with jurisdictions that affect narrow constituencies are unlikely to be supervised by party leaders or given serious problems on the floor.

MAJORITY PARTY STRENGTH. Political scientists have observed that when parties lack cohesiveness because of internal divisions over policy, less authority is extended to party leaders to pursue partisan objectives. Under these conditions, strong-arm tactics are not tolerated and will alienate large numbers of partisans. Committee delegations will recognize party leaders' weakness and operate with little fear of retribution. In contrast, a cohesive majority party will expect its leaders to work pro-actively for party positions and pressure committee chairs and members to support the party.

INSTITUTIONAL CONTEXT. The House and Senate operate under very different rules. The larger, more unwieldy House has a stronger presiding officer and relies more heavily on formal rules than the Senate does. Senate rules protect each senator's right, on most legislation, to offer amendments on any subject and to conduct extended debate. In doing so, Senate rules protect individual initiative and create more opportunities to resist committee- or party-imposed policy choices. As a result, senators have more bargaining leverage with committee and party leaders than do representatives.

The Power of Modern Committees

Committees' power is expressly or implicitly granted to them by the parent chambers and parties. Their continued existence and parliamentary privileges depend on the sufferance of the parent houses and parties. The parent chambers formally approve all committee assignments, but the parties construct the committee lists that are routinely ratified by the chambers. This function gives the parties a source of leverage with committee members and allows the parties – and, most important, the majority parties – to regulate the behavior of committee members through formal and informal rules. For the most part, committees must function procedurally and substantively in ways that are consistent with the expectations of their parent chambers and parties.

The Legislative Power of Committees

Evaluating the power of committees is difficult. It is very difficult to determine the influence of a committee on any given measure without knowing what the outcome would have been in the absence of committee involvement. Nevertheless, it is reasonable to infer that committees exercise real power in the modern Congress. Much of their power stems from the indifference of most members about the details of most legislation. Committees are extended considerable autonomy because most matters over which they have jurisdiction are of some importance to committee members and little, if any, importance to most other members. Parties and leaders focus on the few issues each year that are likely to affect the parties' reputations and electoral prospects. Members do not and cannot take an interest in the details of much, and probably even most, of the legislation that is considered on the floor.

Even when members are not indifferent, committees still have advantages that give their members disproportionate influence over policy outcomes. Mounting real challenges to their power can be difficult. Threats to strip a committee of jurisdiction, funding, or parliamentary privileges or to retract members' committee assignments usually are not credible, if for no other reason than such actions would set precedents that members of other committees would not like to see established (see box "Committee Leaders Complain About Declining Influence"). In this way an implicit, self-enforcing pact among members underpins committee power. The most practical means for keeping committees in check is to reject their policy recommendations.

It is convenient to consider two forms of committee power.

- Positive power is the ability of committees to gain the approval of legislation opposed by others.
- Negative power is the ability of committees to block legislation favored by others.

On both counts, committees have substantial advantages over other players.

POSITIVE POWER. At first glance, committees appear to have no positive power. Under the Constitution, legislation can be enacted only by the full House and Senate. Neither chamber has rules that permit a committee to act on the chamber's behalf with respect to final approval of legislation. Thus, positive power for committees must come from sources other than the explicit provisions of chamber rules.

Standing committees start with considerable discretion in writing and reporting legislation. They are free to act as they see fit on most legislation that is referred to them. They may simply refuse to act, hold hearings but take no legislative action, amend the legislation in any way, or accept the legislation without change. They may also write their own legislation, or they may vote to report legislation with a recommendation that it pass, with no recommendation, or with a recommendation that it be rejected.

Nevertheless, committees are not guaranteed that their legislation will receive favorable consideration on the House and Senate floors. To gain passage of legislation that might not otherwise pass, committees may exploit four sources of potential positive committee power: (1) *persuasion* on the basis of superior argument and information about the merits of legislation, (2) *leverage* acquired through threats of unfavorable action on members' bills if they fail to cooperate with a committee on its agenda, (3) *strategic packaging* of unpopular legislative provisions with more popular provisions to win floor majorities, and (4) *domination of conference committees* to gain chamber endorsement of policy provisions favored by the committee. Each of these deserves a brief mention.

COMMITTEE LEADERS COMPLAIN ABOUT DECLINING INFLUENCE

Early in 2009, Speaker Nancy Pelosi dealt with an open revolt from committee leaders who were upset about major bills, such as the economic stimulus package, being written in Pelosi's office rather than in committee. The stimulus bill was not subject to the "regular order" or committee hearings and markups before a floor vote. This angered top-ranking committee members who see their influence raining on key pieces of legislation. Bart Stupak (D-Michigan) chair of the Energy and Commerce subcommittee said, "The question is: Are we [committees] going to get a chance to legislate?"

Despite the fact that most Democrats supported the general outlines of the legislation crafted in Pelosi's office, many fear that committee power may erode permanently. Referring to the new top-down process, one unnamed Democrat remarked, "One of the problems is that I think the Speaker thinks this is the regular order." For her part, Pelosi urged patience and suggested that these steps were necessary to insure quick action on important legislation such as the stimulus bill.

Source: Jared Allen. "Panel Chairmen Fighting Mad over snubs by Pelosi." The Hill, January 15, 2009.

First, committees can usually gain a tactical edge by being better informed than their opponents. Committee members sit through hearings, participate in discussions with lobbyists and executive branch officials, and often have previous experience with the issues their committee deals with. Committees' large, expert staffs and their extensive networks of allies in the executive branch and interest group community further enhance their informational advantage over competitors. Traditional norms such as serving an apprenticeship before actively participating, developing expertise in the jurisdiction of one's committees, and deferring to committee specialists reflect the importance of informational advantages for committee power.

Second, the ability of committees to obstruct action on some legislation can be used to gain leverage with members whose support is needed on other legislation. Particularly in the House, where circumventing a committee is neither easy nor convenient, obstructing action on legislation can be used as a threat to win support for committee recommendations.

Third, within the bounds of their broad jurisdictions, committees may package provisions addressing multiple subjects in legislation. By doing so, they can combine the unpopular provisions with more popular provisions to win support for bills. In the House, this power is enhanced when a committee can acquire a special rule from the Rules Committee that limits amendments to the unpopular provisions when the legislation is considered on the floor.

Fourth, members of committees gain positive power through their domination of conference committees. Conference negotiations between the House and Senate give conferees considerable flexibility to alter chamber decisions. The conferees know that they are free to exercise such discretion provided that they can attract majority support for the conference report – which cannot be amended on the House or Senate floor – when it is returned to the two chambers for final approval. The ability of conferees to choose any policy outcome that is at least as preferred to no bill by the two chambers often renders opposition to the committee's preferences futile.

NEGATIVE POWER. The negative power of standing committees rests in their ability to control newly introduced legislation and to obstruct alternative routes to the floor. The ability to obstruct action is often called "gatekeeping" in theories of politics. Committees' negative power is much stronger in the House than the Senate.

In the House, negative power is supported by rules that give committees near-monopoly control over newly introduced legislation and make circumventing committees difficult. House Rule 10 requires that all legislation relating to a committee's jurisdiction be referred to that committee, a rule that has been in place since 1880. Before 1975, the single committee with the most relevant jurisdiction would receive the referral, a process that often involved direct conflicts between committees with related jurisdictions. Since 1975, the rule has provided for multiple referral by granting to the Speaker the authority to refer legislation to each committee with relevant jurisdiction. Monopoly control by single committees was broken by the new rule, but the practice of referring nearly all legislation to committee remains in place.

Committees' blocking power is enhanced by their domination of conference committees. The wide latitude extended to conferences to design the final form of legislation gives committee members another opportunity to wield negative powers. Committee members appointed to conference can, and frequently do, delete provisions they find objectionable. Because conference reports cannot be amended when sent to the House and Senate floors, it is difficult to reverse a conference committee's surgical removal of legislative provisions. Conferees also can take the more drastic step of refusing to file a conference report, thus blocking the legislation in its entirety, at least temporarily.

Circumventing House committees is difficult but not impossible under House rules. The House operates under a germaneness rule that requires a floor amendment to be relevant to the section of the bill or resolution it seeks to modify. Thus, it is difficult to bring to the floor as an amendment a policy proposal whose subject has not been addressed in legislation reported by a committee. The germaneness rule can be waived, but only if a special rule from the Rules Committee is approved by a majority on the House floor. The Speaker's control of the Rules Committee means that this approach is unlikely to work without the Speaker's cooperation.

House rules provide additional means for bringing legislation to the floor. At certain times, members may move to suspend the rules to consider a measure blocked by a committee. Going this route is usually not feasible without the consent of the relevant committee because the member must be recognized by the Speaker to make the motion and two-thirds of the House must support it.

A second route is to gain a special rule from the Rules Committee to discharge a measure from committee. This route requires Rules Committee support and majority support in the House for the special rule. The Speaker's cooperation is typically required to gain Rules Committee action on such a rule.

Alternatively, party leaders occasionally circumvent committees by drafting legislation themselves or by delegating this responsibility to task forces or special committees. Task forces are ad hoc panels typically created by party leaders to carry out legislative duties. Party leaders may use task forces if they are concerned that a committee with jurisdiction will perform unsatisfactorily. For example, they may fear that the committee will not reach an agreement in a timely fashion or that it will produce a bill that either cannot pass the chamber or will not satisfy majority party members. When legislation is drafted in a task force, party leaders determine which members are charged with drafting the legislation and, in the House, can and often do exclude minority party members from the process.

Finally, House members may seek to discharge a measure from a committee that fails to report it within thirty days of referral. Any member may file a discharge petition, which requires the signatures of 218 members. Once the petition receives the necessary number of signatures, it is placed on the Discharge Calendar for consideration on the second or fourth Monday of the month following a seven legislative day waiting period. Many members are hesitant to encourage the use of discharge petitions because doing so threatens the power of their own committees. Nevertheless, there has been more interest in discharge petitions since late 1993, when the House voted to make public the names of members who sign them. Public disclosure makes it easier to generate public or interest group pressure on members to sign petitions.

The discharge petition may appear to be the most promising route for circumventing committees because it does not require the assistance of the Rules Committee or the Speaker. In fact, between 1931 and 2002, 563 discharge petitions were filed, but the petitions gained the required number of signatures only 48 times. Of the 48 instances in which discharge petitions gained the necessary 218 signatures, only 19 times did the discharged measure go on to pass the House. However, the threatened use of discharge petitions, special rules, and suspension of the rules occasionally has stimulated committees to act in accordance with the floor majority's preferences. For example, between 1931 and 1994 there were 15 cases in which the needed 218 signatures were acquired on a discharge petition, but the majority leadership called up the legislation for consideration by other means.

The Senate's rules create weaker blocking power for its committees. Senate committees lack much of the negative power that House committees enjoy. Although measures are routinely referred to Senate committees upon their introduction, a senator can easily object to a referral and keep a measure on the calendar for floor consideration. Furthermore, the Senate lacks a germaneness rule for most measures, so senators are able to circumvent committees by offering whole bills as amendments to unrelated legislation. Senators often hesitate to support efforts to bypass a committee in this way, but it is a procedural route that is used much more frequently than are the more complicated House procedures for circumventing committees. Moreover, most conference reports are potentially subject to filibusters in the Senate, giving Senate minorities a source of bargaining leverage over committee members at the conference stage that does not exist in the House.

Nevertheless, in practice, Senate committees do retain some blocking power. Calling up a measure from the calendar requires the cooperation of the majority leader, who usually sides with the committee chair on procedural matters. And if the majority leader cooperates, committee members, like all senators, may filibuster or threaten to filibuster unfriendly legislation. Consequently, successful circumvention of a committee on a controversial matter often requires the support of at least 60 senators, the number needed to invoke cloture.

Nongermane amendments are troublesome for Senate committees, but they can often be set aside by a motion to table. A successful motion to table kills the amendment. Because a tabling motion is not debatable

CIRCUMVENTING UNFRIENDLY COMMITTEES

For Senator Sam Brownback, a Republican from Kansas, banning human cloning became a key legislative objective. Twice in the 107th Congress (2001–2002), Brownback introduced legislation that fell into the unfriendly jurisdiction of the Judiciary Committee. Senator Orrin Hatch (R-Utah), chair of the Judiciary Committee, openly stated that he supported scientific endeavors that could lead to finding cures for diseases.

On his third attempt at passing the legislation calling for a ban on human cloning, however, Senator Brownback manipulated the legislation to circumvent the Judiciary Committee. Knowing that Senator Judd Gregg (R-New Hampshire), chair of the Health, Education, Labor, and Pension (HELP) Committee, was supportive of his legislation, as were other HELP Committee members, Brownback changed the legislation so that a different part of existing law would be modified. Instead of calling upon the U.S. penal code, which falls under the jurisdiction of Judiciary, Brownback altered the legislation so that the ban would be enacted under the Public Service Act, which is under the jurisdiction of the HELP Committee. In response to this maneuver, a GOP senior aide said with understatement, "There are parliamentary conventions that can be used or abused to ensure referral to a more friendly committee."

Source: Emily Pierce, "Leaders Circumvent Hatch," *Roll Call*, February 5, 2003.

(and therefore cannot be filibustered) and is a procedural question, it often attracts more votes than would be cast against the amendment itself. Moreover, the members of conference committees have an opportunity to drop adopted nongermane amendments in conference.

In short, under most circumstances committees in both chambers – but especially in the House – exercise considerable negative power. Circumventing committees requires special effort and is usually possible only with the cooperation of the majority party leadership.

Oversight and the Investigative Power of Modern Committees

Central to the legislative power of committees and vital to the power of Congress as an institution is the ability of committees to oversee and investigate governmental or private activity that is or might be the subject of public policy. Courts have ruled that Congress's power to compel cooperation with its investigations is implicit in its constitutional functions of legislating and appropriating funds. Without broad powers to investigate and compel cooperation, Congress would not be able to exercise its legislative powers effectively.

Congressionally Speaking . . .

As part of their oversight and investigative powers, committees and subcommittees are authorized by House and Senate rules to issue *subpoenas* – formal writs compelling a recipient to testify or produce documents (or both) to the committee or subcommittee from which they originated. Typically committees/subcommittees receive the information they need without forcing compliance. Should the President invoke executive privilege or an official simply refuse to cooperate, however, subpoenas help equip committees to carry out investigations.

The decision rules for issuing a subpoena vary across committees, as they are not codified by chamber rules and parent bodies extend considerable autonomy to committees in determining their internal proceedings. House rules only require that a quorum (majority) be present at the time that the subpoena is agreed to. House rules also allow the committee/subcommittee to delegate subpoena power to full committee chairs. Senate rules provide even less guidance. It is important to note, however, that federal courts have established basic requirements that subpoenas must satisfy in order to be recognized as legitimate.

Throughout the history of Congress, committees have been the vehicle for conducting congressional investigations. Select or special committees have been appointed for many important investigations. In the last three decades, important investigations of the Watergate break-in and cover-up, the involvement of the Central Intelligence Agency in assassinations, and the Iran-Contra affair were conducted by select committees.

Since the passage of the Legislative Reorganization Act of 1946, standing committees have been assigned the duty of maintaining "continuous watchfulness" over executive branch activities within their jurisdictions. The 1946 act also created two committees with governmentwide oversight duties, now called the House Committee on Oversight and Government Reform and the Senate Committee on Homeland Security and Governmental Affairs. Both committees attract members who want to participate in hearings on and investigations into a wide range of government activity.

The 1946 act was reinforced by stronger directives to committees in the Legislative Reorganization Act of 1970, which required most committees to write biennial reports on their oversight activities. Moreover, during the 1970s both chambers assigned oversight responsibility for several broad policy areas to multiple committees to encourage oversight. Furthermore, the

House instructed many committees to create oversight subcommittees and allowed them to add an oversight subcommittee beyond the limit for the number of subcommittees that would otherwise apply. With these developments, committee staffs devoted to oversight expanded greatly in the 1970s, which enabled committees and subcommittees to organize more hearings and more extensive investigations.

Oversight became an increasingly important part of committee activity. In 1961, less than 10 percent of committee meetings and hearings were devoted to oversight; by 1983, more than 25 percent were devoted to oversight. The biggest surge occurred in the 1970s and appears to have been the product of several factors: the new independence of subcommittee chairs to pursue oversight, the expanded capacity of larger committee and subcommittee staffs to conduct oversight activities, tensions between a Democratic Congress and a Republican administration, and a generally more assertive Congress. The proportion of meetings and hearings dedicated to oversight continued to rise throughout most of the 1990s, as congressional Republicans aggressively investigated the Clinton administration. By 1997, nearly 34 percent of all committee hearings and meetings were devoted to oversight.

Declining Committee Autonomy

Committee power has been under siege since the early 1970s. Although committees continue to draft the details of nearly all legislation and their members remain central players in nearly all policy decisions, they have become less autonomous as their parent houses and parties have exercised more control over their operations and policy choices. Change has been most dramatic in the House of Representatives, where committees appeared to have dominated policy making during the middle decades of the twentieth century. The forces producing change in the role of committees in recent decades are similar to the forces that have been active throughout Congress's history – the policy agenda, strength of congressional parties, and the institutional context.

Changing Policy Agenda

Changes in the policy agenda have led to a decline in the autonomy of committees in recent decades. Many new and salient issues arose in the 1960s and 1970s, such as consumer protection, civil rights, and numerous others. Some of the emerging issues, like energy and the environment, were

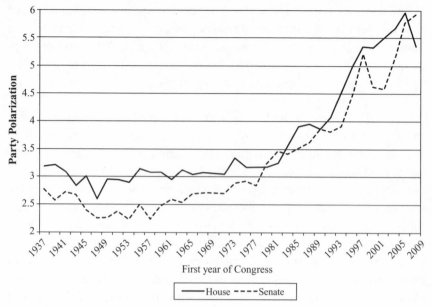

FIGURE 6.1. Party Polarization in the House and Senate, 1937–2008. *Source:* Common space scores from http://voteview.com/dwnl.htm. Calculations by the authors. Note: The measure of polarization is taken from Elizabeth Rybicki, Steven S. Smith, and Ryan Vander Wielen, "Congressional Committee Bias, 1963–2002." Paper presented at the 2003 meetings of the American Political Science Association.

interconnected, sparked controversy, and stimulated the growth of interest groups. They energized outsiders to seek influence over committees' policy choices and pitted powerful committees against one another. As a result, more controversy spilled out of the committee rooms and onto the chamber floors. Since the late 1970s, the struggle with budget deficits led Congress to adopt rules that limited the policy discretion of most congressional commit-tees. As we report in Chapter 12, the effect of the budget rules was a shift in emphasis from authorizing to appropriating committees and increased control over committee action by party and budget leaders.

Changing Party Strength

The increasing polarization of congressional parties (see Figure 6.1) has generated demands for central leaders to become more assertive. Thus, party leaders have clamped down on committee autonomy. Furthermore, the rank-and-file members of the parties, particularly in the House, have become less tolerant of committee and subcommittee chairs' deviating from party policy positions. Following the Republican takeover of 1994, Republican and

Democratic majorities alike have been particularly aggressive in expressing their expectations of committee leaders.

The increase in activity by the party organizations and leaders during recent years is noted in Chapter 5. The party organizations now provide more opportunities for meaningful participation in policy making outside of members' assigned committees. The parties have provided forums, such as task forces, for those outside of committees to challenge the committees and their leaders and even to devise legislation for floor consideration. In the House, party leaders have frequently negotiated legislation after a committee has reported a bill and placed the negotiated provisions in the bill through use of a special rule from the Rules Committee.

Changing Institutional Context

Committee autonomy has been further undermined by rules changes that either directly regulated committee behavior or made it easier for members to challenge committee recommendations. These new rules were pursued by members who were unhappy with the nearly dictatorial control that some full committee chairs exercised over legislative proceedings. They reflected an effort to make committees – and especially committee leaders – more accountable to rank-and-file members of the parent chamber and to make members less dependent on committees for information and advice.

SUNSHINE RULES. Sunshine rules – rules that open congressional activity to public scrutiny – have contributed to the diminishing autonomy of standing committees. One such rule requires that roll-call votes cast in committee be recorded in documents that are open to the public. This rule was amended in 2007 to exclude votes taken in the Rules Committee. Another rule dictates that committee markups be held in public sessions (except for meetings concerned with national security matters) unless a majority of committee members cast a recorded vote in favor of closing a meeting. Even conference committees are required to hold their meetings in open sessions unless, as the House rule requires, a majority of the parent chamber approves the use of closed meetings. The rules were intended to make committee members more accountable, both to outside constituencies and to their colleagues. In recent Congresses, committees have voted more frequently to close meetings to the public, and they have become more creative in their efforts to sidestep the rules. In some cases, members appear to have allowed staff to negotiate legislative details to avoid holding official meetings subject to open-meeting rules. But party leaders have attempted to reinforce the sunshine rules by requiring that committees accommodate television and radio broadcasts and still photographers whenever a meeting is open to the public.

BILL REFERRAL RULES IN THE HOUSE. In 1974, the Speaker of the House was granted the authority to send legislation to committees jointly, sequentially, or in parts. Before 1974, the Speaker was required to assign legislation to the single committee that had the most relevant jurisdiction, a practice that guaranteed monopoly referral rights to a single committee in each policy area. Under the current rule, adopted in 1995, sending a bill jointly to more than one committee is no longer possible, but the Speaker may still establish a sequence of committees for consideration or split a bill into parts that are referred to different committees (sequential and split referral). In fact, in recent Congresses, about one-fourth of the workload for the average House committee has consisted of multiply referred legislation. In the Senate, all three forms of multiple referral are possible upon a joint motion of the majority and minority leaders. Multiple referral remains far less common in the Senate than in the House, perhaps because committees can more easily protect their jurisdictional interests by seeking to amend legislation on the floor.

Multiple referral in the House generates greater interdependence among committees and with the Speaker, reducing committee autonomy. Multiple referral creates more potential conflicts among committees and increases the number of legislators with some role in committee action on the affected bills. Sometimes the conflict among committees spills onto the House floor, where party leaders are asked to intercede. And, perhaps most important, multiple referral substantially strengthens the Speaker's influence over committee decisions. The Speaker determines, without appeal, the referral of legislation to multiple committees and may set deadlines for committee action in such cases. In designing such arrangements, the Speaker is in a position to advantage some committees, speed or delay committee action for strategic purposes, and send strong signals about his or her policy preferences.

VOTING RULES. Weakening committee autonomy and the demise of deference to committees are reflected in the record of floor-amending activity since the mid-1950s. In terms of both the absolute number of floor amendments, the number of amendments per measure, and the proportion of measures amended on the floor, floor-amending activity increased in both chambers during the 1950s and 1960s and surged upward in the 1970s. In the Senate, the number of floor amendments nearly tripled between the mid-1950s and late 1970s, with most of the increase occurring in the 1960s.

The number of House floor amendments more than quadrupled between the mid-1950s and the late 1970s, with most of the increase occurring in the early 1970s after the introduction of recorded electronic voting. Previously, recorded votes were not possible on most amendments, which made it difficult to bring public pressure to bear and enhanced the influence of powerful insiders, particularly committee chairs.

Floor-amending activity was perceived to be a more serious problem in the House and the House majority party could change its practices in response. The most important response was the expanded use of special rules to limit floor amendments. Most rules have not foreclosed floor amendments, but they have required that amendment sponsors notify the Rules Committee in advance, which permits the Rules Committee to arrange for their order of consideration and allows committee leaders to prepare against unfriendly amendments (see Chapters 7 and 8).

No effective constraints on floor-amending activity for the purpose of enhancing committee autonomy are possible in the Senate. The minority would prevent a vote on any reform that would put it at a disadvantage. In only two areas, budget measures and certain trade agreements, has the Senate moved to limit debate and amendments. In general, therefore, a majority of senators have no way to insulate committee bills from unfriendly or nongermane amendments whose sponsors are committed to offering them.

CONFERENCE RULES. The ability of committees to control conference negotiations on behalf of their chambers has long been a vital source of power. In the House of the 1970s and 1980s, challenges to committee autonomy were accompanied by challenges to committees' monopoly over appointments to conference delegations. New rules were adopted imploring the Speaker to appoint delegations that represented House preferences, to include members who had sponsored major components of the legislation in question, and to require conferences to hold their meetings in public sessions. The rules were targeted at senior committee members who had dominated conferences for decades. The Speaker's control over conference delegations was reinforced in 1993 when the House adopted a rule giving the Speaker the power to remove a member from a conference delegation at any time. In spite of these rules, few members not sitting on the standing committees originating legislation are appointed to conference committees.

RANK-AND-FILE RESOURCES. Individual members now have far more sources of information at their disposal than they once did in the mid-twentieth century, so the traditional advantage enjoyed by committee members over rank-and-file members – greater access to expertise and staff assistance – has been reduced. Over the years, changes in House and Senate rules have allowed members to expand their personal staffs. Much of a member's personal staff is devoted to nonlegislative duties such as answering the mail and handling constituents' problems with the federal agencies. Nevertheless, the great expansion in members' personal staffs has allowed legislators to draw on staff for assistance in developing legislative proposals, making arguments, and soliciting support – often in opposition to committee positions. Furthermore, members may draw on the congressional support agencies. These agencies often conduct studies for or delegate staff to congressional committees, but they also respond to requests for information from individual members and their staffs. As a result of the increased availability of these varied sources of information, an enterprising member can equip himself or herself to challenge committee members' arguments. Thus, seldom does a committee now command deference on the basis of policy expertise alone.

Committee Membership

At the start of each new Congress, members of the House and new members of the Senate seek committee assignments that will shape their daily schedules and perhaps their electoral and legislative futures. Returning members are routinely reappointed to their former committees, following the "property right" norm, unless they seek to improve their situation by transferring to other committees, as a few always do. State delegations, intra-party factions, and lobbyists work to maximize their influence over policy by getting friendly members onto the right committees.

Committee Size and Party Ratios

Majority and minority party leaders negotiate the number of Democratic and Republican seats on each committee, with the majority leaders having the upper hand because of their ability to win a floor vote on the resolutions that provide for the allocation of seats to each party. With important exceptions in the House, seats on most committees are allocated roughly in proportion to the size of each party. The exceptions are the House Appropriations, Budget, Rules, and Ways and Means Committees – which are particularly important committees so the majority party reserves a larger-than-proportionate number of seats for themselves (see Table 6.2). The House and Senate ethics committees are the only committees on which there is an equal number of majority and minority party members.

Committee Assignments

In each chamber, committee seats are filled on the basis of recommendations from each party. For example, the House rule states that "the House shall fill a vacancy on a standing committee by election on the nomination of the respective party caucus or conference." To accomplish this, each House and Senate party has its own committee on committees, which is responsible for making committee lists. Assignment decisions depend on the number of vacancies, the number of members competing for assignments, and rules on the number and type of assignments each member may hold. New members and returning members seeking new assignments must compete for support from the members of their party's committee on committees to gain assignment to the committees they want.

THE HOUSE. For the first time in 1995, as proposed by the new Republican majority that year, the House adopted a rule restricting the number of committee assignments its members may hold. The two parties had had internal rules, but the Republicans imposed the new rule and Democrats retained it after gaining a House majority in 2006. The rule prohibits a member from holding more than two standing committee assignments and more than four subcommittee assignments on standing committees. The two parties supplement this restriction by treating four committees (Appropriations, Energy and Commerce, Rules, and Ways and Means) as "exclusive" committees. Members serving on these committees are not permitted to hold seats on other committees. Both parties also identify "exempt" committees (Select Committee on Intelligence and Standards of Official Conduct) that do not count against a member's committee membership limit.

In recent years, both House parties have become less inclined to grant exemptions to their limits on assignments. Traditionally, members have received exemptions with relative ease and have been allowed to maintain them indefinitely. But leaders of both House parties grew frustrated with the number of members who expected to receive exemptions and retain coveted extra seats. Upon becoming leader of the House Democrats at the end of 2002, Nancy Pelosi (D-California) strictly applied party rules limiting committee assignments. In 2005, Pelosi decided against granting John Larson (D-Connecticut) a waiver that would have allowed him to keep his position as ranking member on the House Administration Committee after having been chosen to sit on the Ways and Means Committee. House Republicans approved a party rule in 2004 that requires members who have received a waiver to committee assignment limits to reapply every two years. Moreover,

HOW TO DISCIPLINE A WAYWARD MEMBER?

Senator Joseph Lieberman has had a strained relationship with Senate Democrats in the past few years. First, the former vice-presidential nominee filed and ran as an Independent in 2006 after losing the Democratic primary. He continued to caucus with Democrats after the 2006 election, but openly supported Republican Senator John McCain in the 2008 presidential election. Lieberman made a nationally televised speech at the Republican National Convention and suggested that Democratic nominee Barack Obama was not qualified to serve as president. After the 2008 elections, many Democrats wanted to punish Lieberman by stripping him of the chairmanship of the Senate Homeland Security and Governmental Affairs Committee. Following speculation that Lieberman might decide to caucus with Republicans if he lost his chairmanship, the Senate Democratic Caucus voted 42–13 to allow him to keep that post, but removed him from the Environment and Public Works committee.

the Republicans require members who wish to sit on multiple committees to receive the approval of the chairs of the committees involved in addition to the steering committee. For both parties, restricting exemptions allows party leaders to distribute desirable committee assignments to more members.

THE SENATE. Since the 1970s, Senate rules have restricted the number and type of committee assignments that senators may receive. A senator may sit on no more than two of the 12 most important committees ("A" committees) and is limited to an appointment to only one of five other standing committees, the Special Committee on Aging, or the Joint Economic Committee ("B" committees). There is no restriction for seats on the Select Committee on Ethics, the Committee on Indian Affairs, and the Joint Committee on Taxation ("C" committees). A senator may sit on no more than three subcommittees of any "A" committee (Appropriations members are exempt from this restriction) and no more than two subcommittees of any "B" committee. Both parties have adopted rules that further restrict membership on "A" committees. Senators are not permitted to sit on more than one of the "Super A" or "Big Four" committees, which include Appropriations, Armed Services, Finance, and Foreign Relations. The Senate occasionally grants exemptions to these assignment limitations at the request of the parties. Since the 1950s, both Senate parties have observed the practice of granting every senator a seat on one of the top four committees before any senator gets two such seats. The practice is called the "Johnson rule," after Lyndon Johnson (D-Texas), the Democratic leader who initiated the practice.

INFLUENCES ON ASSIGNMENTS. Many factors influence the committee assignment decisions of party leaders and the committees on committees. The legislators' political needs, claims by individual states or regions for representation on certain committees, geographic considerations, party loyalty, views on specific issues, and seniority are the most important factors. In the House, members supported by the largest state delegations are at a distinct advantage. For example, in 1992 New York's delegation lost all three of its members on House Appropriations through retirement or defeat, but it managed to regain all three seats (two Democratic and one Republican) for its members when new appointments were made. But there are few guarantees – New Jersey Democrats lost their representation on both Appropriations and Ways and Means (one seat each), but failed to gain a replacement.

Only for Senate Republicans has seniority historically been a decisive consideration. In fact, seniority has been the sole determinant in both the allocation of committee seats and the ascension of the committee hierarchy for Senate Republicans. In 2004, reflecting a desire to strengthen their leader's influence with party colleagues, Senate Republicans approved, by narrow margin, a change in party rules to grant the floor leader the authority to make influential committee appointments without regard to seniority. The rule permits the Republican leader to appoint at least half of the party's committee assignments on "A" committees. As a result, the leader has considerable say in the appointments to committees such as Agriculture, Appropriations, Armed Services, Finance, Foreign Relations, and Judiciary. For Senate Democrats, seniority has been an important, but less decisive, factor in committee assignment decisions.

Similar to the Senate Democrats, the House parties consider seniority along with many factors when making committee assignments. Having an established record of party loyalty, trustworthiness, and skill gives a more senior member an edge over newcomers. In recent Congresses, party leaders have increasingly taken into account members' contributions to party campaign efforts when distributing committee seats. Yet, particularly when a large class of new members enters Congress, party leaders make sure that a few freshmen are named to the top committees. The 104th Congress (1995–1996) was particularly unusual in having both a large class of new Republicans and a new Republican majority in the House. The change in party control gave the Republicans 31 new seats on the exclusive committees. The party allocated 19 of those seats to freshmen. In the years following the new Republican majority in 1995, it has become clear that the seniority norm has further weakened in the House.

LEADERSHIP PREROGATIVES. Assignments to the House Committee on Rules and the House Committee on House Administration are unique cases. The Rules Committee's primary function is to consider, devise, and report "special rules," resolutions that provide for the floor consideration of measures – usually reported by other committees – that would otherwise not receive timely consideration under the standing rules. In the 1960s and early 1970s, the independence of Rules Committee members was troubling to the majority party Democrats. Ultimately, both parties transferred the power to appoint Rules members to their top party leaders, making Rules Committee members agents of their party leadership.

In late 1994, both House parties also gave their top leaders similar power to name the members of the House Administration Committee. Because the House Administration Committee has jurisdiction over the internal administrative affairs of the House, including the way important resources are distributed to committees and members, the top leaders wanted to assert more control over it than they had in the past. The committee also has jurisdiction over election and campaign finance law – subjects of the highest partisan significance.

The Pecking Order

The appeal of committees to members varies. We can learn about the value of committees to members by examining the committees that members choose to leave and join. Because members have the ability to stay on the committee that they served on in the previous Congress (because of the norm of "property rights"), we can assume that members transfer to more desirable committees. This is especially likely to be true because of the costs members incur for leaving a committee on which they had accumulated seniority. Table 6.3 shows the ranking of committee values for the House and Senate derived from the study of members' transfers off and on committees.

House Ways and Means (taxes, social security, trade), Appropriations (spending authority), Commerce (health, regulation of interstate commerce), and Rules (special rules) have jurisdictions of exceptional breadth and importance and attract the interest of many members. Competition for assignment to these committees is intense. Because of these committees' importance, party leaders expect loyalty from members assigned to them. In late 1992, a House insider reported that the Democratic leadership was holding applicants to Appropriations and Ways and Means to a high standard of loyalty. Leaders were telling members, "There may be a time your

TABLE 6.3. Ranking of House and Senate Committee Values, 1979–2006.

Ranking	House Committees	Senate Committees
1	Ways and Means	Finance
2	Appropriations	Veterans Affairs
3	Energy and Commerce	Appropriations
4	Rules	Rules and Administration
5	International Relations	Armed Services
6	Armed Services	Foreign Relations
7	Intelligence	Intelligence
8	Judiciary	Judiciary
9	Homeland Security	Budget
10	Transportation and Infrastructure	Commerce, Science, and Transportation
11	District of Columbia	Indian Affairs
12	Government Reform and Oversight	Small Business and Entrepreneurship
13	Budget	Homeland Security and Governmental Affairs
14	Post Office and Civil Service	Agriculture, Nutrition, and Forestry
15	Financial Services	Health, Education, Labor, and Pensions
16	Science	Energy and Natural Resources
17	Resources	Environment and Natural Resources
18	House Administration	Banking, Housing, and Urban Affairs
19	Education and the Workplace	
20	Standards of Official Conduct	
21	Agriculture	
22	Veterans Affairs	
23	Merchant Marine and Fisheries	
24	Small Business	

Source: Keith M. Edwards and Charles Stewart III. "The Value of Committee Assignments in Congress Since 1994." Paper presented at the 2006 Annual Meeting of the Southern Political Science Association.

leader and your president will need your support. It may be difficult for you to vote for it. Will you be with us?"[1] Such anecdotal evidence illustrates the significant role of party as a cue to members on committees of prestige.

As a general rule, freshmen have difficulty gaining assignment to the top committees. Only when an extraordinary number of new members are elected does the leadership become eager to demonstrate a commitment to appointing a fair share of freshmen. And only when their numbers are large, are freshmen emboldened to demand their share of top assignments. At the start of the 103rd Congress (1993–1994), for example, the 63 Democratic freshmen and 47 Republican freshmen gained a total of 13 appointments to Appropriations, Ways and Means, and Commerce. Two years later, with an even larger class of Republican freshmen, 19 of the 31 available slots on the top four committees were given to freshmen by the Republican steering committee.

Beyond the common desire for assignment to one of the top committees, members vary widely in their preferences for committee assignments. Differences among members reflect their personal interests and political goals. As a consequence of these differences, many committees are not very representative of their parent house. Sometimes this imbalance is manifest in the policy preferences held by committee members. For example, the House Armed Services Committee, which attracts members disproportionately from districts with military bases, has been more conservative than the House as a whole for many years. But many committees are distinguished from the rest of their chamber less by their policy views than by their degree of interest in the subject matter. The House Agriculture Committee, for example, attracts legislators from rural farming districts.

Committee Bias?

Differences in the policy preferences of committees and their parent chambers are not easy to measure, but it does appear that the political balance on some committees is quite different from the balance in their parent chamber. Committee medians on a liberal/conservative scale (larger numbers = more conservative) for the Democratically controlled Congress of 2007–2008 are shown along with chamber medians in Figure 6.2. With Democratic majorities, we would expect to observe liberal-leaning committees and they were, but there still is substantial variation among committees. Among House committees, those with a larger proportion of Democrats are among the most liberal – House Administration, Appropriations, Budget, Rules, and Ways and Means.

The biases of congressional committees, as well as subcommittees, are evident in the character of the witnesses they call to their hearings. A study of congressional hearings between 1945 and 1986 on four issues – nuclear power, drug abuse, smoking, and pesticides – found large, predictable bias in the mix of industry and public-interest group representatives appearing before them. Committee majorities chose to listen to more witnesses that confirmed their views than opposed their views.

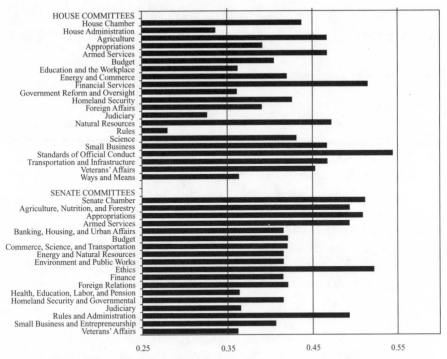

FIGURE 6.2. Median Conservative Score for Standing Committees, 2007–2008. *Source:* Common space scores from http://www.voteview.com. Committee medians calculated by authors.

Committee Leaders

The most powerful member on most committees is the full committee chair. The chair exercises considerable control over the agenda, schedules meetings and hearings of the full committee, and, in recent Congresses, approves the scheduling of subcommittees' meetings and hearings. Furthermore, the committee chair controls the committee budget, offers party leaders recommendations regarding the composition of conference committees for legislation falling under the committee's jurisdiction, supervises a sizable staff, and often serves as a spokesperson for the committee and party on issues under the committee's jurisdiction. The chair also reports legislation to the floor on behalf of the committee and makes requests of the majority leadership and, in the House, the Rules Committee to schedule the legislation for action on the floor. In exercising his or her formal powers, the chair benefits from years of experience in dealing with the policy problems and constituencies of the committee. Consequently, the support of the full committee chair can be critical to bill sponsors and opponents. However, full committee chairs no longer dominate their committees as they once did. Understanding why is important.

The Seniority System

Both the majority and minority parties designate a formal leader for each committee and subcommittee. The majority party names the chair of each committee and subcommittee, and the minority party appoints a ranking minority member for each committee and subcommittee. The seniority norm dictates that the party member with the longest continuous service on the committee serves as chair or ranking minority member, although there are limitations on the number and type of chairmanships a member may hold. Subcommittee chairs and ranking minority members are chosen, in most cases, on the basis of seniority within the committee. Accruing seniority toward leadership posts is one reason members are reluctant to transfer to other committees, where they must start at the bottom of the seniority ladder.

The seniority norm came to be recognized in the House in the late nineteenth century and was observed in both chambers, virtually without exception, in the middle decades of the twentieth century. The norm was weakened in the 1970s by party rules that required a secret ballot election of full committee chairs and ranking minority members. Senate Republicans led the way in 1973 by requiring that their ranking member on each committee be elected by the Republican members of the committee, although the full Republican conference retains the right to reconsider a committee contingent's decision. House Democrats followed by requiring that all committee chairs or ranking members and the chairs or ranking members of subcommittees on the Appropriations Committee stand for election in the Democratic caucus at the start of each Congress. They later required the chairs of Ways and Means subcommittees to stand for caucus election as well. The new rules had an impact. Three full committee chairs were deposed in 1974, an Appropriations subcommittee chair was replaced in 1977, and four more Democratic committee chairs were ousted later. The other two congressional parties, House Republicans and Senate Democrats, adopted rules in the mid-1970s allowing separate votes on the ranking committee members in their conferences.

The reforms have been extended. In 1992, House Republicans, then in the minority, adopted a new party rule to limit the tenure of their full committee and subcommittee leaders to three consecutive Congresses, forcing rotation in the top committee posts every six years. In 1995, the Republicans made this a House rule for committee and subcommittee chairmanships and Democrats retained it after winning a majority in 2006, but have since repealed the rule for the 111th Congress. A Republican conference rule applies the term limits to ranking committee and subcommittee leaders when the party is in the minority. Since the adoption of the term limits, only one exemption has been granted – for David Drier (R-California) to remain the Rules committee chair for the duration of the 109th Congress. Chairs are permitted to move from one chairmanship to another.

Predictions that term limits would lead to more frequent departures from the seniority norm in selecting committee chairs proved accurate. In the first Congress to have forced turnover in committee chairs, the 107th Congress (2001–2002), six of the 13 vacant chairs were won by members who were not the most senior of the remaining members on their committees. In the next two Congresses, there were five vacancies compelled by the term limits and only two were filled by the most senior remaining member of the committee. In one instance, five Republicans with more seniority were skipped over to elect a chair.

In 1996, Senate Republicans adopted a six-year limit on committee chairs. Because the Republican majority status was interrupted in the 107th Congress (2001–2002) following Senator Jim Jeffords' decision to leave the Republican Party, the term limits were enforced for the first time at the beginning of the 109th Congress (2005–2006). The resulting vacancies led to a game of musical chairs, as four term-limited chairs went on to chair other committees. The Senate Democrats have not adopted term limits on committee leaders. However, Senator Robert Byrd (D-West Virginia) agreed to give up the chairmanship of the Senate Appropriations committee prior to the 111th Congress at least in part based on concerns that his advanced age (92) left him unable to perform the duties of the job.

Senate Republicans also adopted a new rule governing the election of committee leaders. Rather than allowing the Republicans on each committee to elect their committee chair or ranking minority member, as they had been doing for many years, the new rule requires secret ballot votes within each committee and then by the full Republican conference, making the chairs and ranking members more accountable to the full conference. The first use of this rule, in early 1997, produced no changes in committee chairs. Nevertheless, two senators, Mark Hatfield (R-Oregon) and Arlen Specter (R-Pennsylvania), had to overcome substantial opposition from within their party conference to retain or gain chairmanships.

THE CHANGING CONGRESS: A HOUSE COMMITTEE CHAIR DEPOSED

The seniority system took a major hit in the 111th Congress as Henry Waxman (D-California) successfully challenged John Dingell (D-Michigan) for the chairmanship of the House Commerce Committee. Dingell, the longest serving House member in history had been either chair or ranking Democrat on Commerce since 1981. Waxman's challenge centered on the theme of "change" and argued that Dingell's policies on energy and the environment were out of touch with the House Democratic Caucus. Dingell is known as a fierce protector of the automobile industry and thus was often opposed to increased fuel efficiency standards and other environmental legislation that could harm automakers. Waxman was seen by some as having views more in line with Speaker Nancy Pelosi and incoming President Barack Obama. For his part, Dingell tried to reassure caucus members by pointing to his experience and ability to shepherd legislation though the House. The weeks-long campaign culminated in both Dingell and Waxman giving impassioned speeches to the caucus urging other members to support them. Democrat George Miller of California said, "It was like Zeus and Thor in there, hurling lightning bolts at each other. You just wanted to get out of the way." Despite his last-minute pleas, Dingell lost the vote by a count of 137–122.

Formal reforms have been reinforced by changes in practice. After the Republicans won a House majority in the 1994 elections, Speaker Newt Gingrich assumed responsibility for appointing committee chairs even before his conference had had an opportunity to meet. For three committees, Gingrich bypassed the most senior committee Republican and backed a more assertive or conservative member as chair. At the same time, House Democratic leader Dick Gephardt chose a close political ally to be ranking member on the House Oversight Committee (now House Administration), dumping the former chairman, who had challenged Gephardt for his leadership post. Speaker Dennis Hastert followed Gingrich's lead by considering member loyalty to be an important element in the selection of committee chairs when vacancies occurred. Speaker Nancy Pelosi made it quite clear prior to the Democratic victory in 2006 that seniority would be only one of the factors considered in determining committee assignments. In fact, the Democratic caucus rules drafted by the House Democratic leaders stated that the Steering committee "shall consider all relevant factors, including but not limited to merit, seniority, length of service on the committee, degree of commitment to Democratic principles and the Democratic agenda, and the diversity of the caucus."

Selecting Subcommittee Chairs

THE HOUSE. The means for selecting House subcommittee chairs have come full circle. Before the 1970s, full committee chairs appointed sub-committees and their chairs. That procedure was transformed into a more egalitarian one in the 1970s. Starting in the mid-1970s, House Democrats required that Democratic committee members bid for subcommittee lead-ership posts, chairs, or ranking minority member status in order of seniority and that appointments be ratified by a majority vote of the party members on the committee. Although seniority generally is observed, this procedure gives party members on a committee the right to reject the most senior member and elect someone else, as has happened more than a dozen times. House Democrats also bar full committee chairs or ranking members from serving as chair or ranking member of a subcommittee. To make the most important subcommittee leaders accountable to the party, House Democrats require subcommittee leaders of three committees – Appropriations, Energy and Commerce, and Ways and Means – to receive majority approval of the full House Democratic Caucus and, since early 2004, require those subcom-mittee leaders to first receive approval of the party's Steering and Policy Committee, which is chaired by the party leader.

In contrast, the House Republicans leave the appointment process to each committee's chair (or ranking minority member), although a majority of the Republican members on the full committee can override the chair's decisions. Like the House Democrats, the Republicans require that subcom-mittee leaders of the Appropriations Committee receive full approval of the party conference. In practice, nearly all of the Republican subcommittee leaders are selected on the basis of committee seniority. As a part of their late 1992 reforms, the House Republicans adopted a party rule prohibiting most chairs or ranking members of full committees from serving as chair or ranking member of any subcommittee. This party rule was made a rule of the House in 1995. These rules spread committee and subcommittee leadership posts among more members and limit the influence that any one member can enjoy by holding multiple leadership posts.

THE SENATE. Both Senate parties allow committee members to select their subcommittee chairs or ranking members in order of seniority. Less con-flict over subcommittee chairs has arisen in the Senate than in the House, perhaps because nearly all senators can count on having at least one sub-committee leadership post. Senate rules merely prohibit any member from holding more than one chair on a single committee. With most senators serving on three standing committees, they may have up to three subcommittee chairs (or two if they hold a full committee chair on one of those standing committees). In the 110th Congress (2007–2008), roughly 80 percent of majority party members held at least one subcommittee chair, and more than one-half held two or three subcommittee leadership posts.

Limiting the Power of Full Committee Chairs

Compared with their predecessors of the 1950s and 1960s, today's full committee chairs face more effective competition for control over policy choices. Rank-and-file legislators are more likely to appeal to central party leaders and their party caucus to hold committee leaders accountable to them, and the parties have adopted changes in their rules to limit service of committee leaders and to force chairs to face party approval periodically. Moreover, as discussed earlier, rank-and-file legislators now have larger staffs and can turn to outside groups for assistance in challenging the handiwork and arguments of committees and their leaders.

House Committee Chairs

We have noted a few of the changes affecting the power of full committee chairs, but it is useful to review the two waves of reforms that altered the role of House committee chairs. First, the House Democratic majority of the early 1970s adopted rules to reduce the influence of full committee chairs over the decisions of their committees:

- Chairs were required to stand for election by the Democratic caucus at the start of each Congress,
- Committees with 15 or more members were required to form at least four subcommittees,
- Subcommittees were empowered with written jurisdictions and provided staffs,
- Proxy voting by chairs and ranking members was restricted (see box "Congressionally Speaking. . . ."),
- The minority party contingents on committees were guaranteed staff,
- Committees were required to open their meetings to the public unless a majority of committee members agreed to close them,
- Committee members were empowered to call meetings (on a majority vote) so that chairs could no longer refuse to hold meetings, and

- Chairs were required to report legislation promptly after it was approved by their committees.

Furthermore, as discussed above, House Democrats adopted a new procedure for subcommittee assignments so that full committee chairs could no longer stack important subcommittees with their supporters. Thus, the ability of full committee chairs to block legislation favored by their committees was curtailed.

Second, following the Republican takeover in 1995, the House passed a series of reforms that would increase the power of the majority party at the expense of both committee and subcommittee chairs. First, and, perhaps most visible, House rules reduced the number of committees by three and the number of subcommittees by 28. The elimination of these committees and subcommittees resulted in a loss of 484 seats. Additional reforms were passed that placed the majority party leadership at the center of decision-making, and further constrained the behavior of committee chairs:

- Six-year term limits on committee chairs (since repealed),
- Committees were limited to forming five subcommittees (some exceptions granted),
- Proxy voting was banned (see box "Congressionally Speaking... "),
- TV and radio coverage had to be accommodated for all committee meetings that were open to the public,
- Overall committee staff budgets were cut.

Senate Committee Chairs

The Senate also adopted rules to provide guidelines for the conduct of committee meetings, hearings, and voting and to require committees to publish additional rules governing committee procedures. But unlike in the House, Senate chamber and party rules have never specified internal committee organization in any detail and are silent on the functions of subcommittees; indeed, most Senate committees' rules are very brief. In the majority of cases, the full committee chair is assumed to have great discretion, although even that is left unstated. For nearly all Senate full committees, the referral of legislation to subcommittees and the discharge of legislation from subcommittees remain under the formal control of the committee chair.

Senate Republican party rules specify limitations on the number and type of committees Republicans can lead. In 1995, after the Senate Republicans

Congressionally Speaking . . .

Attendance at committee meetings has been a problem for many years. Members often have multiple committee meetings or hearings scheduled at the same time and must fulfill other obligations – meet with constituents, vote on the House floor – while their committees are meeting. Thus, members often grant their committee leaders authority to cast proxy votes in their absence.

To control abuses of proxy voting, the House and Senate have adopted rules on their use. An old House rule provided that a majority of committee members must actually be present at the meeting for a committee to report legislation to the floor. If a majority were not present, a point of order could be raised against a bill when it reached the floor, which would lead the Speaker to rule a bill out of order.

But getting a majority of committee members to show up at one time and circumventing points of order can be troublesome. House Democrats moved in 1993 to minimize the problem. Their rule allowed a "rolling quorum." House Rule 11 now counts as "present" members who voted in committee even if no majority was actually present at the same time. Moreover, no point of order could be raised on the House floor unless it was raised at the appropriate time in committee.

House Republicans banned proxy voting and rolling quorums after they gained a majority in the 1994 elections. Since that time, attendance has continued to be a problem for committee chairs, some of whom have suggested returning to some form of proxy voting. Despite persistent problems with committee attendance, the rules remained intact when Democrats took over in 2007.

Furthermore, party leaders have become more involved in committee chairmanship fights and creating task forces and other forums for writing legislation.

regained a majority, they joined their House counterparts in placing even stricter limitations on committee chairs in party rules. The Senate Republicans adopted a party rule prohibiting full committee chairs from chairing any subcommittees and further barring any Republican senator from chairing more than two subcommittees. Both rules were intended to spread chairmanships among as many senators as possible and to limit the special influence that any one senator might enjoy through multiple chairmanships. The rule soon proved to be a hardship for the party, however. On a few committees, the Republicans found themselves without a sufficient number of eligible senators to take another subcommittee chairmanship, so they began to grant waivers to the rule. Senate Democrats have not adopted similar rules.

Subcommittees

Subcommittees became more common after the Legislation Reorganization Act of 1946 consolidated committee jurisdictions and reduced the number of standing committees in both chambers. The number of subcommittees continued to grow into the 1970s, as individual committees responded to new policy problems and as members demanded their own subcommittees. Currently, of the committees with authority to report legislation, the only ones without subcommittees are the House Budget, House Administration, and Standards of Official Conduct Committees and the Senate Budget, Rules and Administration, Indian Affairs, Small Business and Entrepreneurship, Veterans' Affairs, and Intelligence committees.

THE HOUSE. In the House, the resistance of some full committee chairs to efforts to create legislative subcommittees was eventually overcome by a 1974 rule that provides that "each standing committee . . . except the Committee on the Budget . . . that has more than twenty members shall establish at least four subcommittees." As a result, subcommittees proliferated to the extent that over 125 subcommittees existed in 1980. Later, problems associated with the growth in the number of House subcommittees – jurisdictional squabbles between subcommittees, scheduling difficulties, and the burden of subcommittee hearings on executive officials – led the Democratic caucus in 1981 to limit the number of subcommittees. The 1981 rule was supplanted by a new House rule, adopted in 1993, limiting the number of subcommittees to five per committee, unless a committee maintains a subcommittee on oversight (in which case the committee may have six subcommittees). The 1993 rule permitted only two committees to exceed the subcommittee limit – Appropriations (which may have 13 subcommittees) and Government Reform (which may have seven). The rules changes adopted in 1993 required the abolition of 16 subcommittees, and additional changes introduced by the Republicans in 1995 further scaled back the number of subcommittees. Cumulatively, these changes brought the House back to the 1955 level of about 80 subcommittees. The number of subcommittees has crept up since then, reaching 101 in 2007. Contributing to this trend was a 2007 rules change granting additional exemptions to subcommittee limits to Armed Services (which may have seven), Foreign Affairs (which may have seven), and Transportation and Infrastructure (which may have six).

THE SENATE. The Senate and the Senate parties do not have formal rules on the number of subcommittees. Instead, the Senate's limits on the number of subcommittee assignments that individual senators may hold effectively

Congressionally Speaking . . .

The first great book about Congress was Woodrow Wilson's *Congressional Government,* written in 1883 and 1884 when Wilson was a graduate student at Johns Hopkins University. He penned two frequently quoted phrases – "Congressional government is *committee government*" (emphasis added) and "Congress in session is Congress on public exhibition, whilst Congress in its committee-rooms is Congress at work." Wilson later became president of the United States.

The power of subcommittees was enhanced during the early 1970s, leading observers to look for new ways to label Congress. Political scientists Roger Davidson and Walter Oleszek characterized the House as *subcommittee government* in their 1977 book *Congress Against Itself.* Neither Davidson nor Oleszek has exhibited ambitions for high public office.

restricts the number of subcommittees that can be created. In 1985, compliance with the limits on subcommittee assignments led to the elimination of 10 subcommittees. Republicans further reduced the number of subcommittees after taking majority control of the Senate in 1995. In 1997, the Senate had 68 subcommittees, down from nearly 90 ten years earlier. The number of Senate subcommittees has changed little since that time, increasing only to 71 in 2007.

Checking the Power of Subcommittees in the House

In the Democratic House of the 1970s, subcommittees became very important in committee decision making in the House. The House and the Democratic caucus adopted rules in the early 1970s that substantially weakened the ability of full committee chairs to control subcommittees. Consequently, decision-making processes within House committees became more decentralized than they had been in the 1950s and 1960s. Most legislation originated in subcommittees, the vast majority of hearings were held in subcommittees, about half of all committee staff was allocated to subcommittees, and subcommittee chairs usually served as the floor managers for legislation originating in their subcommittees. The House and Democratic party rules together created substantial uniformity across House committees in their reliance on subcommittees for initial action on legislation. The pattern in the House led some observers to label House decision making "subcommittee government."

Subcommittee government evaporated with the new Republican majority in 1995. House subcommittees were no longer guaranteed that legislation sent to their parent committees would be referred to them. In addition, as noted previously, the Republicans forced most House committees to reduce the number of their subcommittees from six to five (with exception to those committees maintaining an oversight subcommittee and those granted explicit exemptions), and they returned to full committee chairs control over subcommittee appointments and over all committee and subcommittee staff. When they cut committee budgets, a disproportionate share of the resulting staff cutbacks occurred in subcommittee staffs. Whereas subcommittee chairs once had the authority to hire one staffer, House rules now give full committee chairs the authority to determine the staff allotted to subcommittees. Subcommittee staff now constitutes less than 40 percent of all committee staff, down nearly 10 percent from the 1980s. The consequence of these changes has been the reemergence of variation across House committees in the way they use subcommittees.

It is too early to determine whether the Democratic majority elected to the House in 2006 will return to greater reliance on subcommittees for initial consideration of legislation. Early signs are that the Democratic full committee chairs are giving subcommittee chairs greater independence than did their Republican predecessors.

The Senate and its parties never adopted rules granting subcommittees the kind of independence that House subcommittees enjoyed under the Democrats in the 1970s and 1980s. The lack of formal rules empowering subcommittees in the Senate has produced great variation among committees in their reliance on subcommittees. Several Senate committees hold no or only a few hearings in subcommittee, and only a few Senate committees use subcommittees to write legislation. "Subcommittee government" never fit the decision-making processes in most Senate committees.

Committee Staff

Committees in the early nineteenth century worked without staff assistance, which meant that committee chairs personally managed the administrative details of committee business. However, the growing workload of the mid-1800s rendered this practice infeasible. In 1856, the House approved committee assistance for the Ways and Means committee, and the Senate did the same for the Finance committee. Expansion in committee assistance following this was slow; it was not until 1890 that the total number of committee employees in both chambers exceeded 100.

The Legislative Reorganization Act of 1946 was a significant turning point in the history of committee staffing as it established statutory provisions for the allocation of staff. Specifically, it granted standing committees in both chambers the authority to hire four professional staff assistants and six clerical aides. The number of professional assistants was raised to six (totaling 12 statutory positions) in 1970 by the second Legislative Reorganization Act. In addition, committees were extended the opportunity to make annual requests for committee staff beyond the statutory allotments. This gave way to a rapid expansion of committee staff, particularly in the non-statutory category (referred to as "investigative"). After the 1970 Legislative Reorganization Act, committee staffing has followed different courses in the two chambers.

THE HOUSE. In 1974, the House increased the personnel limit to 18 professional assistants and 12 clerical aides, where it remains today. The number of committee staff in the House exploded in the 1970s, primarily as a result of the growth in subcommittees. While growth leveled off in the House during the 1980s, the total number of committee staff employed continued to rise through the early 1990s. By 1990, only one House committee had a staff smaller than 40, while six committees had more than 100 assistants.

THE SENATE. Although growth in committee staff was more gradual in the Senate, Senate committees, like their House counterparts, took advantage of the 1970s procedures permitting investigative staff. However, the adoption of a 1980 Senate resolution eliminated the distinction between statutory and investigative staff, and moved to annual funding (changed to biennial funding in 1985) of committee staff. As is now the practice, committees were directed to draft budget requests to be packaged and voted on by the chamber.

REPUBLICAN CUTS RESTORED. As they promised, the Republicans elected in 1994 cut committee budgets and staff. House committee (full and subcommittee) staff dropped from just over 1,700 to under 1,100; Senate committee staff dropped from nearly 1,000 to under 800. Since the mid-1990s, House committee staff has risen to approximately 1,300, and Senate committee staff has grown back to over 900.

Both chambers guarantee the minority party a share of the staff. Senate rules state that the allocation of committee staff "should reflect the relative number of majority and minority members of committees." The standing rules of the House are less favorable to the minority than in the Senate. The

House guarantees to the minority only 10 staff members, or one-third of the committee staff, whichever is less.

Conclusions

Committees are a central but changing feature of legislative policy making. Changes in the role of committees are primarily the products of:

- the emergence of new and salient policy problems,
- fluctuations in the strength of congressional parties, and
- the character of the existing institutional arrangements.

When interest in an issue is narrow, the policy outcome satisfies most members, and the issue has little impact on party fortunes, autonomous committees are tolerated and even revered. However, when an issue is more complex and few members are indifferent to the outcome, as appeared to be the case more frequently in the 1970s, committees become constrained by their parent chambers and must rely on formal procedural safeguards to preserve their control over legislative details. When the parties' electoral fortunes are tied to the issue and the policy outcome, as happened on budget matters in the 1980s, party leaders and their functionaries assume decision-making responsibilities that otherwise would fan to committees.

The direction of change over the last three decades – toward less autonomous committees and a less committee-oriented process – must not be confused with the degree of change. The changes reported in this chapter, particularly those in the House, appear to be quite sweeping. Many of the procedural sources of committee power seem to have been weakened. Developments affecting committee assignments, bill referrals, floor debate, conferences, and the budget process have reduced committee autonomy. Additionally, the informal norm of deference to committee recommendations certainly is much weaker today than it was in the 1950s and 1960s.

But some care must be taken in drawing inferences about these changes. Most legislation comes from a single committee in each chamber, receives few or no floor amendments, and does not require a conference. Necessary conferences are managed by conferees chosen nearly exclusively from the committee of origin. Moreover, committees have devised a remarkable variety of legislative tricks to minimize the effect of budget constraints. With the creative use of special rules and large omnibus measures in the 1980s, committees have actually recovered some of the autonomy they lost in the 1970s.

Above: Sen. Robert Byrd (D-WV) speaks, Monday, during the Senate impeachment trial against President Clinton. Byrd introduced a motion to dismiss the trial. (KRT) PL,KD 1999 (Horiz)
Below: Sen. Christopher Dodd, D-CT, (L) and Sen. Richard Shelby, R-AL, listen to testimony during a Senate Banking, Housing and Urban Affairs Committee hearing on the crises facing investment banks and other financial institutions on Capitol Hill in Washington on September 23, 2008. (UPI Photo/Roger L. Wollenberg)

7

The Rules of the Legislative Game

C ONGRESSIONAL POLITICS OFTEN HAS THE FLAVOR OF A GAME – ALBEIT A
very important game – as the contending factions vie for control over
public policy. The game is characterized by bargaining, procedural maneu-
vers, and close votes. On many issues, the outcome is uncertain. When the
interests and rights of large groups in society are at stake, the game is emo-
tionally charged. And the game is made more compelling by the personalities
of the players. Members of Congress, presidents, staff aides, lobbyists, and
other participants in congressional politics are ambitious people with large
egos. Many of the players hate to lose. Skilled players are masters of the
rules; they are proficient in strategy and tactics and take pleasure in anticipating the moves of their opponents. Their knowledge of the rules and their
aptitude for strategy do not guarantee success, but can give them an advantage. Even for spectators, mastering the rules and strategy is essential to
appreciating and enjoying the game.

The rules of the game change – and legislators do the changing. Each
chamber of Congress is empowered by the Constitution to enact its own
rules. The rules of the House of Representatives extend to more than 60,000
words, while the Senate's rules are less than half that long at around 30,000
words. The differences in the length of the rules reflect not only the differences in the sizes of the two chambers, with the larger House requiring more
formalities to keep order, but also the different paths that the two chambers
took at critical junctures in their parliamentary histories. The Senate, at a
very early point in its history, eliminated the means to limit debate, which
created the possibility of preventing a vote on a measure by refusing to stop
talking. As a result, controversial changes in the rules can be blocked by a
minority in the Senate. The House, in contrast, adopted a means to limit
debate by a simple majority vote, which allowed even small majorities to

impose new rules on that chamber. The result is that the House gradually accumulated a much larger and more detailed set of rules.

Legislative Rules in Perspective

Perhaps the most remarkable feature of the legislative process is how much it is stacked against the enactment of new law. Typically, getting a major bill passed involves attracting majority support in successive stages – first in a subcommittee, then in the full committee, then on the floor, then in conference, and then on the floor again for the conference report. This must be done in both chambers and usually requires the cooperation of both the minority and majority party leadership in the Senate and, in the case of the House, the majority party leadership and the Rules Committee. Once congressional passage is acquired, presidential approval or the support of an extraordinary majority in both chambers must be obtained. Success, then, depends on finding support from multiple groups and subgroups that are not likely to have identical policy preferences. Proponents of a new program or project usually must successfully pilot the necessary legislation through the process twice – once for an authorization bill to create the program and once for the related appropriations bill to fund the program.

Often, the members of Congress and other players in this game take the rules as they are and adjust their strategies accordingly. However, the players also seek to shape and create rules that suit their political needs, which change over time. The existing rules are seldom reevaluated in their entirety. Rather, their weaknesses or biases are considered individually and solutions are adopted piecemeal. New options, limitations, and contingencies have been added incrementally, making the rules more elaborate and altering the strategic context within which legislative factions must compete for majority support. Over the more than two centuries that Congress has been making law, a remarkably complex set of rules, further elaborated by precedents and informal practices, have evolved to shape the legislative process.

It would be a serious mistake to infer that the rules are so detailed and biased that they dictate policy outcomes. They are not. Rules are typically created to facilitate action, not determine outcomes. With a few exceptions, rules do not stipulate the issues to be considered by Congress. National and international events shape those issues, and much of the legislative struggle involves getting new issues on the congressional agenda. Moreover, rules do not determine the policy preferences of the players. Who gets elected is the most important factor in determining what policies will be favored by Congress, although interest groups, presidents, and others influence members' policy choices as well. In addition, the rules do not determine which of the interest groups, local government officials, political commentators, and others exercise the most influence on policy decisions. Larger social forces are more important than the legislative rules in this regard. Generally, the rules are not so detailed and biased that they can compensate for a scarcity of support and votes.

Nevertheless, the rules of the legislative game do matter. Some rules restrict or expand the options available to members by placing certain bills in order on the floor at certain times or by regulating the amendments that may be offered. Other rules set the decision rule – requiring a majority or supermajority for certain kinds of motions or measures – while still others specify which members have the right to make a motion or to speak at certain times. Members know that Congress's rules matter and often regret that the general public does not appreciate their importance. Robert Michel (R-Illinois), the House Republican leader from 1981 to 1994, once lamented the difficulty of attracting public attention to the plight of the minority party under House rules:

> Nothing is so boring to the layman as a litany of complaints over the more obscure provisions of House procedures. It is all "inside baseball." Even among the media, none but the brave seek to attend to the howls of dismay from Republicans [then the minority party] over such esoterica as the kinds of rules under which we are forced to debate. But what is more important to a democracy than the method by which its laws are created?

> We Republicans are all too aware that when we laboriously compile data to demonstrate the abuse of legislative power by the Democrats, we are met by reporters and the public with that familiar symptom best summarized in the acronym "MEGO" – my eyes glaze over. We can't help it if the battles of Capitol Hill are won or lost before the issues get to the floor by the placement of an amendment or the timing of a vote. We have a voice and a vote to fight the disgraceful manipulation of the rules by the Democrats, and we make use of both. All we need now is media attention, properly directed to those boring, but all-important, House procedures.[1]

Representative Michel was well aware that misconceptions about congressional rules abound. Some believe that "if there's a will, there's a way" – legislators' effort, not rules, determine outcomes. Others see congressional procedures as arcane and deeply biased against action – "the outcome is rigged by the rules." Particular rules become critical factors in shaping policy choices only in combination with the preferences of the players. If all members of Congress support a particular bill, it doesn't matter whether only a simple majority or a supermajority is required to pass it. But as divisions emerge, the particular rules under which bills are crafted and brought to a vote may influence the outcomes. The ability to offer an amendment at a crucial moment, to delay action until more support can be attracted, or to gain enactment with a simple majority rather than a supermajority can be critical to the final policy outcome.

Knowledge of the rules can be an important resource. Former House Energy and Commerce Chairman John Dingell (D-Michigan) once said, "If I let you write the substance and you let me write the procedure. I'll screw you every time." In both chambers of Congress, the rules and precedents are sufficiently complex that most members do not master them in their entirety. Instead, they rely on knowledgeable colleagues, staffers, the parliamentarians, and others to advise them. But a member who masters the rules is valuable to other members, more likely to be consulted, and more likely to be viewed as fit for a leadership position.

The rules governing the legislative process have two main sources: the Constitution and Congress itself. The Constitution sets a few basic but critically important rules (see Chapter 2). However, the chambers themselves are a source of rules in three ways. First, the rules adopted by the House and Senate supplement the constitutional requirements. Second, several statutes or laws passed by Congress set procedural requirements for the two chambers of Congress (although most of these allow the House and Senate to supplement or supplant the statutory requirements with their own rules). Third, the two chambers of Congress have a large body of procedural precedents, built up over their more than 200-year history, that govern many aspects of congressional operations that are not addressed elsewhere. This chapter outlines the rules that are critical to understanding legislative politics.

Beyond the Constitution: House and Senate Rules

The Constitution outlines the fundamental rules of the legislative game but leaves out important details. How legislation is to be prepared for a vote in the House and Senate is left undefined, as are the means for resolving differences between the House and Senate. The Constitution makes the vice president the presiding officer of the Senate and specifies that an elected Speaker shall preside over the House, but it does not mention the specific powers of these presiding officers. The Constitution also does not mention how the president is to decide what to recommend to Congress or the degree to which the president will rely on departments and agencies to speak for the executive branch. Moreover, the means for resolving differences between Congress and the executive branch are not discussed.

The details of legislative procedure have been filled in by the evolution of informal practices and the accumulation of recognized precedents. But in both chambers of Congress, a sizable number of formal rules have been established as well. Such rules both reflect and shape the distribution of power within Congress and between Congress and the president.

The framers of the Constitution anticipated the need for rules of procedure. The Constitution's Article I, Section 5, provides that "each house may determine the rules of its proceedings." As a result, each chamber has devised a complex set of standing rules. They concern the committee systems, procedures for amending and voting on legislation, ethics regulations for members and staff, and many other matters. It is important to keep three things in mind: (1) each chamber has its own set of rules, (2) each chamber may change its rules whenever it desires, and (3) each chamber may waive its rules whenever it desires.

Formally, the House dissolves at the end of each two-year Congress and must reestablish its rules as one of its first items of business at the start of each new Congress. In nearly all cases, this is done with a few amendments sponsored by the majority party and approved on a party-line vote. The Senate, in contrast, considers itself to be a continuous body because at least two-thirds of its members continue to serve from one Congress to the next. For that reason, the Senate's rules remain in effect from Congress to Congress unless the Senate votes to change them.

In addition to their own standing rules, the House and Senate are guided by statutes and precedents established by rulings of their presiding officers. When Congress chooses to include certain procedures in new statutes, such as the Congressional Budget and Impoundment Control Act of 1974 (see Chapter 12), these have the force of standing rules. Party rules govern such things as the selection of party leaders and committee appointments. In some cases party rules dictate limits on the use of standing rules by party or committee leaders. Rulings of the presiding officers concern interpretations of statutory or standing rules.

The Standard Legislative Process

The standard legislative process in the modern Congress is outlined in Figure 7.1. It is called the standard process because it is patterned after the typical route legislation follows. The chambers are free to alter it for certain legislation, and they have done so with greater frequency in the last decade or two. Even the standard process involves many options that are used regularly. The standard process involves multiple stages in each chamber, followed by

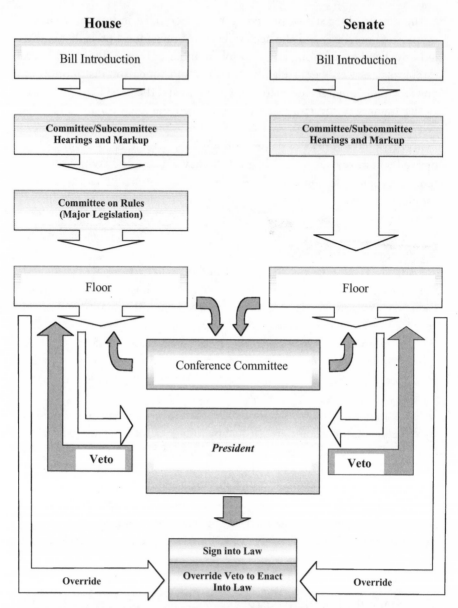

FIGURE 7.1. The Standard Legislative Process for a Major Bill.

steps for resolving House-Senate differences. The Constitution stipulates that after the House and Senate agree on legislation, the president must approve or veto it, and if it is vetoed, Congress may then attempt to override the veto. The standard process is like an obstacle course in which majorities must be created at several stages among different groups of legislators.

Introduction of Legislation

The modern legislative process gives a member who is interested in enacting a new law three basic procedural options. First, she could introduce her own bill and work to gain passage in each chamber. Second, she could seek to have her ideas incorporated into legislation drafted by a committee or by other members. And third, she could offer her proposal as an amendment to someone else's legislation. She might even pursue the three options simultaneously.

Legislation may be drafted by anyone – a member and his or her staff, a committee, lobbyists, executive branch officials, or any combination of insiders and outsiders – but it must be introduced by a member and while Congress is in session. In the House, a member simply places a copy of the draft legislation in a mahogany box, the "hopper," which is located at the front of the House chamber. In the Senate, members hand their draft legislation to a clerk or gain recognition to introduce it orally from the floor. In both chambers, the chief sponsor of a measure may seek cosponsors. Legislation is designated as a bill, a joint resolution, a concurrent resolution, or a resolution, and is numbered as it is introduced (see box, "Types of Legislation").

Although legislation is given a number, it may be known by several names. Each bill is required to have a formal title, which is often quite long. For example, the 2005 Energy Policy Act was "An act to ensure jobs for our future with secure, affordable, and reliable energy." But the bill is known by a more convenient, short title – 2005 Energy Policy Act. Most participants and observers simply called it the energy bill. In addition, bills often come to be known informally by the names of their chief sponsors. The Pell Act, which provided grants to college students, was named after Senator Claiborne Pell (D-Rhode Island), who fought hard for student financial aid.

Because lobbyists and other outsiders cannot introduce legislation, they search for members who are willing to champion their causes and introduce legislation they have drafted. Although they would prefer to have influential members introduce their proposals, they also seek members who have the time and interest to give their legislation some priority. The right mix is often found in a majority party member of mid-level seniority who sits on the committee with jurisdiction over the bill. Usually gaining the sponsorship of several members willing to work together on behalf of the legislation is advantageous. Better still is a group of cosponsors who are known as serious legislators and who represent a range of views in both parties. Of course, sponsors also are sought in both chambers so that companion bills can be introduced at about the same time.

TYPES OF LEGISLATION

There are four types of legislation. In each Congress, legislation of each type is generally numbered in the order it is introduced, although sometimes members request that specific numbers be reserved for their bills.

- **Bills** are designated H.R. (number) or S. (number). Public bills change public law. If enacted into law, public bills are published in a volume entitled *Statutes at Large* and given a public law number, such as P.L. 111. Private bills address matters affecting individuals, such as an immigration case and, if enacted into law, are not reported in *Statutes at Large*.

- **Joint Resolutions** are designated H. J. Res. (number) or S. J. Res. (number). Most joint resolutions are the same as bills for all purposes – they change public law and, if enacted into law, are published in *Statutes at Large* and given a public law number. By tradition, certain kinds of legislation, such as special appropriations measures, are labeled joint resolutions. A special class of joint resolution is proposed constitutional amendments, which if passed by Congress do not go to the president but rather go directly to the states for ratification.

- **Concurrent Resolutions** are designated H. Con. Res. (number) or S. Con. Res. (number) and do not change public law. They concern matters affecting both chambers, such as certain changes in congressional procedures, and so must be adopted by both chambers. They sometimes are used to express the "sense of Congress" about certain issues or events.

- **Resolutions** are designated H. Res. (number) or S. Res. (number) and do not change public law. They concern matters affecting only one chamber, such as most standing rules, and so are adopted only by that chamber. They sometimes are used to express the "sense of the House" or the "sense of the Senate" about certain issues or events.

Members sometimes introduce measures "on request," as a courtesy to the president or someone else. When this is done, it is indicated next to the sponsors' names at the top of the first page of the legislation, signifying that the sponsor does not endorse the provisions of the bill. Similarly, legislation is often introduced by a committee chair on behalf of his or her committee, usually after the committee has drafted and approved the details. The chair is the formal sponsor, but the bill is recognized as a "committee bill."

Referral to Committee

After draft legislation is introduced, the Speaker of the House or the Senate's presiding officer refers it to the appropriate committee(s). In practice, the House and Senate parliamentarians inspect the content of proposed legislation and recommend referral to the committee or committees with the appropriate jurisdiction. Careful drafting of legislation may favorably influence the referral decision.

Legislation may be referred to more than one committee, an action called multiple referral, because committees sometimes share jurisdiction over the content of legislation. Multiple referral has become quite common in the House. Since 1974, the Speaker of the House has been authorized to send legislation to multiple committees. The current rule requires that the Speaker identify a "primary" committee. The Speaker may send a bill, in whole or in part, reflecting the different jurisdictions of committees, to one or more additional committees either before or after consideration by the primary committee. The Speaker also may set time limits for committee action. In recent Congresses, about one in five House measures has been multiply referred, with a higher proportion of important measures, closer to one in four, being so referred.

Most referrals are routine, but occasionally referrals can become controversial. Committee members care about referrals – staking a claim and winning a dispute over jurisdiction may expand a committee's jurisdiction and influence for years to come. Large, complex bills – such as major health care reform and telecommunications bills – often generate competition among committees with jurisdictions relevant to the legislation. Bills dealing with issues not anticipated by the existing rules governing committee jurisdictions are especially likely to stimulate competing jurisdictional claims. On some matters, the composition of the committee that receives a bill may affect the nature of the legislation it eventually reports to the floor, so bill sponsors and outside interests care about which committee receives the referral. On occasion, protracted negotiations among bill sponsors, committee leaders, and party leaders will precede introduction and referral of draft legislation.

Committee Action

Formally, committees have many options concerning how to process most of the legislation referred to them. They may approve the legislation and report it back to the parent chamber, with or without amendments; reject the measure outright; simply not consider it; or set it aside and write a new bill on the same subject. In practice, most proposed legislation does not survive committee consideration. Inaction at the committee stage dooms most legislation. In the 109th Congress (2005–2006), a fairly typical Congress, 4,920 bills and resolutions were introduced in the Senate and 8,154 were introduced in the House. But only 518 and 679 measures were reported by committees of the Senate and House, respectively – 10.5 and 8.3 percent.

Committees may send a bill to a subcommittee for initial action or hold it for the full committee to consider. Although nearly all committees have subcommittees with well-understood jurisdictions, full committee chairs have substantial discretion in deciding whether to refer measures to subcommittees or hold them for full committee consideration. Full committee chairs can also control the scheduling of meetings to expedite or delay action on a bill.

Committees and subcommittees may hold hearings to receive testimony on proposed legislation from members, administration officials, interest-group representatives, outside experts, and others. Hearings may address a general issue related to the legislation or the specifics of the legislation itself. Hearings are perhaps the most important formal information-gathering mechanism for Congress and its committees. Still, some hearings generate little but rhetoric and media coverage – members' questions turn into lengthy statements, celebrity witnesses offer scripted answers, and the television networks later replay a 20-second exchange between an antagonistic committee member and an acerbic witness. Other hearings are designed more to advertise a bill, raise issues, or draw public attention to a problem than to gather information.

If a committee or subcommittee intends to act on a bill, it normally conducts a "markup" on the legislation – a meeting at which the committee or subcommittee reviews the measure line-by-line or section-by-section and considers amendments. Committees may write their own legislation and have it introduced by their chair. When this approach is taken, the chair often proposes a "chair's mark" as the starting point for the markup. Once the markup by the full committee is complete, the measure may be reported to the floor if a majority of the committee votes to do so. Committees are free to report legislation with or without amendments or even without a recommendation that the legislation pass. But most important legislation is amended or written as a "clean" committee bill and then recommended to pass.

In the House, a bill reported to the floor from a committee must be accompanied by a document called a committee report. Senate committees are not required to write these reports but usually do. Committee reports provide the committee's justification for the bill and are usually drafted by staff members as a routine matter. Committee reports may include a statement of minority views on the legislation. On occasion, committee reports are controversial because they provide further interpretations of the bill that might guide later actions on the part of executive agencies or the courts. Committee reports sometimes help non-committee members and their aides explain complicated legislation to constituents. In the House, the Ramseyer rule (named after Rep. John Ramseyer who proposed it years ago) requires that committee reports specify all changes to existing law that the proposed legislation would make.

Circumventing Committees

Proponents of legislation opposed by a committee have a variety of means for gaining floor action on the legislation without having it reported from the committee. These mechanisms are different in the two chambers. Circumventing committees is more difficult in the House.

Circumventing Committees in the House

In the House, the options are to move to suspend the rules, to employ a discharge petition, or to gain a discharge resolution from the Rules Committee. To successfully suspend the rules and pass a bill (one motion), a member must be recognized by the Speaker to make the motion to suspend, and then a two-thirds majority must approve the motion. Because the Speaker is usually supportive of committees dominated by members of his or her own party, this approach is seldom a feasible strategy. Also, a two-thirds majority is unlikely to be obtained for a measure opposed by a committee. In recent decades, committee leaders have used the suspension process to speed floor action or avoid amendments to committee bills.

The discharge procedure allows any member to introduce a motion to discharge or extract a measure from a committee once the measure has been before the committee for 30 legislative days (that is, days on which the House meets). After the motion is filed, a discharge petition is prepared and made available for members to sign. If 218 or more members sign the petition, the motion to discharge becomes privileged business on the second and fourth Mondays of the month (except during the last six days of a session). If the discharge motion is adopted by majority vote, a motion to call up the bill for immediate consideration is in order.

Until 1993, the identity of members signing a discharge petition was not made public until the 218th signature was added. The secrecy of the signatories made it difficult to hold members accountable and undermined lobbyists' efforts to pressure members to sign. Still, both before and after the 1993 rule change, the discharge process has seldom produced House action on a bill. In fact, only 19 bills have been discharged and passed by the House since 1931. Two factors may account for this. First, committees are probably more or less in line with the House majority most of the time.

UNORTHODOX LEGISLATING

The committee process is sometimes circumvented on important legislation in order to facilitate top-level negotiations between party leaders, committee chairs, the administration, and sometimes key representatives of outside groups. In 2008, for example, the $700 billion financial market bailout bill was drafted by the top leaders and administration officials in close consultation with the Federal Reserve chairman and outside financial system experts. The bailout provisions were added to a House bill pending in the Senate. The Senate approved the bill, with a variety of additional provisions on unrelated matters, without committee approval and only eleven hours after the Senate version was posted online. Quick Senate action was made possible by a unanimous consent agreement providing for the bill's consideration. The House approved the bill with the Senate amendments (which added the $700 bailout provisions). The House moved in this way by adopting a special rule for the consideration of the bill that provided for 90 minutes of debate, barred amendments, and waived points of order.

Second, members may prefer to discourage a practice that could be used to discharge legislation from their own committees.

The third approach involves the Rules Committee's authority to report a privileged resolution that, if adopted, brings a bill to the floor for immediate consideration. The majority party members of the Rules Committee are appointed by the Speaker, so the committee is unlikely to use this power without the support of the Speaker. Again, the Speaker usually works to support the actions of committee majorities.

Circumventing Committees in the Senate

In the Senate, committees can be circumvented by introducing nongermane amendments to bills under consideration on the floor, by placing bills directly on the calendar for floor action, by moving to suspend the rules, and by employing the discharge procedure. Unlike the House, which requires that amendments offered to a bill be germane to the content of the bill, Senate rules are silent on the content of amendments offered to most bills. Consequently, a senator is free to offer his or her bill as an amendment to another measure pending before the Senate, thus circumventing a committee that is refusing to report the bill to the floor. There is no guarantee that a majority will support the amendment, of course, but the mechanism is very easy to employ.

Another approach is to object to the standard procedure of referring a bill to committee. Under Senate Rule XIV, a single senator may object and have a bill placed on the calendar, thus avoiding delays that might be caused by an unfriendly committee. But this action may alienate senators who otherwise might support the bill. Senators also may seek to suspend the rules, but doing this requires a two-thirds vote under Senate precedents, which makes it more difficult to use successfully than a nongermane amendment. Alternatively, a senator can move to discharge a committee, but such motions are debatable and thus can be filibustered.

Floor Scheduling

Legislation is listed, in the order it is reported from committee, on one of four calendars in the House and one of two calendars in the Senate. Each chamber has multiple mechanisms for scheduling legislation for floor consideration so that priority legislation will not get backlogged behind less important legislation. Moreover, for certain types of "privileged" legislation – such as budget and appropriations bills – the House allows committee leaders to call up the legislation directly on the floor. In both chambers, the majority party leaders assume primary responsibility for scheduling, but the two chambers have developed very different methods for setting the floor agenda.

Scheduling in the House

Minor legislation and major legislation are treated differently in the House. In recent years, minor bills have been called up most frequently by unanimous consent requests or by motions to suspend the rules. When legislation is called up by unanimous consent, there typically is no discussion. Under a motion to suspend the rules and pass a bill, debate is limited to no more than 40 minutes, no amendments are allowed (unless specified in the motion), and a two-thirds majority is required for approval. Although legislation can only be brought up under suspension of the rules on specified days (typically Monday, Tuesday, and Wednesday only), this has become a very common means for disposing of bills on the House floor. In the 109th House (2005–06), more than 900 measures were passed under suspension of the rules.

Major or controversial legislation is more troublesome. Sponsors of a major or controversial bill usually cannot obtain unanimous or even two-thirds majority support, so they go to the Rules Committee to request a resolution known as a "special rule," or simply a "rule." The following box shows a recent rule adopted by the House for a 2008 bill dealing with wage disparities between men and women. The rule provides for priority consideration of the measure by allowing the Speaker to move the House into the Committee of the Whole, where the bill may be amended (see the section on Floor Consideration). The rule limits general debate on the bill to one hour and allows only those amendments to the committee version that are listed in an accompanying report from the Rules Committee. This rule also sets aside objections (waives points of order) that may be made to the provisions of the bill or to amendments that violate House rules.

Special rules are highly flexible tools for tailoring floor action to individual bills. Amendments may be limited or prohibited. The order of voting on amendments may be structured. For example, the House can adopt a special rule known as a king-of-the-hill rule. First used in 1982, a king-of-the-hill rule provides for a sequence of votes on alternative amendments, usually full substitutes for the bill. The last amendment to receive a majority wins, even if it receives fewer votes than some other amendment. This rule allows members to vote for more than one version of the legislation, which gives them the freedom both to support a version that is easy to defend at home and to vote for the version preferred by their party's leaders. Even more important, the procedure advantages the version voted on last, which is usually the proposal favored by the majority party leadership.

If the Rules Committee grants the rule and a majority of the House supports it, the way is paved for floor debate on the bill. Since the mid-1970s, the Rules Committee has been under the direction of the Speaker. In 1975, after years of struggle to get friendly, timely rules from a Rules Committee dominated by conservatives, the House Democratic Caucus granted the Speaker the power to appoint the committee's Democratic members, subject to its approval. Because the Democrats were the majority party and insisted on firm control of the rules, they reserved nine of the 13 seats on the committee for their part – a ratio that is still in place today. Since the late 1970s, Rules Committee Democrats, often at the direction of the Speaker, have become much more creative in structuring the amendment process on the House floor.

Finally, five House committees (Appropriations, Budget, House Administration, Rules, and Standards of Official Conduct) have direct access to the floor for certain kinds of legislation. Privileged measures – such as appropriations or tax bills – are considered critical to the House as an institution. When other legislation is not pending on the floor, a member authorized by one of these committees can move for immediate consideration of a privileged measure. Special rules from the Rules Committee are the single biggest group of privileged measures. Although privileged bills do not require a special rule from the Rules Committee, their sponsors often seek one anyway to limit or structure debate and amendments or to waive a House rule that might otherwise be used to raise a point of order against the bill.

Resolved. That at any time after the adoption of this resolution the Speaker may, pursuant to clause 2(b) of rule XVIII, declare the House resolved into the Committee of the Whole House on the state of the Union for consideration of the bill (H.R. 1338) to amend the Fair Labor Standards Act of 1938 to provide more effective remedies to victims of discrimination in the payment of wages on the basis of sex, and for other purposes. The first reading of the bill shall be dispensed with. All points of order against consideration of the bill are waived except those arising under clause 9 or 10 of rule XXI. General debate shall be confined to the bill and shall not exceed one hour equally divided and controlled by the chairman and ranking minority member of the Committee on Education and Labor. After general debate the bill shall be considered for amendment under the five-minute rule. It shall be in order to consider as an original bill for the purpose of amendment under the five-minute rule the amendment in the nature of a substitute recommended by the Committee on Education and Labor now printed in the bill. The committee amendment in the nature of a substitute shall be considered as read. All points of order against the committee amendment in the nature of a substitute are waived except those arising under clause 10 of rule XXI. Notwithstanding clause 11 of rule XVIII, no amendment to the committee amendment in the nature of a substitute shall be in order except those printed in the report of the Committee on Rules accompanying this resolution. Each such amendment may be offered only in the order printed in the report, may be offered only by a Member designated in the report, shall be considered as read, shall be debatable for the time specified in the report equally divided and controlled by the proponent and an opponent, shall not be subject to amendment, and shall not be subject to a demand for division of the question in the House or in the Committee of the Whole. All points of order against such amendments are waived except those arising under clause 9 or 10 of rule XXI. At the conclusion of consideration of the bill for amendment the Committee shall rise and report the bill to the House with such amendments as may have been adopted. Any Member may demand a separate vote in the House on any amendment adopted in the Committee of the Whole to the bill or to the committee amendment in the nature of a substitute. The previous question shall be considered as ordered on the bill and amendments thereto to final passage without intervening motion except one motion to recommit with or without instructions.

Scheduling in the Senate

Scheduling is one area, and certainly not the only one, in which the Senate is very different from the House. In some respects, floor scheduling is simple in the Senate. Bringing up a bill is a matter of making a motion to proceed to its consideration. This is done by the majority leader, and though the motion technically requires a majority vote, it usually is approved by unanimous consent. The Senate has no committee empowered to report special rules.

SPECIAL RULES OF THE HOUSE

Since 1979, the House Rules Committee, in partnership with the majority party leadership, has proven remarkably creative in designing special rules to govern floor debate and amendments on major legislation. Different styles of special rules have gained informal names that are widely recognized by the members of the House. All of these creative special rules waive many standing rules of the House governing floor debate and amendments.

• *Restrictive Rules.* Three kinds of rules restricting amending activity were known before the 1980s – modified open, modified closed, and closed rules. Closed rules simply barred all amendments. Modified open rules allowed amendments except for a specific title or section of a bill. Modified closed rules barred amendments except for a specific title or section of a bill. Since the early 1980s, restrictions have come in so many combinations that these traditional categories do not capture their diversity.

• *King-of-the-Hill Rules.* Invented by Democrats in the early 1980s and sometimes called king-of-the-mountain rules, these rules provide that the House will vote on a series of alternative versions of a bill (substitutes) in a specified order and that the last version to receive a majority vote (no matter how large the majority on other versions) wins.

• *Queen-of-the-Hill Rules.* Invented by Republicans in 1995, these rules provide that the House will vote on a series of alternative versions of a bill in a specified order and that the version with the most votes wins. If two versions receive the same number of votes, the last one voted on wins.

• *Time-Limit Rules.* Invented by Republicans in 1995, these rules provide that all debate and amending activity will be completed within a specified period of time.

What appears bizarre to many newcomers to Senate politics is that the motion to proceed is debatable and may be subject to a filibuster (see the accompanying box). That is, senators may refuse to allow the majority leader's motion to come to a vote by conducting extended debate. In fact, they may not even have to conduct the filibuster, because just the threat of doing so is usually enough to keep legislation of only moderate importance off the floor. The reason is that the majority leader usually cannot afford to create a logjam of legislation awaiting floor consideration by subjecting one measure to extended debate. Under Senate Rule XXII, breaking a filibuster is a time-consuming process that requires a three-fifths constitutional majority – if no seat is vacant, 60 senators – willing to invoke cloture. In 1994, a proposal to limit debate on motions to proceed was blocked by Republicans who threatened to filibuster the resolution providing for the change in the rules.

A good example of a bizarre filibuster was the one conducted by Senator Alfonse D'Amato (R-New York) in October 1992. D'Amato objected to the fact that a tax break for a Cortland, New York, typewriter manufacturer had been stricken from a bill in a conference committee, so he filibustered the entire bill. D'Amato held the floor for more than 15 hours, sometimes with the assistance of Senators Patrick Moynihan (D-New York) and John Seymour (R-California). Under the Senate's rules, D'Amato could not sit down or excuse himself to go to the bathroom without yielding the floor. The quality of this extended "debate," which prevented the Senate from completing its business and adjourning for the year, degenerated as time wore on. At one point, D'Amato reported:

> The young lady who works for me in my Syracuse office, Marina Twomey – her parents. She married a young boy who I ran track against in high school – went to Andrew Jackson, met Larry, he went up to Syracuse on a track scholarship, competed. And he married this lovely girl, Marina, who came from Cortland. This is how I came to know Cortland. I visited her and her family.

> Fate and life and what not, circumstances as we talk, Marina is now one of the two people – the other you know for many years, Gretchen Ralph, who used to be the leader of the symphony or the executive director- and a great community person. She and Marina Twomey run my Syracuse office. We talk about Cortland and knowing and having an affinity.[2]

By the time D'Amato gave up, the filibuster consumed a little more than 86 pages of the Congressional Record. This number was not enough to break the record established by Strom Thurmond (R-South Carolina), who spoke for more than 24 hours against a civil rights bill in 1957.

The ever-present threat of a filibuster requires that scheduling be a matter of consultation and negotiation among the majority leader, the minority leader, bill sponsors, and other interested senators. These discussions, conducted in private, often yield bargains about how to proceed and may include compromises about substantive policy matters. The agreement, which may include limitations on debate and amendments, is then presented to the Senate. It requires unanimous approval to take effect. The process contrasts sharply with the formal Rules Committee hearings and majority approval of special rules in the House.

Floor Consideration

For most minor and routine legislation that reaches the House or Senate floor, floor consideration is brief, no amendments are offered, and the

---

Congressionally Speaking ... The Filibuster

The term filibuster is an anglicized version of the Dutch word for "free-booter." A "filibusterer" was a sixteenth- and seventeenth-century pirate. How it came to be the Senate term for talking a bill to death in the nineteenth century is not clear. Political lexicographer William Safire notes that one of the term's first appearances was in 1854, when the Kansas-Nebraska Act was filibustered.

The current Senate Rule XXII provides for cloture (closing of debate) with the approval of a three-fifths majority of all senators present. That is, if all senators are present, at least 60 senators must support a motion for cloture to stop a filibuster. An exception is made for measures changing the Senate rules, for which a vote of two-thirds of those senators present and voting is required.

---

legislation is approved by voice vote or by unanimous consent. On major legislation, many members usually want to speak and offer amendments, creating a need for procedures that will maintain order and expedite action. The two chambers have quite different floor procedures for major legislation.

Floor Action in the House

In the House, committee chairs write a letter to the Rules Committee chair, requesting a hearing and a special rule for major legislation they are about to report to the floor. Once a special rule for a measure is adopted, the House may resolve to convene "the Committee of the Whole House on the State of the Union" to conduct general debate and consider amendments. The Committee of the Whole, as it is usually abbreviated, consists of the full House meeting in the House chamber and operating under a special set of rules. For example, the quorum required to conduct business in the Committee of the Whole is smaller than it is for the House (100 versus 218), making it easier to conduct business while members are busy with other activities.

A chair appointed by the Speaker presides over the Committee of the Whole. The Committee of the Whole first conducts general debate on the bill and then moves to debate and votes on amendments. Legislation is considered section by section. An amendment must be relevant – germane – to the section under consideration, a requirement that is interpreted very restrictively. For example, an amendment to limit abortions cannot be considered when a bill on water treatment plants is being debated. Amendments sponsored by the committee originating the legislation are considered first for each section and are considered under the five-minute rule. That is, members are allowed to speak for five minutes each on an amendment. The special rule providing for the consideration of the measure may – and often does – alter these standard procedures.

Voting on amendments in the Committee of the Whole can take one of three forms: voice vote, standing division vote, or recorded vote. On a voice vote, members yell out "yea" or "nay," and the presiding officer determines whether there were more yeas or nays. On a standing division vote, members voting "yea" stand and are counted, followed by those voting "nay." Since 1971, it has been possible to get a recorded vote, for which each individual member's position is officially and publicly recorded. Under the current rule, a recorded vote in the Committee of the Whole must be demanded by 25 members. Since 1973, recorded voting has been done by a computerized system. Members insert an identification card into a small voting box and push a "yea," "nay," or "present" button. This system is used for recording other voting in the House as well.

Legislation cannot be passed in the Committee of the Whole, so once debate and amending actions are complete, the measure, along with any approved amendments, is reported back to the House. Special rules usually provide that the "previous question" be ordered, preventing additional debate by the House. The amendments approved in the Committee of the Whole may then be subject to separate votes; if no one demands separate votes, however, the amendments are voted on as a group. Next, a motion to recommit the legislation to committee, which by custom is made by a minority party member, is in order. If the motion to recommit is defeated, as it nearly always is, or simply not offered, the House moves to a vote on final passage.

Floor Action in the Senate

The Senate lacks detailed rules or a well-structured process for debating and amending legislation on the floor. What happens after the motion to proceed is adopted depends on whether or not unanimous consent has been obtained to limit or structure debate and amendments. In the absence of a unanimous consent agreement providing otherwise, Senate rules do not limit debate or amendments for most legislation. Debate and amending activity may go on for days. In contrast to the House, the Senate has no five-minute rule or general germaneness rule for amendments. The floor schedule becomes very unpredictable. Normally, the Senate muddles through controversial legislation with one or more unanimous consent agreements that limit debate, organize the consideration of amendments, and lend some predictability to its proceedings.

THE CHANGING CONGRESS: "GOING NUCLEAR"

Going nuclear is a term used in the Senate to describe a strategy for limiting debate on judicial nominations and other matters. In principle, presidential nominations and treaties can be filibustered. If they are, a two-thirds majority is required to invoke cloture in order to get a vote on them. It has been argued that this practice violates the spirit of the Constitution, which provides that the president may make appointments to top executive and judicial positions with "the advice and consent" of the Senate. If the Senate cannot vote on a presidential nomination, the argument goes, it is not meeting its constitutional obligation under the advice and consent clause.

One approach to addressing filibusters is to change the cloture rule, perhaps just for nominations and treaties. However, proposals to change the cloture rule may be filibustered and would themselves require a two-thirds majority to invoke cloture. So Senate majorities have looked for another approach, an approach that Democrats and the media have described as the "nuclear option."

The idea is to get a ruling from the presiding officer (the Vice President, in all likelihood) that would establish the precedent that the Senate must vote on nominations (and maybe treaties). The proposed tactic goes as follows

• A senator makes a point of order that the Constitution implies that a simple majority can bring a nomination to a vote and the presiding officer rules in favor of the point of order;

• the opposition appeals the ruling of the presiding officer to a vote of the Senate, but the senator making the point of order moves to table the appeal, a motion that is not debatable and so receives an immediate vote; and the majority votes to table the appeal and the presiding officer's ruling stands.

Why haven't Senate majorities used this tactic before to get new rules established as precedents? The primary reason is that a minority can retaliate by obstructing action on the majority's larger agenda. Partisanship would become red hot, other legislation would be filibustered, unanimous consent for routine actions would not be given, Senate action would slow to a crawl, and ultimately the majority might be blamed by the public for mismanaging the Senate. All out partisan war – going nuclear – is the likely result. In 2005, then-Senate Majority Leader Bill Frist (R-Tennessee) threatened to use the nuclear option to do away with filibusters of judicial nominations. A showdown was avoided when a group of seven Democrats and seven Republicans agreed to oppose the strategy, support votes on some of the nominations in dispute, and avoid filibusters on nominations during that Congress.

One reason consent may not be acquired for a time limitation on debate is that some senators may want to have the option of filibustering. A filibuster, and sometimes just the threat of one, will force a compromise. If a compromise is not possible, cloture must be invoked, or the majority leader will be compelled to withdraw the measure from the floor. Once cloture is invoked, 30 hours of debate are permitted (under the current rule), and germane amendments submitted before cloture was invoked can be considered. In fact, cloture is sometimes invoked to avoid the inclusion of nongermane amendments that may require embarrassing votes, complicate negotiations with the House, or risk a presidential veto.

To avoid an unanticipated filibuster, Senate floor leaders seek to learn of possible objections to their plans to bring up a bill on the floor. An informal practice has arisen in recent decades that allows senators to register their objections, usually in writing, to floor action on a bill. An objection is known as a "hold." A hold gains its bite when a majority leader refuses to bring up a measure or nomination on which a hold has been placed or when the minority leader indicates his or her objection to the consideration of a measure or nomination on the basis of a hold that has been registered. Since at least the 1970s, holds have been a source of frustration, particularly for majority leaders and bill managers, but rank-and-file senators of both majority and minority parties have voiced concerns about the practice with regularity. Making holds even more frustrating is the practice of keeping secret the identity of the senator placing a hold. While floor leaders do not always observe holds or confidentiality, the practice is difficult to avoid as long as the majority leader needs unanimous consent to take up measures and wants to avoid filibusters that would make the floor schedule unpredictable for all senators.

The Senate attempted to make holds a matter of public record in 2007. The new rule requires that a senator is require to disclose a hold "following the objection to a unanimous consent [sic] to proceeding to, and, or passage of, a measure or matter on their behalf" by the floor leader. This exceptionally poorly phrased rule goes on to say that the disclosure – a "Notice of Intent to Object" – must be published in the *Congressional Record* within six session days. In other words, a senator is required to have his objection to the consideration of a bill published *after* the objection is first exercised by the leader on the floor. This procedure does not force disclosure if a hold is observed by the majority leader without attempting to gain Senate action on the targeted bill. That is, the rule is not enforceable without the cooperation of the floor leaders, who continue to have an incentive to accommodate their colleagues. Only a few notices of holds have been published since the new rule was adopted.

The modern Senate does not use a committee of the whole. Floor voting can take one of three forms: voice vote, division vote, and roll-call vote. Voice and division votes are similar to those in the House, although the Senate very seldom uses division votes. The Senate does not have an electronic voting system, so recorded votes, which can be demanded by 11 senators, are conducted by a name-by-name call of the roll. The vote on final passage of a bill occurs as specified in the unanimous consent agreement or, in the absence of an agreement, whenever senators stop talking about and offering amendments.

Resolving Differences between the Chambers

The Constitution dictates that the two chambers must approve identical bills before legislation can be sent to the president. This can be accomplished in several ways. One chamber can accept a measure passed by the other. The chambers may exchange amendments until they agree on them, or they may agree to hold a conference to resolve matters in dispute and then send the bill back to each chamber for approval. For complex or controversial legislation, such a conference is the only practical approach.

Members of conference committees, known as conferees, are appointed by the presiding officers of the two chambers, usually according to the recommendations of standing committee leaders. Committee leaders take into account potential conference committee delegates' seniority, interest in the legislation, and other factors, and some committees have established traditions concerning who shall serve on conference committees, which the leaders observe. Conference committees may be of any size. Except for the large conferences held for budget measures, the average conference has roughly 24 representatives and 12 senators.

Agreements between House and Senate conferees are written up as conference reports, which must be approved by a majority of each chamber's conferees. Conference reports must then be approved by majority votes in the House and Senate. In the 109th Congress (2005–2006) only 29 conference reports were filed. Plainly, most legislation is routine and noncontroversial and therefore does not require conference action.

House and Senate Rules Compared

The procedures of the House reflect a majoritarian impulse: A simple majority is allowed to take action expeditiously and can do so easily if it is led by the majority party leadership. The House carefully follows established rules

---

Congressionally Speaking . . .

The Constitution stipulates that the vice president serve as president of the Senate. The vice president retains an office in the Capitol, may preside over the Senate, and may cast a vote to break a tie. Because recent vice presidents have had a policy-making role in the administration and travel frequently, they have not used their Capitol office on a regular basis and have seldom presided over the Senate.

Eleven vice presidents never cast a vote in the Senate. In contrast, George Bush, when he was vice president between 1981 and 1989, cast seven votes, and Albert Gore, vice president under President Bill Clinton, cast two votes in 1993. The record belongs to John Adams, the first vice president, who cast 29 tie-breaking votes during the eight-year presidency of George Washington.

---

and practices, which are quite lengthy. The House makes exceptions to its most important floor procedures by granting and adopting special rules by simple majority vote. Procedures dictating internal committee procedures are elaborate. Debate is carefully limited, and the timing and content of amendments are restricted.

The rules of the Senate are relatively brief. They reflect an egalitarian, individualistic outlook. The right of individuals to debate at length and to offer amendments on any subject is generally protected. Only extraordinary majorities can limit debate or amendments. For reasons of practicality, most scheduling is done by unanimous consent. The majority party usually must negotiate with minority party members to schedule floor action and to bring important measures to a vote. Consequently, Senate decision making is more informal and less efficient than House decision making.

In part, these differences (which are highlighted in Table 7.1) are due to the different sizes of the chambers. The large size of the House requires that its rules more explicitly and stringently limit participation on the floor. Scheduling floor action to suit the needs of individuals is out of the question. In contrast, Senate leaders manipulate the floor schedule through unanimous consent agreements to meet the requests of individual senators. The Senate's smaller size allows peer pressure to keep obstructionism in check. A senator who objects frequently to unanimous consent requests risks objections to consideration of his or her own bills.

The differences also reflect the unique parliamentary history of each chamber. In their earliest days, the rules of both the House and Senate contained a previous question motion. In modern times, standard parliamentary rules

TABLE 7.1. Major House-Senate Differences in Rules of Practice.

House	Senate
Does not allow filibusters	Allows filibusters on most legislation
Has a general rule limiting debate	Has no general rule limiting debate
Bars non-germane amendments	Has no general rule barring non-germane amendments
Uses special rules from the Rules Committee to schedule major legislation for floor action	Relies on unanimous consent agreements to schedule major legislation for floor action
Frequently adopts restrictive special rules to limit the number of amendments and limit debate	Must rely on unanimous consent or cloture to restrict debate and amendments
Uses multiple referral frequently	Rarely uses multiple referral
Committees are not easily circumvented	Committees easily circumvented
Rules permit efficient action without minority party cooperation	Rules do not permit efficient action without minority party cooperation
Considers major legislation in the "Committee of the Whole" first	Has no Committee of the Whole
Speaker of the House empowered by House rules	Presiding officer given little power by Senate rules
Records votes by electronic device	No electronic voting system; roll calls are tabulated manually

Source: Collected by authors from House and Senate rules.

such as *Roberts Rules of Order* provide for a motion that, if passed, forces an immediate debate on the issue before the body. In this way, the previous question motion is a means to end debate, but in the early Congresses neither chamber used the previous question motion as a tool to end debate. The question took the form of "shall the main question be now put," which was the traditional parliamentary means of putting off discussion on a controversial measure. If the motion failed, discussion was put off; if it passed, discussion continued. The early Senate rarely invoked the motion and eliminated it from its rules in 1806. The House overturned a ruling of the Speaker in 1807 that a successful previous question motion ended debate on a bill, before reversing this precedent in the face of obstruction in 1811. Thus, from 1811 forward, the House had an effective means for a majority to end debate on a bill or proposed rule change, while the Senate, bound by its lack of a previous question motion, has never been able to develop an efficient means of ending debate.

The previous question played a pivotal role in the development of House and Senate rules. With the previous question motion, House majority parties could get a vote on new rules they wanted adopted. Senate majority parties faced minority filibusters when they proposed rules that advantaged the majority. Consequently House majority parties have regularly modified and elaborated on their chamber's rules, while Senate majority parties seldom seek, let alone achieve, a change in their chamber's rules. The result is that modern House rules are several times as long as Senate rules. When the House and Senate have determined that some limitation on debate is desirable, as for budget measures and trade agreements, special provisions have been written for the Senate to guarantee that debate could be closed. But this has happened only when supermajorities favor the change and often has happened as a part of a much larger legislative package.

Not until 1917, 111 years after the Senate dropped the previous question motion from its rules, did the Senate again adopt a rule that provided a means for closing debate. Rule XXII allowed an extraordinary majority to invoke cloture – that is, to force an end to debate. The 1917 rule provided for a two-thirds majority to invoke cloture. The 1975 reform of the rule reduced the required majority to three-fifths of all elected senators (60 votes with 100 elected senators), except for matters affecting the Senate's rules, which are still subject to a two-thirds majority cloture threshold. As a result, a fairly broad base of support is still required to bring a rules change to a vote in the Senate.

Authorizing and Appropriating

Under congressional rules, most federal government programs are subject to two types of legislation: authorization bills and appropriations bills. Theoretically, an authorization bill sets the program's organization, rules, and spending ceiling, and an appropriations bill provides the money. House and Senate rules require that an authorization bill creating a federal program or agency be passed before an appropriations bill providing spending authority can be adopted. The authorization bill and the appropriations bill for each program or set of programs both follow the standard legislative process. For most programs, a new appropriations bill must be approved each year.

For example, suppose proponents of a bill creating a new financial aid program for college students managed to get the measure enacted into law. They would have taken the bill through the House Committee on Education

---

Congressionally Speaking...

An *engrossed bill* is the final version of a bill passed by one house, including any amendments that may have been approved, as certified by the clerk of the House or the secretary of the Senate.

An *enrolled bill* is the final version of a bill as approved by both houses, printed on parchment, certified by either the clerk of the House or the secretary of the Senate (for the house that first passed it), and signed by the Speaker of the House and the president pro tempore of the Senate; it has a space for the signature of the president.

---

and the Workforce and the Senate Committee on Health, Education, Labor, and Pensions. The bill would specify how the program was to be organized, how financial aid decisions were to be made, and how much – say $400 million – could be spent, at most, on the program in any one year. It is likely that the bill would authorize the program for a specific period of time – say, four or five years. A separate appropriations bill, which would include spending authority for the new program, must be passed before the program could begin operations. The House and Senate appropriations committees might decide that only $250 million should be spent on the program. If the House and Senate went along with the lower figure, the program would be limited to a $250 million budget for the next year.

In the modern Congress, jurisdiction over authorization legislation is fragmented among many standing committees. Jurisdiction over appropriations is consolidated in one appropriations committee in each chamber, although each of the appropriations committees has 13 subcommittees that do most of the work. Jurisdiction over taxes, the major source of federal revenue, falls to one tax-writing committee in each house: the House Committee on Ways and Means and the Senate Committee on Finance. Thus, power over fiscal policy is not only shared between the House, Senate, and president, it is shared among the various committees within House and Senate as well.

The system creates tensions between the congressional committees. Tax committees do not like to pass bills increasing taxes to cover spending other committees have authorized. Authorizing committees often dislike the handiwork of the appropriations committees. A small appropriation can defeat the purpose of the original authorization bill. In response, authorizing committees have pursued a number of tactics, such as including provisions for permanent appropriations for some programs (social security is one), to avoid the appropriations process.

A MAJOR GLITCH

In 2008, the House and Senate passed the conference report to an important farm bill in identical form. President George W. Bush vetoed the bill and returned it to the House, with everyone unaware that Title III concerning international trade had not been included in the papers sent to the president. The omission of the title from the 15-title bill was made by the enrolling clerk of the House in the rush to complete action on renewal of farm programs before they expired. No one in the administration reported the missing title when the bill was vetoed. The error was not discovered and reported to the House leadership until the day of the veto override vote. Minority party members complained, but the House and Senate proceeded to override the veto. To clarify the status of Title III, the two houses repassed the farm bill with all titles in their proper place, the president vetoed the new bill, and the House and Senate again overrode the veto.

Provisions limiting the length of authorizations are known as *sunset* provisions. In principle, sunset provisions force the authorizing committee and Congress to re-pass authorization legislation periodically, which compels the executive branch to justify the continuation of the programs and gives the authorizing committees additional influence over the executive agencies. In recent years, many authorizations have expired but the programs have not died – sometimes out of neglect but often because of conflict over the program. Welfare reform, college student financial aid, and federal highway programs are among the dozens of unauthorized programs in recent years. These programs can continue as long as Congress passes the separate appropriations bills for them. An appropriation is possible by use of a waiver of the House rule, which may be included in the special rule under which the appropriations bills are considered on the House floor. A consequence of this practice is that the authorizing committees do not realize the special influence over the direction of these programs that was expected when the sunset provisions were first enacted.

Evolution of the Legislative Process

For most of the twentieth century, nearly all major and minor legislative measures have followed the path of the standard processes described in this chapter. The House and Senate were always free to modify their processes and have sometimes handled a bill in a special way. In the last three decades of the twentieth century, nonstandard approaches to preparing legislation for a vote have been employed with increasing frequency. Bypassing committees, negotiating details in summits between congressional leaders and representatives of the president, having multiple committees consider bills, and drafting omnibus bills characterize the action on a large share of major legislation considered by recent Congresses. In fact, according to one survey of the processes used by the House and Senate on major legislation since the late 1980s, four out of five measures in the House and two out of three in the Senate were considered under some nonstandard procedure.

Unorthodox legislative procedures have been invented for many reasons. The sheer complexity of some new public policies and legislative measures forces action by many committees – and compels committee and party leaders to find new ways to piece together legislation, negotiating a bewildering array of technical provisions and working with the president to avoid a veto. The reforms of the 1970s – which strengthened the House Speaker's procedural options and reduced the power of full committee chairs – were discovered to have unanticipated uses. Perhaps most important, partisan maneuvering stimulated procedural innovations as first one party and then the other sought parliamentary advantages when pushing legislation.

Furthermore, both chambers of Congress often create new rules in response to new challenges. In some cases the House and Senate have tailored their procedures to particular kinds of legislation or specific issues. In the last two decades, for example, Congress has created "fast-track" procedures for considering trade agreements negotiated by the executive branch with foreign governments. These procedures limit debate and bar amendments to speed congressional approval and limit congressional second-guessing of executive branch decisions.

An even more important class of legislation that has inspired special procedures concerns fiscal policy: decisions about federal spending, taxing, and budget deficits and surpluses. The Congressional Budget and Impoundment Control Act of 1974, often known simply as the Budget Act of 1974, established a process to coordinate congressional decision making affecting fiscal policy. In the 1980s and early 1990s, skyrocketing federal deficits motivated Congress to set tight rules constraining fiscal choices and to adopt unique procedures for enforcing the new constraints.

In other cases, special procedures are invented for an individual bill. In the House, special rules governing floor debate have become more complex, as have the provisions of unanimous consent agreements in the Senate. Task forces, usually appointed by party leaders, have become an everyday part of decision making in the House. Inter-committee negotiations guided by party leaders sometimes occur after committees report but before legislation is taken to the floor. In these ways, the traditional committee-to-floor-to-conference process has become a less accurate description of the increasingly meandering route that major legislation takes through the modern Congress.

Conclusion

Rules matter. Legislative rules, whether they arise from the Constitution or elsewhere, determine procedural advantages among the players, factions, and parties that compete for control over public policy. The rules also are the foundation of Congress's major organizational features, such as its leadership positions and committees, which help the institution manage a large and diverse workload and are generally designed to serve the political needs of its members.

The House and Senate have evolved quite different rules. Compared with Senate rules, House rules make it more difficult to circumvent committees, more strictly limit participation on the floor, and give the majority a greater ability to act when confronted with an obstructionist minority. The House is more majoritarian; the Senate is more egalitarian. The House is more committee oriented; the Senate is more floor oriented.

But the rules do not determine the political and policy objectives of legislators. Those objectives are primarily the product of the electoral processes through which people are selected to serve in Congress. Campaigns and elections connect members to their constituencies and lead many members to take a local, sometimes quite parochial, outlook in legislative politics.

Above: Sen. Olympia Snowe, R-Me., is questioned by reporters on her way to vote on the economic stimulus bill, February 10, 2009.
Below: January 1999: The vote board in the House of Representatives. Rebecca Roth/Roll Call.

8

The Floor and Voting

T HE TALLY WAS STUCK AT 207 IN FAVOR, 226 AGAINST, BUT THE DOW JONES industrial average continued to fall. First, it was 200 points, then 300 points, and finally close to 800 points before the gavel fell – more than 30 minutes after the vote began – with 205 in favor, 228 against. In a dramatic scene that seemed to catch the public, stock traders, and the leaders of both congressional parties by surprise the House had failed to pass a bill that would commit $700 billion to buy up troubled banking assets in an attempt to calm credit markets. In the days that followed, Democratic leaders blamed Republican leaders for not delivering promised votes, while Republican leaders blamed Democrats for poisoning the atmosphere surrounding the vote with partisan rhetoric. A compromise bill passed without drama a few days later, but the failed vote revealed a change in the way congressional leaders manage some controversial bills.

Votes are occasionally held open to allow straggling members to vote or in hopes of changing the outcome, but it is relatively rare to see a surprise outcome on the floor. Both the House and Senate have developed elaborate committee and party systems that can take much of the policy-making process off the chamber floors, but in recent Congresses, Democrats and Republicans alike have not been as hesitant to bring a bill to the floor without having a firm majority in place before hand and then doing enough "arm-twisting" to secure a majority.

During most of Congress's history, responsibility for the details of public policy rested with the standing committees. At times, power over the details of important bills resided in the hands of central party leaders. Most scholars have used this continuum – from decentralized, committee-oriented decision making to centralized, party-oriented decision making – to characterize the decision-making processes and distribution of power within the

237

TABLE 8.1. Possible Patterns of Congressional Decision Making.

Number of units	Number of effective participants	
	Few	Many
Few	Centralized (party leadership)	Collegial (floor)
Many		Decentralized (committees)

two chambers. Everything that goes on within the House and Senate is, in principle, subject to the approval of the parent chambers in floor sessions. In principle, therefore, the details of all legislation could be written and reviewed on the chamber floors, but in modern practice, this rarely happens.

These alternatives are depicted in Table 8.1. If important decisions were made on the chamber floor, all members, in that one place, would have the opportunity to participate effectively in deliberations on all measures. In general, as we saw in Chapter 6, the modern House is more dependent on committees than is the Senate. But there have been times when central party leaders dominated the House. Thus, the House is often characterized as varying along the centralized-decentralized continuum. The Senate is more collegial – more likely to make detailed policy choices on the floor. Both committees and party leaders are important in the Senate, but relative to the House, the Senate has long been far more floor oriented. Neither committees nor party leaders have found the Senate floor predictable or controllable. These differences are obvious every day in the Capitol.

In this chapter, we report on a typical day on the House and Senate floors and explain how differences in floor procedure shape the distribution of power in the two chambers. In addition, the chapter reviews how members' records of floor voting are most commonly analyzed by political scientists, journalists, and interest groups, providing a "consumer's guide" to studies of floor voting. The chapter concludes with a review of the factors that influence the relationship between the parties, committees, and the floor.

A Typical Day on the House and Senate Floors

On a March day in 2007, a fairly typical day while Congress is in session, dozens of committees and subcommittees held morning meetings and hearings in the congressional office buildings while clerks and pages prepared for the opening of the House and Senate floor sessions. In the Senate, this

meant distributing various documents to individual senators' desks, which
are arranged by party (when facing the front, Democrats are on the left and
Republicans are on the right) and seniority (junior members are in the back).
In the House, members do not have desks or assigned seats, although, by
tradition, the Democrats sit on the left and the Republicans on the right.
As the clerks and pages went about their work, tourists went in and out of
the galleries, some disappointed that they did not have a chance to see a
debate before they hurried off to other sites in Washington. As usual, the
Senate session opened before the House session – the Senate at 9:15 A.M.
and the House at 10 A.M.

The Day in the House

The House session began when Speaker pro tempore Jan Schakowsky
(D-Illinois) assumed the chair. The Speaker does not always preside over
House proceedings. She frequently appoints other members (Speakers *pro
tempore*) to take her place presiding over the House so that she can conduct
business in her office or elsewhere. Typically, several members will preside
during the course of the day.

The session opened with a prayer from the Reverend Thomas J. McCarthy
of St. Paul Catholic Church in Salem, Ohio. The Speaker pro tempore then
announced that she had examined the *Journal* of the House and announced
her approval of it. Approval of the *Journal* used to require a vote of the House,
but dilatory requests for votes led House Democrats to push through a rule
allowing the Speaker to approve the *Journal*. A member may still demand a
vote on the *Journal*, but that vote may be postponed until late in the day. Next
came the Pledge of Allegiance, which has been recited since 1989. The practice was started the year the Supreme Court ruled that burning the American flag was constitutionally protected speech, and Congress responded
with legislation to ban flag burning. House Republicans proposed –
and the Democrats did not dare block – a House rule that required that
the Pledge be recited after the prayer. After the Pledge, several members
of the Ohio delegation welcomed Reverend McCarthy to the House and
gave brief speeches on his life and accomplishments. The floor session
was televised (see box, "The Changing Congress: Televising the House and
Senate").

The Speaker pro tempore announced that members of each party would
be recognized to give one-minute speeches. The reservation of time for
one-minute speeches gives legislators a brief period to address the House
and the nation on any matter they choose. Frequently, members use

THE CHANGING CONGRESS: TELEVISING THE HOUSE AND SENATE

The House began televising its floor sessions in 1979. After becoming somewhat jealous of the attention given to the House, the Senate began to televise its sessions in 1986. Congressional employees operate both television systems, and the signal is made available to television networks and individual stations via satellite.

Floor proceedings are carried live on C-SPAN, the Cable-Satellite Public Affairs Network. Most cable television systems carry C-SPAN I, on which House sessions are shown. Many cable systems also carry C-SPAN II, where Senate sessions are broadcast. Many committee hearings, press conferences, and other public affairs programs are shown on C-SPAN when the House and Senate are not in session.

In both chambers, the most obvious consequence of television coverage has been an increase in floor speeches. In the House, one-minute and special-order speeches have become more numerous. One-minute speeches are made at the beginning of the day for about half an hour. Special-order speeches are made after the House finishes its regular business for the day. In 1994, House Democratic and Republican leaders agreed that special-order speeches should be limited to four hours on most days. They also began to experiment with structured, Oxford-style debates. In 1995, "reaction shots" of members on the floor were limited after members complained about being caught in unflattering shots by the floor cameras.

The Senate created a new class of speeches, the aforementioned special-order speeches, which are limited to five minutes. In addition, representatives and senators have made increasing use of large poster charts and graphs to illustrate their points for the television audience. In addition, many senators now address their chamber from the back row, some distance from their personal desks, so that the camera angle will be less steep and, in the case of male senators, will not expose their bald spots to home viewers.

one-minute speeches to respond to the news of the day, and they often use the opportunity to compliment or criticize the president. Occasionally, a group of members will organize themselves to emphasize a particular theme – and being outrageous or flamboyant increases the chance of getting on the evening news. On this day, there was a mix of speeches, some concerned the bill to provide more funding for military operations in Iraq, others addressed the Democrats plans for the federal budget, while others concerned less controversial topics such as prevention of veteran suicides, and honoring U.S. Marshal award winners.

After about a half hour of one-minute speeches, the Speaker pro tempore declared that the House dissolve into the Committee of the Whole House on the state of the Union for further consideration of H.R. 1227, a bill to assist in the provision of affordable housing to low-income families affected by Hurricane Katrina. The Committee of the Whole (COW) is what it sounds like, a committee of which all members of the House are members. The House often dissolves into the COW to debate and vote on amendments to bills. The quorum requirement is reduced to 100 from 218, which makes it easier to transact business. Since 1971, the House has allowed recorded voting on amendments in the COW, but the rules stipulate than any member can request that a vote be taken by the House on any amendments that pass in the COW.

Under the previously adopted special rule governing consideration of the bill, Representative Randy Neugebauer (R-Texas) was recognized to offer an amendment to the bill striking the section of the bill that would allow families to continue receiving housing vouchers after the termination of the Disaster Voucher program. Under the provisions of the special rule (see box "The Special Rule for H.R. 1227"), the amendment was debated for 60 minutes, with the time divided between Rep. Neugebauer and a member opposed to the amendment, in this case Rep. Barney Frank (D-Massachusetts). The debate centered on whether allowing hurricane victims to continue receiving housing vouchers would undermine the Section 8 public housing program. Proponents of the amendment argued that extending the vouchers was too expensive and was the wrong way to solve the region's housing problem. Opponents argued that given the level of destruction of housing in the Gulf region, there was insufficient public housing available. It was, therefore, crucial that the government not disadvantage beneficiaries of this program by putting a time limit on the voucher program.

At the conclusion of debate on the amendment, a voice vote was taken and it was announced that the amendment had failed. Rep. Neugebauer asked for a recorded vote on the amendment. House rules allow the chairperson of the Committee of the Whole to delay requests for recorded votes. This is typically done as a time-saving measure so that debate can continue on amendments. It is common practice for votes to be "stacked," that is occur one after another, so that members who are not on the floor can vote on several items in succession. The COW then debated an amendment offered by Rep. Tom Price (R-Georgia). At the close of debate on the amendment offered by Rep. Price, recorded votes on both the Price amendment and

THE SPECIAL RULE FOR H.R. 1227 (ANNOTATIONS BY THE AUTHORS)

Resolved, That at any time after the adoption of this resolution the Speaker may, pursuant to clause 2(b) of rule XVIII, declare the House resolved into the Committee of the Whole House on the state of the Union for consideration of the bill (H.R. 1227) to assist in the provision of affordable housing to low-income families affected by Hurricane Katrina.

This provision gives the Speaker control over when the bill will be considered.

The first reading of the bill shall be dispensed with. All points of order against consideration of the bill are waived except those arising under clause 9 or 10 of rule X.

This provision bans points of order that might be raised against consideration of the bill on the grounds that its provisions violate some rule or precedent.

General debate shall be confined to the bill and shall not exceed one hour equally divided and controlled by the chairman and ranking minority member of the Committee on Financial Services. After general debate the bill shall be considered for amendment under the five-minute rule.

This provision sets time limits on debate. General debate – that is, debate not directed at a specific amendment – is divided so that the two bill managers control 30 minutes each. They may allocate some time to colleagues by yielding time to them. The five-minute rule refers to a standing rule of the House that governs debate in the Committee of the Whole. The Chair first recognizes the amendment's sponsor to speak for five minutes. Next a Member opposing the amendment can claim five minutes to speak in opposition. Other Members may secure five minutes for debate by offering pro forma amendments. This is done by asking the Chair "to strike the last word."

The amendment in the nature of a substitute recommended by the Committee on Financial Services now printed in the bill, modified by the amendment printed in part A of the report of the Committee on Rules accompanying this resolution, shall be considered as adopted in the House and in the Committee of the Whole. The bill, as amended, shall be considered as the original bill for the purpose of further amendment under the five-minute rule and shall be considered as read. All points of order against provisions in the bill, as amended, are waived.

These provisions provide that the Financial Services Committee's version of the bill, rather than the version originally introduced, will be the subject of floor amending activity. An amendment to the committee's version, which was considered by the Rules Committee, would be automatically adopted upon the adoption of the special rule.

Notwithstanding clause 11 of rule XVIII, no further amendment to the bill, as amended, shall be in order except those printed in part B of the report of the Committee on Rules. Each further amendment may be offered only in the order printed in the report, may be offered only by a Member designated in the report, shall be considered as read, shall be debatable for the time specified in the report equally divided and controlled by the proponent and an opponent, shall not be subject to amendment, and shall not be subject to a demand for division of the question in the House or in the Committee of the Whole. All points of order against such further amendments are waived except those arising under clause 9 or 10 of rule X.

These provisions allow consideration of amendments specified in the accompanying report, which also specifies the order of consideration and the time allowed for debate. Other amendments are prohibited. Points of order against the amendments for violating House rules or precedent are prohibited.

At the conclusion of consideration of the bill for amendment the Committee shall rise and report the bill, as amended, to the House with such further amendments as may have been adopted. The previous question shall be considered as ordered on the bill and amendments thereto to final passage without intervening motion except one motion to recommit with or without instructions.

This provision gives the minority party an opportunity to offer an amendment as "instructions." If the instructions are adopted as a part of a motion to recommit, the bill is amended and immediately considered for final passage.

Sec. 2. During consideration in the House of H.R. 1227 pursuant to this resolution, notwithstanding the operation of the previous question, the Chair may postpone further consideration of the bill to a time designated by the Speaker.

the Neugebauer amendment were taken in succession. The Neugebauer amendment was rejected by a vote of 185–247 and the Price amendment was rejected by a vote of 96–333.

With all amendments having been considered, the COW then "rose" and the Speaker pro tempore resumed presiding over the House. The House then moved into the final stages of consideration of the H.R. 1227. Rep. Price asked for a revote on an amendment that had been adopted in the COW, which subsequently passed by a vote of 242–184. Rep. Bobby Jindal (R-Louisiana) then offered a motion to recommit with instructions that would give priority in public housing to displaced returning residents who were both "law-abiding" and employed. The motion to recommit is reserved for the minority party or someone who is opposed to the bill "in its current form." A motion to recommit with instructions to report forthwith – the type offered by Jindal – is essentially a substantive amendment to the bill. If it is adopted, the bill does not leave the floor at all, the change is reported by

---

Congressionally Speaking...

On the House floor, members engage in a carefully scripted language when debating on the floor. When a bill manager wishes to speak about a bill on the floor they say, "I yield myself such time as I may consume." If another member wishes to interject into debate he or she will say "Will the gentleman [gentle-woman] yield?" If the member holding the floor wishes to yield he/she will say in return, "I yield two minutes [or another block of time] to the gentleman [gentle-woman] from New Hampshire." The interjecting member will then say, "I thank the gentleman [gentlewoman] for yielding. I rise in support/opposition . . . " Once they have concluded they may say, "I yield back to the balance of my time." The bill manager will then begin his/her speech again with "Reclaiming my time . . . " This back and forth between floor managers and other members continues until the time allotted for debate is consumed.[1]

---

the committee immediately. Rep. Jindal's motion passed by a vote of 249–176, with a majority of Democrats voting no, and a majority of Republicans voting yea. During the 12 years of Republican rule it was rare for a motion to recommit with instructions to pass against the will of the Republican Party, but in the early months of the 110th Congress, the Democrats have lost a handful of these votes. The vote on the motion to recommit is the last procedural step before the "final passage" vote on a bill. The House then passed H.R.1227 by a vote of 302–125, with all Democrats voting in favor of passage along with 72 Republicans.

Following passage of H.R. 1227, the House considered several bills under suspension of the rules. This is a procedure in which a member can ask to "suspend the rules and pass" a particular bill. Bills taken up under this procedure are allotted 40 minutes of debate and amendments are not allowed. If two-thirds of the House votes in favor, the bill is passed. This procedure is used for non-controversial bills that typically involve a cost of less than $100 million. On this day, the House considered numerous bills and resolutions under this procedure, including a resolution authorizing the use of the capitol rotunda for a Holocaust remembrance ceremony, a reauthorization of the Hawaiian Homeownership Opportunity Act, the Judicial Disclosure Responsibility Act, and a bill to change the cost of living adjustment for veterans – with six receiving recorded votes – all passing except for the Hawaiian Homeownership Opportunity.

The House then heard a number of special order speeches – most concerning the status of the War in Iraq and what, if any, policy changes the

THE CHANGING CONGRESS: *THE CONGRESSIONAL RECORD*

The proceedings of the House and Senate are published daily in the *Congressional Record*. The *Record* is printed overnight and distributed to Capitol Hill and to many other places, including most large libraries. Hardcover, permanent editions are published and distributed periodically.

The *Record* is much more than a report of the words spoken on the chamber floors. Introduced bills, committee meetings, and many other items are listed in the *Record* each day. The text of bills and conference reports considered on the floor is included, as are the many newspaper articles, scholarly studies, executive agency reports, and other items that members place in the *Record* by gaining unanimous consent of their house. As a general rule, the charts or graphs that members use on the floor cannot be printed in the *Record*, although tabular material may be inserted if the member receives unanimous consent.

The members' ability to alter prose reported in the *Record* after they have spoken has long been a controversial issue. Members are allowed to make non-substantive grammatical changes in their prose. As a result, some members appear far more articulate in the *Record* than they do on the floor. Statements and other insertions in the *Record* are supposed to be distinguished by a bullet (•). In the Senate, members frequently seek, and then always receive, unanimous consent to have their statements placed in the *Record* "as though read." This revision makes distinguishing what was said from what was inserted nearly impossible. Frequently, senators request that their statements be included "at the appropriate place," which is usually done so that the statement does not interrupt the discussion on a pending matter in the *Record*.

The *Congressional Record* tends to be a more faithful record of House proceedings than of Senate proceedings. Representatives frequently seek permission to "revise and extend" their remarks, so many statements reported in the *Record* were not actually read on the floor. But the House has more restrictive rules about including extraneous matter and speeches in the *Record* and requires that newspaper articles and other insertions be printed in a separate section, "Extensions of Remarks." The House also has long required that revisions or extensions that are not "a substantially verbatim" account be distinguished by a different typeface. The House adopted an even tighter rule in 1995 that limits changes to corrections of grammar and typographical errors.

House should adopt as part of the bill providing supplemental funding for the Iraq war. Special orders typically take place at the conclusion of other business that the House is considering that day. Members are allowed to give speeches on topics of their choice regardless of whether the speech concerns pending legislation. Members typically reserve time for special orders through the party leadership and may choose to insert the speech

into the *Congressional Record* without actually delivering the speech – unde-
livered speeches appear in the *Extension of Remarks* section of the *Congressional Record*. The House adjourned at 1:05 A.M. until 10:00 A.M. the same
morning.

The Day in the Senate

The Senate convened at 9:15 A.M. when Senator Sheldon Whitehouse
(D-Rhode Island) called the Senate to order. The vice president is the president of the Senate, but tends to preside only at ceremonial occasions (for
example, when the oath of office is administered to newly elected senators at
the start of a Congress) and when a tie-breaking vote might be needed. The
Constitution provides for a president pro tempore to preside in the absence
of the vice president. But the president pro tempore, who by tradition is
the most senior member of the majority party, is not able to preside on
a full-time basis because of other duties. Consequently, the president pro
tempore's staff arranges for other majority party senators, usually the most
junior ones, to take turns presiding over the Senate.

On this day, following the pledge of allegiance, Senator Whitehouse read
a letter from the president pro tempore, Senator Robert Byrd (D-West
Virginia), appointing Whitehouse as acting president pro tempore. After the
prayer, Senator Kent Conrad (D-North Dakota), serving as acting majority leader in the absence of Majority Leader Harry Reid (D-Nevada), was
recognized and indicated that the Senate immediately resume debate on
the budget resolution for fiscal year 2008. Senator Conrad indicated that
Senator John Ensign (R-Nevada) would be recognized to offer an amendment, followed by an amendment from the majority party. Senator Conrad also informed senators that there would be no recorded votes taken
before 5:00 P.M. Senator Conrad also urged his colleagues to speed up
debate on the budget resolution, warning them that the session could run
to midnight if necessary. Senator Ensign's amendment sought to "ensure
that troops serving in harm's way remain America's top budget priority
by: ensuring full funding for the Department of Defense within the regular appropriations process, reducing reliance on supplemental appropriation bills, and by improving the integrity of the Congressional budget
process." Debate on the Ensign amendment continued with several senators expressing their support or opposition. Then Senator Barack Obama
(D-Illinois) asked for and was granted 10 minutes to discuss the costs –
both monetary and in terms of human life – of the Iraq war and to urge

---

Congressionally Speaking...

On the Senate floor, *quorum calls* are used to get a temporary break in the action – a time out. A senator might say, "Mr. President, I suggest the absence of a quorum," and the presiding officer will respond, "The clerk will call the roll." Technically, if a quorum is not discovered, the Senate will have to adjourn. Indeed, filibustering senators sometimes note the absence of a quorum to force senators to appear on the floor. Most of the time, however, a quorum call is used as a time out that gives absent senators time to come to the floor to offer an amendment or speak. At other times, a quorum call is used to give leaders time to work out agreements on issues or procedure.

---

senators to consider these costs. The speech by Senator Obama highlights the fact that the rules of debate in the Senate are much more casual than in the House. Senators regularly ask for and receive unanimous consent to give speeches that are not related to the bill currently under consideration.

When debate on the Ensign amendment was concluded, the Senate moved on to an amendment offered by Senator Jim Bunning (D-Kentucky) concerning Social Security funding, along with several other amendments. Debate on these amendments continued until late into the afternoon, at which point the Senate moved into "morning business." Despite the name, morning business does not necessarily occur in the morning. During morning business, the Senate conducts routine business such as receiving messages from the House and the president, as well as petitions and memorials, committee reports, and bill introductions.

Following morning business the Senate moved into Executive session to consider a nominee for the post of Assistant Secretary of Preparedness and Response in the Department of Health and Human Services. The nominee was confirmed by unanimous consent. The Senate then adjourned for the day at 7:52 P.M.

House-Senate Differences

The events of this day illustrate many of the differences between the two chambers of Congress. Most of the differences are the by-product of one fact: Floor debate and amendments are governed by strict rules in the House, but are generally limited only by unanimous consent agreements or super-majority votes in the Senate. Representatives must worry that their floor amendments might not be put in order by a special rule from the Rules Committee. Once a bill is on the House floor, representatives are compelled to conform to the schedule laid out by the Speaker and the special rules. In sharp contrast, senators can introduce amendments freely, even on subjects unrelated to the bill at hand, and protect their ability to do so by objecting to requests for unanimous consent to limit amendments. Moving the Senate from amendment to amendment and from bill to bill is a constant struggle for the majority leader and bill managers. The House has a schedule that is followed in the main; scheduling in the Senate is often much like fortune telling.

Voting Procedure

By the end of that March day in 2007, the House had held 12 recorded votes, all using its computerized voting system. The Senate had held seven recorded votes, all on amendments to the budget resolution. When the Senate conducts a roll-call vote, the process is time consuming. It is an old-fashioned roll call for which a clerk calls out the individual names of the senators in alphabetical order ("Mr. Akaka... Mr. Alexander... Mr. Allard... Mr. Baucus," and so on) and waits for senators to arrive on the floor and respond. After calling all of the names, the roll-call clerk starts from the beginning to call the names of senators who have not voted. The clerk is then interrupted by senators appearing during the vote to recognize them and hear their votes. The Constitution provides that "the Yeas and Nays of the Members of either House on any question shall, at the desire of one-fifth of those present, be entered upon the Journal." This rule means that 20 senators or 87 representatives (if all members are present) may demand a vote in which each member's vote is recorded. In practice, with few members being present, usually only 11 senators or 44 representatives are required – one-fifth of a quorum, which is half of the membership of the chamber. Because the quorum requirement is not enforced unless a member makes a point of order that a quorum is not present, the presiding officer will assume that a quorum is present and order the yeas and nays based on the lower threshold. Under the rules of the House, 25 members may demand a recorded vote in the Committee of the Whole, where most votes on amendments to bills take place. The Constitution does not specify how the houses should vote in the absence of a demand for the yeas and nays.

House Voting Procedure

In today's Congress, the House votes by three means: voice vote, division vote, and recorded vote. On most motions, the presiding officer (the chair of the Committee of the Whole or the Speaker) first asks for a voice vote. He or she might say, "The question is on the amendment by the gentlewoman from Illinois. All in favor say 'aye,' all opposed say 'no.' The noes have it, and the amendment is rejected." In many cases, this is spoken so rapidly that it is obvious that the number voting each way had little to do with the announcement of the winning side. Sometimes, the issue is not controversial, and the presiding officer is merely reporting the obvious result. In other cases, the presiding officer knows that his or her announcement will make no difference because a member will demand a recorded vote on the issue.

The division, or standing, vote is used little and is virtually never decisive. Any member may demand such a vote, which is conducted by having members voting aye stand and be counted and then having members voting no stand and be counted. Only the vote tally – the number of ayes and noes – is recorded. Because few members are on the floor for debate on most matters, the result usually shows that less than a quorum of members is present (a quorum is 100 or more in the Committee of the Whole) which leads automatically to a recorded vote. Consequently, this method is seldom used any longer.

Recorded votes are conducted with the assistance of an electronic voting system and nearly always occur upon the demand of the necessary number of members after a voice vote. In the Committee of the Whole, 25 members must demand a recorded vote. (The Constitution's requirement that one-fifth of those present demand a recorded vote applies only to requests for recorded votes in the House, not in the Committee of the Whole.)

Each member is issued a voting card about the size of a credit card. To vote, a member uses his or her card in any one of the nearly 40 voting boxes scattered around the House chamber (most are attached to the back of the chamber's bench-like seats). With the card inserted, the member presses one of three buttons – yea, nay, or present – and his or her vote is recorded by the computer system. As the votes are cast, they are displayed on panels above the gallery at the front of the chamber, and the running totals can be viewed on computer terminals. Under the House rules, recorded votes take 15 minutes, although the presiding officer often holds the vote open a little longer to allow members to make it to the floor and cast their votes. On a few occasions, the Speaker has held open the vote for several minutes to find

THE CHANGING CONGRESS: LONG VOTES LEAD TO CONTROVERSY

On November 23, 2003, the House of Representatives passed a prescription drug benefit for senior citizens under the Medicare programs. Debate on the bill had continued until 3:00 A.M. at which time presiding officer Richard Hastings (R-Washington) announced that the House would have a 15-minute vote. At the end of 15 minutes the bill was losing by 15 votes, and after one hour, the tally stood at 216–218. By most accounts, then-Speaker Dennis Hastert (R-Illinois) was resolved to the fact that the bill would fail, but he, along with then-Majority Leader Tom DeLay (R-Texas) and others, continued to try to convince recalcitrant Republicans to vote for the bill. At 5:00 A.M., then President Bush was awakened to begin calling wayward members. The combination of his encouragement and other persuasive activities was enough to secure victory. Democrats cried foul and called for reform. Upon gaining a majority in House after the 2006 elections, Democrats enacted a rule banning holding a vote open for the "sole purpose of reversing the outcome."

The new rule did not prevent the Democrats from becoming ensnared in their own controversy over vote outcomes in August 2007 on a motion to recommit. Republicans charged that the vote count was reported incorrectly and that the vote had been closed while members were still trying to change their vote. A Select Committee on Voting Irregularities agreed and urged the House to repeal the apparently unenforceable rule on holding votes open.

the last vote or two his or her side needed to win. The rules do permit the Speaker to postpone votes – to "stack" votes is the jargon used – in some circumstances, such as votes on motions to suspend the rules and pass a measure. Stacked votes are cast in rapid succession in periods of five minutes each, usually near the end of a session, to allow members to vote on several matters without having to make multiple trips back-and-forth between their offices and the House floor. By the way, the record for the number of recorded votes cast without missing one belongs to Representative William Natcher (D-Kentucky), who cast 18,401 consecutive votes over 22 years before he became ill and died in 1994.

Senate Voting Procedure

The Senate, too, has voice, division, and recorded votes, but virtually no division votes are cast in the Senate because of its smaller size. On voice and recorded votes, Senate practice is quite different from House practice. On many, perhaps most, "votes," the Senate does not really vote at all. The presiding officer often brings a matter to a vote when debate appears to have ended by saying, "Hearing no further debate, and without objection, the amendment is agreed to." In this way, even the pretense of a voice vote is not observed in the Senate. Recorded roll-call votes often are ordered in advance, upon the successful demand of a senator, so no preliminary voice vote is held, as in the House.

Recorded votes in the Senate are properly called roll-call votes. The names of the senators are called out, one by one, by a clerk, and senators' responses are recorded by hand. Roll-call votes are supposed to take only 15 minutes, as stipulated by a unanimous consent agreement that the majority leader arranges at the beginning of each Congress. Many, if not most, Senate roll-call votes last longer than 15 minutes, however, to accommodate senators who need more time to make it to the floor. At times, these delays have become so burdensome that majority leaders have promised to insist that the 15-minute limit be observed, but the desire to accommodate colleagues seems so overwhelming that votes extending to 20 minutes or more remain common. Senator Robert Byrd (D-West Virginia) cast his 17,000th roll-call vote in April 2004 – a Senate record.

Changes in Floor Decision Making

On the surface, it might seem that the differences in voting procedures between the two chambers matter little. The record suggests otherwise. House voting procedures changed in the early 1970s – and with important consequences. As earlier chapters have discussed, the early 1970s was a period of remarkable change in House politics. Power devolved from full committee chairs to subcommittee chairs, many of whom were inexperienced as bill managers. Personal and subcommittee staffs were growing, which enabled more members to design and promote their own legislation. Also, a new breed of member – more media-oriented and more insistent on having a meaningful role – seemed to be flooding into Congress. In this context, the House changed the voting rules in such a way that encouraged members to pursue floor amendments more frequently and more actively.

The House voting reforms had two components. First, a new rule extended recorded voting to the Committee of the Whole. Before 1971, no recorded votes took place in the House's Committee of the Whole, where action on floor amendments takes place. That meant that members' positions on most floor amendments were not recorded. As is still the case, a roll-call vote could be demanded on amendments approved in the Committee of the Whole just before the vote on final passage of the bill, but rejected amendments could not be considered again.

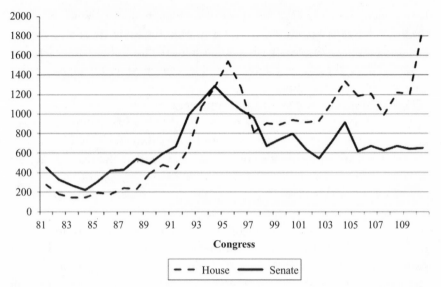

FIGURE 8.1. Number of House and Senate Roll-Call Votes, 1947–2008. *Source: Data collected by the authors.*

Second, the electronic voting system was used for the first time in 1973. Voting "by electronic device," as they call it in the House, nearly completely replaced the old system of teller voting in the Committee of the Whole and the traditional call of the roll in the House. Teller voting was done by having members pass by tellers (members appointed to do the counting), with the yes voters to one side and the no voters to the other. The 1971 reform allowed recorded teller voting, in which members signed green (yes) or red (no) cards, deposited them in a box, and then waited for tellers to count them and turn them over to clerks, who would record each member's individual vote. This cumbersome process discouraged recorded voting in the Committee of the Whole. Automated vote counting by the electronic system allowed the Committee of the Whole and the House to complete a vote and have the results in 15 minutes.

Electronic recorded voting produced a surge in amending activity. Being able to put one's position on a particular issue on the record (and forcing one's opponents to do the same) created new incentives to offer amendments, particularly for the minority party. Electronic voting also reduced the burden imposed on colleagues by demands for recorded votes. The result, as Figure 8.1 illustrates, was an increase in the number of floor votes, most on amendments, beginning in the first Congress (the 93rd, 1973–1974) that used both electronic and recorded voting in the Committee of the Whole. By the late 1970s, the House floor began to look much more like the Senate floor than it had for a century. Longer daily floor sessions, repetitive amendments, and scheduling uncertainty had become the norm. Worse yet for the Democratic leaders, more free-wheeling amending activity made it more difficult for them to enforce deals made in committee and to hold a majority coalition together on the floor.

House Democrats sought relief in new rules and practices. In 1979, after several aborted attempts, they finally increased from 20 to 25 the number of members required to support a request for a recorded vote in the Committee of the Whole. This change seemed to have little effect on amending activity, however. A more important reaction to the increase in amendment votes was an expansion of the number of days each month in which motions to suspend the rules were in order. A motion to suspend the rules simultaneously brings a measure to the floor and passes it. No amendments are allowed and debate is limited to 40 minutes, which makes suspending the rules an attractive procedure for bill managers. Although a successful motion to suspend the rules requires a two-thirds majority, Democrats managed to increase the use of suspension motions during the 1970s, a trend that has continued.

The most important response by the Democrats was to have the Rules Committee design more special rules to restrict floor amendments. The change in the content of special rules in the 1980s was quite dramatic. Most special rules continued to put in order at least some, and often many, amendments (open or modified open rules), but Republicans correctly complained that many special rules had been designed to prevent all or most amendments (closed or modified closed rules). Consequently, Republicans made procedural reforms a centerpiece of the 1994 congressional campaign. As Figure 8.2 reveals, after becoming the majority party following the 1994 elections, Republicans initially kept their campaign promise to offer more open/modified open rules than had the Democrats, although there was a slight increase in the use of restrictive rules under the new Republican majority. This policy has changed dramatically in recent congresses. In 2005–2006, more than half of the special rules (59 percent) were either closed or modified closed, while only 12 percent were open or modified – a complete reversal from the last democratically controlled Congress in 1993–1994. The trend toward more restrictive rules has only accelerated as the House has reached an all time high in the rule restrictiveness in the 109th and 110th Congresses – both with Democratic majorities.

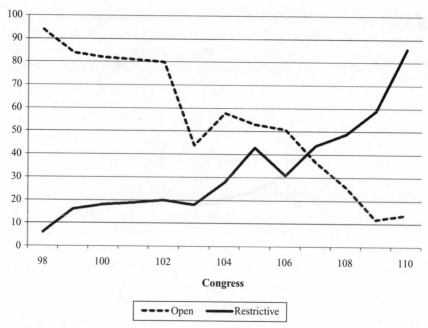

FIGURE 8.2. Restrictiveness of Special Rules, 1983–2008. *Source:* Data collected from reports of the House Committee on Rules.

The net result of the more than two decades of adjustments to the voting reforms of the early 1970s has been a more bifurcated process for managing legislation on the House floor. Legislation that is of little importance is not subject to amendments; it is considered under suspension of the rules or, if it is sufficiently non-controversial, it is brought up by unanimous consent and passed without a recorded vote. Legislation that is likely to attract even a few amendments is likely to be considered under a special rule that limits amending activity in some way, often to the disadvantage of the minority party.

These changes have renewed the distinctiveness of House floor decision-making. While the number of House floor votes has been similar to that of the Senate in recent Congresses, House floor action is more predictable and more carefully controlled to advantage committees' legislation.

Analyzing Votes

Nearly all members participate in recorded floor votes, so floor votes offer a natural basis for comparing members' policy positions. The voting record

is available in the *Congressional Record* and a variety of commercial publications. It can even be examined on personal computers through the use
of THOMAS, a service of the Library of Congress (http://thomas.loc.gov).
Political scientists, journalists, interest groups, challengers to incumbents,
and many others have long analyzed the roll-call record for scientific, educa-
tional, and political purposes. Consequently, the use – and misuse – of the
congressional voting record to make inferences about legislators is a subject
that recurs in nearly every congressional campaign.

The Problems of Interpreting the Roll-Call Vote

A legislator's roll-call vote can be thought of as an act based on (1) a policy
preference and (2) a decision about how to act on that preference. The policy
preference may be influenced by an array of political forces – constituents,
the president, interest groups, party and committee leaders, the legislator's
personal views, and so on. Thus, the personal view of a legislator is not easily
inferred from a roll-call vote. Moreover, whatever the basis for his or her
policy preference, the legislator may hold that preference intensely or only
weakly.

A member's decision about how to vote can be sincere or strategic. For
example, a member may strategically vote against a bill even if she prefers
the bill to no bill at all, if she believes that killing the bill will lead to action
on an alternative that she will like even more. Such "strategic voting" on the
first bill might lead an observer to conclude incorrectly that the member
prefers the status quo to the first bill. A member also might cast a deceptive
vote. An extreme example is a member who holds a strong policy preference
and works hard behind the scenes to push his point of view, yet votes the
other way on the floor to make the folks back home happy.

Plainly, the political and strategic character of members' policy preferences and voting choices is an obstacle to the use of roll-call votes as the
basis for making claims about legislators' intentions or objections in casting
a vote. But the situation is not as hopeless as it might seem. Most votes are
not strategic or deceptive. They reflect the political preference of the member fairly well, which makes political sense. Members know that their votes
on important issues may be used against them, so they have an incentive to
cast votes that are easily explained. Besides, the number of situations that
present an opportunity for strategic or deceptive voting is not nearly as large
as it could be. Nevertheless, caution is required when making inferences
from a particular vote.

The possibility of strategic or deceptive voting is less troublesome in analyzing summary statistics on members' voting records than it is when considering votes individually. Many voting indices summarize members' records over a large number of votes by counting the number of times that they vote in a certain way – for example, in favor of the president's position. Instances of strategic or deceptive voting are not likely to affect the scores assigned to the legislators, but skepticism is in order for scoring based on subsets of the larger voting record.

Common Voting Measures

Political scientists and journalists have relied on several indices to characterize members' voting records. The most widely reported measures are those calculated by the research department of the Congressional Quarterly (CQ), which publishes *Congressional Quarterly Weekly Report*, a news magazine that provides in-depth coverage of Congress. CQ calculates objective indicators of members' support for and opposition to the president, support for and opposition to their party's positions, and support for and opposition to the conservative coalition.

Measures of the role that party plays in members' voting decisions are the most frequently used roll-call statistics. Many of these measures are based on the party vote, which CQ defines as a vote on which a majority of Democrats oppose a majority of Republicans. The percentage of all votes that are party votes is a common measure of the degree of partisanship in the House and Senate. The historical record for party votes – sometimes called party unity votes – is demonstrated in Figure 8.3. An individual member's overall level of support for his or her party is usually determined by the percentage of times he or she has supported the party's position on party votes. CQ calls these party unity scores.

CQ's label is a little misleading. Because a party vote occurs any time a majority of one party votes differently than a majority of the other party, a party vote might occur when the parties actually differ very little. For example, a vote on which 51 percent of Democrats and 49 percent of Republicans voted yea would be a party unity vote. This result would hardly be an indication of unified parties, and party influences or differences might not have played much of a role in the outcome. Of course, any objective measure requires that some standard be used – if not a simple majority, then perhaps a two-thirds or a 90 percent majority. Thus, whereas some caution is required in using CQ's measure, it remains one of the best available for examining the frequency of party alignments in Congress over time.

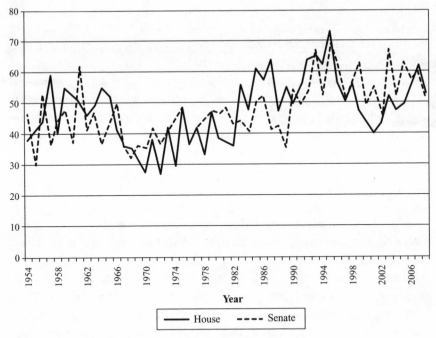

FIGURE 8.3. Percent of All Votes that Were Party Votes, 1954–2008.

CQ also analyzes congressional votes on bills for which the president has taken a position by examining the public statements of the president and administration officials. CQ calculates a success rate for the president, consisting of the percentage of such votes on which the president's position prevails. Analysts using CQ's scores must rely on the CQ staff's ability to accurately identify the votes and the president's position. They must also hope that CQ is consistent in applying its selection criteria over time. Perhaps because CQ says nothing beyond a single sentence about the president's public statements, no one has effectively challenged CQ's work on this score.

The most obvious weakness of the CQ scores is that they do not take into account the varying importance of the issues behind the votes. One way to handle this problem is to use only votes that are contested – those that show a close division. The argument is that lopsided votes – for example, 90 to 10 – are less likely to have been seen as decisive, controversial, or critical to the choices made on issues important to members. Besides, one-sided outcomes do not allow analysts to distinguish among members. Thus, analysts frequently limit their choice of votes to those with less than

75 percent, or perhaps even 60 percent, of the members voting in the majority.

CQ offers a corrective of its own by identifying 15–20 key votes every year for each chamber. The publication first identifies the year's major issues subjectively – identifying those that were highly controversial, a matter of presidential or political power, or had a great impact on the country – and then, for each issue identified, chooses the vote that was the most important in determining an outcome. CQ does not calculate scores based on these key votes, although political scientists have frequently used key votes for the construction of their own voting measures.

The Ratings Game

Dozens of interest groups regularly report ratings for members of Congress. The wide range of groups that do this includes ideological groups, farmers' organizations, environmental and consumer groups, and large labor and business associations. Not surprisingly, the ratings are used for political purposes. Most interest groups send press releases to the news media in members' home states and districts, praising their supporters in Congress and chastising their opponents. They also use their own ratings as a factor in decisions about campaign contributions. Nearly all groups use their scores to enlighten their memberships about their friends and enemies in Congress. Even incumbents and challengers advertise interest group ratings to substantiate their claims about the policy stances of the incumbents.

Interest groups' ratings of legislators are based on a limited number of votes selected by group officials. The processes by which groups select votes on which to base their ratings vary widely. Some groups do not complete their analyses until their board of directors or some other authoritative group approves the list of votes, whereas others allow low-level staff to identify the pertinent votes. Typically, groups have compiled and published their annual lists at the end of a congressional session. However, more recently some groups have begun choosing votes prior to their occurrence and sometimes even at the request of individual members or party leaders. In publicizing that a particular vote will be "scored," interest groups seek to influence wavering members to support the group's position. Upon preselecting a vote for scoring, groups will fax notices to members' offices or distribute cards prior to the vote that are imprinted with the group's logo and position on the vote. Some accounts suggest that the failure in the House to pass a comprehensive bankruptcy reform bill at the end of the

107th Congress was due in part to interest groups announcing that they would be "scoring" the vote on the special rule, which contained a provision concerning the ability of anti-abortion activists to avoid fines by filing for bankruptcy.

Groups vary in how narrowly or broadly they define their interests. The AFL-CIO, for example, includes votes in its ratings that concern issues that "affect working people who are not necessarily union members." The National Farmers Union has included votes on such issues as the MX missile, social security financing, and constitutional amendments requiring a balanced budget in its scales.

Moreover, the number of votes included in interest group scales varies widely as well. Sometimes as few as nine or 10 votes are included in an interest group's scale, which means that just one or two votes can produce great swings in the scores assigned to legislators. Groups sometimes include several votes on the same issue to give that issue greater weight in their calculations, whereas others carefully avoid doing so. And groups have been known to alter their selection of votes to get a certain scale that will benefit friends or make enemies look bad.

Further complicating the interpretation of interest groups' ratings of law-makers is the type of votes these groups select. Quite naturally interest groups want to separate supporters and opponents, so they tend to choose important votes that show close divisions. Because legislators tend to be consistent in their policy positions, the tendency to pick votes with close divisions has the effect of repeatedly counting the same set of members as supporters and another set of members as opponents. As some critics of interest group ratings have noted, this process produces a polarized distribution of scores even when the real distribution of legislators' preferences more closely approximates a normal curve (a bell-shaped curve).

The lesson is that we should be quite skeptical of claims that legislators' interest group ratings are reliable indicators of their support for particular causes. Anyone seriously concerned about legislators' support for a cause should seek additional clues. Using the ratings of two or more groups with similar agendas is a good place to start. Sometimes, a better guide than a legislator's specific percentage rating is how that figure compares with other legislators' ratings. The legislator might have a rating of 85 percent support on a group's rating scale, but places in only the 50th percentile among all legislators on that scale. The latter often is a better indicator of where the member is positioned on the full spectrum of views on a given issue. Moreover, whenever a member's degree of commitment to a cause is at issue, we should look for corroborating evidence – bills sponsored, amendments offered, speeches made, and behind-the-scenes effort – that may be reported in the press or identified by knowledgeable observers.

Yet, interest group ratings retain their special appeal for analysts because collectively they provide a summary of legislators' policy views across a broad array of issue areas. Scholars often argue that the selection of the votes used in the ratings by knowledgeable interest group officials gives the ratings validity as measures of support for various causes. But convenience, rather than a careful judgment about the ratings' validity, seems to underlie many scholars' use of interest group ratings.

Dimensions, Alignments, and Coalitions

Given the limitations of interest group ratings, asking whether legislators' policy positions can be characterized in more objective ways is natural. They can. Political scientists have developed ways to determine the basic attitudes or dimensions that underlie voting patterns and the nature of the voting alignments in Congress (who votes with whom). Three basic concepts – dimensions, alignments, and coalitions – are important to understand.

Political scientists' techniques involve a search for consistency in the voting patterns across a set of roll-call votes. The idea is simple: If the legislators' voting behavior exhibits a discernable pattern for a set of votes, then we might assume that a particular mix of political forces were at work on members for that set of votes. A dimension of political conflict is said to be present when a certain alignment of members is visible throughout a set of votes.

For example, liberal and conservative members are often identified at opposite ends of an ideological dimension. The usual assumption is that each member holds a fairly stable ideological perspective and is guided by that perspective when deciding how to vote. Of course, members' voting behavior also may reflect the political outlook of their home state or district, the influence of party or faction leaders, and other political forces that produce an alignment of members that appears to have a liberal-to-conservative character. This is one reason politicians often resist being labeled liberals or conservatives. Some members may not even have personal views about the policies at issue on most votes and still demonstrate voting patterns that appear to fit neatly on a liberal-conservative continuum.

In principle, many dimensions of conflict may organize voting patterns, perhaps a different dimension for different sets of votes. Indeed, many scholars argue that we should expect many dimensions in congressional voting because Congress operates in a pluralistic political system, one in which a different set of interest groups and constituents wages the legislative battle on each issue. The issues may divide urban and rural Americans, producers and consumers, employers and employees, coastal- and middle-Americans, retired and not-yet-retired people, and, of course, Democrats and Republicans. The number of possible bases for conflict is large. The analyst's task is to find the important dimensions of conflict without arbitrarily limiting the search to a few of the possible alignments, such as party-based alignments.

Two schools of thought about the dimensions and alignments of congressional voting have emerged. The older school adopts the pluralistic view and emphasizes the multidimensionality of congressional voting. A newer school emphasizes the consistent presence and explanatory power of a liberal-conservative dimension. Some of the difference between the schools is due to differences in the statistical techniques they use. Part of the difference is due to differences in judgment or taste – just how much must a voting alignment vary from what is thought to be a liberal-conservative division before we count it as something else?

The difficulty of making a satisfactory interpretation is visible in an analysis of Senate votes during the 109th Congress (2005–2006). Senators' scores on two dimensions, calculated by political scientist Keith Poole, are arrayed in Figure 8.4. The horizontal dimension is related to the general liberal-conservative position on economic, tax, and spending issues; the vertical dimension separates senators according to their behavior on the very few issues that do not cleanly divide senators along liberal/conservative lines, such as free trade, immigration, and abortion. Senators with nearly identical scores on one of the dimensions often have a wide range of scores on the other dimension. However, in recent congresses the first dimension has explained more than 90 percent of the variance in roll-call voting. Party leaders, presidents, and lobbyists do not dare ignore such differences. They see important differences among members who operate in a complex world filled with conflicting pressures on legislators.

The alignment of legislators in Figure 8.4 is clearly partisan. Democratic senators are grouped in the upper left and Republicans are grouped in the lower right. We might be tempted to say that the two parties were strong coalitions on the issues confronting Congress. And yet, both parties show substantial internal variation, with some Democrats and Republicans falling closer to each other than they do to fellow partisans. Ben Nelson (D-Nebraska) and Lincoln Chafee (R-Rhode Island) are virtually indistinguishable on the liberal conservative dimension. Although the parties have

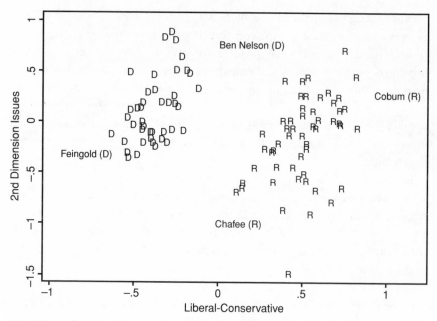

FIGURE 8.4. Ideological Alignments in the Senate, 109th Congress (2005–2006). *Source:* Data provided by Keith Poole and Howard Rosenthal, http://www.pooleandrosenthal.com.

quite different central tendencies, they simply are not tightly knit groups that keep their members from deviating from the position preferred by most party members. To be sure, party leaders and other factors tend to keep party members together, but many other forces lead party members to go their own way from time to time.

The distinction between alignments and coalitions is critical for understanding legislative politics. An alignment merely shows the distribution of policy positions among members, based on their voting behavior. But a group of members may vote the same way for different reasons, and they may vote alike only because they have similar home constituencies. They can be called a coalition only if they consciously coordinate their voting. Thus, we simply cannot determine the presence of active coalitions from voting behavior alone.

During the middle decades of the twentieth century, southern Democrats often voted with Republicans, creating policy victories for what was known as the "conservative coalition." There has been some dispute about how much coordination actually took place between Republican leaders and southern Democratic leaders on these votes. That is, just how much of a coalition was the so-called conservative coalition? The answer seems to be that at times genuine coordination took place that affected members' voting behavior, but at most times the alignment of Republicans and southern Democrats against northern Democrats appeared without coordination as members made largely independent judgments about how to vote.

The Floor, Committees, and Parties

This chapter completes the examination of the three major features of congressional organization – the parties, the committees, and the floors. These three components combine to create the policy-making process in Congress. As we have seen, just how the components are combined varies between the two chambers and, within each chamber, over time. This is a good place to summarize the forces that lie behind those variations – the character of Congress's policy agenda, the distribution of policy preferences among members, and the institutional context.

Issue Agenda

The character of the legislative process is greatly affected by the nature of the issues that Congress confronts. As a general rule, Congress relies more heavily on committees to make policy choices when it must deal with a large number of issues and when the issues it considers are readily separable, recur frequently, or are less salient. Why? A large workload requires a division of labor so that many issues can be addressed simultaneously. A system of standing committees provides such a division of labor. If the issues are separable into distinct categories, then committees with distinct jurisdictions work well. Furthermore, if the same issues arise time and again, then fixing committee jurisdictions can be done without concern that some committees will become superfluous over time. Moreover, if most issues concern only a few members, committees are a natural place for those members to gather and make the detailed policy choices that do not interest other members.

Alignment of Policy Preferences

Because the process by which decisions are made may influence which choices are made, the contending parties and factions in Congress often seek to shape the decision-making process to their liking. Sometimes party divisions predominate; at other times, cross-party coalitions arise to make the important policy choices. When issues are salient to most members and the members of the majority party share similar policy views, the majority party may centralize policy making in the hands of its leaders. When most members care about the issues, but the majority party is not cohesive, neither committees nor majority party leaders may be trusted. Members then turn to the floor as the place where they can shape policy details.

Institutional Context

Differences in the institutional arrangements in the House and Senate are likely to cause different responses to similar changes in issue agendas and policy alignments. The Senate's rules and practices protect the rights of individual senators to offer amendments and conduct debate on the floor. Consequently, the Senate usually retains a more collegial, floor-oriented decision-making process. In contrast, the rules and practices of the House advantage the Speaker and standing committees. If the majority party is united, the Speaker tends to direct policy making with vigor; if not, the committees are more independent. As a result, House decision making is generally less collegial and less floor-oriented. Change in the House tends to come as movement along the centralized-decentralized continuum described previously.

Indeed, the constraints on floor amendments under House special rules are the product of cooperation between the traditional centers of power in the House – committees and majority party leaders. Rules Committee decisions about special rules often represent the terms of an agreement between committee and party leaders. Cohesiveness in the majority party enables agreements between committee and party leaders to gain the majority required to adopt restrictive special rules on the floor. In the Senate, the carefully preserved rights of individual members to debate and offer amendments to legislation stand in the way of committee and party leaders who might otherwise seek to structure floor action in a way that would disadvantage the minority party or individual member.

Conclusion

The floor is not only a place where the full House and Senate conduct business, it also is where the most vital stage in the policy-making process, when members exercise their equal voting rights, occurs. We have seen variations between the House and Senate in the degree to which the details of legislation are devised on the floor, but the possible reaction of the floor to the handiwork of committees and parties has always been a central considera-tion in legislative strategies. Despite similarities in the nature of floor activity in the two chambers, we see obvious inter-chamber differences – the details of legislation are far more likely to be determined on the Senate floor than on the House floor.

Above: President Barack Obama acknowledges applause before his address to a joint session of Congress in the House Chamber of the U.S. Capitol in Washington, D.C., Tuesday, February 24, 2009. (Pablo Martinez Monsivais/Pool/MCT)

Below: President-elect Barack Obama meets with Vice President-elect Joe Biden, Senate Majority Leader Harry Reid (D-NV), House Speaker Nancy Pelosi (D-CA), and Rep. John Boehner (R-OH) Monday, January 5, 2009, on Capitol Hill in Washington, D.C. (Chuck Kennedy/MCT)

9

Congress and the President

T HE PRESIDENT IS AN INTEGRAL PART OF THE LEGISLATIVE PROCESS. THE basic rules of the legislative game specified by the Constitution provide for three institutional players – the House, the Senate, and the president. The president requires Congress to pass legislation for any policy that requires statutory authorization. In turn, the enactment of legislation necessitates presidential approval unless both chambers of Congress can muster a two-thirds majority to override a veto. Moreover, the Senate must ratify treaties negotiated by the president and must approve the president's choices for top executive and judicial posts. Congress must approve all funding for federal programs. Interdependency, based on shared as well as separate powers, characterizes the relationship among the three institutions.

Interdependency would not be important if the House, Senate, and president held similar policy preferences on important issues. Even when one party controls the House, Senate, and presidency, incumbents of the three institutions are not likely to have identical views. Representatives, senators, and presidents are elected on different cycles and they have diverse constituencies. They are likely to anticipate and react to somewhat different political demands and conditions.

To complicate matters, the framers left ambiguities in the Constitution about congressional and presidential functions and powers. For example, the president is instructed to appoint ambassadors and make treaties with the "advice and consent" of the Senate, but it is unclear how the president is to receive and account for senatorial advice. When the framers granted Congress the power to declare war, they did not anticipate the speed of modern military technology and the scope of the threats, which in some circumstances requires the president to make decisions about war without congressional involvement. In addition, when the framers allowed the president to kill a bill after a congressional adjournment by taking no action, they did not define adjournment. In each of these examples of constitutional ambiguity, and in many others, presidents have argued for interpretations that maximize their power at the expense of Congress.

The role of the president in policy making expanded during the twentieth and early twenty-first centuries. Congress has delegated more power to the president and executive agencies by delegating to the executive branch the authority to determine the details and methods of implementing a wide range of policies. Presidents have asserted their ability to make policy through executive orders and other means. In addition, the enhanced role of the United States in foreign affairs, and the increased importance of world events for American life, have given the president, who has important advantages over Congress in foreign affairs, a more powerful role.

While presidents have become more important relative to Congress in policy making over the last century, Congress has moved to reassert its own role, at least to some degree. An expanded staff, restrictions on appropriated funds, new approaches to designing programs, and other developments have helped Congress retain a meaningful role in policy making when faced with aggressive presidents.

The President as a Legislative Player

The president is central to the legislative process, although he does not always assert himself. Many pieces of legislation do not interest the president and are routinely signed into law at the recommendation of trusted administration officials. On some issues, the president chooses to remain silent and inactive for political reasons. Yet, when the president chooses to become involved, he usually can have some influence over the outcome by threatening to use his veto power, employing his unilateral powers, and mobilizing support for his position with his considerable political resources.

The President's Formal Role

The Constitution defines a formal role for the president at both the beginning and the end of the legislative process. With respect to the beginning of the process, the Constitution assigns the president responsibility to recommend a legislative agenda. The Constitution provides that the president "shall from time to time give to the Congress information of the state of the union and recommend to their consideration such measures as he shall judge necessary and expedient; he may, on extraordinary occasions, convene both houses, or either of them, and in case of disagreement between them, with respect to the time of adjournment, he may adjourn them to such time as he shall think proper." This provision is supplemented by various federal laws that require the president to recommend legislation to Congress.

With respect to the end of the legislative process, the Constitution provides that "every order, resolution, or vote to which the concurrence of the Senate and House of Representatives may be necessary (except on a question of adjournment) shall be presented to the President of the United States; and before the same shall take effect, shall be approved by him, or being disapproved by him, shall be repassed by two thirds of the Senate and House of Representatives, according to the rules and limitations prescribed in the Case of a Bill." This veto power is not unambiguous and has been a source of controversy between the branches.

AGENDA SETTING. By requiring the president to report to Congress on the state of the union and recommend legislation, the framers of the Constitution expected the president to energize and focus the legislative process. Of course, Congress is not required to consider matters the president brings to its attention. This is true even if the president calls a special session. Indeed, the president's powers and duties were designed to spur congressional action without giving the president coercive power over the activity of Congress or the ability to impose new laws unilaterally.

Presidents now address a joint session of Congress early in each calendar year with a speech known as the State of the Union Address. The speech is covered on live, prime-time television. It signals the president's priorities and is designed to generate support for his program. Some recent presidents have sent to Congress longer written versions of their addresses to provide more detail and rationale. Since the 1970s, a congressional leader of the opposite party has sought network television time after the speech to respond to the president. The major networks, however, have not always given opposition leaders the requested time.

Federal law requires the president to submit a variety of statements and proposed legislation to Congress. Of particular importance is the requirement that the president submit an annual budget message and an annual economic message to Congress. The budget message, required by the Budget and Accounting Act of 1921, specifies the president's taxation and spending proposals for the forthcoming fiscal year. The economic message, prescribed by the Employment Act of 1946, provides a presidential assessment of the state of the U.S. economy and details the chief executive's

---

Congressionally Speaking . . .

Executive orders are directives issued by the president to require or authorize some action of executive branch agencies. Some executive orders are authorized by law, but in most cases they are issued on the basis of the express or implied constitutional powers of the president. Executive orders can have a significant affect on the structure of the executive branch and public policy. For example, an executive order created the Office of Homeland Security following the 9–11 terrorist attack. Some executive orders establish important policy, particularly in areas, such as civil rights, where Congress did not enact relevant legislation. President Harry Truman desegregated the military by executive order, and President John Kennedy created the Presidential Committee on Equal Employment Opportunity by an executive order in which the term "affirmative action" was first used in federal policy. In recent decades, the use of executive orders has increased, often when an opposition Congress made legislative action impossible. In many cases, presidents justify the use of executive orders by citing previous executive orders as precedents for the assertion of unilateral presidential authority.

---

economic projections for the coming fiscal year. These messages sometimes stir controversy and often shape congressional debate over spending and tax policy each year.

Starting with President Truman in 1948, modern presidents have offered special messages providing additional detail – and often drafts of legislation – for the components of the administration's legislative program outlined by the State of the Union addresses and the budget and economic messages. The administration's legislation usually is introduced by members of the House and Senate as a courtesy to the president. Since Truman, presidents have devised formal processes within the executive branch for generating, synchronizing, and clearing legislative proposals from the administration.

The implied powers of the president under the Constitution also contribute to the president's role in agenda setting. In particular, the president's implied authority to issue regulations and executive orders to subordinates in the executive branch without the direct authorization of Congress boosts the president's ability to influence policy. This positive power becomes particularly controversial when the president seeks to interpret laws in a manner inconsistent with the expectations of members of Congress. Presidential actions often stimulate Congress to clarify its position in new legislation, if such legislation can survive a presidential veto.

In theory, the use of executive orders is constrained by the Constitution and law. Executive orders must be linked to executive authority and must not contradict provisions of the Constitution or a statute passed by Congress. In fact, during most of the eighteenth and nineteenth centuries, executive orders were principally used for routine administrative matters. In recent decades, however, executive orders have become more common, more important, and, at times, inconsistent with statute. In the 1980s, the Supreme Court upheld executive orders provided that they do not directly challenge explicit statutory provisions. Since it is unrealistic for statutes to address all contingencies, these decisions grant the president substantial flexibility in policy making. Furthermore, in a few cases, the courts have sided with the president when executive orders and statutes were directly at odds with each other and the Supreme Court even has found circumstances in which an executive order or proclamation invalidates a law. Thus, step by step over recent decades, the use of executive orders and judicial tolerance has expanded presidential power at the expense of Congress.

Formal constitutional rules also grant the president agenda-setting power in negotiating treaties and international agreements. Specifically, the Constitution authorizes the president to make treaties "by and with the Advice and Consent of the Senate." The executive branch customarily initiates treaties and international agreements, although the president does not have exclusive power over the treaty-making process. The president must submit treaties to the Senate and obtain ratification by a two-thirds majority vote. The Senate, however, is under no obligation to act on treaties presented by the president. Furthermore, the president is often dependent on the House for the appropriation of the necessary funds or to modify domestic law to comply with the terms of a treaty. Nevertheless, the power to determine the starting point for policy bargaining on treaties and international agreements gives the president considerable influence over the outcome. It is exceedingly unusual for the president's proposal to fail, and the Senate accepts a majority of treaties without change.

THE VETO POWER. The power to sign, veto, or take no action on legislation passed by Congress makes the president a critical actor in the legislative process. When the president vetoes a measure (a bill or joint resolution), he returns it to the chamber that first passed it along with a message indicating his objection to the legislation in its present form. If the chamber that first passed the measure is capable of obtaining the votes of two-thirds of the members to override the veto, the measure is then sent to the other chamber.

This chamber also must vote to override the veto by a two-thirds majority before the measure can become law.

The veto power gives the president both the ability to block legislation (subject to a possible override) and a source of leverage with legislators to gain policy concessions. Legislators must necessarily consider both a potential presidential veto and the likelihood of forming a two-thirds coalition to override a veto in their initial legislative decisions. For instance, members interested in passing some form of legislation may choose to make policy concessions to the president if they expect the president to veto their most preferred legislation and they lack sufficient numbers to orchestrate an override. It should be noted, however, that there are instances in which congressional majorities that lack enough support for an override will present the president with legislation they know the president will find unacceptable. Typically, this is a strategic maneuver with the purpose of intensifying partisan differences or forcing the president to expend valuable political capital to win a veto battle.

Congress seldom overrides a presidential veto – since 1789, Congress has overridden just 4 percent of all vetoes (Table 9.1). Recent presidents facing opposing majority parties in Congress have increasingly resorted to vetoes in confronting Congress. President George H.W. Bush (1989–1993) used vetoes rather successfully; only one of his 31 regular vetoes was overridden. Of the 36 regular vetoes issued by President Clinton, all during periods of divided government, only two were overridden. Presidents challenge the House and Senate with vetoes much less frequently when their parties have enjoyed majorities in both houses. While President Clinton issued a number of vetoes during Republican Congresses, he did not veto a single measure passed when Democrats had majorities in both chambers. Republican President George W. Bush (2001-2009) vetoed only one bill when dealing with Republican Congresses for nearly six years, but vetoed 11 bills in the last two years of his administration when dealing with a Democratic Congress. Four of those 11 vetoes were overridden by Congress.

In some circumstances, the veto is a sign of presidential weakness. Failing to persuade Congress to pass legislation to his liking, the president resorts to a veto. For example, President Reagan in 1988 – weakened by revelations of the Iran-Contra scandal – vetoed several bills that had broad congressional support, including measures to overhaul the nation's water pollution control and highway funding programs. The vetoes were swiftly overridden.

At other times, a veto is an interim step in a longer bargaining process as presidents use the veto in the hope of forcing additional concessions from Congress. An analysis of vetoed bills between 1946 and 1991 shows that

TABLE 9.1. Presidential Vetoes, 1947–2007.[1]

Year (Congress)	President (Party)	Total Vetoes	Regular Vetoes	Pocket Vetoes	Vetoes Overridden
1947–1948 (80th)	TRUMAN (D)	75	42	33	6
1949–1950 (81st)	**TRUMAN (D)**	**79**	**70**	**9**	**3**
1951–1952 (82d)	**TRUMAN (D)**	**22**	**14**	**8**	**3**
1953–1954 (83d)	*EISENHOWER (R)*	*52*	*21*	*31*	*0*
1955–1956 (84th)	EISENHOWER (R)	34	12	22	0
1957–1958 (85th)	EISENHOWER (R)	51	18	33	0
1959–1960 (86th)	EISENHOWER (R)	44	22	22	2
1961–1962 (87th)	**KENNEDY (D)**	**20**	**11**	**9**	**0**
1963 (88th)	**KENNEDY (D)**	**1**	**1**	**0**	**0**
1963–1964 (88th)	**JOHNSON (D)**	**8**	**4**	**4**	**0**
1965–1966 (89th)	**JOHNSON (D)**	**14**	**10**	**4**	**0**
1967–1968 (90th)	**JOHNSON (D)**	**8**	**2**	**6**	**0**
1969–1970 (91st)	NIXON (R)	11	7	4	2
1971–1972 (92d)	NIXON (R)	20	6	14	2
1973–1974 (93d)	NIXON (R)	12	11	1	1
1974 (93d)	FORD (R)	27	16	11	4
1975–1976 (94th)	FORD (R)	37	32	5	8
1977–1978 (95th)	**CARTER (D)**	**19**	**6**	**13**	**0**
1979–1980 (96th)	**CARTER (D)**	**12**	**7**	**5**	**2**
1981–1982 (97th)	REAGAN (R)	15	9	6	2
1983–1984 (98th)	REAGAN (R)	24	9	15	2
1985–1986 (99th)	REAGAN (R)	20	13	7	2
1987–1988 (100th)	REAGAN (R)	19	8	11	3
1989–1990 (101st)	GEORGE BUSH (R)	21	16	5	0
1991–1992 (102d)	GEORGE BUSH (R)	25	15	10	1
1993–1994 (103d)	**CLINTON (D)**	**0**	**0**	**0**	**0**
1995–1996 (104th)	CLINTON (D)	17	17	0	1
1997–1998 (105th)	CLINTON (D)	8	8	0	1
1999–2000 (106th)	CLINTON (D)	12	11	1	0
2001–2002 (107th)*	GEORGE W. BUSH (R)	0	0	0	0
2003–2004 (108th)	*GEORGE W. BUSH (R)*	*0*	*0*	*0*	*0*
2005–2006 (109th)	*GEORGE W. BUSH (R)*	*1*	*1*	*0*	*0*
2007–2008 (110th)	GEORGE W. BUSH (R)	11	11	0	4

Democratic presidents facing a unified Democratic Congress appear in **bold**
Republican presidents facing a unified Republican Congress appear in *italics*.
Presidents (D or R) under divided control of government appear in regular typeface.
* Congress was under unified Republican control from January 20, 2001, to June 6, 2001.
Source: http://www.senate.gov/reference/reference_index_subjects/Vetoes_vrd.htm.

Congress re-passed about 35 percent of them in a modified form. Of the re-passed bills, 83 percent became law, which reflects the success of the president in extracting policy concessions following a veto.[2]

The pocket veto deserves special mention. The Constitution allows the president to kill a bill by simply failing to sign it if Congress has adjourned within 10 days (Sundays excepted) of enacting a measure. If Congress has adjourned and therefore is not in session, its absence prevents the president from returning the bill to Congress with an official veto message. The informal name for such a veto is a pocket veto.

The pocket veto has been controversial. What counts as a congressional adjournment has been challenged in several court cases. In response to a lawsuit filed by Senator Edward Kennedy (D-Massachusetts), the Ford administration in 1976 declared that pocket vetoes would be used only after the adjournment at the end of a Congress's second session. This move limited the president's ability to use the pocket veto during vacation recesses and the adjournment period between the first and second sessions of a Congress, provided that Congress had made arrangements for receiving veto messages during the intervening periods. President Reagan maintained that such inter-session pocket vetoes were constitutional. A federal district judge upheld the president's position, but an appeals court reversed the decision. The appeals court ruling stands as the most definitive ruling to date. Fearing an unfavorable ruling from the Supreme Court, the Reagan administration did not appeal further. Since the Supreme Court has yet to rule directly on the issue, presidents continue to argue that mid-session pocket vetoes are valid.

The President's Informal Role

Formal institutions place the president firmly in the legislative game. So too do the expectations of the American public and the president's fellow partisans and presidents' own aspirations.

PARTISAN BONDS. The president's service as the recognized leader of his party positions him as a player in the legislative process. Parties often are a means for bridging the gap between the legislative and executive branches, and much of the responsibility of building this bridge is borne by the president. There are powerful incentives for a president and his Capitol Hill partisans to work together. Presidents usually need the support of fellow partisans in Congress for their legislative program and partisans in Congress know that their own political success is affected by the standing of the president. This mutual dependence means that a president and his congressional partisans can influence each other.

The relative weakness of American political parties makes it difficult for the president to merely command support from his party colleagues in Congress. The president does not determine who represents his party in Congress; legislators gain the ballot through primaries and are elected largely on the basis of their own efforts. The president does not select his party's leaders in the House and Senate; legislators elect their own leaders. Consequently, while the president is expected to and generally wants to take the lead in setting legislative strategy for his party, the president often must bargain with legislators of his own party over priorities and the direction of public policy.

PUBLIC EXPECTATIONS. The American people expect presidential leadership on matters of national importance. The emergence of the president as the focal point of an expanding federal government after the Great Depression and World War II was accompanied by heightened public expectations of the president. Increased media concentration on the chief executive, as well as the president's tendency to resort to public appeals for support, has contributed to the president's standing as the most visible elected official in the country. Since World War II, the American public has increasingly expected the president to be the nation's leading policy maker in both domestic and international affairs.

In response to public expectations, presidential candidates and sitting presidents make many public policy commitments. These pledges help attract political support, but, because violating a commitment is likely to alienate some supporters in the electorate and in Congress, policy pledges also may constrain a president while in office. The president's policy objectives are determined in part by the public commitments he makes during campaigns. Thus, as presidents have become more likely to try to mobilize public pressure on Congress, public policy commitments have become more of a double-edged sword for them.

The chief executive's role as a legislative player also is conditioned on public approval ratings. Members of Congress, primarily for electoral reasons, are more willing to pay heed to the legislative proposals and policy positions of a president who has the confidence of the public. A president with high approval ratings cannot, however, be expected to dominate all policy formation. High approval ratings do not translate to presidential influence on all types of legislation. Instead, scholars have found that approval ratings are related to a president's legislative influence on matters that are both salient and complex. When the public is paying little attention to an issue, legislators do not fear electoral repercussions from opposing a popular president.

PERSONAL ASPIRATIONS. Most presidents, and surely all presidents since the 1920s, have had aspirations that required they take an active role in the legislative process. Whether seeking to move the federal government into new endeavors or modify or repeal existing policy, presidents have had to work with, and often resist, Congress. Presidents' personal interests, political commitments, and circumstances beyond their control compel them to become engaged.

Presidents' Strategies

Presidential strategies for influencing legislative outcomes depend upon the political context. Although executed in a variety of ways, every recent president has confronted decisions about how to structure his legislative agenda, how to generate congressional support, how to employ the veto power, and how to control the bureaucracy in the face of competition from Capitol Hill.

Agenda Setting

Perhaps nothing affects presidential success in Congress as much as a president's decisions about what legislation to recommend to Congress, when to recommend it, and what priority to give each recommendation. Political scientist Paul Light observes that "control of the agenda becomes a primary tool for securing and extending power. Presidents certainly view the agenda as such."[3] The president's legislative choices send a signal to a wide audience – Congress, administration officials, interest groups, the media, and the public – about the president's view of the lessons of the last election, the president's policy preferences, and the president's likely priorities. The president's choices shape the strategies of other legislative players and help set expectations by which the president's own success or failure will be judged.

In most situations, the president cannot force Congress to address his proposals. Rather, he must convince members of Congress to give priority to his legislation. Members of Congress may see national problems differently, give precedence to other issues, or approach problems in a different way. The president must, therefore, motivate Congress by generating support among important members or groups of members, organized interest groups, and the general public. He may employ the full range of presidential resources available to encourage Congress to take his proposals seriously.

Except in times of national crisis, the president's ability to influence the legislative agenda is strongest at the beginning of his first term, followed, perhaps, by the beginning of the second term. At those times, public support, a claim to an electoral mandate, and core congressional support tend to be most in his favor. Opponents of the president's programs are likely to have fewer seats in Congress, be the most disorganized, and suffer low public esteem.

Even in the best of times, the president must carefully calculate which issues to pursue. He or she almost always wants more than Congress is willing to support. The president must not overload Congress and his own staff with too many proposals. Congress and its committees have a finite capacity to produce major legislation quickly. And the administration has a limited ability to formulate detailed proposals, lobby Congress, and negotiate compromises in its first few months in office. The president also is unable to generate media attention and public support for more than a few proposals at a time.

Among recent presidents, Ronald Reagan appears to have used the early months of his first term most effectively. Reagan moved quickly and set his priorities carefully by defining his agenda as two major bills, one for domestic budget cuts and one for tax cuts. Although both were complex, multifaceted proposals, Reagan was successful in leading the media and the public to focus on the broad effects of his proposals. The approach allowed the Reagan administration to concentrate its resources, stimulate public pressure on Congress for widely recognized proposals, and gain legislative action in its first year in office.

Attracting Congressional Support

On important legislation, modern presidents usually pursue a mixed strategy – both bargaining in Washington with members of Congress and lobbyists and soliciting public support to affect legislators' estimates of the public response to their treatment of the president's proposals. In deciding how to allocate resources to inside and outside strategies, the White House takes into account how many and which members of Congress must be persuaded, the strategies of the opposition, whether public opinion currently favors the president's position, the commitment of resources to other issues, and how much time the president has before Congress makes a decision. Daily, even hourly, tactical adjustments are common in the midst of a tough legislative fight.

A president's legislative strategy is often shaped by the demands of members of Congress. Congressional leaders of the president's party regularly consult with the White House and other administration officials about the substance of policy proposals and legislative tactics. In fact, recent presidents have met with their party's congressional leaders at least once a week while Congress is in session. Committee and faction leaders also press the administration to pursue certain strategies. Presidents are compelled to consider these demands so as not to jeopardize the reelection of their party's congressional membership. In addition, cooperating with important members of Congress, as well as with influential interest groups, bureaucrats, and others, may encourage these actors to employ their own resources on behalf of the administration's program.

INSIDE STRATEGIES. The inside strategy is one of bargaining. Although often seen as underhanded, presidents must frequently employ bargaining tactics to accomplish legislative objectives. This is particularly true when presidents are faced with an effective, committed opposition within Congress. Knowing when, where, and how to make a deal with the members and factions of Congress requires information and skill on the part of presidents and their legislative advisors. Successful bargaining also accounts for formal rules of the game, the composition of the Congress, public opinion, and other resources.

The cost to the president of doing business with Congress depends upon the political context. When the president is popular, legislators are more likely to be happy to be associated with the president and his program and fewer legislators will require special attention to get their votes. When the president is unpopular, the cost of attracting votes – whether by making concessions on the substance of policy proposals or in offering other incentives – will be higher.

Presidents may use the stick as well as the carrot. In 2006, Representative Peter King (R-New York) was the target of retribution after refusing to support President George W. Bush's proposal to allow a Dubai company to assume operations at six major U.S. ports. King, who was chair of the House Homeland Security committee, threatened to block Bush's port deal. In a matter of days after King issued the threat, the Pentagon notified him that it would no longer provide an aircraft and military support for his upcoming trip to Iraq – a trip that had been cleared months earlier.

OUTSIDE STRATEGIES. Observers of presidential strategies have noticed that presidents have become more reliant on outside strategies in recent decades. Twentieth-century presidents as early as Theodore Roosevelt sought public support to strengthen their hand against Congress, but only recent presidents have routinely done so. Through such activities as televised prime-time addresses, press conferences, domestic and foreign travel, exclusive interviews, timely leaks, and now television talk shows and call-in programs, presidents are increasingly cultivating external allies to strengthen their position within Washington.

"Going public," as the outside strategy is labeled by political scientist Samuel Kernell, is an attractive strategy for several reasons. First, technological advances, such as transcontinental jets and live satellite feeds, have increased the ease of reaching a wide audience. Second, campaign finance practices and declining presidential coattails have reduced legislators' dependence on support from the president and the parties. Third, the administration's advantage in information and expertise has weakened, as rank-and-file members have benefited from the diffusion of power and staff within Congress. Finally, budgetary constraints have reduced the president's supply of projects and other favors that he can use to trade with individual members.

Fundamentally, going public is about taking credit and issuing blame. With this strategy, the president seeks to increase the benefits to legislators of supporting him and to increase the electoral costs of opposing him. But every move produces counter-moves. Opposition leaders are encouraged to develop public relations strategies of their own, and, in doing so, they are motivated to propose alternatives to the president's program that the president and his supporters would be embarrassed to oppose. In this way, outside strategies encourage early public commitments by legislators, foster partisan maneuvering and grandstanding, and discourage bargaining and compromise that require a softening of positions and a sharing of credit and blame.

A high-profile appeal, such as a special televised address to the nation from the Oval Office, entails risks for a president. Members of Congress sometimes view this approach as an effort by the president to go over their heads, can cause problems of legislators in the home constituencies, and can create tension between Congress and the president. Since the president cannot make such appeals frequently, he must reserve this approach for only those issues of significant importance in which his appeal is likely to generate critical support. Failure to gain more public or congressional support may damage the president's reputation, reducing his effectiveness in future legislative battles and perhaps hurting his own reelection chances. Therefore, more cautious, less publicized, and more narrowly targeted approaches, such as speaking before certain groups and calling on small groups of newspaper editors, may be preferred at times.

President Barak Obama is adding a new direction to the outside strategy. His 2008 campaign organization developed a database of email addresses for about 13 million supporters. The database was given to a group overseen by the Democratic National Committee, which employed it to request that people work in their communities and contact legislators in support of the president's budget proposals. The group, called Organizing for America, was announced by Obama in a YouTube video, another outlet that administration backers exploit.

The Veto

The veto inserts the president into the legislative game. A threatened veto may lead congressional leaders to set aside certain legislation or to make concessions to the president before passing the legislation. Particularly when control of the Congress and presidency is divided between the parties, the veto gives the president a critical source of leverage with legislators. It has been argued that the increasing polarization of Congress has limited the president's ability to bargain directly with Congress, and therefore has elevated the relative importance of the veto within the president's arsenal.

Veto threats are relatively infrequent events, but tend to result in policy changes that are favorable to the president. Veto threats are most common when the legislation under consideration is important and the president is faced with a Congress dominated by the opposing party. One study estimates that presidents threaten to veto roughly 14 percent of important measures; this number increases to 23 percent under divided government.

Moreover, it appears that presidents are often quite successful in extracting policy concessions from Congress when veto threats are issued. In fact, by one approximation, roughly 90 percent of bills that encounter a veto threat are modified, to varying extents, to accommodate the preferences of the president.[4] Given the success of veto threats, why do we not see presidents issuing threats on *all* congressional proposals?

The answer to this question lies largely in the fact that successful veto threats require credibility. It would be neither feasible nor politically prudent for a president to veto all legislation, and therefore threatening to do so would result in the veto threat losing its credibility with members of

---

The Veto Process

To veto a bill, the president signs a veto message that is sent to Congress. The message may contain the president's reasoning. The house of Congress that first passed the legislation acts first on the veto. That house may attempt an override, pass new legislation without an override attempt, or take no further action. The bill dies if a two-thirds majority is not acquired to override the veto. If the first house does override the veto, the other house also may attempt an override, pass new legislation without an override attempt, or take no further action. The bill dies if a two-thirds majority is not also acquired in that house to override the veto. New legislation may reflect concessions to the president. It must be approved by both houses and sent to the president for signature or veto.

Congress. A president who fails to follow through on threats is likely to gain a reputation for bluffing.

Members of Congress are certainly not passive bystanders in the veto game. Members frequently solicit a veto threat from the administration to solidify their bargaining position on Capitol Hill. Sometimes a congressional party will bait the president with a bill that it knows he will find unacceptable in order to force a veto of a popular bill. A well-documented example of this was the 1995–96 legislative struggle in which a Republican-controlled Congress presented Democratic President Bill Clinton with a bill it knew to be unacceptable to him, received the expected veto, approved another virtually identical bill, and received another veto. Congressional Republicans hoped to portray Clinton as an opponent to welfare reform as the 1996 elections approached.

Statistically, attempts to override vetoes are associated with low presidential popularity, a strong opposition party in Congress, and bipartisan support for the legislation. Low presidential popularity and bipartisan support for the legislation also contribute to successful override attempts. Generally, highly partisan legislation, as vetoed legislation tends to be, is not overridden because a two-thirds majority is required. Parties seldom have close to the two-thirds of the seats in both chambers needed to override a veto.

Controlling the Executive Branch

Much of the competition between Congress and the president concerns control of the executive agencies whose responsibility it is to implement policy. Agencies become players in the legislative game once they are established and begin to perform functions that are valuable to others. They have resources of their own to bring to the legislative battle. Much of the information and expertise about federal programs resides in the agencies. That information and expertise can be shared selectively with Congress and the White House. Agencies also have friends within the interest group community and the general public to whom they can appeal for support.

An unfavorable agency policy is not always easy for Congress to change. The need for agreement among all three legislative institutions – House, Senate, and president – makes a formal legislative response difficult and perhaps impossible. Consequently, members of Congress, presidents, and the organized interests seek means other than the legislative process to control agencies. For presidents, the most direct means of control is to appoint department and agency heads who support administration policies. But appointment power is not the only presidential tool.

Presidents seek to control departments and agencies by several means. The primary means of presidential control is the appointment of agency heads who share the president's policy views and are willing to be responsive to directions and suggestions from the White House. In the Small Business Administration, for example, the president appoints the director, assistant directors, and regional administrators, none of whom must be confirmed by the Senate. In cabinet departments, confirmation is required for most top administrators – under 600 overall – but more than 3,000 are "at will" appointees who serve at the president's discretion without Senate confirmation.

The central organizational tool of the president for controlling the executive branch is the Office of Management and Budget (OMB). This agency, like its predecessor, the Bureau of the Budget, constructs the president's budget proposals for the federal government. Furthermore, central clearance – the job of coordinating and approving all executive branch proposals sent to Congress – is the responsibility of the OMB. OMB responsibilities also entail scrutinizing written proposals and even preparing the congressional testimony of executive branch officials to ensure consistency with the president's policy goals. In addition, the OMB reviews enacted legislation to provide the president with a recommendation to sign or veto it.

In recent decades, the OMB has become more politicized and has expanded its bureaucratic control functions. By appointing aides ideologically aligned with himself to run the OMB, and by centralizing the rulemaking process within the OMB, President Reagan turned the OMB into a major instrument in shaping national policy and managing relations between

---

Congressionally Speaking . . .

As Chief Executive, the constitution requires that the president "take care that the laws be faithfully executed." In recent years, the practice of issuing signing statements at the time the president signs legislation has raised questions about whether the president is fulfilling this constitutional obligation.

Signing statements are written declarations issued by the president that indicate to Congress how he intends to direct his administration in the implementation of the law and often to articulate constitutional limits on the implementation of certain provisions. In practice, the signing statement has become reminiscent of the line-item veto. While proponents of signing statements say that they communicate valuable information to Congress, opponents contend that they are used by presidents to pick and choose the provisions they wish to enforce or implement.

Some scholars credit President Ronald Reagan for developing the signing statement into a policy-making tool, but President George W. Bush used signing statements with unprecedented frequency. Through January 2007, one study found that Bush used signing statements to challenge 1,149 provisions in 150 bills.[5] Some observers speculated that the signing statement supplanted the veto in Bush's arsenal. The advantage of the signing statement is that it is far less visible than the veto, allowing the president greater flexibility in shaping policy out of the public eye and without creating a veto override showdown with Congress.

Early in his administration, President Barak Obama issued a memorandum requiring executive agencies to consult with the attorney general before enforcing provisions of his predecessors' signing statements. Obama said that he would use signing statements only to address "constitutional concerns." He soon used a signing statement to list five objections to provisions of a large economic stimulus bill. For example, he observed that Congress lacks power to demand that executive officials reallocate certain money only after gaining approval of congressional committees. Signing statements are likely to remain an important means for presidential objections to provisions of larger bills that a presidential considers unconstitutional.

---

the administration and Congress. By executive order, Reagan authorized the OMB's Office of Information and Regulatory Affairs (OIRA) to review the proposed rules and regulations of executive agencies and to evaluate them by a strict cost-benefit analysis. In practice, granting this authority to OIRA provided a means for the president to make certain that agency activity was in step with his preferences or policy objectives. On numerous occasions during the Reagan administration, OIRA intervened in agency rule making and stopped agencies from issuing congressionally mandated regulations.

This intervention was principally achieved through use of return letters – a letter from the administration that returns a rule for further consideration. These requirements undercut the independence of agency and department heads, delayed action on many regulations, and ultimately led to killing or substantially changing some regulations.

Under the George H.W. Bush administration, the OMB's regulatory review functions were supplanted to some extent by the efforts of the Council on Competitiveness, also created by executive order. The council was officially located in the office of, and headed by, Vice President Dan Quayle. This organizational arrangement protected under the umbrella of executive privilege the council's inner workings from the public and congressional scrutiny to which the OMB is subject. As the administration intended, members of Congress, lobbyists, and the media found it difficult to anticipate or react to unfriendly White House efforts to interpret law and mold regulations required by law (executive privilege is discussed in Chapter 10).

President Clinton did not reestablish the Council on Competitiveness, but instead returned authority to the OMB. Early in the administration, Clinton issued an executive order supplanting the executive order issued by Reagan that had governed regulatory review up to that time. Clinton's executive order preserved the use of cost-benefit analysis in evaluating regulatory rules and their alternatives, it also mandated "the primacy of Federal agencies in the regulatory decision-making process." Although OIRA under Clinton maintained powers of bureaucratic oversight, it reviewed only the most salient regulatory matters. Furthermore, Clinton restructured OIRA to allow for preferred interest groups to gain greater access to the decision-making process.

Under President George W. Bush, OIRA's role in regulatory oversight returned to a state similar to that seen under the Reagan administration. Much like Reagan, George W. Bush has used his broad appointment powers to place individuals with like ideologies in key agency and OIRA positions. The Bush OIRA issued many more return letters than the Clinton OIRA, reflecting Bush administration opposition to agency proposals. Morevoer, the Bush OIRA created a new tool of control over the regulatory process known as a "prompt letter." Whereas return letters require agencies to reevaluate proposed regulations, prompt letters request that agencies reconsider an existing regulation. The addition of the prompt letter gives the president greater ability to curtail regulations according to his preferences. In 2007, President Bush signed an executive order that mandated that all agencies put into place a regulatory policy office to supervise the development of agency rules. The regulatory policy offices were run by appointees of the president. The addition of these offices, imbedded in the agencies, effectively gives the White House another gatekeeper to monitor agency activity and to block, if not preempt, rules that are unfavorable to the administration.

At this writing, it is too early to outline the innovations in regulatory review of the Obama administration. Administration officials made clear that they want to streamline the review process to allow the executive branch to address global warming and other issues more rapidly. Interest in revising the use of cost-benefit analysis was expressed by many experts close to the administration. The result is likely to be a substantial revision of the executive orders that governed OMB's involvement in the rulemaking functions of executive agencies.

Foreign and Defense Policy

The legislative politics of foreign and defense policy are typically different from the politics of domestic affairs. Political scientist Aaron Wildavsky argues that the presidential activities associated with these policy arenas differ substantially. Moreover, the degrees of success that presidents have in foreign and domestic affairs are sufficiently different that the American presidency can be thought of as two distinct presidencies. Although the "two presidencies" thesis is not always useful, it is true that the rules of the game often advantage the president in foreign policy. Under the Constitution, the president more clearly takes initiative and has greater autonomy over action related to foreign and defense matters than he does in domestic affairs. He appoints ambassadors (with the advice and consent of the Senate), makes treaties (subject to the approval of a two-thirds majority in the Senate), receives the ambassadors of other countries, serves as the commander in chief of the armed forces and of state militias when they are called into federal service, and commissions the officers of the United States. Although senators have become increasingly involved in monitoring treaty negotiations, the president largely retains control over U.S. diplomacy.

Congress is not helpless, of course. In fact, the Constitution gives Congress many resources. Because funding is required for much international activity, control of appropriations inserts Congress as a critical factor in foreign and defense policy. The Constitution also gives Congress the power to declare war, create and organize armed forces, regulate foreign commerce, and define offenses against the law of nations. Yet in practice substantial ambiguity exists about the proper role of the two branches. How much discretion is granted to the president in using troops, making minor agreements with other governments, or conducting secret negotiations is not clearly defined in the Constitution. For the most part, the courts have left it to Congress and presidents to work out their differences.

Presidents who claim broad implicit powers argue that they are free to ignore Congress on some matters of foreign and defense policy. This position has been strengthened by the increasing importance of world affairs during the twentieth century. Scientific and technological advances have integrated economies and yielded weapons of mass destruction, increasing the importance of the president's ability to coordinate U.S. policy, act with secrecy, and respond quickly. Presidents often argue that the dangers of the modern world and the prominent role of the United States in international affairs, requires that the president be free to conduct diplomacy, launch secret operations, and even deploy armed forces as he sees fit. Several Supreme Court cases have endorsed an unfettered right of presidents to conduct foreign policy. Chief among these rulings was *United States v. Curtiss-Wright Export Corp.*, a 1936 ruling asserting that even if extensive powers over foreign affairs were not spelled out for the president in the Constitution, the president is best suited to assume those responsibilities.

As international affairs gained importance to the United States, control of national security was increasingly centralized and institutionalized in the White House. The 1947 National Security Act consolidated control of the military in a single Defense Department and created the Central Intelligence Agency and National Security Council. All three organizations are headed by individuals who are directly accountable to the president – the secretary of defense, the director of central intelligence, and the national security adviser. In 2004, new legislation created the position of Director of National Intelligence, appointed by the president, to supervise intelligence activities of the government and serve as the principal intelligence advisor to the president. These developments have enhanced the president's ability to collect and digest information and to act promptly without substantial congressional participation.

Public expectations of presidential leadership also give the president an advantage in the area of foreign policy. Because the electorate supports centralized leadership on national security matters, particularly in times of international crisis, congressional opposition to an assertive president is unpopular with the electorate. The public is especially supportive of the president if the lives of Americans are at stake.

In the decades after World War II, the liberties given to the president to fight world communism led some observers to believe that Congress was

THE CHANGING CONGRESS: EVOLVING WAR POWERS

The Constitution grants Congress the power to declare war (Article I, Section 8), but also makes the president the commander in chief of the armed forces (Article II, Section 2). Congress has formally declared war only five times – the War of 1812, the Mexican War (1846–1848), the Spanish-American War (1898), World War I (1917–1918), and World War II (1941–1945).

Presidents have used the commander-in-chief power, various treaty obligations, resolutions of the United Nations, and their implicit duty to provide for national security as grounds for committing U.S. forces abroad without a declaration of war. By one count, the United States had been involved in 192 military actions without a declaration of war by 1972. At least nine more have occurred since then, including the response to the Iraqi invasion of Kuwait in 1990 (the Persian Gulf War), the use of troops in Somalia beginning in 1992, the military efforts in Afghanistan following the events of September 11, 2001, and the conflict in Iraq beginning in 2003. Many of these commitments were very brief, and Congress had no time to respond. In other cases, such as the Vietnam War, Congress implicitly supported the president by approving the funding he requested for the effort.

The costly Vietnam War in the 1960s and early 1970s stimulated efforts in Congress to limit the war powers that presidents had assumed. In 1973, Congress enacted, over President Richard Nixon's veto, the War Powers Resolution. This law requires that the president notify Congress about any commitment of military forces within 48 hours and terminate the commitment within 60 days unless Congress approves an extension or is unable to meet. The commitment may be extended by the president for another 30 days. Congress may halt the action at any time by concurrent resolution (that is, by a resolution that does not require the president's signature).

No one seems particularly satisfied with the 1973 law. Supporters of broad presidential discretion argue that the act infringes on the president's con-stitutional powers; supporters of a literal interpretation of the Constitution claim that the act gives away Congress's constitutional powers by allowing the president to initiate wars. Since 1973, presidents have observed the reporting requirement, but have sought alternatives to formal congressional approval. In 1983, President Reagan and Speaker O'Neill negotiated a timetable for the involvement of U.S. Marines in Lebanon. In 1991, Congress approved a resolution that authorized President George H.W. Bush to use "all neces-sary means" to enforce the United Nations resolution calling for the removal of Iraqi forces from Kuwait. In 2002, Congress approved a resolution that authorized the use of force against Iraq to "defend the national security of the United States against the continuing threat posed by Iraq" and to "enforce all relevant United Nations Security Council resolutions regarding Iraq,"

(*continued*)

THE CHANGING CONGRESS: EVOLVING WAR POWERS (*continued*)

which concerned weapons of mass destruction. In all three cases, the president avoided endorsing the constitutionality of the War Powers Resolution. In none of the cases did Congress actually declare war, but in the latter two cases Congress indicated that the terms of the War Powers Resolution requirement for congressional authorization were met.

In 2008, a private commission headed by two former secretaries of state, a Democrat and a Republican, recommended new war powers legislation that would (a) require the president to consult with Congress before any military operation that is expected to last more than a week, (b) require discontinuation of the operation if Congress has not approved it by concurrent resolution within 30 days, and (c) allow Congress to approve a joint resolution of disapproval to force discontinuation of the operation, by overriding a presidential veto, if necessary. If the operation required secrecy, the president would have to consult a joint committee of top party and committee leaders within three days after the operation began.

acting as if it ought to defer to the president on matters of foreign affairs. By the early 1970s, as Congress was beginning to assert itself against presidential policies it opposed, views about congressional deference to the president began to change. However, the national consensus about Cold War policy generated a basic agreement between Congress and presidents about international affairs that effectively returned Congress to a state of greater passivity. When that consensus began to disintegrate, members of Congress looked for ways to recapture their influence. In the immediate aftermath of the terrorist attacks of September 11, 2001, however, the president was once again poised to forge the way in foreign and defense policy. With growing discontent over the war in Iraq, and an administration embroiled in controversy, the current shifting balance in power is reminiscent of the early 1970s.

The reassertion of congressional power in the early 1970s represented the beginning of a tug-of-war between congressional Democrats and White House Republicans that is still evident today. Between 1969 and 2006, there were only 10 years in which the president's party controlled both chambers of Congress. Conversely, for 20 years during that period presidents faced a unified Congress of the opposing party. Therefore, partisanship confounded matters by reinforcing institutional conflict between the branches. In addition, legislative action became increasingly central to the making of foreign policy as international economic relations, human rights, environmental problems, and other issues gained a more prominent role in this sphere of policy making. This, in conjunction with the ideological gap between Congress and the president that prevailed for the better part of this period, made deference to the president particularly costly for Congress.

Policies governing the intelligence agencies have been a prime source of conflict between Congress and the president. The tension between the branches increased significantly after the revelations of the Iran-Contra affair. In 1985 and 1986, the administration secretly sold arms to the Iranians in efforts to negotiate the release of American hostages in the Middle East. Furthermore, the administration used the profits from the arms sales to fund the Contras in Nicaragua, which violated congressional restrictions on funding and covert assistance to the Contras.

Presidents' Resources

The strategies adopted by presidents and members of Congress to influence policy outcomes are influenced by the quality and quantity of resources available to each. The president possesses numerous resources that serve to strengthen the role of the presidency in legislative politics. Some of these resources, such as constitutional powers, White House staff, information, and expertise, are relatively secure and may even expand during a president's term of office.

The president has a sizable staff operation to assist him in managing relations with Congress. The president controls the size of his White House staff, although it is subject to congressional appropriations. In recent decades, the White House staff has expanded, particularly in the offices for legislative affairs, communications, and domestic and foreign policy. In addition, presidents have expanded agencies within the larger Executive Office of the President, such as the Office of Management and Budget (OMB) and Council of Economic Advisers, to enhance their policy-making capability. These staffs help the president monitor developments on Capitol Hill, work with committees and leadership, and give the president adequate representation on legislative matters.

Congress has moved to curtail the president's discretion in managing executive office staff. In the 1970s, after the OMB had gained great importance in the development and implementation of policy, Congress required the president to receive Senate confirmation for the director of the agency as for cabinet secretaries. In the 1980s, when President Ronald Reagan was proposing cuts in domestic programs, congressional Democrats made sure that funding for White House staff was constrained as well. In 1992, House Democrats moved to eliminate funding for Vice President Dan Quayle's Council on Competitiveness to show their opposition to its role in disapproving regulations proposed by federal agencies. In general, however, presidents have been able to organize their staffs as they choose and have had adequate funding to do so.

Some resources, such as information and expertise, may increase during a presidency as experience is acquired. For example, a lack of Capitol Hill experience was a serious shortcoming of President Jimmy Carter and his top aides when he entered office in 1977. As time went on, the Carter team gained familiarity with the people and ways of doing business in Congress. But Carter also recognized the limitations of his White House staff and moved to hire more experienced people. An important element of the change was giving more responsibility to Vice President (and former senator) Walter Mondale in the planning of legislative strategies.

In contrast, the president can suffer losses of other resources while in office. One scholar called this the "cycle of decreasing influence." Party strength in Congress and public support often diminish during a president's term. Recent exceptions aside (see Chapter 3), the president's party typically loses congressional seats in midterm elections.

Public support for a president often declines during a presidential term, weakening support for the president in Congress. As President Johnson reportedly once told his staff:

> You've got to give it all you can that first year. Doesn't matter what kind of majority you come in with. You've got just one year when they treat you right and before they start worrying about themselves. The third year, you lose votes. . . . The fourth year's all politics.[6]

This advice, which most presidents take to heart, encourages presidents to try to move quickly on their legislative programs early in their terms.

Presidents eventually run out of time. The two four-year terms that a president may serve under the Twenty-second Amendment are a long time, to be sure, but they are shorter than the legislative careers of many members of Congress and far shorter than the time horizons of many lobbyists and most bureaucrats. In fact, the president often seems to be in more of a hurry than others in Washington. Beyond the diminishing political capital that results from typical patterns of decreasing public and congressional support associated with the natural progression of the presidency, members of Congress, lobbyists, and even bureaucrats tend to limit their relations with the incumbent president nearing the end of his term.

LEGISLATIVE RESOURCES OF PRESIDENTS

Partisan base in Congress. The size of the House and Senate caucuses of the president's party can boost presidential success in enacting their priorities. When a president's partisans in Congress are cohesive and ideologically in step with him, the advantages offered to the president increase.

Formal powers. Presidents gain leverage with legislators by using, or threatening to use, their formal powers. The most obvious power is the power to veto legislation. In addition, the president may issue executive orders that interpret laws or regulate the behavior and decisions of executive branch agencies.

Visibility and public approval. The national media concentrate on the president. Unlike Congress, which finds speaking with one voice difficult, the president can dominate the news and manipulate the types of information Americans receive about his activities. If presidents mobilize public support for their initiatives, members of Congress must weigh carefully the costs of opposing the president.

Expertise and information. Broad policy expertise is available to the president from the agencies of the executive branch.

White House staff. The president has a large personal staff in the White House that allows the president to monitor and communicate with Congress, lobbyists, the media, and others.

Patronage and projects. Presidents and top cabinet officials use personnel appointments to assert control of the bureaucracy and to do favors for members of Congress. Modern presidents make more than 6,000 executive and judicial branch appointments. Presidents and top administration officials can influence decisions about who wins federal contracts and the location of federal installations and buildings.

National party organizations. The president effectively controls the resources of his party's national committees, which can be used to do favors for members of Congress.

Campaign resources. The president may exploit his campaign apparatus to generate support for his program. President Obama did this in using the large email list he developed as a candidate.

Congressional Resources and Strategies

The tendency to see legislative-executive relations as a zero-sum game is strong. Observers tend to think that if the president is gaining power, then Congress must be losing power. That perspective is too simplistic. Both Congress and the president have gained power as the role of the federal government has expanded over the decades. Moreover, neither branch is monolithic. Within the executive branch, power has been distributed in a variety of ways between the White House, departments, and independent regulatory commissions. Within Congress, the somewhat different constitutional responsibilities of the House and Senate have meant that their power has not always shifted in the same direction. Moreover, developments that seem to affect the power of Congress adversely may enhance the power of certain members, factions, or parties within the institution. Since members of Congress and the president represent different audiences with different interests, it also may be the case the changes in the legislative-executive relationship benefit both branches even if one side appears to be gaining an advantage.

Thus, it is wise to keep in mind that Congress does not really use its resources – individual members, groups of members, and legislative parties use the institution's resources as they pursue their political goals. The exercise of congressional power is usually the by-product of the competition among members within the institution. In other words, congressional output is the result of (sometimes intense) competition between members with different preferences. Given the degree to which preferences in Congress diverge, seldom do all members consider themselves to be winners on important matters.

Congress's most fundamental resources are the formal powers granted to it by the Constitution. The ability to exercise those powers effectively depends on the human and technological resources of the institution. The membership's motivation, committee and party structures, parliamentary procedure, staffing arrangements, electronic information systems, relations with outside experts and information sources, and other factors affect Congress's performance. Congress has periodically attempted to better equip itself to compete with the expanding capabilities of the president. The legislative reorganization acts of 1946 and 1970, among many other less-extensive efforts, expanded staff, reorganized committees, and changed procedures. In sum, Congress has developed a battery of resources to support an expanding repertoire of strategies for responding to challenges from the executive branch.

Periodic Authorizations

Historically, most agencies and programs have continued indefinitely once they were created. Although they must receive annual appropriations from Congress, most of the basic laws creating and empowering agencies have been permanent. Delegating authority to an executive branch agency in such a manner increases the difficulty of retracting or altering the authority later.

MULTIPLE USES OF SUNSET PROVISIONS

Although the concept of a sunset provision – a provision in law that requires periodic reauthorization of a program – dates back to the writings of Thomas Jefferson, its use as a legislative tool is a recent phenomenon. Sunset provisions grew in popularity among reformers in the late 1960s and 1970s who argued that programs must be reexamined by Congress from time to time. When the Republicans, who opposed many federal programs, took control of Congress in 1995, the idea of imposing limits on the lifespan of programs.

A prominent example of the recent use of sunset provisions is the Patriot Act, first enacted in 2001. At the time, the Republican leadership added sunset provisions as a concession to Democrats and members within their party who were skeptical about the intelligence-gathering authority granted to law enforcement and national security agencies. The legislation was reauthorized in 2006 and included provisions scheduled to expire again in 2009. Senator Dianne Feinstein (D-California) declared that the sunset provisions were an "important element of the continued vigorous oversight necessary to ensure this law is carried out in an appropriate manner."[7]

Republican majorities used sunset provisions on tax cut bills for a different purpose. By making certain provisions to the bills temporary, they were able to minimize projected costs and present a more favorable long-term estimated budget. Republicans now face the reality that the tax cuts may be reversed if Congress fails to extend them when the expiration dates arrive in 2010.

After all, a new law requires the agreement of the House, Senate, and president, or, in the case of a presidential veto, a two-thirds majority in both houses of Congress.

In recent decades, Congress has moved away from permanent authorizations. When Congress enacts legislation creating a program or establishing a new policy, it may limit the length of the authorization. A "sunset" provision sets an end date for a program, thus requiring new authorizing legislation to continue a program or policy past that date. This approach requires administration officials to return to Congress to justify the continuation of the program and it ensures that Congress will periodically review the law underlying the program. An important case is the authorization for defense programs, which must be passed each year. Before the 1960s, defense programs were authorized for an indefinite period. During the 1960s and 1970s Congress added more defense programs – military personnel, weapons systems, research and development, and so on – to the annual defense authorization bill. The immediate effect was to give members of the armed services committees greater influence over the activities of the Department of

Defense. The long-term effect was to give all members of Congress a regular opportunity to influence the direction of defense policy.

Designing Agencies

In practice, much of the conflict over legislation is about the design of the agencies charged with implementing policy. The line of authority, decision-making and appeals procedures, decision-making criteria, rule-making deadlines, reporting requirements, job definitions, personnel appointment processes and restrictions, and salaries all may affect the ability of Congress, the president, the courts, and outside interests to gain favorable action by agencies. Legislators, responding to political pressures from organized interests and others, generally seek to insulate agencies from unfriendly influences, including future Congresses and presidents, and to guarantee that agencies are guided by their policy preferences. Presidents, on the other hand, generally seek to place new programs in the hierarchy of executive departments to which they can appoint politically loyal individuals to important administrative positions. Thus, congressional and presidential views about the organization and control of agencies are often in conflict.

The effort to elevate the Environmental Protection Agency (EPA) to department-level status – making the head of the EPA a member of the president's cabinet – is a good example of structural politics. Democrats in Congress sought to modify the EPA's status in 1990 to give environmental programs more priority and authority within the executive branch. The bill, passed by the House on a vote of 371 to 55, also called for the creation of a Bureau of Environmental Statistics, which was to be independent of the new department. In addition, the bill would have established a separate Commission on Improving Environmental Protection, with the purpose of coordinating the regulations of the new department and other federal agencies with environmental jurisdiction.

The independent department was designed to be insulated from political manipulation. In fact, the bill required the department to report its findings directly to Congress, without review by the OMB or the new secretary of the environment. Furthermore, the multimember commission would have added a policy-making unit outside of the president-department line of authority. The White House, which wanted a bill that would reinforce President George H.W. Bush's claim to be the "environment president," opposed the bureau and commission on the grounds that they undermined the president's line of authority over agency activities. The bill stalled in the

Senate because of credible threats of a filibuster by Republicans after the administration threatened a veto.

In the next Congress, the bill passed the Senate on a voice vote after its Senate sponsors met the Bush administration's demands by folding the statistics bureau into the new department and restricting the policy-making authority of the commission. House Democrats refused to act on the Senate bill. The bill died in the House Committee on Government Operations because House Democrats wanted to deny President Bush an opportunity to claim credit for pro-environmental legislation in an election year.

The EPA bill is typical of the conflict between Congress and the president over the structure of agencies. Agreement about the general policy was not enough to guarantee enactment because the conflict over presidential control of the agency proved to be too divisive. Conflict over the control of information and personnel in this case was at least as controversial as the policy. Specifically, the point of contention was whether the executive branch official controlling the information going to Congress would be responsible to the president or an independent bureau chief. The president's veto power ultimately forced concessions from Senate Democrats, but House Democrats were more concerned about the political sacrifices than about raising the EPA to cabinet status.

Structural politics is not limited to original authorizations and reauthorizations. The fight is continuous, as the issue of personnel ceilings demonstrates. In recent decades, Congress has become more specific in dictating the design of executive agencies. On occasion, administrations have undermined congressional efforts to bolster agency resources by refusing to hire or replace important personnel. The appropriations committees have responded in committee reports by specifying a minimum number of personnel for agencies, requiring reports on deviations, and insisting on a formal presidential request when an agency seeks to reduce spending with a personnel ceiling. Increasingly, Congress has imposed statutory restrictions on personnel ceilings, thus limiting the administration's control over agencies' personnel resources.

The structure of many executive agencies is the result of compromise. The give-and-take process can produce a variety of outcomes, ranging from agencies that are distant from the president and responsive to Congress to agencies that are firmly under the control of the executive administration. The decision of political actors to make concessions on some aspects of structural policy and not on others is principally a function of the impact that the given agency has upon preferred constituents. Members of Congress and the president are reluctant to relinquish power over an agency when the agency under consideration has a significant direct effect – either positive or negative – on constituents of interest.

The Power of the Purse

A major congressional strategy for controlling policy and its implementation involves Congress's "power of the purse" – the constitutional provision that "no money shall be drawn from the treasury, but in consequence of appropriations made by law." Since laws must originate in Congress, the legislative body can refuse to appropriate funds for certain purposes or condition the use of funds upon certain stipulations. Thus, the authority over appropriations gives Congress the ability to shape the actions of the executive branch in a manner consistent with congressional preferences. Certainly, conditioning appropriations upon specific activity explicitly mandates behavior consistent with the will of Congress. Even the threat that appropriations for an agency or program will be reduced or eliminated may achieve the same end.

In the field of foreign and military affairs, the power of the purse is often the only effective tool for Congress to influence policy. Congress's ability to restrict the uses of appropriated funds is well supported by court decisions, giving Congress a clear avenue of response to a president who asserts broad constitutional powers. By forbidding the executive branch from spending federal monies for certain purposes, Congress can prevent the president from pursuing a policy it opposes.

Committee Reports

Committees often make clear their expectations about the implementation of programs in the reports that are required by House and Senate rules to accompany legislation when it is sent to the floor. Reports usually indicate the objectives of the legislation and sometimes interpret the language used, both of which may guide rule-making decisions by agencies. At times, committee reports indicate that the committee "clearly intends," "expects," or even "anticipates" that an executive branch official or agency will or will not do something. Earmarks for specific projects are sometimes listed in committee reports. Although they are not legally binding, committee reports often guide courts when they seek to interpret ambiguous statutory language. More important, reports make explicit the expectations of important members of Congress who will influence future legislation affecting an agency.

Packaging Strategies

The Constitution requires that the president have an opportunity to sign or veto legislation passed by Congress, but it does not indicate the size or format of the legislation Congress presents to the president. For example, a variety of items are often included in one bill to facilitate bargains among members of Congress, the president, and other interested parties. By using their ability to package legislation, members of Congress may encourage or discourage a presidential veto.

Congress exercises considerable influence over policy outcomes from its ability to package multiple measures and present the president with a single take-it-or-leave-it offer. When several bills or aspects of bills are combined into one package that includes legislation both favored and opposed by the president, Congress reduces the president's capacity to control national policy. Because the president does not have the formal authority to strike from a bill those provisions that he finds unfavorable, he is forced to make a difficult decision. Issuing a veto means losing, at least temporarily, those provisions of the legislation that he does find satisfactory. Of course, a packaged proposal that does encounter a veto may result in Congress losing valued provisions as well.

The advantages and disadvantages of packaging can be seen in the use of omnibus continuing resolutions (called CRs), which combine two or more regular appropriations bills for the coming fiscal year into one giant package. CRs are required when Congress and the president fail to appropriate bills enacted before the beginning of a new fiscal year. If the president vetoes the bill that contains the funding for some executive agencies and no new bill is enacted, those agencies must shut down. Hence, the president needs to weigh carefully how effective a veto would be. Congress also risks losing measures packed into a CR that provoke the president's opposition. For example, Representative John Dingell's attempt in 1987 to codify in the CR the "fairness doctrine" governing broadcasters (a bill previously vetoed by President Reagan) was dropped from the bill after Reagan drew attention to its inclusion in the CR. The bundling strategy on these bills and other "must pass" legislation – such as bills to raise the federal government's debt ceiling – thus have the potential to help Congress reassert influence over the legislative game.

Recent presidents have promoted the line-item veto as a means to combat Congress's packaging strategies in appropriations bills. Adopting the line-item veto, an authority held by 43 state governors, would allow the president to strike out individual provisions nestled in individual or omnibus spending bills. However, creating a line-item veto would require a constitutional amendment. The Supreme Court ruled the line-item veto as passed by Congress in 1996 unconstitutional. Presidential signing statements have been used to register a president's objections to provisions in larger bills, particularly to provisions considered to be unconstitutional, even when the president chooses to sign the bill (see above).

Presidential Nominations

The Senate is given a special opportunity to influence the administration every time the president nominates someone for a top executive branch post. Beyond judges, ambassadors, and "other public ministers and consuls," the Constitution allows Congress to determine by law who must stand for confirmation by the Senate. Currently, the Constitution and public law subject about 3,000 civilian executive branch positions to confirmation by the Senate. Judicial nominations and confirmations are considered in Chapter 10. In addition, the promotions of all military officers are submitted to the Senate.

The Senate tends to defer to the president on executive branch appointments, particularly on positions below the cabinet level. This is not to say, however, that the president's appointments go unchecked. In fact, in 1989 President George H.W. Bush's first nominee for secretary of defense, former senator John Tower, was rejected by the Senate largely because of concerns about the senator's private behavior. The president swiftly moved to nominate House Republican Dick Cheney, a choice calculated to be far more acceptable to the Senate. In 1993, President Bill Clinton's first nomination for attorney general was withdrawn when it was discovered that the nominee, Zoe Baird, had hired illegal aliens as household help. In 2009, President Obama's choices for secretaries of Health and Human Services and a new position, Chief Performance Officer within the Office of Management and Budget, withdrew after irregularities in past tax payments were made public.

Occasionally Congress acts to require that certain executive officials be subject to Senate confirmation. In 1973, Congress required the president to receive Senate confirmation on appointments to director of the OMB. In 1986, Congress extended their authority by requiring that the president also receive Senate confirmation on appointments to head OIRA. When Congress approved legislation to create the Department of Homeland Security in 2002, the new secretary of the department automatically became subject to Senate confirmation.

Moreover, Congress may, and does, get involved in executive branch personnel matters beyond Senate action on presidential nominations. Congress

---

Congressionally Speaking . . .

The Constitution and many statutes require that the president submit the names of certain appointees to the Senate for confirmation. The Constitution also allows the president to make a *recess appointment* when the Senate is not in session. A recess appointment is good until the end of the next session of Congress, which could be more than a year in duration. Presidents have used recess appointments to avoid the regular confirmation process, but they usually announce their intention to forward a regular nomination to the Senate at the time appointments are made. Because recess appointments are a way for the president to circumvent, at least for a short while, the authority of the Senate, this practice can and does create animosity.

President George W. Bush employed the recess appointment with greater frequency than his two predecessors, but lagged slightly behind President Ronald Reagan and eventually was thwarted by a parliamentary maneuver. In his first six years as president, George W. Bush made 167 recess appointments, whereas President Bill Clinton made 140 over two terms and President George H.W. Bush made 77 in his single term. Reagan made 240 recess appointments during his eight years in office.[8] Senate Democrats blocked recess appointments in the last year of the Bush administration by avoiding long recesses. Rather than taking a recess, the Senate could remain officially in session by holding a *pro forma* session every three days. Why three days? The Constitution does not define a recess. A 1993 Justice Department opinion argued that the president may make a recess appointment during a recess of more than three days (that is, more than a long weekend).

In a *pro forma* session (an informal name), the Senate session opens, no business is conducted, and is immediately gaveled closed by the only senator in attendance.

---

is able to specify in law the qualifications required of presidential appointees, and it may even grant department heads, rather than the president, the authority to appoint certain officials. Congress also may limit the ability of the president or agency heads to dismiss employees. In these ways, Congress may seek to insulate certain executive branch officials from White House pressure.

Oversight

A member of Congress dissatisfied with agency performance or with presidential directives to an agency can choose from several oversight strategies to try to bring the bureaucracy into line. Oversight strategies centered on formal hearings include committee or subcommittee hearings, which regularly bring agency heads in front of legislators, special hearings designed to draw attention to a disputed policy or agency action, and more dramatic investigations, such as the Watergate hearings in 1973 and 1974 and the 1987 Iran-Contra hearings, usually conducted by special committees.

Less formal methods of monitoring and influencing agency behavior include written and telephone communications with agency officials, discussions with agency heads and other interested parties during informal office visits, public relations campaigns, and threats to pursue new legislation. Such approaches can be useful in congressional efforts to increase agency responsiveness to the interests of Congress. Although a considerable amount of bureaucratic oversight occurs within the committee forum, there are oversight mechanisms available to members that are independent of committees. Members seeking to influence agency actions in their districts also have recourse to informal visits and more formal inquiries conducted by staff. Often, members acting on behalf of communities in their district will pressure agency officials to respond to local concerns. For example, individual members frequently push the Environmental Protection Agency to investigate hazardous waste sites or to initiate cleanups in their districts. At other times, members will compel the administration not to act in their district when agencies have the potential to adversely affect preferred constituents.

Some observers have distinguished between "police-patrol" and "fire-alarm" oversight. Under police-patrol oversight, Congress pursues routine, systematic surveillance of executive branch agencies on its own initiative. In contrast, fire-alarm oversight is more decentralized. Instead of initiating and maintaining patrols, Congress develops a system that lets others "pull the alarms." Citizens, interest groups, or the media bring agency decisions to the attention of legislators and motivate them to act. Members may prefer fire-alarm oversight because it is more cost efficient and because it allows them to claim credit for acting when the alarm bells ring.

Yet police-patrol oversight appears to have become more common since the early 1970s. Fiscal constraints may have led members to turn away from legislation for new programs and instead to focus on overseeing the implementation of established programs. Expanded committee staffs and the independence of subcommittees, some devoted exclusively to oversight activities, have also facilitated more conventional oversight. Furthermore, the centralization of the executive branch's regulatory process in the OMB and the Council on Competitiveness motivated members to pursue formal oversight hearings more aggressively. Partisan rivalries when there is divided

THE IRAN-CONTRA AFFAIR

A Lebanese newspaper reported in early November 1986 that the Reagan administration had been engaged in trading arms to Iran for release of hostages held by Islamic extremists in Lebanon. When Attorney General Edwin Meese later that month uncovered a memo outlining the diversion of profits from the arms sales to the Nicaraguan Contras, a series of executive and congressional investigations ensued. Together, these events sparked the biggest scandal of President Reagan's two terms in office and helped precipitate Reagan's marked decline in popularity and influence.

An investigation by special House and Senate panels into the Iran-Contra affair uncovered a remarkable series of events, in which officials of the Reagan administration lied to Congress and helped subvert normal democratic decision-making processes. The Reagan administration essentially pursued secret policies that were in direct conflict with public policy objectives. On one hand, the administration's public policies were to ban arms shipments to Iran and to make no concessions for the release of hostages. On the other hand, the administration pursued secret policies of selling sophisticated missiles to Iran and trading weapons to get the hostages back. Although Reagan originally told a special investigatory commission that he approved the shipments, he later reversed this statement. In the end, he testified that he could not remember whether or not he had approved the shipments.

Reagan's advisors admitted to directing the covert arms transactions and the subsequent attempts to divert the profits to the Contras. They confessed to concealing and, at times, outwardly lying about the activities to Congress. The arms sales violated laws requiring that such transactions be reported to Congress. Even though law prohibited military or paramilitary assistance to the Contras, the National Security Council (NSC) staff sought illicit funding from foreign countries and private citizens, and turned over much of the operation to private arms merchants. The private enterprise accumulated approximately $10.6 million, carrying out covert U.S. policies with funds in a way that was entirely unaccountable to Congress.

Eventually, several senior administration officials were convicted of lying to Congress.

party control of Congress and the White House have motivated legislators to be more aggressive in their oversight activities.

Congress has increasingly turned to the Government Accountability Office (GAO) to assist with oversight. The GAO is an agency of Congress and is authorized to examine any federal agency. It gives members of Congress the option of having its expert, nonpartisan staff conduct an investigation of executive branch performance without a large commitment of time on the part of members or their staff. The duties of the GAO were expanded under the Legislative Reorganization Act of 1970, and since then the GAO has significantly increased the range and number of its audits and analyses of program effectiveness.

In recent decades, Congress has more frequently required the president and executive agencies to provide written reports on their actions and performance. In some cases, the requirement is designed to ensure the timely receipt of information – for example, just before Congress must reauthorize a program. In other situations, Congress demands that an agency conduct a special study of a problem and report the results. Executive branch officials often complain that they spend too much time writing reports that few members, if any, read. From Congress's perspective, however, the exercise is another aspect of police-patrol oversight that shifts the burden to agencies themselves.

Beginning in 1978, police-patrol oversight was extended by the creation of offices of inspectors general within major departments and agencies. Inspectors general are given substantial independence from political appointees and agency heads, are authorized to conduct wide-ranging audits and investigations, and are required to submit their reports directly to Congress. With few exceptions, Congress has looked favorably upon having a full-time, on-site bureaucratic oversight mechanism.

Police-patrol oversight also is reflected in Congress's intensified scrutiny of "reprogramming" by agencies. Congress usually appropriates funds for executive branch activities in large lump-sum categories, with the understanding that the funds will be spent in accordance with the more detailed budget justifications that agencies submit each year. Frequently, variation from the budget justifications – reprogramming – is deemed prudent or even necessary because of changing conditions, poor estimates, or new congressional requirements. Agencies and the White House, however, have occasionally taken advantage of reprogramming discretion to spend money for purposes not anticipated – or even opposed – by Congress. Congress has responded by establishing more and more requirements, such as demanding advanced notification of reprogramming actions and even requiring prior approval by the appropriate committees.

National security is an area in which Congress's ability to oversee the executive branch and publicize what it learns is somewhat limited. Several committees, including the appropriations, national security, and intelligence committees, receive classified information from executive agencies and hold hearings on classified matters in executive sessions. Committee reports from hearings or investigations are cleared with executive agencies and frequently must exclude materials that the agencies determine should remain classified. In 2004, as a part of a large intelligence reform package, Congress assigned the Public Interest Declassification Board (PIDB), comprised of members appointed by both Congress and the president, to resolve disputes between Congress and executive agencies about classified material that Congress wishes to publish.

Legislative Veto

A congressional strategy of disputed constitutionality is the use of the legislative veto. A legislative veto is a provision written into legislation that delegates authority for certain actions to the president or agencies, subject to the approval or disapproval of one or both houses of Congress, certain committees, or even designated committee leaders. The legislative veto gives Congress a way to check executive branch action without having to pass new legislation that would require presidential approval. Congress can, then, avoid writing detailed legislation by delegating rule-making power to the executive branch, and still retain the final say over executive decisions. Legislative vetoes may, at first glance, appear to be a strategy used exclusively by congressional players against the president. The origins of the legislative veto, however, convey a different story. In 1932, Congress and President Herbert Hoover reached an agreement on executive branch reorganization that included the first legislative veto. The compact delegated reorganization powers to the president, provided that Congress did not disapprove his plan within 60 days. The agreement effectively gave the president wide latitude in exercising powers delegated to him, but it also gave Congress a chance to control those actions without having to enact another law. The provision seemingly benefited both Congress and the president by expanding the powers of the president, but giving Congress an opportunity to nullify those decisions.

The Supreme Court eventually saw it differently and declared legislative vetoes unconstitutional in 1983 in *Immigration and Naturalization Service v. Chadha*. The majority of the Court noted that some legislative vetoes circumvent constitutional requirements that legislative actions be passed by both chambers. Perhaps more important, the Court said, legislative vetoes violate the constitutional requirement that all measures subject to congressional votes be presented to the president for signature or veto. The Court's position was evident: If Congress wants to limit executive branch use of delegated authority, it must pass new legislation by the traditional route.

Congress has devised no consistent strategy to replace the legislative veto. At times, Congress has written more detailed legislation or committee reports, added new procedural requirements for agencies, or turned to sunset provisions. At other times, it has turned toward informal agency-committee spending agreements, which require agencies to notify certain committees before they act. Although advance notification requirements have been upheld by the courts, committees actually retain an implicit form of veto under these arrangements. Specifically, agencies encountering opposition from the committees that fund them are not likely to proceed with their original plans out of fear of reprisal when their authorizing and appropriations legislation is next before Congress.

Despite the Court's 1983 ruling, Congress has continued to add legislative vetoes to new laws. In just over a year after the Chadha decision, an additional 53 legislative vetoes were enacted into law. By the completion of the 105th Congress (1997–1998), more than 400 new legislative vetoes had been enacted. New forms of legislative vetoes are still being attempted and, in some cases, enacted. These efforts reflect the desire of Congress, the president, and the executive agencies to find mutually acceptable ways to balance the delegation of power with checks on the use of that power. The president and agency officials know that courts would rule in their favor if they chose to challenge legislative vetoes, but they often agree to comply with them because legislative vetoes are a necessary condition for the latitude that accompanies them.

A convenient inference is that the Supreme Court's 1983 decision had little practical effect on inter-branch relations. Such an inference is premature and probably incorrect. A scholarly review of inter-branch relations in the foreign policy arena indicates that the 1983 decision eliminated an important means for resolving conflict. Where Congress and the executive branch are in serious disagreement, the executive branch appears unwilling to accept even symbolic legislative veto provisions, and Congress seems unwilling to delegate power that the executive branch seeks. Thus, changing the rules of the game seems to have affected the ability of the branches to identify cooperative strategies.

Conclusion

This review of congressional and presidential strategies suggests how dynamic and complex the relationship between the legislative and executive branches has become. As political conditions have evolved, senators, representatives, presidents, and bureaucrats have devised new and sometimes ingenious strategies to influence policy outcomes. Dissatisfaction with the likely or realized outcomes of the game has often yielded institutional innovations, such as expanding the responsibilities of the OMB, creating the line-item veto, expanding the use of executive orders, and creating legislative vetoes. Incrementally, the web of statutes, court rulings, and informal understandings produced by this process of innovation has made interbranch relations more complex. On the whole, the separation of powers between Congress and the president has become less clearly defined with the expansion of the president's legislative powers and Congress's administrative capabilities. What keeps the system operating is a minimal level of agreement among the House, Senate, and president, or at least an understanding that compromise is essential to prevent complete gridlock.

The three-institution legislative game of the House, Senate, and presidency generates cooperation and conflict as the policy preferences and political interests of officeholders vary across issues and over time. However, the requirement that the three institutional players agree before new law can be made, in the absence of sufficient congressional support to override a veto, leads to exploitation of extra-statutory tactics and often necessitates informal accommodation. Accommodation is frustrating to players set on gaining outright victories, and it often is possible only after a long struggle. Furthermore, accommodation produces unstable results. New Congresses and presidents seeking new strategies to meet their own political needs frequently alter the state of the institutions. Consequently, relations between the branches seldom remain in equilibrium for long.

Above: Supreme Court Justices arrive at the inauguration of Barack Obama as 44th U.S. President.
Below: Anti-abortion and pro-choice advocates rally in front of the U.S. Supreme Court on the 36th anniversary of the *Roe v. Wade* decision.

10

Congress and the Courts

S UPREME COURT NOMINATIONS WERE AT THE CENTER OF ATTENTION IN
the summer of 2005. Sandra Day O'Connor announced her intentions to resign on July 1, 2005 creating the first vacancy on the Supreme
Court in 11 years. Then, before O'Connor's seat could be filled, Chief Justice William Rehnquist lost his battle with thyroid cancer on September 3,
2005. Rehnquist's death created a second vacancy on the Supreme Court
and gave President George W. Bush an opportunity to shape the ideological
direction of the Court for a generation. Chief Justice Rehnquist was often
considered a reliably conservative vote, while O'Connor was considered the
"swing" justice who often cast the deciding vote in bitterly divided 5–4 decisions. President Bush first nominated John Roberts, a judge on the D.C.
Circuit Court of Appeals, to replace O'Connor, but following Rehnquist's
death, Bush nominated Roberts to become the new Chief Justice. Roberts
was considered a "home run" of a nominee with impeccable credentials
and qualifications. Conservatives were sure he would be a reliable vote on
their side, while liberals could find little in his record to warrant opposing
him. Roberts played his part well in his confirmation hearings as he repeatedly showed off his intellect all the while proclaiming judicial modesty, best
exemplified in his opening statement where he declared:

> Judges are like umpires. Umpires don't make the rules; they apply them. The
> role of an umpire and a judge is critical. They make sure everybody plays by the
> rules. But it is a limited role. Nobody ever went to a ball game to see the umpire.
> Judges have to have the humility to recognize that they operate within a system
> of precedent, shaped by other judges equally striving to live up to the judicial
> oath.

Roberts easily won Senate confirmation by a vote of 78–22, which then
focused the nation's attention on who President Bush would nominate to

replace Justice O'Connor – the first female justice to serve on the Supreme
Court. Bush first nominated White House Counsel Harriet Miers, a longtime ally and loyal soldier in the Bush administration. Unlike Roberts, Miers
immediately came under fire from politicians of all political stripes. Conservatives questioned whether or not she was conservative enough, given her
apparent support for abortion rights in her earlier work as an attorney, while
others questioned her qualifications given that she had never worked as a
judge or served in any posts that would have appeared to prepare her for
the job. Both sides questioned whether President Bush put cronyism above
finding the best nominee for the post. Miers eventually asked to have her
name withdrawn from consideration citing, among other factors, the growing opposition to her nomination.

Bush quickly named a new nominee – 3rd Circuit Court Judge Samuel
Alito – who was cut from the same model as Chief Justice Roberts. Alito
was eminently qualified, having spent 15 years as a judge, and was thought
to be a judicial conservative – in fact, many compared him to current Justice
Antonin Scalia. Alito found the Senate much less receptive to his nomination
than it had been to Roberts. Alito endured grueling confirmation hearings –
that once brought his wife to tears – and an attempted filibuster on the
Senate floor before eventually winning confirmation by a vote of 58–42.

The battle over judicial nominees such as Roberts, Miers, Alito, and scores
of lower court nominees has raged in the past two decades at least in part
because the House, Senate, and president are not the only institutional
players in the policy-making game. Federal judges serve, as Justice Roberts
stated, as "umpires" in encounters between players in the legislative and
executive arenas and help determine the boundaries of each institution's
powers. In separation-of-powers cases, for example, judges often draw lines
between the two branches and specify the constitutional powers on each
side. Judges also consider the scope of legislative powers generally, including
the scope of congressional power to investigate the executive branch and
where the line between federal and state jurisdictions should be drawn.

The courts are not simply umpires in the legislative game, however. They
are both political and legal institutions. In the past generation, judges have
increasingly contributed to making policy – not merely interpreting statutes
already enacted. The growth of judicial activism since the 1970s and the
reactions to judicial activism are an important part of the story of relations
between Congress and the courts.

Congress is not a quiet bystander to the decisions of the courts. Most
important areas of law are the product of interaction between the legislative institutions (Congress and the president) and the courts. The legislative

institutions have a number of ways to influence, at least indirectly, the decisions the courts make, as Congress and the president determine the composition of the courts. The president nominates judges and the Senate must confirm the nominees. Moreover, the size of the Supreme Court and lower courts, the organization and funding for the federal court system, and the Supreme Court's jurisdiction with respect to appeals from lower courts are determined by law, making them subject to the legislative process controlled by the House, Senate, and president. More directly, Congress and the president anticipate and react to court rulings. They sometimes comply with, ignore, or even reverse judicial decisions. They may speed, slow, or even exclude court consideration of certain matters in the way they write law. This chapter takes up each of these subjects – the courts as umpires, the courts as policy makers, and congressional resources and strategies.

Courts as Umpires

The Constitution implicitly grants to the Supreme Court the power to declare actions of state and federal legislatures and executives unconstitutional. This authority inserts the court into the dynamics of the legislative game. First exercised in *Marbury v. Madison* in 1803, the power of *judicial review* – the ability to declare laws unconstitutional – gives the courts a say in the enactment of new legislation.

Most cases come to the courts when a private party, sometimes an interest group, challenges the constitutionality of an act of Congress after an executive agency seeks to implement or enforce the act. Occasionally, members of Congress file suit against the executive branch for its failure to implement laws in a manner consistent with the members' expectations. In fact, members have been plaintiffs in suits filed against the executive branch in more cases during the past two decades than in all previous decades. Issues of great importance are appealed from lower courts to the Supreme Court, although this process might take years after the original enactment of the legislation.

As Figure 10.1 shows, the Supreme Court has overturned federal provisions at an uneven pace over its history. Before 1865, few provisions were overturned. Indeed, for much of its history the Supreme Court has exercised its review powers only intermittently. Intense legislative-judicial conflict is relatively infrequent, occurring in the decades around the New Deal and in more recent decades. Even then, historically the majority of laws and provisions overturned by the Court are actually minor or relatively unimportant, yet this tendency has changed in recent years as the Court has taken on

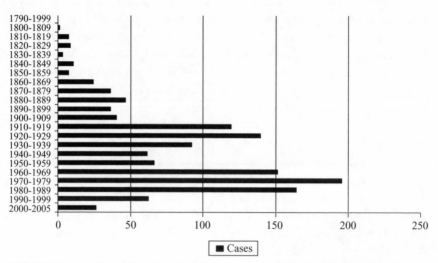

FIGURE 10.1. Number of Provisions Ruled Unconstitutional by the Supreme Court. *Source:* Lawrence Baum, *The Supreme Court,* 9th edition. Washington, D.C.: Congressional Quarterly Press.

high-profile legislation such as the Violence Against Women Act and the Religious Freedom and Restoration Act.

In this section, two types of cases involving the interpretation of the Constitution are discussed: cases involving the separation-of-powers between Congress and the executive branch and cases concerning the scope of congressional powers. The section concludes with a discussion of the role of courts as umpires in disputes about the meaning of statutes.

Separation-of-Powers Cases

In the decades before the 1970s, court involvement in separation-of-powers cases was uncommon. Because Congress was relatively deferential to the executive branch, fewer encounters were likely to provoke conflict over the powers of each branch. That situation changed dramatically during the Nixon administration (1969–1974) and in the following years when Congress moved to reassert itself.

President Richard Nixon asserted broad presidential powers in his conflict with a Congress controlled by the Democrats. The most conspicuous conflict was Nixon's battle with Congress over federal spending. Nixon claimed a right to withhold funds from executive agencies – a process called impoundment – even after the appropriations legislation was enacted into law. For example, Nixon impounded funds appropriated for sewage treatment plants administered by the Environmental Protection Agency. The impoundments were frequently challenged in the courts and Nixon usually lost. In 1973 and 1974 alone, only six of more than 50 cases upheld the president's position on impoundments in any way. Most of the decisions were made at the U.S. district court level and were not appealed by the administration to higher courts. In the sewage-treatment case, the Supreme Court ruled that the president was obligated to follow the law and allocate the funds.

In the 1980s, partisan dissension between the Republican White House and the Democratic House continued to drive each branch to the courts for redress against the perceived excesses of the other branch. For most of the Reagan and G. H. W. Bush presidencies, the Supreme Court followed a "doctrinal notion of separated powers" – the view that a sharp line can be drawn between executive and legislative powers. Two particularly revealing decisions in which the Court decided against Congress during this period were *Immigration and Naturalization Service v. Chadha* (1983) and *Bowsher v. Synar* (1986). These decisions merit attention in light of the ways in which the Court refereed contentious encounters between the branches. A later case, *Clinton v. City of New York* (1998), further demonstrates the Court's willingness to draw sharp distinction even in the absence of inter-branch contention.

In the *Chadha* decision, the Supreme Court ruled 7 to 2 that the legislative veto (see Chapter 9) was unconstitutional. According to the Court, Congress was to present bills to the president, who had the sole power to veto them. Arguments that the legislative veto was a workable means of extending authority to the executive short of formal enactment of a law were rejected. Still, the ban on legislative vetoes has largely been ignored by Congress, with more than 400 legislative vetoes enacted into law after *Chadha* – often with the agreement of the executive branch. Although the *Chadha* decision has forced Congress to be more creative in crafting provisions that give the legislature a potential veto, the response to the decision shows the weakness of the Court as an umpire when Congress and presidents agree on mutually beneficial ways to distribute power between themselves.

Building upon *Chadha*, the *Bowsher* decision advanced a stricter concept of separation of powers. *Bowsher* struck down a provision of the 1985 Gramm-Rudman-Hollings Act that required the President to implement spending reductions determined by the Comptroller General when the budget deficit exceeded a prescribed maximum. A majority of the Court concluded that such budget cuts were a power belonging to the Executive. Furthermore, the Court asserted that the Comptroller General, who can be removed from office by a joint resolution of Congress, was essentially an officer of the legislative branch. Therefore, this provision was deemed an unconstitutional infringement by the legislative branch on the powers of the Executive. While the *Bowsher* decision focused on a relatively narrow legal question, it ultimately forwarded a model of legislative-executive relations in which the legislative branch has a limited role in supervising the implementation of the laws it enacts. The Court wrote, "once Congress makes its choice in enacting legislation, its participation ends. Congress can thereafter control the execution of its enactment only indirectly – by passing new legislation." As discussed in chapter 9, the strict model forwarded by the Court in *Bowsher* has clearly not been practiced by the branches.

The Supreme Court's decision in *Clinton v. City of New York* (1998), striking down the line-item veto, demonstrated that the Court will enforce the separation of powers between Congress and the President even when the two branches are not in conflict. In 1996, Congress passed and President Clinton signed the line-item veto, which gave the President the power to remove or veto specific spending or tax breaks from bills while signing the underlying bill, with the law taking effect after the presidential election of 1996. Presidents had long sought this power to control federal spending, while many in Congress were eager to let the President help control it and take the blame for cutting popular programs. In striking down the line-item veto, the Court ruled that allowing the modification of a bill before signing it violated the constitutionally prescribed legislative process, specifically the "presentment" clause of Article I. During the presidency of G. W. Bush, he and many members of Congress expressed their desire to reenact a version of the line-item veto, but the Court's ruling has made it clear that it will guard the constitutionally prescribed separation-of-powers.

It has been noted by some observers that the modern Court has increasingly taken cases that pit the principle of separation of powers against that of checks and balances – related, yet not wholly compatible principles. While neither of these principles is spelled out in detail by the Constitution, they are nonetheless implicit. On the one hand, a strict view of separation of powers, as expressed in the *Bowsher* decision, confines the branches to their own designated arena, which may be inferred from the separate articles that outline the powers of the branches. Conversely, the principle of checks and balances, implied by the powers granted to the branches to prevent overreaching by other branches, requires that the branches occasionally engage in activities that extend beyond the strict definition of their role. Given that the Constitution offers little guidance regarding the details of these principles, it is silent as to when one principle should prevail over the other. In other words, the Constitution offers no roadmap as to when the branches should be confined to their own arena or granted shared powers for the sake of oversight.

Several actions of the G. W. Bush administration, many related to the War on Terror, have brought the tensions between these principles to the forefront, particularly regarding the limits of legislative oversight of the executive branch. And it appears that the Court will someday be the final arbiter on a number of these issues. Of particular interest in legislative-executive relations, is how the courts will rule on questions relating to executive privilege. G. W. Bush's broad claims of executive privilege on sensitive matters marked some of the most expansive use of the privilege in history, which enraged many in congress.

Perhaps the most controversial use of executive privilege came when Bush instructed former White House Counsel Harriet Miers and White House Chief of Staff Joshua Bolten to ignore congressional subpoenas relating to the investigation of the firing of nine U.S. attorneys, thought by some in congress to be politically motivated. On July 31, 2008, a U.S. District Court for the District of Columbia ruled in favor of Congress, holding that Miers and Bolten must comply with the subpoenas. However, the U.S. Court of Appeals for the District of Columbia later stayed that ruling, stating that the matter could not be resolved before the completion of the session of Congress. It was left to the next Congress to determine whether it would pursue the matter. The House rules package for the 111th Congress (2009–10) subsequently authorized the House to continue its lawsuit against Miers and Bolten, indicating that the Democratic-led Congress did not intend to put the issue to rest. However, members were increasingly concerned about letting judges determine the limitations of executive privilege, especially considering that a Democrat had recently entered the White House. Consequently, a deal was struck that required Miers (and former Deputy Chief of Staff, Karl Rove) to be interviewed under oath by the House Judiciary Committee in closed depositions. This agreement averted an almost certain path to the Supreme Court.

Should the rather delicate matter of executive privilege be resolved in the courts at some future date, the decision will have significant consequences for legislative-executive relations. A ruling against Congress would certainly enforce a vision that the branches are to operate in mutually exclusive spheres, thereby severely limiting congress's ability to check the executive branch. Conversely, a decision in Congress's favor would support the view that checks and balances are to be a central aspect in the relationship between Congress and the president.

Congressional Powers

The courts also referee the legislative game by their involvement in questions of congressional powers. Although Article I of the Constitution specifies in some detail the powers of Congress, the Supreme Court has often ruled on whether certain acts of Congress are permissible. In contrast, the Supreme Court has heard relatively few cases on Congress's authority over its internal affairs. On questions of membership qualifications, Congress's ability to punish its members, and speech privileges of members, the Court has generally given Congress a good deal of leeway. A few examples show how difficult the issues can be and how much the role of the courts as umpire can change in particular areas of the law.

THE COMMERCE CLAUSE. The most frequent way that the courts have refereed legislative politics is by interpreting the limits of congressional power under the Constitution. Perhaps the best examples are Supreme Court rulings that interpret the commerce clause of the Constitution (Article I, Section 8). The commerce clause allows Congress to enact legislation that regulates interstate commerce, and it has been used by Congress to regulate many aspects of American life that are related, however indirectly, to interstate commerce. Over the years, the Supreme Court has decided many cases that affect the limits of what activities are related to interstate commerce. As the national economy became more integrated and as Congress sought to establish more uniform policies for the nation in the late 1800s and early 1900s, congressional powers under the commerce clause became a controversial issue.

In the late 1800s and early 1900s, the Supreme Court took a narrow view of interstate commerce. If an activity concerned production or manufacturing, concerned only intrastate exchange, and did not directly affect interstate commerce, the Court tended to protect it from federal regulation. This interpretation greatly limited the ability of Congress and the president to respond to the rapidly changing national economy. In fact, the Court's narrow view of the commerce clause led it to strike down Franklin Roosevelt's New Deal legislation in the early 1930s, which was enacted in response to the Great Depression. After Roosevelt requested, but failed to get, congressional approval to enlarge the Court so that he could change the balance of opinion on the Court, two justices changed their views on the commerce clause, and the Court reversed itself on several major decisions.

Since the 1930s, step-by-step, the Court has allowed Congress to determine what activities are related to interstate commerce. In the 1960s, the Court affirmed the right of Congress to forbid owners of public accommodations with an interstate commerce connection (e.g., hotels, restaurants, etc.) from denying access on the basis of race or color. In the 1980s and early 1990s, the Court upheld laws that ban threats and extortion to collect on loans, set minimum wages for employees of state and local governments, and prohibited age discrimination by agencies of state government. Until recently, Court action appeared to erase the line between intrastate and interstate commerce and leave very broad powers for Congress under the commerce clause.

In 1995, led by conservative justices, the Supreme Court changed the direction of 70 years of rulings in favor of congressional discretion to determine the breadth of the commerce clause. In *United States v. Lopez*, the Court struck down a 1990 law that prohibited anyone from knowingly carrying a firearm in a school zone. The government argued that Congress had implicit authority, from its ability to interpret the commerce clause, to regulate firearms for such a public purpose. The Court ruled that nothing in the commerce clause or other constitutional provisions authorizes Congress to regulate such behavior, absent compelling evidence that the presence of firearms in school zones had an adverse effect on interstate commerce.

The Court continued its efforts to set limits on Congress's ability to stretch the commerce clause by striking down parts of the Violence Against Women Act in *U.S. v. Morrison* (2000). The 5–4 ruling invalidated a portion of the statute allowing women who were victims of sexual assault to sue their attackers in federal court. Congress had granted women this power citing numerous studies indicating that fear of violence had a chilling effect on the mobility of female students and employees. The majority opinion in *U.S. v. Morrison* held that Congress's attempt to regulate crimes against women in this manner could, "obliterate the Constitution's distinction between national and local authority" while the dissent held that Congress had adequately demonstrated the link between violence against women and interstate commerce.

The conservative majority that had seemed intent on limiting the power of Congress under the commerce clause splintered in *Gonzales v. Raich* (2005). The case dealt with whether or not the federal government could prohibit states from enacting laws sanctioning the use of medicinal marijuana. The government argued that the Controlled Substances Act – a law regulating the use of drugs such as marijuana – did not allow the use of the drug for medicinal purposes. The defendants argued that the Controlled Substances Act was unconstitutional because the drug was homegrown, did not cross state lines, and was not sold; hence did not involve interstate commerce. A 6–3 majority of the Supreme Court disagreed, finding that Congress did have the power to regulate medicinal marijuana under the commerce clause, signaling a reversal in the Court's tightening of Congress's powers under the commerce clause.

POWER TO INVESTIGATE. One area in which the courts have been more active in interpreting congressional powers has been Congress's power to investigate. Although the power to investigate is not mentioned explicitly in the Constitution, investigatory authority has traditionally been considered an implied power of Congress. In general, the authority to acquire information is usually seen as necessary for the proper functioning of a legislature. For example, the investigative and contempt powers of the English Parliament are exempt from judicial review. Although most investigations by the U.S. Congress are carried out without ending up in court, the Supreme Court has on occasion reached some rather controversial decisions about the scope of congressional investigatory authority. In particular, the Court has refereed cases contesting the subjects Congress can investigate and the rights that congressional witnesses retain. The Court originally took a narrow view of congressional investigative and contempt authority in *Kilbourn v. Thompson*, decided in 1881. In overturning the arrest of Hallet Kilbourn, who refused to provide information to the House about certain real estate deals, the Supreme Court limited Congress's ability to investigate private matters. The Court also delineated several principles concerning the proper scope of congressional powers to investigate. Specifically, the Court limited the scope of congressional authority to matters on which Congress could legitimately legislate and on which the chamber had indicated its intent to legislate.

Those standards stood for nearly 50 years, until the Supreme Court broadened congressional authority in *McGrain v. Daugherty* in 1927. The Court ruled that Congress had no general power to investigate private matters, but the Court extended the scope of congressional authority to any subject of *potential* legislation. The Court also affirmed Congress's power to compel private individuals to testify. Still, the Court did reserve for individuals the right to refuse to answer certain questions if they were not pertinent to the general investigation. Reserving a right for individuals to refuse to testify was to become central to Senator Joseph McCarthy's investigations of subversive activities in the 1950s.

In the 1950s and 1960s, the Warren Court moved to protect the right of private individuals to refuse to answer questions, based on their Fifth Amendment privilege against self-incrimination (*Watkins v. United States*, 1957; *Bernblatt v. United States*, 1959). *Watkins* concerned the rights of persons convicted of contempt of Congress for failing to answer questions about their association with the Communist Party that were posed by the House Un-American Activities Committee. In this case, the Court ruled that the committee did not have a sufficiently well-defined legislative purpose to justify requiring an individual to respond to questions. Chief Justice Earl Warren, writing for the Court, noted that "there is no congressional power to expose for the sake of exposure."

REGULATING CAMPAIGN SPENDING. In overturning parts of campaign finance legislation passed in 1974, the Supreme Court ruled in *Buckley* v. *Valeo* (1976) that Congress cannot limit individual or group expenditures in a political campaign when those expenditures are made independently of a particular candidate or party. The Court said that the First Amendment of the Constitution, which guarantees freedom of speech, prevents the government from regulating political speech – in this case, speech funded by an individual on her own behalf.

The Court said that limitations on campaign expenditures, as for any restraint on political speech, are constitutional only if some compelling government interest exists. The determination of what constitutes a compelling interest requires the courts to exercise discretion and judgment. In this case, the Supreme Court decided that the goal of limiting the electoral influence of wealthy individuals or groups was insufficient and ran directly counter to the intent of the First Amendment.

The Court reached a different conclusion in a case regarding the constitutionality of the 1974 law restricting the amount of money that political parties could spend directly on behalf of candidates. In reversing a previous decision by a circuit court, the Supreme Court held in *FEC* v. *Colorado Republican Federal Campaign Committee* (1996), that coordinated spending by political parties was not protected by the First Amendment and thus could be constitutionally regulated. Further, a majority of the Court found that there was a compelling government interest in regulating the spending activities of political parties. The Supreme Court upheld Congress's most recent attempt to regulate campaign finance, the 2002 Bipartisan Campaign Reform Act, in *McConnell* v. *FEC* (2003). As we describe in detail in Chapter 3, the Court allowed Congress to ban soft money and set restrictions on issue advocacy ads placed on television.

The Politics of Statutory Interpretation

When courts act as umpires in the legislative game, they often make judgments about the meaning of statutes. The imprecision of language,

THE AMERICAN CONGRESS

inconsistencies among various laws adopted at different times, and evolving circumstances to which a statute must be applied guarantee that the courts will face difficult decisions about the interpretation of laws. Compounding matters is that the legislators and presidents responsible for drafting legislation may have disagreed about the legislation's meaning or even deliberately left certain provisions vague to smooth over differences among themselves that would have been obstacles to enactment. Judges, when asked to resolve disputes about the interpretation of statutes, may affect the direction of public policy and sometimes alter the strategies of legislators, presidents, and others who care about policy.

Judges and legal scholars have developed several approaches to interpreting statutes, each reflecting a different view about how Congress functions, how legislative outcomes are reached, and how capable judges are of understanding congressional intent. The most traditional approach to interpreting statutes relies on the "canons of statutory construction." The canons outline for judges how to interpret the language of laws and are often stated in Latin. For example, one canon – *inclusio unius est exclusio alterius* – means that the inclusion of one thing indicates the exclusion of another. Other canons apply to specific subjects. For example, the "rule of lenity" stipulates that statutes that make certain conduct unlawful and impose penalties must be construed to apply narrowly to the conduct specified.

Unfortunately canons often conflict and there is no canon to help judges choose the appropriate canon. One school of legal scholars advocates that judges determine the objective or purpose of the statute and then deduce the outcome most consistent with the law's purpose. Another school insists that judges should determine how legislators, motivated by the special interests influencing them, would decide a question if asked to do so. Yet others contend that judges should be free to interpret and reinterpret statutes as the societal or legal context changes. Not surprisingly, some scholars argue that judges should refuse to resolve ambiguities and insist that they be resolved in the legislative process.

Perhaps the most important issue in statutory interpretation is being waged over the relevance and content of legislative histories. A few purists argue for strict construction of statutes. Rather than turning to committee reports and floor debates to interpret legislative intent, supporters of this approach urge courts to restrict themselves to the "plain meaning," or intrinsic meaning, of a statute's text. This view seems to be gaining support in the federal judiciary. Its most prominent proponent is Supreme Court Justice Antonin Scalia.

In practice, most judges still gladly accept guidance from committee reports, the record of floor debate, statements of bill or amendment sponsors, presidential messages, and other documented evidence of the intent of a bill's authors. Yet, because legislative histories often encapsulate conflicting views, they are not straightforward guides to statutory interpretation for judges. Further, members of Congress can try to add things to the legislative history to influence the decisions of judges. Most judges seem willing to exercise some judgment about which views should be considered most authoritative. Some effort has been made in recent years to improve communication between the federal judiciary and Congress so that problems of statutory interpretation can be minimized.

In recent years, a majority of justices on the Supreme Court have begun to look more carefully at legislative histories in the context of federalism cases. In striking down major provisions of the Americans with Disabilities Act, the Violence Against Women Act, and the Religious Freedom and Restoration Act, and upholding provisions of the Family and Medical Leave Act, the Court has cited legislative histories extensively in their opinions. The Court in these cases has used the content of legislative histories to determine whether or not Congress has generated a record of mistreatment of individuals by the States. The Court has reasoned that a substantial legislative record is necessary for Congress to abridge states' Eleventh Amendment protection against lawsuits in order to enforce the equal protection clause of the Fourteenth Amendment. This new line of reasoning by the Court has altered the balance of power between Congress and the States, and raised new questions about the quality and content of legislative deliberation, such as what standards of evidence Congress should be held to in demonstrating the need for new laws.

Members, lobbyists, and administrations often anticipate that legislative history may be important when issues are taken to the courts. Sometimes, the language of committee reports is the subject of as intense a fight as the bill language itself. For example, after the House Energy and Commerce Committee voted to approve a major overhaul of clean air laws in 1990, it took nearly a month for committee staff to hammer out report language that was acceptable to all sides. On most matters, carefully prepared statements by committee chairs and bill sponsors are made on the floors of the two chambers to give weight to a particular interpretation of major provisions of legislation and to set a record that judges cannot easily ignore.

Judges as Policy Makers

Although the courts' primary role is to serve as an umpire for disputes about legislative authority and procedure, the relationship between courts and the legislative institutions is more complex than that. In recent decades, federal

---

Congressionally Speaking...

Members frequently attempt to establish a clear record about how certain provisions of a bill should be interpreted. One way of doing this is to discuss the provisions in the *committee report* that accompanies the bill. Committee reports provide the background and justification for the bill and its provisions and often provide detailed sections on the meaning of key words or phrases. They are drafted by committee staffs and approved by committees, sometimes after long debate. Members also engage in *colloquies* – scripted exchanges on the floor among two or more members to clarify the interpretation of a bill or an amendment. Colloquies, of course, are transcribed in the *Congressional Record*, where judges, executive branch officials, and others can find floor statements.

In recent years, presidents have used *signing statements*, issued at the time they sign legislation, to offer their interpretation of controversial provisions. These statements send a message to administrative agencies about the interpretation of the law. Courts have not yet placed much weight on signing statements in their reading of legislative histories. They have tended to place greater weight on *veto statements* when the veto is not overridden by Congress and the legislation is modified in the direction suggested by the president.

---

judges have been seen as policy makers, that is, as players and not just umpires. At times, judges have even moved aggressively to place themselves at the center of political disputes. But in many areas, Congress and the president have encouraged courts' policy-making activities in the legislation they have enacted.

The assertiveness of the Warren Court in the 1950s in addressing racial desegregation marked a considerably more active and aggressive involvement of the courts in national policy making. Although the Burger Court impeded somewhat the extent of judicial involvement in policy making, the Rehnquist Court was the most "activist" ever (see Figure 10.1).

In the 1970s and 1980s, the mix of liberal, conservative, and moderate judges on the Supreme Court further fueled the expansion of court involvement in policy making. Reading statutes broadly and sometimes creatively enabled the two sides to sidestep controversial constitutional issues, which as a by-product expanded court involvement in the creation of national policy. In lower courts, judges often found that they were much less likely to evoke criticism from the Supreme Court if they misread statutes than if they misread the Constitution.

Judicial activism was reinforced by legislative activism on the part of Congress and the president. The wave of legislation between the mid-1960s and mid-1970s created new civil rights, broadened eligibility for welfare and health benefits, established new consumer rights, and set new public health, safety, and environmental standards. Much of the legislation required administrative agencies to design new regulations. Other legislation required agencies to account formally for additional factors in making their decisions. And some new laws were enacted that assigned the executive branch the duty to achieve certain policy goals. At the same time, new and often complex procedures were imposed on agencies by new legislation – the Freedom of Information Act, the Privacy Act, Government in the Sunshine Act, and other legislation. These procedural requirements were designed to open agency decision making to public scrutiny, protect individual rights, and ensure that agency officials heard all interests and views.

Although the role of the courts in the administrative process is, in part, the result of judges' assertiveness, it is much more than that. The creation of new substantive and procedural rights is often the direct product of interest group politics. Interest groups that lack confidence in decisions by regulatory agencies often view litigation as an alternative route for securing favorable policy outcomes. The type of agency decisions that are reviewable by courts, the actions courts may take, the parties who have standing to sue, and other issues are subject to the give-and-take of legislative politics.

The result is that courts are often left to enforce new rights and procedures, determine whether certain factors were given adequate weight in decisions, and evaluate the effectiveness of agency strategies for achieving specified goals. On the procedural side, judicial review sometimes encourages or even requires agencies to elaborate decision-making processes in ways unanticipated by Congress. Political scientist William Gormley[1] notes that

> by stressing the need for due process and by defining due process very broadly indeed, many federal courts have encouraged administrative agencies to adopt cumbersome procedures when handling individual cases, such as welfare or social security cases. A similar development in rule-making review has stimulated the growth of "hybrid ruling-making" procedures, including opportunities to cross-examine witnesses and other procedural guarantees. In practice, hybrid rule-making often benefits special interest groups, who need little additional protection. That is because such groups can afford the legal representation that hybrid rule-making requires.

The courts have often taken the step from procedural matters to the substance of agency decisions. In some cases, the law provides explicitly for the appeal of agency decisions to the courts. For example, the law requiring public schools to provide education for children with disabilities provides appeals to give local groups a chance to challenge federal, state, and local decisions affecting education in their communities. In such cases, courts are called on to judge what constitutes adequate education. In doing so, the courts are asked to direct public policy, even to influence the spending priorities of government.

In other cases, lawsuits pursued by affected parties or interest groups unhappy with agency decisions have led courts to make policy judgments. Gormley explains:

> Citing the "hard look doctrine" popularized by the late Judge Harold Leventhal, [courts] have insisted that agencies take a hard look at the available evidence, engage in reasoned decision-making, and give careful consideration to alternatives. All of this sounds rather innocuous. In practice, however, the hard-look doctrine enables judges to substitute their judgment for that of administrative officials who possess far greater technical expertise.

Thus, by applying judicially derived doctrine for situations in which agencies have been delegated substantial policy-making discretion, the courts sometimes have become policy makers themselves.

The question of why Congress has tended to devolve quasi-legislative powers to agencies and the courts remains. Plainly, institutional politics has become quite complex. Some commentators argue that members of Congress often use the agencies and the courts to avoid difficult choices and political blame. Members, according to this view, often are unable or unwilling to resolve their differences, so they give up and leave legislation ambiguous or include contradictory provisions, a practice which sometimes leaves interested parties no option but to take the matter to court. Other observers note that Congress and the courts have largely been willing allies in the expansion of the federal bench into the legislative arena. Unwilling to trust agency regulators under Republican administrations, Democratic majorities in Congress repeatedly turned to the courts to help put teeth into increasingly complex and detailed legislation in the 1970s and 1980s. Yet other analysts emphasize the influence of interest groups to whom Congress and the president are responding when they approve legislation.

Each of these interpretations seems to fit at least some major legislation. Members of Congress have certainly tried to use the courts when they have lacked the political support to secure policy goals through legislation. As just discussed, failed efforts by members to enforce the War Powers Resolution in the courts show the limits of enticing the courts to resolve political controversies. But Congress's tendency to draw the courts into the policy arena also reflects the cumbersome nature of legislating under divided government. Unable to procure favorable outcomes from regulators, members of Congress and organized groups have deliberately sought the assistance of the courts in battling administrators.

Congressional Resources and Strategies

Congress has formidable tools for dealing with an unfriendly federal judiciary. The framers of the Constitution left several tools for Congress and the president to check the actions of the courts. Lifetime tenure of federal judges is intended to provide some autonomy to the courts, as is the prohibition against reducing the compensation of judges. But neither Congress nor the president has been willing to give a free hand to the federal judiciary. Congress has used its constitutional authority to impeach federal judges, change the number of judges and courts, set the courts' budgets, and alter the appellate jurisdiction of the Supreme Court. Perhaps most familiar to even casual observers of American politics, the president and Congress frequently struggle over appointments to the federal bench.

In addition, Congress has responded legislatively to court decisions. Congress often enacts new legislation that is adapted to court rulings. For example, in 1993 Congress enacted the Religious Freedom and Restoration Act – a direct refutation of the Court's decision in *Oregon v. Smith* (1990), which dealt with religious practice and federal unemployment benefits. When Congress objects to a court's interpretation of a law, Congress sometimes passes a new bill that clarifies its intentions. In some cases, Congress adjusts the new legislation to take into account a court's ruling about the constitutionality of certain kinds of provisions. In recent years, several bills have been introduced in Congress to remove federal court jurisdiction from certain policy areas. And, of course, Congress may propose a constitutional amendment to overrule the courts' interpretation of an existing provision.

Congress and the Structure of the Federal Judiciary

The Constitution vests judicial power in the Supreme Court but grants to Congress the authority to establish inferior courts when it chooses. The size, budget, and appellate jurisdiction of the Supreme Court, as well as the structure, size, budget, and jurisdiction of lower courts, are determined by law and are therefore subject to the normal legislative process. In addition,

Congress is authorized by the Constitution to create what are known as Article I courts, or legislative courts – the military courts, tax court, customs courts, and bankruptcy courts. These courts are located in either the executive or judicial branches, the judges are appointed by the president with Senate confirmation, and the judges serve fixed, limited terms.

Partisan politics has been an ever-present condition in Congress's handling of the judiciary. The first major effort to structure the courts for political purposes occurred in 1801, when the defeated president John Adams and his Federalist supporters in Congress created new circuit court judgeships to be filled with Federalists. The effort to influence the character of the federal bench failed, however, when the new Republican Congress repealed the act and abolished the judgeships. Even though Congress postponed the next meeting of the Supreme Court to prevent it from hearing a challenge to its repeal, the Court upheld Congress's power to repeal the Federalists' Judiciary Act of 1801 a year later.

Congress has only once limited the jurisdiction of the Supreme Court. In 1868, striking down parts of Reconstruction legislation in 1866, the court was scheduled to hear another case on Reconstruction law – the Habeas Corpus Act, which concerned the rights of individuals held in detention. Anticipating that the Court would use the occasion to find all Reconstruction laws unconstitutional, Congress enacted a law to prevent the Court from hearing cases related to the Habeas Corpus Act. The Supreme Court, incidentally, backed down from any confrontation with Congress when it upheld the constitutionality of the repeal of its jurisdiction a year later.

With the exception of the Reconstruction-era episode, efforts to curb the Supreme Court's jurisdiction have failed. This result is not too surprising. After all, the House, Senate, and president, or two-thirds of both houses of Congress, must agree to legislation curbing Court jurisdiction before it is enacted. Nevertheless, members of Congress continue to introduce bills that would restrict the jurisdiction of the Supreme Court or all federal courts. Between 1975 and 2002, according to one count, 132 bills were introduced to limit the federal judiciary's jurisdiction in some way. While none of these efforts were successful, and none have been since then, many members see them as an opportunity to demonstrate to judges that Congress can limit jurisdiction, and these efforts are often popular with constituents.

Congress also has had a mixed record in efforts to control the Supreme Court by changing its size. In the nineteenth century, Congress used its power over the size of the Court several times to exert pressure on the Court and to help change its ideological shape. Although Presidents James Madison, James Monroe, and John Quincy Adams each claimed that a growing nation needed a larger Supreme Court (that started with just six members), Congress did not change the Court's size until 1837. Even then, it postponed the change to nine members until the last day of President Andrew Jackson's term that year. Later, by increasing the size of the Court to ten justices, Congress gave President Abraham Lincoln an opportunity to solidify a pro-Union majority on the Court. Soon thereafter, Congress reduced the number of justices from ten to eight to prevent President Andrew Johnson from filling any vacancies. When Johnson's successor, Ulysses S. Grant, took office, Congress changed the number of justices to nine, where it has remained.

The best-known attempt to influence Supreme Court decisions by altering its size was the "court-packing" plan of President Franklin Roosevelt. Roosevelt, disturbed by rulings that struck down important parts of his New Deal legislation, proposed in 1937 that the Supreme Court be expanded from nine to 15 justices so that he could appoint new justices and change the balance of opinion. Congressional resistance, as well as a series of Supreme Court decisions more favorable to Roosevelt's New Deal legislation, led Roosevelt to drop his plan. But the uproar over the Roosevelt plan has had a chilling effect on other presidents and Congresses that might have pushed legislation to alter the size of the Court for political purposes.

The Senate and Judicial Nominations

The shared power of appointment remains the primary means by which senators and presidents influence federal courts. Needless to say, the president and the Senate do not always agree on what course federal courts ought to take. Historically, this battle was largely fought over presidential nominations to the Supreme Court, with the nominations of Judge Robert H. Bork in 1987 and Judge Clarence Thomas in 1991 standing out as particularly controversial. As we explore in the following section, recent years have seen the controversies extend to appointments to the lower courts.

LOWER COURT NOMINATIONS. Senators of a president's party typically have had a great deal of influence over the president's appointments to federal district courts and the courts of appeal. These senators usually play an active role in the nominating process by suggesting acceptable candidates to the administration. But only a few senators usually play an active role in Senate deliberations considering judicial appointments at the district level. Unlike nominations to the Supreme Court, and more recently circuit courts, which elicit much broader interest, district court seats generally draw fairly localized interest from the Senate body. In most cases, the Senate's Judiciary Committee staff studies lower-court nominees, receives reports from the American Bar Association and the Federal Bureau of Investigation, and routinely recommends approval to the full Senate, which confirms the nominees with little or no discussion.

The record of judicial appointments during the Reagan and G. H. W. Bush presidencies continued the pattern of routine approval for most nominees, but with the addition of a few very controversial cases. During the course of the Reagan and G. H. W. Bush presidencies, more than 460 appointments were made to appeals and district courts, meaning that by the end of the Bush administration, more than 70 percent of sitting federal judges had been appointed during the Reagan and Bush years. These appointments have produced a much more conservative federal bench. Although the Democrats controlled the Senate for more than half the period, they largely acquiesced to presidential preferences for more conservative, younger, white federal judges. Not until the few months before the 1992 presidential election did Senator Joseph Biden (D-Delaware) and the Judiciary Committee take a more aggressive stance against the administration's nominees, apparently emboldened by the possibility that Democrat Bill Clinton would win the presidency. After suggesting that he would be more selective about which Bush nominees would receive hearings before the election, Biden and the Judiciary Committee slowed down the pace of confirmation hearings for appellate court appointments.

When Bill Clinton assumed the presidency, he had 99 seats on the federal bench to fill – seats that observers expected would be filled by a greater proportion of minorities and women than were those filled by Bush and Reagan. With a Democratic majority in the Senate during his first two years in office, Clinton was successful in getting rapid confirmations. But after the Republicans took majority control of the Senate in 1995, the speed of Senate confirmations declined markedly. In 1998, Chief Justice William Rehnquist complained about the slow pace, noting that 101 judicial nominees had been confirmed in 1994 but only 17 were confirmed in 1996 and 36 in 1997.

Many vacancies had gone unfilled for more than 18 months, with some going up to four years between nomination and confirmation. Senate Judiciary Committee Chairman Orrin Hatch (R-Utah) insisted that the Republican Senate had been just as responsive as the Democrats had been for President G. H. W. Bush, and the battle continued into the administration of G. W. Bush. In all, the confirmation rate for lower court judges has declined somewhat in the past two decades amidst increasing partisan polarization, yet remains quite high. Some variation has occurred in the

THE CHANGING CONGRESS: "REVERSE FILIBUSTER" HIGHLIGHTS INCREASED PARTISANSHIP ON JUDICIAL NOMINEES

Lacking a majority on the Senate Judiciary Committee, Senate Democrats in 2003 refused to allow a floor vote on some of President G. W. Bush's lower court nominees. Senate Republicans, who had the slimmest of majorities in the 108th Senate (51), were short of the 60 votes needed to invoke cloture, or end debate, on these nominees. Although they pursued several options to change Senate rules regarding filibusters on judicial nominees, Senate Republicans remained frustrated by their inability to gain up or down votes on some judicial nominations. In an attempt to raise public awareness of the impasse on these nominations, in November 2003 Senate Republicans staged a 39-hour continuous debate seeking to highlight Democratic obstruction. The marathon debate, labeled a "reverse filibuster" by its organizers, was ironic in that it used extended debate to highlight real or threatened obstruction by some members of the Democratic Party. Senate Republican leaders hoped that the event would attract enough publicity to increase public pressure on Senate Democrats to agree to vote on the stalled nominees and would increase public support for their efforts to reform the filibuster rule.

Instead, the event turned into political theatre, with lots of melodrama, but nothing of substance was accomplished. Republicans labeled the session a "Justice for Judges" marathon, complete with T-shirts and signs bearing the slogan, while Democrats countered with a large sign emblazoned "168–4"– representing the number of Bush's judges confirmed (168) and the number blocked (4). Cots were set up for tired senators, beer was provided for the reporters covering the event, Democrat Tom Harkin posted a sign reading, "I'll Be Home Watching 'The Bachelor'," and a filibuster bingo game was unveiled. At the end of the marathon session, it did not appear that much had changed; none of the judges in question received a vote in the Senate, and there was no noticeable public outcry. In fact, one of the police officers standing guard outside the Senate summed up the likely opinion of most of the public, stating: "I could see if it was something important like the budget or Iraq, but who cares about judicial appointments?"

confirmation rate for district court nominees, however there has been a more appreciable decline in circuit court confirmations. The confirmation rate for district court nominees has generally centered around 90 percent among recent presidents, with G. W. Bush having the lowest rate of approximately 79 percent. On the other hand, there has been a reasonably consistent drop in the circuit court confirmation rate over this period. The Carter administration enjoyed an approximately 92 percent confirmation rate for circuit court nominees, which fell to 71 and 73 percent for the Clinton and G. W. Bush administrations respectively.

Congressionally Speaking . . .

Senatorial courtesy is the practice of conferring with senators of the president's party whenever a vacancy in a position subject to presidential appointment is located within the senators' state. The practice applies to vacancies in federal district courts. For many years, senators could exercise a virtual veto over appointments affecting their states. The practice rests on the willingness of the Senate and its Judiciary Committee to refuse to act on nominees opposed by those senators. It gives senators a form of patronage with which to reward political friends.

Senatorial courtesy is institutionalized through the use of *blue slips* – blue sheets of paper sent out by the Judiciary Committee asking senators from a nominee's home state his or her opinion of the nominee. A home state senator who objects to a nominee will often write on the blue slip that the nominee is "personally offensive." This practice has existed since the early 1910s, with negative blue slips usually meaning that the Judiciary Committee will not act on a nominee. Although not always the case today, a negative blue slip usually makes confirmation of the nominee extremely difficult.

The influence of partisanship in appointment to the lower courts is clear. More than 90 percent of nominees to the lower courts are affiliated with the party of the president nominating them. Moreover, lower-court nominees in the fourth year of a four-year presidential term are much less likely to be confirmed than are nominees sent to the Senate in other years, and the confirmation process typically takes much longer when the Senate and presidency are controlled by different parties. At the end of a president's term, senators of the opposition party often prefer to leave judgeships vacant until they see which party wins the presidency. If their party wins the presidency, the new president can submit new names – presumably more to their liking.

SUPREME COURT NOMINATIONS. As the Miers/Alito spectacle described in the introduction points out, Supreme Court nominations are not routine. Unlike the appointment process for district court seats, presidential nominations to the Supreme Court garner a much broader spectrum of interest across the Senate. In fact, lower court nominees are often screened more carefully if they are thought to be potential Supreme Court nominees. After a president makes a nomination, the Senate Judiciary Committee has the nominee complete a lengthy questionnaire, orders its staff to conduct an extensive background investigation on the nominee, receives an evaluation from the American Bar Association, and then holds several days of hearings. Recently interest groups have actively lobbied senators and generated publicity for the groups' views. The administration, which sometimes discusses a list of possible nominees with senators in advance of the nomination, coaches the nominee in preparation for the hearings.

The outcomes of Supreme Court confirmation efforts hinge on numerous factors. First, the partisan makeup of the Senate matters. When the president's party has been in the majority, close to 90 percent of nominees have been confirmed. In contrast, during times of divided government, only 59 percent of nominees have been approved by the Senate. Second, the timing of the nomination also has implications. Not only does partisanship in Congress tend to increase in election years, but the president's influence in the legislative arena usually declines during the course of his term in office. Presidents also appear to be more successful when they make public statements on behalf of their nominees. Overall weakness of a president clearly affects his ability to get a nominee approved by the Senate. Reagan nominated Robert Bork in 1987 after the revelations of the Iran-Contra scandal had significantly weakened the president's standing in Congress and public approval. Bork was turned down by the Senate.

Timing is important from other perspectives as well. Many argue that senators up for reelection give greater weight to public opinion than do senators who do not face reelection in the near future. But most senators appear to take into account the qualifications and ideological outlook of nominees. The greater distance the nominee's positions are from the senator and the less qualified the nominee is, the lower the probability of the senator voting in favor of the president's choice. The appearance of one or more of these factors – partisan balance, presidential popularity, proximity to the end of the presidential term, ideological placement, or nominee qualifications – increases the likelihood of conflict in the Senate during the confirmation process. On many confirmation votes, individual senators are also likely to be influenced by constituency concerns. In the case of Thurgood Marshall and Clarence Thomas's nominations to the Court, state racial composition had a determinative effect on votes by senators representing states with large African American populations.

The Senate has failed to confirm only 26, or about 20 percent, of presidents' nominations to the Supreme Court. Twentieth-century presidents have had better luck than their predecessors, but even recent presidents have stumbled. President Lyndon Johnson was forced to withdraw two nominations, two nominees of President Richard Nixon were rejected, President Reagan withdrew one nomination and one nominee was rejected, and both Presidents G. H. W. and G. W. Bush withdrew one name. Two nominations deserve special mention: President Reagan's nomination of Robert Bork, which was rejected by the Senate, and President G. H. W. Bush's nomination of Clarence Thomas, which was approved by a narrow margin, 52 to 48.

In 1987, President Reagan faced a Democratic Senate when he nominated Judge Bork, then a judge on the U.S. Court of Appeals for the District of Columbia and a former solicitor general and law school professor. Bork's longstanding and well-published opposition to affirmative action and the established ruling on abortion, along with his judicial activism, stimulated an extraordinary and influential effort by civil rights groups and others to prevent his confirmation by the Senate. Interest in his nomination stimulated unprecedented scrutiny by the media – the media even reported Bork's videotape rentals. The Senate voted 58 to 42 against his confirmation.

Four years later, President Bush nominated Clarence Thomas, also a sitting judge on the U.S. Court of Appeals for the District of Columbia, and a former chair of the Equal Employment Opportunity Commission (EEOC). Thomas had relatively little judicial experience: He had been on the appeals court for only 18 months and had never argued a case before a court. The American Bar Association's review committee rated him "qualified" on their three-point scale (highly qualified, qualified, and not qualified), with two members of the committee voting "not qualified," making Thomas the only Supreme Court nominee rated by the Bar Association to receive such a weak evaluation. Thomas had a record of commitment to conservative views on many issues, leading liberal groups to mobilize against him and drawing tough questions from the liberal Democrats on the Judiciary Committee.

Nevertheless, Thomas's confirmation seemed likely until the eve of the scheduled vote by the full Senate. National Public Radio reported that a complaint of sexual misconduct against Thomas had been disclosed to Judiciary Committee staff and noted in an FBI report, although it had not been mentioned in the initial committee hearings. The committee reopened the hearings to listen to the testimony of Anita Hill, a University of Oklahoma law professor who had worked for Thomas at the EEOC. At the hearings, she repeated her charges against Thomas. He responded, and the committee heard character witnesses for both Thomas and Hill, all before a very large national television audience.

After Thomas was confirmed by the full Senate by a vote of 52–48, the committee and the Senate were criticized for the manner in which they had conducted the hearings. Senator Arlen Specter ran into difficulty in his 1992 reelection bid because of the way he had grilled Professor Hill. In response to the criticism, Senator Biden announced changes in Judiciary Committee practice guaranteeing that all information received by a committee and its staff would be placed in the nominee's FBI file to ensure all senators access to FBI reports and provide for closed briefings for all senators so that any charges against nominees, if there were any, could be reviewed. And, in a conspicuous move to make sure that any sexism on the committee would be held in check, two women – Senators Dianne Feinstein (D-California) and Carol Moseley-Braun (D-Illinois) – were appointed to the committee in 1993.

Congress and the Impeachment of Judges

Under the Constitution, judges "shall hold their offices during good behaviour," but the House is empowered to bring and vote on impeachment charges against judges. If a judge is impeached by the House, the Senate conducts a trial on the charges. A two-thirds vote of the senators present is required to convict and remove a judge – the same number required for removing a president from office. Removal of a judge by House impeachment and Senate conviction is rare. Over the course of the history of the federal bench, no Supreme Court justice has been removed from office by Congress. In 1804, Republicans tried to impeach justice Samuel Chase on several charges, but they failed to get a two-thirds vote to convict. Thirteen lower federal judges have been impeached by the House, and only seven have been convicted by the Senate. Of the seven judicial convictions, three have occurred since 1986.

Congress's impeachment power has not proven to be a source of leverage over the courts. Even the threat of impeachment has only once been credited with inducing a change in Supreme Court membership: Justice Abe Fortas resigned in 1969 after revelations of questionable financial practices. Impeachment trials do pose certain challenges for a Senate already having trouble managing its time and discharging its duties. Any trial procedure involving the full Senate inevitably distracts the Senate from its legislative agenda. To address this problem, the Senate moved in 1986 to form a special 12-member committee to gather and review evidence on behalf of the full Senate.

Legislative Responses to the Courts

Interaction between Congress and the courts does not necessarily end with judicial action. Congress can, of course, use its traditional legislative powers to respond to court decisions. For example, after the Supreme Court decided in 1988 that burning the U.S. flag in protest of government policy should be afforded First Amendment protection as a form of political speech,

Congress eventually enacted a statute designed to strip flag burning of its constitutional protection. In another case, Congress overrode a presidential veto to reverse a Supreme Court decision concerning sex discrimination in colleges and universities.

But successful reversals of unpopular Supreme Court decisions are not automatic. On some occasions, efforts to reverse decisions pass one chamber and get stalled in the other. Other efforts often get stymied at the committee level, after hearings are held on possible legislation to reverse the decision.

Studies show that Congress responds to about one-third of these Supreme Court moves to nullify a federal law. Why? The three-institution legislative game makes a response to the Court difficult. All three institutions must agree, or at least two-thirds of both chambers must agree, to any legislative response. If the committees with jurisdiction over the affected legislation recognize that gaining the approval of the House, Senate, and president is impossible, they may choose to take no action. Nevertheless, Congress sometimes does respond to court decisions. Several factors appear to motivate congressional efforts to respond to court decisions. One study emphasizes the important role of public opinion in motivating Congress to act. If the majority of public opinion is in favor of action by Congress, the probability of a congressional response increases dramatically. Salience of the issue to organized interest groups, sometimes indicated by the participation of groups in the case before the Supreme Court, also appears to influence congressional decisions to respond. In many cases, however, members seem to have been motivated to take preliminary steps to respond to demands, but they did not push the legislation to the point of passage.

Not surprisingly, Congress is also more likely to respond to Supreme Court decisions when invited to do so by judges on the bench. On occasion, the Court rules that although particular provisions are unconstitutional, Congress could remedy the problem by rewriting the provision. In effect, the Supreme Court outlines the boundaries of what changes would be considered constitutional. Such guidance by the courts markedly increases the chances that Congress will undertake efforts to respond to or reverse the nullifying decision. Judicial invitations to review give a different cast to relations between Congress and the courts. Far from the conflict that many normally assume exists when the Court overturns a federal law, these invitations to reverse reflect a more cooperative relationship between the branches.

Amending the Constitution

A frequent response of members to court decisions is to propose a constitutional amendment. Since the Supreme Court's decision in *Roe v. Wade*

(1973), for example, many members have supported a constitutional amendment that would reserve to the states the power to regulate abortions. The constitutional requirement that an amendment receive the support of two-thirds of both chambers before it is sent to the states for ratification sets a high threshold that has seldom been met. Only four amendments to the Constitution were adopted in direct response to Supreme Court decisions: the Eleventh Amendment, on the ability of citizens of one state to bring suit against another state; the Fourteenth Amendment, on the application of the first 10 amendments to the states; the Sixteenth Amendment, on the federal income tax; and the Twenty-sixth Amendment, on the right of 18-year-olds to vote.

Conclusion

The courts occupy a critical, but often overlooked, place in forming national policy. The roles played by the courts vary widely – from separation-of-powers umpire to congressional overseer and partner in policy making.

Relationships between the branches clearly depend on the rules of the game. But those rules, as we have seen, are themselves often the product of political battles. The rules of the policy-making process can be ambiguous, and this ambiguity gives the courts an opening into the legislative game. As a result, members of Congress have an incentive to watch over the actions of courts carefully and, on occasion, to enlist judges in their campaigns against a recalcitrant executive branch.

Judges, however, are not always willing to take the bait. Sometimes, the courts smell a political contest and send the dispute back to congressional players to resolve themselves. Other times, judges simply define respective powers of each contending actor and set boundaries for future interactions between the players. Although Congress and the president can shape the membership of the bench, other congressional tools rarely give members enough leverage over the courts to limit judicial independence and discretion. When the courts have chosen to enter the policy process, however, major changes in policy making have often occurred. Whether expanding procedural rights of individuals or forcing executive agencies to work more assiduously to follow congressional intent, federal courts in recent decades have made inroads into the legislative arena. Attention to the interactions of judges, legislators, and executives thus markedly affects our understanding of how separate branches are indeed sharing power to shape national policy.

Above: Senator Roger Wicker (R-Mississippi), right, walks with lobbyists on his way from a meeting to the Senate floor for a vote.
Below: Former-Senator Ted Stevens (R-Alaska) departs the Senate floor for the last time after being convicted on seven counts of corruption relating to false statements he made on Senate ethics forms to cover up hundreds of thousands of dollars he received in gifts. Stevens was defeated by Mark Begich, the former-mayor of Anchorage, in his bid for an eighth term.

11

Congress, Lobbyists, and Interest Groups

T HE FIRST AMENDMENT TO THE CONSTITUTION PROVIDES THAT CONGRESS may make no law abridging the right of the people to petition the government for a redress of grievances. Court rulings interpret the Amendment broadly to include organized and paid representatives of the people, therefore limiting Congress's ability to regulate lobbying. In practice, interest groups and their lobbyists are a very important means by which the public conveys their expectations and demands to Congress. Nevertheless, Americans believe that members of Congress are beholden to special interests and lobbyists. A 2008 survey conducted by the Center on Congress at Indiana University found that 71 percent of Americans gave Congress a grade of D or F when asked to assess Congress's representation of the American people; over 76 percent of those surveyed gave Congress a D or F on its ability to control the influence of special interests.[1] A 2006 CBS/*New York Times* survey found that 75 percent of Americans agreed that most members of Congress are more interested in serving special interest groups than the people they represent.[2]

These contrasting views – that lobbyists are essential to democracy and yet reviled by the public – give interest groups and lobbyists an uneasy place in congressional politics. In earlier chapters, we have noted that representation of organized interests is a rapidly growing industry in Washington. In this chapter, we reemphasize this theme, discuss the evolving strategies of interest groups, and review the limited efforts of Congress to regulate lobbying. Congress, in accordance with the Constitution, has been able to put in place only minimal regulations on lobbying. As an alternative, Congress has placed more severe restrictions on legislators, as it is allowed to do, with respect to their relations with organized interests. Restrictions on campaign contributions from organized interests were detailed in Chapter 3. In this chapter, we concentrate on developments in the legislative strategies of groups and lobbyists.

The Expanding Community of Lobbyists and Interest Groups

Lobbyists have been present since the first congresses. The wide reach of federal policy and Congress's central role in shaping it motivates many citizens, organized groups, and lobbyists to converge on Washington (see box "Congressionally Speaking..."). Congress's internal decision-making processes are largely responsible for this. Reliance on committees and subcommittees for writing the details of most legislation gives outsiders many points of contact with legislators and staff. Even congressional parties are quite permeable. Many legislators influence party strategies through their participation in party caucuses, committees, and task forces. If legislators can be influenced, so too can party strategies. The vast institutional partitioning of Congress (i.e., bicameralism, parties, committees, subcommittees, etc.) gives lobbyists more opportunities for influence than they find in most other national legislatures. The more complex the legislative process and the more places that interests can be protected, the more valuable the experienced lobbyist is to the average citizen.

Generalizing about lobbyists is difficult. Some lobbyists are officials of organized interest groups such as the U.S. Chamber of Commerce, the Sierra Club, and the National Cable Television Association. Other lobbyists are lawyers, former members or staff of Congress, or public relations specialists who have their own lobbying firms that are hired by interest groups, corporations, or other organizations to represent their interests, sometimes on a specific bill or issue. Many lobbyists work for universities and colleges, state and local governments, and even foreign governments that seek to influence federal policy. Frequently, lobbyists are citizens who have made the trip to Washington to make their case in person. As discussed later in this chapter, important legal distinctions are made between those hired to lobby for a person or organization and concerned citizens that lobby on their own behalf.

Most interest groups represent occupational or organizational communities. Occupational groups include organizations representing doctors, teachers, accountants, and even association executives. Government employees have many specialized interest groups – the American Association of State Highway and Transportation Officials, for example. Many, perhaps most, interest groups are associations comprised of organizations. Most trade associations, such as the American Petroleum Institute, the Association of American Railroads, and the National Association of Wholesaler-Distributors, represent corporations in a particular sector of the economy. But associations representing member unions, universities, local governments, and other organizations are important as well. The Association of American Universities and the National League of Cities are prominent examples.

Congressionally Speaking...

Lobbyist is a term that referred originally to reporters waiting in the lobby of the British House of Commons to speak to members of Parliament. In the mid-nineteenth century, the term came to be used for people seeking to influence legislators and soon gained quite negative connotations because of the money and other resources with which lobbyists plied legislators.

Today, a lobbyist has a more technical meaning in federal law – someone who is paid to communicate with Congress on behalf of others. And lobbyists now see themselves as specialized professionals. They even have their own professional association, the American League of Lobbyists.

Citizens' groups compose about 20 percent of the interest group community. Their members generally are individuals rather than representatives of organizations or institutions. Political scientist Jack Walker observed that these groups usually arise in the wake of broad social movements concerned with such problems as the level of environmental pollution, threats to civil rights, or changes in the status of women. Citizens' groups include Citizens for Tax Justice, Common Cause, the National Association for the Advancement of Colored People, the National Organization for Women, and Ralph Nader's Public Citizen.

Citizens' groups often are created by political entrepreneurs operating with the support of wealthy individuals, private foundations, or elected political leaders who act as their protectors, financial supporters, and patrons. It is common to see a few individuals bearing much of the cost of group formation. Such an arrangement is often essential to overcoming the numerous obstacles associated with collective action.

The greatest dilemma that interest groups encounter in the formation process is that of free riders – individuals who consume the benefits of a public good without paying a fair share of the costs of its production. All groups seek to attract members by appealing to a sense of obligation to support a cause, but often that is not enough to attract and retain members. Some groups overcome this problem by offering selective benefits restricted to those who contribute. For example, members of the AARP (formerly the American Association of Retired Persons but now using just the initials) receive a variety of benefits including discounts on airfare, car rentals, hotels, and cruises, as well as reasonably priced legal services and health care. Others offer special events, club memberships, or other social benefits to attract members.

The size of the lobbying and interest group community has expanded tremendously in recent decades. The *Encyclopedia of Associations* listed more than 22,500 organizations in 2008, which marks a more than 50 percent increase in the number of interest groups since 1980 and an almost 400 percent increase since 1955. The most rapid documented growth in interest groups occurred between the 1960s and 1980s, during which many federal programs were created and expanded. During this period, the interest group community became significantly more diverse as well. Along with the rapid expansion and diversification of the interest group community came a proliferation of organizations settling in Washington. A 1982 survey of 2,800 organizations that had lobbying offices in Washington found that 40 percent had been created since 1960 and an additional 25 percent since 1970.[3] One analyst found that the number of Washington offices for trade associations – the National Association of Manufacturers and the National Independent Retail Jewelers, for example – nearly tripled from about 1,200 in 1960 to 3,500 in 1986. Even greater proportionate growth in the number of corporations with offices in Washington occurred in the same period.[4]

Since the 1990s, the size of the interest group community has remained relatively stable. Nevertheless, the number of groups with Washington representation continues to grow, which points to the significance of lobbying in modern-day politics. Today, nearly 5,000 organizations have some kind of representation in Washington. In 2009, the privately published directory *Washington Representatives* listed more than 18,000 "persons working to influence government policies and actions" – a number that has more than quadrupled since the early 1970s. Even with these soaring numbers, it appears that there is no shortage of demand for their services. Between 2000 and 2005, by one account, D.C. lobbyists increased their fees to new clients by as much as 100 percent.[5]

Many factors have contributed to the proliferation of the interest group community and lobbying activity. Among the most important factors is the rapid social and economic change characteristic of recent decades. The expanding role of federal programs and regulation motivated individuals, firms, and local governments to organize and lobby. A series of social movements, such as civil rights, women's rights, environmental protection, and consumer rights, swept the country, redefined the nation's policy agenda, and spawned lasting interest groups. And organization spurred counter-organization. For example, Planned Parenthood was challenged by the National Right to Life Committee. The consequence of organization and counter-organization was the proliferation of strongly issue-oriented citizens' groups and greater diversity in the kinds of groups found in Washington.

While citizens' groups have changed the contours of Washington lobbying, the interest group community remains dominated, at least numerically, by business groups. By one estimate, 70 percent of organized interests in

Washington are business groups. Nevertheless, the growth of citizens' groups does mean that business interests are more likely to be challenged and challenged successfully.

An enlarged middle class and technological advances also contributed to the growth of the Washington interest group community. The middle class has become an important base of support for occupational and citizens' groups that depend on membership dues and other contributions for financial support. Technological advances in communications and computer-generated mailings have facilitated the growth of groups that require support from the general public. Also, advances in communication and transportation have made it more convenient and affordable for groups to headquarter in Washington, far from concentrations of their members.

Finally, the federal government is responsible for directly stimulating the creation of some groups and underwriting their costs of operations. Much of the domestic legislation of the 1960s and 1970s required some kind of citizen participation in executive agency rule making or provided for the creation of community-based groups. Many interest groups representing citizen, environmental action groups, and legal and health care organizations for the poor were stimulated by these public policies. Indeed, the activists running many of the new social programs vigorously promoted the creation of new organizations to represent their clients' interests. In other cases, federal agencies encouraged the formation of groups to facilitate communication between the agencies and the sector they served and to build a base of support for their own programs and budgets. Additionally, as federal domestic programs expanded, many more citizens' groups received grants or contracts from the federal government to conduct studies or perform services for executive agencies.

The enlarged community of lobbyists and interest groups has altered the political environment of members of Congress in important ways. The most obvious effect is that the expanded lobbying community has increased the diversity and intensity of demands placed on members of Congress. Issues of even modest importance are more likely to generate conflict among groups, and no one group is as likely to dominate policy making as was often the case at mid-twentieth century. There is now greater uncertainty about the mix of organized interests that will seek to influence congressional action and hold members accountable for their individual actions.

Developments in Interest Group Strategies

Influencing Congress involves much more than gaining the votes of individual members. Lobbyists work hard to find legislators who are willing to

FAMILY MEMBERS AS LOBBYISTS

A recent trend among organized interest groups is to hire the relatives of key congressional members and their top aides as lobbyists on a variety of issues. A 2007 report identified 63 sitting members of Congress with relatives who had "lobbied or consulted on government relations at the federal or the state level in recent years." This number is likely a conservative estimate, considering that it fails to account for relatives of members who are corporate or nonprofit board members or political consultants. Some estimates from political insiders put the number of members with relatives in the lobbying community closer to 100.

At least a portion of these cases can be attributed to the fact that members are increasingly entering the lobbying profession following public service, and some of these members are being succeeded in office by a relative. In addition, some members meet their spouses, who are already lobbyists, through political circles. However, a substantial number of these cases result from lobbying firms actively pursuing the relatives of sitting members. Relatives, after all, have certain inside advantages, such as access, that can substitute for experience working on the Hill. GOP attorney, Randy Evans, commented, "It's about access, but equally important is the degree to which folks know each other. That can be a product of time: You can have been around 10 Congresses and gotten to know enough members to make a difference, or you can just have grown up in Congress and gotten to know it that way."

The obvious concern with such an arrangement is the possibility that relatives will have undue influence over legislative outcomes, and there is some evidence to suggest that this is a legitimate concern. For instance, a 2005 study of the 94 members of the House and Senate appropriations committees and their 250 top staffers found that spending bills reflected the lobbying efforts of family members. Specifically, the study found 30 instances in which a relative lobbied for money in an appropriations bill that his or her family member or family member's boss helped write. In 22 of these cases, the relative was successful in obtaining funds – a total of roughly $750 million in projects.

To curb the influence family members can have on legislative outcomes, the Honest Leadership and Open Government Act of 2007 placed greater restrictions on the interaction that can take place between a member's office and relatives of that member who are registered as lobbyists. The Senate rules were changed to prohibit all staff from having any official contact with the member's spouse or immediate family if the relative is a registered lobbyist. Moreover, Senate rules prohibit staff from officially contacting the spouse of any Senator who is a lobbyist. An exception is granted to the spouse of a Senator who served as a registered lobbyist at least one year prior to the member's election or at least one year prior to marrying the member. House rules changes were less extensive, and only require a member to instruct his or her staff to refrain from official contact with that member's spouse if the spouse is a registered lobbyist. While these rules changes do, indeed, limit the influence that family members can have in their capacity as lobbyists, critics of the legislation claim that loopholes prevent the rules changes from being truly effective.

Source: Based on information from Matt Kelley and Peter Eisler, "Relatives Have 'Inside Track' in Lobbying for Tax Dollars," *USA Today*, October 17, 2006; Marisa Katz, "Family Ties," *National Journal Magazine*, March 31, 2007.

champion their causes. Lobbyists need members to introduce their proposals as legislation, to offer amendments in committee and on the floor, and to help them get issues on, or keep issues off, the agendas of committees and subcommittees.

Moreover, lobbyists spend more time gathering, digesting, and reporting information to their clients than they do trying to influence Congress. They help their clients anticipate and track legislative developments that are difficult for people not experienced in congressional politics to follow. Because congressional politics and federal policy are so much more complex and important than they were a few decades ago, corporations and other organizations need the assistance of experienced insiders to observe and interpret congressional activity that might affect their interests. A good lobbyist seeks to develop access to well-placed members and staff on Capitol Hill to meet the demands of his or her clients for information.

Lobbyists employ a wide range of techniques, which have evolved as lobbyists have adapted to changes in technology, society, and Congress. The empowerment of House subcommittees in the 1970s, the greater individualism in the membership, and expansion of congressional staffs since the mid-twentieth century have forced lobbyists to develop relationships with more members and staff and follow the activity of more committees and subcommittees. At the same time, developments in electronic communications and computers have enabled lobbyists and interest groups to reach people throughout the country with ease.

These developments have stimulated important changes in the way lobbyists do their work. Many observers of Washington politics have noted the change from inside lobbying, or face-to-face efforts to influence a few important legislators, to outside strategies, or public relations efforts to generate public support for special interest causes. Perhaps more accurately, outside strategies have supplemented the old-style inside strategies that once dominated Washington lobbying.

Inside Lobbying

The more traditional form of lobbying – inside lobbying – involves personal contact between a lobbyist and members of Congress. Successful lobbyists use access to important decision makers, a network of contacts, mastery of the process, policy expertise, Washington experience, and money to develop strong ties to legislators and their staffs. Their success often depends on their being able to phone a prominent member of Congress, get the call returned promptly, and gather critical intelligence about when an issue will be raised or which member is wavering on an important provision. An aide to a former House Speaker characterized the work of the inside lobbyist this way:

> They know members of Congress are here three nights a week, alone, without their families. So they say, "Let's have dinner. Let's go see a ballgame." Shmooze with them. Make friends. And they don't lean on it all the time. Every once in a while, they call up – maybe once or twice a year – ask a few questions. Call you up and say, "Say, what's Danny [Rostenkowski, chair of the House Ways and Means Committee] going to do on this tax-reform bill?" Anne Wexler [a former official in the Carter White House, and now a lobbyist] will call up and spend half an hour talking about left-wing politics, and suddenly she'll pop a question, pick up something. They want that little bit of access. That's what does it. You can hear it. It clicks home. They'll call their chief executive officer, and they've delivered. That's how it works. It's not illegal. They work on a personal basis.[6]

Career Washingtonians – former members, former executive branch officials, and even some family members of prominent public officials who have developed personal friendships with members and their staffs – are greatly advantaged in direct lobbying. Former members are particularly advantaged because they retain special privileges of access on Capitol Hill – access to the House and Senate floors, gyms, and dining rooms. They also benefit from the political and policy expertise gained from service in Congress, a certain visibility in Washington and in the country, and their established contacts with people and organizations with money. In 2006, the Center for Responsive Politics identified 155 registered lobbyists as former members of Congress.

Former congressional staff aides and federal employees share many of the advantages and knowledge enjoyed by former members, so they also make ideal lobbyists. In 2008, for instance, more than one-third of the top congressional staffers who left their positions that year went on to work for lobbying firms or other groups seeking to influence the government.[7] Because staff aides and federal employees develop contacts and skills that make them attractive to law firms, corporations, and lobbying firms, many individuals enter jobs on the Hill with the intent of going to these other more lucrative positions (see box, "Limits on Lobbying after Leaving Capitol Hill").

Beyond personal relations, money and information are essential ingredients of successful inside strategies. Money, of course, can be used as an outright bribe, though it seldom is any longer. But money has been a vital asset to gaining access to legislators. In recent years, money has allowed lobbyists to arrange for members to take trips to exclusive resorts to attend conferences or charity functions that are also attended by lobbyists and corporate leaders, to host outings to golf courses, ball games, and

LIMITS ON LOBBYING AFTER LEAVING CAPITOL HILL

The exchange of personnel between high-level public and private sector positions is commonly referred to as the *revolving door*. Upon leaving their positions within government, former members of Congress as well as congressional staffers and employees of the federal government frequently enter private sector positions to serve as lobbyists. Furthermore, it is often the case that individuals in top positions within industries are called upon to fill key roles within the government, such as agency directors.

The heightened access that former members, congressional staffers, and federal employees have does not, however, go unchecked. As established by the Lobbying Disclosure Act of 1995 (LDA), exiting members of Congress are banned from lobbying in Congress for a duration of time, known as a "cooling off" period. The cooling off period for House members is currently one year, which is the duration originally set by the LDA. In 2007, the Senate changed its rules to extend the cooling off period for Senators to two years. Congressional staff whose salaries are at least 75 percent of members' salaries (or $130,500 in 2009) are also prohibited from lobbying in Congress immediately after leaving their positions. In the House, there is a one-year ban on senior staff lobbying the committee or member for whom they worked. The 2007 rules changes prohibit senior Senate staff from lobbying *any* Senator or employee of the Senate for a period of one year. In addition, former members and senior staff are prohibited from lobbying the executive branch on behalf of another party for one year as well.

concerts, and to sponsor lunches, dinners, and receptions in Washington. However, such behavior was severely curtailed after the House and Senate passed rules changes in 2007 in response to a series of high-profile scandals linking several members of congress to lobbyist Jack Abramoff (see box, "The DeLay-Abramoff Scandal"). Both chambers placed heavy restrictions on gifts from lobbyists and imposed more extensive oversight of member-lobbyist relations. Although gifts from lobbyists valued at less than $50 were permitted by the former rules, both chambers eliminated this exception to the gifts restriction. Moreover, the rules changes now require members to gain prior approval from the appropriate ethics committee before accepting travel paid for by an outside, private source. It is important to note, though, that money allows lobbyists to do more than simply dole out goodies. With adequate financial means, lobbyists are also able to acquire other resources, such as the assistance of policy experts, which are often critical in dealing with legislators and their staffs.

The most obvious, and perhaps most important, use of money is for campaign contributions. Some lobbyists are able to make considerable

THE DELAY-ABRAMOFF SCANDAL

In May 2000, then-House Majority Whip Tom DeLay (R-Texas) took a 10-day vacation to Great Britain coordinated by lobbyist Jack Abramoff. DeLay, his wife, and two aides, stayed at lavish hotels, ate at the best restaurants, went to the theater, and took a four-day side trip to play golf at the historic links at St. Andrews golf course. DeLay's financial disclosures reported that the $70,000 trip was paid for by a nonprofit conservative organization, the National Center for Public Policy Research. It was later discovered that a Native American tribe and a gambling services company that had hired Abramoff had each contributed $25,000 to the National Center for the purpose of the trip. Large portions of the trip were found to have been paid with a credit card under Abramoff's name. And this was not the only such trip. DeLay accepted a similarly extravagant trip from Abramoff to the Northern Mariana Islands as well.

House ethics rules permit members and their staff to have travel expenses paid for only when travel is connected to official business and only by organizations directly connected to the trip. House ethics rules also prohibit travel paid for by registered lobbyists. Finally, rules require that members accurately report the cost of a trip and the names of the people and organizations that paid for it. Given the facts that were uncovered, the trip was in violation of each of these rules. To make matters worse, email correspondences later confirmed that DeLay's office was aware of the infractions and was perhaps even concerned "if someone starts asking questions."

Although we cannot be certain what DeLay's motivations were in making policy decisions, we do know that following the trip DeLay helped kill legislation opposed by the tribe and the gambling services company that were represented by Abramoff. In addition, DeLay was a key player in blocking legislation that would have required the Northern Mariana Islands, a U.S. territory, to comply with U.S. labor laws. According to reports, Abramoff received $1.36 million from the Northern Mariana Islands to block this legislation, which would have ended the territory's ability to produce goods with the "Made in the USA" label in sweatshop conditions. A similar bill subsequently passed in 2008, after DeLay had vacated his seat.

Sources: Jeffrey Smith, "DeLay Airfare Was Charged to Lobbyist's Credit Card," *Washington Post*, April 24, 2005; James V. Grimaldi and Jeffrey Smith, "Gambling Interests Funded DeLay Trip," *Washington Post*, March 12, 2005; John Solomon, "E-mails: DeLay Staff Knew Lobbyist Paid for Golf Trip," *The Associated Press*, May 7, 2006; Mark Shields, "The Real Scandal of Tom DeLay," *CNN*, May 9, 2005.

contributions themselves. And many are in a position to orchestrate contributions from numerous political action committees and wealthy individuals to maximize their influence with a few legislators.

Just how much influence is exercised through campaign contributions is an open question. Most campaign contributions appear to flow to members who already support the positions of the contributors – the money follows the votes, the saying goes. But measuring the influence of campaign contributions is very difficult. Some contributions are intended to encourage members to remain inactive, or at least not to challenge policies favored by groups. Other contributions are designed to generate action at less visible stages of the legislative process – to offer an amendment in a subcommittee markup, to hold to a policy position in private negotiations in conference, and so on. Of course, members in key positions, such as party leaders or committee chairs, attract substantial contributions. In her first congress as House Speaker, contributions to Nancy Pelosi (D-California) increased by more than one million dollars compared to her previous two years of service ($1.68 million in 2005–06 and $2.86 million in 2007–08).

Despite the difficulties in gauging the influence of campaign contributions, few doubt that contributions are an important link between members and those lobbyists who can generate large sums for the members' campaigns. We can infer from interest group behavior that there are returns to making contributions (see box, "Fannie and Freddie Launch Targeted Attack"). In recent years, members have increasingly called upon lobbyists to organize fundraising activities on their behalf. Lobbyists often do not dare refuse, because they fear losing access that they have worked so hard to gain.

Information is a critical resource for the lobbyist engaged in inside lobbying. Legislators appear to have an insatiable desire for information about the policy and political consequences of their actions. Political scientists David Austen-Smith and John R. Wright contend that legislators are imperfectly informed about constituency preferences and, therefore, lobbyists provide an important source of information. Furthermore, they argue that competition among interests induces truthful behavior from the interest groups. Lobbyists who develop a reputation for having reliable information at hand are called on more frequently by legislators and are more likely to gain the access necessary for exercising influence. Of course, the amount of technical information a professional lobbyist is likely to have is limited, so success depends on having a network of contacts in research institutes, universities, executive agencies, corporations, or wherever expertise relevant to the lobbyist's interests is found. In fact, many lobbying firms and interest groups hire technical specialists such as lawyers and social and physical scientists

TABLE 11.1. Percent of Interest Groups that Reported Using a Lobbying Technique.

Testify at hearings	99
Contact government officials directly to present your point of view	98
Engage in informal contacts with officials – at conventions, over lunch, etc.	95
Present research results or technical information	92
Send letters to members of your organization to inform them about your activities	92
Enter into coalitions with other organizations	90
Attempt to shape the implementation of policies	89
Talk with people from the press and the media	86
Consult with government officials to plan legislative strategy	85
Help draft legislation	85
Inspire letter-writing or telegram campaigns	84
Mount grassroots lobbying efforts	80
Have influential constituents contact their congressman's office	80
Make financial contributions to electoral campaigns	58
Publicize candidates' voting records	44
Run advertisements in the media about your position on issues	31

Source: TABLE (Adapted) – "Percent of Interest Groups That..." from *Organized Interest and American Democracy* by Kay Lehman Schlozman and John T. Tierney 150. Copyright ©1986 by Kay Lehman Schlozman and John T. Tierney. Reprinted by permission of HarperCollins Publishers, Inc.

so that they can provide timely information to decision makers and even conduct original research of their own.

Outside Lobbying

The most dramatic change in the lobbying business in recent decades has been the increase in outside, or grassroots, lobbying. Rather than relying solely on Washington lobbyists to make appeals on behalf of a cause, groups often attempt to mobilize their membership or the general public to generate outside pressure on members of Congress. Successful mobilization of members' constituents increases the stakes for members by increasing the likelihood that their actions will have electoral consequences. The survey of lobbying groups reported in Table 11.1 shows that more than 80 percent of groups inspired letter-writing or telegram campaigns, 80 percent mounted grassroots lobbying efforts and prodded influential constituents to contact their congressional representatives, and about one-third ran advertisements

FANNIE AND FREDDIE LAUNCH TARGETED ATTACK

In September 2008, the U.S. federal government took over control of Fannie Mae and Freddie Mac, the nation's two largest mortgage finance companies. Marking one of the largest corporate rescues in U.S. history, the federal government's decision to bail out Fannie and Freddie came as a response to the impending failure of the mortgage giants amidst the financial crisis. Together, Fannie and Freddie hold about half of the nation's $9.5 trillion of mortgage debt, and the collapse of the companies would have a catastrophic effect on the economy.

How did Fannie and Freddie end up in such a precarious situation? Some economists argue that it was risky lending behavior backed by the federal government that was responsible, while others point to the companies' excessive borrowing to generate capital. In all likelihood both are partially to blame. What we can be certain of is that both explanations are rooted in myopic corporate strategies that pay dividends when economic times are good and can prove disastrous when times are bad. For years, though, government officials had been aware of these dangerous practices and their possible consequences and did nothing.

Why, then, did the government not intervene? In part the answer to this question is that Fannie and Freddie were able to stave off regulation through well-orchestrated lobbying efforts. Senator Chuck Hagel's (R-Nebraska) attempt to regulate the companies in 2005 was a particularly telling incident. Hagel sponsored legislation that, among other things, would have instituted independent oversight of the companies, and would have required the companies to sell off hundreds of billions of dollars of assets. Despite overwhelming Republican support, at a time when the Republicans had a 10-seat advantage in the Senate, the bill never made it to the floor for final consideration. The Democrats opposed the legislation, citing concerns that the forced sale of portfolio assets would make it difficult for low- and moderate-income families to buy houses, but the Republicans remained only a few votes short of a majority. It was later discovered that Freddie had spent $2 million on a stealth lobbying campaign that strategically targeted 17 Republican senators, many of whom were vulnerable in the upcoming election. Nine of the targeted senators indicated that they would not back the bill, and therefore the bill was never brought to the floor due to lack of sufficient support.

Hagel's struggle to overcome the efforts of Freddie and Fannie is not an isolated story. Freddie ranks in the top 20 lobbying spenders over the period of 1998 to 2008, having spent a total of more than $96.1 million on lobbying. Fannie was close behind with a total of more than $80.4 million in lobbying expenditures over the same period.

Sources: Yost, Pete, "AP IMPACT: How Freddie Mac Halted Regulatory Drive," *Washington Post*, December 7, 2008; Yost, Pete, "AP IMPACT: Mortgage Firm Arranged Stealth Campaign," *Washington Post*, October 19, 2008; Center for Responsive Politics at opensecrets.org.

in the media about their positions on the issues. And evidence suggests that grassroots campaigns do influence legislators' decisions, which we might expect considering the widespread use of this technique.

Technology and money have driven innovations in outside lobbying. Throughout the history of Congress, groups of people from around the country have converged on Washington to demand action on their programs. Improved means of transportation have increased the frequency with which groups mobilize their members or the general public for marches, special lobbying days, and other events in Washington that are designed to heighten congressional interest and support for their causes. Mass marches have always been the necessary strategy of large groups without the money and experienced Washington lobbyists essential to execute effective inside strategies. But today, many groups, even well-established groups, bring large numbers of people from around the country on special occasions to pressure members of Congress.

By the 1970s, computer-generated mailings allowed groups to send "legislative alert" letters to group members or targeted groups in the general public to stimulate an avalanche of mail and waves of phone calls to congressional offices. Members of Congress soon learned to identify and discount orchestrated letter-writing campaigns. Nevertheless, as lobbyist Bill Murphy observes, "The congressman has to care that *somebody* out there in his district has enough power to get hundreds of people to sit down and write a postcard or a letter – because if the guy can get them to do *that*, he might be able to influence them in other ways. So, a member has no choice but to pay attention."[8] At a minimum, a member must worry that those same constituents could be motivated, by the same means used to stimulate their letter writing, to contribute their money to or cast their votes for a member's opponent.

Today's lobbyists take outside strategies several steps further. For example, Washington-based firms have adapted telemarketing strategies to congressional politics. Working from computer-generated lists of Americans likely to support a particular point of view, telephone operators dial homes, ask a few questions, and then transfer the call to the appropriate congressional offices so that constituents' views can be registered with their representatives and senators. Particular geographic constituencies can be targeted to maximize the pressure on a few members of Congress.

The internet also serves as a valuable, low-cost resource for interest groups looking to engage the public. Large-scale email campaigns have become a common grassroots strategy among organized interests. And considering the minimal cost of the approach, the returns tend to be sizeable. In one instance, an email campaign organized by the National Education

Association (NEA) encouraged public education advocates to pressure members of Congress to back a class-size reduction and a 15 percent increase in education funding – an ambitious proposal. The effort prompted 20,000 emails and resulted in a 12 percent increase in the education budget.

Media advertising has become an increasingly integral part of lobbying strategies. Most advertising of this variety is intended to increase the visibility of an issue or cause and shape opinion in the general public. For the most part, the media ads are designed and produced by the same people who produce election campaign ads. One group, the U.S. Chamber of Commerce, produces its own television programs that are shown on local stations throughout the country. It uses its production and satellite facilities to link its Washington studios (which are just one block from the White House) with corporate sponsors.

A particular advantage of outside lobbying is that there are few registration and disclosure requirements. Under current law, organized interests and representatives of organized interests that engage exclusively in grassroots lobbying are not obligated to register as lobbyists or file any disclosure statements. Disclosure of grassroots lobbying is only triggered by participation in direct, or inside, lobbying. Groups that have limited lobbying ambitions may, therefore, adopt grassroots strategies to avoid undue reporting burdens. This loophole has, however, led to the emergence of massive grassroots lobbying organizations whose practices go largely unchecked. There have been a number of recent efforts by reformers to close this loophole by extending disclosure requirements to grassroots lobbyists. In fact, the Honest Leadership and Open Government Act of 2007 – the major lobbying and ethics reform legislation passed at the outset of the 110th Congress (2007–08) – contained such a provision, but the legislation was later amended to remove all disclosure requirements for grassroots lobbyists.

The growing importance of outside strategies has led to the proliferation of "full-service" lobbying firms. These large firms combine traditional insider lobbyists with policy experts, specialists in public relations, graphic arts, and electronic media, speechwriters, fundraisers, communications and computer technicians, and pollsters. The model is Hill & Knowlton Public Affairs, a firm with more than 180 employees that boasts its own broadcast studio. The firm includes former members of Congress, staff assistants, and executive officials from both parties. Firms, like Hill & Knowlton, with the capacity to effectively employ both inside and outside strategies must determine the mix of strategies that will position them to best meet their goals. According to political scientists Marie Hojnacki and David Kimball, organized interests are likely to use inside lobbying to target allies in committee, so as to influence the content of legislative proposals. Outside lobbying, on

GRASSROOTS VS. ASTROTURF

New technologies and strategies have greatly expanded efforts to influence members of Congress by generating an avalanche of phone calls and letters to Capitol Hill. A type of grassroots lobbying, astroturf lobbying refers to seemingly spontaneous citizen-based lobbying efforts that are in reality orchestrated by organized groups.

Sometimes these strategies are too obvious to succeed. For example, a group called the Health Care Coalition had operators call small business owners who were likely to be affected by an amendment pending in the House, tell them that the amendment would be bad for managed health care, and then offer to connect them to the office of the member from their district. Dozens of calls were targeted at critical members.

In another case, hundreds of telegrams were dumped onto the floor of the House Commerce Committee to show public opposition to a telecommunications bill. Perhaps thousands more were sent directly to members. Suspicious congressional aides discovered that many of the telegrams were sent without the signatories' permission by a group called the Seniors Coalition. The public relations firm in charge of the effort blamed shoddy work by a mass marketing subcontractor. Some of the signatories proved to be deceased.

Legislators are likely to discount communications that are so heavily coordinated, but they cannot ignore such communications altogether. It is possible that the citizens who acquiesced to the astroturf scheme could also be motivated to vote against the member in the future.

Source: Juliet Eilperin, "Dingell Takes on Bogus Mailgram," *Roll Call,* October 16, 1995, 1, 20. Reprinted by permission.

the other hand, has the broader goal of maintaining and expanding the base of legislative support, and, therefore, is used to influence members irrespective of their policy position. Outside lobbying, however, has less potential to affect meaningful policy change (also see box, "The Choice of Strategies").

Coalitions

Whatever an interest group's mix of inside and outside strategies, it seldom stands alone in major legislative battles. Many coalitions are created for specific issues and then disappear once congressional action on certain legislation is complete. Other coalitions are more enduring. Some coalitions have formal names; others do not. Coalitions are a means for pooling the resources of lobbyists and groups. They also are a means for lobbyists and groups to demonstrate a broad base of support for their cause and to make

THE CHOICE OF STRATEGIES

In an effort to learn more about interest group strategies, political scientist Jack Walker conducted a detailed survey of the top officers in 734 national interest groups. Walker found that:

most groups adopt a preferred style of political action early in their histories, and, when these early choices are made, group leaders naturally emulate the tactics being employed at that time by the most successful groups. Once either an inside or outside strategy becomes the association's dominant approach, it is very difficult to move in a new direction. Choices made early in the history of a group establish a strategic style that restricts innovation, largely because political strategies are so intertwined with other basic organizational decisions.

Not surprisingly, Walker discovered that groups facing organized opposition to their goals tend to more aggressively pursue both inside and outside strategies than do other groups. Outside strategies, however, are more frequently the choice of groups with many local chapters or subunits, citizens' groups, and groups from the nonprofit sector (local governments, universities, nonprofit professions, and so on). Inside strategies are more likely to be the choice of groups representing business and groups that have established large central office staffs, usually in Washington.

Source: Based on information from Jack L. Walker, Jr., *Mobilizing Interest Groups in America: Patrons, Professions, and Social Movements* (Ann Arbor: University of Michigan Press, 1991), 103–121; quote from 119–120.

their effort appear to be as public-spirited as possible. Some coalitions are the creation of lobbyists looking to manufacture a new client.

An impressive example of an interest group coalition was the Archer MSA (medical savings account) Coalition, which played a prominent role in shaping the 2003 Medicare Prescription Drug, Improvement, and Modernization Act. The coalition was comprised of 49 interest groups, including such notable organizations as the American Medical Association (AMA) and the Christian Coalition of America. It was a vocal proponent of tax-preferred health savings accounts (HSAs). Although there was some resistance to the inclusion of HSAs among Republicans, the coalition made its presence felt. The final version of the legislation included the HSAs and passed by narrow margins in both chambers, handing the Archer MSA Coalition a major victory.

Much remains unanswered about interest group coalitions. There is, for instance, no clear-cut answer for why coalitions emerge when they do. There is a tremendous amount of variation across issues in terms of the number and size of coalitions that form. Scholars have suggested that the emergence of coalitions is systematically related to such factors as issue conflict and salience. There is, however, only tentative support for these hypotheses. Also it is somewhat unclear whether interest groups in coalitions are actually more successful than ones acting alone. While the Archer MSA Coalition appears to have been successful in 2003, not all coalitions are so fortunate. Moreover, there were interest groups that acted alone on the Medicare legislation, such as the AARP (formerly the American Association of Retired Persons), that also were successful in achieving their policy objectives. One study of coalition success found that a mere 58 percent of coalitions accomplished any of their goals.[9] This lackluster rate could reflect some of the disadvantages to coalition formation – namely, greater collective action problems to overcome. While the comparative advantages of belonging to a coalition are not entirely clear, there is some evidence that coalition formation leads to greater success when seeking to defend the status quo.

Legislators Influencing Organized Interests

The path of influence between lobbyists and members is a two-way street. Plainly, lobbyists seek to influence outcomes in the legislative process by persuading at least a few members to support or even champion their cause that would not have done so otherwise. But legislators often want something from lobbyists, too. And because lobbyists want to cultivate or maintain good relations with key legislators, they are often quite responsive to legislators' demands. Legislators frequently pressure interest groups to generate campaign contributions for them. They ask lobbyists for assistance in attracting support from other legislators, the public, or others on issues not directly of concern to the lobbyists. Legislators may enlist the support of lobbyists on matters before the executive branch or encourage lobbyists to take action in the courts. Lobbyists may resist these pressures. After all, the requests may not be compatible with other objectives the lobbyists pursue. But lobbyists must assess how important the legislator is, or will be in the future, to their groups' or their personal interests. Ignoring senior party and committee leaders can come at a significant cost.

When congressional Republicans gained majority party status in 1995, GOP leaders launched a project to pressure Washington lobbying firms to hire Republicans for top positions. Called the K Street Project, Republican leaders tracked the party affiliation of Washington lobbyists and rewarded those that were loyal. With like-minded individuals in key lobbying positions, congressional Republicans could limit the power of opposing interests. With unified control of Congress and the White House between 2000 and 2006, lobbying firms had to stay in the good graces of Republicans if they wished to exert influence over legislative outcomes. Whereas lobbying firms have historically hired lobbyists from both parties to accommodate changes in party control, there is reason to believe that lobbying firms predicted lasting Republican dominance. This, along with the strict oversight of the K Street Project, led many lobbying firms to pass up Democrats for important lobbying positions. In 2004, the Capitol Hill newspaper, *The Hill*, reported that "retiring House Democrats are feeling a cold draft from K Street as they seek post-congressional employment at lobbying firms, trade groups and corporations. By contrast, K Street is aggressively courting GOP lawmakers who have announced their retirements."[10]

Things began to change in the months leading up to the 2006 elections, as lobbying firms sensed a Democratic takeover of one or both houses of Congress. The same firms that, months earlier, had shunned Democrats were now embracing them with open arms. The eventual Democratic victory led to a rush to hire Democratic lobbyists. One prominent lobbyist reported that the average annual salary for Republican lobbyists plummeted $50,000 upon the election returns. Shortly after taking control, House and Senate Democrats addressed the practices of the K Street Project that had burdened them for the past decade. Both chambers adopted rules in 2007 that expressly prohibit members from influencing "on the basis of partisan political affiliation, an employment decision or employment practice of any private entity."

Regulating Lobbying

Modern lobbying is remarkably clean and ethical, at least when compared with lobbying during most of American history. In the nineteenth century, lobbyists ran gambling establishments to put legislators in their debt and openly paid members for representing their interests on Capitol Hill. With few (recent) exceptions, the retainers and bribes are gone. In fact, lobbyists now have their own professional code of ethics.

At various points throughout history, congressional, journalistic, and criminal investigations have exposed remarkably corrupt lobbying practices, but on only a few occasions did Congress or either house impose any restrictions on lobbying. In 1876, for example, Congress for the first time required that lobbyists register, but the rule was in effect for only one Congress. Congress did not pass its first comprehensive lobbying regulations until 1946, when the Federal Regulation of Lobbying Act was adopted as a part of the Legislative Reorganization Act.

The central feature of the 1946 law was the requirement that people who solicit or receive money for the purpose of influencing legislation must register with the clerk of the House or the secretary of the Senate. Lobbyists were required to file quarterly reports on the money they received for and spent on lobbying. The authors of the 1946 act hoped that disclosure of lobbyists' clients and legislative purposes would put members, reporters, and the public in a better position to evaluate lobbyists' influence.

The law proved to be unenforceable. In 1954, the Supreme Court ruled in *United States v. Harriss* that the registration and reporting requirements applied only to those persons who are paid by others to lobby, who contact members directly, and whose "principal purpose" is to influence legislation. The Court argued that the First Amendment to the Constitution, which prohibits Congress from making a law that abridges the right "to petition the Government for a redress of grievances," limits Congress's ability to regulate an individual's right to represent him or herself before Congress and to organize others with the intent of influencing Congress. By confining the force of the 1946 act to those lobbyists whose principal purpose is to influence legislation, the Court created a large loophole for anyone who wanted to claim that influencing legislation was not his or her principal purpose.

Interest in creating meaningful registration and reporting requirements was renewed in the early 1990s. Ross Perot gave great emphasis to the influence of "special interests" in his 1992 presidential campaign. Perot's theme was reinforced by television reports about members' all-expenses-paid trips to vacation resorts where they fraternized with lobbyists. In response to the heightened public scrutiny of the relationship between lobbyists and members of Congress, a large number of members elected for the first time in the 1990s had promised to reduce the influence of special interests in Washington. The result was the consideration of significant lobbying reforms.

In late 1995, Congress enacted new legislation designed to close some of the loopholes in the 1946 law. The new law, titled the Lobbying Disclosure Act of 1995 (LDA), extended the 1946 law that covered only people who lobbied members of Congress, to also include those who seek to influence congressional staff and top executive branch officials. The LDA formally defines a lobbyist as:

> Any individual who is employed or retained by a client for financial or other compensation for services that include more than one lobbying contact [Defined as any oral or written communication (including an electronic communication) to a covered executive branch official or a covered legislative branch official that

is made on behalf of a client], other than an individual whose lobbying activities constitute less than 20 percent of the time engaged in the services provided by such individual to the client over a six month period.

Anyone who is hired to lobby a covered public official and spends 20 percent or more of his or her time in paid lobbying, must register with the clerk of the House and the secretary of the Senate within 45 days of being hired or making the first contact, whichever is earlier. Under the LDA, individuals who received $5,000 or less in a six-month period and organizations that spent less than $20,000 in a six-month period were not required to register. This exception was included to allow average citizens to have their voices heard without needing to register. Lobbyists are required to file reports that disclose who their clients are, the general issue area they were hired to influence, and a good faith estimate of the total amount paid by clients. The LDA originally required these reports to be filed on a semiannual basis. Lobbyists for foreign governments or organizations must also register. The registration requirement excludes grassroots lobbying, such as efforts to persuade people to write members of Congress.

Due to the introduction of these registration requirements, the LDA had the effect of more than doubling the number of registered lobbyists. Among the newly registered were a variety of lobbying coalitions – organized groups of lobbyists, associations, and lobbying firms – that had not been registered under the old law. Even still, the law fell short of registering many individuals that acted as lobbyists.

Separately, the House and Senate also adopted rules limiting lobbyists' gifts to members and staff. The rules banned gifts valued at more than $50, including meals and entertainment. Gifts from any one source could not exceed $100 in value for a year, with gifts under $10 excluded from the calculation. Gifts from family members and gifts of token value (T-shirts, mugs) were also excluded. In addition, chamber rules permitted privately funded trips but banned travel paid for directly by a lobbyist.

In the months leading up to the 2006 elections, the public witnessed an inordinate number of lobbying scandals. In March 2006, former Representative Randall "Duke" Cunningham (R-California) was convicted of accepting $2.4 million in bribes primarily from defense contractors in return for securing contracts. In May 2006, the FBI raided the home of Representative William Jefferson (D-Louisiana) to find $90,000 in his freezer. The government claimed that Jefferson took in excess of $400,000 in bribes. He was later indicted on 16 charges of corruption. In October 2006, former Representative Bob Ney (R-Ohio) pled guilty to accepting gifts in exchange for favorable action on behalf of convicted lobbyist Jack Abramoff's clients.

The election outcomes were, at least in part, a reaction to the many scandals. In a CNN exit poll of voters in the 2006 congressional elections, corruption was more frequently cited by voters as "extremely important" than any other issue, including terrorism, the economy, and Iraq.[11]

After gaining majorities in the House and Senate in the 2006 elections, the Democrats set out to fulfill promises of ethics and lobbying reform. House Democrats did so immediately by including reforms in their chamber rules. The Senate opted to pursue statutory reforms, and passed legislation containing rules changes similar to those the House passed days earlier. In August 2007, the House and Senate approved the Honest Leadership and Open Government Act of 2007, and President Bush then signed the legislation into law the following month. The newly passed Act amended the LDA of 1995 in several important areas, including, but not limited to, disclosure requirements, revolving door restrictions, and gift limitations.

The Act requires quarterly instead of semiannual filing of lobbying disclosure reports, and reduces the monetary thresholds by half to conform to the new quarterly periods. Reports must identify if a client is a state or local government, department, agency, or other instrumentality, and must be filed electronically to facilitate transparency. For former senators, the Act bans directly lobbying in Congress for two years after leaving office, rather than one year under the LDA. The House retained the one-year "cooling off" period specified by the LDA. The Act also prohibits senior Senate staff from lobbying any Senator or employee of the Senate for a one-year period. In addition, the Act prohibits Senate staff from having official contact with the Senator's spouse or immediate family member, should the relative be a registered lobbyist. Senate staff are also prohibited from contacting the spouse of any Senator who is a lobbyist. Legislators are furthermore banned from negotiating private employment until after their successor is elected, unless they file a report disclosing the name(s) of the entity involved in the negotiations.

Perhaps the most pertinent reforms, considering the events leading up to the elections, related to restrictions on gifts from lobbyists to members and their staff. The Act sharply limits gifts to Senators, striking the exception that previously permitted Senators and their staff to receive gifts under $50. The House passed the identical rule. According to the Act, Senators and their staff are not permitted to accept privately financed travel from lobbyists or entities that employ lobbyists. Moreover, Senators and their staff are prohibited from traveling with lobbyists present on any segment of the trip. The rules do allow travel for one day and one night to locations where there is minimal lobbyist involvement. The House adopted substantially similar rules. The Act requires Senators to receive advanced approval for all travel paid for by an outside, private source. To promote adherence to the lobbying laws, the Act increases the maximum civil penalty for violations of the provisions from $50,000 to $200,000, and provides for criminal penalties of imprisonment for deliberate noncompliance.

Members' Groups and Legislative Service Organizations

Groups of members frequently coalesce or even formally organize to pursue specific political interests. In fact, informal groups of members have been prominent features of Washington politics since the early Congresses. In the early nineteenth century, members tended to find lodging in boarding houses where they found like-minded colleagues. Informal but conspicuous intra-party factions, such as southern Democrats, have been quite important from time to time. And state delegations, particularly those of the larger states, have been the building blocks for coalitions throughout the history of Congress. Two developments of recent decades have altered the character of membership groups.

The first is that intra-party factions developed formal organizations with formal memberships, elected leaders, staff, offices, and even membership dues. The prototype, and still the largest such group, is the Democratic Study Group (DSG). The DSG was formed in 1959 by House Democratic liberals to counter the strength of the conservative coalition of Republicans and southern Democrats. The services of the DSG – especially issuing and scheduling reports – eventually became so highly valued that nearly all Democrats joined and contributed dues to take advantage of the group's work. Nevertheless, the DSG remains the organizational focal point for liberal activists in the House.

Since the 1970s there has been a remarkable increase in the number of single-issue caucuses. Today there are over 200 such caucuses, and many have bipartisan memberships. The Congressional Arts Caucus and the Congressional Sportsmen's Caucus formed to promote certain public funding for the arts and to oppose many proposed regulations on fire arms, respectively; regional interests are promoted by the Northeast-Midwest Congressional Coalition and the Congressional Western Caucus. Both constituency concerns and personal circumstances provide a foundation for the Congressional Black Caucus, the Congressional Hispanic Caucus, and the Congressional Caucus for Women's Issues. District economic interests are reflected in the Congressional Coastal Caucus, Congressional Steel Caucus, and the Congressional Tourism and Travel Caucus.

Caucuses, now officially called congressional members organizations in the House, are a way for members to become involved in and demonstrate a commitment to a particular cause or issue that falls outside of the scope of their regular committee duties. This is particularly true in the House, where most members are limited to two committee assignments. In fact, about 90 percent of caucuses are found in the House. In most cases, a caucus is a basis for publicizing a cause or an issue and building policy coalitions within Congress. Outside interest groups seeking to cultivate congressional support for their interests have stimulated the creation of many congressional caucuses.

Until recently, many caucuses were formally recognized in the House as "legislative service organizations," or LSOs, and were subject to audits and a few regulations. LSOs were controversial because they received dues from members' office accounts and gained office space in the House office buildings. Critics charged that this practice allowed money from office accounts to be spent indirectly for purposes, such as dinners, for which office account funds cannot be spent directly. Moreover, many LSOs bridged the gap between interest groups and congressional caucuses by creating foundations and institutes with close ties to both external groups and internal caucuses. In the view of some critics, the ability of lobbyists and interest groups to contribute money to these new foundations was just another way for special interests to support travel and social events for members and congressional staff participating in the work of the foundations. These critiques of LSOs paved the way for the second significant development in membership groups in recent decades.

The newly elected Republican majority of 1995 fundamentally changed the character of membership groups by banning LSOs. Membership groups lost several special privileges – the ability to receive dues paid from official budgets and office space in House buildings. Slowly, congressional member organizations, or CMOs, replaced LSOs and are granted more limited privileges. Members of CMOs may jointly pay for staff and other functions, but they do not pay dues for separate staff and activities. Dozens of member organizations have been created and, among other activities, serve to advertise legislators' interests in subjects important to key groups in their districts and states.

The Influence of Lobbyists and Interest Groups

Even experienced and insightful watchers of the lobbying and interest group community have mixed views about the influence of special interest lobbying. A popular view in the 1950s and 1960s was that policy making was dominated by "subgovernments" or "iron triangles" – tightly bound sets of interest groups, executive agencies, and committees. According to this view, cozy relationships among lobbyists, bureaucrats, and members prevented other interests from influencing policy choices and implementation. The subgovernments perspective was always recognized as an overly stylized view, but it captured an important feature of Washington politics: In many policy areas, only a few groups, agencies, and members took an interest in the issues, so they dominated the policy choices that were made.

The classic case of subgovernment policy making was mid-twentieth century agriculture policy politics. Generally, only those agriculture groups directly affected by certain federal commodities programs, the Agriculture Department bureaus that ran the programs, and a few members sitting on the agriculture committees of Congress took an active interest in farm policy. Those groups, bureaucrats, and members interested in the various farm commodities assisted each other in gaining congressional approval of the periodic legislation that supported federal programs. Although federal taxpayers paid for these programs, the costs were not so high as to breed resistance. And the lack of conflict among agriculture sector groups and decision makers helped keep others from paying attention.

Many political scientists responded to the subgovernments' perspective by noting the special conditions that allow a subgovernment to develop and dominate policy making. The most important feature is little conflict. Conflict among the interested groups and members would encourage the contending forces to recruit supporters from a broader range of groups, legislators, executive branch officials, and even the general public. Expanding the scope of the conflict in this way usually alters the balance of forces and the policy outcome. The low level of conflict, in turn, is the product of the concentrated benefits and widely distributed costs of some programs. The beneficiaries are motivated to organize and lobby to protect their interests, and the fairly small burden on taxpayers stimulates little opposition. But the number of people affected by policy choices, distribution of costs and benefits, and the scope and intensity of conflict varies greatly across policy areas. The result is significant variation in the role of groups in shaping policy choices.

Political scientist Hugh Heclo noticed that policy areas once dominated by subgovernments had lost their insular character by the 1970s. Heclo coined the term *issue networks* to capture the more diverse, mutually antagonistic, and fluid character of the lobbying and interest group community found in many policy areas. Many factors contributed to the change. In the 1960s and 1970s, new citizens' groups, many of which were by-products of broad-based social movements, challenged established groups. Groups representing economic interests proliferated, partly in response to new government policies and regulations, which led to a fragmentation of Washington representation in many policy areas that were once dominated by just one or two groups. In addition, congressional reforms made Congress more open, accessible, and democratic, which encouraged new groups to lobby and stimulated more members of Congress to champion the cause of once-neglected interests.

Analysts are divided over the political implications of the expansion of the interest group community and the breakdown of subgovernments. Tierney and Schlozman emphasize the continuing numerical advantage of business-oriented groups. They also observe that the explosion of interest group activity has

> introduced a potentially dysfunctional particularism into national politics. If policymakers in Congress are forced to find an appropriate balance between deference to the exigencies of the short run and the consideration of consequences for the long run, between acquiescence to the clearly expressed wishes of narrow groups that care intensely and respect for the frequently unexpressed needs of larger publics, the balance may have shifted too far in the direction of the near-term and the narrow.[12]

Political scientist Robert Salisbury disagrees. He insists that the large number of corporate lobbyists and the tremendous resources of business groups should not lead us to conclude

> that business interests or even self-serving groups invariably prevail. The total system of policy advocacy is far broader than the array, vast as it is, of organized interest groups. Every holder of public office – indeed, every candidate for public office – is or may be an advocate of some policy alternatives. Members of Congress do not wait passively for lobbyists to persuade them one way or the other; they too are advocates, as are the more prominent members of the administration, the editorialists and commentators in the mass media, the academic pundits and writers, and a host of other citizens who write letters, attend rallies, argue with each other, and generally make their views known on policy questions of the day.[13]

Besides, Salisbury contends, most business-group resources are devoted to monitoring government activity important to business decisions rather than to influencing policy choices.

It seems fair to say that Tierney and Schlozman's critical view is more widely shared among sophisticated observers of congressional politics than is Salisbury's more forgiving perspective. Nevertheless, Salisbury's note of caution is important. Lobbyists and interest groups are not the only source of pressure on members, nor are they the only important source of change in the nature of congressional politics. Communications and transportation technologies, electoral campaigns, the structure of the legislative process, the distribution of power within Congress, and other factors affect the balance of forces influencing congressional policy choices as well.

Conclusion

Lobbyists and interest groups are among the most controversial and least well-understood features of the legislative game. They appear to be both an essential part of the representation of interests before Congress and a potential source of bias in the policy choices made by Congress. Generally, they direct members' attention to narrow and parochial issues that might otherwise not be addressed. Whatever their consequences, the relationship that lobbyists and interest groups have with members of Congress has changed markedly over the years. In particular, transformations in Congress have caused lobbyists and interest groups to evolve. They are now:

- a much larger and more diverse community than just a few decades ago,
- more professional, with increasingly developed infrastructures,
- a more central player in congressional elections, both in terms of direct contributions and advocacy efforts, and
- better able to provide legislators with quick and accurate information.

These developments have sensitized the general public about the influence of special interests and produced new efforts to regulate lobbyists and lobbying.

Above: Representative Paul Ryan (R-Wisconsin), left, and Senator Judd Gregg (R-New Hampshire), right, the ranking House and Senate Budget Committee members, react to the fiscal 2010 budget proposed by President Obama.

Below: Senate Budget Chairman Kent Conrad (D-North Dakota), left, and House Budget Chairman John Spratt, Jr. (D-South Carolina), right, during a news conference on President Obama's fiscal 2010 budget request.

12

Congress and Budget Politics

THE FEDERAL BUDGET IS OFTEN THE CENTER OF CONGRESSIONAL politics. For fiscal year 2009, the federal government's spending will exceed $3 trillion, or approximately $10,000 for every American.[1] And estimates for fiscal year 2010 project an even larger number. Although many people are bored to tears when the details of spending and tax policy are discussed, the budget reflects fundamental choices about the role of government in American life. Action on the annual budget tends to generate the most partisan fights in Washington. The twists and turns of budget politics have strongly influenced winners and losers in elections, shaped the political careers of the most prominent politicians, reshaped congressional decision-making processes, and altered the distribution of power within Congress.

Federal budgeting since the 1970s has been a roller coaster ride. Beginning in the late 1970s and continuing for more than a decade, presidents and Congress struggled with annual deficits. In fiscal year 1992, the federal government spent about $290 billion more than it received from taxes and other revenues. To pay the interest on the debt that had accumulated over the years (nearly $4 trillion by that point), the federal government spent a little more than $200 billion – about 14 percent of its $1.5 trillion budget for fiscal year 1992. By 1998, the budget picture had improved markedly. Fiscal year 1998 ended with a small surplus, and annual surpluses were achieved in the three following years. Deficits returned by late 2001 during an economic recession. The fight against terrorism and the war in Iraq prompted increases in defense and homeland security spending, while tax cuts enacted in 2001 and 2003 cut into revenues. Deficits were looming again by 2002 and have continued through to the present. A deficit of nearly $1.2 trillion was projected for fiscal year 2009, a record high.

During the past four decades, political battles stimulated by budget deficits have produced a series of procedural innovations in the way

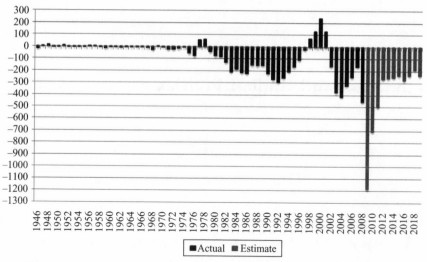

FIGURE 12.1. Annual Surplus (+) or Deficit (−) in Billions of Dollars, for Fiscal Years 1946–2019. *Source: Congressional Budget Office.*

Congress drafts the budget. In the 1970s and early 1980s, the process was modified to force congressional committees to write legislation that would either reduce spending or raise more revenue. Since then, the emphasis has been on enforcing multiyear budget plans. Each new effort to enforce deficit and spending agreements was a response to legislators, whose votes were often pivotal to passing budget legislation, to take credible action against deficits.

This is an important story. Step-by-step, the changes in rules reshaped the congressional decision-making process, contributed to heightened partisanship, and shifted the relative power of party and committee leaders. Cumulatively, these changes proved so important that they warrant special attention in this chapter.

Overview of the Federal Budget

Figure 12.1 shows the history of the federal deficit since the end of World War II. In the aftermath of the war, the federal government managed small annual budget surpluses about as often as it experienced budget deficits. In the 1960s, small deficits were the norm. Deficits crept upward during the 1970s and became a dominant issue in the 1980 presidential campaign, which ended with the election of the Republican candidate, Ronald Reagan, and a Republican majority in the Senate. During the 1980s and early 1990s,

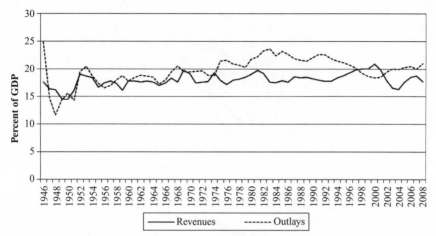

FIGURE 12.2. Federal Receipts and Outlays as a Percent of Gross Domestic Product, Fiscal Years 1946–2008. *Source: Congressional Budget Office.*

the deficit never approached the level experienced in 1980, Jimmy Carter's last year as president. The deficit contracted a little in the mid-1980s, but returned to a pattern of continued growth thereafter. President Clinton confronted this situation when he entered office in 1993. Clinton left office after surpluses had returned and his successor, George W. Bush, served while deficits expanded. Estimates from the Congressional Budget Office suggest that President Obama's first year in office will mark the largest deficit in history, followed by gradually receding levels.

The federal deficit must be seen in the context of the overall size of the U.S. economy, which has grown a great deal in the last half century. Figure 12.2 shows the size of federal expenditures and revenues as percentages of the gross domestic product (GDP), an annual measure of all of the goods and services produced in the United States. The figure demonstrates that federal revenues as a percentage of GDP have been fairly stable since World War II, seldom reaching 20 percent of GDP. It also shows that the deficit since 2002 is due to both higher spending and generally low revenues.

The increase in federal outlays that has put spending over 20 percent of GDP in most years since the early 1980s is due to both defense and domestic spending. Higher defense spending accounted for about half of the overall increase in expenditures between 1979 and 1983 and again after 2001. Most of the rest of the increase – and nearly all of it since the mid-1980s – is due to the rising cost of entitlement programs.

Entitlements are provisions in law that guarantee individuals certain benefits if they meet eligibility requirements. The spending is considered

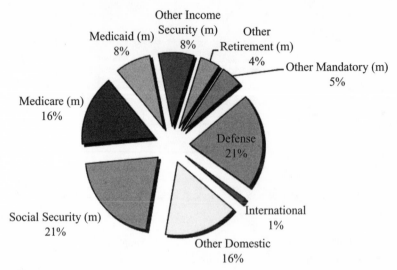

FIGURE 12.3. Major Categories of Federal Spending, Fiscal 2008. Mandatory programs designated with (*m*), others are discretionary. *Source: Congressional Budget Office.*

mandatory – unless Congress changes the law it must provide the required funding. In contrast, for *discretionary* programs, year-to-year spending is not dictated by eligibility requirements but rather is determined by Congress. Social security, Medicare (health care for the elderly), Medicaid (health care for the poor), veterans' benefits, and other income-security programs such as pensions are examples of entitlement programs with mandatory spending. Defense, education, environmental protection, medical research, and space programs are examples of discretionary spending. Entitlements have grown so much that they now account for over 60 percent of federal expenditures, as Figure 12.3 shows.

Creating a Congressional Budget Process: 1974

In the early 1970s, interest in budget reform was spurred by chronic deficits and political tensions between the Democratic Congress and a Republican president. In retrospect, the deficits of that period seem small, but they were unprecedented for a time without a declared war. The shortfall was largely the result of new and expensive domestic initiatives (President Lyndon Johnson's Great Society program) and the Vietnam War. Promising to gain control of the budget, Republican Richard Nixon won the 1968 presidential election and then proceeded to engage in intense battles with

---

Congressionally Speaking . . .

The *fiscal year* for the federal government begins on October 1 and runs through September of the following year. For example, fiscal year 2010 starts on October 1, 2009, and ends on September 30, 2010. Thus, Congress aims to have spending and tax bills for the next fiscal year enacted by October 1 of each year. The president proposes a budget in February, leaving Congress less than eight months to act on it. Failure to pass bills that approve spending for federal agencies, called *appropriations bills*, may force a shutdown of some government agencies. In most such cases, Congress passes *continuing resolutions*, which are joint resolutions of Congress that authorize temporary spending authority at the last year's level or at some percentage of that level.

---

the Democratic Congress over spending and taxes. These battles motivated Congress to strengthen its own budget-making capacities by adopting the Congressional Budget and Impoundment Control Act of 1974, usually called the Budget Act of 1974.[2]

The Budget Act created a process for coordinating the actions of the appropriations, authorizing, and tax committees. Each May, Congress would pass a preliminary budget resolution setting nonbinding targets for expenditures and revenues. During the summer, Congress would pass the individual bills authorizing and appropriating funds for federal programs, as well as any new tax legislation. Then, in September, Congress would adopt a second budget resolution, providing final spending ceilings. This resolution might require adjustments to some of the decisions made during the summer months. Those adjustments would be reflected in the second resolution, and additional legislation, written by the proper committees, would then be drafted to make the necessary changes. This process of adjustment was labeled "reconciliation," to reflect the need to reconcile the earlier decisions with the second budget resolution. The reconciliation legislation was to be enacted by October 1, the first day of the federal government's fiscal year.

The Budget Act provided for two new committees, the House and Senate Budget Committees. The budget committees write the budget resolutions and package reconciliation legislation from various committees ordered to adjust the programs under their jurisdiction. The Congressional Budget Office (CBO) was created by the act to provide Congress with nonpartisan, expert analyses of the economy and budget.

The Budget Act also modified Senate floor procedures in a critical way. The act barred nongermane amendments and set a limit of 20 hours on debate over budget resolutions and reconciliation legislation. These rules mean that budget measures cannot be loaded with extraneous floor amendments or killed by a Senate filibuster. However, the rules did not restrict the kinds of provisions committees could write into budget measures. Consequently, the door was left open for committees to include in reconciliation bills legislation unrelated to spending cuts. This became a common practice once reconciliation bills became a central feature of the budget-making process in the 1980s.

Reducing the Discretion of Committees: 1980 and 1981

The new budget process worked smoothly during its first four years, primarily because congressional Democrats did not use budget resolutions to constrain or compel action from appropriations, authorizing, or tax committees. But in 1979 and 1980, the last two years of the Carter administration, escalating deficits spurred a search for new means to control spending. An effort in 1979 to include reconciliation instructions to committees in the second budget resolution ended in failure, in part because of resistance from some committees to reducing spending on programs under their jurisdiction. Confronting projections of a rapidly rising deficit and a reelection campaign in 1980, President Carter and Democratic congressional leaders agreed to include reconciliation instructions in the first budget resolution, adopted in May. That is, they decided to order some committees to report legislation that would reduce spending at a point in the process before the usual authorization and appropriations legislation was considered. This switch meant that the initiative would shift from the various authorizing committees to the budget and party leaders, who together with administration officials would devise the reconciliation instructions. The innovation worked. The 1980 reconciliation legislation reduced the deficit by $8.2 billion, through a combination of spending cuts and tax increases. Strangely, the term reconciliation was and still is used, even though it ostensibly refers to the process of reconciling the decisions of the summer months with the second budget resolution.

Republicans learned from the experience of the Carter years and used reconciliation instructions to force much deeper cuts in domestic programs once they took over the White House and the Senate after the 1980 elections. The Republicans managed to gain adoption of reconciliation instructions

IMPOUNDMENT

During the early 1970s, the Nixon administration began to cut off funds for programs opposed by the president. That is, the president unilaterally stopped spending for programs for which funds had been appropriated by law. The practice, known as *impoundment*, created a constitutional crisis. Many members of Congress charged the president with violating his constitutional responsibility to see that the laws are faithfully executed. The courts agreed, for the most part, although some programs had been irreparably harmed by the time a court had ruled on the issue.

Congress responded in its 1974 budget reforms by providing for two types of impoundments – rescissions and deferrals. To withhold funds permanently for a particular purpose (make a rescission), a president would have to gain prior approval from both houses of Congress. To temporarily delay spending (make a deferral), a president would only have to notify Congress, and the president could defer spending unless either house specifically disapproved.

In 1983, the Supreme Court ruled that the legislative veto was unconstitutional because it allowed Congress to check an executive action without passing a regular bill. The ruling implied that the deferral process of the 1974 reforms was unconstitutional. Congress responded in 1987 by formally limiting the deferral authority to routine administrative matters.

Rescission authority continues to be used but it has involved only a very small fraction of total federal spending. Between 1976 and 2005, presidents requested nearly $73 billion in rescissions but Congress approved only about $25 billion.

and pass a reconciliation bill that cut spending for fiscal year 1982 by about $37 billion.

Figure 12.4 illustrates how the inclusion of reconciliation instructions in the first budget resolution has altered the budget process. Reconciliation, authorization, and appropriations legislation now proceed simultaneously, so there is no need for a second budget resolution.

Sequestration: 1985 and 1987

The savings achieved by the 1981 reconciliation bill were more than offset by a large tax cut enacted in separate legislation that year, continued increases in entitlement spending, and the budget crisis which intensified in the early 1980s. A tax increase in 1982 – initiated by Senate Republicans and quietly accepted by President Reagan – helped reduce the deficit a little, but it was not enough to change its long-term upward trajectory.

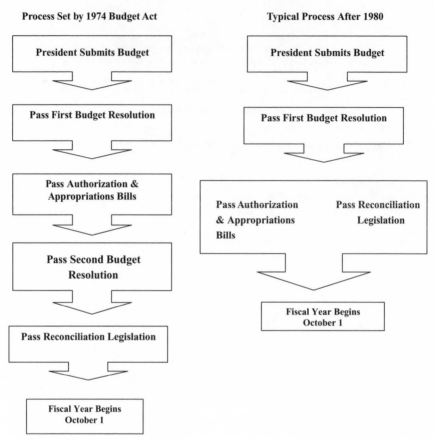

FIGURE 12.4. Steps in Budget Process.

In 1985, a trio of senators – Phil Gramm (R-Texas), Warren Rudman (R-New Hampshire), and Ernest Hollings (D-South Carolina) – pushed a seemingly irresistible amendment to a debt-ceiling bill, establishing the amount of outstanding debt the federal government is permitted to carry. The Gramm-Rudman-Hollings proposal was adopted as the Balanced Budget and Emergency Deficit Control Act of 1985. It provided for reducing the deficit by $36 billion in each of the following five years, so that the deficit would drop from about $172 billion in fiscal year 1986 to zero in fiscal year 1991. If Congress failed to meet any year's deficit target by more than $10 billion, as determined by the comptroller general (who headed the General Accounting Office, now called the Government Accountability Office), across-the-board cuts in spending would be ordered by an amount necessary to reduce the deficit to the specified level. This process of withholding a certain percentage of funding from programs was called "sequestration." Sequestration, it was argued, would be so distasteful to lawmakers that Congress and the president would be motivated to find a way to reduce the deficit without triggering the automatic cuts. If Congress and the president failed to do the job, sequestration would do it for them.

To reinforce this deficit-reduction scheme, the 1985 law barred floor amendments to budget resolutions and reconciliation measures that would raise the projected deficit beyond specified levels. A point of order could be made against any ineligible amendment. But the Senate had a history of overruling its presiding officer on points of order and dozens of popular nongermane amendments were proposed to the reconciliation bill considered in the fall of 1985. Senator Robert Byrd (D-West Virginia) therefore proposed, and the Senate approved, a new rule that provided that the presiding officer's ruling on the germaneness of an amendment to a reconciliation bill could not be overturned unless a three-fifths majority agreed. The "Byrd rule" reinforced the 1974 Budget Act's restrictions on floor amendments and debate and made Senate rules governing the content of budget measures and amendments to them even more restrictive than those in the House.

On paper, Congress and the president met the deficit targets in the next three fiscal years. But, in each case, this goal was accomplished through a remarkable combination of creative accounting and absurdly optimistic estimates about the economy, future demands on federal programs, and the next year's revenues. "Blue smoke and mirrors" became the catch phrase used to describe federal budgeting. As a result of this budgetary legerdemain, the actual deficit in fiscal 1988 turned out to be $155 billion rather than the targeted $108 billion.

In the fall of 1987, another debt-ceiling bill presented an opportunity to restart the Gramm-Rudman-Hollings process. Congress attached to the bill a new set of targets, this time moving the zero-deficit deadline back from 1991 to 1993. The measure also made it more difficult for the Senate to waive the deficit targets, by requiring a three-fifths rather than a simple majority vote. But many observers, including stock market investors, thought that merely restarting the Gramm-Rudman-Hollings process was woefully inadequate, a view that appeared to contribute to a crash in the stock market in October 1987.

The crisis of the stock market crash and the November 20 sequester deadline propelled Congress and President Reagan to reach a new agreement. The agreement was unique because it provided separate spending ceilings for defense and nondefense spending for a two-year period – fiscal 1987 and 1988. This compromise allowed the Reagan administration to end with a

---

Congressionally Speaking...

Only a few congressional rules are known by the name of their original author. One of them is the Byrd rule, named after Senator Robert C. Byrd (D-West Virginia), the former majority leader and former Appropriations Committee chair.

The *Byrd rule* bars extraneous matter from reconciliation bills. A provision is considered to be extraneous if it does not change spending or revenues, concerns issues that lie outside of the jurisdiction of the committee reporting it, or leads to a net increase in spending or decrease in revenues for the years beyond those covered by the bill. In addition, strangely, any change in social security, Washington's political sacred cow, is considered a violation of the Byrd rule.

The rule is enforced by points of order raised by senators from the floor and upheld by a ruling of the chair, who depends on the advice of the Senate parliamentarian. The Senate may overturn the ruling of the chair as long as 60 senators agree. If a point of order is successful, either through a ruling of the presiding officer or by a vote, the entire bill falls. The rule gives a sizable minority the ability to force certain kinds of provisions from reconciliation bills. It is one of the few places in which Senate rules are more restrictive than House rules.

---

truce with Congress on the budget. Neither party was eager to continue the battle into the election year of 1988.

PAYGO: 1990

The partisan war over the budget resumed in 1989, the first year of the Republican George H. W. Bush administration. By late 1989, it was clear that the Gramm-Rudman-Hollings procedure had been a failure. Instead of a $100 billion deficit, as targeted in the 1987 Gramm-Rudman-Hollings Act, the deficit turned out to be a record $221 billion because of a slumping economy. The Gramm-Rudman-Hollings procedure was shown to have a major weakness: the absence of a means for forcing further reductions during a fiscal year for which the original deficit estimates had been too optimistic.[3]

The 1990 budget package set a new direction for enforcing agreements, as indicated by its title – the Budget Enforcement Act (BEA). The 1990 BEA focused on spending limits rather than deficit reduction *per se*. For fiscal years 1991 to 1993, the BEA provided for three categories of non-entitlement spending (defense, international, and domestic) and established spending ceilings for each. These ceilings were to be adjusted for inflation each year so that economic conditions would not make them more or less onerous. If a category's ceiling was exceeded, sequestration would apply only to programs within that category – thus, this process is called categorical sequestration. "Firewalls" were established; that is, it became a violation of the rules to transfer funds between the three categories. In this way, Republicans would not fear a raid on defense funding to increase domestic spending, and Democrats did not have to worry about transfers in the opposite direction.

The 1990 BEA added teeth to the budget-making process by requiring that all tax and direct spending legislation be deficit-neutral. That is, if a bill cut taxes or increased spending, it also would have to provide fully offsetting tax increases or spending cuts. This pay-as-you-go mechanism – known as PAYGO – was enforced by a provision allowing any member to raise a point of order against a bill on the grounds that it was not deficit-neutral. If a bill that was not deficit-neutral were to sneak through, a sequester on spending in the appropriate category would be applied.

The PAYGO focus on spending ceilings rather than deficit-reduction targets meant that Congress and the president had given up on the Gramm-Rudman-Hollings approach. Of course, if the economy slumped and revenues declined, the deficit would go up even if the spending ceilings were obeyed. But if the economy performed better than expected, spending would be controlled as expected, revenues would flow into the Treasury faster than expected, and the increased revenues would reduce the deficit.

The 1990 budget deal made it more difficult for authorizing and tax committees to propose new policy initiatives. Legislation that would create a new program that entailed spending would have to provide for spending cuts somewhere else. Tax-writing committees could not propose legislation to grant tax breaks to some groups or industries unless they increased taxes or cut spending for other programs under their jurisdiction. The net winners under the 1990 rules seemed to be the appropriations committees. Although they had to operate under the spending ceilings, the ceilings were viewed as reasonably generous, given the programs that had to be funded, and would be adjusted for inflation. The appropriators also had substantial flexibility on how to set priorities within the broad categories.

Unfortunately for President G. H. W. Bush, deficits shot upward in 1991 and 1992, despite the fact that domestic discretionary spending was constrained. The economy did not perform well, which reduced revenues over those two years by nearly $90 billion from what had been predicted in 1990. The slow economy contributed to increased spending on entitlements – particularly Medicare, Medicaid, and farm price supports – outside of the discretionary spending ceilings. Unanticipated expenditures for the Persian

Gulf War and disaster aid to help Florida and Hawaii recover from hurricanes added to the deficit. The 1992 deficit of $290 billion was nearly $140 billion larger than the deficit in 1989, Bush's first year in office. Bush failed to win election to a second term.

Deficit-Reducing Trust Fund and Entitlement Review: 1993

Congress demonstrated remarkable creativity in devising new rules and processes for budgeting during the 1970s, 1980s, and early 1990s. But the impressive array of budgetary enforcement devices – reconciliation, sequestration, points of order, spending ceilings, PAYGO, and firewalls – did not seem to improve the bottom line. Deficits were never put on a downward path during the Reagan and G. H. W. Bush administrations, as the major deficit-reduction packages had promised. By the time Bill Clinton was sworn in as president in January 1993, the public was deeply cynical about federal budgetary politics, the annual deficit was at a record high, and the deficit was a major obstacle to the new president's other policy objectives.

Entitlement spending, particularly health care spending, spurred large annual increases in the budget. As Figure 12.5 demonstrates, the escalating costs of health care programs poses serious threats to deficit control. The major government health care programs, Medicare and Medicaid, are entitlement programs for the elderly and the poor. Cutting those programs entails either reducing the number of eligible people, which is an unpopular option, or cutting payments to hospitals, doctors, and state governments. Reducing payments, however, leads hospitals and doctors to shift their costs to people with private insurance, thereby increasing the cost of health care for everyone else.

Domestic programs that do not involve entitlements – most education, law enforcement, transportation, housing, energy, research, construction, and space programs – have declined as a percentage of GDP since 1980. Most federal programs were cut or frozen, in terms of constant dollars, during the 1980s. In most cases, further cuts would mean a basic change in the direction of public policies that are popular or have strong constituencies. Moreover, defense spending has been on a downward path for several years.

In 1993, President Clinton sought increases for some domestic programs, cuts in others and in defense, and some tax increases, all in the hope of reducing the deficit by $500 billion over five years. The Democrats decided to move budget measures at a more rapid pace and to incorporate Clinton's proposed tax increases in the reconciliation bill. Placing the tax increases in

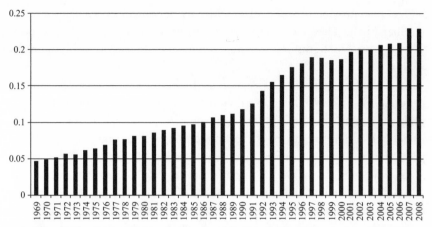

FIGURE 12.5. Health Spending as a Percent of Total Federal Outlays, 1962–2008. *Source: Congressional Budget Office.*

the reconciliation bill had important advantages for the Democrats. Selling never-popular tax increases might be easier as a part of a larger deficit-reduction package. Furthermore, reconciliation instructions to committees set deadlines on reporting legislation. This change meant that the two tax-writing committees, House Ways and Means and Senate Finance, could not indefinitely delay the tough decisions about taxes. And just as important, reconciliation bills are subject to a 20-hour limit on debate in the Senate, which protects them from filibusters and nongermane amendments. These special budget procedures meant that Republican opponents of the tax legislation could not delay Senate action.

The administration's plan ran into serious difficulty with conservative Democrats and, as had happened in previous years, the president's plan was adopted only once. New procedural devices – a deficit-reduction trust fund and a mandatory review of entitlement spending – were invented to satisfy legislators who lacked confidence in the legislation's goals. The trust fund plan provided that an amount equal to the projected deficit reduction from the bill be placed in a trust fund that could be used only to pay maturing public debt obligations, thereby reducing the national debt. The trust fund innovation proved insufficient to satisfy many conservative Democrats, however, so an agreement was reached between Democratic leaders and leading conservatives to make highly privileged legislation to address entitlement spending if such spending ultimately exceeded levels specified in the budget bill. In this way, the conservatives were assured that Congress would consider more serious entitlement reform if the budget plan proved too optimistic. With this agreement in place, a sufficient number of the Democrats supported the reconciliation bill for it to pass, 219 to 213. No Republicans voted for it, and 38 Democrats still voted against it.

After the Senate passed its version of the bill, the conference committee negotiations on the bill occurred almost entirely among Democrats. Their problem was a common one for the Democrats – how to keep liberals satisfied with commitments for domestic spending without raising taxes to the point that the party's conservatives would object. To make matters worse, a deadline of sorts loomed for approving the bill. The August recess was scheduled to begin at the end of the week of August 2. The Democrats did not want their internal divisions to delay the recess and give Republicans an opportunity to score political points by claiming that the Democrats had failed to end gridlock in Washington. Protecting the party's public image, as well as its policy objectives, appeared to motivate the Democratic leaders, and the conference's many staff assistants labored through several nights to produce the 1,800-page conference report.

As House and Senate leaders began to reveal the compromises they were making on various details of the conference report, some conservative Democrats who had supported the reconciliation bill indicated their intention to vote against the conference report. To appease at least some of them, President Clinton acted unilaterally to add credibility to the promise that the new tax revenues would be used to reduce the deficit rather than to increase spending. By executive order, he created the deficit trust fund and established an entitlement review process to measure whether legislators were abiding by the budget plan's requirements. Moreover, the House would adopt, as a part of a special rule for the conference report, a requirement that it act on new legislation to address any overages in entitlement spending when they occur. No provisions were made to bind the Senate to the same process, but House action on entitlement spending in future budget resolutions would force the Senate to confront the issue.

Even with these last-minute concessions, the outcome eventually turned on the vote of a freshman member, Marjorie Margolies-Mezvinsky, a Democrat from a Republican-leaning district just outside Philadelphia. She had voted against the president's position on the budget resolution and on passage of the House bill, but reportedly she had promised her support if her vote turned out to be pivotal – no doubt hoping it would not be. Early in the 15-minute period for the vote, Margolies-Mezvinsky cast a no vote. But with no time left in the vote, the Democrats had only 216 votes – two votes short of a majority – so the Speaker held the vote open. Ray Thorton (D-Arkansas), who had not yet voted, signed a red voting card to vote no. Only if both Margolies-Mezvinsky and Pat Williams (D-Montana) changed their votes to yes would the conference report pass. Williams was a 14-year veteran Democrat from Montana who had made the same promise as Margolies-Mezvinsky. Williams changed his vote first, and then all eyes fell on Margolies-Mezvinsky, who was being ushered to the front desk by a group of colleagues. The Republicans chanted, "Goodbye, Marjorie," referring to her reelection prospects if she voted against them. She signed a green card to vote yes, and the Speaker gaveled the vote closed.

Margolies-Mezvinsky spent the next few days explaining her vote. She appeared on local television and radio; was interviewed on National Public Radio, the MacNeil/Lehrer News Hour, and CNN's Moneyline; and immediately aired radio ads in her district to explain her vote. Her explanation was that she had extracted an important promise from the president. Minutes before the vote, she was called to the phone to talk to the president. Asked what it would take to get her vote, she told the president that she wanted a high-level conference for a serious discussion of cutting entitlement spending. Clinton agreed, so she agreed to vote yes. The next week, Secretary of Health and Human Services Donna Shalala traveled to Philadelphia to discuss plans for the conference. The full conference finally took place in December, with the president in attendance. Margolies-Mezvinsky lost her bid for reelection in 1994.

The Senate outcome came down to the decision of Senator Bob Kerrey, a Nebraska Democrat. Kerrey, who had acquired the nickname "Cosmic Bob" during his failed 1992 presidential bid, frustrated the White House because there were no particular provisions or promises of future action that he was looking for that could be used to get him to vote yes. Several talks with Clinton did not clarify Kerrey's position. Finally, hours before the Senate vote, Kerrey went to the Senate floor to announce his decision in favor of his party. He said, in part, "President Clinton, if you are watching now, as I suspect you are, I tell you this: I could not and should not cast a vote that brings down your Presidency. You have made mistakes and know it far better than I. But you do not deserve, and America cannot afford, to have you spend the next sixty days quibbling over whether or not we should have this cut or this tax increase." His Democratic colleagues rose in applause. The Republicans watched in silence. With Kerrey staying with his party, another tie vote was ensured. Once again Vice President Gore cast the deciding vote, and the conference report was approved, 51 to 50.

Tax Bill Certification: 1995–1996

Budget legislation became the central battleground for the new Republican majorities elected to the House and Senate in 1994. In 1995, the Republicans failed to gain congressional approval of a constitutional amendment to require an annually balanced budget, but in 1996 they gave the president the line-item veto for spending bills (although it was later struck down by the courts). In the interim, the Republicans pursued a strategy that they thought would compel the president to accept a budget reconciliation bill representing a far different mix of spending and taxing priorities than those contained in the 1993 bill. They failed miserably. The result contributed to the demise of Speaker Newt Gingrich's House career and bolstered President Clinton's chances for reelection in 1996. It also proved to be a lesson about political brinksmanship that congressional majority parties would carry into future Congresses.

In designing their budget resolution and reconciliation bill in 1995, the congressional Republican majorities largely ignored the proposals of the Clinton administration. They combined the goal of achieving a balanced budget by 2002 – which had been jettisoned in the fight over the 1993 bill – with a plan to cut taxes by $245 billion over seven years, which meant that federal spending had to be cut deeply. They sought to limit Medicaid spending and to give the states administrative responsibility for the program, stem the growth of Medicare, eliminate three executive departments (the Departments of Education, Commerce, and Energy), cut welfare spending, limit environmental regulations, and eliminate dozens of federal programs.

Procedural innovations were once again used to help bridge policy differences. Many senators were concerned that the deep tax cuts proposed would undermine the effort to balance the budget. To gain their support for the budget resolution, a provision was included that required the Finance Committee to wait to mark up tax cut provisions for the reconciliation bill until the Congressional Budget Office had officially certified that the bill would actually balance the federal budget by 2002. In this way, a nonpartisan staff arm of Congress, the CBO, had to approve estimates of the long-term effects of the budget package *before* a committee could act on the budget package.

By the time Congress approved the budget resolution, in the early summer of 1995, the House Republican leadership had devised a strategy that they hoped would gain the president's signature for their reconciliation bill, which would incorporate their spending and tax legislation. The Republicans would refuse to pass two critical sets of legislation – appropriations bills and a debt-ceiling increase – until the president agreed to approve their reconciliation bill. Failure to enact appropriations bills would force many departments to shut down at the end of the fiscal year (at midnight on September 30). Failure to increase the debt ceiling when needed would force the government to stop borrowing and possibly default on its debt obligations. The ceiling would be reached sometime in the fall. The strategy was predicated on the assumption that the Republican budget plan would be popular with the public. The Republicans' view, articulated by Speaker Gingrich, was that the president would not dare to shut down federal services or allow the government to default on its loans and would feel compelled to sign their legislation.

As the October 1 deadline approached, talk of the "train wreck" that would occur if the appropriations bills were not enacted began to dominate Washington. The reconciliation bill was due on September 22, but that date slipped by as Republicans struggled to resolve differences within their own ranks and finish writing the huge bill. Unfortunately for the Republicans, public enthusiasm for their budget plan had weakened. By November 13, Congress had failed to pass any appropriations bills or the reconciliation bill and the debt ceiling was about to be reached. The need for the debt-ceiling bill was eased when the administration found ways to juggle money in trust funds to create cash for the government to continue to pay its debt-service obligations.

The Republicans remained eager to force a showdown with the president. They passed an extension of appropriations authority through December 15 and a temporary debt-ceiling increase measure extending the government's borrowing authority to December 12. The debt-ceiling bill included provisions that prevented the president from juggling the trust funds and would revert the debt ceiling to its previous level on December 12. The continuing resolution was designed to be unpalatable to the president – it reduced spending in the affected agencies to just 60 percent of the previous year's level and canceled a scheduled reduction in Medicare premiums.

To the Republicans' surprise, Clinton vetoed both bills. As the administration knew, the Republicans lacked the two-thirds majority in each house required to override a presidential veto. The result was a shutdown of the unfunded federal agencies, forcing about 800,000 "nonessential" federal workers to be furloughed. Additional accounting moves made the veto of the debt-ceiling bill inconsequential, but the shutdown caused by the veto of the continuing resolution proved politically costly – for the Republicans. Although the Republicans blamed the shutdown on Clinton's unwillingness to bargain, the public blamed the Republicans over Clinton by a two-to-one margin. The fact that Republicans had made their strategy so conspicuous but still didn't have a reconciliation bill ready to pass hurt their cause. Worse yet for the Republicans, the president's willingness to take a stand enhanced his popularity with the public, giving the president a stronger bargaining position. The Republicans had misjudged Clinton's willingness to veto the bills and had badly miscalculated the general public's response.

Scrambling to determine what to do next, the Republicans adopted another continuing resolution – which ended a six-day shutdown – and soon approved a conference report on the reconciliation bill. It was expected that the reconciliation bill would be vetoed as well, so the issue was how to conduct negotiations to find a version acceptable to the president and to both houses of Congress. The second continuing resolution included a new feature: It stipulated that the president and Congress must agree to a plan to balance the federal budget within seven years – by 2002 – using economic estimates provided by the Congressional Budget Office. The Republicans viewed the commitment to a balanced budget as a large victory, but the details of a new budget plan were yet to be negotiated.

Partisan rhetoric sharpened. Differences between the parties over the reconciliation bill continued to concern the size of spending cuts in domestic programs and the size of tax cuts. A handful of regular appropriations bills passed and received presidential approval, but several others remained unfinished by December 15, again forcing a shutdown of many federal agencies, this time involving approximately 260,000 workers. House Speaker Gingrich and Senate Majority Leader Bob Dole appeared to be willing to pass another continuing resolution, but hard-line House Republicans made it plain that they would not support another resolution. Before they would agree to fund certain federal agencies, they wanted concessions from the president that the president was simply unwilling to grant. The result was that this shutdown lasted 21 days.

News stories of hardships suffered by government workers over the holidays worsened the standing of the congressional Republicans in the polls. By the first week of January, Clinton's poll ratings were heading up, and the Republicans were eager to pass continuing resolutions. In fact, they passed three measures – one narrow appropriations bill, to keep the most popular programs funded through September 1996; a second appropriations bill, to fund a couple of other programs through March 15; and a continuing resolution to keep the remaining programs and agencies open until January 26. Meanwhile, deep divisions among Republicans concerning the efficacy and political costs of their strategy began to emerge.

MAJOR DEVELOPMENTS IN THE BUDGET PROCESS, 1974–2007

1974 Congressional Budget and Impoundment Control Act

Created the modern budgeting process, established the budget committees, and provided for congressional review of presidential rescissions and deferrals.

1980 Reconciliation Bill

Provided that (for the first time) reconciliation be used at the start of the budget process. Committees were required to forward legislation drafted specifically to reduce spending as required by the first budget resolution.

1985 and 1987 Gramm-Rudman-Hollings Bill

Set fixed annual targets for deficit reduction and established a sequestration process to bring spending down to levels required to meet targets.

1990 Budget Enforcement Act

Dropped the fixed deficit targets of the Gramm-Rudman-Hollings approach and replaced them with caps on spending in domestic, defense, and international budgetary categories; pay-as-you-go rules for spending and revenues; and restrictions on loans and indirect spending.

1993 Omnibus Budget Reconciliation Act

Modified spending priorities and extended the enforcement provisions of the 1990 act through 1998.

1996 Balanced Budget Act

Modified spending priorities, extended the enforcement provisions of the 1993 act through 2002, and projected a balanced budget in fiscal year 2002.

2002

PAYGO enforcement provisions allowed to expire.

2007

PAYGO rule adopted; rules requiring sponsors of earmarks to be identified; House rule provides a "trigger" that establishes a point of order against tax-cut legislation that does not require that the OMB certify that the tax cuts cost less than $179.8 billion through fiscal 2012 or more than 80 percent of any surplus projected for 2012 at the time.

2009

PAYGO rule changed in the House to align it with the rule in the Senate so that both chambers use the same CBO baseline to assess compliance, to allow separate House-passed bills to be considered collectively deficit-neutral provided they are linked at engrossment, and to include an emergency exception to the PAYGO rule; rule providing a point of order against any earmark inserted in a general appropriations conference report.

The debt ceiling loomed on the horizon yet again. The financial adjustments that had allowed the administration to avoid defaulting on the country's debt obligations were just about exhausted. To avoid being blamed for playing games with the debt ceiling, Republican leaders wrote President Clinton that they intended to increase the debt ceiling when required. No progress had been made on the reconciliation bill by January 26, however, so another continuing resolution was enacted. It was now four months after the start of the fiscal year, and still no budget was in place. The process for drafting a budget for the next fiscal year began on February 5, when the president submitted his budget proposals to Congress. Plainly, those proposals meant little in the absence of a budget for the current fiscal year.

Just before March 15, for the fifth time since September of the previous year, a continuing resolution was passed to avoid a shutdown of federal agencies, this time for only a week. This practice of passing short-term continuing resolutions went on for several more weeks. Eventually, late in the evening of April 24, nearly seven months late and after a total of 14 limited spending bills and short-term continuing resolutions, the president and congressional Republican leaders agreed on a budget. The next day, Republican leaders rushed through to passage an appropriations bill to fund government agencies for the rest of the fiscal year. Compromise spending and tax cuts were quickly enacted.

Dropping and Reinstating PAYGO Rules: 1997–2009

With the 1996 budget plan in place, the Republicans did not challenge President Clinton on the budget again; instead, they turned to tactical fights on individual appropriations bills. They had no interest in repeating the political disaster of the 1995–1996 budget fight. Many Republican conservatives did not like Speaker Gingrich's willingness to compromise with Clinton, but, at least in the Speaker's view, there was little to be gained by laying down more ultimatums for the president. By the end of 1997, a strong economy, which yielded both reduced spending and increased tax revenues, had cut the deficit much faster than expected. In fact, a balanced budget was achieved in 1998, four years earlier than predicted in the 1996 budget. The large strategic moves of deficit politics were replaced with the less visible, tactical moves of surplus politics, with congressional Republicans and the Democratic president fighting over the details of appropriations bills.

Partisan differences caused four straight years of gamesmanship with appropriations bills. Sparring over spending details routinely led to delays in passing appropriations bills, which required that Congress pass numerous continuing resolutions. Moreover, when agreement was finally reached, compromises often extended over several appropriations bills and many extraneous measures that were packaged in large omnibus appropriations bills. In 1998, for example, eight of the 13 regular appropriations bills and over 30 non-appropriations measures were included in the omnibus appropriations bills for fiscal 1999. In 2000, 21 continuing resolutions were adopted before an omnibus appropriations bill was passed a few days before Christmas. That bill included the provisions of three regular appropriations bills, some new emergency spending, and non-appropriations legislation on Medicare, Medicaid, medical savings accounts and other tax provisions, immigration, and commodities regulation. This multidimensional bill represented many bargains and reflected members' realization that it was the last opportunity to address some issues before that Congress ended.

The political tables had turned in Washington after Republican President George W. Bush was elected in 2000. Bush was in office for less than a year when the 9–11 terrorist attack occurred. The subsequent airline and New York subsidies, homeland security, war on terrorism, and Afghan and Iraqi wars cost many hundreds of billions for the federal government, contributing to the creation of the first deficit after four years of surpluses. A prolonged recession and spending on national security contributed to the deficits, as did a tax cut enacted in 2001 when surpluses were still projected. Despite significant loss of revenue, the 2001 Bush tax cuts were passed without sequestration due to some shrewd maneuvering. Fearing that PAYGO may prevent the tax cuts from becoming permanent, congressional Republicans allowed it to expire in 2002. The Senate did, however, adopt its own PAYGO rule shortly after the statute expired.

In February 2003, President Bush proposed a budget deficit of over $300 billion for fiscal 2004. He proposed more tax cuts, some of which were opposed by at least a few Senate Republicans, and some spending increases. The administration argued that much of the tax proposal and some of the spending hikes were needed to boost the economy. The proposals, if adopted, would require Congress to adjust spending ceilings in the budget enforcement mechanisms.

The return of deficits was accompanied by failure to pass appropriations bills on time. From 2001 through 2004, most appropriations bills were not enacted until after the October 1 deadline and most were wrapped into large omnibus bills. For example, in 2002, when the appropriations bills for fiscal 2003 were considered, no appropriations bill was enacted by October 1 and eventually 10 continuing resolutions were adopted. Democrats argued that Republicans deliberately delayed action on a few of the bills so that Republicans would not have to cast potentially embarrassing votes just before the 2002 election. Not until January 2003, more than four months after the bills were due to be passed and after a new Congress was in place, did the House and Senate pass an omnibus bill that incorporated 11 of the 13 regular appropriations bills. Conference committee negotiations over the bill were not complete until February – six months late and halfway through the fiscal year. The Republican Congress passed all appropriations bills in 2005 and 2006 before adjourning. Although many were passed long after the October deadline, Republicans were confronted with difficult choices in the 2006 election year, leaving work on nine of 11 appropriations bills incomplete after they lost their House and Senate majorities.

The new House Democratic majority of 2007 reinstated the PAYGO rule, having scored political points against Republicans in the 2006 campaign for letting the deficit drift upward. House Democrats did not include a sequestration process, so the more recent adoption lacks the tough enforcement mechanism that was included in the 1990, 1993, and 1996 versions. Instead, they provided for only a point of order, which can be waived by approving a special rule, to be raised against a bill or amendment that increases the deficit. The Senate had implemented its own PAYGO rule in 2002 following the expiration of the statute, and extended the rule with some revisions in 2007. The latest versions of the PAYGO rules in the House and Senate closely resemble one another. Similar to the House rule, the Senate rule likewise enforces PAYGO requirements by point of order. In the Senate, points of order raised against a bill for PAYGO violations can be waived with 60 votes. Since PAYGO now exists only in the form of chamber rules, the houses have greater flexibility to set aside the rules when they prove to be an obstacle. For this reason, President Obama has advocated statutory PAYGO, but has received some resistance from within Congress. As of the time of this writing, Congress has taken no such action.

In 2007, both houses also moved to put in place new rules governing earmarks, the term used to describe funding for specific projects. The rules do not ban earmarks but rather require the disclosure of the name of the legislator sponsoring each project, publication of a justification for the project, and certification that the project does not benefit the legislator or his or her spouse. In addition to spending on construction projects, the rule applies to tax and tariff provisions geared to individual firms or organizations.

THE BATTLE OVER EARMARKS

In early 2006, Republicans found themselves embarrassed by the volume of earmarks – totaling about $20 billion – included in a supplemental appropriations bill, which President George W. Bush threatened to veto. Earmarks are provisions to fund individual projects that are championed by individual members, often in collaboration with outside interests and lobbyists. Republican leaders passed the bill only after promising earmark reform. The promised reform included a requirement that the names of earmarks' sponsors be made public. Members of the Appropriations committees believed that they were being singled out for earmarks when members of the tax-writing committees used legislation to write into law narrow provisions for tax breaks or tariff protection. As a consequence of the bad publicity for the bill and other developments, particularly a lobbying scandal, Republicans started but never completed work on an ethics reform bill that addressed earmarks.

House Democrats, after gaining a majority in the 2006 elections, incorporated earmark reform, including provisions that Republicans invented but did not adopt in the previous Congress. In response to the reform, House committees must keep a record of requests for earmarks. Critics of the reform approved of the provision requiring publication of sponsors' names but preferred that floor votes be guaranteed on individual earmarks. The Senate adopted similar rules included in the passage of the Honest Leadership and Open Government Act of 2007.

The reforms appear to have limited the number of earmarks, but legislators and lobbyists have looked for ways to circumvent the new requirements. Lobbyists have increasingly turned their attention to persuading executive branch officials to include specific projects in the president's budget requests so that legislators do not have to file requests with committees. Executive officials are also lobbied to use their discretion to favor certain projects after receiving appropriations.

The House passed some changes to its PAYGO rule in 2009. One such change aligns the House rules with those of the Senate, so that both chambers use the same Congressional Budget Office baselines when estimating the costs of bills. Another change allows the House to pass one bill that offsets the spending in another bill, provided that both are linked at engrossment. Previous rules required all bills passed by the House to be independently deficit-neutral over a one- and five-year period. Finally, the House inserted an exception that permits the House to waive the PAYGO rule for provisions designated as emergency spending. In addition to the PAYGO rules, the 2009 rules changes also prohibit conference committees from inserting earmarks into general appropriations bills that did not appear in either of the chamber bills.

Conclusion

The history of budgetary politics discussed in this chapter illustrates several important features of congressional politics that have been recurrent themes throughout this book:

1. Legislative outcomes in the United States are the product of a three-player legislative process in which the House, the Senate, and the president must negotiate and reach compromises. In the budget battles described in this chapter, differences in policy preferences among the three institutional players, combined with the necessity of gaining the consent of all three, produced compromised efforts to reduce the deficit and procedural innovations designed to force other players to act.

2. The president is a central player in congressional politics. When the president proposes a change in direction in budget policy, it usually changes Congress's agenda. The president's proposals may be set aside by the majority party in Congress, as they were initially in 1995. Doing so entails great political risks, however. For the party controlling the White House, the president, not the party's congressional leaders, tends to be the chief strategist for the party.

3. Rules matter. The constitutional requirement of a two-thirds majority in each house to override a presidential veto prevented the majority party in Congress from imposing its budget priorities in 1995 and 1996. Statutory limits on appropriations authority and the debt ceiling proved vital. The Senate rule that prevents extraneous amendments from being attached to budget bills (the Byrd rule) limited the options of House and Senate committees. Also, enforcement provisions included in previous budget agreements were essential to crafting compromises that the players could trust would be honored. Except for the basic rules outlined in the Constitution, all of these rules were subject to change and became a part of the debate over budget policy.

4. The Budget Act, and how the different players made use of it, altered the traditional relationship between the parent houses and their committees. Historically, committees had taken the initiative in setting the policy agenda and designing legislation within their jurisdictions. The new budget process, however, allowed top party and budget leaders to present comprehensive budget resolutions to the parent houses and required committees to produce legislation, after the fact, that

they most certainly would not have drafted had they been left to their own discretion.

5. The rules of the legislative game are changed by the players. The players often turned to new procedural rules to guarantee that promises critical to achieving a compromise would be kept in the future. New enforcement mechanisms were invented on several occasions to convince key groups of legislators that uncertainties about the future would not work to their disadvantage.

6. Elections have clear and powerful effects on policy making. In the history described in this chapter, elections produced realignments in the preferences of key players – the president and members of Congress – concerning budgetary policy. Divided party control of the House, Senate, and White House was the direct product of elections and shaped the players' strategies in basic ways. Less significant, but clearly present, were the effects of election timing. On several occasions, approaching elections tended to dampen partisanship and encourage compromise on the part of the party with the greater public relations problem. In addition, public opinion polls, which are taken as a gauge of the potential electoral consequences of political events and policy positions, appeared to alter players' strategies on many occasions.

7. Parties are the primary building blocks for creating voting coalitions, but party discipline is far from perfect. Leaders of both the Democratic and the Republican parties, when in the majority in Congress, first attempted to satisfy enough fellow party members to create a majority before soliciting support from the other party. In the end, voting on the budget plans, which typically encapsulated the major policy priorities of the majority party, was very partisan. Those party members who voted against the position of their own party leaders were criticized but ultimately faced no formal punishment.

8. Party leaders are important players in Congress, but they are not all-powerful. In the budget negotiations described in this chapter, the distribution of power within Congress showed a fairly centralized pattern that was partly the result of the rules governing the budget process and partly a reflection of the need for high-level negotiations to work out differences of great importance to the parties and the two branches. The large differences in the two parties' budgetary policy preferences and each party's fairly great internal cohesiveness encouraged party leaders to be assertive strategists on behalf of their party. But party leaders, it appears, were more than mere agents of

their parties. They focused agendas, made good and poor tactical decisions, and shaped their parties' images with the general public in ways that had consequences for the eventual legislative outcome. Some reliance on party leaders is inevitable, given the difficulty of producing collective action among the dozens of members in each of the four congressional parties. Still, as was most obvious in the 1995–1996 budget battle, even the most aggressive leader is constrained by what his or her party colleagues are willing to accept in terms of strategy and policy.

9. Committees play a central role in the legislative process, but their influence is not constant. Budgetary politics since the late 1970s has tended to push key decisions up to central budget and party leaders, and to reduce the independence of committees and their chairs. And yet, it is important to qualify this important consequence of budgetary politics by observing that committees were still responsible for writing the details of most of the legislative provisions of budget packages, even if they were highly constrained by agreements negotiated elsewhere. Even when the top party leaders and administration officials were hammering out the overall shape of the budget deals, most of the language of the budget packages was written by committees, and hundreds of specific policy provisions were negotiated by committee representatives.

The importance of parties, leaders, and committees in congressional policy making will continue to be shaped by the alignment of members' policy preferences, the nature of the issues, and the inherited rules of the game. Perceptions and preferences about budgetary issues are particularly important because of the pervasive effect of the budget on policy initiatives throughout the government. If budget issues begin to lose salience as the deficit fades from memory, then more policy initiatives originating from interest groups and creative members may rejuvenate the committees.

Appendix

Introduction to the Spatial Theory of Legislating

Much of congressional politics has geometric characteristics. When we speak of most Democrats as liberals, most Republicans as conservatives, and some legislators as moderates, we have in mind an ideological or policy spectrum – a line or dimension – along which we can place legislators. In recent Congresses, the parties have been sharply divided, with very little overlap between the parties. Figure A-1 illustrates this for the 109th Congress (2005–2006) for senators. Using a statistical technique, senators were scored on the basis of their overall voting record in the Congress. Democrats and Republicans were concentrated on opposite sides of the spectrum, creating one of the most polarized Senates in history.

Legislators' policy positions also can be represented in two or more dimensions, when appropriate. In Figure A-2, senators' policy positions are identified in two dimensions for a debate on an immigration reform bill in 2006. Their locations are identified with the help of a statistical analysis of their votes on about three dozen amendments and other motions that were considered on the Senate floor. The most significant issue during the debate concerned the standards for allowing illegal immigrants to gain legal entry to the United States. Senators who opposed special arrangements for reentry lined up on the far right, while senators who favored standards that would ease reentry for work or citizenship were located on the left (the horizontal dimension). Other issues, such as the ceiling on the number of legal immigrants allowed, were debated, too, and sometimes divided senators differently than the votes related to the treatment of current illegal immigrants (the vertical dimension). Democrats tended to favor both standards that facilitated reentry and larger quotas, while Republicans were split on reentry standards and tended to favor smaller quotas.[1]

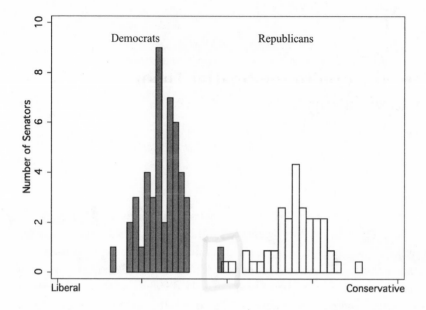

FIGURE A-1. Distribution of Senators on Liberal-Conservative Dimension, 2005–2006 (Democrats on left; Republicans on right). *Source:* Optimal Classification scores; www.voteview.com.

Basic Concepts for Analyzing a Legislative Body

Political scientists have taken advantage of geometric representations to develop spatial theories of legislative politics. The theories provide a way to conceptualize the location of legislators, policy alternatives, and policy outcomes. Like all scientific theories, spatial theories are based on assumptions that allow us to draw inferences about expected behavior. With a few assumptions about legislators, the policy space, and the rules governing

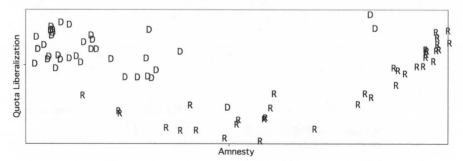

FIGURE A-2. Senators' Policy Positions on 2006 Immigration Bill in Two Dimensions (Democrats, D; Republicans, R). *Source:* Optimal Classification scores on Senate votes related to S2611, 109th Congress.

Median

FIGURE A-3. Illustration of the Median Voter Theorem.

decisions, we can deduce remarkably useful and usually intuitive proposi-
tions about the location of legislative outcomes. Non-intuitive predictions
are particularly useful because they often yield insights that even the close
observer of legislative politics might overlook.

Preferences and the Policy Space

Spatial theories assume the legislators, presidents, and other players have
preferences about policy outcomes. Preferences may reflect personal beliefs
or political influences. The preferences are assumed to be consistent. For
example, if a legislator prefers policy A over policy B and also prefers B
over C, then she favors A over C (transitive preferences, we say). When
a legislator's preference is depicted geometrically, as in the figures, it is
usually assumed that alternatives that are closer to the legislator's ideal
point are preferred to more distant points (a Euclidean policy space, we
say). Furthermore, it is assumed that each legislator chooses a strategy that
she believes will yield the best possible outcome – that is, minimizes the
distance between her ideal point and the outcome.

Simple Majority Rule and the Median Voter Theorem

Spatial theorists define "institutions" as a set of rules that govern decision
making. Rules may concern who has the right to participate, the "weight"
that each participant has in determining the outcome, the way in which
policy proposals are constructed, the order in which policy proposals are
considered, the standard for a final decision, and so on. Here, we assume
that each legislator has the right to cast one vote and, to begin, that a simple
majority of legislators is required for a proposal to be adopted.

In Figure A-3, a small legislature with five legislators is illustrated. With a
simple majority decision rule, a winning majority will always include legislator C. As the median legislator, C can join two other legislators – to the left
with A and B, to the right with D and E, or in the middle with B and D – to
form a three-vote majority. Of course, larger majorities could form, but they
will always include C. A spatial theorist would say that C is pivotal – C must
be included in a majority and so can demand that the outcome be located
at her ideal point. The *median voter theorem*, which we will not formally prove

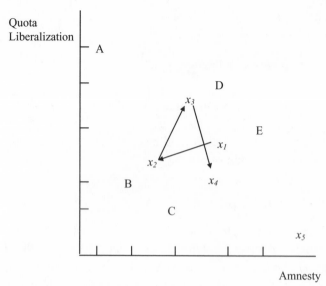

FIGURE A-4. Illustration of the Chaos Theorem.

here, provides that if C's position is adopted it cannot be defeated by another proposal. A corollary is that if two alternatives are presented, a majority will always prefer the alternative closer to the median legislator.

The median voter theorem means that when a median exists we can predict the outcome by knowing only the median legislator's ideal point. Spatial theorists refer to the stable prediction of the median outcome as an *equilibrium*. When a new legislature is elected, a new median location would lead us to predict a change in the outcome. That is, a new equilibrium is expected.

Multidimensional Spaces and the Chaos Theorem

A multidimensional policy space, such as the one in Figure A-4, creates important complications for predicting legislative outcomes. No legislator is the median on both dimensions. C is the median on the amnesty dimension but E is the median on the quota liberalization dimension. What is the expected outcome? In fact, political scientists have demonstrated mathematically that in most cases there is no single predicted outcome, no equilibrium, as there is in the unidimensional case.

A thought experiment will demonstrate an important point. Let us assume that current policy is located at x_1. Legislator B might propose a policy at x_2 and would win the support of A and C, both of whom are closer to x_1 than to x_2 and so would join B to form a majority to vote for x_2 and defeat x_1. But then D might offer x_3 and win the support of A and E. This process can continue indefinitely with a new majority of three forming at each step. If the rules allow a continuous flow of new proposals, there is no single outcome that cannot be defeated by some other proposal. This illustrates the *chaos theorem*. The theorem provides that, as a general rule, we cannot expect a stable outcome from simple majority rule in two (or more) dimensions.

Agenda Setting, Structure-Induced Equilibria, and Political Power

The chaos result – or majority rule cycling – may seem surprising. Legislatures regularly make final decisions without endless cycling through proposals. Why that is the case is the subject of a vast literature in political science. We do not want to review the complexities here, but three important points about legislative politics need to be understood.

First, legislative rules may not allow multidimensional proposals or may limit the number of proposals that may be considered. Such rules would limit the range of possible outcomes and make those outcomes more predictable. If only unidimensional proposals may be considered, the median voter theorem applies and majority rule chaos is avoided. Theorists use the label *structure-induced equilibria* for constraints on outcomes that are imposed by the rules. Thus, even if legislators' preferences are multidimensional, the rules may generate median outcomes by either limiting the range of proposals that are allowed or imposing unidimensionality on the proposals that may be considered.

Second, special influence over the agenda, either granted under the rules or gained through informal means, may control the alternatives subject to a vote and further limit the possible outcomes. A Speaker or presiding officer may be able to limit who is recognized to offer a motion. A coalition of legislators, such as members of the majority party, may agree to support only those proposals that a majority of the coalition endorses, thus limiting the set of proposals that can win majority support.

Three, introducing a proposal that creates a new dimension can transform a situation that would produce a median outcome into one with no predictable outcome. A legislator who dislikes the median outcome might be motivated to offer a proposal on an issue that divides his colleagues in a new way in order to avoid the certain, but undesirable outcome. The original median legislator would be motivated to create an agenda that prevents the proposal on the new issue from being considered.

In practice, then, rules and legislative strategies can contract or expand the range of possible outcomes. Real politics is often played in this way. Political scientists have studied many of the consequences of a variety of rules and

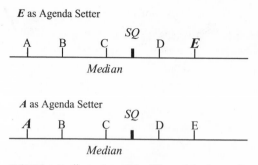

FIGURE A-5. Illustration of the Effect of the Status Quo and an Agenda Setter, the Unidimensional Case.

strategies, but continue to pursue research on the relationship between rules, strategies, and outcomes.

The Status Quo and Agenda Setting

A legislature often inherits policy from past legislatures. In most cases, the inherited policy, which we call the *status quo* (*SQ*), remains in place until a new policy is adopted. That is, the *SQ* is the default outcome if it is not defeated by a new proposal. The set of proposals that can defeat the *SQ* is called the *win set of SQ*. When there are no proposals that can defeat the *SQ*, we say that the win set is empty and predict that the outcome will remain at *SQ*.

The effect of the *SQ* on legislative strategies is important and intuitive. In Figure A-5, five legislators are arrayed on a single dimension. In the figure's top panel, let's assume that no proposal can be considered unless legislator E approves, but if a proposal is offered it can be amended. E, of course, wants the outcome at her own ideal point and might make a proposal there. However, A, B, or C might offer an amendment to move the outcome away from E and to the other side of *SQ*. Such an amendment would win a majority and E would be worse off than if he left the policy at *SQ*. Consequently, we would expect E to refuse to make an initial proposal. In this case, the agenda setter, E, protects the status quo. In contrast, in the lower panel in Figure A-5, legislator A is the agenda setter. Because A prefers the median's position over the *SQ*, A is willing to allow the legislature to consider a proposal and have it amended to C, the expected outcome.

Thus, the location of the status quo relative to the median determines the agenda setter's strategy. With the same agenda setter and median, different issues can generate different outcomes – the median or the *SQ*.

The same logic applies to the multidimensional case, as in Figure A-6. Legislators will support a proposal that improves on the status quo, *SQ*. In

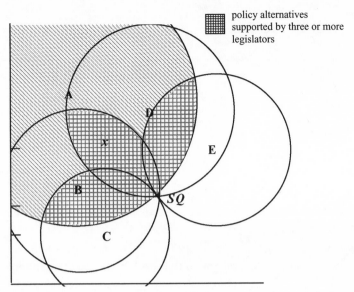

policy alternatives
supported by three or more
legislators

FIGURE A-6. Illustration of the Effect of the Status Quo and an Agenda Setter, the Multidimensional Case.

the figure, these *preferred-to* sets are denoted by the partial or full circles. For example, within the shaded circle centered on legislator A is the preferred-to set for A. The double shaded areas are the sets of locations preferred by at least three of the five legislators over *SQ*. Because points in the double shaded areas attract majority support for a proposal over the *SQ*, they define the win set of *SQ*. A large number of locations will not defeat *SQ* so majority rule narrowed the possible outcomes considerably. But, in this two-dimensional space, the win set includes a wide range of possibilities, many of which are less preferred to the *SQ* by one or two of the legislators. A, B, and D might agree to an outcome at *x*, which would make C and E worse off than leaving the policy at *SQ*.

Bicameralism, Separation of Powers, Agency Decisions, and Legislative Outcomes

Bicameralism

In the previous section, we considered a single legislative body. Congress and many other legislatures are bicameral, and usually require that a majority of each chamber approve legislation before it is sent to the president or chief executive. Spatially, this means that we must consider the relationship between the outcomes in the two chambers.

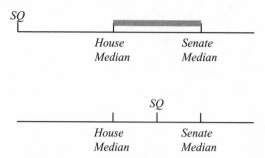

FIGURE A-7. Illustration of a Bicameral Outcome in One Dimension.

In unidimensional space, shown in Figure A-7, the outcome would be negotiated between the House and Senate medians. If both medians favor some of the same proposals over SQ, as they do in the top panel, they will negotiate an outcome among the range of proposals that they both prefer to SQ. If SQ falls between the two medians so that each house median prefers SQ to anything the other house would prefer to SQ, as in the figure's lower panel, the houses will not agree to a new policy and the outcome will be SQ.

In multidimensional space, as depicted in Figure A-6, we would define the bicameral win set as the intersection of the win sets in the two houses. We do not show that situation here. The overlap in the win sets for the two houses can be very small or very large. Little overlap greatly narrows the range of possible outcomes. Large overlap creates the possibility that a conference committee charged with finding compromise legislation will be able to exercise great discretion in determining the location of the final bill and still be able to attract majority support in both houses for the final version.

The President and the Veto

Under the Constitution, the president may veto legislation and a veto can be overridden only with the support of a two-thirds majority in each house of Congress. The threshold of a two-thirds majority in each house makes it necessary to appeal to more legislators than the requirement of a simple majority for initial approval of legislation. In our five-legislators illustrations, this means attracting the support of four of the five legislators (three of five would be less than the two-thirds required).

The president will veto any legislation that makes him worse off than SQ. In one dimension, several possibilities arise. In Figure A-8, the president's ideal point is P and the House and Senate medians are M_H and M_S, respectively. The two houses of Congress negotiate a bill at B somewhere between their medians. The president prefers SQ to B so he vetoes the bill. Both

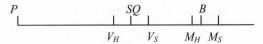

FIGURE A-8. Illustration of Upholding a Presidential Veto, in One Dimension.

House and Senate medians would like to override the veto but they must gain the support of two thirds of their colleagues. V_H and V_S are the *veto pivots*. That is, they are the legislators who are the leftmost members of the two-thirds majority that is required to override a veto. Without their support for the bill over the SQ, the veto cannot be overridden. In this case, V_H prefers SQ to B and so votes against the override. SQ is the outcome. Thus, the general rule is that a presidential veto will kill a bill whenever at least one of the veto pivots is on the same side of SQ as the president.

Other scenarios are easy to understand without illustration. Whenever the chamber medians are on the same side of SQ as the president, the president will sign the bill with a veto. Whenever V_H and V_S are on the same side of SQ opposite the president (not shown), the two houses of Congress can override the veto of the president.

As always, the multidimensional case is more complicated but it is still easy to visualize. In Figure A-9, there are two regions in which four of the five legislators of one house would favor the bill over the SQ. Consequently, a veto would be overridden any time the president vetoes a bill that is located in those regions. The bill also would have to be located in similar regions in the other house for both houses to override a president's veto. A bill that is located in the *veto win set of SQ* is one for which a veto can be overridden in both houses.

Plainly, the two-thirds majority requirement for a veto override shrinks the region of bill locations that can survive a veto to one that is smaller than the region of bill locations that can receive simple majority support in both houses. The implication is that the threat of a veto requires more careful negotiations within Congress and may have implications for legislators who win and lose. In Figure A-9, for example, the bill at x_2 survives a veto but a bill at x_1 does not, although both would receive simple majority support. But the outcome at x_2 is less favorable to legislators A and D and more favorable to B and C.

Agency Decisions

Political scientists often think of executive branch agencies as having policy preferences of their own. Staffed by people who have personal or

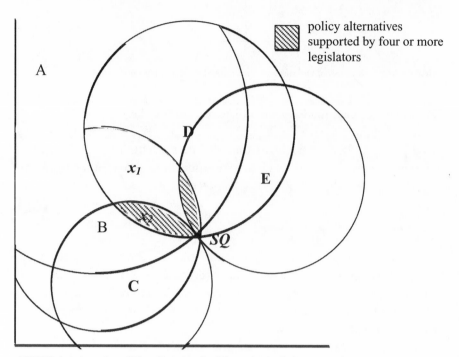

FIGURE A-9. Location of Veto Override Coalitions, the Multidimensional Case.

professional experience in a policy field, agencies are likely to devise rules and regulations that implement law in a manner that reflects their own preferences. Congress and presidents may seek to control the independence of agencies, but agency officials know that it may not be easy for Congress and the president to enact new legislation to place additional constraints on them. After all, new legislation requires the approval of the House, Senate, and president, or, in the case of a veto, a two-thirds majority in both houses. This is a high threshold. If a House majority, Senate majority, or president favors the direction an agency is taking, it can block legislation that would place new constraints in statute. (We have reported on other congressional strategies in Chapter 9.)

The strategic setting of agency decision making can be treated spatially, as we do in Figure A-10. To simplify, we characterize the House and Senate as having specific locations in multidimensional space just as the president does. If an agency took action to move a policy from a_1 (the current policy) to a_2, the Senate would like the move and block any effort by the House to enact legislation to require that the policy be returned to a_1. In this case, the agency, knowing that the Senate will protect its move, is free to shift policy without fear that the law will be changed. In contrast, if the agency

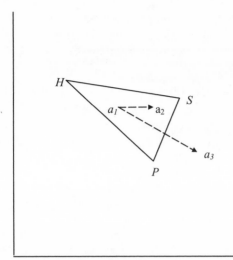

FIGURE A-10. Illustration of Agency Discretion, in Multidimensional Space.

sought to move policy as far as a_3, all three of the policy-making institutions would be better off by enacting legislation located on the line between S and P.

These scenarios demonstrate that the autonomy of an agency is limited to the range of policy moves that will not generate a new law. The farther apart the House, Senate, and president, the greater the discretion the agency enjoys. In fact, the triangle formed by the House, Senate, and president defines the limits of agency discretion. Any move that yields policy inside or to the edge of the triangle will be defended by at least one of the House, Senate, or president. Any move outside of the triangle will stimulate new legislation.

Advanced Theory and the Limits of Spatial Theory

We have presented a rudimentary introduction to the spatial theory of legislative politics. Political scientists have extended the theory in many directions. They have developed additional theory on the conditions that limit the range of possible outcomes under majority rule, explored the effect of agenda control rules that advantage parties or committees, and considered the effects of different assumptions about legislators' preferences and decision rules. We encourage our readers to pursue these important subjects elsewhere.

Spatial theory is not the ultimate theory of legislative politics. The spatial theorist assumes that legislators' policy preferences are known and invariant and theorizes only about how they motivate strategies. The determinants of legislators' policy preferences are beyond the scope of spatial theory.

The effects of nonpolicy motivations, such as the desire for reelection or to serve in the majority party, also are beyond the scope of spatial theory. Such motivations may be the overriding consideration in some circumstances. A legislator whose bill is rejected by the House of Representatives might be seen as a loser by some observers, but she may benefit from favorable press coverage and an appreciative home constituency for putting up a good fight. A legislative majority that fails to override a presidential veto may use the issue in a campaign to get more fellow partisans elected in the next Congress. Winning and losing in politics is sometimes hard to judge, at least in the short term.

Nevertheless, spatial theory is a powerful tool for predicting behavior and legislative outcomes. It often establishes a baseline expectation for outcomes against which the effects of other considerations can be measured. We can better judge the effects of persuasion by party leaders or presidents once we have a prediction for the outcome expected on the basis of legislators' prior policy preferences. It also shows that policy preferences and parliamentary rules often do not yield very specific predictions and define sometimes large ranges of possible outcomes that can be influenced by other political forces at work. Most important, spatial theory yields important insights about the effects of institutions – the rules of the game – that are so transparent in legislative decision making.

Notes

1. The American Congress

1. Paul Boller, *Congressional Anecdotes* (New York: Oxford University Press, 1991), 18.
2. Norman J. Ornstein, "Congress Inside Out: Here's Why Life on the Hill Is Meaner Than Ever," *Roll Call*, September 20, 1993, 27.
3. Robert A. Dahl, "Americans Struggle to Cope with a New Political Order That Works in Opaque and Mysterious Ways," *Public Affairs Report* (Institute of Governmental Studies, University of California, Berkeley, September 1993), 1, 4–6.
4. Robert H. Salisbury, "The Paradox of Interest Groups in Washington–More Groups, Less Clout," in *The New American Political System*, 2nd ed., ed. Anthony King, 203–229 (Washington, D.C.: American Enterprise Institute, 1990). For an analysis of the effects of these developments on Congress, see Barbara Sinclair, *The Transformation of the U.S. Senate* (Baltimore: Johns Hopkins University Press, 1989), 57–64.
5. See Theodore J. Lowi, "Toward a Legislature of the First Kind," in *Knowledge, Power, and the Congress*, ed. William H. Robinson and Clay H. Wellborn, 9–36 (Washington, D.C.: Congressional Quarterly Press, 1991).
6. Lawrence C. Dodd, "Congress and the Politics of Renewal: Redressing the Crisis of Legitimation," in *Congress Reconsidered*, 5th ed., ed. Lawrence C. Dodd and Bruce I. Oppenheimer, 426 (Washington, D.C.: Congressional Quarterly Press, 1993).
7. David E. Price, "Comment," in *Knowledge, Power, and the Congress*, 128.
8. Richard F. Fenno, Jr. *Learning to Govern: An Institutional View of the 104th Congress* (Washington, D.C.: Brookings Institution, 1997). On the consequences of alternating party control of Congress, also see Lawrence C. Dodd and Bruce I. Oppenheimer, "Congress and the Emerging Order: Conditional Party Government or Constructive Partisanship?" in *Congress Reconsidered*, 6th ed., 390–413.
9. "Capitol Hill's Uncertainty Principle," *National Journal*, November 2, 1996: 2365.

2. Representation and Lawmaking in Congress

1. Robert S. Weissberg, "Collective vs. Dyadic Representation in Congress," *American Political Science Review* 72 (1978): 535–547.

2. Jane J. Mansbridge, *Beyond Adversarial Democracy* (Chicago: University of Chicago Press, 1983).

4. Members, Goals, Resources, and Strategies

1. David E. Price, *The Congressional Experience: A View from the Hill* (Boston: Little, Brown, 1973), 146.
2. Quoted in Craig Winneker, "That Was The Year That Was...Whew!" *Roll Call*, December 21, 1992, 15.
3. As quoted in Deering and Smith, *Committees in Congress*, 67.
4. Richard F. Fenno, Jr., *The Making of a Senator: Dan Quayle* (Washington, D.C.: Congressional Quarterly Press, 1989), 29.
5. From Neil MacNeil, *Forge of Democracy: The House of Representatives* (NewYork: D. McKay, 1963), 141.
6. Adapted from Richard F. Fenno, Jr., *Home Style: House Members in Their Districts* (Boston: Little, Brown, 1978), 1–30.
7. Michael J. Malbin, *Unelected Representatives: Congressional Staff and the Future of Representative Government* (New York: Basic Books, 1980), 5.
8. Lori Montgomery and Paul Kane, "Sweeping Bailout Bill Unveiled," *Washington Post*, September 29, 2008.
9. John W. Kingdon, *Congressmen's Voting Decisions*, 2nd ed. (New York: Harper & Row, 1981), 96.
10. Richard F. Fenno, Jr., *The Emergence of a Senate Leader: Pete Domenici and the Reagan Budget* (Washington, D.C.: Congressional Quarterly Press, 1991), 134.
11. A report on the Senate aides' responses can be found in Steven S. Smith, "Informal Leadership in the Senate," in *Leading Congress*, ed. John Kornacki (Washington, D.C.: Congressional Quarterly Press, 1990), 71–83. Most respondents were members' legislative directors or administrative assistants.
12. Press release, "U.S. Senator Dan Quayle: Effective Leadership for Indiana," November 3, 1986.

5. Parties and Leaders

1. *Majority and Minority Leaders of the Senate*. U.S. Senate No. 91–20 (Washington, D.C.: Government Printing Office, 1969), 13.

6. The Standing Committees

1. Joel D. Aberbach, "What Has Happened to the Watchful Eye?" *Congress and the Presidency* 29 (2002): 3–23.

7. The Rules of the Legislative Game

1. Robert H. Michel, "The Minority Leader Replies," *Washington Post*, December 29, 1987, A14.
2. *Congressional Record*, October 5, 1992, S16894.

8. The Floor and Voting

1. Information taken from "Pocket Guide to Common Parliamentary Phrases in the House of Representatives." Congressional Research Service.
2. Some rules do not affect amending activity, so percentages do not sum to 100.

9. Congress and the President

1. Charles M. Cameron, *Veto Bargaining: Presidents and the Politics of Negative Power* (New York: Cambridge University Press, 2000), 188.
2. Paul Light, *The President's Agenda*, revised edition (Baltimore: Johns Hopkins University Press, 1991), 2.
3. Citing a study by Christopher Kelley, Charlie Savage, "House Panel Probing Bush's Record on Signing Statements," *The Boston Globe*, February 1, 2007.
4. Quoted in Light, *President's Agenda*, 13.
5. *Congressional Record*, February 16, 2006: S1402.
6. Henry B. Hogue, "Recess Appointments: Frequently Asked Questions," CRS Report, Congressional Research Services, September 10, 2002; Henry B. Hogue, "Recess Appointments: Frequently Asked Questions," CRS Report, Congressional Research Services, January 16, 2007.

10. Congress and the Courts

1. William T. Gormley, Jr. "The Bureaucracy and its Masters: The New Madisonian System in the U.S." *Governance*, January 1991, 10–11.

11. Congress, Lobbyists, and Interest Groups

1. Survey conducted by The Center on Congress at Indiana University in March 2008. Available at http://www.centeroncongress.org/learn_about/feature/survey_public_attitudes_detail_march_2008.php.
2. CBS New/*New York Times Poll* conducted September 15–19, 2006. Available at http://www. pollingreport. com/congress.htm#misc.

3. Kay Lehman Schlozman and John T. Tierney, *Organized Interests and American Democracy* (New York: Harper & Row, 1986), 74–82.
4. Jeffrey M. Berry, *The Interest Group Society*, 2nd ed. (Glenview, IL: Scott, Foresman, 1989), 20–21.
5. Jeffrey H. Birnbaum, "The Road to Riches is Called K Street," *The Washington Post*, June 22, 2005.
6. Hedrick Smith, *The Power Game* (New York: Ballantine Books, 1988), 232.
7. Matt Kelley, "Third of Top Aides Become Lobbyists," *USA Today*, December 26, 2008.
8. Quoted in John T. Tierney and Kay Lehman Schlozman, "Congress and Organized Interests," in *Congressional Politics*, ed. Christopher J. Deering (Chicago: Dorsey Press, 1989), 212.
9. Christine Mahoney and Frank Baumgartner, "When To Go It Alone: The Determinants and Effects of Interest-Group Coalitions," Working Paper.
10. Hans Nichols, "K Street Freezes out Dems," *The Hill*, September15, 2004.
11. "Corruption Named as Key Issue by Voters in Exit Polls." Available at CNN.com http://www.cnn.com/2006/POLITICS/11/07/election.exitpolls/index.html.
12. Tierney and Schlozman, "Congress and Organized Interests," 216.
13. Robert H. Salisbury, "Putting Interests Back into Interest Groups," in *Interest Group Politics*, 3rd ed., ed. Allan J. Cigler and Burdett A. Loomis (Washington, D.C.: Congressional Quarterly Press, 1991), 382–383.

12. Congress and Budget Politics

1. The most current budget figures and estimates are available in the current budget projections section of the Congressional Budget Office's website, http://www.cbo.gov.
2. On the developments leading up to the enactment of budget reform in 1974, see Allen Schick, *Congress and Money: Budgeting, Spending and Taxing* (Washington, D.C.: The Urban Institute, 1980), 17–81.
3. On the 1989 budget battle, see Lawrence J. Hass, *Running on Empty: Bush, Congress, and the Politics of a Bankrupt Government* (Homewood, IL: Business One-Irwin, 1990).

Appendix. Introduction to the Spatial Theory of Legislating

1. Figure A-2 is drawn to show greater variance on the first dimension, which explains far more the variance in voting behavior than the second dimension.

Suggested Readings

1. The American Congress: Modern Trends

Burrell, Barbara C. *A Woman's Place Is in the House*. Ann Arbor: University of Michigan Press, 1994.

Carroll, Susan J. *The Impact of Women in Public Office*. Bloomington: Indiana University Press, 2001.

Cook, Elizabeth Adell, Sue Thomas, and Clyde Wilcox, eds. *The Year of the Woman: Myths and Reality*. Boulder: Westview, 1994.

Cooper, Joseph, ed. *Congress and the Decline of Public Trust: Why Can't the Government Do What's Right*. Boulder: Westview Press, 1999.

Dodson, Debra L. 2006. *The Impact of Women in Congress*. Oxford; New York: Oxford University Press.

Gamble, Katrina L. "Black Political Representation: An Examination of Legislative Activity Within U.S. House Committees." *Legislative Studies Quarterly* 32, no. 3 (2007): 421–443.

Gertzog, Irwin N. *Women and Power on Capitol Hill: Reconstructing the Congressional Women's Caucus*. Boulder: Lynne Reinner Publishers, 2004.

Hibbing, John R., and Elizabeth Theiss-Morse *Congress as Public Enemy*. Cambridge: Cambridge University Press, 1995.

Hibbing, John R. *Congressional Careers: Contours of Life in the U.S. House of Representatives*. Chapel Hill: University of North Carolina Press, 1991.

Kean, Thomas H., Lee Hamilton, and Benjamin Rhodes. *Without Precedent: The Inside Story of the 9/11 Commission*. 1st ed. New York: Alfred A. Knopf, 2006.

Lawless, Jennifer L., and Richard Logan Fox. *It Takes a Candidate: Why Women Don't Run for Office*. Cambridge; New York: Cambridge University Press, 2005.

Loomis, Burdett A. *The New American Politician: Ambition, Entrepreneurship, and the Changing Face of Political Life*. New York: Basic Books, 1988.

Mann, Thomas E., and Norman J. Ornstein. *The Broken Branch: How Congress is Failing America and How to Get It Back on Track*. Oxford; New York: Oxford University Press, 2006.

Mayhew, David R. *America's Congress: Actions in the Public Sphere-James Madison through Newt Gingrich*. New Haven: Yale University Press, 2000.

Mikulski, Barbara. et al. *Nine and Counting: The Women of the Senate*. William Morris and Company, 2000.

Mondak, Jeffery J., Edward G. Carmines, Robert Huckfeldt, Dona-Gene Mitchell, and Scot Schraufnagel. "Does Familiarity Breed Contempt? The Impact of Information on Mass Attitudes toward Congress." *American Journal of Political Science* 51, no. 1 (2007): 34–48.

Ornstein, Norman J., Thomas E. Mann, and Michael Malbin. *Vital Statistics on Congress, 2001–2002*. Washington, D.C.: AEI Press, 2002.

Povich, Elaine S. *Nancy Pelosi: a biography. Greenwood biographies*. Westport, Conn.: Greenwood Press, 2008.

Rosenthal, Cindy S., ed. *Women Transforming Congress*. Norman: University of Oklahoma Press, 2002.

Schaffner, Brian F, Wendy J. Schiller, and Patrick J. Sellers. "Tactical and Contextual Determinants of U.S. Senators' Approval Ratings." *Legislative Studies Quarterly* 28, no. 2 (2003): 203–223.

Schwindt-Bayer, Leslie A., and Renatto Corbetta. "Gender Turnover and Roll-Call Voting in the U.S. House of Representatives." *Legislative Studies Quarterly* 29, no. 2 (2004): 215–229.

Shepsle, Kenneth. "*The Changing Textbook Congress*," In *Can the Government Govern?*, John E. Chubb and Paul E. Peterson, eds. Washington, D.C.: Brookings Institution Press, 1989.

Sinclair, Barbara. *The Transformation of the U.S. Senate*. Baltimore: Johns Hopkins University Press, 1989.

Swain, Carol. *Black Faces, Black Interests: The Representation of African Americans in Congress*. Cambridge: Harvard University Press, 1993.

Swers, Michele L. *The Difference Women Make: The Policy Impact of Women in Congress*. Chicago: University of Chicago Press, 2002.

Thomas, Sue. *How Women Legislate*. New York: Oxford University Press, 1994.

Tolchin, Susan, and Martin Tolchin. *Glass Houses: Congressional Ethics and the Politics of Venom*. Boulder: Westview Press, 2003.

United States. Congress. House. Committee on House Administration., and United States. Congress. House. Office of History and Preservation. 2008. *Black Americans in Congress, 1870–2007*. Washington, D.C.: U.S. G.P.O.

Whitby, Kenny J. *The Color of Representation: Congressional Behavior and Black Interests*. Ann Arbor: University of Michigan Press, 1998.

2. Representation and Lawmaking in Congress: The Constitutional and Historical Context

Anderson, Thorton. *Creating the Constitution: The Convention of 1787 and the First Congress*. University Park: Pennsylvania State University Press, 1993.

Baker, Richard A., Nancy Erickson, and United States. *Congress. Senate. 2007. Traditions of the United States Senate.* Washington, D.C.: U.S. Senate, 2007.

Barclay, John M. *Constitution of the United States of America with the Amendments thereto: To Which are Added Jefferson's Manual of Parliamentary Practice, The Standing Rules and Orders for Conducting Business in The House of Representatives and Senate of the United States and Barclay's Digest of the Rules of Proceeding in the House of Representatives of the United States.* Washington, D.C.: Government Printing Office. 1860, 1863, 1867, 1868, 1872.

Bates, Ernest S. *The Story of Congress: 1789–1935.* New York: Harper and Brothers, 1936.

Bessette, Joseph M. *The Mild Voice of Reason: Deliberative Democracy and American National Government.* Chicago: University of Chicago Press, 1994.

Binder, Sarah. "Dynamics of Legislative Gridlock, 1947–96." *American Political Science Review* 93 (1999): 519–534.

Byrd, Robert C. The Senate, 1789–1989. Vol. 4. Historical Statistics, 1789–1992. 100th Congress, 1st session.S. Doc. 100–20. Washington, D.C.: Government Printing Office, 1993.

Cooper, Joseph. *Congress and its Committees: A Historical Approach to the Role of Committees in the Legislative Process.* New York: Garland Publishing, Inc., 1988.

Cooper, Joseph. *The Origins of the Standing Committees and the Development of the Modern House.* Houston: William Marsh Rice University, 1970.

Currie, David P. *The Constitution Congress: The Federalist Period, 1789–1801.* Chicago: University of Chicago Press, 1997.

Davidson, Roger, and Walter Oleszek. *Congress Against Itself.* Bloomington: Indiana University Press, 1977.

Devins, Neal, and Keith E. Whittington. *Congress and the Constitution.* Durham: Duke University Press, 2005.

Fenno, Richard, Jr. *The United States Senate: A Bicameral Perspective.* Washington, D.C.: American Enterprise Institute, 1982.

Grant, J. Tobin, and Thomas J. Rudolph. "The Job of Representation in Congress: Public Expectations and Representative Approval." *Legislative Studies Quarterly* 29, no. 3 (2004): 431–445.

Haynes, George H. *The Election of Senators.* New York: Henry Holt and Company, 1906.

Haynes, George H. *The Senate of the United States: Its History and Practice.* 2 vols. Boston: Houghton Mifflin, 1938.

Hoffer, William James. 2007. *To Enlarge the Machinery of Government: Congressional Debates and the Growth of the American State, 1858–1891, Reconfiguring American Political History.* Baltimore: Johns Hopkins University Press.

Jefferson, Thomas. *A Manual of Parliamentary Practice for the Use of the Senate of the United States.* First Edition 1801 With Annotations by the Author. Washington, D.C.: Samuel Harrison Smith, 1801. Reprint, Washington, D.C.: Government Printing Office (page references are to the reprint edition), 1993.

Jillson, Calvin, and Rick Wilson. *Congressional Dynamics: Structure, Coordination, and Choice in the First American Congress, 1774–1789.* Stanford: Stanford University Press, 1994.

Lapinski, John S. "Policy Substance and Performance in American Lawmaking, 1877–1994." *American Journal of Political Science* 52, no. 2 (2008): 235–251.

Morgan, Donald. *Congress and the Constitution*. Cambridge: Harvard University Press, 1966.

Polsby, Nelson W. *How Congress Evolves: Social Bases of Institutional Change*. Oxford; New York: Oxford University Press, 2004.

Rakove, Jack N. *Original Meanings: Politics and Ideas in the Making of the Constitution*. New York: Vintage, 1997.

Remini, Robert V. and the Library of Congress. *The House: The History of the House of Representatives*. New York: Harper Collins, 2006.

Riker, William H. "The Senate and American Federalism." *American Political Science Review* 49, no. 2 (1955): 452–469.

Rothman, David J. *Politics and Power: The United States Senate, 1869–1901*. Cambridge: Harvard University Press, 1966.

Schickler, Eric. *Disjointed Pluralism*. Princeton: Princeton University Press, 2001.

Schiller, Wendy. *Partners and Rivals: Representation in U.S. Senate Delegations*. Princeton: Princeton University Press, 2000.

Swift, Elaine K. *The Making of an American Senate: Reconstitutive Change in Congress, 1787–1841*. Ann Arbor: University of Michigan Press, 1996.

Wilson, Woodrow. *Congressional Government: A Study in American Politics*. Boston: Houghton Mifflin Company, 1885 [1985].

Wilson, Woodrow, and Walter Lippmann. *Congressional Government: A Study in American Politics*. Mineola, NY: Dover Publication, 2006.

Wirls, Daniel, and Stephen Wirls. *The Invention of the United States Senate*. Baltimore: Johns Hopkins University Press, 2004.

Young, James S. *The Washington Community, 1800–1828*. New York: Columbia University Press, 1966.

Zelizer, Julian E. 2006. *On Capitol Hill: The Struggle to Reform Congress and Its Consequences, 1948–2000*. 1st pbk. ed. Cambridge; New York: Cambridge University Press.
Websites:

U.S. Senate History. http://www.senate.gov/pagelayout/history/g three sections with teasers/origins.htm

3. Congressional Elections and Policy Alignments

Abramowitz, Alan I., and Jeffrey Segal. *Senate Elections*. Ann Arbor: University of Michigan Press, 1992.

Baretto, Matt A., Gary M. Segura, and Nathan D. Woods. "The Mobilizing Effect of Majority-Minority Districts on Latino Turnout." *American Political Science Review* 98, no. 1 (2004): 65–76.

Benoit, Kenneth, and Michael Marsh. "The Campaign Value of Incumbency: A New Solution to the Puzzle of Less Effective Incumbent Spending." *American Journal of Political Science* 52, no. 4 (2008): 874–890.

Bickerstaff, Steve. 2007. *Lines in the sand: congressional redistricting in Texas and the downfall of Tom DeLay.* 1st ed. Austin, Tex.: University of Texas Press.

Biersack, Robert, John Green, Paul Herrnson, Lynda Powell and Clyde Wilcox. *The Financiers of Congressional Elections: Investors, Ideologues, and Intimates.* New York: Columbia University Press, 2003.

Brady, David W. *Critical Elections and Congressional Policy Making.* Stanford: Stanford University Press, 1988.

Brady, David W., Hahrie Han, and Jeremy C. Pope. "Primary Elections and Candidate Ideology: Out of Step with the Primary Electorate?" *Legislative Studies Quarterly* 32, no. 1 (2007): 79–105.

Burden, Barry, and David Kimball. *Why Americans Split Their Tickets: Campaigns, Competition, and Divided Government.* Ann Arbor: The University of Michigan Press, 2002.

Campbell, James E. *The Presidential Pulse of Congressional Elections.* Lexington, KY: University of Kentucky Press, 1993.

Canon, David T. *Race, Redistricting, and Representation.* Chicago: University of Chicago Press, 1991.

Canon, David. *Race, Redistricting, and Representation: The Unintended Consequences of Black Majority Districts.* Chicago: University of Chicago Press, 1999.

Carson, Jamie L., Erik J. Engstrom, and Jason M. Roberts. "Candidate Quality, the Personal Vote, and the Incumbency Advantage in Congress." *American Political Science Review* 101, no. 2 (2007): 289–301.

Citrin, J, Eric Schickler, and John Sides. "What if Everyone Voted? Simulating the Impact of Increased Turnout in Senate Elections." *American Journal of Political Science* 47, no. 1 (2003): 75–90.

Corrado, Anthony, Thomas E. Mann, and Trevor Potter, eds. *Inside the Campaign Finance Battle: Court Testimony on the New Reforms.* Washington, D.C.: Brookings Institution Press, 2003.

Currinder, Marian L. "Leadership PAC Contributions Strategies and House Member Ambitions." *Legislative Studies Quarterly* 28, no. 4 (2003): 551–577.

Currinder, Marian. *Money in the House: Campaign Funds and Congressional Party Politics.* 1st ed. Boulder, CO: Westview Press, 2008.

Dion, Douglas. *Turning the Legislative Thumbscrew.* Ann Arbor: University of Michigan Press, 1997.

Dwyer, Diane, and Victoria Farrar-Meyers. *Legislative Labyrinth: Congress and Campaign Finance Reform.* Washington, D.C.: Congressional Quarterly Press, 2000.

Fenno, Richard, Jr. *Congress at the Grassroots: Representational Change in the South, 1970–1998.* Chapel Hill: University of North Carolina Press, 2000.

Fenno, Richard, Jr. *Senators on the Campaign Trail: The Politics of Representation.* Norman: University of Oklahoma Press, 1996.

Fiorina, Morris P. *Congress: Keystone of the Washington Establishment,* 2nd ed. New Haven: Yale University Press, 1989.

Fowler, Linda, and Robert McClure. *Political Ambition: Who Decides to Run for Congress.* New Haven: Yale University Press, 1989.

Glazer, Amihai, and Bernard Grofman. "Two Plus Two Plus Two Equals Six: Tenure of Office of Senators and Representatives, 1953–1983." *Legislative Studies Quarterly* 12, no. 4 (1987): 555–63.

Gronke, Paul. *The Electorate, the Campaign, and the Office: A Unified Approach to Senate and House Elections.* Ann Arbor: University of Michigan Press, 2000.

Gross, Christian, and Antoine Yoshinaka. "The Electoral Consequences of Party Switching by Incumbent Members of Congress, 1947–2000." *Legislative Studies Quarterly* 28, no. 1 (2003): 55–76.

Herrnson, Paul S. *Congressional Elections: Campaigning at Home and in Washington,* 3rd ed. Washington, D.C.: Congressional Quarterly Press, 2000.

Jacobson, Gary C. *The Politics of Congressional Elections.* 6th ed. New York: Longman, 2004.

Jacobson, G. and S. Kernell. *Strategy and Choice in Congressional Elections.* New Haven: Yale University Press, 1983.

Jacobson, Gary, Samuel Kernell, and Jeffrey Lazarus. "Assessing the President's Role as Party Agent in Congressional Elections: The Case of Bill Clinton in 2000." *Legislative Studies Quarterly* 29, no. 2 (2004): 159–184.

Jones, David R., and Monika L. McDermott. "The Responsible Party Government Model in House and Senate Elections." *American Journal of Political Science* 48, no. 1 (2004): 1–12.

Kahn, Kim F., and Patrick J. Kenney. *The Spectacle of U.S. Senate Campaigns.* Princeton: Princeton University Press, 1999.

Kazee, Thomas, ed. *Who Runs for Congress? Ambition, Context, and Candidate Emergence.* Washington, D.C.: Congressional Quarterly Press, 1994.

Lewis-Beck, Michael, and Tom Rice. *Forecasting Elections.* Washington, D.C.: Congressional Quarterly Press, 1992.

Lipinski, Daniel L., William T. Bianco, and Ryan Work. "What Happens When House Members 'Run with Congress'? Consequences of Institutional Loyalty." *Legislative Studies Quarterly* 28, no. 3 (2003): 413–429.

Maestas, Cherie, Sarah Fulton, L. Sandy Maisel, and Walter Stone. "When to Risk It? Institutions, Ambitions, and the Decision to Run for the U.S. House." *American Political Science Review* 100 (2) (2006): 195–208.

Maestas, Cherie D., and Cynthia R. Rugeley. "Assessing the 'Experience Bonus' Through Examining Strategic Entry, Candidate Quality, and Campaign Receipts in U.S. House Elections." *American Journal of Political Science* 52, no. 3 (2008): 520–535.

Magleby, David B., J. Quin Monson, and Kelly D. Patterson. *Electing Congress: New Rules for an Old Game: Real Politics in America.* Upper Saddle River, NJ: Pearson Prentice Hall, 2007.

Maisel, L. Sandy. *From Obscurity to Oblivion: Running in the Congressional Primary.* Knoxville: University of Tennessee Press, 1982.

Mann, Thomas E. *Unsafe at Any Margin: Interpreting Congressional Elections.* Washington, D.C.: American Enterprise Institute Press, 1978.

Nelson, Candice J., David A. Dulio, and Stephen K. Medvic. *Shades of Gray: Perspectives on Campaign Ethics.* Washington, D.C.: Brookings Institution Press, 2002.

Peterson, David, et al. "Congressional Response to Mandate Elections." *American Journal of Political Science* 47, no. 3 (2003): 411–426.

Stone, Walter, L. Sandy Maisel, and Cherie Maestas. "Quality Counts: Extending the Strategic Politician Model of Incumbent Deterrence." *American Journal of Political Science* 48, no. 3 (2004): 479–495.

Sulkin, Tracy. *Issue Politics in Congress.* Cambridge; New York: Cambridge University Press, 2005.

Tate, Katherine. "Black Opinion on the Legitimacy of Racial Redistricting and Minority-Majority Districts." *American Political Science Review* 97, no. 1 (2003): 45–56.

Thurber, James. ed. *The Battle for Congress: Consultants, Candidates, and Voters.* Washington, D.C.: Brookings Institution Press, 2000.

West, Darrell M. *Air Wars: Television Advertising in Election Campaigns* 1952–1996. Washington, D.C.: Congressional Quarterly Press, 1997.

Wolfensberger, Donald. *Congress and the People: Deliberative Democracy on Trial.* Baltimore: Johns Hopkins University Press, 1999.

Websites:

Federal Election Commission. http://www.fec.gov/

Census Bureau (Districts and Apportionment). http://fastfacts.census.gov/home/cws/main.html

4. Members, Goals, Resources, and Strategies

Abramson, Paul, John Aldrich, and David Rohde. "Progressive Ambition Among United States Senators: 1972–1988." *Journal of Politics* 49, no. 1 (1987): 3–55.

Baker, Ross K. *Friend and Foe in the U.S. Senate.* New York: Free Press, 1980.

Bianco, William. *Trust: Representatives and Constituents.* Ann Arbor: University of Michigan Press, 1994.

Burden, Barry C. *Personal Roots of Representation.* Princeton: Princeton University Press, 2007.

Cain, Bruce, John Ferejohn, and Morris Fiorina. *The Personal Vote: Constituency Service and Electoral Independence.* Cambridge: Harvard University Press, 1987.

Canon, David. *Actors, Athletes, and Astronauts: Political Amateurs in the United States Congress.* Chicago: University of Chicago Press, 1990.

Cook, Timothy E. *Making Laws and Making News: Media Strategies in the U.S. House of Representatives.* Washington, D.C.: Brookings Institution Press, 1989.

Davidson, Roger H. *The Role of the Congressman.* Indianapolis: Bobbs-Merrill, 1969.

Dodd, Lawrence C. 1977. "Congress and the Quest for Power." In *Congress Reconsidered,* L.C. Dodd and B. Oppenheimer, eds. New York: Praeger.

Fenno, Richard, Jr. *Going Home: Black Representatives and Their Constituents.* Chicago: University of Chicago Press, 2003.

Fenno, Richard, Jr. *Home Style: House Members in Their Districts.* Boston: Little, Brown, 1978.

Fowler, Linda, and Robert McClure. *Political Ambition: Who Decides to Run for Congress?* New Haven: Yale University Press, 1989.

Fox, Harrison, Jr., and Susan W. Hammond. *Congressional Staffs: The Invisible Force in American Lawmaking*. New York: Free Press, 1977.

Lee, Frances E., *and Brice I. Oppenheimer. Sizing Up the Senate: The Unequal Consequences of Equal Representation*. Chicago: University of Chicago Press, 1999.

Lee, Frances E. "Bicameralism and Geographic Politics: Allocating Funds in the House and Senate." *Legislative Studies Quarterly* 29, no. 2 (2004): 185–213.

Loomis, Burdett. The New American Politician. New York: Basic Books, 1988.

Matthews, Donald. *U.S. Senators and their World*. Chapel Hill: University of North Carolina Press, 1960.

Miller, Warren E., and Donald E. Stokes. "Constituency Influence in Congress." *American Political Science Review* 57, no. 1 (1963): 45–56.

Parker, Glenn R. *Homeward Bound: Explaining Changes in Congressional Behavior*. Pittsburgh: University of Pittsburgh Press, 1986.

Price, David E. *The Congressional Experience: A View from the Hill*, 2nd ed. Boulder: Westview Press, 2000.

Rocca, Michael S. "Military Base Closures and the 1996 Congressional Elections." *Legislative Studies Quarterly* 28, no. 4 (2003): 529–550.

Sidlow, Ed. *Freshman Orientation: House Style and Home Style*. Washington, D.C.: CQ Press, 2006.

Wawro, Gregory. *Legislative Entrepreneurship in the U.S. House of Representatives*. Ann Arbor: University of Michigan Press, 2000.

Websites:

Current Representatives. http://www.house.gov/house/MemberWWW.shtml

Current Senators. http://www.senate.gov/general/contact information/senators cfm.cfm

Congressional Budget Office. http://www.cbo.gov/

Government Accountability Office. http://www.gao.gov/

5. Parties and Leaders

Aldrich, John, and David Rohde. "The Transition to Republican Rule in the House: Implications for Theories of Congressional Politics." *Political Science Quarterly* 112, no. 4 (1997): 541–567.

Aldrich, John, Mark Berger, and David Rohde. *"The Historical Variability in Conditional Party Government, 1877–1994."* In *Parties, Procedure and Policy: Essays on the History of Congress*, D. Brady and M. McCubbins, eds. Stanford: Stanford University Press, 2002.

Aldrich, John H. *Why Parties? The Origin and Transformation of Political Parties in America*. Chicago: University of Chicago Press, 1995.

Ansolabehere, Stephen, James Snyder, Jr., and Charles Stewart III. "The Effects of Party and Preferences on Congressional Roll Call Voting." *Legislative Studies Quarterly* 26, no. 4 (2001): 533–572.

Bawn, Kathleen. "Congressional Party Leadership: Utilitarian versus Majoritarian Incentives." *Legislative Studies Quarterly* 23, no. 2 (1998): 219–243.

Brady, David, David Epstein, and Mathew McCubbins, eds. *Party, Process, and Political Change in Congress*. Stanford: Stanford University Press, 2002.

Brady, David W., and Mathew D. McCubbins. Party, Process, and Political Change in Congress. v. 2: *Further New Perspectives on the History of Congress, Social Science History*. Stanford, Calif.: Stanford University Press, 2007.

Burden, Barry C., and Tammy N, Frisby. "Preferences, Partisanship, and Whip Activity in the U.S. House of Representatives." *Legislative Studies Quarterly* 29, no. 4 (2004): 569–590.

Caro, Robert A. *The Years of Lyndon Johnson: Master of the Senate*. New York: Alfred A. Knopf, 2002.

Connelly, William, Jr. and John Pitney. *Congress' Permanent Minority? Republicans in the U.S. House*. Lanham, MD: Rowman and Littlefield, 1994.

Cox, Gary, and Mathew McCubbins. *Legislative Leviathan: Party Government in the House*. Berkeley: University of California Press, 1993.

Cox, Gary W., and Mathew D. McCubbins. *Setting the Agenda: Responsible Party Government in the U.S. House of Representatives*. Cambridge: Cambridge University Press, 2005.

Cox, Gary W., and Mathew D. McCubbins. *Legislative Leviathan : Party Government in the House*. 2nd ed. Cambridge; New York: Cambridge University Press, 2007.

Currinder, Marian. *Money in the House: Campaign Funds and Congressional Party Politics*. 1st ed. Boulder, CO: Westview Press, 2008.

Finocchiaro, Charles J., and David W. Rohde. "War for the Floor: Partisan Theory and Agenda Control in the U.S. House of Representatives." *Legislative Studies Quarterly* 33, no. 1 (2008): 35–61.

Forgette, Richard. "Party Caucuses and Coordination: Assessing Caucus Activity and Party Effects." *Legislative Studies Quarterly* 29, no. 3 (2004): 407–430.

Frohman, Lewis, Jr., and Randall Ripley. "Conditions for Party Leadership: The Case of the House Democrats." *American Political Science Review* 59, no. 1 (1965): 52–63.

Gamm, Gerald, and Steven S. Smith. *"The Dynamics of Party Government in Congress."* In *Congress Reconsidered*, 7th ed., edited by Lawrence C. Dodd and Bruce I. Oppenheimer. Washington, D.C.: Congressional Quarterly Press, 2001.

Gamm, Gerald, and Steven S. Smith. The Emergence of Senate Party Leadership, in *Senate Exceptionalism*, edited by Bruce I. Oppenheimer. Columbus: Ohio State University Press, 2002.

Hasbrouck, Paul D. *Party Government in the House of Representatives*. New York: Macmillan, 1927.

Hess, Stephen. *The Ultimate Insiders*. Washington, D.C.: Brookings Institution Press, 1986.

Jacobson, Gary C. "Party Polarization in National Politics: The Electoral Connection," in *Polarized Politics: Congress and the President in a Partisan Era*, edited by J. Bond and R. Fleischer. Washington, D.C.: Congressional Quarterly Press, 2000.

Jenkins, Jeffrey, and Charles Stewart III. "Out in the Open: The Emergence of Viva Voce Voting in House Speakership Elections." *Legislative Studies Quarterly* 28, no. 4 (2003): 481–508.

Jenkins, Jeffrey A., Michael H. Crespin, and Jamie L. Carson. "Parties as Procedural Coalitions in Congress: An Examination of Differing Career Tracks." *Legislative Studies Quarterly* 30, no. 3 (2005): 365–389.

Jones, Charles O. *The Minority Party in Congress*. Boston: Little, Brown, 1970.

Kolodny, Robin. *Pursuing Majorities: Congress Campaign Committees in American Politics*. Norman: University of Oklahoma Press, 1998.

Lawrence, Eric, Forrest Maltzman, and Steven S. Smith. "Who Wins? Party Effects in Legislative Voting." *Legislative Studies Quarterly* 31, no. 1 (2006): 33–69.

Lebo, Matthew J., Adam J. McGlynn, and Gregory Koger. "Strategic Party Government: Party Influence in Congress, 1789–2000." *American Journal of Political Science* 51, no. 3 (2007): 464–481.

Lee, Frances E. "Agreeing to Disagree: Agenda Content and Senate Partisanship, 1981–2004." *Legislative Studies Quarterly* 33, no. 2 (2008): 199–222.

Maltzman, Forrest. *Competing Principals: Committees, Parties, and the Organization of Congress*. Ann Arbor: University of Michigan Press, 1997.

Manley, John F. The Politics of Finance. Boston: Little, Brown, 1970. Nokken, Timothy, and Keith Poole. "Congressional Party Defection in American History." *Legislative Studies Quarterly* 29, no. 4 (2004): 545–568.

Peabody, Robert. *Leadership in Congress: Stability, Succession, and Change*. Boston: Little, Brown, 1976.

Peters, Ronald M. *The American Speakership: The Office in Historical Perspective*, 2nd ed. Baltimore: Johns Hopkins University Press, 1997.

Ripley, Randall B. *Majority Party Leadership in Congress*. Boston: Little, Brown, 1969.

Rohde, David W. *Parties and Leaders in the Postreform House*. Chicago: University of Chicago Press, 1991.

Sinclair, Barbara. *Legislators, Leaders, and Lawmaking: The U.S. House of Representatives in the Postreform Era*. Baltimore: Johns Hopkins University Press, 1995.

Sinclair, Barbara. *Majority Leadership in the U.S. House*. Baltimore: Johns Hopkins University Press, 1983.

Sinclair, Barbara. *Party wars: Polarization and the Politics of National Policy Making*, The Julian J. Rothbaum *distinguished lecture series; v.* 10. Norman: University of Oklahoma Press, 2006.

Smith, Steven S. Parties and Leadership in the Senate. In The Legislative Branch, P. J. Quirk and S. A. Binder, eds. New York: Oxford University Press, 2005.

Smith, Steven S. *Party Influence in Congress*. New York: Cambridge University Press, 2007.

Smith, Steven S., and Gerald Gamm. 2001. *The Dynamics of Party Government in Congress*. In *Congress Reconsidered*, Lawrence C. Dodd and Bruce I. Oppenheimer, eds. Washington, D.C.: Congressional Quarterly Press.

Strahan, Randall. 2007. *Leading Representatives: The Agency of Leaders in the U.S. House*. Baltimore: Johns Hopkins University Press.

Taylor, Andrew J., and Norman J. Ornstein. *Elephant's Edge: The Republicans as a Ruling Party*. Westport, CT: Praeger Publishers, 2005.

Theriault, Sean M. *Party Polarization in Congress*. Cambridge; New York: Cambridge University Press, 2008.

Websites:

House Party Leaders & Organizations.

http://www.house.gov/house/orgs pub hse ldr www.shtml

Senate Party Leaders & Organizations.

http://www.senate.gov/pagelayout/senators/a three sections with teasers/leadership.htm

6. The Standing Committees

Adler, E. Scott, and John D. Wilkerson. "Intended Consequences: Jurisdictional Reform and Issue Control in the U.S. House of Representatives." *Legislative Studies Quarterly* 33, no. 1 (2008): 85–114.

Aldrich, John, and David W. Rohde. "The Republican Revolution and the House Appropriations Committee." *Journal of Politics* 62, no. 1 (2000): 1–33.

Baumgartner, Frank., Brad. Jones, and Michael. MacLeod. "The Evolution of Legislative Jurisdictions." *Journal of Politics* 62, no. 2 (2000): 321–349.

Crombez, Christophe, Keith Krehbiel, and Tim Groseclose. "Gatekeeping." *Journal of Politics* 68, no. 2 (2006): 322–334.

Davidson, Roger H. *Subcommittee Government: New Channels for Policy Making*. In The New Congress, Thomas Mann and Norman Ornstein, eds. Washington, D.C.: American Enterprise Institute Press, 1981.

Deering, Christopher J., and Steven S. Smith. *Committees in Congress*, 3rd ed. Washington, D.C.: Congressional Quarterly Press, 1997.

Evans, C. Lawrence, and Walter Olezsek. *Congress under Fire: Reform Politics and the Republican Majority*. Boston: Houghton Mifflin, 1997.

Evans, C. Lawrence. *Leadership in Committee: A Comparative Analysis of Leadership Behavior in the U.S. Senate*. Ann Arbor: University of Michigan Press, 1991.

Fenno, Richard, Jr. *Congressmen in Committees*. Boston: Little, Brown, 1973.

Fenno, Richard, Jr. *The Power of the Purse*. Boston: Little, Brown, 1966.

Fowler, Linda L., and R. Brian Law. "Seen but Not Heard: Committee Visibility and Institutional Change in the Senate National Security Committees, 1947–2006." *Legislative Studies Quarterly* 33, no. 3 (2008): 357–385.

Frisch, Scott A., and Sean Q. Kelly. *Committee Assignment Politics in the U.S. House of Representatives*. Norman: University of Oklahoma Press, 2006.

Goodwin, George. *The Little Legislatures: Committees of Congress*. Amherst: University of Massachusetts Press. 1970.

Hall, Richard I. *Participation in Congress*. New Haven: Yale University Press, 1996.

Kiewiet, D. Roderick, and Mathew McCubbins. *The Logic of Delegation: Congressional Parties and the Appropriations Process*. Chicago: University of Chicago Press, 1991.

King, David. *Turf Wars: How Congressional Committees Claim Jurisdiction*. Chicago: University of Chicago Press, 1997.

Krehbiel, Keith. *Information and Legislative Organization*. Ann Arbor: University of Michigan Press, 1991.

Kriner, Douglas, and Liam Schwartz. "Divided Government and Congressional Investigations." *Legislative Studies Quarterly* 33, no. 2 (2008): 295–321.

Longley, Lawrence, and Walter Oleszek. *Bicameral Politics: Conference Committees in Congress*. New Haven: Yale University Press, 1989.

Mayhew, David R. *Congress: The Electoral Connection*. New Haven: Yale University Press, 1974.

McConachie, Lauros G. *Congressional Committees: A Study of the Origins and Development of Our National and Local Legislative Methods*. New York: Thomas Y. Crowell, 1898.

Schickler, Eric, Eric McGhee, and John Sides. "Remaking the House and Senate: Personal Power, Ideology, and the 1970s Reforms." *Legislative Studies Quarterly* 28, no. 3 (2003): 297–331.

Shepsle, Kenneth. *The Giant Jigsaw Puzzle*. Chicago: University of Chicago Press, 1978.

Smith, Steven S. *Call to Order: Floor Politics in the House and Senate*. Washington, D.C.: Brookings Institution Press, 1989.

Strahan, Randall. *New Ways and Means: Reform and Change in a Congressional Committee*. Chapel Hill: University of North Carolina Press, 1990.

Vander Wielen, Ryan. "Conference Committees and Bias in Legislative Outcomes." Ph.D. Dissertation, Political Science, Washington University, St. Louis, 2006.

Websites:

House Committees. http://www.house.gov/house/CommitteeWWW.shtml

Senate Committees. http://www.senate.gov/pagelayout/committees/d three sections with teasers/committees home.htm

Historical Committees. http://web.mit.edu/17.251/www/data page.html#1

7. The Rules of the Legislative Game

Adler, E. Scott. *Why Congressional Reforms Fail*. Chicago: Chicago University Press, 2002.

Alexander, DeAlva S. *History and Procedure of the House of Representatives*. Boston: Houghton Mifflin, 1916.

Bach, Stanley, and Steven S. Smith. *Managing Uncertainty in the House of Representatives: Adaptation and Innovation in Special Rules*. Washington, D.C.: Brookings Institution Press, 1988.

Beeman, Richard R. "Unlimited Debate in the Senate: The First Phase." *Political Science Quarterly* 83, no. 3 (1968): 419–34.

Binder, Sarah. "Partisanship and Procedural Choice: Institutional Change in the Early Congress, 1789–1823." *Journal of Politics* 57, no. 4 (1995): 1093–1118.

Binder, Sarah. *Minority Rights, Majority Rule: Partisanship and the Development of Congress*. Cambridge, U.K.; New York: Cambridge University Press, 1997.

Binder, Sarah. "Parties and Institutional Choice Revisited." *Legislative Studies Quarterly* 31, no. 4 (2006): 413–532.

Binder, Sarah, and Steven S. Smith. *Politics or Principle? Filibustering in the United States Senate*. Washington, D.C.: Brookings Institution Press, 1997.

Burdette, Franklin L. *Filibustering in the Senate*. Princeton: Princeton University Press, 1940.

Foley, Michael. *The New Senate: Liberal Influence on a Conservative Institution, 1959–1972*. New Haven: Yale University Press, 1980.

Lawrence, Eric D. Essays on Procedural Development in the U.S. Congress. Ph.D. Dissertation, *University of Minnesota*, 2004.

Oleszek, Walter J. *Congressional Procedures and the Policy Process*. 7th ed. Washington, D.C.: CQ Press, 2007.

Roberts, Jason M. Minority Rights and Majority Power: Conditional Party Government and the Motion to Recommit in the House. *Legislative Studies Quarterly* 30, no. 2 (2005): 219–234.

Shepsle, Kenneth, and Barry Weingast. "When Do Rules of Procedure Matter?" *Journal of Politics* 46, no. 1 (1984): 206–221.

Sinclair, Barbara. *Unorthodox Lawmaking: New Legislative Processes in the U.S. Congress*, 2nd ed. Washington, D.C.: Congressional Quarterly Press, 2000.

Tiefer, Charles. *Congressional Practice and Procedure*. Westport, CT: Greenwood Press, 1989.

Wawro, Gregory, and Eric Schickler. *Filibuster: Obstruction and Lawmaking in the U.S. Senate, Princeton Studies in American Politics*. Princeton, NJ: Princeton University Press, 2006.

Wolfensberger, Donald. *Congress and the People: Deliberative Democracy on Trial*. Washington, D.C.: Woodrow Wilson Center Press, 2000.

Websites:

House Rules. http://www.house.gov/rules Senate Rules.

http://www.senate.gov/reference/reference index subjects/Rules and Procedure vrd. htm

Library of Congress (Thomas). http://thomas.loc.gov/

Bill Process (brief). http://www.house.gov/house/Tying it all.shtml

Bill Process (long). http://thomas.loc.gov/home/holam.txt

8. The Floor and Voting

Anderson, William, Janet Box-Steffensmeier, and Valeria Sinclair-Chapman. "The Keys to Legislative Success in the U.S. House of Representatives." *Legislative Studies Quarterly* 28, no. 3 (2003): 357–386.

Arnold, R. Douglas. *The Logic of Congressional Action*. New Haven: Yale University Press, 1990.

Bach, Stanley, and Steven S. Smith. *Managing Uncertainty in the House of Representatives: Adaptation and Innovation in Special Rules*. Washington, D.C.: Brookings Institution Press, 1988.

Binder, Sarah, and Steven S. Smith. *Politics or Principle? Filibustering in the United States Senate*. Washington, D.C.: Brookings Institution Press, 1997.

Calvert, Randall, and Richard F. Fenno, Jr. "Strategy and Sophisticated Voting in the Senate." *Journal of Politics* 56, no. 2 (1994): 349–376.

Clausen, Aage. *How Congressmen Decide*. New York: St. Martin's Press, 1973.

Clinton, Joshua, Simon Jackman, and Douglas Rivers. "The Statistical Analysis of Roll Call Data." *American Political Science Review* 98, no. 2 (2004): 355–370.

Frantzich, Stephen, and John Sullivan. *The C-SPAN Revolution*. Norman: University of Oklahoma Press, 1999.

Gamm, Gerald, and Steven S. Smith. *Last Among Equals: The Presiding Officer of the Senate*. In *Esteemed Colleagues: Civility and Deliberation in the United States Senate*, edited by B. Loomis. Washington, D.C.: Brookings Institution Press, 2000.

Jackson, John, and John Kingdon. "Ideology, Interest Group Score, and Legislative Votes." *American Journal of Political Science* 36, no. 3 (1992): 805–823.

King, David C., and Richard L. Zeckhauser. "Congressional Vote Options." *Legislative Studies Quarterly* 28, no. 3 (2003): 387–411.

Kingdon, John W. *Congressmen's Voting Decisions*, 3rd ed. Ann Arbor: University Of Michigan Press, 1989.

Krehbiel, Keith. *Pivotal Politics: A Theory of U.S. Lawmaking*. Chicago: University of Chicago Press, 1998.

Loomis, Burdette, ed. *Esteemed Colleagues: Civility and Deliberation in the U.S. Senate*. Washington, D.C.: Congressional Quarterly Press, 2001.

Poole, Keith T. *Spatial Models of Parliamentary Voting, Analytical methods for social research*. Cambridge; New York: Cambridge University Press, 2005.

Poole, Keith, and Howard Rosenthal. *Congress: A Political-Economic History of Roll Call Voting*. New York: Oxford University Press, 1996.

Poole, Keith T., Howard Rosenthal, and Keith T. Poole. *Ideology and Congress*. New Brunswick, NJ: Transaction Publishers, 2007.

Roberts, Jason M., and Seven S. Smith. "Procedural Contexts, Party Strategy, and Conditional Party Voting in the U.S. House of Representatives: 1971–2000." *American Journal of Political Science* 47, no. 2 (2003): 305–317.

Smith, Steven S. *Call to Order: Floor Politics in the House and Senate*. Washington, D.C.: Brookings Institution Press, 1989.

Young, Garry, and Vicky Wilkins. "Vote Switchers and Party Influence in the U.S. House." *Legislative Studies Quarterly* 32, no. 1 (2007): 59–77.

Websites:

Library of Congress (Thomas). http://thomas.loc.gov

Roll-Call Voting Data, NOMINATE Scores. http://www.voteview.com

Recent Roll-Call Voting Data, Raw Voting Files. http://web.mit.edu/17.251/www/data page.html#3

House Committee on Rules. http://www.house.gov/rules/

9. Congress and the President

Aberbach, Joel D. *Keeping a Watchful Eye: The Politics of Congressional Oversight*. Washington, D.C.: Brookings Institution Press, 1990.

Barrett, David M. The CIA and Congress: The Untold Story from Truman to Kennedy. Lawrence, Kan.: University Press of Kansas, 2005.

Binder, Sarah. "The Dynamics of Legislative Gridlock, 1947–1996." *American Political Science Review* 93, no. 3 (1999): 519–533.

Binder, Sarah. *Stalemate: Causes and Consequences of Legislative Gridlock*. Washington, D.C.: Brookings Institution Press, 2003.

Binkley, Wilfred. *President and Congress*. New York: Knopf, 1947.

Bond, Jon R., and Richard Fleisher. *The President and the Congress in a Partisan Era*. Washington, D.C.: Congressional Quarterly Press, 2000.

Bond, Jon R., and Richard Fleisher. *The President in the Legislative Arena*. Chicago: University of Chicago Press, 1990.

Brady, David W., and Craig Volden. *Revolving Gridlock: Politics and Policy from Jimmy Carter to George W. Bush (Transforming American Politics)*, 2nd ed. Boulder, CO: Westview Press, 2005.

Cameron, Charles. *Veto Bargaining: Presidents and the Politics of Negative Power*. Cambridge: Cambridge University Press, 2000.

Collier, Kenneth E. *Between the Branches: The White House Office of Legislative Affairs*. Pittsburgh: University of Pittsburgh Press, 1997.

Dodd, Lawrence C., and Richard Schott. *Congress and the Administrative State*, 2nd ed. Boulder: Westview, 1994.

Edwards, George C. *At the Margins: Presidential Leadership of Congress*. New Haven: Yale University Press, 1989.

Epstein, David, and Sharon O'Halloran. *Delegating Powers: A Transaction Cost Politics Approach to Policy Making Under Separate Powers*. Cambridge: Cambridge University Press, 1999.

Fenno, Richard F., Jr. *Divided Government*. New York: Allyn & Bacon, 1995.

Fiorina, Morris P. *Divided Government*, 2nd ed. Needham Heights: Allyn & Bacon, 1996.

Fisher, Louis. *Congressional Abdication on War and Spending*. College Station: Texas A&M University Press, 2000.

Fisher, Louis. *Constitutional Conflicts Between Congress and the President*, 4th ed. Lawrence: University Press of Kansas, 1997

Fisher, Louis. *The Constitution Between Friends: Congress, the President, and the Law*. New York: St. Martin's, 1978.

Fisher, Louis. *The Politics of Shared Power: Congress and the Executive*. College Station: Texas A&M Press, 1998.

Foreman, Christopher J., Jr. *Signals from the Hill: Congressional Oversight and the Challenge of Social Regulation*. New Haven: Yale University Press, 1988.

Gilmour, John B. *Strategic Disagreement: Stalemate in American Politics*. Pittsburgh: University of Pittsburgh Press, 1995.

Hersman, Rebecca K.C. *Friends and Foes: How Congress and the President Really Make Foreign Policy*. Washington, D.C.: Brookings Institution Press, 2000.

Hinckley, Barbara. *Less Than Meets the Eye: Foreign Policy Making and the Myth of the Assertive Congress*. Chicago: University of Chicago Press, 1994.

Howell, William G., and Jon. C. Pevehouse. *While Dangers Gather: Congressional Checks on Presidential War Powers*. Princeton: Princeton University Press, 2007.

Jones, Charles O. *Separate but Equal Branches: Congress and the Presidency*, 2nd ed. New York: Chatham House, 1999.

Kernell, Samuel. *Going Public: New Strategies of Presidential Leadership*. Washington, D.C.: Congressional Quarterly Press, 1986.

Krehbiel, Keith. *Pivotal Politics: A Theory of U.S. Lawmaking*. Chicago: University of Chicago Press, 1998.

Larocca, Roger T. *The Presidential Agenda: Sources of Executive Influence in Congress*. Columbus: Ohio State University Press, 2006.

Lindsay, James. *Congress and the Politics of U.S. Foreign Policy*. Baltimore: Johns Hopkins University Press, 1994.

Light, Paul. *The President's Agenda*. Rev. ed. Baltimore: Johns Hopkins University Press, 1991.

Lowenthal, Mark M. *Intelligence: From Secrets to Policy*. Washington, D.C.: Congressional Quarterly Press, 1999.

MacDonald, Jason A. "The U.S. Congress and the Institutional Design of Agencies." *Legislative Studies Quarterly* 32, no. 3 (2007): 395–420.

Mann, Thomas, ed. *A Question of Balance: The President, the Congress, and Foreign Policy*. Washington, D.C.: Brookings Institution, 1990.

Marshall, Bryan W., and Brandon C. Prins. "Strategic Position Taking and Presidential Influence in Congress." *Legislative Studies Quarterly* 32, no. 2 (2007): 257–284.

Mayer, Kenneth R. *With the Stroke of a Pen: Executive Orders and Presidential Power*. Princeton: Princeton University Press, 2001.

Mayhew, David. *Divided We Govern: Party Control, Lawmaking, and Investigating: 1946–1990*. New Haven: Yale University Press, 1992.

McCarty, Nolan. "The Appointments Dilemma." *American Journal of Political Science* 48, no. 3 (2004): 413–428.

Mezey, Michael L. *Congress, the President, and Public Policy*. Boulder: Westview, 1989.

Miller, Russell A., ed. *U.S. National Security, Intelligence and Democracy: From the Church Committee and the War on Terror*. Milton Park, Abingdon, Oxon; New York: Routledge.

Moe, Terry. "An Assessment of the Positive Theory of 'Congressional Dominance.'" *Legislative Studies Quarterly* 12, no. 4 (1987): 475–520.

Moe, Terry. The Presidency and the Bureaucracy: The Presidential Advantage. In *The Presidency and the Political System*, M. Nelson, ed. Washington, D.C.: Congressional Quarterly Press, 2003.

Neustadt, Richard E. *Presidential Power*. New York: John Wiley and Sons, 1980.

Peterson, Mark A. *Legislating Together: The White House and Capitol Hill from Eisenhower to Reagan*. Cambridge: Harvard University Press, 1990.

Ripley, Randall, and James Lindsay, eds. *Congress Resurgent: Foreign and Defense Policy on Capitol Hill*. Ann Arbor: University of Michigan Press, 1993.

Sollenberger, Michael A. *The President Shall Nominate: How Congress Trumps Executive Power*. Lawrence, Kan.: University Press of Kansas, 2008.

Spitzer, Robert J. *President and Congress: Executive Hegemony at the Crossroads of American Government*. New York: McGraw Hill, 1993.

Stevenson, Charles A. *Congress at War: The Politics of Conflict Since 1789*. Dulles, VA: Potomac Books, 2007.

Thurber, James, ed. *Rivals for Power: Presidential-Congressional Relations*. Washington, D.C.: Congressional Quarterly Press, 1996.

Wayne, Stephen J. *The Legislative Presidency*. New York: Harper, 1978.

Wildavsky, Aaron. "*The Two Presidencies*." In Perspectives on the Presidency, edited by A. Wildavsky. Boston: Little, Brown, 1975.

Websites:

White House and Executive Agencies. http://www.whitehouse.gov/government/

10.   Congress and the Courts

Abraham, Henry J. *Justices, Presidents, and Senators: A History of the U.S. Supreme Court Appointments from Washington to Clinton*. Lanham: Rowman and Littlefield, 1999.

Barnes, Jeb. *Overruled?: Legislative Overrides, Pluralism, and Contemporary Court-Congress Relations*. Stanford: Stanford University Press, 2004.

Berger, Raoul. *Congress v. The Supreme Court*. Cambridge: Harvard University Press, 1969.

Binder, Sarah, and Forrest Maltzman. "The Limits of Senatorial Courtesy." *Legislative Studies Quarterly* 29, no. 1 (2004): 5–22.

Cameron, Charles, Albert Cover, and Jeffrey Segal. "Senate Voting on Supreme Court Nominees: A Neoinstitutional Model." *American Political Science Review* 84, no. 2 (1990): 525–534.

Carson, Jamie L, and Benjamin A. Kleinerman. "A Switch in Time Saves Nine: Institutions, Strategic Actors, and FDR's Court-Packing Plan." *Public Choice* 113 (2002): 301–324.

Cohen Bell, Lauren. *Warring Factions: Interest Groups, Money, and the New Politics of Senate Confirmation*. Columbus: Ohio State University Press, 2002.

Frickey, Philip, and Seven S. Smith. "Judicial Review, the Congressional Process, and the Federalism Cases: An Interdisciplinary Critique." *The Yale Law Journal* 111, no. 7 (2002): 1707–1756.

Geyh, Charles Gardner. *When Courts and Congress Collide: The Struggle for Control of America's Judicial System*. Ann Arbor: University of Michigan Press, 2006.

Hoekstra, Valerie J. *Public Reaction to Supreme Court Decisions*. New York: Cambridge University Press, 2003.

Katzmann, Robert A. *Courts and Congress*. Washington, D.C.: Brookings Institution, 1997.

Lovell, George I. *Legislative Deferrals: Statutory Ambiguity, Judicial Power, and American Democracy*. New York: Cambridge University Press, 2003.

Maltzman, Forrest, James F. Spriggs, and Paul J. Wahlbeck. *Crafting Law on the Supreme Court: The Collegial Game*. New York: Cambridge University Press, 2000.

Moraski, Byron J., and Charles R. Shipan. "The Politics of Supreme Court Nominations: A Theory of Institutional Constraints and Choices." *American Journal of Political Science* 43, no. 4 (1999): 1069–1095.

Shipan, Charles R. *Designing Judicial Review: Interest Groups, Congress, and Communications Policy*. Ann Arbor: University of Michigan Press, 1997.

Solberg, Rorie L. Spill and Eric S. Heberlig. "Communicating to the Courts and Beyond: Why Members of Congress Participate in *Amici Curiae*." *Legislative Studies Quarterly* 29, no. 4 (2004): 591–610.

Urofsky, Melvin I. *Money and Free Speech: Campaign Finance Reform and the Courts.* Lawrence, KS: University Press of Kansas, 2005.

Wittes, Benjamin. *Confirmation Wars: Preserving Independent Courts in Angry Times.* Lanham, MD: Rowman & Littlefield, 2006.

Yalof, David. *Pursuit of Justices: Presidential Politics and the Selection of Supreme Court Nominees.* Chicago: University of Chicago Press, 1999.

Websites:

Supreme Court. http://www.supremecourtus.gov

Federal Court System. http://www.uscourts.gov/

Supreme Court Opinions. http://www.findlaw.com/casecode/supreme.html

11. Congress, Lobbyists, and Interest Groups

Austen-Smith, David, and John R. Wright. "Counteractive Lobbying." *American Journal of Political Science* 38, no. 1 (1994): 25–44.

Austen-Smith, David, "Campaign Contributions and Access." *American Political Science Review* 89, no. 3 (1995): 566–581.

Balla, Steven J., and John R. Wright. "Interest Groups, Advisory Committees, and Congressional Control of the Bureaucracy," *American Journal of Political Science* 45, no. 4 (2001): 799–812.

Baumgartner, Frank, and Beth Leech, "The Multiple Ambiguities of 'Counteractive Lobbying.'" *American Journal of Political Science* 40, no. 2 (1996): 521–542.

Biersack, Robert, Paul Herrnson, and Clyde Wilcox, eds. *After the Revolution: PACs, Lobbies, and the Republican Congress.* Boston: Allyn & Bacon, 1999.

Birnbaum, Jeffrey, and Alan S. Murray. *Showdown at Gucci Gulch: Lawmakers, Lobbyists, and the Unlikely Triumph of Tax Reform.* New York: Random House, 1987.

Caldeira, Greg, and John R. Wright, "Lobbying for Justice: Organized Interests, Supreme Court Nominations, and United States Senate." *American Journal of Political Science* 42, no. 2 (1998): 499–523.

Campbell, Colton, and John S, Stack, Jr., eds. *Congress Confronts the Court: The Struggle for Legitimacy and Authority in Lawmaking.* Lanham, MD: Rowman and Littlefield, 2001.

Cater, Douglas. *Power in Washington.* New York: Random House, 1964.

Cigler, Alan J., and Burdette A. Loomis. Always Involved, Rarely Central: Organized Interests in American Politics. In *Interest Group Politics*, 6th ed., Alan Cigler and Burdette Loomis, eds. Washington, D.C.: Congressional Quarterly Press, 2002.

Dexter, Lewis A. *How Organizations Are Represented in Washington.* Indianapolis: Bobbs-Merrill, 1969.

Hall, Richard L. and F.W. Wayman. "Buying Time: Moneyed Interests and the Mobilization of Bias in Congressional Committees." *American Political Science Review* 84, no. 3 (1990): 797–820.

Hammond, Susan W. *Congressional Caucuses in National Policymaking.* Baltimore: Johns Hopkins University Press, 1997.

Hansen, John Mark. *Gaining Access: Congress and the Farm Lobby, 1919–1981.* Chicago: University of Chicago Press, 1991.

Heclo, Hugh. *Issue Networks and the Executive Establishment*. In *The New American Political System*, Anthony King, ed. Washington, D.C.: American Enterprise Institute Press, 1978.

Hojnacki, Marie, and David C. Kimball. "Organized Interests and the Decision of Whom to Lobby in Congress." *American Political Science Review* 92, no. 4 (1998): 775–790.

Cigler, Allan, and Burdette Loomis, eds. *Interest Group Politics*, 6th ed. Washington, D.C.: Congressional Quarterly Press, 2002.

Loomis, B. and A. Cigler. The Changing Nature of Interest Groups. In *Interest Group Politics*, 6th ed. Washington, D.C.: Congressional Quarterly Press, 2002.

Lowi, Theodore J. *The End of Liberalism*. New York: Norton, 1979.

Lupia, Arthur and Mathew McCubbins. "Who Controls? Information and the Structure of Legislative Decision Making." *Legislative Studies Quarterly* 19, no. 3 (1994): 361–384.

Mackenzie, G.C., with Michael Hafken. *Scandal Proof: Do Ethics Laws Make Government Ethical?* Washington, D.C.: Brookings Institution Press, 2002.

McCubbins, Mathew, and Thomas Schwartz. "Congressional Oversight Overlooked: Police Patrols versus Fire Alarms." *American Journal of Political Science* 28, no. 1 (1984): 59–82.

McCubbins, Mathew, Roger Noll and Barry Weingast. "Administrative Procedures as Instruments of Political Control." *Journal of Law, Economics and Organization* 10, no. 2 (1987): 243–277.

McCune, Wesley. *The Farm Bloc*. New York: Doubleday, Doran, and Company, 1943.

Moe, Terry M. "Control and Feedback in Economic Regulation: The Case of the NLRB." *American Political Science Review* 79, no. 4 (1985): 1094–1116.

Olson, Mancur. *The Logic of Collective Action: Public Goods and the Theory of Groups*. Cambridge: Harvard University Press, 1965.

Ornstein, Norman, and Shirley Elder. *Interest Groups, Lobbying, and Policymaking*. Washington, D.C.: Congressional Quarterly Press, 1978.

Salisbury, Robert H., et al. "Who You Know Versus What You Know: The Uses of Government Experience for Washington Lobbyists." *American Journal of Political Science* 33, no. 1 (1989): 175–195.

Salisbury, Robert H. "An Exchange Theory of Interest Groups." *Midwest Journal of Political Science* 13, no. 1 (1969): 1–32.

Schlozman, Kay, and John Tierney. *Organized Interests and American Democracy*. New York: Harper & Row, 1986.

Shipan, Charles R. *Designing Judicial Review: Interest Groups, Congress, and Communications Policy*. Ann Arbor: University of Michigan Press, 2000.

Truman, David. *The Governmental Process*, 2nd ed. New York: Knopf, 1971.

United States. Congress. Senate. Committee on Homeland Security and Governmental Affairs. 2006. *Lobbying Reform: Proposals and Issues: Hearing Before the Committee on Homeland Security and Governmental Affairs, United States Senate, One Hundred Ninth Congress, Second Session, January 25, 2006*. Washington, D.C.: Government Printing Office.

Walker, Jack L., Jr. *Mobilizing Interest Groups in America*. Ann Arbor: University of Michigan Press, 1991.

Wright, John R. *Interest Groups and Congress: Lobbying, Contributions, and Influence*. Boston: Allyn & Bacon, 1996.

Websites:

Federal Election Commission. http://www.fec.gov/

House Lobbying Disclosure. http://clerk.house.gov/pd/index.html

Senate Lobbying Disclosure. http://www.senate.gov/pagelayout/legislative/g_three_sections_with_teasers/lobbyingdisc.htm

12. Congress and Budget Politics

Farrier, Jasmine. *Passing the Buck: Congress, the Budget, and Deficits*. Lexington: University Press of Kentucky, 2004.

Keith, Robert, and Allen Schick. *The Federal Budget Process*. New York: Nova Science Publishers, 2003.

Krutz, Glen S. *Hitching a Ride: Omnibus Legislating in the U.S. Congress*. Columbus: Ohio State University Press, 2001.

LeLoup, Lance T. *Parties, Rules, and the Evolution of Congressional Budgeting*. Pullman, WA: Washington State University, 2005.

Primo, David M. *Rules and Restraint: Government Spending and the Design of Institutions*. Chicago: University of Chicago Press, 2007.

Rubin, Irene S. *Balancing the Federal Budget*. New York: Chatham House, 2003.

Schick, Allen. *Congress and Money*. Washington, D.C.: Urban Institute Press, 1980.

Schick, Allen. *The Federal Budget: Politics, Policy Process*. Rev. ed. Washington, D.C.: Brookings Institution Press, 2000.

Sinclair, Barbara. *Unorthodox Lawmaking: New Legislative Processes in the U.S. Congress*, 2nd ed. Washington, D.C.: Congressional Quarterly Press, 2000.

United States. Congress. House. Committee on the Budget. 2007. Perspective on Renewing Statutory PAYGO: Hearing Before the Committee on the Budget, House of Representatives, One Hundred Tenth Congress, First Session July 25, 2007. Washington, D.C.: Government Printing Office.

Index

Note to the Index: An *f* following a page number denotes a figure on that page; a *t* following a page number denotes a table on that page.